Windmills of the Gods
The Sands of Time
The Doomsday Conspiracy

Sidney Sheldon

Diamond Books
an imprint of HarperCollins*Publishers*,
77–85 Fulham Palace Road,
Hammersmith, London W6 8JB

This Diamond Books Omnibus edition first published 1993
9 8 7 6 5 4 3 2 1

Windmills of the Gods © Sheldon Literary Trust 1987
The Sands of Time © Sheldon Literary Trust 1988
The Doomsday Conspiracy © Sheldon Literary Trust 1991

ISBN 1 85813 253 3 (UK)
ISBN Diamond Books 0 261 66153 1 (international edition)

Photoset in Linotron Times by Rowland Phototypesetting Ltd,
Bury St Edmunds, Suffolk

Printed in France by Maury-Eurolivres

Contents

Windmills of the Gods

For Jorja

We are all victims, Anselmo. Our destinies are decided by a cosmic roll of the dice, the whims of the stars, the vagrant breezes of fortune that blow from the windmills of the gods.

A Final Destiny H. L. Dietrich

PROLOGUE

Ilomantsi, Finland

The meeting took place in a comfortable, weather-proofed cabin in a remote, wooded area some 200 miles from Helsinki. The members of the Western Branch of the Committee had arrived discreetly at irregular intervals. They came from eight different countries, but their visit had been quietly arranged by a senior minister in the Valtioneuvosto, the Finnish Council of State, and there was no record of entry in their passports. Upon their arrival, armed guards escorted them into the cabin, and when the last visitor appeared, the cabin door was locked and the guards took up positions in the full-throated January winds, alert for any sign of intruders.

The members seated around the large, rectangular table were men in powerful positions, high in the councils of their respective governments. They had met before and under less clandestine circumstances, and they trusted one another because they had no choice. For added security, each had been assigned a code name.

The meeting lasted almost five hours, and the discussion was heated.

Finally, the chairman decided the time had come to call for a vote. He rose, standing tall, and turned to the man seated at his right. 'Sigurd?'

'Yes.'

'Odin?'

'Yes.'

'Balder?'

'We're moving too hastily. If this should be exposed, our lives would be –'

'Yes, or no, please?'

'No . . .'

'Freyr?'

'Yes.'

'Sigmund?'

'Nein. The danger –'

'Thor?'

'Yes.'

'Tyr?'

'Yes.'

'I vote "yes". The resolution is passed. I will so inform the Controller.

At our next meeting, I will give you his recommendation for the person best qualified to carry out the motion. We will observe the usual precautions and leave at twenty-minute intervals. Thank you, gentlemen.'

Two hours and forty-five minutes later, the cabin was deserted. A crew of experts carrying kerosene moved in and set the cabin on fire, the red flames licked by the hungry winds.

When the Palokunta, the fire brigade from Ilomantsi, finally reached the scene, there was nothing left to see but the smouldering embers that outlined the cabin against the hissing snow.

The assistant to the fire chief approached the ashes, bent down and sniffed. 'Kerosene,' he said. 'Arson.'

The fire chief was staring at the ruins, a puzzled expression on his face. 'That's strange,' he muttered.

'What?'

'I was hunting in these woods last week. There was no cabin.'

BOOK ONE

1

Stanton Rogers was destined to be President of the United States.
He was a charismatic politician, highly visible to an approving public,
and backed by powerful friends. Unfortunately for Rogers, his libido
got in the way of his career. Or, as the Washington mavens put it:
'Old Stanton fucked himself out of the Presidency.'

It was not that Stanton Rogers fancied himself a Casanova. On
the contrary, until that one fatal bedroom escapade, he had been a
model husband. He was handsome, wealthy, and on his way to one
of the most important positions in the world, and although he had
had ample opportunity to cheat on his wife, he had never given
another woman a thought.

There was a second, perhaps greater irony: Stanton Rogers' wife,
Elizabeth, was social, beautiful and intelligent, and the two of them
shared a common interest in almost everything, whereas Barbara,
the woman Rogers fell in love with and eventually married after a
much-headlined divorce, was five years older than Stanton, pleasant-
faced, rather than pretty, and seemed to have nothing in common
with him. Stanton was athletic; Barbara hated all forms of exercise.
Stanton was gregarious; Barbara preferred to be alone with her
husband or to entertain small groups. The biggest surprise to those
who knew Stanton Rogers was the political differences. Stanton was a
liberal, while Barbara had grown up in a family of arch-conservatives.

Paul Ellison, Stanton's closest friend, had said, 'You must be out
of your mind, chum! You and Liz are practically in the *Guinness
Book of Records* as the perfect married couple. You can't throw that
away for some quick lay.'

Stanton Rogers had replied tightly, 'Back off, Paul. I'm in love
with Barbara. As soon as I get a divorce, we're getting married.'

'Do you have any idea what this is going to do to your career?'

'Half the marriages in this country end in divorce. It won't do
anything,' Stanton Rogers replied.

He had proved to be a poor prophet. News of the bitterly fought
divorce was manna for the press, and the gossip papers played it up
as luridly as possible, with pictures of Stanton Rogers' love nest, and
stories of secret midnight trysts. The newspapers kept the story alive

as long as they could, and when the furore died down, the powerful friends who had backed Stanton Rogers for the Presidency quietly disappeared. They found a new white knight to champion: Paul Ellison.

Ellison was a sound choice. While he had neither Stanton Rogers' good looks nor his charisma, he was intelligent, likeable and had the right background. He was short in stature, with regular, even features and candid blue eyes. He had been happily married for ten years to the daughter of a steel magnate, and he and Alice were known as a warm and loving couple.

Like Stanton Rogers, Paul Ellison had attended Yale and was graduated from Harvard Law School. The two men had grown up together. Their families had adjoining summer homes at Southampton, and the boys swam together, organized baseball teams, and later, double-dated. They were in the same class at Harvard. Paul Ellison did well, but it was Stanton Rogers who was the star pupil. As editor of the *Harvard Law Review*, he saw to it that his friend Paul became assistant editor. Stanton Rogers' father was a senior partner in a prestigious Wall Street law firm, and when Stanton worked there summers, he arranged for Paul to be there. Once out of law school, Stanton Rogers' political star began rising meteorically, and if he was the comet, Paul Ellison was the tail.

The divorce changed everything. It was now Stanton Rogers who became the appendage to Paul Ellison. The trail leading to the top of the mountain took almost fifteen years. Ellison lost an election for the Senate, won the following one, and in the next few years became a highly visible, articulate lawmaker. He fought against waste in government and Washington bureaucracy. He was a populist, and believed in international détente. He was asked to give the nominating speech for the incumbent president running for re-election. It was a brilliant, impassioned speech that made everyone sit up and take notice. Four years later, Paul Ellison was elected President of the United States. His first appointment was Stanton Rogers as Presidential Foreign Affairs Adviser.

Marshall McLuhan's theory that television would turn the world into a global village had become a reality. The inauguration of the forty-second President of the United States was carried by satellite to more than 190 countries.

In the Black Rooster, a Washington, D.C. hangout for newsmen, Ben Cohn, a veteran political reporter for the *Washington Post*, was seated at a table with four colleagues, watching the inauguration on the large television set over the bar.

'The son-of-a-bitch cost me fifty bucks,' one of the reporters complained.

'I warned you not to bet against Ellison,' Ben Cohn chided. 'He's got the magic, baby. You'd better believe it.'

The camera panned to show the massive crowds gathered on Pennsylvania Avenue, huddled inside their overcoats against the bitter January wind, listening to the ceremony on loudspeakers set up around the podium. Jason Merlin, Chief Justice of the United States Supreme Court, finished the swearing-in oath, and the new President shook his hand and stepped up to the microphone.

'Look at those idiots standing out there freezing their asses off,' Ben Cohn commented. 'Do you know why they aren't home, like normal human beings, watching it on television?'

'Why?'

'Because a man is making history, my friends. One day all those people are going to tell their children and grandchildren that they were there the day Paul Ellison was sworn in. And they're all going to brag "I was so close to him I could have touched him."'

'You're a cynic, Cohn.'

'And proud of it. Every politician in the world comes out of the same cookie cutter. They're all in it for what they can get out of it. Face it, fellas, our new President is a liberal and an idealist. That's enough to give any intelligent man nightmares. My definition of a liberal is a man who has his ass firmly stuck in clouds of cotton wool.'

The truth was that Ben Cohn was not as cynical as he sounded. He had covered Paul Ellison's career from the beginning and, while it was true that Cohn had not been impressed at first, as Ellison moved up the political ladder, Ben Cohn began to change his opinion. This politician was nobody's 'yes' man. He was an oak in a forest of willows.

Outside, the sky exploded into icy sheets of rain. Ben Cohn hoped the weather was not an omen of the four years that lay ahead. He turned his attention back to the television set.

'The Presidency of the United States is a torch lit by the American people and passed from hand to hand every four years. The torch that has been entrusted to my care is the most powerful weapon in the world. It is powerful enough to burn down civilization as we know it, or to be a beacon that will light the future for us and for the rest of the world. It is our choice to make. I speak today not only to our allies, but to those countries in the Soviet camp. I say to them now, as we prepare to move into the twenty-first century, that there is no longer any room for confrontation, that we must learn to make the phrase "one world" become a reality. Any other

15

course can only create a holocaust from which no nation would ever recover. I am well aware of the vast chasms that lie between us and the Iron Curtain countries, but the first priority of this administration will be to build unshakeable bridges across those chasms.'

His words rang out with a deep, heartfelt sincerity. *He means it,* Ben Cohn thought. *I hope no one assassinates the bastard.*

In Junction City, Kansas it was a pot-bellied stove kind of day, bleak and raw, and snowing so hard that the visibility on Highway 6 was almost zero. Mary Ashley cautiously steered her old station wagon towards the centre of the highway, where the snowploughs had been at work. The storm was going to make her late for the class she was teaching. She drove slowly, careful not to let the car go into a skid.

From the car radio came the President's voice: '. . . are many in government as well as in private life who insist that America build more moats instead of bridges. My answer to that is that we can no longer afford to condemn ourselves or our children to a future threatened by global confrontations and nuclear war.'

Mary Ashley thought: *I'm glad I voted for him. Paul Ellison is going to make a great President.*

Her grip tightened on the wheel as the snow became a blinding white whirlwind.

In St Croix, a tropical sun was shining in a cloudless, azure sky, but Harry Lantz had no intention of going outside. He was having too much fun indoors. He was in bed, naked, sandwiched between the Dolly sisters. Lantz had empirical evidence that they were not truly sisters. Annette was a tall, natural brunette, and Sally was a tall, natural blonde. Not that Harry Lantz gave a damn whether they were blood relatives. What was important was that they were both expert at what they did, and what they were doing made Lantz groan aloud with pleasure.

At the far end of the motel room, the image of the President flickered on the television set.

'. . . because I believe that there is no problem that cannot be solved by genuine goodwill on both sides, the concrete wall around East Berlin and the Iron Curtain that surrounds the other Soviet Union satellite countries must come down.'

Sally stopped her activities long enough to ask, 'Do you want me to turn that fuckin' thing off, hon?'

'Leave it alone. I wanna hear what he has to say.'

Annette raised her head. 'Did you vote for him?'

Harry Lantz yelled, 'Hey, you two! Get back to work . . .'

16

'As you are aware, three years ago, upon the death of Romania's President, Nicolae Ceausescu, Romania broke off diplomatic relations with the United States. I want to inform you now that we have approached the government of Romania and its President, Alexandros Ionescu, and he has agreed to re-establish diplomatic relations with our country.'

There was a cheer from the crowd on Pennsylvania Avenue.

Harry Lantz sat upright so suddenly that Annette's teeth sank into his penis. 'Jesus Christ!' Lantz screamed. 'I've already been circumcised! What the fuck are you trying to do?'

'What did you move for, hon?'

Lantz did not hear her. His eyes were glued to the television set.

'One of our first official acts,' the President was saying, 'will be to send an Ambassador to Romania. And that is merely the beginning . . .'

In Bucharest, it was evening. The winter weather had turned unexpectedly mild and the streets of the late marketplaces were crowded with citizens lined up to shop in the unseasonably warm weather.

Romanian President Alexandros Ionescu sat in his office in Peles, the old palace, on Calea Victoriei, surrounded by half a dozen aides, listening to the broadcast on a short-wave radio.

'. . . I have no intention of stopping there,' the American President was saying. 'Albania broke off all diplomatic relations with the United States in 1946. I intend to re-establish those ties. In addition, I intend to strengthen our diplomatic relations with Bulgaria, with Czechoslovakia, and with East Germany.'

Over the radio came the sounds of cheers and applause.

'Sending our Ambassador to Romania is the beginning of a worldwide people-to-people movement. Let us never forget that all mankind shares a common origin, common problems, and a common ultimate fate. Let us remember that the problems we share are greater than the problems that divide us, and that what divides us is of our own making.'

In a heavily guarded villa in Neuilly, a suburb of Paris, the Romanian revolutionary leader, Marin Groza, was watching the President on Chaine 2 Television.

'. . . I promise you now, that I will do my best, and that I will seek out the best in others . . .'

The applause lasted fully five minutes.

Marin Groza said thoughtfully, 'I think our time has come, Lev. He really means it.'

Lev Pasternak, his security chief, replied, 'Won't this help Ionescu?'

17

Marin Groza shook his head. 'Ionescu is a tyrant, so in the end, nothing will help him. But I must be very careful with my timing. I failed when I tried to overthrow Ceausescu. I must not fail again.'

Pete Connors was not drunk – not as drunk as he intended to get. He had finished almost a fifth of Scotch when Nancy, the secretary he lived with, said, 'Don't you think you've had enough, Pete?' He smiled and slapped her.

'Our President's talkin'. You gotta show some respect.' He turned to look at the image on the television set. 'You communist son-of-a-bitch,' he yelled at the screen. 'This is my country, and the CIA's not gonna let you give it away. We're gonna stop you, Charlie. You can bet your ass on it.'

2

Paul Ellison said, 'I'm going to need a lot of help from you, old friend.'

'You'll get it,' Stanton Rogers replied quietly.

They were seated in the Oval Office, the President at his desk with the American flag behind him. It was their first meeting together in this office, and President Ellison was uncomfortable.

If Stanton hadn't made that one mistake, Paul Ellison thought, *he would be sitting at this desk instead of me.*

As though reading his mind, Stanton Rogers said, 'I have a confession to make. The day you were nominated for the Presidency, I was as jealous as hell, Paul. It was *my* dream, and you were living it. But do you know something? I finally came to realize that if I couldn't sit in that chair, there was no one else in the world I would want to sit there but you. That chair suits you.'

Paul Ellison smiled at his friend and said, 'To tell you the truth, Stan, this room scares the hell out of me. I feel the ghosts of Washington and Lincoln and Jefferson.'

'We've also had Presidents who –'

'I know. But it's the great ones we have to try to live up to.'

He pressed the button on his desk, and seconds later a white-jacketed steward came into the room.

'Yes, Mr President?'

Paul Ellison turned to Rogers. 'Coffee?'

'Sounds good.'

'Want anything with it?'

'No, thanks. Barbara wants me to watch my waistline.'

The President nodded to Henry, the steward, and he quietly left the room.

Barbara. She had surprised everyone. The gossip around Washington was that the marriage would not last out the first year. But it had been almost fifteen years now, and it was a success. Stanton Rogers had built up a prestigious law practice in Washington, and Barbara had earned the reputation of being a gracious hostess.

Paul Ellison rose and began to pace. 'My people-to-people speech seems to have caused quite an uproar. I suppose you've seen all the newspapers.'

Stanton Rogers shrugged. 'You know how they are. They love to build up heroes so they can knock them down.'

'Frankly, I don't give a damn what the papers say. I'm interested in what *people* are saying.'

'Quite candidly, you're putting the fear of God into a lot of people, Paul. The armed forces are against your plan, and some powerful movers and shakers would like to see it fail.'

'It's not going to fail.' He leaned back in his chair. 'Do you know the biggest problem with the world today? There are no more statesmen. Countries are being run by politicians. There was a time not too long ago when this earth was peopled with giants. Some were good, and some were evil – but, by God, they were giants. Roosevelt and Churchill, Hitler and Mussolini, Charles de Gaulle and Joseph Stalin. Why did they all live at that one particular time? Why aren't there any statesmen today?'

'It's pretty hard to be a world giant on a twenty-one inch screen.'

The door opened and the steward appeared, bearing a silver tray with a pot of coffee and two cups, each imprinted with the Presidential seal. He skilfully poured the coffee. 'Can I get you something else, Mr President?'

'No. That's it, Henry. Thank you.'

The President waited until the steward had gone. 'I want to talk to you about finding the right Ambassador to Romania.'

'Right.'

'I don't have to tell you how important this is. I want you to move on it as quickly as possible.'

Stanton Rogers took a sip of his coffee and rose to his feet. 'I'll get State on it right away.'

*

In the little suburb of Neuilly, it was 2 a.m. Marin Groza's villa lay in ebon darkness, the moon nested in a thick layer of storm clouds. The streets were hushed at this hour, with only the sound of an occasional passer-by rippling the silence. A black-clad figure moved noiselessly through the trees towards the brick wall that surrounded the villa. Over one shoulder he carried a rope and a blanket, and in his arms was cradled an Uzi with a silencer and a dart gun. When he reached the wall, he stopped and listened. He waited, motionless, for five minutes. Finally, satisfied, he uncoiled the nylon rope and tossed up the scaling hook attached to the end of it until it caught on the far edge of the wall. Swiftly, the man began to climb. When he reached the top of the wall, he flung the blanket across it to protect himself against the poisoned-tip metal spikes embedded on top. He stopped again to listen. He reversed the hook, shifting the rope to the inside of the wall, and slid down into the grounds. He checked the balisong at his waist; the deadly Filipino folding knife that could be flicked open or closed with one hand.

The attack dogs would be next. The intruder crouched there, waiting for them to pick up his scent. There were three Dobermans, trained to

20

kill. But they were only the first obstacle. The grounds and the villa were filled with electronic devices, and continuously monitored by television cameras. All mail and packages were received at the gatehouse and opened there by the guards. The doors of the villa were bomb-proof. The villa had its own water supply, and Marin Groza had a food taster. The villa was impregnable. Supposedly. The figure in black was here this night to prove that it was not.

He heard the sounds of the dogs rushing at him before he saw them. They came flying out of the darkness, charging at his throat. There were two of them. He aimed the dart gun and shot the nearest one on his left first, and then the one on his right, dodging out of the way of their hurtling bodies. He spun around, alert for the third dog, and when it came, he fired again, and then there was only stillness.

The intruder knew where the sonic traps were buried in the ground, and he skirted them. He silently glided through the areas of the grounds that the television cameras did not cover, and in less than two minutes after he had gone over the wall, he was at the back door of the villa.

As he reached for the handle of the door, he was caught in the sudden glare of half a dozen floodlights. A voice called out, 'Freeze! Drop your gun and raise your hands.'

The figure in black carefully dropped his gun and looked up. There were half a dozen men spread out on the roof, with a variety of weapons pointed at him.

The man in black growled, 'What the fuck took you so long? I never should have got this far.'

'You didn't,' the head guard informed him. 'We started tracking you before you got over the wall.'

Lev Pasternak was not mollified. 'Then you should have stopped me sooner. I could have been on a suicide mission with a load of grenades or a god-damn mortar. I want a meeting of the entire staff tomorrow morning, eight o'clock sharp. The dogs have been stunned. Have someone keep an eye on them until they wake up.'

Lev Pasternak prided himself on being the best security guard in the world. He had been a pilot in the Israeli six-day war and, after the war, had become a top agent in Mossad, one of Israeli's five secret services.

He would never forget the morning, two years earlier, when his colonel had called him into his office.

'Lev, someone wants to borrow you for a few weeks.'

'I hope it's a blonde,' Lev quipped.

'It's Marin Groza.'

Mossad had a complete file on the Romanian dissident. Groza had been the leader of a popular Romanian movement to depose Alexandros Ionescu and was about to stage a coup when he had been betrayed by one of his men. More than two dozen underground fighters had been executed, and Groza had barely escaped the country with his

21

life. France had given him sanctuary. Ionescu denounced Marin Groza as a traitor to his country and put a price on his head. So far half a dozen attempts to assassinate Groza had failed, but he had been wounded in the latest attack.

'What does he want with me?' Pasternak asked. 'He has government protection.'

'Not good enough. He needs someone to set up a fool-proof security system. He came to us. I recommended you.'

'I'd have to go to France?'

'It will only take you a few weeks.'

'I don't –'

'Lev, we're talking about a *mensch*. He's the guy in the white hat. Our information is that he has enough popular support in his home country to knock over Ionescu. When the timing is right, he'll make his move. Meanwhile, we have to keep the man alive.'

Lev Pasternak thought about it. 'A few weeks, you said?'

'That's all.'

The Colonel had been wrong about the time, but he had been right about Marin Groza. He was a thin, fragile-looking man with an ascetic air about him and a face etched with sorrow. He had an aquiline nose, a firm chin, and a broad forehead, topped by a spray of white hair. He had deep, black eyes, and when he spoke, they blazed with passion.

'I don't give a damn whether I live or die,' he told Lev at their first meeting. 'We're all going to die. It's the *when* that I'm concerned about. I have to stay alive for another year or two. That's all the time I need to drive Ionescu out of my country.' He ran his hand absently across a livid scar on his cheek. 'No man has the right to enslave a country. We have to free Romania and let the people decide their own fate.'

Lev Pasternak went to work on the security system at the villa in Neuilly. He used some of his own men, and the outsiders he hired were checked out thoroughly. Every single piece of equipment was state-of-the-art.

Pasternak saw the Romanian rebel leader every day, and the more time he spent with him, the more he came to admire him. When Marin Groza asked Pasternak to stay on as his security chief, Pasternak did not hesitate.

'I'll do it,' he said, 'until you're ready to make your move. Then I will return to Israel.'

They struck a deal.

At irregular intervals, Pasternak staged surprise attacks on the villa, testing its security. Now, he thought: *Some of the guards are getting careless. I'll have to replace them.*

22

He walked through the hallways, carefully checking the heat sensors, the electronic warning systems, and the infrared beams at the sill of each door. As he reached Marin Groza's bedroom, he heard a loud crash, and a moment later Groza began screaming out in agony.

Lev Pasternak passed Groza's room and kept walking.

3

Headquarters for the Central Intelligence Agency is located in Langley, Virginia, seven miles southwest of Washington, D.C. At the approach road to the Agency is a flashing red beacon on top of a gate. The gatehouse is guarded twenty-four hours a day, and authorized visitors are issued coloured badges giving them access only to the particular department with which they have business. Outside the grey seven-storey headquarters building, whimsically called the 'Toy Factory', is a large statue of Nathan Hale. Inside, on the ground floor, a glass corridor wall faces an inner courtyard with a landscaped garden dotted with magnolia trees. Above the reception desk a verse is carved in marble:

> And ye shall know the truth and
> the truth shall set ye free.

The public is never admitted inside the building, and there are no facilities for visitors. For those who wish to enter the compound 'black' – unseen – there is a tunnel that emerges onto a foyer facing a mahogany elevator door, watched around the clock by a squad of grey-flannelled sentries.

In the seventh-floor conference room, guarded by security aides armed with snub-nosed .38 revolvers under their business suits, the Monday morning executive staff meeting was under way. Seated around the large, oak table were Ned Tillingast, Director of the CIA; General Oliver Brooks, Army Chief of Staff; Secretary of State Floyd Baker; Pete Connors, Chief of Counterintelligence; and Stanton Rogers.

Ned Tillingast, the CIA Director, was in his sixties, a cold, taciturn man, burdened with maleficent secrets. There is a light branch and a dark branch of the CIA. The dark branch handles clandestine operations, and for the past seven years, Tillingast had been in charge of the 4,500 employees working in that section.

General Oliver Brooks was a West Point soldier who conducted his personal and professional life by the book. He was a company man, and the company he worked for was the United States Army.

Floyd Baker, the Secretary of State, was an anachronism, a throwback to an earlier era. He was of southern vintage, tall, silver-haired and distinguished-looking, with an old-fashioned gallantry. He was a man who wore mental spats. He owned a chain of influential newspapers

24

around the country, and was reputed to be enormously wealthy. There was no one in Washington with a keener political sense, and Baker's antennae were constantly tuned to the changing signals around the halls of Congress.

Pete Connors was black-Irish, a stubborn, bulldog of a man, hard-drinking and fearless. This was his last year with the CIA. He faced compulsory retirement in June. Connors was chief of the counterintelligence staff, the most secret, highly compartmentalized branch of the CIA. He had worked his way up through the various intelligence divisions, and had been around in the good old days when CIA agents were the golden boys. Pete Connors had been a golden boy himself. He had taken part in the coup that restored the Shah to the Peacock Throne in Iran, and he had been involved in Operation Mongoose, the attempt to topple Castro's government, in 1961.

'After the Bay of Pigs, everything changed,' Pete mourned. The length of his diatribe usually depended upon how drunk he was. 'The bleeding hearts attacked us on the front pages of every newspaper in the world. They called us a bunch of lying, sneaking clowns who couldn't get out of our own way. Some anti-CIA bastard published the names of our agents, and Dick Welch, our Chief of Station in Athens, was murdered.'

Pete Connors had gone through three miserable marriages because of the pressures and secrecy of his work, but as far as he was concerned, no sacrifice was too great to make for his country.

Now, in the middle of the meeting, his face was red with anger. 'If we let the President get away with his fucking people-to-people programme, he's going to give the country away. It has to be stopped. We can't allow –'

Floyd Baker interrupted. 'The President has been in office less than a week. We're all here to carry out his policies and –'

'I'm not here to hand over my country to the damned commies, Mister. The President never even mentioned his plan before his speech. He sprang it on all of us. We didn't have a chance to get together a rebuttal.'

'Perhaps that's what he had in mind,' Baker suggested.

Pete Connors stared at him. 'By God, you agree with it!'

'He's my President,' Floyd Baker said firmly. 'Just as he's yours.'

Ned Tillingast turned to Stanton Rogers. 'Connors has a point. The President is actually planning to *invite* Romania, Albania, Bulgaria, and the other communist countries to send their spies here posing as cultural attachés and chauffeurs and secretaries and maids. We're spending billions of dollars to guard the back door, and the President wants to throw open the front door.'

General Brooks nodded agreement. 'I wasn't consulted, either. In my opinion, the President's plan could damn well destroy this country.'

Stanton Rogers said, 'Gentlemen, some of us may disagree with the

President, but let's not forget that the people voted for Paul Ellison to run this country.' His eyes flicked across the men seated around him. 'We're all part of the President's team and we have to follow his lead and support him in every way we can.' His words were followed by a reluctant silence. 'All right, then. The President wants an immediate update on the current situation in Romania. Everything you have.'

'Including our covert stuff?' Pete Connors asked.

'Everything. Give it to me straight. What's the situation in Romania with Alexandros Ionescu?'

'Ionescu's riding high in the saddle,' Ned Tillingast replied. 'Once he got rid of the Ceausescu family, all of Ceausescu's allies were assassinated, jailed, or exiled. Since he seized power, Ionescu's been bleeding the country dry. The people hate his guts.'

'What about the prospects for a revolution?'

Tillingast said, 'Ah. That's rather interesting. Remember a couple of years back when Marin Groza almost toppled the Ionescu government?'

'Yes. Groza got out of the country by the skin of his butt.'

'With our help. Our information is that there's a popular groundswell to bring him back. Groza would be good for Romania and, if he got in, it would be good for us. We're keeping a close watch on the situation.'

Stanton Rogers turned to the Secretary of State. 'Do you have that list of candidates for the Romanian post?'

Floyd Baker opened a leather attaché case, took some papers from it, and handed a copy to Rogers. 'These are our top prospects. They're all qualified career diplomats. Each one of them has been cleared. No security problems, no financial problems, no embarrassing skeletons in the closet.'

As Stanton Rogers took the list, the Secretary of State added, 'Naturally, the State Department favours a career diplomat, rather than a political appointee. Someone who's been trained for this kind of job. In this situation, particularly. Romania is an extremely sensitive post. It has to be handled very carefully.'

'I agree.' Stanton Rogers rose to his feet. 'I'll discuss these names with the President and get back to you. He's anxious to fill the appointment as quickly as possible.'

As the others got up to leave, Ned Tillingast said, 'Stay here, Pete. I want to talk to you.'

When Tillingast and Connors were alone, Tillingast said, 'You came on pretty strong, Pete.'

'But I'm right,' Pete Connors said stubbornly. 'The President is trying to sell out the country. What are we supposed to do?'

'Keep your mouth shut.'

'Ned, we're trained to find the enemy and kill him. What if the enemy is behind our lines – sitting in the Oval Office?'

'Be careful. Be very careful.'

Tillingast had been around longer than Pete Connors. He had been

26

a member of Wild Bill Donovan's OSS before it became the CIA. He, too, hated what the bleeding hearts in Congress were doing to the organization he loved. In fact, there was a deep split within the ranks of the CIA between the hard-liners and those who believed the Russian bear could be tamed into a harmless pet. *We have to fight for every single dollar*, Tillingast thought. *In Moscow, the Komitet Gosudarstvennoi Bezopasnosti – the KGB – trains a thousand agents at a time.*

Ned Tillingast had recruited Pete Connors out of college, and Connors had turned out to be one of the best. But in the last few years, Connors had become a cowboy – a little too independent, a little too quick on the trigger. Dangerous.

'Pete – have you heard anything about an underground organization calling itself Patriots for Freedom?' Tillingast asked.

Connors frowned. 'No. Can't say that I have. Who are they?'

'So far they're just a rumour. All I have is smoke. See if you can get a lead on them.'

'Will do.'

An hour later, Pete Connors was making a phone call from a public booth at Hain's Point.

'I have a message for Odin.'

'This is Odin,' General Oliver Brooks said.

Riding back to the office in his limousine, Stanton Rogers opened the envelope containing the names of the candidates for the ambassadorship and studied them. It was an excellent list. The Secretary of State had done his homework. The candidates had all served in Eastern and Western European countries, and a few of them had additional experience in the Far East or Africa. *The President's going to be pleased*, Stanton thought.

*

'They're dinosaurs,' Paul Ellison snapped. He threw the list down on his desk. 'Every one of them.'

'Paul,' Stanton protested, 'these people are all experienced career diplomats.'

'And hide-bound by State Department tradition. You remember how we lost Romania three years ago? Our experienced career diplomat in Bucharest screwed up and we were out in the cold. The pin-striped boys worry me. They're all out to cover their asses. When I talked about a people-to-people programme, I meant every word of it. We need to make a positive impression on a country that at this moment is very wary of us.'

27

'But if you put an amateur in there – someone with no experience – you're taking a big risk.'

'Maybe we need someone with a different kind of experience. Romania is going to be a test case, Stan. A pilot run for my whole programme, if you will.' He hesitated. 'I'm not kidding myself. My credibility is on the line. I know that there are a lot of powerful people who don't want to see this work. If it fails, I'm going to get cut off at the knees. I'll have to forget about Bulgaria, Albania, Czechoslovakia, and the rest of the Iron Curtain countries. And I don't intend for that to happen.'

'I can check out some of our political appointees who –'

President Ellison shook his head. 'Same problem. I want someone with a completely fresh point of view. Someone who can thaw the ice. The opposite of the ugly American.'

Stanton Rogers was studying the President, puzzled. 'Paul – I get the impression that you already have someone in mind. Do you?'

Paul Ellison took a cigar from the humidor on his desk and lit it. 'As a matter of fact,' he said slowly, 'I think I may have.'

'Who is he?'

'She. Did you happen to see the article in the current issue of *Foreign Affairs* called "Détente Now"?'

'Yes.'

'What did you think of it?'

'I thought it was interesting. The author believes that we're in a position to try to seduce the communist countries into coming into our camp by offering them economic aid –' He broke off. 'It was a lot like your inaugural speech.'

'Only it was written six months earlier. She's published brilliant articles in *Commentary* and *Public Affairs*. Last year I read a book of hers on Eastern European politics, and I must admit it helped clarify some of my ideas.'

'All right. So she agrees with your theories. That's no reason to consider her for a post as impor –'

'Stan – she went further than my theory. She outlined a detailed plan that's fascinating. She wants to take the four major world economic pacts and combine them.'

'How can we –?'

'It would take time, but it could be done. Look, you know that in 1949, the Eastern bloc countries formed a pact for mutual economic assistance, called COMECON, and in 1958 the other European countries formed the EEC – the Common Market.'

'Right.'

'We have the Organization for Economic Cooperation and Development, which includes the United States, some Western bloc countries and Yugoslavia. And don't forget that the third world countries have formed a non-aligned movement that excludes us.' The President's voice was charged with excitement. 'Think of the possibilities. If we could combine all these plans and form one big marketplace – my God, it could be awesome! It would mean *real* world trade. And it could bring peace.'

Stanton Rogers said cautiously, 'It's an interesting idea, but it's a long way off.'

'You know the old Chinese saying, "A journey of a thousand miles starts with but a single step . . ."'

'She's an amateur, Paul.'

'Some of our finest ambassadors have been amateurs. Anne Armstrong, the former Ambassador to Great Britain was an educator with no political experience. Perle Mesta was appointed to Denmark, Clare Boothe Luce was Ambassador to Italy. John Gavin, an actor, was the Ambassador to Mexico. One-third of our current ambassadors are what you call "amateurs".'

'But you don't know anything about this woman.'

'Except that she's damned bright, and that we're on the same wavelength. I want you to find out everything you can about her.' He picked up a copy of *Foreign Affairs* and glanced at the table of contents. 'Her name is Mary Ashley.'

*

Two days later, President Ellison and Stanton Rogers breakfasted together.

'I got the information you asked for.' Stanton Rogers pulled a paper from his pocket. 'Mary Elizabeth Ashley, Twenty-Seven Old Milford Road, Junction City, Kansas. Age, almost thirty-five, married to Dr Edward Ashley – two children, Beth twelve, and Tim ten. Chairman of the Junction City Chapter of the League of Women Voters. Assistant Professor, East European Political Science, Kansas State University. Grandfather born in Romania.' He looked up. 'The more I've thought about this, the more sense it makes. She probably knows more about Romania than most ambassadors know about the countries they're going to serve in.'

'I'm glad you feel that way, Stan. I'd like to have a full security check run on her.'

'I'll see that it's done.'

29

4

'I disagree, Professor Ashley.'

Barry Dylan, the brightest and youngest of the students in Mary Ashley's political science seminar, looked around defiantly. 'Alexandros Ionescu is worse than Ceausescu ever was.'

'Can you give us some facts to back up that statement?' Mary Ashley asked.

There were twelve graduate students in the seminar being held in Kansas State University's Dykstra Hall. The students were seated in a semicircle facing Mary. The waiting lists to get into her classes were longer than any other professor's at the University. She was a superb teacher, with an easy sense of humour and a warmth that made being around her a pleasure. She had an oval face that changed from interesting to beautiful, depending on her mood. She had the high cheekbones of a model and almond-shaped, hazel eyes. Her hair was dark and thick. She had a figure that made her female students envious, and the males fantasize, yet she was unaware of how beautiful she was.

Barry was wondering if she was happy with her husband. He reluctantly brought his attention back to the problem at hand.

'Well, when Ionescu took over Romania, he cracked down on all the pro-Groza elements and re-established a hardline, pro-Soviet position. Even Ceausescu wasn't that bad.'

Another student spoke up. 'Then why is President Ellison so anxious to establish diplomatic relations with him?'

'Because we want to woo him into the Western orbit.'

'Remember,' Mary said, 'Nicolae Ceausescu also had a foot in both camps. What year did that start?'

Barry again. 'In 1960 when Romania took sides in the dispute between Russia and China to show its independence in international affairs.'

'What about Romania's current relationship with the other Warsaw Pact countries, and Russia in particular?' Mary asked.

'I'd say it's stronger now.'

Another voice. 'I don't agree. Romania criticized Russia's invasion of Afghanistan, and they criticized the Russians' arrangement with the EEC. Also, Professor Ashley –'

The bell sounded. The time was up.

Mary said, 'Monday we'll talk about the basic factors that affect the Soviet attitude towards Eastern Europe, and we'll discuss the possible consequences of President Ellison's plan to penetrate the Eastern bloc. Have a good weekend.'

Mary watched the students rise and head for the door.

'You, too, Professor.'

Mary Ashley loved the give and take of the seminars. History and geography came alive in the heated discussions among the bright young graduate students. Foreign names and places became real, and historical events took on flesh and blood. This was her fifth year on the faculty of Kansas State University, and teaching still excited her. She taught five political science classes a year in addition to the graduate seminars, and each of them dealt with the Soviet Union and its satellite countries. At times she felt like a fraud. *I've never been to any of the countries I teach about*, she thought. *I've never even been outside the United States.*

Mary Ashley had been born in Junction City, as had her parents. The only member of her family who had known Europe was her grandfather, who had come from the small Romanian village of Voronet.

Mary had planned a trip abroad when she received her Master's Degree, but that summer she met Edward Ashley, and the European trip had turned into a three-day honeymoon at Waterville, 55 miles from Junction City, where Edward was taking care of a critical heart patient.

'We really must travel next year,' Mary said to Edward shortly after they were married. 'I'm dying to see Rome and Paris and Romania.'

'So am I. It's a date. Next summer.'

But that following summer Beth was born, and Edward was caught up in his work at the Geary Community Hospital. Two years later, Tim was born. Mary had taken her Ph.D. and gone back to teaching at Kansas State University, and somehow the years had melted away. Except for brief trips to Chicago, Atlanta and Denver, Mary had never been out of the State of Kansas.

One day, she promised herself. *One day . . .*

Mary gathered her notes together and glanced out of the window. Frost had painted the window a winter grey, and it was beginning to snow again. Mary put on her lined leather coat and a red, woollen scarf and headed towards the Vattier Street entrance, where she parked her car.

The campus was huge, 315 acres, dotted with 87 buildings, including laboratories, theatres and chapels, amid a rustic setting of trees and grass. From a distance, the brown limestone buildings of the University resembled ancient castles, with turrets at the top, ready to repel enemy hordes. As Mary passed Denison Hall, a stranger with a Nikon camera was walking towards her. He aimed the camera at the building and

31

pressed the shutter. Mary was in the foreground of the picture. *I should have got out of his way*, she thought. *I've spoiled his picture.*

One hour later, the negative of the photograph was on its way to Washington, D.C.

Every town has its own distinctive rhythm, a life pulse that springs from the people and the land. Junction City, in Geary County, is a farm community (population 20,381), 130 miles west of Kansas City, priding itself on being the geographical centre of the continental United States. It has a newspaper – the *Daily Union* – a radio station, and a television station. The downtown shopping area consists of a series of scattered stores and gas stations along 6th Street and on Washington. There is a Penney's, the First National Bank, a Domino Pizza, Flower Jeweller's, and a Woolworth's. There are fast food chains, a bus station, a menswear shop, and a liquor store – the type of establishments that are xeroxed in hundreds of small towns across the United States. But the residents of Junction City loved it for its bucolic peace and tranquillity. On weekdays, at least. Weekends, Junction City became the Rest and Recreation Centre for the soldiers at nearby Fort Riley.

Mary Ashley stopped to shop for dinner at Dillon's Market on her way home and then headed north towards Old Milford Road, a lovely residential area overlooking a lake. Oak and elm trees lined the left side of the road, while on the right side were beautiful houses variously made of stone, brick or wood.

The Ashley house was a two-storey stone house set in the middle of gently rolling hills. The house had been bought by Dr Edward Ashley and his bride thirteen years earlier. It consisted of a large living room, a dining room, library, breakfast room and kitchen downstairs and a master suite and two additional bedrooms upstairs.

'It's awfully large for just two people,' Mary Ashley had protested.

Edward had taken her into his arms and held her close. 'Who said it's going to be for only two people?'

When Mary arrived home from the University, Tim and Beth were waiting to greet her.

'Guess what?' Tim said. 'We're going to have our pictures in the paper!'

'Help me put away the groceries,' Mary said. 'What paper?'

'The man didn't say, but he took our pictures and he said we'd hear from him.'

Mary stopped and turned to look at her son. 'Did this man say why?'

'No,' Tim said, 'but he sure had a nifty Nikon.'

On Sunday, Mary celebrated – although that was not the word that sprang to mind – her thirty-fifth birthday. Edward had arranged for a surprise party for her at the country club. Their neighbours, Florence and Douglas Schiffer, and four other couples were waiting for her. Edward was as delighted as a small child at the look of amazement on Mary's face when she walked into the club and saw the festive table and the happy birthday banner. She did not have the heart to tell him that she had known about the party for the past two weeks. She adored Edward. *And why not? Who wouldn't?* He was attractive and intelligent and caring. His grandfather and father had been doctors, and it had never occurred to Edward to be anything else. He was the best surgeon in Junction City, a good father, and a wonderful husband.

As Mary blew out the candles on her birthday cake, she looked across at Edward and thought: *How lucky can a lady be?*

Monday morning, Mary awoke with a hangover. There had been a lot of champagne toasts the night before, and she was not used to drinking alcohol. It took an effort to get out of bed. *That champagne done me in. Never again*, she promised herself.

She eased her way downstairs and gingerly set about preparing breakfast for the children, trying to ignore the pounding in her head.

'Champagne,' Mary groaned, 'is France's vengeance against us.'

Beth walked into the room carrying an armful of books. 'Who are you talking to, Mother?'

'Myself.'

'That's weird.'

'When you're right, you're right.' Mary put a box of cereal on the table. 'I bought a new cereal for you. You're going to like it.'

Beth sat down at the kitchen table and studied the label on the cereal box. 'I can't eat this. You're trying to kill me.'

'Don't put any ideas in my head,' her mother cautioned. 'Would you please eat your breakfast?'

Tim, her ten-year-old, ran into the kitchen. He slid into a chair at the table and said, 'I'll have bacon and eggs.'

'Whatever happened to good morning?' Mary asked.

'Good morning. I'll have bacon and eggs.'

'Please.'

'Aw, come on, Mom. I'm going to be late for school.'

'I'm glad you mentioned that. Mrs Reynolds called me. You're failing maths. What do you say to that?'

'It figures.'

'Tim, is that supposed to be a joke?'

'I personally don't think it's funny,' Beth sniffed.

He made a face at his sister. 'If you want funny, look in the mirror.'

'That's enough,' Mary said. 'Behave yourselves.'

'Her headache was getting worse.

Tim asked, 'Can I go to the skating rink after school, Mom?'

'You're already skating on thin ice. You're to come right home and study. How do you think it looks for a college professor to have a son who's failing maths?'

'It looks okay. You don't teach maths.'

They talk about the terrible twos, Mary thought grimly. *What about the terrible nines, tens, elevens and twelves?*

Beth said, 'Did Tim tell you he got a "D" in spelling?'

He glared at his sister. 'Haven't you ever heard of Mark Twain?'

'What does Mark Twain have to do with this?' Mary asked.

'Mark Twain said he has no respect for a man who can only spell a word one way.'

We can't win, Mary thought. *They're smarter than we are.*

She had packed a lunch for each of them, but she was concerned about Beth, who was on some kind of crazy new diet.

'Please, Beth, eat all of your lunch today.'

'If it has no artificial preservatives. I'm not going to let the greed of the food industry ruin my health.'

Whatever happened to the good old days of junk food? Mary wondered.

Tim plucked a loose paper from one of Beth's notebooks. 'Look at this!' he yelled. 'Dear Beth, let's sit together during study period. I thought of you all day yesterday and –'

'Give that back to me!' Beth screamed. 'That's mine.' She made a grab for Tim, and he jumped out of her reach.

He read the signature at the bottom of the note. 'Hey! It's signed Virgil. I thought you were in love with Arnold.'

Beth snatched the note away from him. 'What would you know about love?' Mary's twelve-year-old daughter demanded. 'You're a child.'

The pounding in Mary's head was becoming unbearable.

'Kids – give me a break.'

She heard the horn of the school bus outside. Tim and Beth started towards the door.

'Wait! You haven't eaten your breakfasts,' Mary said.

She followed them out into the hallway.

'No time, Mother. Got to go.'

''Bye, Mom.'

'It's freezing outside. Put on your coats and scarves.'

'I can't. I lost my scarf,' Tim said.

And they were gone. Mary felt drained. *Motherhood is living in the eye of a hurricane.*

She looked up as Edward came down the stairs, and she felt a glow. *Even after all these years*, Mary thought, *he's still the most attractive man I've ever known.* It was his gentleness that had first caught Mary's interest. His eyes were a soft grey, reflecting a warm intelligence, but they could turn into twin blazes when he became impassioned about something.

'Morning, darling.' He gave her a kiss. They walked into the kitchen.

'Sweetheart – would you do me a favour?'

'Sure, beautiful. Anything.'

'I want to sell the children.'

'Both of them?'

'Both of them.'

'When?'

'Today.'

'Who'd buy them?'

'Strangers. They've reached the age where I can't do anything right. Beth has become a health food freak, and your son is turning into a world-class dunce.'

Edward said thoughtfully, 'Maybe they're not our kids.'

'I hope not. I'm making oatmeal for you.'

He looked at his watch. 'Sorry, darling. No time. I'm due in surgery in half an hour. Hank Cates got tangled up in some machinery. He may lose a few fingers.'

'Isn't he too old to still be farming?'

'Don't let him hear you say that.'

Mary knew that Hank Cates had not paid her husband's bills in three years. Like most of the farmers in the community, Hank Cates was suffering from the low farm prices and the Farm Credit Administration's indifferent attitude towards the farmers. A lot of them were losing farms they had worked on all of their lives. Edward never pressed any of his patients for money, and many of them paid him with crops. The Ashleys had a cellar full of corn, potatoes and wheat. One farmer had offered to give Edward a cow in payment, but when Edward told Mary about it, she said, 'For heaven's sake, tell him the treatment is on the house.'

Mary looked at her husband now and thought again: *How lucky I am*.

'Okay,' she said. 'I may decide to keep the kids. I like their father a lot.'

'To tell you the truth, I'm rather fond of their mother.' He took her in his arms and held her close. 'Happy Birthday, plus one.'

'Do you still love me now that I'm an older woman?'

'I like older women.'

'Thanks.' Mary suddenly remembered something. 'I've got to get home early today and prepare dinner. It's our turn to have the Schiffers over.'

Bridge with their neighbours was a Monday night ritual. The fact that Douglas Schiffer was a doctor and worked with Edward at the hospital made them even closer.

Mary and Edward left the house together, bowing their heads against the relentless wind. Edward strapped himself into his Ford Granada, and watched Mary as she got behind the wheel of the station wagon.

'The highway is probably icy,' Edward called. 'Drive carefully.'

'You, too, darling.'

She blew him a kiss, and the two cars drove away from the house, Edward heading towards the hospital, and Mary driving towards the town of Manhattan, where the University was located, 16 miles away.

Two men in an automobile parked half a block from the Ashley house watched the cars leave. They waited until the vehicles were out of sight.

'Let's go.'

They drove up to the house next door to the Ashleys. Rex Olds, the driver, sat in the car while his companion walked up to the front door and rang the bell. The door was opened by an attractive brunette in her middle thirties.

'Yes? Can I help you?'

'Mrs Douglas Schiffer?'

'Yes . . . ?'

The man reached into his jacket pocket and pulled out an identification card. 'My name is Donald Zamlock. I'm with the Security Agency of the State Department.'

'Good God! Don't tell me Doug has robbed a bank!'

The agent smiled politely. 'No, ma'am. Not that we know of. I wanted to ask you a few questions about your neighbour, Mrs Ashley.'

She looked at him with sudden concern. 'Mary? What about her?'

'May I come in?'

'Yes. Of course.' Florence Schiffer led him into the living room. 'Sit down. Would you like some coffee?'

'No, thanks. I'll only take a few minutes of your time.'

'Why would you be asking about Mary?'

He smiled reassuringly. 'This is just a routine check. She's not suspected of any wrong-doing.'

'I should hope not,' Florence Schiffer said indignantly. 'Mary Ashley is one of the nicest persons you'll ever meet.' She added, '*Have* you met her?'

'No, ma'am. This visit is confidential, and I would appreciate it if you kept it that way. How long have you known Mrs Ashley?'

'About thirteen years. Since the day she moved in next door.'

'Would you say that you know Mrs Ashley well?'

'Of course I would. Mary's my closest friend. What –?'

'Do she and her husband get along well?'

'Next to Douglas and me, they're the happiest couple I've ever known.' She thought a moment. 'I take that back. They *are* the happiest couple I've ever known.'

'I understand Mrs Ashley has two children. A girl twelve and a boy ten?'

'That's right. Beth and Tim.'

'Would you say she's a good mother?'

'She's a *great* mother. What's – ?'

'Mrs Schiffer, in your opinion, is Mrs Ashley an emotionally stable person?'

'Of course she is.'

'She has no emotional problems that you are aware of?'

'Certainly not.'

'Does she drink?'

'No. She doesn't like alcohol.'

'What about drugs?'

'You've come to the wrong town, Mister. We don't have a drug problem in Junction City.'

'Mrs Ashley is married to a doctor?'

'Yes.'

'If she wanted to get drugs –'

'You're way off base. She doesn't do drugs. She doesn't snort, and she doesn't shoot up.'

He studied her a moment. 'You seem to know all the terminology.'

'I watch *Miami Vice*, like everybody else.' Florence Schiffer was getting angry. 'Do you have any more questions?'

'Mary Ashley's grandfather was born in Romania. Have you ever heard her discuss Romania?'

'Oh, once in a while she'll tell stories her grandfather told her about the old country. Her grandfather was born in Romania but he came over here when he was in his teens.'

'Have you ever heard Mrs Ashley express a negative opinion about the present Romanian government?'

'No. Not that I can remember.'

'One last question. Have you ever heard Mrs Ashley or Dr Ashley say anything against the United States government?'

'Absolutely not!'

'Then in your estimation, they're both loyal Americans?'

'You bet they are. Would you mind telling me – ?'

The man rose. 'I want to thank you for your time, Mrs Schiffer. And I'd like to impress upon you again that this matter is highly confidential. I would appreciate it if you didn't discuss it with anyone – not even your husband.'

A moment later he was out of the door. Florence Schiffer stood there staring after him. 'I don't believe this whole conversation took place,' she said aloud.

The two agents drove down Washington Street, heading north. They passed a billboard that read: 'Enjoy yourself in the land of Ah's.'

'Cute,' Rex Olds grunted.

They went by the Chamber of Commerce and the Royal Order of the Elks building, Irma's Pet Grooming and a bar called 'The Fat Chance'. The commercial buildings came to an abrupt end.

Donald Zamlock said, 'Jesus, the main street is only two blocks long. This isn't a town. It's a pit stop.'

Rex Olds said, 'To you it's a pit stop, and to me it's a pit stop, but to these people it's a town.'

Zamlock shook his head. 'It's probably a nice place to live, but I sure as hell wouldn't want to visit here.'

The sedan pulled up in front of the State Bank and Rex Olds went inside.

He returned twenty minutes later. 'Clean,' he said, getting into the car. 'The Ashleys have seven thousand dollars in the bank, a mortgage on their house, and they pay their bills on time. The president of the bank thinks the doctor is too soft-hearted to be a good businessman, but as far as he's concerned, he's a top credit risk.'

Zamlock looked at a clipboard at his side. 'Let's check out a few more names and get back to civilization before I begin to moo.'

Douglas Schiffer was normally a pleasant, easygoing man, but at the moment there was a grim expression on his face. The Schiffers and the Ashleys were in the middle of their weekly bridge game, and the Schiffers were 10,000 points behind. For the fourth time that evening, Florence Schiffer had reneged.

Douglas Schiffer slammed down his cards. 'Florence!' he exploded, 'which side are you playing on? Do you know how much we're down?'

'I'm sorry,' she said nervously. 'I – I just can't seem to concentrate.'

'Obviously,' her husband snorted.

'Is anything bothering you?' Edward Ashley asked Florence.

'I can't tell you.'

They all looked at her in surprise. 'What does *that* mean?' her husband asked.

Florence Schiffer took a deep breath. 'Mary – it's about you.'

'What about me?'

'You're in some sort of trouble, aren't you?'

Mary stared at her. 'Trouble? No. I – what makes you think that?'

'I'm not supposed to tell. I promised.'

'You promised who?' Edward asked.

'A federal agent from Washington. He was at the house this morning asking me all kinds of questions about Mary. He made her sound like some kind of international spy.'

'What kind of questions?' Edward demanded.

'Oh, you know. Was she a loyal American? Was she a good wife and mother? Was she on drugs?'

'Why the devil would they be asking you questions like that?'

'Wait a minute,' Mary said excitedly. 'I think I know. It's about my tenure.'

'What?' Florence asked.

'I'm up for tenure at the University. The University does some sensitive government research on campus, so I suppose they have to check everyone pretty thoroughly.'

'Well, thank God that's all it is.' Florence Schiffer breathed a sigh of relief. 'I thought they were going to lock you up.'

'I hope they do,' Mary smiled. 'At Kansas State.'

'Well, now that that's out of the way,' Douglas Schiffer said, 'can we get on with the game?' He turned to his wife. 'If you renege one more time, I'm going to put you over my knee.'

'Promises, promises.'

5

Abbeywood, England

'We are meeting under the usual rules,' the chairman announced. 'No records will be kept, this meeting will never be discussed, and we will refer to one another by the code names we have been assigned.'

There were eight men inside the library of the fifteenth-century Claymore Castle. Two armed men in plainclothes, bundled up in heavy overcoats, kept vigil outside, while a third man guarded the door to the library. The eight men inside the room had arrived at the site separately, a short time earlier.

The chairman continued. 'The Controller has received some disturbing information. Marin Groza is preparing a coup against Alexandros Ionescu. A group of senior army officers in Romania has decided to back Groza. This time he could very well be successful.'

Odin spoke up. 'How would that affect our plan?'

'It could destroy it. It would open too many bridges to the West.'

Freyr said, 'Then we must prevent it from happening.'

Balder asked, 'How?'

'We assassinate Groza,' the chairman replied.

'That's impossible. Ionescu's men have made half a dozen attempts that we know of, and they've all failed. His villa seems to be impregnable. Anyway, no one in this room can afford to be involved in an assassination attempt.'

'We wouldn't be directly involved,' the chairman said.

'Then how?'

'The Controller discovered a confidential dossier that concerns an international terrorist who's for hire.'

'Abul Abbas, the man who organized the hijacking of the *Achille Lauro*?'

'No. There's a new gun in town, gentlemen. A better one. He's called Angel.'

'Never heard of him,' Sigmund said.

'Exactly. His credentials are most impressive. According to the Controller's file, Angel was involved in the *Sikh Khalistan* assassination in India. He helped the *Macheteros* terrorists in Puerto Rico, and the *Khmer Rouge* in Cambodia. He's master-minded the assassination of half a dozen army officers in Israel and the Israelis have offered a million-dollar reward for him, dead or alive.'

'He sounds promising,' Thor said. 'Can we get him?'

'He's expensive. If he agrees to take the contract, it will cost us two million dollars.'

Freyr whistled, then shrugged. 'That can be handled. We'll take it from the general fund we've set up.'

'How do we get to this Angel person?' Sigmund asked.

'All his contacts are handled through his mistress, a woman named Neusa Muñez.'

'Where do we find her?'

'She lives in Argentina. Angel has set her up in an apartment in Buenos Aires.'

Thor said, 'What would the next step be? Who would get in touch with her for us?'

The chairman replied, 'The Controller has suggested a man named Harry Lantz.'

'That name sounds familiar.'

The chairman said drily, 'Yes. He's been in the newspapers. Harry Lantz is a maverick. He was thrown out of the CIA for setting up his own drug business in Viet Nam. While he was with the CIA, he did a tour in South America, so he knows the territory. He'd be a perfect go-between.' He paused. 'I suggest we take a vote. All those in favour of hiring Angel please raise your hands.'

Eight well-manicured hands went into the air.

'Then it's settled.' The chairman rose. 'The meeting is adjourned. Please observe the usual precautions.'

It was a Monday, and Constable Leslie Hanson was having a picnic in the greenhouse on the castle's grounds, where he had no right to be. He was not alone, he later had to explain to his superiors. It was warm in the greenhouse, and his companion, Annie, a buxom country lass, had prevailed upon the good constable to bring a picnic hamper.

'You supply the food,' Annie giggled, 'and I'll supply the dessert.'

The 'dessert' was five feet six inches, with beautiful, shapely breasts and hips that a man could sink his teeth into.

Unfortunately, in the middle of dessert Constable Hanson's concentration was distracted by a limousine driving out of the castle gate.

'This bloody place is supposed to be closed on Mondays,' he muttered.

'Don't lose your place,' Annie coaxed.

'Not likely, pet.'

Twenty minutes later, the constable heard a second car leaving. This time he was curious enough to get up and peer out of the window. It looked like an official limousine, with darkened windows that concealed the passengers.

'Are you comin', then, Leslie?'

41

'Right. I just can't figure out who could be in the castle. Except for tour days, it's closed down.'

'Exactly what's going to happen to me, love, if you don't hop it.'

Twenty minutes later when Constable Hanson heard the third car leave, his libido lost out to his instincts as a policeman. There were five more vehicles, all limousines, all spaced twenty minutes apart. Because one of the cars stopped long enough to let a deer run by, Constable Hanson was able to note the licence-plate number.

'It's supposed to be your bloody day off,' Annie complained.

'This could be important,' the Constable said. And even as he said it, he wondered whether he was going to report it.

'What were you doing at Claymore Castle?' Sergeant Twill demanded.

'Sight-seeing, sir.'

'The castle was closed.'

'Yes, sir. The greenhouse was open.'

'So you decided to sight-see in the greenhouse?'

'Yes, sir.'

'Alone, of course?'

'Well, to tell the truth –'

'Spare me the grotty details, Constable. What made you suspicious of the cars?'

'Their behaviour, sir.'

'Cars don't behave, Hanson. Drivers do.'

'Of course, sir. The drivers seemed very cautious. The cars left at intervals of twenty minutes.'

'You are aware, of course, that there are probably a thousand innocent explanations. In fact, Hanson, the only one who doesn't seem to have an innocent explanation is yourself.'

'Yes, sir. But I thought I should report this.'

'Right. Is this the licence number you got?'

'Yes, sir.'

'Very well. Be off with you.' He thought of one witticism to add. 'Remember – it's dangerous to throw stones at people if you're in a glass house.' He chuckled at his *bon mot* all morning.

When the report on the licence plate came back, Sergeant Twill decided that Hanson had made a mistake. He took his information upstairs to Inspector Pakula and explained the background.

'I wouldn't have bothered you with this, Inspector, but the licence-plate number –'

'Yes. I see. I'll take care of it.'

'Thank you, sir.'

At SIS Headquarters, Inspector Pakula had a brief meeting with one of the senior heads of the British Secret Intelligence Service, a beefy, florid-faced man, Sir Alex Hyde-White.

'You were quite right to bring this to my attention,' Sir Alex smiled, 'but I'm afraid it's nothing more sinister than trying to arrange a Royal vacation trip without the press being aware of it.'

'I'm sorry to have bothered you about this, sir.' Inspector Pakula rose to his feet.

'Not at all, Inspector. Shows your branch is on its toes. What did you say the name of that young constable was?'

'Hanson, sir. Leslie Hanson.'

When the door closed behind Inspector Pakula, Sir Alex Hyde-White picked up a red telephone on his desk. 'I have a message for Balder. We have a small problem. I'll explain it at the next meeting. Meanwhile, I want you to arrange for three transfers. Police Sergeant Twill, an Inspector Pakula, and Constable Leslie Hanson. Spread them out a few days. I want them sent to separate posts, as far from London as possible. I'll inform the Controller and see if he wants to take any further action.'

In his hotel room in New York, Harry Lantz was awakened in the middle of the night by the ringing of the telephone.

Who the hell knows I'm here? he wondered. He looked blearily at the bedside clock, then snatched up the phone. 'It's four o'fucking clock in the morning? Who the – ?'

A soft voice at the other end of the line began speaking, and Lantz sat upright in bed, his heart beginning to pound. 'Yes, sir,' he said. 'Yes, sir . . . No, sir, but I can arrange to make myself free.' He listened for a long time. Finally he said, 'Yes, sir. I understand. I'll be on the first plane to Buenos Aires. Thank you, sir.'

He replaced the receiver, reached over to the bedside table and lit a cigarette. His hands were trembling. The man he had just spoken to was one of the most powerful men in the world, and what he had asked Harry to do . . . *What the hell is going down?* Harry Lantz asked himself. *Something big.* The man was going to pay him $50,000 to deliver a message. It would be fun going back to Argentina. Harry Lantz loved the South American women. *I know a dozen bitches there with hot pants who would rather fuck than eat.*

The day was starting out great.

At 9 a.m. Lantz picked up the telephone and dialled the number of Aerolineas Argentinas. 'What time is your first flight to Buenos Aires?'

43

The 747 arrived at the Ezeiza Airport in Buenos Aires at 5 p.m. the following afternoon. It had been a long flight, but Harry Lantz had not minded it. *Fifty thousand dollars for delivering a message.* He felt a surge of excitement as the wheels lightly kissed the ground. He had not been to Argentina for almost five years. It would be fun to renew old acquaintances.

As Harry Lantz stepped out of the plane, the blast of hot air startled him for a moment. *Of course. It's summer here.*

During the taxi ride into the city, Lantz was amused to see that the graffiti scrawled on the sides of buildings and sidewalks had not changed. *Plebiscito las pelotas* (Fuck the Plebiscite). *Militares, Asesinos* (Army, Assassins). *Tenemos hambre* (We are hungry). *Marihuana na libre* (Free pot). *Droga, sexo y muncho rock* (Drugs, sex and rock 'n' roll). *Juicio y castigo a los culpables* (Trial and punishment for the guilty).

Yes, it was good to be back.

Siesta was over and the streets were crowded with people lazily walking to and from appointments. When the taxi arrived at the Hotel El Conquistador in the heart of the fashionable Barrio Norte sector, Lantz paid the driver with a million peso note.

'Keep the change,' he said. Their money was a joke.

He registered at the desk in the huge, modern lobby, picked up a copy of the *Buenos Aires Herald* and *La Prensa*, and let the assistant manager show him to his suite. Sixty dollars a day for a bedroom, bathroom, living room and kitchen, air-conditioned, with television. *In Washington, this set-up would cost an arm and a leg,* Harry Lantz thought. *I'll take care of my business with this Neusa broad tomorrow, and stay around a few days and enjoy myself.*

It was more than two weeks before Harry Lantz was able to track down Neusa Muñez.

His search began with the city telephone directories. Lantz started with the places in the heart of the city: Plaza Constitución, Plaza San Martin, Barrio Norte, Catalinas Norte. None of them had a listing for a Neusa Muñez. Nor was there any listing in the outlying areas of Bahia Blanca or Mar del Plaza.

Where the hell is she? Lantz wondered. He took to the streets, looking up old contacts.

He walked into La Biela, and the bartender cried out, '*Señor* Lantz! *Por dios* – I heard you were dead.'

Lantz grinned. 'I was, but I missed you so much, Antonio, I came back.'

'What are you doing in Buenos Aires?'

Lantz let his voice grow pensive. 'I came here to find an old girl friend. We were supposed to get married, but her family moved away and I lost track of her. Her name is Neusa Muñez.'

The bartender scratched his head. 'Never heard of her. *Lo siento*.'

'Would you ask around, Antonio?'

'*Por qué no?*'

Lantz's next stop was to see a friend at police headquarters.

'Lantz! Harry Lantz! *Dios! Qué pasa?*'

'Hello, Jorge. Nice to see you, *amigo*.'

'Last I heard about you, the CIA kicked you out.'

Harry Lantz laughed. 'No way, my friend. They begged me to stay. I quit to go into business for myself.'

'*Si?* What business are you in?'

'I opened up my own detective agency. As a matter of fact, that's what brings me to Buenos Aires. A client of mine died a few weeks ago. He left his daughter a bundle of money, and I'm trying to locate her. All the information I have on her is that she lives in an apartment somewhere in Buenos Aires.'

'What's her name?'

'Neusa Muñez.'

'Wait here a moment.'

The moment stretched into half an hour.

'Sorry, *amigo*. I can't help you. She is not in our computer or in any of our files.'

'Oh, well. If you should come across any information about her, I'm at the El Conquistador.'

'*Bueno*.'

The bars were next. Old familiar haunts. The Pepe Gonzalez and Almeida, Café Tabac.

'*Buenas tardes, amigo. Soy de los Estados Unidos. Estoy buscando una mujer. El nombre es* Neusa Muñez. *Es una emergencia.*'

'*Lo siento, señor. No la conozco.*'

The answer was the same everywhere. *No one has ever heard of the fucking broad.*

Harry Lantz wandered around La Boca, the colourful waterfront area where one could see old ships rusting at anchor in the river. No one around there knew of Neusa Muñez. For the first time, Harry Lantz began to feel he might be on a wild goose chase.

It was at the Pilar, a small bar in the barrios of Flores, that his luck suddenly changed. It was a Friday night, and the bar was filled with working men. It took Lantz ten minutes to get the bartender's attention. Before Lantz was half way through his prepared speech, the bartender said, 'Neusa Muñez? *Si*. I know her. If she wishes to talk to you, she will come here *mañana*, about midnight.'

The following evening, Harry Lantz returned to the Pilar at eleven o'clock, watching the bar gradually fill up. As midnight approached, he found himself getting more and more nervous. What if she did not show up? What if it was the wrong Neusa Muñez?

Lantz watched as a group of giggling young women came into the bar. They joined some men at a table. *She's got to show up*, Lantz thought. *If she doesn't, I can kiss the fifty grand goodbye.*

He wondered what she looked like. She had to be a stunner. He was authorized to offer her boyfriend, Angel, a cool two million dollars to assassinate someone, so Angel was probably up to his ass in millions. He would be well able to afford a beautiful young mistress. Hell, he could probably afford a dozen of them. This Neusa had to be an actress or model. *Who knows, maybe I can have a little fun with her before I leave town. Nothing like combining business and pleasure*, Harry Lantz thought happily.

The door opened and Lantz looked up expectantly. A woman was walking in alone. She was middle-aged and unattractive, with a fat, bloated body and huge, pendulous breasts that swayed as she walked. Her face was pockmarked, and she had dyed blonde hair, but her dark complexion indicated *mestizo* blood inherited from an Indian ancestor who had been bedded by a Spaniard. She was dressed in an ill-fitting skirt and sweater meant for a much younger woman. *A hooker down on her luck*, Lantz decided. *But who the hell would want to fuck her?*

The woman looked around the bar with vacant, listless eyes. She nodded vaguely to several people and then pushed her way through the crowd. She walked up to the bar.

'Wanna buy me a drink?' She had a heavy Spanish accent, and up close she was even more unattractive.

She looks like a fat, unmilked cow, Lantz thought. *And she's drunk.* 'Get lost, sister.'

'Esteban say you are lookin' for me, no?'

He stared at her. 'Who?'

'Esteban. The bartender.'

Harry Lantz still could not accept it. 'He must have made a mistake. I'm looking for Neusa Muñez.'

'*Si. Yo soy* Neusa Muñez.'

But the wrong one, Harry Lantz thought. *Shit!* 'Are you Angel's friend?'

She smiled drunkenly. '*Si*.'

Harry Lantz recovered swiftly. 'Well, well.' He forced a smile. 'Can we go to a corner table and talk?'

She nodded indifferently. 'Ess okay.'

They fought their way across the smoky bar, and when they were seated, Harry Lantz said, 'I'd like to talk about –'

'You buy me a rum, *si*?'

Lantz nodded. 'Sure thing.'

A waiter appeared, wearing a filthy apron, and Lantz said, 'One rum and a scotch and soda.'

Muñez said, 'Make mine a double, huh?'

When the waiter left, Lantz turned to the woman seated beside him. 'I want to meet with Angel.'

She studied him with her dull, watery eyes. 'Wha' for?'

Lantz lowered his voice. 'I have a little present for him.'

'*Si?* What kin' a presen'?'

'Two million dollars.' Their drinks arrived. Harry Lantz raised his glass and said, 'Cheers.'

'Yeah.' She downed her drink in one gulp. 'Wha' for you wanna give Angel two million dollars?'

'That's something I'll have to discuss with him in person.'

'Tha's not possible. Angel, he don' talk to nobody.'

'Lady, for two million dollars –'

'Kin I have 'nother rum? A double, huh?'

My God, she already looks like she's about to pass out. 'Sure.' Lantz summoned the waiter and ordered the drink. 'Have you known Angel a long time?' He made his tone casual.

She shrugged. 'Yeah.'

'He must be an interesting man.'

Her vacant eyes were fixed on a spot on the table in front of her.

Jesus! Harry Lantz thought. *It's like trying to have a conversation with a fucking wall.*

Her drink arrived, and she finished it in one long swallow.

She has the body of a cow and the manners of a pig. 'How soon can I talk to Angel?'

Neusa Muñez struggled to her feet. 'I tol' you, he don' talk to nobody. *Adios.*'

Harry Lantz was filled with a sudden panic. 'Hey! Wait a minute! Don't go.'

She stopped and looked down at him with bleary eyes. 'Wha' you wan'?'

'Sit down,' Lantz said slowly, 'and I'll tell you what I want.'

She sat down heavily. 'I need a rum, huh?'

Harry Lantz was baffled. *What the fuck kind of man is this Angel? His mistress is not only the ugliest broad in all of South America, but she's a lush.*

Lantz did not like dealing with drunks. They were too unreliable. On the other hand, he hated the thought of losing his $50,000 commission. He watched as Muñez gulped her drink. He wondered how many she had had before coming to meet him.

47

Lantz smiled and said reasonably, 'Neusa, if I can't talk to Angel, how can I do business with him?'

'Ess simple. You tell me what you wan'. I tell Angel. If he say *si*, I tell you *si*. If he say *no*, I tell you *no*.'

Harry Lantz distrusted using her as a go-between, but he had no choice. 'You've heard of Marin Groza.'

'No.'

Of course she hadn't. Because it wasn't the name of a rum. This stupid bitch was going to get the message all wrong and screw up the deal for him.

'I need a drink, huh?'

He patted her fat hand. 'Certainly.' He ordered another double rum. 'Angel will know who Groza is. You just say Marin Groza. He'll know.'

'Yeah? Then wha'?'

She was even stupider than she looked. What the fuck did she think Angel was supposed to do for two millions dollar? Kiss the guy? Harry Lantz said carefully, 'The people who sent me want him blown away.'

She blinked. 'Wha's "blown away"?'

Christ! 'Killed.'

'Oh.' She nodded indifferently. 'I'll ass' Angel.' Her voice was beginning to slur even more. 'Wha' you say the man's name is?'

He wanted to shake her. 'Groza. Marin Groza.'

'Yeah. My baby's outta town. I'll call him tonight 'n meet you here tomorrow. Kin I have 'nother rum?'

Neusa Muñez was turning out to be a nightmare.

The following evening, Harry Lantz sat at the same table in the bar from midnight until four in the morning, when the bar closed. Muñez did not appear.

'Do you know where she lives?' Lantz asked the bartender.

The bartender looked at him with innocent eyes. *'Quien sabe?'*

The bitch had fouled everything up. How could a man who was supposed to be as smart as Angel get hooked up with such a rum dummy? Harry Lantz prided himself on being a pro. He was too smart to walk into a deal like this without first checking it out. He had cautiously asked around, and the information that impressed him most was that the Israelis had put a price of a million dollars on Angel's head. A million bucks would buy a lifetime's worth of booze and young hookers. Well, he could forget about that and he could forget about his $50,000. His only link to Angel had been broken. He would have to call The Man and tell him he had failed.

I won't call him yet, Harry Lantz decided. *Maybe she'll come back here. Maybe the other bars will run out of rum. Maybe I should have had my ass kicked for saying yes to this fucking assignment.*

6

The following night at eleven o'clock, Harry Lantz was seated at the same table in the Pilar, intermittently chewing peanuts and his fingernails. At 2 a.m. he saw Neusa Muñez stumble in the door, and Harry's heart soared. He watched as she made her way over to his table.

'Hi,' she mumbled, and slumped into a chair.

'What happened to you?' Harry demanded. It was all he could do to control his anger.

She blinked. 'Huh?'

'You were supposed to meet me here last night.'

'Yeah?'

'We had a date, Neusa.'

'Oh. I went to a movie with a girl frien'. There's this new movie, see? Ess 'bout this man who falls in love with this fuckin' nun an' –'

Lantz was so frustrated he could have wept. *What could Angel possibly see in this dumb, drunken bitch? She must have a golden pussy*, Lantz decided. 'Neusa – did you remember to talk to Angel?'

She looked at him vacantly, trying to understand the question. 'Angel? *Si*. Kin I have a drink, huh?'

He ordered a double rum for her and a double scotch for himself. He needed it desperately. 'What did Angel say, Neusa?'

'Angel? Oh, he say yeah. Ess okay.'

Harry Lantz felt a surge of relief. 'That's wonderful!' He no longer gave a damn about his messenger boy mission. He had thought of a better idea. This drunken bitch was going to lead him to Angel. One million dollars reward money.

He watched her slop down her drink, spilling some of it down her already soiled blouse. 'What else did Angel say?'

Her brow knit in concentration. 'Angel, he say he wanna know who your people are.'

Lantz gave her a winning smile. 'You tell him that's confidential, Neusa. I can't give him that information.'

She nodded, indifferent. 'Then Angel say to tell you to fuck off. Kin I have a rum 'fore I go?'

Harry Lantz's mind started working at top speed. If she left, he was sure he would never see her again. 'I'll tell you what I'll do, Neusa. I'll telephone the people I'm working for, and if they give me permission, I'll give you a name. Okay?'

She shrugged. 'I don' care.'

49

'No,' Lantz explained patiently, 'but Angel does. So you tell him I'll have an answer for him by tomorrow. Is there some place I can reach you?'

'I guess so.'

He was making progress. 'Where?'

'Here.'

Her drink arrived, and he watched her gulp it down like an animal. Lantz wanted to kill her.

Lantz made the telephone call collect, so it could not be traced, from a public telephone booth on Calvo Street. It had taken him one hour to get through.

'No,' the Controller said. 'I told you that no names are to be mentioned.'

'Yes, sir. But there's a problem. Neusa Muñez, Angel's mistress, says he's willing to make a deal, but he won't move without knowing who he's dealing with. Naturally, I told her I had to check it out with you first.'

'What is this woman like?'

The Controller was not a man to play games with. 'She's fat and ugly and stupid, sir.'

'It's much too dangerous for my name to be used.'

Harry Lantz could feel the deal slipping away from him. 'Yes, sir,' he said earnestly. 'I understand. The only thing is, sir, Angel's reputation is based on his being able to keep his mouth shut. If he ever started talking, he wouldn't last five minutes in his business.'

There was a long silence. 'You have a point.' There was another silence, even longer. 'Very well. You may give Angel my name. But he is never to divulge it, and never to contact me directly. He'll work only through you.'

Harry Lantz could have danced. 'Yes, sir. I'll tell him. Thank you, sir.' He hung up, a big grin on his face. He was going to collect the fifty thousand dollars.

And then the million-dollar reward.

When Harry Lantz met Neusa Muñez late that evening, he immediately ordered a double rum for her and said, happily, 'Everything's set. I got permission.'

She looked at him indifferently. 'Yeah?'

He told her the name of his employer. It was a household word, and he expected her to be impressed.

She shrugged. 'Never heard'a him.'

'Neusa, the people I work for want this done as quickly as possible. Marin Groza is hiding out in a villa in Neuilly, and –'

50

'Where?'

God Almighty! He was trying to communicate with a drunken moron. He said patiently, 'It's a little town outside of Paris. Angel will know.'

'I need 'nother drink.'

An hour later, Neusa was still drinking. And this time Harry Lantz was encouraging her. *Not that she needs much encouragement*, Lantz thought. *When she's drunk enough, she's going to lead me to her boy-friend. The rest will be easy.*

He looked over at Neusa Muñez staring filmy-eyed into her drink.

It shouldn't be hard to catch Angel. He may be tough, but he can't be very bright. 'When is Angel coming back to town?'

She focused her watery eyes on him. 'Nex' week.'

Harry Lantz took her hand and stroked it. 'Why don't you and I go back to your place?' he asked softly.

'Okay.'

He was in.

Neusa Muñez lived in a shabby, two-room apartment in the Belgrano district of Buenos Aires. The apartment was messy and unkempt, like its tenant. When they walked through the door, Neusa made straight for the little bar in the corner. She was unsteady on her feet.

'How 'bout a drink?'

'Not for me,' Lantz said. 'You go ahead.' He watched as she poured out a drink and downed it. *She's the most ugly, repulsive bitch I've ever met*, he thought, *but the million dollars is going to be beautiful.*

He looked around the apartment. There were some books piled on a coffee table. He picked them up, one by one, hoping to get an insight into Angel's mind. The titles surprised him: *Gabriela*, by Jorge Amado; *Fire From The Mountain*, by Omar Cabezas; *One Hundred Years of Solitude*, by Garcia Marquez; *At Night The Cats*, by Antonio Cisneros. So Angel was an intellectual. The books did not fit with the apartment or the woman.

Lantz walked over to her and put his arms around her huge, flabby waist. 'You're damned cute, do you know that?' He reached up and stroked her breasts. They were the size of watermelons. Lantz hated big-breasted women. 'You've got a really great body.'

'Huh?' Her eyes were glazed.

Lantz's arms moved down and stroked her fat thighs through the thin cotton dress she wore. 'How does that feel?' he whispered.

'Wha'?'

He was getting nowhere. He had to think of an approach that would get this amazon into bed. But he knew he had to make his move care-fully. If he offended her, she might go back and report him to Angel, and that would be the end of the deal. He could try to sweet talk her, but she was too drunk to know what he was saying.

As Lantz was desperately trying to think of a clever gambit, Neusa mumbled, 'Wanna fuck?'

He grinned in relief. 'That's a great idea, baby.'

'Come on 'n the bedroom.'

She was stumbling as Lantz followed her into the small bedroom. It contained one closet with the door ajar, a large unmade bed, two chairs and a bureau with a cracked mirror above it. It was the closet that caught Harry Lantz's attention. In it he glimpsed a row of men's suits hanging on a rack.

Neusa was at the side of the bed, fumbling with the buttons on her blouse. Under ordinary circumstances, Harry Lantz would have been at her side, undressing her, caressing her body and murmuring exciting indecencies into her ear. But the sight of Muñez sickened him. He stood there watching as her skirt dropped to the floor. She was wearing nothing under it. Naked, she was uglier than when dressed. Her huge breasts sagged, and her protruding stomach shook like jelly as she moved. Her fat thighs were a mass of cellulite. *She's the grossest thing I've ever seen*, Lantz thought. *Think positively*, Lantz told himself. *This will be over in a few minutes. The million bucks will last forever.*

Slowly, he forced himself to get undressed. She was propped up in bed, like a leviathan, waiting for him, and he crawled in beside her.

'What do you like?' he asked.

'Huh? Choc'late. I like choc'late.'

She was drunker than he had thought. *That's good. It will make things easier.* He began to caress her flabby, fish-white body. 'You're a very pretty woman, hon. You know that?'

'Yeah?'

'I like you a lot, Neusa.' His hands moved down towards the hairy mound between her fat legs, and he began to make small, titillating circles. 'I'll bet you live an exciting life.'

'Huh?'

'I mean – being Angel's girl friend. That must be really interesting. Tell me, baby, what's Angel like?'

There was a silence, and he wondered if Neusa had fallen asleep. He inserted his fingers in the soft, damp cleft between her legs, and felt her stir.

'Don't go to sleep, sweetheart. Not yet. What kind of man is Angel? Is he handsome?'

'Rich. Angel, he's rich.'

Lantz's hand continued its work. 'Is he good to you?'

'Yeah. Angel's good t' me.'

'I'm going to be good to you, too, baby.' His voice was soft. His problem was that everything was soft. What he needed was a million-dollar erection. He started thinking about the Dolly sisters and some of the things they had done to him. He visualized them working on his naked body with their tongues and fingers and nipples, and his penis began to grow hard. He quickly rolled over on top of Neusa and inserted himself into her. *God, it's like sticking it in a fucking pudding*, Harry Lantz thought. 'Does that feel good?'

'Ess okay, I guess.'

He could have strangled her. There were dozens of beautiful women around the world who were thrilled by his lovemaking, and this fat bitch was saying *Ess okay, I guess*.

He began moving his hips back and forth. 'Tell me about Angel. Who are his friends?'

Her voice was drowsy. 'Angel got no fren's. I'm his fren'.'

'Of course you are, babe. Does Angel live here with you, or does he have his own place?'

Neusa closed her eyes. 'Hey, I'm sleepy. When you gonna come?'

Never, he thought. *Not with this cow*. 'I already came,' Lantz lied.

'Then le's go to sleep.'

He rolled off her and lay at her side, fuming. *Why couldn't Angel have had a normal mistress? Someone young and beautiful and hot-blooded*. Then he would have had no trouble getting the information he needed. But this stupid bitch –! Still . . . there were other ways.

Lantz lay there quietly for a long time, until he was certain Neusa was asleep. Then he carefully arose from the bed and padded over to the closet. He switched the closet light on and closed the door so the light would not awaken the snoring behemoth.

There were a dozen suits and sports outfits hanging on the rack, and six pairs of men's shoes on the floor. Lantz opened the jackets and examined the labels. The suits were all custom-made by Herrera, Avenue La Plata. The shoes were made by Vill. *I've hit the jackpot!* Lantz gloated. *They'll have a record of Angel's address. I'll go to the shop first thing in the morning and ask a few questions.* A warning sounded in his mind. *No. No questions.* He had to be more clever than that. He was, after all, dealing with a world-class assassin. It would be safer to let Neusa lead him to Angel. *Then all I have to do is tip off my friends in the Mossad and collect the reward. I'll show Ned Tillingast and the rest of the fucking CIA bunch that old Harry Lantz hasn't lost his touch. All the bright boys have been chasing their asses trying to find Angel, and I'm the only one smart enough to pull it off.*

He thought he heard a sound from the bed. He carefully peeked out of the closet door, but Neusa was still asleep.

Lantz turned out the closet light and walked over to the bed. Muñez's eyes were closed. Lantz tiptoed to the bureau and began looking through the drawers, hoping to find a photograph of Angel. That would be a help. No luck. He crept back into bed. Neusa was snoring loudly.

When Harry Lantz finally drifted off to sleep, his dreams were filled

53

with visions of a white yacht crowded with beautiful, naked girls with small, firm breasts.

In the morning when Harry Lantz awakened, Neusa was gone. For an instant, Lantz panicked. Had she already left to meet Angel? He heard noises in the kitchen. He hurried out of bed and slipped into his clothes. Neusa was at the stove.

'*Buenos dias*,' Lantz said.

'Wan' coffee?' Neusa mumbled. 'I can't fix no breakfast. I got 'n appointment.'

With Angel. Harry Lantz tried to hide his excitement. 'That's fine. I'm not hungry. Why don't you go and keep your appointment and we'll meet for dinner tonight.' He put his arms around her, fondling her pendulous breasts. 'Where would you like to have dinner? Nothing but the best for my girl.' *I should have been an actor*, Lantz thought.

'I don' care.'

'Do you know Chiquin on Cangallo Street?'

'No.'

'You'll like it. Why don't I pick you up here at eight o'clock? I have a lot of business to attend to today.' He had no business to attend to.

'Okay.'

It took all his willpower to lean over and kiss Neusa goodbye. Her lips were flabby and wet and disgusting. 'Eight o'clock.'

Lantz walked out of the apartment and hailed a taxi. He hoped Neusa was watching from the window.

'Turn right at the next corner,' he instructed the driver.

When they had turned the corner, Harry Lantz said, 'I'll get out here.'

The driver looked at him in surprise. 'You wish to ride only one block, *señor*?'

'Right. I have a bad leg. War wound.'

Harry Lantz paid him, then hurried back to a tobacconist's shop across from Neusa's apartment building. He lit a cigarette and waited.

Twenty minutes later, Neusa came out of the apartment building. Harry watched as she waddled down the street, and he followed her at a careful distance. There was no chance of his losing her. It was like following the Lusitania.

Neusa Muñez seemed to be in no hurry. She moved down Florida Street, past the Spanish Library, and plodded along the Avenida Cordoba. Lantz watched as she walked into Berenes, a leather shop on San Martin. He stood across the street and observed her chatting with a male clerk. Lantz wondered whether the shop could be a connection with Angel. He made a mental note of it.

Neusa came out a few minutes later carrying a small package. Her next stop was at a *heladeria* on Corrientes, for an ice cream. She walked down San Martin, moving slowly. She seemed to be strolling aimlessly with no particular destination in mind.

What the hell happened to her appointment? Lantz wondered. *Where is Angel?* He did not believe Neusa's statement that Angel was out of town. His instincts told him that Angel was somewhere nearby.

Lantz suddenly realized that Neusa Muñez was not in sight. She had turned a corner ahead and disappeared. He quickened his step. When Lantz rounded the corner, she was nowhere to be seen. There were small shops on both sides of the street, and Lantz moved carefully, his eyes searching everywhere, fearful that Neusa might see him before he saw her.

He finally spied her in a *fiambreria*, a delicatessen, buying groceries. Were they for her, or was she expecting someone at her apartment for lunch? Someone named Angel.

From a distance, Lantz watched Neusa enter a *verduleria* and buy fruit and vegetables. He trailed her back to her apartment building. As far as he could tell, there had been no suspicious contacts.

Harry Lantz watched Neusa's building from across the street for the next four hours, moving around to make himself as inconspicuous as possible. Finally he decided that Angel was not going to show up. *Maybe I can get some more information out of her tonight*, Lantz thought, *without fucking her*. The idea of having to make love to Neusa again sickened him.

*

In the Oval Office at the White House, it was evening. It had been a long day for Paul Ellison. The entire world seemed to be composed of committees and councils and urgent cables and conclaves and sessions and he had not had a moment to himself until now. Well, *almost* to himself. Stanton Rogers was sitting across from him, and the President found himself relaxing for the first time that day.

'I'm keeping you from your family, Stan.'

'That's all right, Paul.'

'I wanted to talk to you about the Mary Ashley investigation. How is it coming?'

'It's almost completed. We'll have a final check on her by tomorrow or the next day. So far it looks very good. I'm getting excited about the idea. I think it's going to work.'

'We'll make it work. Would you like another drink?'

'No, thanks. Unless you need me for anything else, I'm taking Barbara to an opening at the Kennedy Center.'

'You go ahead,' Paul Ellison said. 'Alice and I are due to entertain some relatives of hers.'

'Please give my love to Alice,' Stanton Rogers said. He rose.

'And you give mine to Barbara.' He watched Stanton Rogers leave. The President's thoughts turned to Mary Ashley.

When Harry Lantz arrived at Neusa's apartment that evening to take her out to dinner, there was no answer to his knock. He felt a moment of consternation. Had she walked out on him?

He tried the door, and it was unlocked. Was Angel here to meet him? Perhaps he had decided to discuss the contract face to face. Harry assumed a brisk, businesslike manner and walked in.

The room was empty. 'Hello.' Only an echo. He went into the bedroom. Neusa was lying across the bed, drunk.

'You dumb –' He caught himself. He must not forget that this stupid, drunken broad was his gold mine. He put his hands on her shoulders and tried to rouse her.

She opened her eyes. 'Wha'sa matter?'

'I'm worried about you,' Lantz said. His voice throbbed with sincerity. 'I hate to see you unhappy, and I think you're drinking because someone is making you unhappy. I'm your friend. You can tell me all about it. It's Angel, isn't it?'

'Angel,' she mumbled.

'I'm sure he's a nice man,' Harry Lantz said soothingly. 'You two probably had a little misunderstanding, right?'

He tried to straighten her out on the bed. *It's like beaching a whale*, Lantz thought.

Lantz sat down beside her. 'Tell me about Angel,' Lantz said. 'What's he doing to you?'

Neusa stared up at him, bleary-eyed, trying to focus on him. 'Le's fuck.'

Oh, Jesus! It was going to be a long night. 'Sure. Great idea.' Reluctantly, Lantz began to undress.

*

When Harry Lantz awoke in the morning alone in bed, memories came flooding into his brain, and he felt sick to his stomach.

Neusa had awakened him in the middle of the night. 'You know wha' I wan' you to do to me?' she mumbled. She told him.

He had listened in disbelief, but he had done the things she asked him to do. He could not afford to antagonize her. She was a sick, wild animal, and Lantz wondered whether Angel had ever done those things for her. The thought of what he had gone through made Lantz want to vomit.

He heard Neusa singing off-key in the bathroom. He was not sure he could face her. *I've had enough*, Lantz thought. *If she doesn't tell me this morning where Angel is, I'm going to his tailor and shoemaker.*

He threw back the covers and went in to Neusa. She was standing in front of the bathroom mirror. Her hair was in fat curlers, and she looked, if possible, even more unattractive than before.

'You and I are going to have a talk,' Lantz said firmly.

'Sure.' Neusa pointed to the bathtub full of water. 'I fix a bath for you. When you're finish', I fix breakfast.'

Lantz was impatient, but he knew he must not press too hard.

'You like omelettes?'

He had no appetite. 'Yeah. Sounds great.'

'I make good omelettes. Angel teach me.'

Lantz watched as she started to take the huge, lumpy curlers out of her hair. He stepped into the bathtub.

Neusa picked up a large, electric dryer, plugged it in, and began drying her hair.

Lantz lay back in the warm tub thinking: *Maybe I should get a gun and take Angel myself. If I let the Israelis do it, there'll probably be a fucking inquiry into who gets the reward. This way there won't be any question. I'll just tell them where to pick up his body.*

Neusa said something, but Harry Lantz could barely hear her over the roar of the hair dryer.

'What did you say?' he called out.

Neusa moved to the side of the tub. 'I got a presen' for you from Angel.'

She dropped the electric hair dryer into the water and stood there watching as Lantz's body twitched in a dance of death.

7

President Paul Ellison put down the last security report on Mary Ashley and said, 'Not a blemish, Stan.'

'I know. I think she's the perfect candidate. Of course, State isn't going to be happy.'

'We'll send them a crying towel. Now let's hope the Senate will back us up.'

*

Mary Ashley's office in Kedzie Hall was a small, pleasant room lined with bookcases crammed with reference books on Middle European countries. The furniture was sparse, consisting of a battered desk with a swivel chair, a small table at the window, piled with examination papers, a ladder-back chair, and a reading lamp. On the wall behind the desk was a map of the Balkans. An ancient photograph of Mary's grandfather hung on the wall. It had been taken around the turn of the century, and the figure in the photograph was standing in a stiff, unnatural pose, dressed in the clothes of the period. The picture was one of Mary's treasures. It had been her grandfather who had instilled in her a deep curiosity about Romania. He had told her romantic stories of Queen Marie, and baronesses and princesses; tales of Albert, the Prince Consort of England, and Alexander II, Tsar of Russia, and dozens of other thrilling characters.

Somewhere in our background there is royal blood. If the revolution had not come, you would have been a princess.

She used to have dreams about it.

Mary was in the middle of grading examination papers when the door opened and Dean Hunter walked in.

'Good morning, Mrs Ashley. Do you have a moment?' It was the first time the Dean had ever visited her office.

Mary felt a sudden sense of elation. There could be only one reason for the Dean coming here himself: He was going to tell her that the University was giving her tenure.

'Of course,' she said. 'Won't you sit down?'

He sat down on the ladder-back chair. 'How are your classes going?'

'Very well, I think.' She could not wait to relay the news to Edward. He would be so proud. It was seldom that someone her age received tenure from a university.

Dean Hunter seemed ill at ease. 'Are you in some kind of trouble, Mrs Ashley?'

The question caught her completely off guard. 'Trouble? I – No. Why?'

'Some men from Washington have been to see me, asking questions about you.'

Mary Ashley heard the echo of Florence Schiffer's words: *Some federal agent from Washington . . . He was asking all kinds of questions about Mary. He made her sound like some kind of international spy . . . Was she a loyal American? Was she a good wife and a good mother . . . ?*

So it had not been about her tenure, after all. She suddenly found it difficult to speak. 'What – what did they want to know, Dean Hunter?'

'They inquired about your reputation as a professor, and they asked questions about your personal life.'

'I can't explain it. I really don't know what's going on. I'm in no kind of trouble at all. As far as I know,' she added lamely.

He was watching her with obvious scepticism.

'Didn't they tell you *why* they were asking questions about me?'

'No. As a matter of fact, I was asked to keep the conversation in strict confidence. But I have a loyalty to my staff, and I felt it only fair that you should be informed about this. If there is something I should know, I would prefer to hear it from you. Any scandal involving one of our professors would reflect badly on the University.'

She shook her head, helplessly. 'I – I really can't think of anything.'

He looked at her a moment, as though about to say something else, then nodded. 'So be it, Mrs Ashley.'

She watched him walk out of her office and wondered: *What in God's name could I have done?*

Mary was very quiet during dinner. She wanted to wait until Edward finished eating before she broke the news of this latest development. They would try to figure out the problem together. The children were being impossible again. Beth refused to touch her dinner.

'No one eats meat any more. It's a barbaric custom carried over from the caveman. Civilized people don't eat live animals.'

'It's not alive,' Tim argued. 'It's dead, so you might as well eat it.'

'Children!' Mary's nerves were on edge. 'Not another word. Beth, go make yourself a salad.'

'She could go graze in the field,' Tim offered.

'Tim! You finish your dinner.' Her head was beginning to pound. 'Edward –'

The telephone rang.

'That's for me,' Beth said. She leaped out of her chair and raced towards the telephone. She picked it up and said seductively, 'Virgil?' She listened a moment, and her expression changed. 'Oh, sure,' she

59

said disgustedly. She slammed down the receiver and returned to the table.

'What was that all about?' Edward asked.

'Some practical joker. He said it was the White House calling Mom.'

'*The White House?*' Edward asked.

The telephone rang again.

'I'll get it,' Mary said. She rose and walked over to the telephone. 'Hello.' As she listened, her face grew grim. 'We're in the middle of dinner, and I don't happen to think this is funny. You can just – what? . . . Who? The President?' There was a sudden hush in the room. 'Wait a – I – oh, good evening, Mr President.' There was a dazed expression on her face. Her family was watching her, wide-eyed. 'Yes, sir. I do. I recognize your voice. I – I'm sorry about hanging up a moment ago. Beth thought it was Virgil, and – yes, sir. Thank you.' She stood there listening. 'Would I be willing to serve as *what*?' Her face suddenly flushed.

Edward was on his feet, moving towards the phone, the children close behind him.

'There must be some mistake, Mr President. My name is Mary Ashley. I'm a professor at Kansas State University, and – You read it? Thank you, sir . . . That's very kind of you . . . Yes, I believe it is . . .' She listened for a long time. 'Yes, sir, I agree. But that doesn't mean that I . . . Yes, sir. Yes, sir. I see. Well, I'm certainly flattered. I'm sure it's a wonderful opportunity, but I . . . Of course I will. I'll talk it over with my husband and get back to you.' She picked up a pen and wrote down a number. 'Yes, sir. I have it. Thank you, Mr President. Goodbye.'

She slowly replaced the receiver and stood there in shock.

'What in God's name was that all about?' Edward demanded.

'Was that *really* the President?' Tim asked.

Mary sank into a chair. 'Yes. It really was.'

Edward took Mary's hand in his. 'Mary – what did he say? What did he want?'

Mary sat there, numb, thinking: *So that's what all the questioning has been about.*

She looked up at Edward and the children and said slowly, 'The President read my book and the article of mine in *Foreign Affairs* Magazine, and he thought they were brilliant. He said that's the kind of thinking he wants for his people-to-people programme. He wants to nominate me as Ambassador to Romania.'

There was a look of total disbelief on Edward's face.

'*You? Why you?*'

It was exactly what Mary had asked herself, but she felt that Edward could have been more tactful. He could have said, *How wonderful! You'd make a great ambassador.* But he was being realistic. *Why me, indeed?*

'You haven't had any political experience.'

'I'm well aware of that,' Mary responded tartly. 'I agree that the whole thing is ridiculous.'

'Are you going to be the Ambassador?' Tim asked. 'Are we moving to Rome?'

'Romania.'

'Where's Romania?'

Edward turned to the children. 'You two finish your dinner. Your mother and I would like to have a little talk.'

'Don't we get a vote?' Tim asked.

'By absentee ballot.'

Edward took Mary's arm and led her into the library. He turned to her and said, 'I'm sorry if I sounded like a pompous ass in there. It was just such a –'

'No. You were perfectly right, Edward. Why on earth *should* they have chosen me?'

When Mary called him Edward, he knew he was in trouble.

'Honey, you'd probably make a great ambassador, or ambassadress, or whatever they call it these days. But you must admit it came as a bit of a shock.'

Mary softened. 'Try thunderbolt.' She sounded like a little girl. 'I still can't believe it.' She laughed. 'Wait until I tell Florence. She'll die.'

Edward was watching her closely. 'You're really excited about this, aren't you?'

She looked at him in surprise. 'Of course I am. Wouldn't you be?'

Edward chose his words carefully. 'It *is* a great honour, honey, and I'm sure it's not one they would offer lightly. They must have had good reason for choosing you.' He hesitated. 'We have to think about this very carefully. About what it would do to our lives.'

She knew what he was going to say, and she thought: *Edward's right. Of course he's right.*

'I can't just leave my practice and walk out on my patients. I have to stay here. I don't know how long you'd have to be away, but if it really means a lot to you, well, maybe we could work out some way where you could go over there with the children and I could join you whenever –'

Mary said softly, 'You crazy man. Do you think I could live away from you?'

'Well – it's an awfully big honour, and –'

'So is being your wife. Nothing means as much to me as you and the children. I would never leave you. This town can't find another doctor like you, but all the government has to do to find a better ambassador than me is to look in the yellow pages.'

He took her in his arms. 'Are you sure?'

'I'm positive. It was exciting being asked. That's enough for –'

The door flew open and Beth and Tim hurried in. Beth said, 'I just called Virgil and told him you're going to be an ambassador.'

'Then you'd better call him back and tell him I'm not.'

'Why not?' Beth asked.

'Your mother has decided she's going to stay here.'

'Why?' Beth wailed. 'I've never been to Romania. I've never been anywhere.'

'Me neither,' Tim said. He turned to Beth. 'I told you we're never going to escape from this place.'

'The subject is closed,' Mary informed them.

The following morning Mary dialled the telephone number that the President had given her. When an operator answered, Mary said, 'This is Mrs Edward Ashley. I think the President's assistant – a Mr Greene – is expecting my call.'

'One moment, please.'

A male voice on the other end said, 'Hello. Mrs Ashley?'

'Yes,' Mary said. 'Would you please give the President a message for me?'

'Certainly.'

'Would you please tell him that I'm very, very flattered by his offer, but my husband's profession ties him down here, so I'm afraid it would be impossible for me to accept. I hope he understands.'

'I'll pass on your message,' the voice said noncommittally. 'Thank you, Mrs Ashley.' The line went dead.

Mary slowly replaced the receiver. It was done. For one brief moment, a tantalizing dream had been offered her. But that was all it was. A dream. *This is my real world. I'd better get ready for my fourth period history class.*

*

Manama, Bahrain

The whitewashed stone house was anonymous, hidden among dozens of identical houses, a short walk from the *souks*, the large, colourful outdoor markets. It was owned by a merchant sympathetic to the cause of the organization known as the Patriots for Freedom.

'We will need it for only one day,' a voice over the telephone told him.

It was arranged. Now the chairman was speaking to the men gathered in the living room.

'A problem has arisen,' the chairman said. 'The motion that was recently passed has run into difficulty.'

'What sort of difficulty?' Balder asked.

'The go-between we selected – Harry Lantz – is dead.'

'Dead? Dead, how?'

'He was murdered. His body was found floating in the harbour in Buenos Aires.'

'Do the police have any idea who did it? I mean – can they connect this to us in any way?'

'No. We're perfectly safe.'

Thor asked, 'What about our plan? Can we go ahead with it?'

'Not at the moment. We have no idea how to reach Angel. However, the Controller gave Harry Lantz permission to reveal his name to him. If Angel is interested in our proposition, he will find a way to get in touch with him. All we can do now is wait.'

*

The banner headline in the Junction City *Daily Union* read: JUNCTION CITY'S MARY ASHLEY DECLINES AMBASSADORSHIP.

There was a two-column story about Mary, and a photograph of her. On KJCK, the afternoon and evening broadcasts carried feature stories on the town's new celebrity. The fact that Mary Ashley had rejected the President's offer made the story even bigger than if she had accepted it. In the eyes of its proud citizens, Junction City, Kansas, was a lot more important than Bucharest, Romania.

When Mary Ashley drove into town to shop for dinner, she kept hearing her name on the car radio.

'. . . Earlier, President Ellison had announced that the Ambassadorship to Romania would be the beginning of his people-to-people programme, the cornerstone of his foreign policy. How Mary Ashley's refusal to accept the post will reflect on –'

She switched to another station.

'. . . is married to Dr Edward Ashley, and it is believed that –'

Mary switched off the radio. She had received at least three dozen phone calls that morning from friends, neighbours, students and curious strangers. Reporters had called from as far away as London and Tokyo. *They're building this up all out of proportion*, Mary thought. *It's not my fault that the President decided to base the success of his foreign policy on Romania. I wonder how long this pandemonium is going to last? It will probably be over in a day or two.*

She drove the station wagon into a Derby gas station and pulled up in front of the self-service pump.

As Mary got out of the car, Mr Blount, the station manager, hurried over to her. 'Mornin', Mrs Ashley. An ambassador lady ain't got no call to be pumpin' her own gas. Let me give you a hand.'

Mary smiled. 'Thanks. I'm used to doing it.'

'No, no. I insist.'

When the tank was filled, Mary drove down Washington Street and parked in front of the Shoe Box.

'Mornin', Mrs Ashley,' the clerk greeted her. 'How's the ambassador this mornin'?'

This is going to get tiresome, Mary thought. Aloud, she said, 'I'm not an ambassador, but I'm fine, thank you.' She handed him a pair of shoes. 'I'd like to have Tim's shoes re-soled.'

The clerk examined them. 'Ain't these the ones we did last week?'

Mary sighed. 'And the week before.'

Mary's next stop was at Long's Department Store. Mrs Hacker, the manager of the dress department, said to her, 'I jest heard your name on the radio. You're puttin' Junction City on the map. Yes, sir. I guess you and Eisenhower and Alf Landon are Kansas' only political big shots, Mrs Ambassador.'

'I'm not an ambassador,' Mary said patiently. 'I turned it down.'

'That's what I mean.'

It was no use. Mary said, 'I need some jeans for Beth. Preferably something in iron.'

'How old is Beth now? About ten?'

'She's twelve.'

'Land's sake, they grow so fast these days, don't they? She'll be a teenager before you know it.'

'Beth was born a teenager, Mrs Hacker.'

'How's Tim?'

'He's a lot like Beth.'

The shopping took Mary twice as long as usual. Everyone had some comment to make about the big news. She went into Dillon's to buy some groceries, and was studying the shelves when Mrs Dillon approached.

'Mornin', Mrs Ashley.'

'Good morning, Mrs Dillon. Do you have a breakfast food that has nothing in it?'

'What?'

Mary consulted a list in her hand. 'No artificial sweeteners, no sodium, fats, carbohydrates, caffeine, caramel colouring, folic acid or flavourites.'

Mrs Dillon studied the paper. 'Is this some kind of medical experiment?'

'In a sense. It's for Beth. She'll only eat natural foods.'

'Why don't you just put her out to pasture and let her graze?'

Mary laughed. 'That's what my son suggested.' Mary picked up a package and studied the label. 'It's my fault. I never should have taught Beth how to read.'

Mary drove home carefully, climbing the winding hill towards Milford Lake. It was a few degrees above zero, but the wind chill factor brought the temperature down to well below zero, for there was nothing to stop the winds from their biting sweep across the endless plains. The lawns were covered with snow, and Mary remembered the previous winter when an ice storm had swept the county and the ice snapped the power lines. They had no electricity for almost a week. She and Edward made love every night. *Maybe we'll get lucky again this winter*, she grinned to herself.

When Mary arrived home, Edward was still at the hospital. Tim was in the study watching a science fiction programme. Mary put away the groceries and went in to confront her son.

'Aren't you supposed to be doing your homework?'

'I can't.'

'And why not?'

'Because I don't understand it.'

'You're not going to understand it any better by watching *Star Trek*. Let me see your lesson.'

Tim showed her his fifth grade mathematics book. 'These are dumb problems,' Tim said.

'There are no such things as dumb problems. There are only dumb students. Now let's take a look at this.'

Mary read the problem aloud. 'A train leaving Minneapolis had one hundred and forty-nine people on board. In Atlanta more people boarded the train. Then there were two hundred and twenty-three on the train. How many people boarded in Atlanta?' She looked up. 'That's simple, Tim. You just subtract one hundred and forty-nine from two hundred and twenty-three.'

'No, you don't,' Tim said glumly. 'It has to be an equation. One hundred and forty-nine plus n equals two hundred and twenty-three. n equals two hundred and twenty-three minus one hundred and forty-nine. n equals seventy-four.'

'That's dumb,' Mary said.

*

As Mary passed Beth's room, she heard noises. Mary went in. Beth was seated on the floor, cross-legged, watching television, listening to a rock record, and doing her homework.

'How can you concentrate with all this noise?' Mary shouted.

She walked over to the television set and turned it off and then turned off the record player.

Beth looked up in surprise. 'What did you do that for? That was George Michael.'

Beth's room was wallpapered with posters of musicians. There was

Kiss and Van Halen, Motley Crue and Aldo Nova and David Lee Roth. The bed was covered with magazines: *Seventeen* and *Teen Idol* and half a dozen others. Beth's clothes were scattered over the floor.

Mary looked around the messy room in despair. 'Beth – how can you live like this?'

Beth looked up at her mother, puzzled. 'Live like what?'

Mary gritted her teeth. 'Nothing.'

She looked at an envelope on her daughter's desk. 'You're writing to Rick Springfield?'

'I'm in love with him.'

'I thought you were in love with George Michael.'

'I *burn* for George Michael. I'm in *love* with Rick Springfield. Mother, in your day didn't you ever *burn* for anybody?'

'In my day we were too busy trying to get the covered wagons across the country.'

Beth sighed. 'Did you know Rick Springfield had a rotten childhood?'

'To be perfectly honest, Beth, I was not aware of that.'

'It was awful. His father was in the military and they moved around a lot. He's a vegetarian, too. Like me. He's awesome.'

So that's what's behind Beth's crazy diet!

'Mother, may I go to a movie Saturday night with Virgil?'

'Virgil? What happened to Arnold?'

There was a pause. 'Arnold wanted to fool around. He's dorky.'

Mary forced herself to sound calm. 'By "fooling around", you mean –?'

'Just because I'm starting to get breasts the boys think I'm easy. Mom, did you ever feel uncomfortable about your body?'

Mary moved up behind Beth and put her arms around her. 'Yes, my darling. When I was about your age, I felt very uncomfortable.'

'I hate having my period and getting breasts and hair all over. Why?'

'It happens to every girl, and you'll get used to it.'

'No, I won't.' She pulled away and said fiercely, 'I don't mind being in love, but I'm never going to have sex. No one's going to make me. Not Arnold or Virgil or Kevin Bacon.'

Mary said solemnly, 'Well, if that's your decision . . .'

'Definitely. Mom, what did President Ellison say when you told him you weren't going to be his ambassador?'

'He was very brave about it,' Mary assured her. 'I think I'd better get dinner started.'

Cooking was Mary Ashley's secret *bête noire*. She hated to cook, and consequently was not very good at it, and because she liked to be good at everything she did, she hated it even more. It was a vicious circle that had partly been solved by having Lucinda come in three times a week to cook and clean the house. This was one of Lucinda's days off.

When Edward came home from the hospital, Mary was in the kitchen, burning some peas. She turned off the stove and gave Edward a kiss. 'Hello, darling. How was your day? Dorky?'

'You've been communicating with our daughter,' Edward said. 'As a matter of fact, it *was* dorky. I treated a thirteen-year-old girl this afternoon who had genital herpes.'

'Oh, darling!' She threw out the peas and opened a can of tomatoes.

'You know, it makes me worry about Beth.'

'You don't have to,' Mary assured him. 'She's planning to die a virgin.'

At dinner Tim asked, 'Dad, can I have a surf board for my birthday?'

'Tim – I don't want to rain on your parade, but you happen to live in *Kansas*.'

'I know that. Johnny invited me to go to Hawaii with him next summer. His folks have a beach house in Maui.'

'Well,' Edward said reasonably, 'if Johnny has a beach house, then he probably has a surf board.'

Tim turned to his mother. 'Can I go?'

'We'll see. Please don't eat so fast, Tim. Beth, you're not eating anything.'

'There's nothing here that's fit for human consumption.' She looked at her parents. 'I have an announcement to make. I'm going to change my name.'

Edward asked carefully, 'Any particular reason?'

'I've decided to go into show business.'

Mary and Edward exchanged a long, pained look.

Edward said, 'Okay. Find out how much you can get for them.'

8

In a scandal that had rocked the international secret service organizations, Mehdi Ben Barka, an opponent of King Hussan II of Morocco, was abducted from his exile in Paris and murdered with the help of the French Secret Service. It was following that incident that President Charles de Gaulle took the Secret Service from the control of the Premier's Office and placed it under the aegis of the Ministry of Defence. Thus it was that the current Minister of Defence, Roland Passy, was responsible for the safety of Marin Groza, who had been granted sanctuary by the French government. Gendarmes were stationed in front of the villa in Neuilly on twenty-four hour shifts, but it was the knowledge that Lev Pasternak was in charge of the villa's inner security that gave Passy confidence. He had seen the security arrangements himself and was firmly convinced that the house was impregnable.

In recent weeks, rumours had been sweeping the diplomatic world that a coup was imminent; that Marin Groza was planning to return to Romania; and that Alexandros Ionescu was going to be deposed by his senior military officers.

Lev Pasternak knocked on the door and entered the book-crammed library that served as Marin Groza's office. Groza was seated behind his desk, working. He looked up as Lev Pasternak came in.

'Everybody wants to know when the revolution is going to happen,' Pasternak said. 'It's the world's worst kept secret.'

'Tell them to be patient. Will you come to Bucharest with me, Lev?'

More than anything, Lev Pasternak yearned to return to Israel. *I'll only take this job temporarily*, he had told Marin Groza. *Until you're ready to make your move. Temporarily* had turned into weeks and months, and finally into three years. And now it was time to make another decision.

In a world peopled with pygmies, Lev Pasternak thought, *I have been given the privilege of serving a giant.* Marin Groza was the most selfless and idealistic man Lev Pasternak had ever known.

When Pasternak had come to work for Groza, he had wondered about the man's family. Groza would never speak of them, but the officer who had arranged for Pasternak to meet Groza told him the story.

'Groza was betrayed. The *Securitate* picked him up and tortured him for five days. They promised to free him if he would give them the names of his associates in the underground. He wouldn't talk. They arrested his wife and his fourteen-year-old daughter and brought them to the interrogation room. Groza was given a choice: Talk or watch them die. It was the hardest decision any man ever had to make. It was the life of his beloved wife and child against the lives of hundreds of people who believed in him.' The man paused, then went on more slowly. 'I think in the end what made Groza decide the way he did was that he was convinced that he and his family were going to be killed, anyway. He refused to give them the names. The guards strapped him in a chair and forced him to watch his wife and daughter being gang-raped until they died. But they weren't through with Groza yet. When it was over and their bloody bodies were lying at his feet, they castrated him.'

'Oh, my God!'

The officer looked into Lev Pasternak's eyes and said, 'The most important thing for you to understand is that Marin Groza does not want to return to Romania to seek vengeance. He wants to go back to free his people. He wants to make certain that such things can never again happen.'

Lev Pasternak had been with Groza from that day on, and the more time he spent with the revolutionary, the more he came to love him. Now, he would have to decide whether to give up his return to Israel and go to Romania with Groza.

*

Pasternak was walking down the hallway that evening, and as he passed Marin Groza's bedroom door, he heard the familiar screams of pain ring out. *So it's Friday*, Pasternak thought. The day the prostitutes came. They were selected from England, North America, Brazil, Japan, Thailand, and half a dozen other countries, chosen at random. They had no idea what their destination was, or who they were going to see. They were met at Charles de Gaulle Airport, driven directly to the villa, and, after a few hours, taken back to the airport and put on a return flight. Every Friday night the halls resounded with Marin Groza's screams. The staff assumed that kinky sex was going on. The only one who knew what was really happening behind the bedroom door was Lev Pasternak. For the visits with the prostitutes had nothing to do with sex. They were a penance. Once a week Groza stripped himself naked and had a woman tie him to a chair and whip him mercilessly, until his blood flowed, and each time he was whipped he would see his wife and daughter being raped to death, screaming for help. And he cried out, 'I'm sorry! I'll talk. Oh, God, please let me talk . . .'

*

The telephone call came ten days after Harry Lantz's body was found. The Controller was in the middle of a staff meeting in the conference room when the intercom buzzer sounded.

'I know you asked not to be disturbed, sir, but there's an overseas call for you. It sounds urgent. A Miss Neusa Muñez is calling from Buenos Aires. I told her –'

'It's all right.' He kept his emotions under tight control. 'I'll take the call in my private office.' He excused himself, went into his office, and locked the door. He picked up the telephone. 'Hello. Is this Miss Muñez?'

'Yeah.' It was a voice with a South American accent, coarse and uneducated. 'I got a message for you from Angel. He din' like the nosey messenger you sent.'

He had to choose his words carefully. 'I'm sorry. But we would still like Angel to go ahead with our arrangement. Would that be possible?'

'Yeah. He say he wanna do it.'

The man held back a sigh of relief. 'Excellent. How shall I arrange his advance?'

The woman laughed. 'Angel, he don' need no advance. Nobody cheats Angel.' Somehow the words were chilling. 'When the job is finished, he say you put the money in – wait a minute – I got it wrote down – here it is – the State Bank of Zürich. Tha's some place in Switzerland.' She sounded like a moron.

'I'll need the account number.'

'Oh, yeah. The number is – Jesus. I forgot. Hol' on. I got it here somewhere.' He heard the rustle of papers, and finally she was back on the telephone. 'Here it is. J-three four nine-zero seven seven.'

He repeated the number. 'How soon can he handle the matter?'

'When he's ready, *señor*. Angel say you'll know when 'ees done. You'll read 'bout it in the newspapers.'

'Very well. I'm going to give you my private telephone number in case Angel needs to reach me.'

He gave it to her slowly.

*

Tbilisi, Russia

The meeting was being held in an isolated dacha bordering on the River Kura.

The chairman said, 'Two urgent matters have arisen. The first is good news. The Controller has had word from Angel. The contract is moving forward.'

'That's *very* good news!' Freyr exclaimed. 'What's the bad news?'

'I'm afraid it concerns the President's candidate for the Ambassadorship to Romania, but the situation can be handled . . .'

It was difficult for Mary Ashley to keep her mind on the class. Something had changed. In the eyes of her students, she had become a celebrity. It was a heady feeling. She could feel the class hanging on her words.

'As we know, 1956 was a watershed year for many of the Eastern European countries. With Gomulka's return to power, national communism emerged in Poland. In Czechoslovakia Antonin Mavorony led the Communist Party. There were no major political changes in Romania that year . . .'

Romania . . . Bucharest . . . From the photographs Mary had seen, it had to be one of the most beautiful cities in Europe. She had not forgotten any of the stories her grandfather had told her about Romania. She remembered how terrified she had been as a little girl by his tales of the horrible Prince Vlad of Transylvania. *He was a vampire, Mary, living in his huge castle high in the mountains of Braşov, sucking the blood of his innocent victims.*

Mary was suddenly aware of a deep silence in the room. The class was staring at her. *How long have I been standing here daydreaming?* she wondered. She hurriedly continued her lecture. 'In Romania, Gheorgiu-Dej was consolidating his power in the Workers' Party . . .'

The class seemed to go on endlessly, but mercifully, it was almost over.

'Your homework assignment will be to write an essay on the USSR's economic planning and management, describing the basic organization of the government organs, and the CPSU control. I want you to analyse the internal and external dimensions of Soviet policy, with emphasis on its positions on Poland, Czechoslovakia and Romania.'

Romania . . . Welcome to Romania, Madam Ambassador. Your limousine is here to drive you to your embassy. Her embassy. She had been invited to live in one of the most exciting capitals of the world, reporting to the President, being in the centre of his people-to-people concept. *I could have been a part of history.*

She was roused from her reverie by the sound of the bell. Class was over. Time to go home and change. Edward would be back from the hospital early. He was taking her out to the country club for dinner.

As befitted an almost-Ambassador.

'Code Blue! Code Blue!' the crackling voice sounded over the loudspeaker throughout the hospital corridors. Even as the emergency crew began to converge on the ambulance entrance, the sound of an approaching siren could be heard. The Geary Community Hospital is an austere-looking, three-storey brown building perched on a hill on St Mary's Road in the southwest section of Junction City. The

71

hospital holds 92 beds, has two modern operating rooms, and a series of examining rooms and administrative offices.

It had been a busy Friday, and the ward on the top floor was already filled with injured servicemen who had come to town from nearby Fort Riley, home of the First Infantry Division, known as The Big Red One, for their weekend R & R.

Dr Edward Ashley was sewing up the scalp of a soldier who had lost a bar fight. Edward Ashley had been a doctor at Geary Community Hospital for thirteen years, and before going into private practice, he had been an Air Force flight surgeon with the rank of Captain. Several prestigious hospitals in large cities had tried to lure him away, but he preferred to stay where he was.

He finished with the patient he was working on, and looked around. There were at least a dozen soldiers waiting to be patched up. He heard the sound of the approaching ambulance siren. 'They're playing our song.'

Dr Douglas Schiffer, who was tending a gunshot wound victim, nodded. 'It looks like MASH in here. You'd think we were in some kind of war.'

Edward Ashley said, 'It's the only war they have, Doug. That's why they come into town every weekend and go a little nuts. They're frustrated.' He finished the last stitch. 'There you are, soldier. You're as good as new.' He turned to Douglas Schiffer. 'We'd better get down to emergency.'

The patient wore the uniform of a private, and he looked to be no more than eighteen years old. He was in shock. He was sweating profusely and his breathing was laboured. Dr Ashley felt his pulse. It was weak and thready. A splotch of blood stained the front of his uniform jacket. Edward Ashley turned to one of the paramedics who had brought in the patient.

'What do we have here?'

'A knife wound to the chest, doctor.'

'Let's see if his lung is collapsed.' He turned to a nurse. 'I want a stat chest x-ray. You've got three minutes.'

Dr Douglas Schiffer was observing the jugular vein. It was raised. He looked over at Edward. 'It's distended. The pericardium's probably been penetrated.' Which meant that the sac which protected the heart was filled with blood, pressing against the heart so that it could not beat properly.

The nurse who was taking the patient's blood pressure said, 'Blood pressure's dropping fast.'

The monitor measuring the patient's electrocardiogram began to slow. They were losing the patient.

Another nurse hurried in with the chest x-ray. Edward scanned it. 'Pericardial tamponade.'

The heart had a hole in it. The lung was collapsed.

'Get a tube in him and expand the lung.' His voice was quiet, but there was no mistaking the urgency in it. 'Get an anaesthesiologist. We're going to open him up. Intubate him.'

A nurse handed Dr Schiffer an endotracheal tube. Edward Ashley nodded at him. 'Now.'

Carefully Douglas Schiffer began to push the tube into the unconscious soldier's windpipe. There was a bag at the end of the tube, and Schiffer began to squeeze it in a steady rhythm, ventilating the lungs. The monitor began to slow, and the curve on the monitor was completely flat. The smell of death was in the room.

'He's gone.'

There was no time to wheel the patient up to the operating room. Dr Ashley had to make an instant decision.

'We're going to do a thoracotomy. Scalpel.'

The instant the knife was in his hand, Edward reached down and slashed it across the patient's chest. There was almost no blood, because the heart was trapped in the pericardium.

'Retractor!'

The instrument was put in his hands, and he inserted it into the patient's chest to spread the ribs apart.

'Scissors. Stand back!'

He moved closer so that he could reach the pericardial sac. He snipped the scissors into it, and the blood released from the imprisonment of the heart sac spurted out, hitting the nurses and Dr Ashley. Dr Ashley reached in and began to massage the heart. The monitor began to beep, and the pulse became palpable. There was a small laceration at the apex of the left ventricle.

'Get him up to the operating room.'

Three minutes later the patient was on the operating table.

'Transfusion – a thousand cc's.'

There was no time to match blood type, so 'O Negative' – the universal donor – was used.

As the blood transfusion began, Dr Ashley said, 'A thirty-two chest tube.'

A nurse handed it to him.

Dr Schiffer said, 'I'll close, Ed. Why don't you get cleaned up?'

Edward Ashley's surgical gown was stained with blood. He looked at the monitor. The heart was strong and steady.

'Thanks.'

Edward Ashley had showered and changed clothes and was in his office writing up the required medical report. It was a pleasant office, filled with bookcases containing medical tomes and athletic trophies. It contained a desk, an easy chair and a small table with two straight chairs. On the walls were his diplomas, neatly framed.

Edward's body felt stiff and tired from the tension he had just gone through. At the same time, he felt sexually aroused, as he always did after major surgery. *It's coming face to face with death that magnifies the values of the life force*, a psychiatrist had once explained to Edward. *Making love is the affirmation of nature's continuum. Whatever the reason*, Edward thought, *I wish Mary were here.*

He selected a pipe from the pipe rack on his desk, lighted it, and sank into the easy chair and stretched out his legs. Thinking about Mary made him feel guilty. He was responsible for her turning down the President's offer, and his reasons were valid. *But there's more to it than that*, Edward admitted to himself. *I was jealous. I reacted like a spoiled brat. What would have happened if the President had made me an offer like that? I'd probably have jumped at it. Jesus! All I could think of was that I wanted Mary to stay home and take care of me and the kids. Talk about your genuine male chauvinist pig!*

He sat there, smoking his pipe, upset with himself. *Too late*, he thought. *But I'll make it up to her. I'll surprise her this summer with a trip to Paris and London. Maybe I'll take her to Romania. We'll have a real honeymoon.*

The Junction City Country Club is a three-level, limestone building set in the midst of lush hills. The club has an eighteen-hole golf course, two tennis courts, a swimming pool, and a bar and dining room with a large fireplace at one end, a card room upstairs and locker rooms downstairs.

Edward's father had belonged to the club, as had Mary's father, and Edward and Mary had been taken there since they were children. The town was a closely knit community, and the country club was its symbol.

When Edward and Mary arrived, it was late, and there was only a sprinkling of guests left in the dining room. They stared, watching as Mary sat down, and whispered to one another. Mary was getting used to it.

Edward looked at his wife. 'Any regrets?'

Of course there were regrets. But they were castles-in-Spain regrets about the kind of glamorous, impossible dreams that everyone has. *If I had been born a princess; if I were a millionairess; if I received the Nobel prize for curing cancer; if . . . if . . . if . . .*

Mary smiled. 'None, darling. It was a fluke that they even asked me. Anyhow, there's no way I would ever leave you or the children.'

She took his hand in hers. 'No regrets. I'm glad I refused the offer.'

He leaned across to her and whispered, 'I'm going to make you an offer you can't refuse.'

'Let's go,' Mary smiled.

In the beginning, when they were first married, their lovemaking had been fierce and demanding. They had a constant physical need for each other that could not be satisfied until they were both completely spent. The urgency had mellowed with time, but the emotions were still there, constant and sweet and fulfilling.

When they returned home now, they undressed without haste and got into bed. Edward held her close to him, then began to stroke her body gently, playing with her breasts, teasing the nipples with his fingers, moving his hand down towards the velvety softness.

Mary moaned with pleasure. 'That feels wonderful.'

She moved on top of him and began flicking her tongue down his body, feeling him become hard. When they were both ready, they made love until they were exhausted. Edward held his wife tightly in his arms. 'I love you so much, Mary.'

'I love you twice as much. Good night, darling.'

At three o'clock in the morning, the phone exploded into sound. Edward sleepily reached for the instrument and brought it to his ear. 'Hello . . .'

A woman's urgent voice said, 'Dr Ashley?'

'Yes . . .'

'Pete Grimes is havin' a heart attack. He's in pain somethin' awful. I think he's dying. I don't know what to do.'

Edward sat up in bed, trying to blink the sleep away. 'Don't do anything. Keep him still. I'll be there in half an hour.' He replaced the receiver, slid out of bed and started to dress.

'Edward . . .'

He looked over at Mary. Her eyes were half open.

'What's wrong?'

'Everything's fine. Go back to sleep.'

'Wake me up when you come back,' Mary mumbled. 'I think I'm going to feel sexy again.'

Edward grinned. 'I'll hurry.'

Five minutes later, he was on his way to the Grimes' farm.

He drove down the hill on Old Milford Road towards J Hill Road. It was a cold and raw morning, with a northwesterly wind driving the temperature well below zero. Edward turned up the car heater. As he drove, he wondered whether he should have called for an ambulance before he left the house. The last two 'heart attacks' Pete Grimes

75

had had turned out to be bleeding ulcers. No. He would check it out first.

He turned the car onto Route 18, the two lane highway that went through Junction City. The town was asleep, its houses huddled against the bitter, frigid wind.

When Edward came to the end of 6th Street, he made the turn that took him onto Route 57, and headed towards Grandview Plaza. How many times had he driven over these roads on hot summer days with the sweet smell of corn and prairie hay in the air, past miniature forests of cottonwood trees and cedars and Russian olive trees, and August haystacks piled up alongside the roads? The fields had been filled then with the odour of burning cedar trees that had to be regularly destroyed because they kept taking over the crops. And how many winters had he driven on this road through a frosted landscape with power lines delicately laced with ice, and lonely smoke from far-off chimneys? There was an exhilarating feeling of isolation, being encapsulated in the morning darkness, watching fields and trees fly silently past.

Edward drove as fast as possible, mindful of the treacherous road beneath the wheels. He thought of Mary lying in their warm bed, waiting for him. *Wake me up when you come back. I think I'm going to feel sexy again.*

He was so lucky. *I'll make everything up to her,* Edward promised himself. *I'll give her the damnedest honeymoon any woman ever had.*

Ahead, at the intersection of Highways 57 and 77 was a stop sign. Edward turned at Route 77, and as he started into the intersection, a truck appeared out of nowhere. He heard a sudden roar, and his car was pinned by two bright headlights racing towards him. He caught a glimpse of the giant five-ton Army truck bearing down on him, and the last sound he heard was his own voice screaming.

*

In Neuilly, it was Sunday and church bells pealed out across the quiet noon air. The gendarmes guarding Marin Groza's villa had no reason to pay attention to the dusty Renault cruising by. Angel drove slowly, but not slowly enough to arouse suspicion, taking everything in. Two guards in front, a high wall, probably electrified, and inside, of course, the usual electronic nonsense of beams, sensors and alarms. It would take an army to storm the villa. *But I don't need an army,* Angel thought. *Only my genius. Marin Groza is a dead man. If only my mother were alive to see how rich I have become. How happy it would have made her.*

In Argentina, poor families were very poor indeed, and Angel's mother had been one of the unfortunate *descamidos*. No one knew

76

or cared who the father had been. Through the years Angel had watched friends and relatives die of hunger and sickness and disease. Death was a way of life, and Angel thought philosophically: *Since it is going to happen anyway, why not make a profit from it?* In the beginning, there were those who doubted Angel's lethal talents, but those who tried to put roadblocks in the way had a habit of disappearing. Angel's reputation as an assassin grew. *I have never failed,* Angel thought. *I am Angel. The Angel of Death.*

9

The snow-covered Kansas highway was ablaze with vehicles with flashing red lights that turned the frosty air blood-red. A fire truck, ambulance, tow truck, four highway patrol cars, a sheriff's car, and in the centre, ringed by headlights, the five-ton M871 Army tractor-trailer, and partially beneath it, Edward Ashley's crumpled car. A dozen police officers and firemen were milling around, swinging their arms and stamping their feet, trying to keep warm in the pre-dawn freeze. In the middle of the highway, covered by a tarpaulin, was a body. A sheriff's car was approaching, and as it skidded to a stop, Mary Ashley ran out of it. She was trembling so hard that she could barely stand. She saw the tarpaulin and started towards it.

Sheriff Munster grabbed her arm. 'I wouldn't look at him if I were you, Mrs Ashley.'

'Let go of me.' She was screaming. She shook loose from his grasp and moved towards the tarpaulin.

'Please, Mrs Ashley. You don't want to see what he looks like.'

He caught her as she fainted.

*

She woke up in the back seat of the sheriff's car. Sheriff Munster was sitting in the front seat, watching her. The heater was on, and the car was stifling.

'What happened?' Mary asked dully.

'You fainted.'

She suddenly remembered. *You don't want to see what he looks like.*

Mary stared out of the window at all the emergency vehicles and flashing red lights and thought: *It's a scene from hell.* In spite of the heat in the police car, her teeth were chattering.

'How did –' She found it difficult to get the words out. 'How did it h-happen?'

'Your husband ran the stop sign. An Army truck was comin' along 77 and tried to avoid him, but your husband drove right out in front of him.'

She closed her eyes and watched the accident happen in her mind. She saw the truck bearing down on Edward and felt his last second panic.

All she could think of to say was, 'Edward was a c-careful driver. He would n-never go through a stop sign.'

The sheriff said sympathetically, 'Mrs Ashley, we have eye-witnesses.

A priest and two nuns saw it happen, and a Colonel Jenkins from Fort Riley. They all said the same thing. Your husband ran the stop sign.'

Everything after that seemed to happen in slow motion. She watched Edward's body being lifted into the ambulance. Police were questioning a priest and two nuns, and Mary thought: *They're going to catch cold standing out there like that.*

Sheriff Munster said, 'They're takin' the body to the morgue.'

The body. 'Thank you,' Mary said politely.

He was looking at her strangely. 'I'd best get you back home,' he said. 'What's the name of your family doctor?'

'Edward Ashley,' Mary said. 'Edward Ashley is my family doctor.'

Later, she remembered walking up to the house and Sheriff Munster leading her inside. Florence and Douglas Schiffer were waiting for her in the living room. The children were still asleep.

Florence threw her arms around her. 'Oh, darling, I'm so terribly, terribly sorry.'

'It's all right,' Mary said calmly. 'Edward had an accident.' She giggled.

Douglas was watching her closely. 'Let me take you upstairs.'

'I'm fine, thank you. Would you care for some tea?'

Douglas said, 'Come on, I'm putting you to bed.'

'I'm not sleepy. Are you sure you wouldn't care for something?'

As Douglas led her upstairs into the bedroom, Mary said to him, 'It was an accident. Edward was in an accident.'

Douglas Schiffer looked into her eyes. They were wide and vacant. He felt a chill go through him.

He went downstairs to get his medical bag. When he returned, Mary had not moved. 'I'm going to give you something to make you sleep.' He gave her a sedative, helped her into bed, and sat at her side. An hour later, Mary was still awake. He gave her another sedative. Then a third. Finally, she slept.

In Junction City there are strict investigative procedures involved in the report of a 1048 – an injury accident. An ambulance is dispatched from the County Ambulance Service, and a sheriff's officer is sent to the scene. If army personnel are involved in the accident, the CID – the Criminal Investigating Division of the Army – conducts an investigation along with the sheriff's office.

Shel Planchard, a plainclothes officer from the CID headquarters at

Fort Riley, and the sheriff and a deputy were examining the accident report in the sheriff's office on 9th Street.

'It beats me,' Sheriff Munster said.

'What's the problem, Sheriff?' Planchard asked.

'Well, looky here. There were five witnesses to the accident, right? A priest and two nuns, Colonel Jenkins and the truck driver, Sergeant Wallis. Every single one of them says Doc Ashley's car turned into the highway, ran the stop sign and was hit by the Army truck.'

'Right,' the CID man said. 'What's bothering you?'

Sheriff Munster scratched his head. 'Mister, have you ever seen an accident report where even *two* eyewitnesses said the same thing?' He slammed a fist against the papers. 'What bothers the hell out of me is that every one of these witnesses says *exactly* the same thing.'

The CID man shrugged. 'It just shows that what happened was pretty obvious.'

The sheriff said, 'There's somethin' else nigglin' at me.'

'Yeah?'

'What were a priest and two nuns and a colonel doin' out on Highway 77 at 4 a.m. in the mornin'?'

'Nothing mysterious about that. The priest and the sisters were on their way to Leonardville, and the colonel was returning to Fort Riley.'

The sheriff said, 'I checked with the DMV. The last ticket Doc Ashley got was six years ago for illegal parking. He had no accident record.'

The CID man was studying him. 'Sheriff, just what are you suggesting?'

Munster shrugged. 'I'm not suggestin' anythin'. I jest have a funny feelin' about this.'

'We're talking about an accident seen by five witnesses. If you think there's some kind of conspiracy involved, there's a big hole in your theory. If –'

The sheriff sighed. 'I know. If it wasn't an accident, all the Army truck had to do was knock him off and keep goin'. There wouldn't be any reason for all these witnesses and rigmarole.'

'Exactly.' The CID man rose and stretched. 'Well, I've got to get back to the base. As far as I'm concerned, the driver of the truck, Sergeant Wallis, is cleared.' He looked at the sheriff. 'Are we in agreement?'

Sheriff Munster said reluctantly, 'Yeah. It musta been an accident.'

*

Mary was awakened by the sound of the children crying. She lay still, her eyes tightly closed, thinking: *This is a part of my nightmare. I'm asleep, and when I wake up, Edward will be alive.*

But the crying continued. When she could stand it no longer, she opened her eyes and lay there, staring at the ceiling. Finally, reluctantly, she forced herself to get out of bed. She felt drugged. She walked into

Tim's bedroom. Florence and Beth were there with him. The three of them were crying. *I wish I could cry,* Mary thought. *Oh, I wish I could cry.*

Beth looked up at Mary. 'Is – is Daddy really d-dead?'

Mary nodded, unable to speak the words. She sat on the edge of the bed.

'I had to tell them,' Florence apologized. 'They were going to go off to play with some friends.'

'It's all right.' Mary stroked Tim's hair. 'Don't cry, darling. Everything is going to be all right.'

Nothing was going to be all right again.
Ever.

The United States Army CID Command at Fort Riley is headquartered at Building Number 169, in an old limestone structure, surrounded by trees, with steps leading up to the porch of the building. In an office on the first floor, Shel Planchard, the CID officer, was talking to Colonel Jenkins.

'I'm afraid I have some bad news, sir. Sergeant Wallis, the driver of the truck that killed the civilian doctor –'

'Yes?'

'He had a fatal heart attack this morning.'

'That's a shame.'

The CID man said tonelessly, 'Yes, sir. His body is being cremated this morning. It was very sudden.'

'Unfortunate.' The Colonel rose. 'I'm being transferred overseas.' He allowed himself a small smile. 'A rather important promotion.'

'Congratulations, sir. You've earned it.'

Mary Ashley decided later that the only thing that saved her sanity was being in a state of shock. Everything that happened seemed to be happening to someone else. She was under water, moving slowly, hearing voices from a distance, filtered through cotton wool.

The funeral service was held at the Mass-Hinitt Alexander Funeral Home on Jefferson Street. It was a blue building with a white portico and a large white clock hanging above the entrance. The funeral parlour was filled to overflowing with friends and colleagues of Edward. There were dozens of wreaths and bouquets. One of the largest wreaths had a card that read simply: 'My deepest sympathy. Paul Ellison.'

Mary and Beth and Tim sat alone in the small family room off to one side of the parlour, the children red-eyed and still.

The casket with Edward's body in it was closed. She could not bear to think about the reason.

The minister was speaking: 'Lord, thou hast been our dwelling place.

In all generations, before the mountains were brought forth, or ever thou hadst formed the earth and the world, ever from everlasting to everlasting, thou art God. Therefore, we will not fear, though the earth doth change, and though the mountains be shaken into the heart of the seas . . .'

She and Edward were in the small sailboat on Milford Lake.

'Do you like to sail?' he had asked her the first night they dated.

'I've never been sailing.'

'Saturday,' he said. 'We have a date.'

They were married one week later.

'Do you know why I married you, lady?' Edward teased. 'You passed the test. You laughed a lot and you didn't fall overboard.'

When the service ended, Mary and the children got into the long, black limousine that led the funeral procession to the cemetery.

Highland Cemetery on Ash Street is a vast park, with a gravelled road circling it. It is the oldest cemetery in Junction City, and many of the headstones have long since been eroded by time and weather. Because of the numbing cold, the graveside ceremony was kept brief.

'I am the resurrection and the life; he that believeth in me, though he were dead, yet shall he live; and whosoever liveth and believeth in me shall never die. I am he that liveth and was dead; and, behold, I am alive for evermore.'

Finally, mercifully, it was over. Mary and the children stood in the howling wind watching the casket being lowered into the frozen, uncaring earth.

Goodbye, my darling.

*

Death is supposed to be an ending, but for Mary Ashley it was the beginning of an unbearable hell. She and Edward had talked about death, and Mary had thought she had come to terms with it, but now death had suddenly assumed a reality that was immediate and terrifying. It was no longer a vague event that would happen on some far, distant day. There was no way to cope with it. Everything within Mary screamed to deny what had happened to Edward. When he died, everything wonderful died with him. The reality kept hitting her in fresh waves of shock. She wanted to be alone. She cowered deep within herself, feeling like a small, terrified child abandoned by an adult. She found herself raging against God. *Why didn't you take me first?* she demanded. She was furious with Edward for deserting her, furious with the children, furious with herself.

I'm a thirty-five-year-old woman with two children, and I don't know who I am. When I was Mrs Edward Ashley, I had an identity, I belonged to someone who belonged to me.

Time was spinning by, mocking her emptiness. Her life was like a runaway train over which she had no control.

Florence and Douglas and other friends stayed with her, trying to make things easier, but Mary wished they would go away and leave her alone. Florence came in one afternoon and found Mary in front of the television set watching a Kansas State football game.

'She didn't even know I was there,' Florence told her husband that evening. 'She was concentrating so desperately on that game.' She shivered. 'It was spooky.'

'Why?'

'Mary hates football. It was Edward who watched every game.'

It took Mary's last ounce of willpower to handle the detritus left by Edward's death. There was the will, and insurance, bank accounts and taxes and bills due and Edward's medical corporation and loans and assets and deficits, and she wanted to scream at the lawyers and bankers and accountants to leave her in peace.

I don't want to cope, she wept. Edward was gone, and all anyone wanted to talk about was money.

Finally, she was forced to discuss it.

Frank Dunphy, Edward's accountant, said, 'I'm afraid the bills and death taxes are going to use up a lot of the life insurance money, Mrs Ashley. Your husband was pretty lax about his patients paying him. He's owed a lot of money. I'll arrange for a collection agency to go after the people who owe –'

'No,' Mary said fiercely. 'Edward wouldn't want that.'

Dunphy was at a loss. 'Well, then, I guess the bottom line is that your assets are thirty thousand dollars in cash and this house, which has a mortgage on it. If you sold the house –'

'Edward wouldn't want me to sell it.'

She sat there, stiff and rigid, holding in her misery, and Dunphy thought: *I wish to God my wife cared that much about me.*

*

The worst was yet to come. It was time to dispose of Edward's personal things. Florence offered to help her, but Mary said, 'No. Edward would have wanted me to do it.'

There were so many small, intimate things. A dozen pipes, a fresh can of tobacco, two pairs of reading glasses, notes for a medical lecture he would never give. She went into Edward's closet and ran her fingers over suits he would never wear again. The blue tie he had worn on their last night together. His gloves and scarf that kept him warm against the winter winds. He would not need them in his cold grave. She carefully put away his razor and toothbrushes, moving like an automaton.

She found love notes they had written to each other, bringing back memories of the lean days when Edward started his own practice, a Thanksgiving dinner without a turkey, summer picnics and winter sleigh rides, and her first pregnancy and both of them reading to Beth and playing classical music for her while she was in the womb, and the love letter Edward wrote when Tim was born, and the gold-plated apple Edward had given her when she began teaching, and a hundred other wonderful things that brought tears to her eyes. His death was like some cruel magician's trick. One moment Edward was there, alive, talking, smiling, loving, and the next moment he had vanished into the cold earth.

I'm a mature person. I have to accept reality. I'm not mature. I can't accept it. I don't want to live.

She lay awake through the long night, thinking how simple it would be to join Edward, to stop the unbearable agony, to be at peace. *We're brought up to expect a happy ending*, Mary thought. *But there are no happy endings. There's only death waiting for us. We find love and happiness, and it's snatched away from us without rhyme or reason. We're on a deserted space ship careening mindlessly among the stars. The world is Dachau, and we're all Jews.*

She finally dozed off, and in the middle of the night, her wild screams awakened the children, and they ran to her bedside and crawled into bed with her, hugging her.

'You're not going to die, are you?' Tim whispered.

Mary thought: *I can't kill myself. They need me. Edward would never forgive me.*

She had to go on living. For them. She had to give them the love Edward would not be able to give them. *We're all so needy without Edward. We need one another so terribly. It's ironic that Edward's death is harder to bear because we had such a wonderful life together. There are so many more reasons to miss him, so many memories of things that will never happen again. Where are you, God? Are you listening to me? Help me. Please help me.*

Ring Lardner said, 'Three out of three are going to die, so shut up and deal.' *I have to deal. I'm being terribly selfish. I'm behaving badly, as if I'm the only person in the world who is suffering. God isn't trying to punish me. Life is a cosmic grab-bag. At this moment, somewhere in the world, someone is losing a child, skiing down a mountain, having an orgasm, getting a haircut, lying on a bed of pain, singing on a stage, drowning, getting married, starving in a gutter. In the end, aren't we all that same person? An aeon is a thousand million years, and an aeon ago every atom in our bodies was a part of a star. Pay attention to me, God. We are all a part of your universe, and if we die, part of your universe dies with us.*

Edward was everywhere.

He was in the songs Mary heard on the radio, in the hills they had driven through together. He was in bed at her side when she awoke at sunrise.

Got to get up early this morning, honey. I have a hysterectomy and a hip operation.

His voice came to her clearly. She began to talk to him: *I'm worried about the children, Edward. They don't want to go to school. Beth says they're afraid that when they get home I won't be here.*

Mary went to visit the cemetery every day, standing in the icy air, mourning for what was lost to her forever. But it gave her no comfort. *You're not here*, Mary thought. *Tell me where you are. Please.*

She thought of the story by Marguerite Yourcenar, 'How Want-Fo Was Saved'. It was the tale of a Chinese artist condemned to be put to death by his emperor for lying, for creating pictures of a world whose beauty was contradicted by reality. But the artist cheated the emperor by painting a boat and sailing away in it. *I want to escape, too*, Mary thought. *I can't stand it here without you, darling.*

Florence and Douglas tried to comfort her. 'He's at peace,' they told Mary. And a hundred other clichés. The easy words of solace, except that there was no solace. *Not now. Not ever.*

She would wake in the middle of the night and rush into the children's rooms to make sure they were safe. *My children are going to die*, Mary thought. *We're all going to die.* People were calmly walking the streets. *Idiots, laughing, happy – and they were all dying.* Their hours were numbered, and they wasted them playing stupid card games and going to silly movies and pointless football games. *Wake up!* she wanted to scream. *The earth is God's slaughterhouse, and we're his cattle. Didn't they know what was going to happen to them and to everyone they loved?*

The answer came to her, slowly, painfully, through the heavy black veils of grief. Of course they knew. Their games were a form of defiance, their laughter an act of bravado – a bravado born from the knowledge that life was finite, that everyone faced the same fate; and slowly her fear and anger melted and turned to wonder at the courage of her fellow human beings. *I'm ashamed of myself. I have to find my own way through the maze of time. In the end, each of us is alone, but in the meantime, we must all huddle together to give one another comfort and warmth.*

The Bible said that death was not a final ending; it was merely a transition. Edward would never leave her and the children. He was there, somewhere.

She carried on conversations with him. 'I talked to Tim's teacher today. His grades are improving. Beth is in bed with a cold. Remember how she usually gets them this time of the year? We're all having dinner over at Florence and Douglas' tonight. They've been wonderful, darling.'

And, in the middle of the black night, 'The Dean stopped by the house. He wanted to know whether I planned to go back to teaching at the University. I told him not now. I don't want to leave the children alone, even for a little while. They need me so much. Do you think I should go back one day?'

A few days later: 'Douglas got a promotion, Edward. He was made chief of staff at the hospital.'

Could Edward hear her? She did not know. Was there a God, and was there a hereafter? Or was it a fable? T. S. Eliot said: 'Without some kind of God, man is not even very interesting.'

*

President Paul Ellison, Stanton Rogers and Floyd Baker were meeting in the Oval Office. The Secretary of State said, 'Mr President, we're both getting a lot of pressure. I don't think we can hold off any longer on naming an Ambassador to Romania. I'd like you to look over the list I gave you and select –'

'Thanks, Floyd. I appreciate your efforts. I still think Mary Ashley would be ideal. Her domestic situation has changed. What was rotten luck for her may turn out to be good luck for us. I want to try her again.'

Stanton Rogers said, 'Mr President, why don't I fly out there and see if I can persuade her?'

'Let's try it.'

Mary was preparing dinner when the telephone rang, and when she picked it up, an operator said, 'This is the White House. The President is calling Mrs Edward Ashley.'

Not now, she thought. *I don't want to speak to him or anyone.*

She remembered how excited his call had once made her. Now it was meaningless. She said, 'This is Mrs Ashley, but –'

'Would you please hold?'

Moments later, the familiar voice came on the line. 'Mrs Ashley, this is Paul Ellison. I just want you to know how terribly sorry we are about your husband. I understand he was a fine man.'

'Thank you, Mr President. It was kind of you to send flowers.'

'I don't want to intrude on your privacy, Mrs Ashley, and I know it's been a very short time, but now that your domestic situation has changed, I'm asking you to reconsider my offer of an ambassadorship.'

'Thank you, but I couldn't possibly –'

'Hear me out, please. I'm having someone fly out there to talk to you. His name is Stanton Rogers. I would appreciate it if you would at least meet with him.'

She did not know what to say. How could she explain that her world had been turned upside down, that her life had been shattered? All that mattered now were Beth and Tim. She decided that in all courtesy, she would see the man and then refuse as gracefully as possible.

'I'll meet with him, Mr President, but I won't change my mind.'

*

There was a popular bar on the Boulevard Bineau that Marin Groza's guards frequented when they were not on duty at the villa in Neuilly. Even Lev Pasternak occasionally visited the bar. Angel selected a table in an area of the room where conversations could be overheard. The guards, away from the rigid routine of the villa, liked to drink, and when they drank, they talked. Angel listened, seeking the villa's vulnerable point. There was always a vulnerable point. One simply had to be clever enough to find it.

It was three days before Angel overheard a conversation that gave the clue to the solution of the problem.

A guard was saying, 'I don't know what Groza is doing to the whores he brings in there, but they're sure whipping the hell out of him. You should hear the screaming that goes on. Last week I got a look at the whips he keeps in his closet . . .'

And the next night. '. . . The hookers our fearless leader gets up at the villa are real beauties. They bring them in from all over the world. Lev arranges it himself. He's smart. He never uses the same girl twice. That way, no one can use the girls to get at Marin Groza.'

It was all Angel needed.

Early the following morning, Angel changed rental cars and drove a Fiat into Paris. The sex shop was in Montmartre, on the Place Pigalle, in the middle of a section populated by whores and pimps. Angel went inside, walking slowly along the aisles, carefully studying the merchandise for sale. There were shackles and chains and iron-studded helmets, leather pants with slits in front, penis massagers and joy jelly, inflatable rubber dolls and porno video tapes. There were male douches and anal cream and six-foot-long braided-leather whips with thongs at the end.

Angel bought a whip, paid cash for it and left.

The following morning, Angel brought the whip back to the shop. The manager looked up and growled, 'No refunds.'

'I don't want a refund,' Angel explained. 'I feel awkward carrying this around. I would appreciate it if you would mail it for me. I'll pay extra, of course.'

Late that afternoon, Angel was on a plane to Buenos Aires.

The whip, carefully wrapped, arrived at the villa in Neuilly the following day. It was intercepted by the guard at the gatehouse. He read the store label on the package, opened it and examined the whip with great care. *You would think the old man had enough of these already.*

He passed it through, and a guard took it to Marin Groza's bedroom closet, where he placed it with the other whips.

10

Fort Riley, the oldest Army fort in the United States, was constructed in 1853 when Kansas was still referred to as 'Indian Territory'. It was built to protect wagon trains from Indian war parties. Today it is used primarily as a helicopter base and a landing field for smaller military fixed-wing planes.

When Stanton Rogers landed in a DC-7, he was welcomed by the base commander and his staff. A limousine was standing by, waiting to drive Stanton to the Ashley home. He had telephoned Mary after the President's call.

'I promise to make my visit as brief as possible, Mrs Ashley. I plan to fly in Monday afternoon to see you, if that's all right?'

He's being so polite. And he's such an important man. Why is the President sending him to talk to me? 'That will be fine.' In a reflex action, Mary asked, 'Would you care to have dinner with us?'

He hesitated. 'Thank you.' *It's going to be a long, boring evening*, Stanton thought.

When Florence Schiffer heard the news, she was thrilled. 'The President's Foreign Affairs Adviser is coming to dinner *here*? That means you're going to accept the appointment!'

'Florence, it means nothing of the kind. I promised the President I would talk to him. That's all.'

Florence put her arms around Mary and hugged her. 'I just want you to do whatever makes you happy.'

'I know that.'

*

Stanton Rogers was a formidable man, Mary decided. Mary had seen him on *Meet the Press*, and had seen photographs of him in *Time* Magazine, but she thought: *He looks bigger in person.* He was polite, but there was something distant about him.

'Permit me to convey again the President's sincere regrets about your terrible tragedy, Mrs Ashley.'

'Thank you.'

She introduced him to Beth and Tim. Mary went into the kitchen to see how Lucinda was getting along with the dinner.

'Whenever you're ready,' Lucinda said, 'but he'll hate it.'

When Mary had told Lucinda that Stanton Rogers was coming to the house for dinner, and that she wanted Lucinda to make a pot roast, Lucinda had said, 'People like Mr Rogers don't eat pot roast.'

'Oh. What do they eat?'

'Chateaubriand and crêpes suzettes.'

'We're having pot roast.'

'All right,' Lucinda said stubbornly, 'but it's the wrong dinner.'

Along with the pot roast she had prepared creamed mashed potatoes, fresh vegetables and a salad. She had baked a pumpkin pie for dessert. Stanton Rogers finished everything on his plate. During dinner Mary and Stanton Rogers discussed the problems of the farmers.

'The farmers in the mid-west are caught in a terrible squeeze between low prices and overproduction,' Mary said earnestly. 'They're too poor to paint, and too proud to whitewash.'

They talked about the colourful history of Junction City, and Stanton Rogers finally brought the discussion around to Romania.

'What is your opinion of President Ionescu's government?' he asked Mary.

'There is no government in Romania, in the real sense of the word,' Mary replied. 'Ionescu is the government. He's in total control.'

'Do you think there will be a revolution there?'

'Not in the present circumstances. The only man powerful enough to depose him is Marin Groza, who's in exile in France.'

The questioning went on. She was an expert on the Iron Curtain countries, and Stanton Rogers was visibly impressed. Mary had the uncomfortable feeling that he had been examining her under a microscope all evening. She was closer to the mark than she knew.

Paul was right, Stanton Rogers thought. *She really is an authority on Romania.* And there was something more. *We need the opposite of the Ugly American. She's beautiful. And she and the children make an all-American package that will sell.* Stanton found himself getting more and more excited by the prospect. *She can be more useful than she realizes.*

At the end of the evening, Stanton Rogers said, 'Mrs Ashley, I'm going to be frank with you. I was against the President appointing you to a post as sensitive as Romania. I told him as much. I tell you this now because I've changed my mind. I think you may very well make an excellent ambassador.'

Mary shook her head. 'I'm sorry, Mr Rogers. I'm no politician. I'm just an amateur.'

'As President Ellison pointed out to me, some of our finest ambassadors have been amateurs. That is to say, their experience was not in the Foreign Service. Walter Annenberg, our former Ambassador to the United Kingdom of Great Britain, was a publisher.'

'I'm not –'

'Arthur Burns, our former Ambassador to the Federal Republic of Germany, was an assistant professor, and John Kenneth Galbraith, our

90

Ambassador to India, was also a professor. Mike Mansfield started out as a reporter before he became a Senator and then was appointed our Ambassador to Japan. I could give you a dozen more examples. These people were all what you would call "amateurs". What they had, Mrs Ashley, was intelligence, a love for their country, and goodwill towards the people of the country where they were sent to serve.'

'You make it sound so simple.'

'As you're probably aware, you've already been investigated very thoroughly. You've been approved for a security clearance, you have no problem with the IRS, and there's no conflict of interest. According to Dean Hunter, you're an excellent teacher, and of course you're an expert on Romania. You've got a running start. And last, but not least, you have the kind of image the President wants to project in the Iron Curtain countries, where they're fed so much adverse propaganda about us.'

Mary listened, a thoughtful expression on her face. 'Mr Rogers, I want you and the President to know that I appreciate everything you've said. But I couldn't accept it. I have Beth and Tim to think about. I can't just uproot them like –'

'There's a fine school for diplomats' children in Bucharest,' Rogers informed her. 'It would be a wonderful education for Tim and Beth to spend time in a foreign country. They'd learn things they could never learn in school here.'

The conversation was not going the way Mary had planned.

'I don't – I'll think about it.'

'I'm staying in town overnight,' Stanton Rogers said. 'I'll be at the All Seasons Motel. Believe me, Mrs Ashley, I know what a big decision this is for you. But this programme is important not only to the President, but to our country. Please think about that.'

When Stanton Rogers left, Mary went upstairs. The children were waiting for her, wide awake and excited.

'Are you going to take the job?' Beth asked.

'We have to have a talk. If I did decide to accept it, it would mean that you would have to leave school and all your friends. You would be living in a foreign country where we don't speak the language, and you would be going to a strange school.'

'Tim and I talked about all that,' Beth said, 'and you know what we think?'

'What?'

'That any country would be really lucky to have you as an ambassador, Mom.'

*

91

She talked to Edward that night: *You should have heard him, darling. He made it sound as though the President really needed me. There are probably a million people who could do a better job than I could, but he was very flattering. Do you remember how you and I talked about how exciting it would be? Well, I have the chance again, and I don't know what to do. To tell you the truth, I'm terrified. This is our home. How can I bear to leave it? There's so much of you here.* She found that she was crying. *This is all I have left of you. Help me decide. Please help me . . .*

She sat by the window, in her robe, looking out at the trees shivering in the howling, restless wind.

At dawn she made her decision.

At nine o'clock in the morning, Mary telephoned the All Seasons Motel and asked for Stanton Rogers.

When he came on the line, she said, 'Mr Rogers, would you please tell the President that I will be honoured to accept his nomination for the ambassadorship.'

11

This one's even more beautiful than the others, the guard thought. She did not look like a prostitute. She could have been a movie actress or a model. She was in her early twenties, with long blonde hair and a clear, milky complexion. She wore a designer dress.

Lev Pasternak came to the gate himself to conduct her to the house. The girl, Bisera, was a Yugoslavian, and it was her first trip to France. The sight of all the armed security guards made her nervous. *I wonder what I've got myself into?* All Bisera knew was that her pimp had handed her a round-trip plane ticket and told her she would be paid $2,000 for an hour's work.

Lev Pasternak knocked at a bedroom door and Groza's voice called out, 'Come in.'

Pasternak opened the door and ushered the girl inside. Marin Groza was standing at the foot of the bed. He had on a robe, and she could tell he was naked under it.

Lev Pasternak said, 'This is Bisera.' He did not mention Marin Groza's name.

'Good evening, my dear. Come in.'

Pasternak left, carefully closing the door behind him, and Marin Groza was alone with the girl.

She moved towards him and smiled seductively. 'You look comfortable. Why don't I get undressed and we can both be comfortable?' She started to get out of her dress.

'No. Keep your clothes on, please.'

She looked at him in surprise. 'Don't you want me to – ?'

Groza walked over to the closet and selected a whip. 'I want you to use this.'

So that was it. A slave fetish. Strange. He did not look the type. *You never know*, Bisera thought. 'Sure, honey. Whatever turns you on.'

Marin Groza took off his robe and turned around. Bisera was shocked by the sight of his scarred body. It was covered with cruel welts. There was something in his expression that puzzled her, and when she realized what it was, she was even more perplexed. It was anguish. The man was in an enormous amount of pain. Why did he want to be whipped? She watched him as he walked over to a stool and sat on it.

'Hard,' he commanded. 'Whip me very hard.'

'All right.' Bisera picked up the long leather whip. Sado-masochism was not new to her, but there was something different here that she did

93

not understand. *Well, it's none of my business,* Bisera thought. *Take the money and run.*

She raised the whip and cracked it down against his naked back.

'Harder,' he urged. 'Harder.'

He flinched with pain as the tough leather beat against his skin. Once . . . and twice . . . and again . . . and again, harder and harder. The vision he had been waiting for came to him then. Scenes of his wife and his daughter being raped seared through his brain. It was a gang-rape, and the laughing soldiers went from the woman to the child, their pants pulled down, waiting in line for their turn. Marin Groza strained against the stool as though bound to it. As the whip fell again and again, he could hear the screams of his wife and daughter begging for mercy, choking on the men's penises in their mouths, being raped and sodomized at the same time, until the blood started pouring out and their cries finally trailed off.

And Marin Groza groaned, 'Harder!' And with each crack of the whip, he felt the sharp blade of the knife tearing into his genitals, castrating him. He was having difficulty breathing. 'Get – get –' His voice was a croak. His lungs felt paralysed.

The girl stopped, holding the whip in mid-air. 'Hey! Are you all right? I –?'

She watched as he toppled to the floor, his eyes open, staring at nothing.

Bisera screamed, '*Help! Help!*'

Lev Pasternak came running in, gun in hand. He saw the figure on the floor. 'What happened?'

Bisera was hysterical. 'He's dead. He's dead! I didn't do anything. I just whipped him like he told me to. I swear!'

The doctor, who lived in the villa, came into the room within seconds. He looked at Marin Groza's body, and bent down to examine him. The skin had turned blue, and the muscles were rigid.

He picked up the whip and smelled it.

'What?'

'Damn! Curare. It's an extract from a South American plant. The Incas used it on darts to kill their enemies. Within three minutes the entire nervous system is paralysed.'

The two men stood there, staring helplessly at their dead leader.

The news of Marin Groza's assassination was carried all over the world by satellite. Lev Pasternak was able to keep the sordid details away from the press. In Washington, D.C., the President had a meeting with Stanton Rogers.

'Who do you think is behind it, Stan?'

'Either the Russians or Ionescu. In the end, it comes to the same thing, doesn't it? They didn't want the status quo disturbed.'

'So we'll be dealing with Ionescu. Very well. Let's push the Mary Ashley appointment through as quickly as possible.'

'She's on her way here, Paul.'

'Good.'

On hearing the news, Angel smiled. *It happened sooner than I thought.*

At 10 p.m. the private phone rang and the Controller picked it up. 'Hello.'

He heard the sound of Neusa Muñez's guttural voice. 'Angel saw this mornin's paper. He say to depos't the money in his bank account.'

'Inform him that it will be taken care of immediately. And Miss Muñez, tell Angel how pleased I am. Also tell him that I may need him again very soon. Do you have a telephone number where I can reach you?'

There was a long pause, then: 'I guess so.' She gave it to him.

'Fine. If Angel –'

The line went dead.

Damn the stupid bitch.

The money was deposited in a numbered account in Zürich that morning, and one hour after it was received, it was transferred to a Saudi Arabian bank in Geneva. *A person can't be too careful these days*, Angel thought. *The god-damned bankers will cheat you every chance they get.*

12

It was more than packing up a household. It was packing up a life. It was bidding farewell to thirteen years of dreams, memories, love. It was saying a final goodbye to Edward. This had been their home, and now it would become merely a house again, occupied by strangers with no awareness of the joys and sorrows and tears and laughter that had happened within these walls.

Douglas and Florence Schiffer were delighted that Mary had decided to accept the post.

'You'll be fantastic,' Florence assured Mary. 'Doug and I will miss you and the kids.'

'Promise that you'll come to Romania to visit us.'

'Promise.'

Mary was overwhelmed by the practical details that had to be taken care of, the multitude of unfamiliar responsibilities. She made a list:

> Call the storage company to pick up personal things that we're leaving.
> Cancel milkman.
> Cancel newspaper.
> Give postman new mailing address.
> Sign lease on house.
> Arrange for insurance.
> Change over utilities.
> Pay all bills.
> *Don't Panic!*

An indefinite leave of absence from the University had been arranged with Dean Hunter.

'I'll have someone take over your undergraduate classes. That's no problem. But your seminar students are certainly going to miss you.' He smiled. 'I'm sure you'll do us all proud, Mrs Ashley. Good luck.'

'Thank you.'

Mary withdrew the children from their school. There were travel arrangements to be made and airline tickets to be bought. In the past, Mary had taken all the financial transactions for granted, because Edward had been there to handle them. Now there was no Edward, except in her mind and in her heart, where he would always be.

Mary was worried about Beth and Tim. In the beginning, they had been enthusiastic about living in a foreign country, but now that they

96

were face to face with the reality, they were filled with apprehension. They each came to Mary separately.

'Mother,' Beth said, 'I can't just leave all my friends. I may never see Virgil again. Could I stay here until the end of the semester?'

Tim said, 'I just got into little league. If I go away, they'll find another third baseman. Maybe we can go after next summer, when the season's over. Please, Mom!'

They're frightened. Like their mother. Stanton Rogers had been so convincing. But alone with her fears in the middle of the night, Mary thought: *I don't know anything about being an ambassador. I'm a Kansas housewife pretending to be some kind of statesman. Everyone's going to know I'm a fraud. I was insane ever to agree to this.*

Finally, miraculously, everything was ready. The house had been rented on a long lease to a family that had just moved to Junction City.

It was time to leave.

'Doug and I will drive you to the airport,' Florence insisted.

The airport where they would catch the six-passenger commuter plane to Kansas City, Missouri, was located in Manhattan, Kansas. In Kansas City, they would transfer to a larger plane to Washington, D.C.

'Just give me a minute,' Mary said. She walked upstairs to the bedroom she and Edward had shared for so many wonderful years. She stood there, taking a long, last look.

I'm leaving now, my dearest. I just wanted to say goodbye. I think I'm doing what you would have liked me to do. I hope I am. The only thing that really bothers me is that I have a feeling we may never come back here. I feel as though I'm deserting you. But you'll be with me wherever I go. I need you now more than I've ever needed you. Stay with me. Help me. I love you so much. Sometimes I don't think I can stand it without you. Can you hear me, darling? Are you there . . . ?

Douglas Schiffer saw to it that their baggage was checked onto the little commuter plane. When Mary saw the plane sitting on the tarmac, she froze in her tracks. 'Oh, my God!'

'What's the matter?' Florence asked.

'I – I've been so busy, I forgot all about it.'

'About what?'

'Flying! Florence, I've never been up in a plane in my life! I can't go up in that little thing!'

'Mary – the odds are a million to one against anything happening.'

'I don't like the odds,' Mary said flatly. 'We'll take the train.'

'You can't. They're expecting you in Washington this afternoon.'

'*Alive*. I'm not going to be any good to them *dead*.'

It took the Schiffers fifteen minutes to persuade Mary to board the plane. Half an hour later, she and the children were strapped aboard Air Mid-West Flight Number 826. As the motors revved up and the plane began racing down the runway, Mary closed her eyes and gripped the arms of her seat. Seconds later, they were airborne.

'Mama –'

'Sh! Don't talk!'

She sat rigid, refusing to look out of the window, concentrating on keeping the plane in the air. The children were pointing out the sights below, having a wonderful time.

Children, thought Mary bitterly. *What do they know!*

At the Kansas City Airport, they changed to a DC-10 and took off for Washington, D.C. Beth and Tim were seated together, and Mary was across the aisle from them. An elderly lady sat next to Mary.

'To tell you the truth, I'm a little nervous,' Mary's seatmate confessed. 'I've never flown before.'

Mary patted her hand and smiled. 'There's nothing to be nervous about. The odds are a million to one against anything happening.'

BOOK TWO

13

When their plane landed at Washington's Dulles Airport, Mary and the children were met by a young man from the State Department.

'Welcome to Washington, Mrs Ashley. My name is John Burns. Mr Rogers asked me to meet you and see that you get to your hotel safely. I've checked you in at the Riverdale Towers. I think you'll all be comfortable there.'

'Thank you.'

Mary introduced Beth and Tim.

'If you'll give me your baggage claim checks, Mrs Ashley, I'll see that everything is taken care of.'

Twenty minutes later they were all seated in a chauffeur-driven limousine, heading towards the centre of Washington.

Tim was staring out of the car window, awed. 'Look!' he exclaimed. 'There's the Lincoln Memorial!'

Beth was looking out of the other window. 'There's the Washington Monument!'

Mary looked at John Burns in embarrassment. 'I'm afraid the children aren't very sophisticated,' she apologized. 'You see, they've never been away from –' She glanced out of the window, and her eyes widened. 'Oh, my goodness!' she cried. 'Look! It's the White House!'

The limousine moved up Pennsylvania Avenue, surrounded by some of the most stirring landmarks in the world. Mary thought excitedly: *This is the city that rules the world. This is where the power is. And in a small way, I'm going to be a part of it.*

As the limousine approached the hotel, Mary asked, 'When will I see Mr Rogers?'

'He'll be in touch with you in the morning.'

Pete Connors, head of KUDESK, the counterintelligence section of the CIA, was working late, and his day was far from over. Every morning at 3 a.m. a team reported to prepare the President's daily intelligence checklist, collected from overnight cables. The report, codenamed 'Pickles', had to be ready by 6 a.m. so that it could be on the President's desk at the start of his day. An armed courier carried the list to the White House, entering at the west gate. Pete Connors had a renewed interest in the intercepted cable traffic coming from behind the Iron Curtain, because much of it concerned the appointment of Mary Ashley as the American Ambassador to Romania.

The Soviet Union was worried that President Ellison's plan was a ploy to penetrate their satellite countries, to spy on them or seduce them.

The commies aren't as worried as I am, Pete Connors thought grimly. *If the President's idea works this whole country is going to be open house for their fucking spies.*

Pete Connors had been informed the moment Mary Ashley landed in Washington. He had seen photographs of her and the children. *They're going to be perfect*, Connors thought happily.

The Riverdale Towers, one block away from the Watergate Complex, is a small family hotel with comfortable, nicely decorated suites.

A bellhop brought up the luggage, and as Mary started unpacking, the telephone rang. Mary picked it up. 'Hello.'

A masculine voice said, 'Mrs Ashley?'

'Yes.'

'My name is Ben Cohn. I'm a reporter with the *Washington Post*. I wonder if we could talk for a few minutes.'

Mary hesitated. 'We just checked in and I'm –'

'It will only take five minutes. I really just wanted to say hello.'

'Well, I – I suppose –'

'I'm on my way up.'

Ben Cohn was short and stocky, with a muscular body and the battered face of a prize fighter. *He looks like a sports reporter*, Mary thought.

He sat in an easy chair across from Mary. 'Your first time in Washington, Mrs Ashley?' Ben Cohn asked.

'Yes.' She noticed that he had no notebook or tape recorder.

'I won't ask you the dumb question.'

She frowned. 'What's the "dumb question"?'

'"How do you like Washington?" Whenever a celebrity steps off an airplane somewhere, the first thing they're asked is, "How do you like this place?" '

Mary laughed. 'I'm not a celebrity, but I think I'm going to like Washington a lot.'

'You were a professor at Kansas State University?'

'Yes. I taught a course called "Eastern Europe: Today's Politics".'

'I understand that the President first learned about you when he read a book of yours on Eastern Europe. And the magazine articles.'

'Yes.'

'And the rest, as they say, is history.'

'I suppose it *is* an unusual way to –'

'Not that unusual. Jeane Kirkpatrick came to President Reagan's attention in the same way, and he made her Ambassador to the UN.' He smiled at her. 'So you see, there's precedent. That's one of the big

102

buzz words in Washington. Precedent. Your grandparents were Romanian?'

'My grandfather. That's right.'

Ben Cohn stayed for another fifteen minutes, getting information on Mary's background.

Mary asked, 'When will this interview appear in the paper?' She wanted to be sure to send copies to Florence and Douglas and her other friends back home.

Ben Cohn rose and said evasively, 'I'm going to save it for now.' There was something about the situation that puzzled him. The problem was that he was not sure what it was. 'We'll be talking again later.'

After he left, Beth and Tim came into the living room. 'Was he nice, Mom?'

'Yes.' She hesitated, unsure. 'I think so.'

The following morning Stanton Rogers telephoned.

'Good morning, Mrs Ashley. It's Stanton Rogers.'

It was like hearing the voice of an old friend. *Maybe it's because he's the only person in town I know,* Mary thought. 'Good morning, Mr Rogers. Thank you for having Mr Burns meet us at the airport, and for arranging our hotel.'

'I trust it's satisfactory?'

'It's lovely.'

'I thought it would be a good idea if we met to discuss some of the procedures you'll be going through.'

'I would like that.'

'Why don't we make it lunch today at the Grand? It's not far from your hotel. One o'clock?'

'Fine.'

'I'll meet you in the downstairs dining room.'

It was starting.

Mary arranged for the children to have room service, and at one o'clock a taxi dropped her off at the Grand Hotel. Mary looked at it in awe. The Grand Hotel is its own centre of power. Heads of State and diplomats from all over the world stay there, and it is easy to see why. It is an elegant building, with an imposing lobby with Italian marble floors and gracious columns under a circular ceiling. There was a landscaped courtyard, with a fountain and an outdoor swimming pool. A marble staircase led down to the promenade restaurant, where Stanton Rogers was waiting for her.

'Good afternoon, Mrs Ashley.'

'Good afternoon, Mr Rogers.'

He laughed. 'That sounds so formal. What about Stan and Mary?'

She was pleased. 'That would be nice.'

Stanton Rogers seemed different somehow, and the change was hard for Mary to define. In Junction City there had been an aloofness about him, almost a resentment towards her. Now that seemed to have completely vanished. He was warm and friendly. *The difference is that he's accepted me*, Mary thought happily.

'Would you like a drink?'

'Thank you, no.'

They ordered lunch. The entrées seemed very expensive to her. *It's not like the prices in Junction City.* Her hotel suite was $250 a day. *At that rate, my money's not going to last very long*, Mary thought.

'Stan, I don't want to seem rude, but can you tell me how much an ambassador is paid?'

He laughed. 'That's a fair question. Your salary will be sixty-five thousand dollars a year, plus a housing allowance.'

'When does that begin?'

'The moment you're sworn in.'

'And until then?'

'You'll be paid seventy-five dollars a day.'

Her heart sank. That would not even take care of her hotel bill, let alone all the other expenses.

'Will I be in Washington long?' Mary asked.

'About a month. We'll do everything we can to expedite your move. The Secretary of State has cabled the Romanian government for approval of your appointment. Just between us, there have already been private discussions between the two governments. There will be no problem with the Romanians, but you still have to pass the Senate.'

So the Romanian government is going to accept me, Mary thought wonderingly. *Perhaps I'm better qualified than I realized.*

'I've set up an informal consultation for you with the Chairman of the Senate Foreign Relations Committee. The next stop after that will be an open hearing of the full committee. They'll ask you questions about your background, your loyalty to this country, your perceptions of the job, and what you hope to accomplish.'

'What happens after that?'

'The committee votes, and when they turn in their report, the full Senate votes.'

Mary said slowly, 'Nominations have been voted down in the past, haven't they?'

'The President's prestige is on the line with this one. You'll have the full backing of the White House. The President is eager to push your appointment through as quickly as possible. Incidentally, I thought you and the children might like to do some sightseeing in the next few days, so I've arranged for a car and driver for you, and a private tour of the White House.'

'Oh! Thank you so much.'

104

Stanton Rogers smiled. 'My pleasure.'

The private tour of the White House was arranged for the following morning. A guide escorted them. They were taken through the Jacqueline Kennedy Rose Garden and the sixteenth-century-style American Garden containing a pool, trees and herbs for use in the White House kitchen.

'Just ahead,' the guide announced, 'is the East Wing. It houses military offices, Congressional liaisons to the President, a visitor's office, and the First Lady's office.'

They went through the West Wing and looked into the President's Oval Office.

'How many rooms have they got in this place?' Tim asked.

'There are one hundred and thirty-two rooms, sixty-nine closets, twenty-nine fireplaces and seventeen bathrooms.'

'They sure must go to the bathroom a lot.'

'President Washington helped supervise much of the construction of the White House. He is the only President who never resided here.'

'I don't blame him,' Tim muttered. 'It's too darned big.'

Mary nudged him, red-faced.

The tour took almost two hours, and by the end of it the Ashley family was exhausted and impressed.

This is where it all began, Mary thought. *And now I'm going to be a part of it.*

'Mom?'

'Yes, Beth?'

'You have a funny look on your face.'

The call from the President's office came the following morning.

'Good morning, Mrs Ashley. President Ellison wondered whether you could make yourself available this afternoon to meet with him?'

Mary swallowed. 'Yes, I – of course.'

'Would three o'clock be convenient?'

'That would be fine.'

'A limousine will be downstairs for you at two forty-five.'

Paul Ellison rose as Mary was ushered into the Oval Office. He walked over to shake her hand, grinned and said, 'Gotcha!'

Mary laughed. 'I'm glad you did, Mr President. This is a great honour for me.'

'Sit down, Mrs Ashley. May I call you Mary?'

'Please.'

They sat down on the couch.

President Ellison said, 'You're going to be my doppelgänger. Do you know what that is?'

'It's a kind of identical spirit of a living person.'

'Right. And that's us. I can't tell you how excited I was when I read your latest article, Mary. It was as though I were reading something I had written. There are a lot of people who don't believe our people-to-people plan can work, but you and I are going to fool them.'

Our people-to-people plan. *We're* going to fool them. *He's a charmer*, Mary thought. Aloud, she said, 'I want to do everything I can to help, Mr President.'

'I'm counting on you. Very heavily. Romania is the testing ground. Since Groza was assassinated, your job is going to be more difficult. If we can pull it off there, we can make it work in the other communist countries.'

They spent the next thirty minutes discussing some of the problems that lay ahead, and then Paul Ellison said, 'Stan Rogers will keep in close touch with you. He's become a big fan of yours.' He held out his hand. 'Good luck, doppelgänger.'

The next afternoon Stanton Rogers telephoned Mary. 'You have an appointment at nine o'clock tomorrow morning with the Chairman of the Senate Foreign Relations Committee.'

The Committee on Foreign Relations has offices in the Russell Building, the oldest government building in Washington. A plaque in the hallway at the right side of the door reads: COMMITTEE ON FOREIGN RELATIONS SD-419.

The Chairman was a rotund, grey-haired man with sharp green eyes and the easy manner of a professional politician.

He greeted Mary at the door. 'Charlie Campbell. It's a pleasure to meet you, Mrs Ashley. I've certainly been hearing a lot about you.'

Good or bad? Mary wondered.

He led her to a chair. 'Some coffee?'

'No, thank you, Senator.' She was too nervous to hold a cup in her hand.

'Well, then, let's get right down to business. The President is eager to have you represent us in Romania. Naturally, we all want to give him our full support in every way possible. The question is – do you think you're qualified to handle that position, Mrs Ashley?'

'No, sir.'

Her answer caught him off guard. 'I beg your pardon?'

'If you mean have I had any diplomatic experience in dealing with foreign countries, then I'm not qualified. However, I've been told that one-third of the country's ambassadors are also people without previous experience. What I would bring to my job is a knowledge of Romania. I'm familiar with its economic and sociological problems and with its political background. I believe I could project a positive image of our country to the Romanians.'

Well, Charlie Campbell thought in surprise. *I expected a bubble-head.* In fact, Campbell had resented Mary Ashley even before meeting her. He had been given orders from the top to see that Mary Ashley got his committee's approval, no matter what they thought of her. A lot of snickering was going on in the corridors of power about what a gaffe the President had made by selecting an unknown hayseed from a place called Junction City, Kansas. *But, by God,* Campbell thought, *I think the boys may be in for a little surprise.*

Aloud, he said, 'The full Hearing Committee meets at nine o'clock Wednesday morning.'

The night before the hearing, Mary was in a panic. *Darling, when they question me about my experience, what am I going to tell them? That in Junction City I was homecoming queen, and that I won the ice skating contest three years in a row? I'm panicky. Oh, how I wish you were here with me.*

But once again, the irony struck her. If Edward were alive, *she* would not be here. *I'd be safe and warm at home with my husband and children, where I belong.*

She lay awake all night.

The hearing was held in the Senate Foreign Relations Committee Room, with the full fifteen members of the Committee present, seated on a dais in front of a wall that held four large world maps. Along the left side of the room was the press table, filled with reporters, and in the centre, seats for 200 spectators. The corners were brightly lit for television cameras. The room was filled to overflowing. Pete Connors sat in a back row. There was a sudden hush as Mary entered with Beth and Tim.

Mary was wearing a dark, tailored suit and a white blouse. The children had been forced out of their jeans and sweaters and were in their Sunday best.

Ben Cohn, seated at the press table, watched as they came in. *Jesus*, he thought, *they look like a Norman Rockwell cover.*

An attendant seated the children in a front row, and Mary was escorted to the witness chair facing the Committee. She sat under the glare of the hot lights, trying to conceal her nervousness.

The hearing began. Charlie Campbell smiled down at Mary. 'Good morning, Mrs Ashley. We thank you for appearing before this Committee. We will proceed to the questions.'

They started innocently enough.

'Name . . . ?'

'Widow . . . ?'

'Children . . . ?'

The questions were gentle and supportive.

'According to the biography we've been furnished, Mrs Ashley, for the last several years you've taught political science at Kansas State University. Is that correct?'

'Yes, sir.'

'You're a native of Kansas?'

'Yes, Senator.'

'Your grandparents were Romanian?'

'My grandfather. Yes, sir.'

'You've written a book and articles on rapprochement between the United States and Soviet bloc countries?'

'Yes, sir.'

'The latest article was printed in *Foreign Affairs* Magazine and came to the attention of the President?'

'That's my understanding.'

'Mrs Ashley, would you kindly tell this Committee what the basic premise of your article is?'

Her nervousness was rapidly disappearing. She was on sure ground now, discussing a subject on which she was an authority. She felt as though she were conducting a seminar at school.

'Several regional economic pacts currently exist in the world, and because they are mutually exclusive, they serve to divide the world into antagonistic and competitive blocs, instead of uniting it. Europe has the Common Market, the Eastern bloc has COMECON, and then there is the OECD, consisting of the free market countries and the non-aligned movement of third world states. My premise is very simple: I would like to see all the various and discrete organizations linked together by economic ties. Individuals who are engaged in a profitable partnership don't kill one another. I believe that the same principle applies to countries. I would like to see our country spearhead a movement to form a common market that includes allies and adversaries alike. Today, as an example, we're paying billions of dollars to store surplus grain in grain elevators while people in dozens of countries are starving. The one-world common market could solve that. It could cure inequities of distribution, at fair market prices for everyone. I would like to try to help make that happen.'

Senator Harold Turkel, a senior member of the Foreign Relations Committee, and a member of the opposition party, spoke up. 'I'd like to ask the nominee a few questions.'

Ben Cohn leaned forward in his seat. *Here we go.*

Senator Turkel was in his seventies, tough and abrasive, a noted curmudgeon. 'Is this your first time in Washington, Mrs Ashley?'

'Yes, sir. I think it's one of the most –'

'I suppose you've done a good deal of travelling?'

'Well, no. My husband and I had planned to travel, but –'

'Have you ever been to New York?'

'No, sir.'

'California?'

'No, sir.'

'Been to Europe?'

'No. As I said, we planned to –'

'Have you, in fact, ever been outside the State of Kansas, Mrs Ashley?'

'Yes. I gave a lecture at the University of Chicago and a series of talks in Denver and Atlanta.'

Turkel said drily, 'That must have been very exciting for you, Mrs Ashley. I can't recall when this Committee has been asked to approve a less qualified candidate for an ambassadorial post. You expect to represent the United States of America in a sensitive Iron Curtain country, and you're telling us that your entire knowledge of the world comes from living in Junction City, Kansas, and spending a few days in Chicago and Denver and Atlanta. Is that true?'

Mary was aware of the television cameras focused on her, and she held back her temper. 'No, sir. My knowledge of the world comes from studying it. I have a Ph.D. in political science and I've been teaching at Kansas State University for five years, with an emphasis on the Iron Curtain countries. I'm familiar with the current problems of the Romanian people and what their government thinks of the United States, and why.' Her voice was stronger now. 'All they know about this country is what their propaganda machines tell them. I would like to go over there and try to convince them that the United States is not a greedy, war-hungry country. I would like to show them what a typical American family is like. I –'

She broke off, afraid she had gone too far in her anger. And then, to her surprise, the members of the committee started to applaud. All except Turkel.

The questioning went on.

One hour later, Charlie Campbell asked, 'Are there any more questions?'

'I think the nominee has expressed herself very clearly,' one of the senators commented.

'I agree. Thank you, Mrs Ashley. This session is adjourned.'

Pete Connors studied Mary thoughtfully for a moment, then quietly left as the members of the press swarmed around her.

'Was the President's appointment a surprise to you?'

'Do you think they're going to approve your appointment, Mrs Ashley?'

'Do you really believe that teaching about a country qualifies you to –?'

'Turn this way, Mrs Ashley. Smile, please. One more.'

'Mrs Ashley –'

Ben Cohn stood apart from the others, watching and listening. *She's good*, he thought. *She has all the right answers. I wish to hell I knew the right questions.*

When Mary arrived back at the hotel, emotionally drained, Stanton Rogers was on the telephone.

'Hello, Madam Ambassador.'

She felt giddy with relief. 'You mean I *made* it? Oh, Stan. Thank you so much. I can't tell you how excited I am.'

'So am I, Mary.' His voice was filled with pride. 'So am I.'

When Mary told the children, they hugged her.

'I knew you'd make it!' Tim screamed.

Beth asked quietly, 'Do you think Daddy knows?'

'I'm sure he does, darling.' Mary smiled. 'I wouldn't be surprised if he gave the committee a little nudge . . .'

Mary telephoned Florence, and when she heard the news, she began to cry. 'Fantastic! Wait until I spread this around town!'

Mary laughed. 'I'll have a room at the Embassy ready for you and Douglas.'

'When do you leave for Romania?'

'Well, first the full Senate has to vote, but Stan says it's just a formality.'

'What happens next?'

'I have to go through a few weeks of briefing sessions in Washington, and then the children and I are on our way to Romania.'

'I can't wait to call the *Daily Union*!' Florence exclaimed. 'The town will probably put up a statue to you. I've got to go now. I'm too excited to talk. I'll call you tomorrow.'

Ben Cohn heard the results of the confirmation hearing when he returned to his office. He was still bothered. And he did not know why.

14

As Stanton Rogers predicted, the full Senate vote was a formality. Mary was voted in by a comfortable majority. When President Ellison heard the news, he said to Stanton Rogers, 'Our plan is under way, Stan. Nothing can stop us now.'

Stanton Rogers nodded. 'Nothing,' he agreed.

Pete Connors was in his office when he received the news. He immediately wrote out a message and encoded it. One of his men was on duty in the CIA cable room.

'I want to use the Roger Channel,' Connors said. 'Wait outside.'

The Roger Channel is the CIA's ultra-private cable system, available only for use by top-level executives. Messages are sent by a laser transmitter, on an ultrahigh frequency in a fraction of a second. When Connors was alone, he dispatched the cable. It was addressed to Sigmund.

During the next week, Mary called on the Deputy Secretary for Political Affairs, the head of the CIA, the Secretary of Commerce, the directors of the New York Chase Manhattan Bank, and several important Jewish organizations. Each of them had admonitions, advice and requests.

Ned Tillingast, at the CIA, was enthusiastic. 'It will be great to get our people back into action there, Madam Ambassador. Romania's been a blind spot for us since we became *personae non gratae*. I'll assign a man to your embassy as one of your attachés.' He gave her a meaningful look. 'I'm sure you'll give him your full cooperation.'

Mary wondered exactly what that meant. *Don't ask*, she decided.

The swearing-in ceremony of new ambassadors is customarily presided over by the Secretary of State, and there are usually twenty-five to thirty candidates sworn in at the same time. The morning the ceremony was to take place, Stanton Rogers telephoned Mary.

'Mary, President Ellison has asked that you be at the White House at noon. The President himself is going to swear you in. Bring Tim and Beth.'

The Oval Office was filled with members of the press. When President Ellison walked in with Mary and her children, television cameras began to turn and still cameras began to flash. Mary had spent the previous half hour with the President, and he had been warm and reassuring.

'You're perfect for this assignment,' he told her, 'or I would never have chosen you. You and I are going to make this dream come true.'

And it does seem like a dream, Mary thought as she faced the battery of cameras.

'Raise your right hand, please.'

Mary repeated after the President: 'I, Mary Elizabeth Ashley, do solemnly swear that I will support and defend the Constitution of the United States against all enemies foreign and domestic, that I will bear true faith and allegiance to the same, that I take this obligation freely and without any mental reservation or purpose of evasion, that I will well and faithfully discharge the duties of the office on which I am about to enter, so help me God.'

And it was done. She was the Ambassador to the Socialist Republic of Romania.

The treadmill began. Mary was ordered to report to the European and Yugoslavian Affairs Section at the State Department, located in the Mall Building that overlooked the Washington and Lincoln Memorials. There she was assigned a small, temporary, box-like office next to the Romanian Desk.

James Stickley, the Romanian Desk Officer, was a career diplomat with twenty-five years in the service. He was in his late fifties, of medium height, with a vulpine face and small, thin lips. His eyes were a pale, cold brown. He looked with disdain on the political appointees who were invading his world. He was considered the foremost expert on the Romanian desk, and when President Ellison had announced his plan to support an Ambassador to Romania, Stickley had been ecstatic, fully expecting that the post would be given to him. The news about Mary Ashley was a bitter blow. It was bad enough to have been passed over, but to have lost out to a political appointee – a nobody from Kansas – was galling.

'Can you believe it?' he asked Bruce, his closest friend. 'Half of our ambassadors are fucking appointees. That could never happen in England or France, chum. *They* use professional career officers. Would the Army ask an amateur to be a general? Well, overseas our fucking amateur ambassadors are generals.'

'You're drunk, Jimbo.'

'I'm gonna get drunker.'

He studied Mary Ashley now, as she sat across from his desk.

Mary was also studying Stickley. There was something mean-looking about him. *I wouldn't want to have him as an enemy*, Mary thought.

'You're aware that you're being sent to an extremely sensitive post, Mrs Ashley?'

'Yes, of course. I –'

'Our last Ambassador to Romania put one wrong foot forward and the whole relationship exploded in our faces. It's taken us three years to get back in the door. The President would be damned mad if we blew it again.'

If I blew it, he means.

'We're going to have to make an instant expert out of you. We don't have a lot of time.' He handed her an armful of files. 'You can start by reading these reports.'

'I'll dedicate my morning to it.'

'No. In thirty minutes you're scheduled to begin a language course in Romanian. The course usually takes months, but I have orders to push you through the mill.'

Time became a blur, a whirlwind of activity that left Mary exhausted. Every morning she and Stickley went through the daily files of the Romanian desk together.

'I'll be reading the cables you send in,' Stickley informed her. 'They will be yellow copies for action, or white copies for information. Duplicates of your cables will go to Defence, the CIA, the USIA, the Treasury Department, and a dozen other departments. One of the first issues you'll be expected to resolve is Americans being held in Romanian prisons. We want their release.'

'What are they charged with?'

'Espionage, drugs, theft – anything the Romanians want to charge them with.'

Mary wondered how on earth one went about getting a charge of espionage dismissed. *I'll find a way.*

'Right,' she said briskly.

'Remember – Romania is one of the more independent Iron Curtain countries. We have to encourage that attitude.'

Exactly.

Stickley said, 'I'm going to give you a package. Don't let it out of your hands. It's for your eyes only. When you've read it and digested it, I want you to return it to me personally tomorrow morning. Any questions?'

'No, sir.'

He handed Mary a thick manila envelope sealed with red tape. 'Sign for it, please.'

She signed.

During the ride on the way back to the hotel, Mary clutched it to her lap, feeling like a character in a James Bond movie.

The children were dressed up and waiting for her.

Oh dear, Mary remembered. *I promised to take them out to a Chinese dinner and a movie.*

'Fellas,' she said. 'There's been a change of plans. We'll have to make our excursion another evening. Tonight we're going to stay in and have room service. I have some urgent work to do.'

'Sure, Mom.'

'Okay.'

And Mary thought: *Before Edward died, they would have screamed like banshees. But they've had to grow up. We've all had to grow up.*

She took them both in her arms. 'I'll make it up to you,' she promised.

The material James Stickley had given her was incredible. *No wonder he wants this right back*, Mary thought. There were detailed reports on every important Romanian official, from the President to the Minister of Commerce. There was a dossier on their sex habits, financial dealings, friendships, personal traits and prejudices. Some of the reading was lurid. The Minister of Commerce, for example, was sleeping with his mistress and his chauffeur, while his wife was having an affair with her maid.

Mary was up half the night memorizing the names and peccadilloes of the people with whom she would be dealing. *I wonder if I'll be able to keep a straight face when I meet them?*

In the morning, she returned the secret documents.

Stickley said, 'All right, now you know everything you should know about the Romanian leaders.'

'And then some,' Mary murmured.

'There's something you should bear in mind: By now the Romanians know everything there is to know about *you*.'

'That won't get them far,' Mary said.

'No?' Stickley leaned back in his chair. 'You're a woman, and you're alone. You can be sure they've already marked you as an easy target. They'll play on your loneliness. Every move you make will be watched and recorded. The Embassy and the Residence will be bugged. In communist countries, we're forced to use local staffs, so every servant in the Residence will be a member of the Romanian security police.'

He's trying to frighten me, Mary thought. *Well, it won't work.*

Every hour of Mary's day seemed to be accounted for, and most of the evenings. Besides Romanian language lessons, her schedule included a course at the Foreign Service Institute in Rosslyn, briefings at the Defence Intelligence Agency, meetings with the Secretary of the ISA – International Security Affairs – and with Senate committees. They all had demands, advice, questions.

Mary felt guilty about Beth and Tim. With Stanton Rogers' help, she had found a tutor for the children. In addition, Beth and Tim had met some other children living in the hotel, so at least they had playmates; still, she hated leaving them on their own so much.

Mary made it a point to have breakfast with them every morning before she went off to her 8 a.m. language course at the Institute. The language was impossible. *I'm surprised even Romanians can speak it.* She studied the phrases aloud:

'Good morning.'	*Bună Dimineaţa*
'Thank you.'	*Mulţumésc*
'You're welcome.'	*Cu Plăcére*
'I don't understand.'	*Nu Inteleg*
'Sir.'	*Domnule*
'Miss.'	*Domnisoara*

And none of the words was pronounced the way it was spelled.

Beth and Tim sat watching her struggle over her homework, and Beth grinned. 'This is our revenge for your making us learn the multiplication tables.'

James Stickley said, 'I want you to meet your military attaché, Madam Ambassador, Colonel William McKinney.'

Bill McKinney wore mufti, but his military bearing was like a uniform. He was a tall, middle-aged man with a seamed, weathered face.

'Madam Ambassador.' His voice was rough and gravelly, as though his throat had suffered an injury.

'I'm pleased to meet you,' Mary said.

Colonel McKinney was her first staff member, and meeting him gave her a sense of excitement. It seemed to bring her new position much closer. 'I look forward to working with you in Romania,' he said.

'Have you been to Romania before?'

The Colonel and James Stickley exchanged a look.

'He's been there before,' Stickley replied.

Every Monday afternoon diplomatic sessions for new ambassadors were held in a conference room on the eighth floor of the State Department.

'In the Foreign Service, we have a strict chain of command,' the class was told. 'At the top is the Ambassador. Under him – (*under her*, Mary automatically thought) – is the DCM – the Deputy Chief of Mission.

Under him – (*under her*) – are the political consular, economic consular, administrative consular, and public affairs consular. Then you have agriculture, commerce and the military attaché.' *That's Colonel McKinney*, Mary thought. 'When you are at your new posts, you will have diplomatic immunity. You cannot be arrested for speeding, drunken driving, burning down a house, or even for murder. When you die, no one can touch your body or examine any note you may have left. You don't have to pay your bills – the stores can't sue you.'

Someone in the class called out, 'Don't let my wife hear that!'

The instructor glanced at his watch. 'Before our next session, I suggest you study the Foreign Affairs Manual, Volume Two, Section Three Hundred, which talks about social relationships. Thank you.'

Mary and Stanton Rogers were having lunch at the Watergate Hotel.

'President Ellison would like you to do some public relations for him,' Rogers said.

'What kind of public relations?'

'We'll set up some national things. Press interviews, radio, television –'

'I've never – well, if it's important. I'll try.'

'Good. We'll have to get you a new wardrobe. You can't pose in the same dress twice.'

'Stan, that would cost a fortune! Besides, I don't have time to shop. I'm busy from early morning until late at night. If –'

'No problem. Helen Moody.'

'What?'

'She's one of Washington's top professional shoppers. Just leave everything to her.'

Helen Moody was an attractive, outgoing black woman who had been a successful model before she started her own personal shopping service. She appeared at Mary's hotel room early one morning and spent an hour going through her wardrobe.

'Very nice, for Junction City,' she said frankly, 'but we have to wow Washington, D.C. Right?'

'I don't have much money to –'

Helen Moody grinned. 'I know where the bargains are. And we'll do it fast. You're going to need a floor-length evening gown, a dress for cocktail parties and evening receptions, an afternoon dress for tea parties and lunch parties, a suit for street or office wear, a black dress, and an appropriate head covering for official mournings or funerals.'

116

The shopping took three days. When it was finished, Helen Moody studied Mary Ashley. 'You're a pretty lady, but I think we can do even better for you. I want you to see Susan at Rainbow for makeup and then I'll send you to Billy at Sunshine for your hair.'

A few evenings later Mary ran into Stanton Rogers at a formal dinner given at the Corcoran Gallery. He looked at Mary and smiled. 'You look absolutely ravishing.'

The media blitz began. It was orchestrated by Ian Villiers, Chief of Press Relations for the State Department. Villiers was in his late forties, a dynamic ex-newspaperman who seemed to know everybody in the media.

Mary found herself in front of the cameras on *Good Morning America*, *Meet the Press*, and *Firing Line*. She was interviewed by the *Washington Post*, the *New York Times*, and half a dozen other important daily papers. She did interviews for the London *Times, Der Spiegel, Oggi,* and *Le Monde. Time* Magazine and *People* did feature articles on her and the children. Mary Ashley's photograph seemed to be every-where, and whenever there was a news break about an event in some far-off corner of the world, she was asked for her comments. Overnight, Mary Ashley and her children became celebrities.

Tim said, 'Mom, it's really spooky seeing our pictures on the covers of all the magazines.'

'*Spooky* is the word,' Mary agreed.

Somehow she felt uneasy about all the publicity. She spoke to Stanton Rogers about it.

'Look on it as a part of your job. The President is trying to create an image. By the time you arrive in Europe, everyone there will know who you are.'

Ben Cohn and Akiko were lying in bed, naked. Akiko was a lovely Japanese girl, ten years younger than the reporter. They had met a few years earlier, when he was writing a story on models, and they had been together ever since.

Cohn was having a problem.

'What's the matter, baby?' Akiko asked softly. 'Would you like me to work on you some more?'

His thoughts were far away. 'No. I've already got a hard-on.'

'I don't see it,' she teased.

'It's in my mind, Akiko. I've got a hard-on for a story. There's some-thing weird happening in this town.'

'So what else is new?'

117

'This is different. I can't figure it out.'

'Do you want to talk about it?'

'It's Mary Ashley. I've seen her on the covers of six magazines in the last two weeks, and she hasn't even taken up her post yet! Akiko, someone is giving Mrs Ashley a movie-star buildup. She and her two kids are being splashed all over the newspapers and magazines. Why?'

'I'm supposed to be the one with the devious Oriental mind. I think you're complicating that which is very simple.'

Ben Cohn lit a cigarette and took an angry puff on it. 'You could be right,' he grumbled.

She reached down and began to stroke him. 'How about putting out that cigarette and lighting me . . . ?'

'There's a party being given for Vice President Bradford,' Stanton Rogers informed Mary, 'and I've arranged for you to be invited. It's on Friday night at the Pan American Union.'

The Pan American Union was a large, sedate building with a huge courtyard, and was frequently used for diplomatic functions. The dinner for the Vice President was an elaborate affair, with tables holding gleaming antique silverware and sparkling Baccarat glasses. There was a small orchestra. The guest list consisted of the capital's elite. Besides the Vice President and his wife, there were senators, ambassadors and celebrities from all walks of life.

Mary looked around at the glamorous gathering. *I must remember everything so I can tell Beth and Tim about it*, she thought.

When dinner was announced, Mary found herself at a table with an interesting mix of senators, State Department officials and diplomats. The people were charming and the dinner was excellent.

At eleven o'clock, Mary looked at her watch and said to the senator on her right, 'I didn't realize it was so late. I promised the children I'd be back early.'

She rose and nodded to the people seated at her table. 'It's been lovely meeting you all. Good night.'

There was a stunned silence, and everyone in the huge banquet hall turned to watch Mary as she walked across the dance floor and exited.

'Oh, my God!' Stanton Rogers whispered. 'No one told her!'

Stanton Rogers had breakfast with Mary the following morning.

'Mary,' he said, 'this is a town that takes its rules seriously. A lot of them are stupid, but we all have to live by them.'

'Oh, oh. What did I do?'

He sighed. 'You broke rule number one: No one – but no one – ever leaves a party before the guest of honour. Last night it happened to be the Vice President of the United States.'

'Oh, dear.'

'Half the telephones in Washington have been ringing off the hook.'

'I'm sorry, Stan. I didn't know. Anyway, I had promised the children –'

'There are no children in Washington – only young voters. This town is about power. Never forget that.'

Money was proving to be a problem. Living expenses were horrendous. The price of everything in Washington seemed to Mary to be outrageous. She gave some laundry and pressing to the hotel's valet service, and when she got the bill, she was shocked. 'Five dollars and fifty cents to wash a blouse,' she said. 'And a dollar ninety-five for a brassiere!' *No more*, she vowed. *From now on I'll do the laundry myself.*

She soaked her pantihose in cold water, and then put them in the freezer. They lasted much longer that way. She washed the children's socks and handkerchiefs and underpants along with her bras in the bathroom sink. She spread the handkerchiefs against the mirror to dry, and then carefully folded them so that they did not have to be ironed. She steamed out her dresses and Tim's trousers by hanging them on the shower curtain rack, turning the hot water of the shower on full force, and closing the bathroom door. When Beth opened the door one morning, she was hit by a wall of steam.

'Mother – what are you *doing*?'

'Saving money,' Mary informed her loftily. 'The laundry charges a fortune.'

'What if the President walked in? How would it look? He'd think we were Okies.'

'The President's not going to walk in. And close the bathroom door, please. You're wasting money.'

Okies, indeed! If the President walked in and saw what she was doing, he would be proud of her. She would show him the hotel laundry list and let him see how much she was saving by using a little yankee ingenuity. He would be impressed. *If more people in government had your imagination, Madam Ambassador, the economy of this country would be in a lot better shape than it is. We've lost the pioneering spirit that made this country great. Our people have gone soft. We rely too much on time-saving electrical appliances and not enough on ourselves. I would like to use you as a shining example to some of the spendthrifts*

119

in Washington who think this country is made of money. You could teach them all a lesson. As a matter of fact, I have a wonderful idea. Mary Ashley, I'm going to make you Secretary of the Treasury.

Steam was seeping out from under the bathroom door. Dreamily, Mary opened the door. A cloud of steam poured into the living room.

There was the sound of the doorbell, and a moment later Beth said, 'Mother, James Stickley is here to see you.'

15

'The whole thing gets weirder and weirder,' Ben Cohn said. He was sitting up in bed, nude, his young mistress, Akiko Hadaka, at his side. They were watching Mary Ashley on *Meet the Press*.

She was saying, 'I believe that mainland China is heading for a more humane, individualistic communist society with its incorporation of Hong Kong and Macao.'

'Now what the fuck does that lady know about China?' Ben Cohn muttered. He turned to Akiko. 'You're looking at a housewife from Kansas who's become an expert on everything overnight.'

'She seems very bright,' Akiko said.

'Bright is beside the point. Every time she gives an interview, the reporters go crazy. It's like a feeding frenzy. How did she get on *Meet the Press?* I'll tell you how. Someone decided that Mary Ashley was going to be a celebrity. Who? Why? Charles Lindbergh never had a build-up like this.'

'Who's Charles Lindbergh?'

Ben Cohn sighed. 'That's the problem with the generation gap. There's no communication.'

Akiko said softly, 'There are other ways to communicate.'

She pushed him gently down on the bed and moved on top of him. She worked her way down his body, flicking her long, silken hair across his chest and his stomach and his groin, watching him grow hard. She stroked him and said, 'Hello, Arthur.'

'Arthur wants to get inside you.'

'Not yet. I'll be back to him.'

She rose and padded off to the kitchen. Ben Cohn watched her as she moved out of the room. He looked at the television set and thought: *That lady gives me shpilkes. There's a hell of a lot less there than meets the eye, and I'm damned well going to find out what it is.*

'Akiko!' he shouted. 'What're you doing? Arthur's falling asleep.'

'Tell him to wait up,' she called. 'I'll be right there.'

A few minutes later, she returned, carrying a dish filled with ice cream, whipped cream and a cherry.

'For God's sake,' he said. 'I'm not hungry. I'm horny.'

'Lie back.' She put a towel under him, took the ice cream from the dish and started spreading it around his testicles.

He yelled, 'Hey! That's cold.'

'Sh!' Akiko put the whipped cream over the ice cream and then put his penis in her mouth until it became turgid.

'Oh, my God,' Ben moaned. 'Don't stop.'

Akiko put the cherry on top of his now rigid penis. 'I love banana splits,' she whispered.

And as she began to eat it, Ben felt an incredible mixture of sensations, all of them wonderful. When he could stand it no longer, he rolled Akiko over and plunged inside her.

On the television set Mary Ashley was saying, 'One of the best ways to prevent war with countries opposed to the American ideology is to increase our trade with them . . .'

Later that evening, Ben Cohn telephoned Ian Villiers.

'Hi, Ian.'

'Benjie, my boy – what can I do for you?'

'I need a favour.'

'Name it, and you've got it.'

'I understand you're in charge of press relations for our new Ambassador to Romania.'

A cautious, 'Yes . . . ?'

'Who's behind her build-up, Ian? I'm interested in –'

'I'm sorry, Ben. That's State Department business. I'm just a hired hand. You might drop a note to the Secretary of State.'

Hanging up, Ben said, 'Why didn't he just tell me to go fuck myself?' He made a decision. 'I think I'm going to have to go out of town for a few days.'

'Where are you going, baby?'

'Junction City, Kansas.'

As it turned out, Ben Cohn was in Junction City for only one day. He spent an hour talking to Sheriff Munster and one of his deputies, then drove a rental car to Fort Riley, where he visited the CID office. He caught a late afternoon plane to Manhattan, Kansas, and a connecting flight home.

As Ben Cohn's plane took off, a person-to-person telephone call was placed from the Fort to a number in Washington, D.C.

Mary Ashley was walking down the long corridor of the Foreign Service Building on her way to report to James Stickley when she heard a deep, male voice behind her say, 'Now *that's* what I call a perfect ten.'

Mary spun around. A tall stranger was leaning against a wall, openly staring at her, an insolent grin on his face. He was rugged-looking, dressed in jeans, T-shirt and tennis shoes, and he looked scruffy and unshaven. There were laugh lines around his mouth, and his eyes were a bright, mocking blue. There was an air of arrogance about him that was infuriating. Mary turned on her heel and angrily walked away, conscious of his eyes following her.

The conference with James Stickley lasted for more than an hour. When Mary returned to her office, the stranger was seated in her chair, his feet on her desk, looking through her papers. She could feel the blood rising to her face.

'What the devil do you think you're doing?'

The man gave her a long, lazy look and slowly got to his feet. 'I'm Mike Slade. My friends call me Michael.'

She said icily, 'What can I do for you, Mr Slade?'

'Nothing, really,' he said easily. 'We're neighbours. I work here in the department, so I thought I'd come by and say hello.'

'You've said it. And if you really are in the department, I assume you have your own desk. So in the future you won't have to sit at my desk and snoop.'

'God, it has a temper! I heard the Kansians, or whatever you people call yourselves, were supposed to be friendly folks.'

She gritted her teeth. 'Mr Slade, I'll give you two seconds to get out of my office before I call a guard.'

'I must have heard wrong,' he mumbled to himself.

'And if you really work in this department, I'd suggest you go home and shave and put on some proper clothing.'

'I used to have a wife who talked like that,' Mike Slade sighed. 'I don't have her any more.'

Mary felt her face getting redder. 'Out.'

He waved his hand at her. ''Bye, honey. I'll be seeing you.'

Oh, no, Mary thought. *No, you won't.*

The whole morning was a series of unpleasant experiences. James Stickley was openly antagonistic. By noon, Mary was too upset to eat. She decided to spend her lunch hour riding around Washington, getting the anger out of her system.

Her limousine was sitting at the kerb in front of the Foreign Service Building.

'Good morning, Madam Ambassador,' the chauffeur said. 'Where would you like to go?'

'Anywhere, Marvin. Let's just drive around.'

'Yes, ma'am.' The car pulled smoothly away from the kerb. 'Would you like to see Embassy Row?'

'Fine.' Anything to get the taste of the morning out of her mouth.

He made a left turn at the corner and headed for Massachusetts Avenue.

123

'It begins here,' Marvin said as he turned onto the wide street. He slowed the car down and began to point out the various embassies.

Mary recognized the Japanese Embassy because of the rising sun flag in front of it. The Indian Embassy had an elephant over the door.

They passed a beautiful Islamic mosque. There were people in the front courtyard kneeling in prayer.

They reached the corner of 23rd Street and passed a white stone building with pillars on each side of the three steps.

'That's the Romanian Embassy,' Marvin said. 'Next to it is –'

'Stop, please!'

The limousine swung to the kerb. Mary looked out of the car window at a plaque on the outside of the building. It read: EMBASSY OF THE SOCIALIST REPUBLIC OF ROMANIA.

On an impulse, Mary said, 'Wait here, please. I'm going inside.'

Her heart began to beat faster. This was going to be her first real contact with the country she had been teaching about – the country that was going to be her home for the next few years.

She took a deep breath and pressed the doorbell. Silence. She tried the door. It was unlocked. She opened it and stepped inside. The reception hall was dark and freezing cold. There was a red couch in an alcove and next to it two chairs placed in front of a small television set. She heard footsteps and turned. A tall, thin man was hurrying down the stairs.

'Yes, yes?' he called. 'What is it? What is it?'

Mary beamed. 'Good morning. I'm Mary Ashley. I'm the new Ambassador to Rom –'

The man slapped his hand to his face. 'Oh, my God!'

She was startled. 'What's wrong?'

'What's wrong is that we are not expecting you, Madam Ambassador.'

'Oh, I know that. I was just driving by and I –'

'Ambassador Corbescue is going to be terribly, terribly upset!'

'Upset? Why? I just thought I'd say hello and –'

'Of course, of course. Forgive me. My name is Gabriel Stoica. I am the Deputy Chief of Mission. Please let me put on the lights and some heat. We were not expecting guests, as you can see. Not at all.'

He was so obviously in a panic that all Mary wanted to do was leave, but it was too late. She watched as Gabriel Stoica ran around turning on overhead lights and lamps until the reception hall was brightly lit.

'It will take a few minutes for the heat to come on,' he apologized. 'We try to save as much on fuel costs as we can. Washington is very expensive.'

She wished she could have disappeared into the floor. 'If I had realized . . .'

'No, no! It is nothing, nothing. The Ambassador is upstairs. I will inform him you are here.'

'Don't bother –'

Stoica was racing upstairs.

124

Five minutes later, Stoica returned. 'Please come. The Ambassador is delighted that you are here. Delighted.'

'Are you sure that –?'

'He is waiting for you.'

He escorted Mary upstairs. At the top of the stairs was a conference room with fourteen chairs around a long table. Against the wall was a cabinet filled with crafts and sculptures from Romania, and on the wall was a relief map of Romania. There was a fireplace with the Romanian flag above it. Coming forward to greet her was Ambassador Radu Corbescue, in shirt sleeves, hastily pulling on a jacket. He was a tall, heavy-set man with a dark complexion. A servant was hurriedly turning on lights and adjusting the heating.

'Madam Ambassador!' Corbescue cried. 'What an unexpected honour! Forgive us for receiving you so informally. Your State Department did not notify us that you were coming.'

'It's my fault,' Mary said apologetically. 'I was in the neighbourhood and I –'

'It is a pleasure to meet you! A pleasure! We have seen so much of you on television and in newspapers and magazines. We have been very curious about the new Ambassador to our country. You will have some tea?'

'Well, I – if you're sure it isn't too much trouble.'

'Trouble? Of course, not! I apologize because we have not prepared a formal luncheon for you. Forgive me! I am so embarrassed.'

I'm the one who's embarrassed, Mary thought. *What made me do this crazy thing? Dumb, dumb, dumb. I'm not even going to tell the children about this. It will be my secret 'til the grave.*

When the tea was brought, the Ambassador from Romania was so nervous that he spilled it. 'How clumsy of me! Forgive me!'

Mary wished he would stop saying that.

The Ambassador tried to make small talk, but that only made the situation worse. It was obvious that he was miserably uncomfortable. As soon as she discreetly could, Mary rose.

'Thank you so much, your Excellency. It was very nice meeting you. Goodbye.'

And she fled.

When Mary returned to the office, James Stickley immediately sent for her.

'Mrs Ashley,' he said coldly, 'would you mind explaining to me exactly what you thought you were doing?'

I guess it's not going to be a secret I'll carry to the grave, Mary decided. 'Oh. You mean about the Romanian Embassy? I – I just thought I'd drop in and say hello and –'

'This is not a cosy little back-home get-together,' Stickley snapped.

'In Washington, you don't just *drop in* on an embassy. When an Ambassador makes a call on another Ambassador, it's by invitation only. You've embarrassed the hell out of Corbescue. I had to talk him out of making a formal protest to the State Department. He believes that you went there to spy on him and catch him off guard.'

'What! Well, of all the –'

'Just try to remember you're no longer a private citizen – you're a representative of the United States Government. The next time you have an impulse less personal than brushing your teeth, you'll check with me first. Is that clear – I mean *very* clear?'

Mary swallowed. 'That's fine.'

'Good.' He picked up the telephone and dialled a number. 'Mrs Ashley is with me now. Would you like to come in? Right.' He replaced the receiver.

Mary sat there in silence, feeling like a small child being chastised. The door opened and Mike Slade walked in.

He looked at Mary and grinned. 'Hi. I took your advice and shaved.'

Stickley looked from one to the other. 'You two have met?'

Mary was glaring at Slade. 'Not really. I found him snooping at my desk.'

James Stickley said, 'Mrs Ashley, Mike Slade. Mr Slade is going to be your Deputy Chief of Mission.'

Mary stared at him. '*He's what?*'

'Mr Slade is on the East European Desk. He usually works out of Washington, but it's been decided to assign him to Romania as your Deputy Chief.'

Mary found herself springing out of her chair. 'No!' she protested. 'That's impossible.'

Mike said mildly, 'I promise to shave every day.'

Mary turned to Stickley. 'I thought an ambassador was permitted to choose her own Deputy Chief of Mission.'

'That is correct, but –'

'Then I am unchoosing Mr Slade. I don't want him.'

'Under ordinary circumstances, you would be within your rights, but in this case, I'm afraid you have no choice. The order came from the White House.'

Mary could not seem to avoid Mike Slade. The man was everywhere. She ran into him in the Pentagon, in the Senate dining room, in the corridors of the State Department. He was always dressed in either denims and a T-shirt or in sports clothes. Mary wondered how he got away with it in an environment that was so formal.

One day Mary saw him having lunch with Colonel McKinney. They were engaged in an earnest conversation, and Mary wondered how close the two men were. *Could they be old friends? And could they be planning*

126

to gang up on me? I'm getting paranoid, Mary told herself. *And I'm not even in Romania yet.*

Charlie Campbell, head of the Senate Foreign Relations Committee, hosted a party in Mary's honour at the Corcoran Gallery. When Mary walked into the room and saw all the elegantly gowned women, she thought: *I don't even belong here. They look like they were all born chic.*

She had no idea how lovely she looked.

There were more than a dozen photographers present, and Mary was the most photographed woman of the evening. She danced with half a dozen men, some married, and some unmarried, and was asked for her telephone number by almost all of them. She was neither offended nor interested.

'I'm sorry,' she said to each of them, 'my work and my family keep me too busy to think about going out.'

The idea of being with anyone but Edward was unthinkable. There could never be another man for her.

She was at a table with Charlie Campbell and his wife and half a dozen people from the State Department. The conversation turned to anecdotes about ambassadors.

'A few years ago in Madrid,' one of the guests recounted, 'hundreds of rioting students were clamouring for the return of Gibraltar in front of the British Embassy. As they were on the verge of breaking into the building, one of General Franco's ministers telephoned. "I'm deeply distressed to hear what's happening at your embassy," he said. "Shall I send more police?" "No," the Ambassador said, "just send fewer students." '

Someone asked, 'Wasn't it Hermes who was regarded by the ancient Greeks as the patron of ambassadors?'

'Yes,' came the rejoinder. 'And he was also the protector of vagabonds, thieves and liars.'

Mary was enjoying the evening tremendously. The people were bright and witty and interesting. She could have stayed all night.

The man next to her said, 'Don't you have to get up early for appointments tomorrow?'

'No,' Mary said. 'It's Sunday. I can sleep late.'

A little later, a woman yawned. 'Excuse me. I've had a long day.'

'So have I,' Mary said brightly.

It seemed to her that the room was abnormally quiet. She looked around, and everyone seemed to be staring at her. *What on earth –?* She glanced at her watch. It was 2.30 a.m. And with horror, she suddenly remembered something Stanton Rogers had told her: *At a dinner party, the guest of honour always leaves first.*

And *she* was the guest of honour! *Oh, my God*, Mary thought. *I'm keeping everybody up.*

She rose to her feet and said in a choked voice, 'Good night, everybody. It's been a lovely evening.'

She turned and hurried out of the door, and behind her she could hear the other guests scrambling to leave.

Next morning she ran into Mike Slade in the hallway. He grinned and said, 'I hear you kept half of Washington up Saturday night.'

His supercilious air infuriated her.

She brushed past him and went into James Stickley's office.

'Mr Stickley, I really don't think it would serve the best interests of our embassy in Romania for Mr Slade and me to try working together.'

He looked up from the paper he was reading. 'Really? What's the problem?'

'It's his – his attitude. I find Mr Slade to be rude and arrogant. Frankly, I don't like Mr Slade.'

'Oh, I know Mike has his little idiosyncrasies, but –'

'*Idiosyncrasies?* He's a rhinestone in the rough. I'm officially requesting that you send someone else in his place.'

'Are you finished?'

'Yes.'

'Mrs Ashley, Mike Slade happens to be our top field expert on East European affairs. Your job is to make friends with the natives. My job is to see to it that you get all the help I can give you. And his name is Mike Slade. I really don't want to hear any more about it. Do I make myself clear?'

It's no use, Mary thought. *No use at all.*

She returned to her office, frustrated and angry. *I could talk to Stan*, she thought. *He would understand. But that would be a sign of weakness. I'm going to have to handle Mike Slade myself.*

'Daydreaming?'

Mary looked up, startled. Mike Slade was standing in front of her desk, holding a large stack of memos.

'This should keep you out of trouble tonight,' he said. He laid them on her desk.

'*Knock* next time you want to come into my office.'

His eyes were mocking her. 'Why do I get the feeling you're not crazy about me?'

She felt her temper rising again. 'I'll tell you why, Mr Slade. Because I think you're an arrogant, nasty, conceited –'

He raised a finger. 'You're being tautological.'

'Don't you dare make fun of me.' She found herself yelling.

His voice dropped to a dangerous level. 'You mean I can't join the others? What do you think everyone in Washington is saying about you?'

'I don't really care what they're saying.'

'Oh, but you should.' He leaned over her desk. 'Everybody is asking what right you have to be sitting at an ambassador's desk. I spent four years in Romania, lady. It's a piece of dynamite ready to explode, and the government is sending in a dumb kid from the sticks to play with it.'

Mary sat there listening, gritting her teeth.

'You're an amateur, Mrs Ashley. If someone wanted to pay you off, they should have made you Ambassador to Iceland.'

Mary lost control. She sprang to her feet and slapped him hard across the face.

Mike Slade sighed. 'You're never stuck for an answer, are you?'

16

The invitation read: 'The Ambassador of the Socialist Republic of Romania requests your presence for cocktails and dinner at the Embassy, 1607 23rd Street, N.W., at 7.30 p.m., Black Tie, RSVP 232–6593.'

Mary thought of the last time she had visited that embassy and what a fool she had made of herself. *Well, that won't happen again. I'm past all that. I'm part of the Washington scene now.*

She put on one of the new outfits she had bought, a black, cut-velvet evening dress, with long sleeves. She wore black silk high-heel shoes and a pearl necklace.

Beth said, 'You look prettier than Madonna.'

Mary hugged her. 'I'm overwhelmed. You two have dinner in the dining room downstairs and then you may come up and watch television. I'll be home early. Tomorrow we're all going to visit President Washington's home at Mount Vernon.'

'Have a good time, Mom.'

The telephone rang. It was the desk clerk. 'Madam Ambassador, Mr Stickley is waiting for you in the lobby.'

I wish I could have gone alone, Mary thought. *I don't need him or anyone else to keep me out of trouble.*

The Romanian Embassy looked completely different from the last time Mary had seen it. There was a festive air about it that had been totally missing on her first visit. They were greeted at the door by Gabriel Stoica, the Deputy Chief of Mission.

'Good evening, Mr Stickley. How nice to see you.'

James Stickley nodded towards Mary. 'May I present our Ambassador to your country?'

There was no flicker of recognition on Stoica's face. 'It is a pleasure to meet you, Madam Ambassador. Please follow me.'

As they walked down the hallway, Mary noticed that all the rooms were brightly lit and well-heated. From upstairs she could hear the strains of a small orchestra. There were vases of flowers everywhere.

Ambassador Corbescue was talking to a group of people when he saw James Stickley and Mary Ashley approach.

'Ah, good evening, Mr Stickley.'

'Good evening, Ambassador. May I present the United States Ambassador to Romania?'

Corbescue looked at Mary and said tonelessly, 'I am happy to meet you.'

Mary waited for the twinkle in his eye. It never came.

There were a hundred people at dinner. The men wore dinner jackets and the women were beautifully gowned in dresses by Luis Estévez and Oscar de la Renta. The large table Mary had seen upstairs on her earlier visit had been augmented by half a dozen smaller tables around it. Liveried butlers circled the room with trays of champagne.

'Would you like a drink?' Stickley asked.

'No, thank you,' Mary said. 'I don't drink.'

'*Really?* That's a pity.'

She looked at him, puzzled. 'Why?'

'Because it's part of the job. At every diplomatic dinner party you attend, there will be toasts. If you don't drink, you'll offend your host. You have to take a sip now and then.'

'I'll remember,' Mary said.

She looked across the room, and there was Mike Slade. She did not recognize him for a moment. He was wearing a dinner jacket, and she had to admit that he was not unattractive in evening clothes. His arm was draped over a voluptuous blonde who was about to fall out of her dress. *Cheap*, Mary thought. *Just his taste. I wonder how many girl friends he has waiting for him in Bucharest?*

Mary remembered Mike's words: *You're an amateur, Mrs Ashley. If someone wanted to pay you off, they should have made you Ambassador to Iceland.* The bastard.

As Mary watched, Colonel McKinney, in full dress uniform, walked up to Mike. Mike excused himself from the blonde and walked over to a corner with the Colonel. *I'm going to have to watch them both*, Mary thought.

A servant was passing by with champagne. 'I think I *will* have a glass,' Mary said.

James Stickley watched her as she drank it down. 'Okay. It's time to start working the room.'

'Working the room?'

'A lot of business gets done at these parties. That's why embassies give them.'

Mary spent the next hour being introduced to ambassadors, senators, governors and some of Washington's most powerful political figures. Romania had become a hot ticket, and nearly everyone of importance had managed to get an invitation to the Embassy dinner. Mike Slade approached James Stickley and Mary, holding the blonde in tow.

'Good evening,' Mike said genially. 'I'd like you to meet Debbie Dennison. This is James Stickley and Mary Ashley.'

It was a deliberate slap. Mary said coolly, 'It's *Ambassador* Ashley.'

Mike clapped his hand to his forehead. 'Sorry. *Ambassador* Ashley. Miss Dennison's father happens to be an Ambassador, too. He's a career diplomat, of course. He's served in half a dozen countries for the last twenty-five years.'

Debbie Dennison said, 'It's a wonderful way to grow up.'

Mike said, 'Debbie's been around a lot.'

'Yes,' Mary said evenly. 'I'm sure she has.'

Mary prayed she would not be seated next to Mike at dinner, and her prayers were granted. He was at another table, next to the half-naked blonde. There were a dozen people at Mary's table. Some of them were familiar faces she had seen on magazine covers and on television. James Stickley was seated across from Mary. The man to Mary's left spoke a mysterious language that Mary was unable to identify. To her right was a tall, thin, middle-aged blond man, with an attractive, sensitive face.

'I am delighted to be your dinner companion,' he said to Mary. 'I am an ardent fan of yours.' He spoke with a slight Scandinavian accent.

'Thank you.' *A fan of my what?* Mary wondered. *I haven't done anything.*

'I am Olaf Peterson. I am the Cultural Attaché from Sweden.'

'I'm very happy to meet you, Mr Peterson.'

'Have you been to Sweden?'

'No. To tell you the truth, I really haven't been anywhere.'

Olaf Peterson smiled. 'Then so many places have a treat in store for them.'

'Perhaps one day the children and I will visit your country.'

'Ah, you have children? How old are they?'

'Tim is ten and Beth is twelve. I'll show you.' Mary opened her purse and took out snapshots of the children. Across the table, James Stickley was shaking his head disapprovingly.

Olaf Peterson examined the snapshots. 'They are beautiful children!' he exclaimed. 'They take after their mother.'

'They have their father's eyes.'

They used to have mock arguments about which one of them the children resembled.

Beth is going to be a beauty, like you, Edward would say. *I don't know who Tim looks like. Are you sure he's mine?*

And their play-argument would end in lovemaking.

Olaf Peterson was saying something to her.

'I beg your pardon?'

'I said I read about your husband being killed in a motor accident. I am sorry. It must be very difficult for a woman to be alone without a man.' His voice was filled with sympathy.

Mary picked up the glass of wine in front of her and took a sip. It was cold and refreshing. She drained the glass. It was immediately refilled by a white-gloved waiter hovering behind the guests.

'When do you take up your post in Romania?' Peterson asked.

'I was told we'll be leaving within the next few weeks.' Mary picked up her wine glass. 'To Bucharest.' She drank. The wine was really quite delicious, and everyone knew that wine had a low alcoholic content.

When the waiter offered to fill her glass again, she nodded happily. She looked around the room at all the beautifully dressed guests speaking in a dozen different tongues and thought: *They don't have banquets like this in good old Junction City. No, sir. Kansas is as dry as a bone. Washington is as wet as a – what was Washington as wet as?* She frowned, trying to think.

'Are you all right?' Olaf Peterson asked.

She patted him on the arm. 'Great. I'm just great. I'd like another glass of wine, Olaf.'

'Certainly.'

He motioned to the waiter, and Mary's wine glass was refilled.

'At home,' Mary said confidentially, 'I never drank wine.' She lifted her glass and took a swallow. 'In fact, I never drank anything.' Her words were beginning to slur. 'That doesn' 'clude water, of course.'

Olaf Peterson was studying her, smiling.

At the centre table, Romanian Ambassador Corbescue rose to his feet. 'Ladies and gentlemen – distinguished guests – I would like to propose a toast.'

The ritual began. There were toasts to Alexandros Ionescu, the President of Romania. There were toasts to Madam Alexandros Ionescu. There were toasts to the President of the United States, and to the Vice President, to the Romanian flag and to the American flag. It seemed to Mary that there were thousands of toasts. She drank to every one of them. *I'm a 'bassador*, she reminded herself. *'s my duty.*

In the middle of the toasts, the Romanian Ambassador said, 'I am sure we would all like to hear a few words from the United States' charming new Ambassador to Romania.'

Mary raised her glass and started to drink a toast, when she suddenly realized she was being called upon. She sat there for a moment, then managed to get to her feet. She stood up, holding on to the table for support. She looked out at the throng of people and waved. 'Hi, everybody. Having a good time?'

She had never felt happier in her life. Everyone in the room was so friendly. They were all smiling at her. Some were even laughing. She looked over at James Stickley and grinned.

'It's a great party,' Mary said. 'I'm delighted you could all come.'

She sat down heavily and turned to Olaf Peterson. 'They put somethin' in my wine.'

He pressed her hand. 'I think what you need is a little fresh air. It is very stuffy in here.'

'Yeah. Stuffy. To tell you the truth, I'm feelin' a l'l dizzy.'

'Let me take you outside.'

He helped Mary to her feet, and to her surprise, she found it difficult to walk. James Stickley was engaged in an earnest conversation with his dinner partner and did not see Mary leave. Mary and Olaf Peterson passed Mike Slade's table, and he was watching her with a frown of disapproval.

He's jealous, Mary thought. *They didn' ask him to make a speech.*

She said to Peterson, 'You know his problem, don' you? He wan's 'a be Ambassador. He can't stand it that I got the job.'

'Who are you talking about?' Olaf Peterson asked.

' 's not importan'. He's not importan'.'

They were outside in the cold night air. Mary was grateful for the support of Peterson's arm. Everything seemed blurred.

'I have a limousine here somewhere,' Mary said.

'Let's send it away,' Olaf Peterson suggested. 'We'll go up to my place for a little nightcap.'

'No more wine.'

'No, no. Just a little brandy to settle your stomach.'

Brandy. In books, all the sophisticated people drank brandy. Brandy and soda. It was a Cary Grant kind of drink.

'With soda?'

'Of course.'

Olaf Peterson helped Mary into a taxi and gave the driver an address. When they stopped in front of a large apartment building, Mary looked at Peterson, puzzled. 'Where are we?'

'We're home,' Olaf Peterson said. He supported Mary as she stepped out of the taxi, holding on to her as she started to fall.

' 'm I drunk?' Mary asked.

'Of course not,' he said soothingly.

'I feel funny.'

Peterson led her into the lobby of the building and rang for the elevator. 'A little brandy will fix you up.'

They stepped into the elevator and he pressed a button.

'Did you know I'm a toeteetler? I mean – teetotler?'

'No. I did not know that.'

' 's a fact.'

Peterson was stroking her bare arm.

The elevator door opened, and Peterson helped Mary out of the elevator.

'Did anyone ever tell you the floor's uneven?'

'I'll have it taken care of,' Olaf promised.

He held her up with one hand while he fumbled for the key to his apartment and unlocked the door. They stepped inside. The apartment was dimly lit.

' 's dark in here,' Mary said.

Olaf Peterson took her in his arms. 'I like the dark, don't you?'

Did she? She was not sure.

'You are a very beautiful woman, do you know that?'

'Thank you. You're a beaut'ful man.'

He led her to the couch and sat her down. She was feeling giddy. His lips pressed against hers, and she felt his hand sliding up her thigh.

'What're you doing?'

'Just relax, darling. It's going to feel lovely.'

It *did* feel lovely. His hands were very gentle, like Edward's.

'He was a won'erful doctor,' Mary said.

'I'm sure he was.' He pressed his body against hers.

'Oh, yes. 'never anyone needed an operation, they always asked for Edward.'

She was lying on the couch on her back, and soft hands had pushed her dress up and were gently massaging her. Edward's hands. Mary closed her eyes and felt his lips moving down her body – soft lips, and a gentle tongue. Edward had such a gentle tongue. It was blissful. And she wanted it never to stop.

'That's so good, my darling,' she said. 'Take me. Please take me.'

'I will. Now.' His voice was husky. Suddenly harsh. Not at all like Edward's voice.

Mary opened her eyes, and she was staring into the face of a stranger. As she felt the man start to thrust inside her, she screamed, 'No! Stop it!'

She rolled away from him and fell to the floor. She stumbled to her feet.

Olaf Peterson was staring at her. 'But –'

'No!'

She looked around the apartment wildly. 'I'm sorry,' she said. 'I made a mistake. I don't want you to think I –'

She turned and ran towards the door.

'Wait! Let me at least take you home.'

She was gone.

She walked down the deserted streets, bracing herself against the icy wind, filled with a deep, bruising mortification. There was no explanation for what she had done. And there was no excuse. She had disgraced her position. And in what a stupid way! She had got drunk in front of half the diplomatic corps in Washington, had gone to a stranger's apartment, and had almost let him seduce her. In the morning she was going to be the target for every gossip columnist in Washington.

Ben Cohn heard the story from three people who had attended the dinner at the Romanian Embassy. He searched through the columns of the Washington and New York newspapers. There was not one word about the incident. Someone had killed the story. It had to be someone very important.

Cohn sat in the small cubicle that the newspaper called an office, thinking. He dialled Ian Villiers' number. 'Hello, is Mr Villiers in?'

'Yes. Who's calling?'

'Ben Cohn.'

'One moment, please.' She was back on the line one minute later. 'I'm terribly sorry, Mr Cohn. Mr Villiers seems to have stepped out.'

'When can I reach him?'

'I'm afraid he's fully booked up all day.'

'Right.' He replaced the receiver and dialled the number of a gossip columnist who worked on another newspaper. Nothing happened in Washington without her knowing about it.

'Linda,' he said, 'how goes the daily battle?'

'*Plus ça change, plus c'est la même chose.*'

'Anything exciting happening around this gilded watering hole?'

'Not really, Ben. It's deadly quiet.'

He said casually, 'I understand the Romanian Embassy had a big wing-ding last night.'

'Did they?' There was a sudden caution in her voice.

'Uh huh. Did you happen to hear anything about our new Ambassador to Romania?'

'No. I've got to go now, Ben. I have a long distance call.'

The line went dead.

He dialled the number of a friend in the State Department. When the secretary put him through, he said, 'Hello, Alfred'.

'Benjie! What's cooking?'

'It's been a long time. I thought we might get together for lunch.'

'Fine. What are you working on?'

'Why don't I tell you about it when I see you?'

'Fair enough. My calendar is pretty light today. Do you want to meet me at the Watergate?'

Ben Cohn hesitated. 'Why don't we make it Mama Regina's in Silver Springs?'

'That's a little out of the way, isn't it?'

Ben said, 'Yes.'

There was a pause. 'I see.'

'One o'clock?'

'Fine.'

Ben Cohn was seated at a table in the corner when his guest, Alfred Shuttleworth, arrived. The host, Tony Sergio, seated him.

'Would you care for a drink, gentlemen?'

Shuttleworth ordered a martini.

'Nothing for me,' Ben Cohn said.

Alfred Shuttleworth was a sallow-looking, middle-aged man who worked in the European Section of the State Department. A few years earlier, he had been involved in a drunken driving accident that Ben Cohn had covered for his newspaper. Shuttleworth's career was at stake. Cohn had killed the story, and Shuttleworth had shown his appreciation by giving him news tips from time to time.

'I need your help, Al.'

'Name it, and you've got it.'

'I'd like the inside information on our new Ambassador to Romania.'

Alfred Shuttleworth frowned. 'What do you mean?'

'Three people called to tell me that she got so stoned at the Romanian Ambassador's party last night that she made a horse's ass of herself in front of Washington's who's who. Have you seen the morning papers today, or the early editions of the afternoon papers?'

'Yes. They mentioned the Embassy party, but there was no mention of Mary Ashley.'

'Exactly. *Silver Blaze.*'

'I beg your pardon?'

'Sherlock Holmes. The dog didn't bark. It was silent. So are the newspapers. Why would the gossip columnists skip over a juicy story like that? Someone had that story killed. Someone important. If it had been any other VIP who publicly disgraced herself, the press would have had a Roman holiday.'

'That doesn't necessarily follow, Ben.'

'Al, there's this Cinderella who comes out of nowhere, is touched by the magic wand of our President, and suddenly becomes Grace Kelly, Princess Di and Jacqueline Kennedy rolled into one. Now, I'll admit the lady is pretty – but she isn't *that* pretty. The lady is bright – but she isn't *that* bright. In my humble opinion, teaching a political science course at Kansas State University doesn't exactly qualify anyone to be the Ambassador to one of the world's hot spots. I'll tell you something else that's out of kilter. I flew to Junction City and talked to the sheriff there.'

Alfred Shuttleworth drained the remainder of his martini. 'I think I'd like another one. You're making me nervous.'

'Join the club.' Ben Cohn ordered a martini.

'Go on,' Shuttleworth said.

'Mrs Ashley turned down the President because her husband couldn't leave his medical practice. Then he was killed in a convenient auto accident. Voilà! The lady's in Washington, on her way to Bucharest. Exactly as someone had planned from the beginning.'

'Someone? Who?'

'That's the jackpot question.'

137

'Ben – what are you suggesting?'

'I'm not suggesting anything. Let me tell you what Sheriff Munster suggested. He thought it was peculiar that half a dozen witnesses showed up out of nowhere in the middle of a freezing winter night just in time to witness the accident. And do you want to hear something even more peculiar? They've all disappeared. Every one of them.'

'Go on.'

'I went over to Fort Riley to talk to the driver of the Army truck that killed Dr Ashley.'

'And what did he have to say?'

'Not much. He was dead. Heart attack. Twenty-seven years old.'

Shuttleworth was toying with the stem of his glass. 'I assume there's more?'

'Oh, yes. There's more. I went over to the CID office at Fort Riley to interview Colonel Jenkins, the officer in charge of the Army investigation, as well as being one of the witnesses to the accident. The Colonel wasn't there. He's been promoted and transferred. He's a Major General now, overseas somewhere. No one seems to know where.'

Alfred Shuttleworth shook his head. 'Ben, I know you're a hell of a reporter, but I honestly think this time you've gone off the track. You're building a few coincidences into a Hitchcock scenario. People *do* get killed in auto accidents. People *do* have heart attacks, and officers *do* get promoted. You're looking for some kind of conspiracy where there is none.'

'Al, have you heard of an organization called Patriots for Freedom?'

'No. Is it something like the DAR?'

Ben Cohn said quietly, 'It's nothing like the DAR. I keep hearing rumours, but there's nothing I can pin down.'

'What kind of rumours?'

'It's supposed to be a cabal of high-level right wing and left wing fanatics from a dozen Eastern and Western countries. Their ideologies are diametrically opposed, but what brings them together is fear. The communist members think President Ellison's plan is a capitalist trick to destroy the Eastern bloc. The right wingers believe his plan is an open door that will let the communists destroy us. So they've formed this unholy alliance.'

'Jesus! I don't believe it.'

'There's more. Besides the VIPs, splinter groups from various national security agencies are said to be involved. Do you think you could check it out for me?'

'I don't know. I'll try.'

'I would suggest you do it discreetly. If the organization really exists, they won't be too thrilled to have anyone nosing around.'

'I'll get back to you, Ben.'

'Thanks. Let's order lunch.'

The spaghetti carbonara was superb.

Alfred Shuttleworth was sceptical about Ben Cohn's theory. *Reporters are always looking for sensational angles,* Shuttleworth thought. He liked Ben Cohn, but Shuttleworth had no idea how to go about tracking down a probably mythical organization. If it really did exist, it would be in some government computer. He himself had no access to the computers. *But I know someone who does,* Alfred Shuttleworth remembered. *I'll give him a call.*

Alfred Shuttleworth was on his second martini when Pete Connors walked into the bar.

'Sorry I'm late,' Connors said. 'A minor problem at the pickle factory.'

Pete Connors ordered a straight scotch, and Shuttleworth ordered another martini.

The two men had met because Connors' girl friend and Shuttleworth's wife worked for the same company and had become friends. Connors and Shuttleworth were complete opposites; one was involved in deadly games of espionage, and the other functioned as a desk-bound bureaucrat. It was this dissimilarity that made them enjoy each other's company, and from time to time they exchanged useful information. When Shuttleworth had first met him, Pete Connors had been an amusing and interesting companion. Somewhere along the line, something had soured him. He had become a bitter reactionary.

Shuttleworth took a sip of his martini. 'Pete – I need a favour. Could you look up something for me in the CIA computer? It may not be in there, but I promised a friend I'd try.'

Connors smiled inwardly. *The poor schmuck probably wants to find out if someone is banging his wife.* 'Sure. I owe you a few. Who do you want to know about?'

'It's not a "who", it's a "what". And it probably doesn't even exist. It's an organization called Patriots for Freedom. Have you heard of it?'

Pete Connors carefully set down his drink. 'I can't say that I have, Al. What's the name of your friend?'

'Ben Cohn. He's a reporter for the *Post*.'

The following morning, Ben Cohn made a decision. He said to Akiko, 'I either have the story of the century, or I have nothing. It's time I found out.'

'Thank God!' Akiko exclaimed. 'Arthur's going to be very happy.'

Ben Cohn reached Mary Ashley at her office. 'Good morning, Ambassador. Ben Cohn. Remember me?'

'Yes, Mr Cohn. Have you written that story yet?'

'That's what I'm calling you about, Ambassador. I went to Junction City and picked up some information that I think will interest you.'

139

'What kind of information?'

'I'd rather not discuss it over the phone. I wonder if we could meet somewhere?'

'I have a ridiculously full schedule. Let me see . . . I have half an hour free on Friday morning. Would that be all right?'

Three days away. 'I guess it can wait until then.'

'Do you want to come up to my office?'

'There's a coffee shop downstairs in your building. Why don't we meet there?'

'All right. I'll see you Friday.'

They said goodbye and hung up. A moment later there was a third click on the line.

There was no way to get directly in touch with the Controller. He had organized and financed the Patriots for Freedom, but he never attended committee meetings, and he was completely anonymous. He was a telephone number – untraceable (Connors had tried) – and a recording that said, 'You have sixty seconds in which to leave your message.' The number was to be used only in case of emergency. Connors stopped at a public telephone booth to make the call. He talked to the recording.

The message was received at 6 p.m.

In Buenos Aires, it was 8 p.m.

The Controller listened to the message twice, then dialled a number. He waited for three full minutes before Neusa Muñez's voice came on.

'*Si?*'

The Controller said, 'This is the man who made arrangements with you before about Angel. I have another contract for him. Can you get in touch with him right away?'

'I don' know.' She sounded drunk.

He kept the impatience out of his voice. 'When do you expect to hear from him?'

'I don' know.'

Damn the woman. 'Listen to me.' He spoke slowly and carefully, as though addressing a small child. 'Tell Angel I need this done immediately. I want him to –'

'Wait a minute. I gotta go to the toilet.'

He heard her drop the phone. The Controller sat there, filled with frustration.

Three minutes later, she was back on the line. 'A lotta beer makes you pee,' she announced.

He gritted his teeth. 'This is very important.' He was afraid she was going to remember none of it. 'I want you to get a pencil and write this down. I'll speak slowly.'

That evening Mary attended a dinner party given by the Canadian Embassy. As she was leaving the office to go home and dress, James Stickley said, 'I would suggest that you *sip* the toasts this time.'

He and Mike Slade make a wonderful pair.

Now she was at the party, and she wished she were home with Beth and Tim. The faces at her table were unfamiliar. On her right was a Greek shipping magnate. On her left was an English diplomat.

A Philadelphia socialite dripping with diamonds said to Mary, 'Are you enjoying Washington, Madam Ambassador?'

'Very much, thank you.'

'You must be thrilled to have made your escape from Kansas.'

Mary looked at her, not understanding. 'Escape from Kansas?'

The woman went on. 'I've never been to middle America, but I imagine it must be dreadful. All those farmers and nothing but dreary fields of corn and wheat. It's a wonder you could bear it as long as you did.'

Mary felt a surge of anger, but she kept her voice under control. 'That corn and wheat you're talking about,' she said politely, 'feeds the world.'

The woman's tone was patronizing. 'Our automobiles run on gasoline, but I wouldn't want to live in the oilfields. Culturally speaking, I think one has to live in the East, don't you? Quite honestly now – in Kansas unless you're out harvesting in the fields all day, there really isn't anything to do, is there?'

The others at the table were all listening closely.

There really isn't anything to do, is there? Mary thought of August hayrides and county fairs and exciting classical dramas at the University Theatre. Sunday picnics in Milford Park and softball tournaments, and fishing in the clear lake. The band playing on the green and town hall meetings and block parties and barn dances and the excitement of harvest time . . . winter sleigh rides and fourth of July fireworks rainbowing the soft, Kansas sky.

Mary said to the woman, 'If you've never been to middle America, you really don't know what you're talking about, do you? Because that's what this country is all about. America isn't Washington or Los Angeles or New York. It's thousands of small towns that you'll never even see or hear of that make this country great. It's the miners and the farmers and the blue collar workers. And yes, in Kansas we have ballets and symphonies and theatre. And, for your information, we raise a lot more than corn and wheat – we raise honest-to-God human beings.'

'You know, of course, that you insulted the sister of a very important senator,' James Stickley informed Mary the following morning.

'Not enough,' Mary said defiantly. 'Not enough.'

141

Thursday morning. Angel was in a bad mood. The flight from Buenos Aires to Washington, D.C. had been delayed because of a telephoned bomb threat. *The world isn't safe any more*, Angel thought angrily.

The hotel room that had been reserved in Washington was too modern, too – what was the word? *Plastic. That was it.* In Buenos Aires, everything was *auténtico*.

I'll finish this contract and get back home. The job is simple, almost an insult to my talent. But the money is excellent. I've got to get laid tonight. I wonder why killing always makes me horny.

Angel's first stop was at an electrical supply store, then a paint store, and finally a supermarket, where Angel's only purchase was six light bulbs. The rest of the equipment was waiting in the hotel room in two sealed boxes marked 'Fragile – Handle With Care'. Inside the first box were four carefully packed army-green hand grenades. In the second box was soldering equipment.

Working very slowly, with exquisite care, Angel cut off the top of the first grenade, then painted the bottom of it the same colour as the light bulbs. The next step was to scoop out the explosive from the grenade and replace it with a seismic explosive. When it was tightly packed, Angel added lead and metallic shrapnel to it. Angel shattered a light bulb against the table, preserving the filament and threaded base. It took less than a minute to solder the filament of the bulb to an electrically activated detonator. The final step was to insert the filament into a gel to keep it stable and then gently place it inside the painted grenade. When Angel was finished, it looked exactly like a normal light bulb.

Angel began to work on the remaining light bulbs. After that, there was nothing to do but wait for the phone call.

The telephone rang at eight o'clock that evening. Angel picked up the phone and listened, without speaking. After a moment, a voice said, 'He's gone.'

Angel replaced the receiver. Carefully, very carefully, the light bulbs were packed into an excelsior padded container and placed in a suitcase, along with all the scraps of discarded materials.

The taxi ride to the apartment building took seventeen minutes.

There was no doorman in the lobby, but if there had been, Angel was prepared to deal with him. The target apartment was on the fifth floor, at the far end of the corridor. The lock was an early model Schlage, childishly simple to manipulate. Angel was inside the dark apartment within seconds, standing stock still, listening. There was no one there.

It was the work of a few minutes to replace six light bulbs in the

142

living room of the apartment. Afterwards, Angel headed for Dulles airport to catch a midnight flight back to Buenos Aires.

It had been a long day for Ben Cohn. He had covered a morning press conference by the Secretary of State, a luncheon for the retiring Secretary of the Interior, and had been given an off-the-record briefing from a friend in the Defence Department. He had gone home to shower and change, and then left again to have dinner with a senior *Post* editor. It was almost midnight when he returned to his apartment building. *I have to prepare my notes for the meeting with Ambassador Ashley tomorrow*, Ben thought.

Akiko was out of town and would not be returning until tomorrow. *It's just as well. I can use the rest. But Jesus*, he thought with a grin, *the lady sure knows how to eat a banana split.*

He put the key in the lock and opened the door. The apartment was pitch black. He reached for the light switch and pressed it. There was a sudden bright flash of light, and the room exploded like an atomic bomb, splashing pieces of his body against the four walls.

The following day, Alfred Shuttleworth's wife reported him missing. He was never found.

17

'We just received official word,' Stanton Rogers said. 'The Romanian government has approved you as the new Ambassador from the United States.'

It was one of the most thrilling moments of Mary Ashley's life. *Grandfather would have been so proud.*

'I wanted to bring you the good news in person, Mary. The President would like to see you. I'll take you over to the White House.'

'I – I don't know how to thank you for everything you've done, Stan.'

'I haven't done anything,' Rogers protested. 'It was the President who selected you.' He grinned. 'And I must say, he made the perfect choice.'

Mary thought of Mike Slade. 'There are some people who don't agree.'

'They're wrong. You can do more for our country over there than anyone else I can think of.'

'Thank you,' she said soberly. 'I'll try to live up to that.'

She was tempted to bring up the subject of Mike Slade. Stanton Rogers had a lot of power. Perhaps he could arrange to have Slade stay in Washington. *No*, Mary thought. *I mustn't impose on Stan. He's done enough already.*

'I have a suggestion. Instead of flying directly to Bucharest, why don't you and the children stop first in Paris and Rome for a few days? Tarom Airlines flies directly from Rome to Bucharest.'

She looked at him and said, 'Oh, Stan – that would be heaven! But would I have time?'

He winked. 'I have friends in high places. Let me work it out for you.'

Impulsively, she hugged him. He had become such a dear friend. The dreams she and Edward had talked about so often were about to come true. But without Edward. It was a bittersweet thought.

Mary and Stanton Rogers were ushered into the Green Room, where President Ellison was waiting for them.

'I want to apologize for the delay in setting things in motion, Mary. Stanton has told you that you've been approved by the Romanian government. Here are your credentials.'

He handed her a letter. She read it slowly:

Mrs Mary Ashley is herewith appointed to be Chief Representative of the President of the United States in Romania, and every United States government employee there is herewith subject to her authority.

'This goes along with it.' The President handed Mary a passport. It had a black cover instead of the usual blue one. On the front, in gold letters, was printed 'Diplomatic Passport'.

Mary had been anticipating this for weeks, but now that the time had come, she could scarcely believe it.

Paris!

Rome!

Bucharest!

It seemed almost too good to be true. And for no reason, something that Mary's mother used to tell her popped into her mind: *If something seems to be too good to be true, Mary, it probably is.*

There was a brief item in the afternoon press that *Washington Post* reporter Ben Cohn had been killed by a gas explosion in his apartment. The explosion was attributed to a leaky stove.

Mary did not see the news item. When Ben Cohn did not show up for their appointment, Mary decided that the reporter had either forgotten, or was no longer interested. She returned to her office and went back to work.

The relationship between Mary and Mike Slade became steadily more irritating to her. *He's the most arrogant man I've ever met*, Mary thought. *I'm going to have to talk to Stan about him.*

Stanton Rogers accompanied Mary and the children to Dulles Airport in a State Department limousine. During the ride, Stanton said, 'The embassies in Paris and Rome have been alerted to your arrival. They'll see to it that the three of you are well taken care of.'

'Thank you, Stan. You've been wonderful.'

He smiled. 'I can't tell you how much pleasure it's given me.'

'Can I see the catacombs in Rome?' Tim asked.

Stanton warned, 'It's pretty scary down there, Tim.'

'That's why I want to see it.'

At the airport, Ian Villiers was waiting with a dozen photographers and reporters. They surrounded Mary and Beth and Tim, and called out all the usual questions.

Finally, Stanton Rogers said, 'That's enough.'

Two men from the State Department and a representative of the

145

airline ushered the party into a private lounge. The children wandered off to the magazine stand.

Mary said, 'Stan – I hate to burden you with this, but James Stickley told me that Mike Slade is going to be my Deputy Chief of Mission. Is there any way to change that?'

He looked at her in surprise. 'Are you having some kind of problem with Slade?'

'Quite honestly, I don't like him. And I don't trust him – I can't tell you why. Isn't there someone who could replace him?'

Stanton Rogers said thoughtfully, 'I don't know Mike Slade well, but I know he has a magnificent record. He's served brilliantly in posts in the Middle East and Europe. He can give you exactly the kind of expertise you're going to need.'

She sighed. 'That's what Mr Stickley said.'

'I'm afraid I have to agree with him, Mary. Slade's a trouble-shooter.' *Wrong. Slade's trouble. Period.*

'If you have any problem with him, I want you to let me know. In fact, if you have problems with *anyone*, I want you to let me know. I intend to make sure that you get every bit of help I can give you.'

'I appreciate that.'

'One last thing. You know that all your communications will be copied and sent to various departments in Washington?'

'Yes.'

'Well, if you have any messages that you want to send to me without anyone else reading them, the code at the top of the message is three x's. I'll be the only one to receive that message.'

'I'll remember.'

The Charles de Gaulle Airport was something out of science fiction, a kaleidoscope of stone columns and what seemed to Mary like hundreds of escalators running wild. The airport was crowded with travellers.

'Stay close to me, children,' Mary urged.

When they got off the escalator, she looked around helplessly. She stopped a Frenchman passing by, and summoning up one of the few French phrases she knew, she asked haltingly, '*Pardon, monsieur, où sont les bagages?*'

In a heavy French accent, he said witheringly, 'Sorry, Madame. I don't speak English.' He walked away, leaving Mary staring after him.

At that moment, a well-dressed young American hurried up to Mary and the children.

'Madam Ambassador, forgive me! I was instructed to meet you at the plane, but I was delayed by a traffic accident. My name is Peter Callas. I'm with the American Embassy.'

'I'm really glad to see you,' Mary said. 'I think I'm lost.' She introduced the children. 'Where do we find our luggage?'

'No problem,' Peter Callas assured her. 'Everything will be taken care of for you.'

He was true to his word. Fifteen minutes later, while the other passengers were starting to wend their way through Customs and passport control, Mary, Beth and Tim were heading for the airport exit.

Inspector Henri Durand from the General Directorate of External Security, the French Intelligence Agency, watched as they got into the waiting limousine. When the car pulled away, the Inspector walked over to a bank of phone booths and entered one. He closed the door, inserted a jeton, and dialled.

When a voice answered, he said, '*Veuillez dire à Thor que son paquet est arrivé à Paris.*'

When the limousine pulled up in front of the American Embassy, the French press was waiting in force.

Peter Callas watched out of the car window. 'My God! It looks like a riot.'

Waiting for them inside was Hugh Simon, the American Ambassador to France. He was a Texan, middle-aged, with inquisitive eyes in a round face, topped by a wave of bright red hair.

'Everyone's sure eager to meet you, Madam Ambassador. The press has been snapping at my heels all morning.'

Mary's press conference ran longer than an hour, and when it was over she was exhausted. Mary and the children were taken to Ambassador Simon's office.

'Well,' he said, 'I'm glad that's over. When I arrived here to take up this job, I think it got one paragraph on the back page of *Le Monde*.' He smiled. 'Of course, I'm not as pretty as you are.' He remembered something. 'I received a telephone call from Stanton Rogers. I have life and death instructions from the White House to see that you and Beth and Tim enjoy every moment that you're in Paris.'

'*Really* life and death?' Tim asked.

Ambassador Simon nodded. 'His words. He's very fond of you all.'

'We're very fond of him,' Mary assured him.

'I've arranged a suite for you at the Ritz. It's a lovely hotel off the Place de la Concorde. I'm sure you'll be quite comfortable there.'

'Thank you.' Then she added, nervously, 'Is it very expensive?'

'Yes – but not for you. Stanton Rogers has arranged for the State Department to pick up all your expenses.'

Mary said, 'He's incredible.'

'According to him, so are you.'

147

The afternoon and evening newspapers carried glowing stories of the arrival of the President's first ambassador in his people-to-people programme. The event was given full coverage on the evening television news programme, and in the morning papers the following day.

Inspector Durand looked at the pile of newspapers and smiled. Everything was proceeding as planned. The build-up was even better than expected. He could have predicted the Ashleys' itinerary during the next three days. *They'll go to all the mindless tourist places that Americans want to see*, he thought.

Mary and the children had lunch at the Jules Verne Restaurant in the Tour Eiffel, and later they went to the top of the Arc de Triomphe.

They spent the following morning gazing at the treasures of the Louvre, had lunch near Versailles, and dinner at the Tour d'Argent.

Tim stared out of the restaurant window at Notre Dame and asked, 'Where do they keep the hunchback?'

Every moment in Paris was a joy. Mary kept thinking how much she wished Edward were there.

The next day after lunch, they were driven to the airport. Inspector Durand watched them as they checked in for their flight to Rome.

The woman is attractive – quite lovely, in fact. An intelligent face. Good body, great legs and derrière. I wonder what she would be like in bed? The children were a surprise. They were very well-mannered for Americans.

When the plane took off, Inspector Durand went to a telephone booth. '*Veuillez dire à Thor que son paquet est en route à Rome.*'

In Rome, the *paparazzi* were waiting at the Michelangelo Airport. As Mary and the children disembarked, Tim said, 'Look, Mom, they followed us!'

Indeed, it seemed to Mary that the only difference was the Italian accents.

The first question the reporters asked was, 'How do you like Italy . . . ?'

Ambassador Oscar Viner was as puzzled as Ambassador Simon had been.

'Frank Sinatra didn't get this big a reception. Is there something about you I don't know, Madam Ambassador?'

'I think I can explain,' Mary replied. 'It isn't *me* the press is interested in. They're interested in the President's people-to-people programme. We'll soon have representatives in every Iron Curtain country. It will be an enormous step towards peace. I think *that's* what the press is excited about.'

After a moment, Ambassador Viner said, 'A lot is riding on you, isn't it?'

Captain Caesar Barzini, the head of the Italian Secret Police, was also able to predict accurately the places Mary and her children would visit during their brief stay.

The captain assigned two men to watch the Ashleys, and each day when they reported back, it was almost exactly as he had anticipated.

'They had ice cream sodas at Doney's, walked along the Via Veneto, and toured the Colosseum.'

'They went to see the Trevi Fountain. Threw in coins.'

'Visited Terme di Caracalla and then the Catacombs. Boy became ill and was taken back to hotel.'

'Subjects went for a carriage ride in Borghese Park and walked along the Piazza Navona.'

Enjoy yourselves, Captain Barzini thought sardonically.

Ambassador Viner accompanied Mary and the children to the airport.

'I have a diplomatic pouch to go to the Romanian Embassy. Would you mind taking it along with your luggage?'

'Of course not,' Mary said.

Captain Barzini was at the airport to watch the Ashley family board the Tarom Airlines plane bound for Bucharest. He stayed until the plane took off, and then made a telephone call. 'I have a message for Balder. Everything went perfectly. The press coverage was tremendous.'

It was only after they were airborne that the enormity of what was about to happen really struck Mary Ashley. It was so incredible that she had to say it aloud. 'We're on our way to Romania, where I'm going to take up my post as Ambassador from the United States.'

Beth was looking at her strangely. 'Yes, Mother. We know that. That's why we're here.'

But how could Mary explain her excitement to them?

The closer the plane got to Bucharest, the more her excitement increased.

I'm going to be the best damned ambassador they've ever seen, she thought. *Before I'm finished, the United States and Romania are going to be close allies.*

149

The NO SMOKING sign flashed on, and Mary's euphoric dreams of great statesmanship evaporated.

We can't be landing already, Mary thought in a panic. *We just took off. Why is the flight so short?*

She felt the pressure on her ears as the plane began to descend, and a few moments later the wheels touched the ground. *It's really happening*, Mary thought incredulously. *I'm not an ambassador. I'm a fake. I'm going to get us into a war. God help us. Dorothy and I should never have left Kansas.*

BOOK THREE

BOOK THREE

18

Otopeni Airport, twenty-five miles from the heart of Bucharest, is a modern airport, built to facilitate the flow of travellers from nearby Iron Curtain countries, as well as to take care of the lesser number of western tourists who visit Romania each year.

Inside the terminal were soldiers in brown uniforms, armed with rifles and pistols, and there was a stark air of coldness about the building that had nothing to do with the frigid temperature. Tim and Beth unconsciously moved closer to Mary. *So they feel it, too*, she thought.

Two men were approaching. One of them was a slim, athletic, American-looking man, and the other was older and dressed in an ill-fitting foreign-looking suit.

The American introduced himself. 'Welcome to Romania, Madam Ambassador. I'm Jerry Davis, your Public Affairs Consular. This is Tudor Costache, the Romanian Chief of Protocol.'

'It is a pleasure to have you and your children with us,' Costache said. 'Welcome to our country.'

In a way, Mary thought, *it's going to be my country, too.* '*Mulţu-mésc, domnule,*' Mary said.

'You speak Romanian!' Costache cried. '*Cu plăcére!*'

Mary hoped the man was not going to get carried away. 'A few words,' she replied hastily.

Tim said, '*Bună dimineaţa.*'

And Mary was so proud she could have burst.

She introduced Tim and Beth.

Jerry Davis said, 'Your limousine is waiting for you, Madam Ambassador. Colonel McKinney is outside.'

Colonel McKinney. Colonel McKinney and Mike Slade. She wondered whether Slade was here, too, but she refused to ask.

There was a long line waiting to go through Customs, but Mary and the children were outside the building in a matter of minutes. There were reporters and photographers waiting again, but instead of the free-for-alls that Mary had encountered earlier, they were orderly and controlled. When they had finished, they thanked Mary and departed in a body.

Colonel McKinney, in Army uniform, was waiting at the kerb. He held out his hand. 'Good morning, Madam Ambassador. Did you have a pleasant trip?'

'Yes, thank you.'

'Mike Slade wanted to be here, but there was some important business he had to take care of.'

Mary wondered whether it was a redhead or a blonde.

A long, black limousine with an American flag on the right front wing pulled up. A cheerful-looking man in a chauffeur's uniform held the door open.

'This is Florian.'

The chauffeur grinned, baring beautiful white teeth. 'Welcome, Madam Ambassador. Master Tim. Miss Beth. It will be my pleasure to serve all of you.'

'Thank you,' Mary said.

'Florian will be at your disposal twenty-four hours a day. I thought we would go directly to the Residence, so you can unpack and relax. Later, perhaps you would like to drive around the city a bit. In the morning, Florian will take you to the American Embassy.'

'That sounds fine,' Mary said.

She wondered again where Mike Slade was.

The drive from the airport to the city was fascinating. They drove on a two-lane highway, heavily used by cars and lorries, but every few miles the traffic would be held up by little gypsy carts plodding along the road. On both sides of the highway were modern factories, next to ancient huts. The car passed farm after farm, with women working in the fields, colourful bandanas knotted around their heads.

They drove by Baneasa, Bucharest's domestic airport. Just beyond it, off the main highway, was a low, blue and grey, two-storey building with an ominous look about it.

'What is that?' Mary asked.

Florian grimaced. 'The Ivan Stelian Prison. That is where they put anyone who disagrees with the Romanian government.'

During the drive, Colonel McKinney pointed to a red button near the door. 'This is an emergency switch,' he explained. 'If you're ever in trouble – attacked by terrorists or whomever – just press this button. It activates a radio transmitter in the car that's monitored at the Embassy, and turns on a red light on the roof of the car. We're able to triangulate your position within minutes.'

Mary said fervently, 'I hope I'll never have to use it.'

'I hope so, too, Madam Ambassador.'

The centre of Bucharest was beautiful. There were parks and monuments and fountains everywhere one looked. Mary remembered her grandfather saying, 'Bucharest is a miniature Paris, Mary. They even have a replica of the Eiffel Tower.' And there it was. She was in the homeland of her forefathers.

The streets were crowded with people and buses and streetcars. The limousine honked its way through the traffic, the pedestrians scurrying out of the way, as the car turned into a small, tree-lined street.

'The Residence is just ahead,' the Colonel said. 'The street is named after a Russian general. Ironic, eh?'

The Ambassador's Residence was a large and beautiful, old-fashioned three-storey house surrounded by acres of lovely grounds.

The staff was lined up outside the Residence, awaiting the arrival of the new ambassador. When Mary stepped out of the car, Jerry Davis made the introductions.

'Madam Ambassador, your staff. Mihai, your butler; Sabina, your social secretary; Rosica, your housekeeper; Cosma, your chef; and Delia and Carmen, your maids.'

Mary moved down the line, receiving their bows and curtsies, thinking: *Oh, my God. What am I going to do with all of them? At home I had Lucinda come in three times a week to cook and clean.*

'We are very honoured to meet you, Madam Ambassador,' Sabina, the social secretary said.

They all seemed to be staring at her, waiting for her to say something. She took a deep breath. '*Bună ziua. Mulţumésc. Nu vorbésc –*' Every bit of Romanian she had learned flew out of her head. She stared at them, helplessly.

Mihai, the butler, stepped forward and bowed. 'We all speak English, ma'am. We welcome you and shall be most happy to serve your every need.'

Mary sighed with relief. 'Thank you.'

There was iced champagne waiting inside the house, along with a table loaded with tempting-looking foods.

'That looks delicious!' Mary exclaimed. They were watching her hungrily. She wondered whether she should offer them anything. Did one do that with servants? She did not want to start out by making a mistake. *Did you hear what the new American Ambassador did? She invited the servants to eat with her, and they were so shocked that they quit.*

Did you hear what the new American Ambassador did? She gorged herself in front of the starving servants and didn't offer them a bite.

'On second thoughts,' Mary said, 'I'm not hungry right now. I'll – I'll have something later.'

'Let me show you around,' Jerry Davis said.

They followed him eagerly.

The Residence was a lovely house. It was pleasant and charming, in an old-fashioned way. On the ground floor were an entry-way, a library filled with books, music room, living room, and a large dining room, with a kitchen and pantry adjoining. All the rooms were comfortably furnished. A terrace ran the length of the building outside the dining room, facing a large park.

155

Towards the rear of the house was an indoor swimming pool with an attached sauna, and dressing rooms.

'We have our own swimming pool!' Tim exclaimed. 'Can I go swimming?'

'Later, darling. Let's get settled in first.'

The *pièce de résistance* downstairs was the ballroom, built near the garden. It was enormous. Glistening Baccarat sconces lined the walls, which were done in flocked paper.

Jerry Davis said, 'This is where the Embassy parties are given. Watch this.' He pressed a switch on the wall. There was a grinding noise, and the ceiling began to split in the centre, opening up, until the sky became visible. 'It can also be operated manually.'

'Hey, that's neat!' Tim exclaimed.

'I'm afraid it's called the "Ambassador's folly",' Jerry Davis said apologetically. 'It's too hot to keep open in the summer and too cold in the winter. We use it in April and September.'

'It's still neat,' Tim insisted.

As the cold air started to descend, Jerry Davis pressed the switch again, and the ceiling closed.

'Let me show you to your quarters upstairs.'

They followed Jerry Davis up the staircase to a large, central hall with two bedrooms separated by a bathroom. Farther down the hallway were the master bedroom with a sitting room, a boudoir and bath; a smaller bedroom and bath; plus a sewing and utility room. There was a terrace on the roof, with its separate stairway.

Jerry Davis said, 'The third floor has servants' quarters, a laundry room, and a storage area. In the basement is a wine cellar, and the servants' dining and rest area.'

'It's – it's enormous,' Mary said.

The children were running from room to room.

'Which is my bedroom?' Beth asked.

'You and Tim can decide that between yourselves.'

'You can have this one,' Tim offered. 'It's frilly. Girls like frilly things.'

The master bedroom was lovely, with a queen-sized bed with a goose-down comforter, two couches around a fireplace, an easy chair, dressing table with an antique mirror, an armoire, a luxurious bathroom and a wonderful view of the gardens.

Delia and Carmen had already unpacked Mary's suitcases. On the bed was the diplomatic pouch that Ambassador Viner had asked her to bring to Romania. *I must take it to the Embassy tomorrow morning*, Mary thought. She walked over to pick it up, and took a closer look at it. The red seals had been broken and clumsily taped together again. *When could it have happened?* she wondered. *At the airport? Here? And who did it?*

Sabina came into the bedroom. 'Is everything satisfactory, ma'am?'

'Yes. I've never had a social secretary,' Mary confessed. 'I'm not sure exactly what it is you do.'

'It is my job to see that your life runs smoothly, Madam Ambassador. I keep track of your social engagements, dinners, luncheons, and so on. I also see that the house runs well. With so many servants, there are always problems.'

'Yes, of course,' Mary said, off-handedly.

'Is there anything I can do for you this afternoon?'

You can tell me about that broken seal, Mary thought. Aloud, she said, 'No, thank you. I think I'll rest a while.' She suddenly felt drained.

She lay awake most of that first night, filled with a deep, cold loneliness mingled with a growing feeling of excitement about starting her new job.

It's up to me now, my darling. I don't have anyone to lean on. I wish you were here with me, telling me not to be afraid, telling me I won't fail. I mustn't fail.

When she finally drifted off to sleep, she dreamed of Mike Slade saying: *I hate amateurs. Why don't you go home?*

The American Embassy in Bucharest, at 21 Soseava Kiseieff, is a white, semi-Gothic, two-storey building, with an iron gate in front, patrolled by a uniformed officer with a grey coat and a red hat. A second guard sits inside a security booth at the side of the gate. There is a *porte-cochère* for cars to drive through, and rose marble steps leading up to the lobby.

Inside, the lobby is ornate. It has a marble floor, two closed circuit television sets at a desk guarded by a Marine, and a fireplace with a firescreen on which is painted a dragon breathing smoke. The corridors are lined with portraits of Presidents. A winding staircase leads to the second floor, where a conference room and offices are located.

A Marine guard was waiting for Mary. 'Good morning, Madam Ambassador,' he said. 'I'm Sergeant Hughes. They call me Gunny.'

'Good morning, Gunny.'

'They're waiting for you in your office. I'll escort you there.'

'Thank you.'

She followed him upstairs to a reception room where a middle-aged woman sat behind a desk.

She rose. 'Good morning, Madam Ambassador. I'm Dorothy Stone, your secretary.'

'How do you do?'

Dorothy said, 'I'm afraid you have quite a crowd in there.'

She opened the office door, and Mary walked into the room. There were nine people seated around a large conference table. They rose as Mary entered. They were all staring at her, and Mary felt a wave of animosity that was almost palpable. The first person she saw was Mike Slade. She thought of the dream she had had.

'I see you got here safely,' Mike said. 'Let me introduce you to your department heads. This is Lucas Janklow, Administrative Consular; Eddie Maltz, Political Consular; Patricia Hatfield, your Economic Consular; David Wallace, Head of Administration; Ted Thompson, Agriculture. You've already met Jerry Davis, your Public Affairs Consular, David Victor, Commerce Consular, and you already know Colonel Bill McKinney.'

'Please be seated,' Mary said. She moved to the seat at the head of the table and surveyed the group. *Hostility comes in all ages, sizes and shapes*, Mary thought.

Patricia Hatfield had a fat body and an attractive face. Lucas Janklow, the youngest member of the team, looked and dressed Ivy League. The other men were older, grey-haired, bald, thin, fat. *It's going to take time to sort them all out.*

Mike Slade was saying, 'All of us are serving at your discretion. You can replace any of us at any time.'

That's a lie, Mary thought angrily, *I tried to replace you.*

The meeting lasted for fifteen minutes. There was general, inconsequential conversation. Mike Slade finally said, 'Dorothy will set up individual meetings for all of you with the Ambassador later in the day. Thank you.'

Mary resented his taking charge. When she and Mike Slade were alone, Mary asked, 'Which one of them is the CIA agent attached to the Embassy?'

Mike looked at her a moment and said, 'Why don't you come with me?'

He walked out of the office. Mary hesitated a moment, and then went after him. She followed him down a long corridor, past a rabbit warren of offices. He came to a large door with a Marine guard standing in front of it. The guard stepped aside as Mike pushed the door open. He turned and gestured for Mary to enter.

She stepped inside and looked around. The room was an incredible combination of metal and glass, covering the floor, the walls and the ceiling.

Mike Slade closed the heavy door behind them. 'This is the Bubble Room. Every embassy in an Iron Curtain country has one. It's the only room in the Embassy that can't be bugged.'

He saw her look of disbelief.

'Madam Ambassador, not only is the Embassy bugged, but you

can bet your last dollar that your Residence is bugged, and that if you go out to a restaurant for dinner, your table will be bugged. You're in enemy territory.'

Mary sank into a chair. 'How do you handle that?' she asked. 'I mean not ever being able to talk freely?'

'We do an electronic sweep every morning. We find their bugs and pull them out. Then they replace them, and we pull *those* out.'

'Why do we permit Romanians to work in the Embassy?'

'It's their playground. They're the home team. We play by their rules, or blow the ball game. They can't get their microphones into this room because there are Marine guards on duty in front of that door twenty-four hours a day. Now – what are your questions?'

'I just wondered who the CIA man was.'

'Eddie Maltz, your Political Consular.'

She tried to recall what Eddie Maltz looked like. Grey-haired and heavy. No, that was the Agriculture Consular. Eddie Maltz . . . Ah, he was the middle-aged one, very thin, a sinister face. Or did she think that now in retrospect because she was told he was CIA?

'Is he the only CIA man on the staff?'

'Yes.'

Was there a hesitation in his voice?

Mike Slade looked at his watch. 'You're due to present your credentials in thirty minutes. Florian is waiting for you outside. Take your Letter of Credence. You'll give the original to President Ionescu and put a copy in our safe.'

Mary found that she was gritting her teeth. 'I *know* that, Mr Slade.'

'He requested that you bring the children with you. I've sent a car for them.'

Without consulting her. 'Thank you.'

Headquarters for the Romanian government is a forbidding-looking building made of blocks of sandstone, in the centre of Bucharest. It is protected by a steel wall, with armed guards in front of it. There were more guards at the entrance to the building. An aide escorted Mary and the children upstairs.

President Alexandros Ionescu greeted Mary and the children in a long, rectangular-shaped room on the second floor. The President of Romania had a powerful presence. He was dark, with hawk-like features, and curly black hair. He had one of the most imperious noses she had ever seen. His eyes were blazing, mesmerizing.

The aide said, 'Your Excellency, may I present Madam Ambassador from the United States?'

The President took Mary's hand and gave it a lingering kiss. 'You are even more beautiful than your photographs.'

'Thank you, your Excellency. This is my daughter Beth and my son Tim.'

'Fine-looking children,' Ionescu said. He looked at her expectantly. 'You have something for me?'

Mary had almost forgotten. She quickly opened her purse and took out the Letter of Credence from President Ellison.

Alexandros Ionescu gave it a careless glance. 'Thank you. I accept it on behalf of the Romanian government. You are now officially the American Ambassador to my country.' He beamed at her. 'I have arranged a reception this evening for you. You will meet some of our people who will be working with you.'

'That's very kind of you,' Mary said.

He took her hand in his again and said, 'We have a saying here. "An ambassador arrives in tears because he knows he will be spending years in a foreign place, away from his friends, but when he leaves, he leaves in tears because he must leave his new friends in a country he has grown fond of." I hope you will grow to love our country, Madam Ambassador.' He massaged her hand.

'I'm sure I will.' *He thinks I'm just another pretty face*, Mary thought grimly. *I'll have to do something about that.*

Mary sent the children home and spent the rest of the day at the Embassy, in the large conference room, meeting with the section heads, the Political, Economic, Agriculture and Administrative Consulars, as well as the Commerce Consular. Colonel McKinney was present as the military attaché.

They were all seated around a long, rectangular table. Against the back walls were a dozen junior members of the various departments.

The Commerce Consular, a small, pompous man, spoke, rattling off a string of facts and figures. Mary was looking around the room, thinking: *I'll have to remember all their names.*

Then it was the turn of Ted Thompson, the Agriculture Consular. 'The Romanian Agriculture Minister is in worse trouble than he's admitting. They're going to have a disastrous crop this year, and we can't afford to let them go under.'

The Economic Consular, Patricia Hatfield, protested, 'We've given them enough aid, Ted. Romania's already operating under a favoured nations treaty. It's a GSP country.' She looked at Mary, covertly.

She's doing this deliberately, Mary thought, *trying to embarrass me.*

Patricia Hatfield said, patronizingly, 'A GSP country is –'

'– is a generalized system of preferences,' Mary cut in. 'We treat Romania as a less developed country so that they get import and export advantages.'

Hatfield's expression changed. 'That's right,' she said. 'We're already giving the store away and –'

160

David Victor, the Commerce Consular, interrupted, 'We're not giving it away – we're just trying to keep it open so we can shop there. They need more credit in order to buy corn from us. If *we* don't sell it to them, they're going to buy it from Argentina.' He turned to Mary. 'It looks like we're going to lose out on soy beans. The Brazilians are trying to undercut us. I would appreciate it if you'd talk to the Prime Minister as soon as possible and try to make a package deal before we're shut out.'

Mary looked over at Mike Slade, who was seated at the opposite end of the table, slouched in his chair, doodling on a pad, seemingly paying no attention. 'I'll see what I can do,' Mary promised.

She made a note to send a cable to the Head of the Commerce Department in Washington asking permission to offer more credit to the Romanian government. The money would come from American banks, but they would make the loans only with government approval.

Eddie Maltz, the Political Consular, as well as the CIA agent, spoke up. 'I have a rather urgent problem, Madam Ambassador. A nineteen-year-old American student was arrested last night for possession of drugs. That's an extremely serious offence here.'

'What kind of drugs did he have on him?'

'Her. It's a young girl. Marijuana. Just a few ounces.'

'What's the girl like?'

'Bright, a college student, rather pretty.'

'What do you think they'll do to her?'

'The usual penalty is a five-year prison sentence.'

My God, Mary thought. *What will she be like when she gets out?* 'What can we do about it?'

Mike Slade said lazily, 'You can try your charm on the head of *Securitate*. His name is Istrase. He has a lot of power.'

Eddie Maltz went on. 'The girl says she was framed, and she may have a point. She was stupid enough to have an affair with a Romanian policeman. After he fu – took her to bed, he turned her in.'

Mary was horrified. 'How could he?'

Mike Slade said drily, 'Madam Ambassador, here, we're the enemy – not them. Romania is playing patty cake with us, and we're all buddies, and it's smiles and hands across the sea. We let them sell to us and buy from us at bargain basement discounts, because we're trying to woo them away from Russia. But when it comes right down to it, they're still communists.'

Mary made another note. 'All right. I'll see what I can do.' She turned to the Public Affairs Consular, Jerry Davis. 'What are your problems?'

'My department is having trouble getting approvals for repairs on the apartments our Embassy staff live in. Their quarters are in a disgraceful condition.'

'Can't they just go ahead and have their own repairs made?'

'Unfortunately, no. The Romanian government has to approve all repairs. Some of our people are without heat, and in several of the apartments, the toilets don't work and there's no running water.'

'Have you complained about this?'

'Yes, ma'am. Every day for the last three months.'

'Then why – ?'

'It's called harassment,' Mike Slade explained. 'It's a war of nerves they like to play with us.'

Mary made another note.

'Madam Ambassador, I have an extremely urgent problem,' Jack Chancelor, the head of the American Library said. 'Only yesterday some very important reference books were stolen from . . .'

Ambassador Ashley was beginning to get a headache.

The afternoon was spent in listening to a series of complaints. Everyone seemed unhappy. And then there was the reading. On her desk was a blizzard of white paper. There were the English translations of newspaper items that had appeared the day before in Romanian papers and magazines. Most of the stories in the popular newspaper *Scinteia Tineretului*, were about the daily activities of President Ionescu, with three or four pictures of him on every single page. *The incredible ego of the man*, Mary thought.

There were other condensations to read: the *Romania Liberă*, the weekly *Flacăra* magazine, and *Magafinul*. And that was only the beginning. There was the wireless file and the summary of news developments reported in the United States. There was a file of the full texts of important American officials' speeches, a thick report on arms control negotiations, and an update on the state of the United States economy.

There's enough reading material in one day, Mary thought, *to keep me busy for years, and I'm going to get this every morning.*

But the problem that disturbed Mary most was the feeling of antagonism from her staff. That had to be handled immediately.

She sent for Harriet Kruger, her Protocol Officer.

'How long have you worked here at the Embassy?' Mary asked.

'Four years before our break with Romania, and now three glorious months.' There was a note of irony in her voice.

'Don't you like it here?'

'I'm a McDonald's and Coney Island girl. Like the song says, "Show Me The Way To Go Home".'

'May we have an off-the-record conversation?'

'No, ma'am.'

Mary had forgotten. 'Why don't we adjourn to the Bubble Room?' she suggested.

When Mary and Harriet Kruger were seated at the table in the Bubble Room, with the heavy door safely closed behind them, Mary said, 'Something just occurred to me. Our meeting today was held in the conference room. Isn't that bugged?'

'Probably,' Kruger said cheerfully. 'But it doesn't matter. Mike Slade wouldn't let anything be discussed that the Romanians aren't already aware of.'

Mike Slade again.

'What do you think of Slade?'

'He's the best.'

Mary decided not to express her opinion. 'The reason I wanted to talk to you is because I got the feeling today that the morale around here isn't very good. Everyone's complaining. No one seems happy. I would like to know whether it's because of me, or whether it's always that way.'

Harriet Kruger studied her for a moment. 'You want an honest answer?'

'Please.'

'It's a combination of both. The Americans working here are in a pressure cooker. We break the rules, and we're in big trouble. We're afraid to make friends with Romanians because they'll probably turn out to belong to the *Securitate*, so we stick with the Americans. We're a small group, so pretty soon that gets boring and incestuous.' She shrugged. 'The pay is small, the food is lousy, and the weather is bad.' She studied Mary. 'None of that is your fault, Madam Ambassador. You have two problems: The first is that you're a political appointee, and you're in charge of an embassy manned by career diplomats.' She stopped. 'Am I coming on too strong?'

'No, please go on.'

'Most of them were against you before you even got here. Career workers in an embassy tend not to rock the boat. Political appointees like to change things. To them, you're an amateur telling professionals how to run their business. The second problem is that you're a woman. Romania should have a big symbol on its flag: a male chauvinist pig. The American men in the Embassy don't like taking orders from a woman, and the Romanians are a lot worse.'

'I see.'

Harriet Kruger smiled. 'But you sure have a great publicity agent. I've never seen so many magazine cover stories in my life. How do you do it?'

Mary had no answer to that.

Harriet Kruger glanced at her watch. 'Oops! You're going to be late. Florian's waiting to take you home so you can change.'

'Change for what?' Mary asked.

'Haven't you looked at the schedule I put on your desk?'

'I'm afraid I haven't had time. Don't tell me I'm supposed to go to some party!'

'*Parties*. Three of them tonight. You have twenty-one parties altogether this week.'

Mary was staring at her. 'That's impossible. I have too much to –'

'It goes with the territory. There are seventy-five embassies in Bucharest, and on any given night, some of them are celebrating something.'

'Can't I say "no"?'

'That would be the United States saying "no" to them. They would be offended.'

Mary sighed. 'I guess I'd better go and change.'

The cocktail party that afternoon was held at the Romanian State Palace for a visiting dignitary from East Germany.

As soon as Mary arrived, President Ionescu walked over to her. He kissed her hand and said, 'I have been looking forward to seeing you again.'

'Thank you, your Excellency. I, too.'

She had a feeling he had been drinking heavily. She recalled the dossier on him: *Married. One son, fourteen, the heir apparent, and three daughters. Is a womanizer. Drinks a lot. A shrewd peasant mentality. Charming when it suits him. Generous to his friends. Dangerous and ruthless to his enemies.* Mary thought: *A man to beware of.*

Ionescu took Mary's arm and led her off to a deserted corner. 'You will find us Romanians interesting.' He squeezed her arm. 'We are a very passionate people.' He looked at her for a reaction, and when he got none, he went on. 'We are descendants of the ancient Dacians and their conquerors, the Romans, going back to the year A.D. 106. For centuries, we have been Europe's doormat. The country with rubber borders. The Huns, Goths, Avars, Slavs and Mongols wiped their feet on us, but Romania survived. And do you know how?' He leaned closer to her, and she could smell the liquor on his breath. 'By giving our people a strong, firm leadership. They trust me, and I rule them well.'

Mary thought of some of the stories she had heard. The arrests in the middle of the night, the kangaroo court, the atrocities, the disappearances.

As Ionescu went on talking, Mary looked over his shoulder at the people in the crowded room. There were at least two hundred, and Mary was sure they represented every embassy in Romania. She would meet them all soon. She had glanced at Harriet Kruger's appointment list and was interested to see that one of her first duties would be to make a formal duty call on every one of the seventy-five embassies. In addition to that, there were the multiple cocktail parties and dinners scheduled for six nights of the week.

When am I going to have time to be an ambassador? Mary wondered. And even as she thought it, she realized that all this was part of being an ambassador.

A man came up to President Ionescu and whispered in his ear. The expression on Ionescu's face turned cold. He hissed something in Romanian, and the man nodded and hurried off. The dictator turned back to Mary, oozing charm again. 'I must leave you now. I look forward to seeing you again soon.'

And Ionescu was gone.

19

To get a head start on the crowded days that faced her, Mary had Florian pick her up at 6.30. During the ride to the Embassy, she read the reports and the communiqués from other embassies that had been delivered to the Residence during the night.

As Mary walked down the corridor of the Embassy, past Mike Slade's office, she stopped in surprise. He was at his desk, working. He was unshaven. She wondered if he had been out all night.

'You're in early,' Mary said.

He looked up. 'Morning. I'd like to have a word with you.'

'All right.' She started to walk in.

'Not here. Your office.'

He followed Mary through the connecting door to her office, and she watched as he walked over to an instrument in the corner of the room. 'This is a shredder,' Mike informed her.

'I know that.'

'Really? When you went out last night, you left some papers on top of your desk. By now they've been photographed and sent to Moscow.'

'Oh, my God! I must have forgotten. Which papers were they?'

'A list of cosmetics, toilet paper, and other personal feminine things you wanted to order. But that's beside the point. The cleaning women work for the *Securitate*. The Romanians are grateful for every scrap of information they can get, and they're great at putting things together. Lesson number one: At night everything must be locked in your safe, or shredded.'

'What's lesson number two?' Mary asked coldly.

Mike grinned. 'The Ambassador always starts the day by having coffee with her Deputy Chief of Mission. How do you take yours?'

She had no desire to have coffee with this arrogant bastard. 'I – black.'

'Good. You have to watch your figure around here. The food is fattening.' He rose and started towards the door that led to his office. 'I make my own brew. You'll like it.'

She sat there, furious with him. *I have to be careful how I handle him*, Mary decided. *I want him out of here as quickly as possible.*

He returned with two steaming mugs of coffee and set them down on her desk.

'How do I arrange for Beth and Tim to start at the American school here?' Mary asked.

'I've already arranged it. Florian will deliver them mornings and pick them up afternoons.'

She was taken aback. 'I – thank you.'

'You should take a look at the school when you get a chance. It's a small school, about a hundred pupils. Each class has eight or nine students. They come from all over – Canadians, Israelis, Nigerians – you name it. The teachers are excellent.'

'I'll stop by there.'

Mike took a sip of his coffee. 'I understand that you had a nice chat with our fearless leader last night.'

'President Ionescu? Yes. He seemed very pleasant.'

'Oh, he is. He's a lovely fellow. Until he gets annoyed with somebody. Then he chops your head off.'

Mary said nervously, 'Shouldn't we talk about this in the Bubble Room?'

'Not necessary. I had your office swept for bugs this morning. It's clean. After the janitors and cleaning people come in, then watch out. By the way, don't let Ionescu's charm fool you. He's a dyed-in-the-wool son-of-a-bitch. His people despise him, but there's nothing they can do about it. The secret police are everywhere. It's the KGB and police force wrapped into one. The general rule of thumb here is that one out of every three persons works for *Securitate* or the KGB. Romanians have orders not to have any contact with foreigners. If a foreigner wants to have dinner at a Romanian's apartment, it has to be approved first by the State.'

Mary felt a shiver go through her.

'A Romanian can be arrested for signing a petition, criticizing the government, writing graffiti . . .'

Mary had read newspaper and magazine articles about repression in communist countries, but living in the midst of it gave her a feeling of unreality.

'They do have trials here,' Mary said.

'Oh, occasionally they'll have a show trial, where reporters from the West are allowed to watch. But most of the people arrested manage to have fatal accidents while they're in police custody. There are gulags in Romania that we're not allowed to see. They're in the Delta area, and in the Danube near the Black Sea. I've talked to people who have seen them. The conditions there are horrifying.'

'And there's no place they can escape to,' Mary said, thinking aloud. 'They have the Black Sea to the east, Bulgaria to the south, and Yugoslavia, Hungary and Czechoslovakia on their other borders. They're right in the middle of the Iron Curtain.'

'Have you heard about the Typewriter Decree?'

'No.'

'It's Ionescu's latest brainstorm. He ordered every typewriter and copy machine in the country registered. As soon as they were registered, he had them confiscated. Now Ionescu controls all the information that's disseminated. More coffee?'

'No, thanks.'

'Ionescu is squeezing the people where it hurts. They're afraid to strike because they know they'll be shot. The standard of living here is one of the lowest in Europe. There's a shortage of everything. If the people see a line in front of a store, they'll join in and buy whatever it is that's for sale while they have the chance.'

'It seems to me,' Mary said slowly, 'that all these things add up to a wonderful opportunity for us to help them.'

Mike Slade looked at her. 'Sure,' he said drily. 'Wonderful.'

*

As Mary was going through some newly arrived cables from Washington that afternoon, she thought about Mike Slade. He was a strange man. Arrogant and rude, and yet: *I've arranged for the children's school. Florian will deliver them mornings and pick them up afternoons.* And he seemed to really care about the Romanian people and their problems. *He may be more complex than I thought*, Mary decided.

I still don't trust him.

It was by sheer accident that Mary learned of the meetings going on behind her back. She had left the office to have lunch with the Romanian Minister of Agriculture. When she arrived at the Ministry, she was told he had been called away by the President. Mary decided to return to the Embassy and have a working lunch. She said to her secretary, 'Tell Lucas Janklow, David Wallace and Eddie Maltz that I would like to see them.'

Dorothy Stone hesitated. 'They're in a conference, ma'am.'

There was something evasive in her tone.

'In a conference with whom?'

Dorothy Stone took a deep breath. 'With all the other consulars.'

It took a moment for it to sink in. 'Are you saying that there's a staff meeting going on without me?'

'Yes, Madam Ambassador.'

It was outrageous! 'I gather that this isn't the first time?'

'No, ma'am.'

'What else is going on here that I should know about and don't?'

Dorothy Stone took a deep breath. 'They're all sending out cables without your authorization.'

Forget about a revolution brewing in Romania, Mary thought. *There's a revolution brewing right here in the Embassy.* 'Dorothy – call a meeting of all department heads for three o'clock this afternoon. That means *everybody*.'

'Yes, ma'am.'

Mary was seated at the head of the table, watching as the staff entered the conference room. The senior members seated themselves at the conference table and the junior members took chairs against the wall.

'Good afternoon,' Mary said crisply. 'I won't take up much of your time. I know how busy you all are. It has come to my attention that senior staff meetings have been called without my knowledge or sanction. From this moment on, anyone attending such a meeting will be instantly dismissed.' Out of the corner of her eye, she saw Dorothy taking notes. 'It has also come to my attention that some of you are sending cables without informing me. According to State Department protocol, each ambassador has the right to hire and fire any member of the Embassy staff at his or her discretion.' Mary turned to Ted Thompson, the Agriculture Consular. 'Yesterday, you sent an unauthorized cable to the State Department. I've made reservations for you on a plane leaving for Washington at noon tomorrow. You are no longer a member of this Embassy.' She looked around the room. 'The next time anyone in this room sends a cable without my knowledge, or fails to give me full support, that person will be on the next plane back to the United States. That's all, ladies and gentlemen.'

There was a stunned silence. Then, slowly, the people began to rise and file out of the room. There was an intrigued expression on Mike Slade's face as he walked out.

Mary and Dorothy Stone were alone in the room. Mary said, 'What do you think?'

Dorothy grinned. 'Neat, but not gaudy. That's the shortest and most effective staff meeting I've ever seen.'

'Good. Now it's time to enlighten the cable office.'

All messages sent from embassies in Eastern Europe are sent in code. They are typed on a special typewriter, read by an electronic scanner in the code room, and automatically encoded there. The codes are changed every day, and have five designations: Top Secret; Secret; Confidential; Limited Official Use; and Unclassified. The cable office itself was a barred, windowless back room filled with the latest electronic equipment, and was closely guarded.

Sandy Palance, the officer in charge, was seated in the cable room behind a cage. He rose as Mary approached. 'Good afternoon, Madam Ambassador. May I help you?'

'No. I'm going to help *you*.'

There was a puzzled look on Palance's face. 'Ma'am?'

'You've been sending out cables without my signature. That means they're unauthorized cables.'

He was suddenly defensive. 'Well, the consulars told me that –'

'From now on, if you are asked by anyone to send a cable that does not have my signature on it, it is to be brought directly to me. Is that understood?' There was steel in her voice.

Palance thought: *Jesus! They sure had this one pegged wrong.* 'Yes, ma'am. I understand.'

'Good.'

Mary turned and walked away. She knew that the cable room was used by the CIA to send messages through a 'black channel'. There was no way she could stop that. She wondered how many members of the Embassy were part of the CIA, and she wondered if Mike Slade had told her the whole truth about it. She had the feeling he had not.

That night, Mary made notes of the day's events, and jotted down the problems that needed to be acted upon. She put them at her bedside, on top of a small table. In the morning she went into the bathroom to shower. When she was dressed, she picked up her notes. They were in a different order. *You can be sure that the Embassy and the Residence are bugged.* Mary stood there for a moment, thinking.

At breakfast, when she and Beth and Tim were alone in the dining room, Mary said, in a loud voice, 'The Romanians are such a wonderful people. But I have a feeling they're far behind the United States in some ways. Did you know that a lot of the apartments our Embassy staff live in have no heat or running water, and that the toilets don't work?'

Beth and Tim were looking at her strangely.

'I suppose we'll have to teach the Romanians how to fix things like that.'

The following morning, Jerry Davis said, 'I don't know how you did it, but there are workmen all over the place, fixing up our apartments.'

Mary grinned. 'You just have to speak nicely to them.'

At the end of a staff meeting, Mike Slade said, 'You have a lot of embassies to pay respects to. You'd better get started today.'

She resented his tone. Besides, it was none of his business; Harriet Kruger was the Protocol Officer, and she was away from the Embassy for the day.

Mike went on. 'It's important that you call on the embassies according to priority. The most important –'

'– is the Russian Embassy. I know that.'

'I would advise you –'

'Mr Slade – if I need any advice from you about my duties here, I'll let you know.'

Mike let out a deep sigh. 'Right.' He rose. 'Whatever you say, Madam Ambassador.'

After her visit to the Russian Embassy, the rest of Mary's day was taken up with interviews, a senator from New York who wanted inside information about dissidents, and a meeting with the new Agriculture Consular.

As Mary was about to leave the office, Dorothy Stone buzzed her. 'There's an urgent call for you, Madam Ambassador. James Stickley from Washington.'

Mary picked up the telephone. 'Hello, Mr Stickley.'

Stickley's voice came burning over the wire. 'Would you mind telling me what in God's name you're doing?'

'I – I don't know what you mean.'

'*Obviously.* The Secretary of State has just received a formal protest from the Ambassador of Gabon about your behaviour.'

'Just a minute!' Mary replied. 'There's some mistake. I haven't even *talked* to the Ambassador of Gabon.'

'Exactly,' Stickley snapped. 'But you talked to the Ambassador of the Soviet Union.'

'Well – yes. I made my courtesy call this morning.'

'Aren't you aware that foreign embassies take precedence according to the date they presented their credentials?'

'Yes, but –'

'For your information, in Romania, Gabon is the first, the Estonian Embassy is last, and there are about seventy more embassies in between. Any questions?'

'No, sir. I'm sorry if I –'

'Please see that it doesn't happen again.'

When Mike Slade heard the news, he came into Mary's office. 'I tried to tell you.'

'Mr Slade –'

'They take things like that very seriously in the diplomacy business. As a matter of fact, in 1661 the attendants of the Spanish Ambassador in London attacked the French Ambassador's coach, killed the postilion, beat up the coachman and hamstrung two horses just to make sure that the Spanish Ambassador's coach arrived first. I would suggest that you send a note of apology.'

Mary knew what she would be having for dinner. *Crow.*

Mary was disturbed by the comments she kept hearing about the amount of publicity she and the children were getting. 'There's even an article in *Pravda* about the three of you.'

At midnight Mary placed a call to Stanton Rogers. He would just be getting into his office. He came onto the line immediately.

'How's my favourite ambassador?'

'I'm fine. How are you, Stan?'

'Aside from a forty-eight hour day schedule, I can't complain. As a matter of fact, I'm enjoying every minute of it. How are you getting along? Any problems I can help you with?'

'It's not a problem, really. It's just something I'm curious about.' She hesitated, trying to phrase it so he would not misunderstand. 'I presume you saw the photograph of the children and me in *Pravda* last week?'

'Yes, it's wonderful!' Stanton Rogers exclaimed. 'We're finally getting through to them.'

'Do other ambassadors get as much publicity as I've been getting?'

'Frankly, no. But the boss decided to go all out with you, Mary. You're our showcase. President Ellison meant it when he said he was looking for the opposite of the ugly American. We've got you and we intend to flaunt you. We want the whole world to get a good look at the best of our country.'

'I – I'm really flattered.'

'Keep up the good work.'

They exchanged pleasantries for a few more minutes and said goodbye.

So it's the President who's behind this build-up, Mary thought. *No wonder he's been able to arrange so much publicity.*

The inside of the Ivan Stelian Prison was even more forbidding than its exterior. The corridors were narrow, painted a dull grey. There was a jungle of crowded, black-barred cells downstairs and on an upper tier, patrolled by uniformed guards armed with machine guns. The stench in the crowded cell area was overpowering.

A guard led Mary to a small visitor's room at the rear of the prison. 'She's in there. You have ten minutes.'

'Thank you.' Mary stepped inside the room, and the door closed behind her.

Hannah Murphy was seated at a small, battle-scarred table. She was handcuffed, and wearing prison garb. Eddie Maltz had referred to her as a pretty, nineteen-year-old student. She looked ten years older. Her face was pale and gaunt, and her eyes were red and swollen. Her hair was uncombed.

'Hi,' Mary said. 'I'm the American Ambassador.'

Hannah Murphy looked at her and began to sob uncontrollably.

Mary put her arms around her and said, soothingly, 'Sh! It's going to be all right.'

'N-no it's not,' the girl moaned. 'I'm going to be sentenced next week. I'll die if I have to stay in this place five years. I'll die!'

Mary held her for a moment. 'All right, tell me what happened.'

Hannah Murphy took a deep breath, and after a few moments she said, 'I met this man – he was a Romanian – and I was lonely. He was

172

nice to me and we – we made love. A girl friend had given me a couple of sticks of marijuana. I shared one with him. We made love again and I went to sleep. When I woke up in the morning, he was gone, but the police were there. I was naked. They – they stood around watching me get dressed and they brought me to this hell-hole.' She shook her head helplessly. 'They told me five years.'

'Not if I can help it.'

Mary thought of what Lucas Janklow had said to her as she was leaving for the prison. 'There's nothing you can do for her, Madam Ambassador. We've tried before. A five-year sentence for a foreigner is standard. If she were a Romanian, they'd probably give her life.'

Now Mary looked at Hannah Murphy and said, 'I'll do everything in my power to help you.'

Mary had examined the official police report on Hannah Murphy's arrest. It was signed by Captain Aurel Istrase, head of *Securitate*. It was brief and unhelpful, but there was no doubt of the girl's guilt. *I'll have to find another way*, Mary thought. *Aurel Istrase*. The name had a familiar ring. She thought back to the confidential dossier James Stickley had showed her in Washington. There had been something in there about Captain Istrase. Something about – she remembered.

Mary arranged to have a meeting with the Captain the following morning.

'You're wasting your time,' Mike Slade told her bluntly. 'Istrase is a mountain. He can't be moved.'

Aurel Istrase was a short, swarthy man with a scarred face, a shiny, bald head and stained teeth. Earlier in his career, someone had broken his nose, and it had failed to heal properly. Istrase had come to the Embassy for the meeting. He was curious about the new American Ambassador.

'You wished to talk to me, Madam Ambassador?'

'Yes. Thank you for coming. I want to discuss the case of Hannah Murphy.'

'Ah, yes. The drug peddler. In Romania, we have strict laws about people who sell drugs. They go to jail.'

'Excellent,' Mary said. 'I'm pleased to hear that. I wish we had stricter drug laws in the United States.'

Istrase was watching her, puzzled. 'Then you agree with me?'

'Absolutely. Anyone who sells drugs deserves jail. Hannah Murphy, however, did not sell drugs. She offered to *give* some marijuana to her lover.'

'It is the same thing. If –'

'Not quite, Captain. Her lover was a lieutenant on your police force. He smoked marijuana, too. Has he been punished?'

173

'Why should he be? He was merely gathering evidence of a criminal act.'

'Your lieutenant has a wife and three children?'

Captain Istrase frowned. 'Yes. The American girl tricked him into bed.'

'Captain – Hannah Murphy is a nineteen-year-old student. Your lieutenant is forty-five. Now who tricked whom?'

'Age has nothing to do with this,' the Captain said stubbornly.

'Does the lieutenant's wife know about her husband's affair?'

Captain Istrase stared at her. 'Why should she?'

'Because it sounds to me like a clear case of entrapment. I think we had better make this whole thing public. The international press will be fascinated.'

'There would be no point to that,' he said.

She sprang her ace. 'Because the lieutenant happens to be your son-in-law?'

'Certainly not!' the Captain said angrily. 'I just want to see justice done.'

'So do I,' Mary assured him.

According to the dossier she had seen, the son-in-law specialized in making the acquaintance of young tourists – male or female – sleeping with them, suggesting places where they could trade in the black market or buy dope, and then turning them in.

Mary said in a conciliatory tone, 'I see no need for your daughter to know how her husband conducts himself. I think it would be much better for all concerned if you quietly released Hannah Murphy from jail, and I shipped her back to the States. What do you say, Captain?'

He sat there, fuming, thinking it over. 'You are a very interesting lady,' he said finally.

'Thank you. You're a very interesting man. I'll expect Miss Murphy in my office this afternoon. I'll see that she's put on the first plane out of Bucharest.'

He shrugged. 'I will use what little influence I have.'

'I'm sure you will, Captain Istrase. Thank you.'

The following morning a grateful Hannah Murphy was on her way home.

'How did you do it?' Mike Slade asked, unbelievingly.

'I followed your advice. I charmed him.'

20

The day Beth and Tim were to start school, Mary got a call at 5 a.m. from the Embassy that a NIACT – a night action cable – had come in and required an immediate answer. It was the start of a long and busy day, and by the time Mary returned to the Residence it was after 7.00. The children were waiting for her.

'Well,' Mary asked, 'how was school?'

'I like it,' Beth replied. 'Did you know there are kids there from twenty-two different countries? This neat Italian boy kept staring at me all through class. It's a great school.'

'They've got a keen science laboratory,' Tim added. 'Tomorrow we're going to take some Romanian frogs apart.'

'It's so weird,' Beth said. 'They all speak English with such funny accents.'

'Just remember,' Mary told the children, 'when someone has an accent, it means that he knows one more language than you do. Well, I'm glad you had no problems.'

Beth said, 'No. Mike took care of us.'

'Who?'

'Mr Slade. He told us to call him Mike.'

'What does Mike Slade have to do with your going to school?'

'Didn't he tell you? He picked us up and drove Tim and me there and took us in and introduced us to our teachers. He knows them all.'

'He knows a lot of kids there, too,' Tim said. 'And he introduced us to them. Everybody likes him. He's a neat guy.'

A little too neat, Mary thought.

The following morning when Mike walked into Mary's office, she said, 'I understand you took Beth and Tim to school.'

He nodded. 'It's tough for youngsters trying to adjust in a foreign country. They're good kids.'

Did he have children? Mary suddenly realized how little she knew about Mike Slade's personal life. *It's probably better that way*, she decided. *He intends to see that I fail.*

She intended to succeed.

175

Saturday afternoon Mary took the children to the private Diplomatic Club, where members of the diplomatic community gathered to exchange gossip.

As Mary looked across the patio, she saw Mike Slade having a drink with someone, and when the woman turned, Mary realized that it was Dorothy Stone. Mary felt a momentary shock. It was as though her secretary were collaborating with the enemy. She wondered how close Dorothy and Mike Slade were. *I must be careful not to trust her too much*, Mary thought. *Or anyone.*

Harriet Kruger was seated at a table alone. Mary walked over. 'Do you mind if I join you?'

'I'd be delighted.' Harriet pulled out a package of American cigarettes. 'Cigarette?'

'Thank you, no. I don't smoke.'

'A person can't live in this country without cigarettes,' Harriet said.

'I don't understand.'

'Kent's One Hundred soft packs make the economy go around. I mean – literally. If you want to see a doctor, you give the nurse cigarettes. If you want meat from the butcher, a mechanic to fix your automobile, or an electrician to fix a lamp – you bribe them with cigarettes. I had an Italian friend who needed a small operation. She had to bribe the nurse in charge to use a new razor blade when she prepped her, and she had to bribe the other nurses to put on clean bandages after they had cleansed the wounds, instead of using all the old bandages again.'

'But why – ?'

Harriet Kruger said, 'This country's short on bandages and every kind of medication you can name. It's the same everywhere in the Eastern bloc. Last month there was a plague of botulism in East Germany. They had to get all their anti-serum from the West.'

'And the people have no way of complaining,' Mary commented.

'Oh, they have their ways. Haven't you heard of Bula?'

'No.'

'He's a mythical character the Romanians use to let off steam. There's a story about people standing in line for meat one day and the line was barely moving. After five hours, Bula gets mad and says, "I'm going over to the palace and kill Ionescu!" Two hours later, he comes back to the line and his friends ask, "What happened – did you kill him?" Bula says, "No. There was a long line there, too." '

Mary laughed.

Harriet Kruger said, 'Do you know what one of the biggest black market items here is? Our home video cassettes.'

'They like to watch our movies?'

'No – it's the commercials they're interested in. All the things we take for granted – washing machines, vacuum cleaners, automobiles, television sets – those things are out of their reach. They're fascinated by them. When the movie starts again, they go to the john.'

Mary looked up in time to see Mike Slade and Dorothy Stone leaving the club. She wondered where they were going.

When Mary came home at night after a hard, long day at the Embassy, all she wanted to do was bathe and change clothes and shed the day. At the Embassy every minute seemed to be filled, and she never had any time to herself. But she soon found that the Residence was just as bad. Wherever Mary went, there were the servants, and she had the uncomfortable feeling they were constantly spying on her.

One night she got up at 2 a.m. and went downstairs to the kitchen. As she opened the refrigerator, she heard a noise. She turned around, and Mihai, the butler, in his robe, and Rosica and Delia and Carmen were standing there.

'What can I get you, Madam?' Mihai asked.

'Nothing,' Mary said. 'I just wanted a little something to eat.'

Cosma, the chef, came in and said in a hurt voice, 'All Madam had to do was tell me she was hungry and I would have prepared something.'

They were staring at her reprovingly.

Mary said, 'I don't think I'm really hungry. Thank you.' And she fled back to her room.

The next day she told the children what had happened. 'Do you know,' she said to Tim and Beth, 'I felt like the second wife in *Rebecca*.'

'What's *Rebecca*?' Beth asked.

'It's a lovely book you'll read one day.'

When Mary walked into her office, Mike Slade was waiting for her.

'We have a sick kid you'd better take a look at,' he said.

He led her to one of the small offices down the corridor. On the couch was a white-faced young Marine, groaning in pain.

'What happened?' Mary asked.

'My guess is appendicitis.'

'Then we'd better get him to a hospital right away.'

Mike turned and looked at her. 'Not here.'

'What do you mean?'

'He has to be flown either to Rome or Zürich.'

'That's ridiculous,' Mary snapped. She lowered her voice, so the boy would not hear. 'Can't you see how sick he is?'

'Ridiculous or not, no one from an American embassy goes to a hospital in an Iron Curtain country.'

'But, why –?'

'Because we're vulnerable. We'd be at the mercy of the Romanian government and the *Securitate*. We could be put under ether, or given scopolamine – they could extract all kinds of information from us. It's a State Department rule – we fly him out.'

177

'Why doesn't our Embassy have its own doctor?'

'Because we're a "C" category embassy. We haven't the budget for our own doctor. An American doctor pays us a visit here once every three months. In the meantime, we have a pharmacist for minor aches and pains.' Mike walked over to a desk and picked up a piece of paper. 'Just sign this, and he's on his way. I'll arrange for a special plane to fly him out.'

'Very well.' Mary signed the paper. She walked over to the young Marine and took his hand in hers. 'You're going to be fine,' she said softly. 'Just fine.'

Two hours later, the Marine was on a plane to Zürich.

The following morning when Mary asked Mike how the young Marine was, he shrugged. 'They operated,' he said indifferently. 'He'll be all right.'

What a cold man, Mary thought. *I wonder if anything ever touches him.*

21

No matter what time in the morning Mary arrived at the Embassy, Mike Slade was always there ahead of her. She saw him at very few of the embassy parties, and she had a feeling he had his own private entertainment every night.

He was a constant surprise. One afternoon Mary agreed to let Florian take Beth and Tim ice-skating at Floreasca Park. Mary left the Embassy early to join them, and when she arrived, she saw that Mike Slade was with them. The three of them were skating together, obviously having a wonderful time. He was patiently teaching them figure eights. *I must warn the children about him*, Mary thought. But she was not sure exactly what the warning should be.

The following morning when Mary arrived at her office, Mike walked in. 'A codel is arriving in two hours. I thought –'

'A codel?'

'That's diplomatese for a congressional delegation. Four senators with their wives and aides. They'll expect you to meet with them. I'll set up an appointment with President Ionescu and have Harriet see that their shopping and sight-seeing are taken care of.'

'Thank you.'

'Some of my home-brewed coffee?'

'Fine.'

She watched him as he walked through the connecting door into his office. A strange man. Rough, rude. And yet, there was his patience with Beth and Tim.

When he returned with two cups of coffee, Mary said, 'Do you have children?'

The question caught Mike Slade off guard. 'I have two boys.'

'Where – ?'

'They're in the custody of my ex-wife.' He abruptly changed the subject. 'Let's see if I can set up that appointment with Ionescu.'

The coffee was delicious. Mary was later to remember that this was the day she realized that having coffee with Mike Slade had become a morning ritual.

*

Angel picked her up in the evening at La Boca, near the waterfront, where she was standing with the other *putas*, dressed in a tight-fitting

179

blouse and jeans that were cut off at the thighs, showing off her wares. She looked no older than fifteen. She was not pretty, but that did not bother Angel.

'*Vámonos, querida.* We will entertain each other.'

The girl lived in a cheap, walk-up apartment nearby, consisting of one dirty room with a bed, two chairs, a lamp and a sink.

'Get undressed, *estrelita.* I want to see you naked.'

The girl hesitated. There was something about Angel that frightened her. But it had been a slow day, and she had to bring money to Pepe, or she knew she would be beaten. Slowly, she began to undress.

Angel stood watching. Off came the blouse and then the jeans. The girl was wearing nothing underneath. Her body was pale and thin.

'Keep your shoes on. Come over here and kneel down.'

The girl obeyed.

'Now here is what I want you to do.'

She listened, and looked up with frightened eyes. 'I've never done –'

Angel kicked her in the head. She lay on the floor, moaning. Angel picked her up by the hair and threw her on the bed. As the girl started to scream, Angel punched her hard across the face. She moaned.

'Good,' Angel said. 'I want to hear you moan.'

A huge fist slammed into her nose and broke it. When Angel was finished with her thirty minutes later, the girl lay on the bed, unconscious.

Angel smiled down at the battered figure of the girl and threw a few pesos on the bed. '*Gracias.*'

Mary spent every possible moment she could with the children. They did a lot of sight-seeing. There were dozens of museums and old churches to visit, but for the children the highlight was the trip to Braşov, to Dracula's castle, located in the heart of Transylvania, a hundred miles from Bucharest.

'The count was really a Prince,' Florian explained on the drive up. 'Prince Vlad Tepes. He was a great hero who stopped the Turkish invasion.'

'I thought he just liked to suck blood and kill people,' Tim said.

Florian nodded. 'Yes. Unfortunately, after the war Vlad's power went to his head. He became a dictator and he impaled his enemies on stakes. The legend grew that he was a vampire. An Irishman, named Bram Stoker, wrote a book based on the legend. A silly book, but it has done wonders for tourism.'

Bram Castle was a huge, stone monument high in the mountains. They were all exhausted by the time they climbed the steep stone stairs leading to the castle. They went into a low-ceilinged room containing guns and ancient artefacts.

'This is where Count Dracula murdered his victims and drank their blood,' the guide said in a sepulchral voice.

The room was damp and eerie. A spiderweb brushed across Tim's face. 'I'm not scared of anything,' he said to his mother, 'but can we get out of here?'

Every six weeks an American Air Force C-130 plane landed at a small airfield on the outskirts of Bucharest. The plane was loaded with food and luxuries unavailable in Bucharest, that had been ordered by members of the American Embassy through the military commissary in Frankfurt.

One morning, while Mary and Mike Slade were having coffee, Mike said, 'Our commissary plane is due in today. Why don't you take a ride out to the airport with me?'

Mary started to say no. She had a great deal of work to do, and it seemed a pointless invitation. Still, Mike Slade was not a man given to wasting time. Her curiosity got the better of her.

'All right.'

They drove to the airfield, and on the way discussed various Embassy problems that had to be dealt with. The conversation was kept on a cool, impersonal level.

When they arrived at the airport, an armed Marine sergeant opened a gate to allow the limousine to pass through. Ten minutes later, they watched the C-130 land.

Behind the fence, on the boundary of the airport, hundreds of Romanians had gathered. They watched hungrily as the crew began unloading the aircraft.

'What is that crowd doing here?'

'Dreaming. They're looking at some of the things they can never have. They know we're getting steak and soap and perfume. A crowd is always here when the plane lands. It's some kind of mysterious underground telegraph.'

Mary studied the avid faces behind the fence. 'It's unbelievable.'

'That plane is a symbol to them. It's not just the cargo – it represents a free country that takes care of its citizens.'

Mary turned to look at him. 'Why did you bring me here?'

'Because I don't want you to get carried away by President Ionescu's sweet talk. This is the real Romania.'

Every morning when Mary rode to work, she noticed long queues of people outside the gates waiting to get into the consular section of the Embassy. She had taken it for granted that they were people with minor problems they hoped the consul could solve. But on this particular morning, she went to the window to take a closer look, and the expressions she saw on their faces compelled her to go into Mike's office.

'Who are all those people waiting in line outside?'

Mike walked with her to the window. 'They're mostly Romanian Jews. They're waiting to file applications for visas.'

'But there's an Israeli Embassy in Bucharest. Why don't they go there?'

'Two reasons,' Mike explained. 'First of all, they think the United States government has a greater chance of assisting them to get to Israel than the Israeli government. And secondly, they think there's less of a chance of the Romanian security people finding out their intention if they come to us. They're wrong, of course.' He pointed out the window. 'There's an apartment house directly across from the Embassy that has several flats filled with agents using telescopic lenses, photographing everybody who goes in and out of the Embassy.'

'That's terrible!'

'That's the way they play the game. When a Jewish family applies for a visa to emigrate, they lose their green job cards and they're thrown out of their apartments. Their neighbours are instructed to turn their backs on them. Then it takes three to four years before the government will tell them whether they'll even get their exit papers, and the answer is usually "no".'

'Can't we do something about it?'

'We try all the time. But Ionescu enjoys playing a cat-and-mouse game with the Jews. Very few of them are ever allowed to leave the country.'

Mary looked out at the expressions of hopelessness painted on their faces. 'There has to be a way,' Mary said.

'Don't break your heart,' Mike told her.

The time zone problem was exhausting. When it was daylight in Washington, it was the middle of the night in Bucharest, and Mary was constantly being awakened by telegrams and telephone calls at three and four in the morning. Every time a night cable came in, the Marine on duty at the Embassy would call the day officer, who would send a staff assistant to the Residence to awaken Mary. After that, she would be too keyed up to go back to sleep.

It's exciting, Edward. I really think I can make a difference here. Anyway, I'm trying. I couldn't bear to fail. Everyone is counting on me. I wish you were here to say 'you can do it, old girl'. I miss you so much. Can you hear me, Edward? Are you here somewhere where I can't see you? Sometimes not knowing the answer to that makes me crazy . . .

They were having their morning coffee.

'We have a problem,' Mike Slade began.

'Yes?'

'A delegation of a dozen Romanian church officials wants to see you. A church in Utah has invited them for a visit. The Romanian government won't issue them an exit visa.'

'Why not?'

'Very few Romanians are allowed to leave the country. They have a joke about the day Ionescu took power. He went to the east wing of the palace and saw the sun rising. "Good morning, comrade sun," Ionescu said. "Good morning," the sun said. "Everyone is so happy that you are Romania's new President." That evening, Ionescu went to the west wing of the palace to watch the sun set. He said, "Good evening, comrade sun." The sun didn't answer. "How is it that you spoke to me so nicely this morning, and now you won't speak to me at all?" "I'm in the west now," the sun said. "You can go to hell." Ionescu is afraid that once they get out, the church officials will tell the government to go to hell.'

'I'll talk to the Foreign Minister and see what I can do.'

Mike rose. 'Do you like folk-dancing?' he asked.

'Why?'

'There's a Romanian dance company opening tonight. They're supposed to be pretty good. Would you like to go?'

Mary was taken by surprise. The last thing she had expected was for Mike to invite her out.

And now, even more incredibly, she found herself saying, 'Yes.'

'Good.' Mike handed her a small envelope. 'There are three tickets here. You can take Beth and Tim, courtesy of the Romanian government. We get tickets to most of their openings.'

Mary sat there, her face flushed, feeling like a fool. 'Thank you,' she said stiffly.

'I'll have Florian pick you up at eight o'clock.'

Beth and Tim were not interested in going to the theatre. Beth had invited a schoolmate for dinner.

'It's my Italian friend,' Beth said. 'Is it okay?'

'To tell you the truth, I've never really cared much for folk-dancing,' Tim added.

Mary laughed. 'All right. I'll let you two off the hook this time.'

She wondered if the children were as lonely as she was. She thought about who she could invite to go with her. She mentally ran down the list: Colonel McKinney, Jerry Davis, Harriet Kruger? There was no one she really wanted to be with. *I'll go alone*, she decided.

Florian was waiting for Mary when she stepped out of the front door.

'Good evening, Madam Ambassador.' He bowed and opened the car door.

'You seem very cheerful tonight, Florian.'

He grinned. 'I am always cheerful, Madam.' He closed the door and got behind the wheel. 'We Romanians have a saying: "Kiss the hand you cannot bite." '

Mary decided to take a chance. 'Are you happy living here, Florian?'

He studied her in the rear-view mirror. 'Shall I give you the official party line answer, Madam Ambassador, or would you like the truth?'

'The truth, please.'

'I could be shot for saying this, but no Romanian is happy here. Only foreigners. You are free to come and go as you please. We are prisoners. There is not enough of anything here.' They were driving by a long queue of people in front of a butcher's shop. 'Do you see that? They will wait in line for three or four hours to get a lamb chop or two, and half the people in line will be disappointed. It is the same for everything. But do you know how many homes Ionescu has hidden away? Twelve! I have driven many Romanian officials to them. Each one is like a palace. Meanwhile, three or four families are forced to live together in tiny apartments without heat.' Florian stopped suddenly, as though afraid he had said too much. 'You will not mention this conversation, please?'

'Of course not.'

'Thank you. I would hate to have my wife become a widow. She is young. And Jewish. There is the anti-semitism problem here.'

Mary knew that already.

'There is a story about a store that was promised fresh eggs. At five o'clock in the morning, there was a long line waiting in the freezing cold. By eight o'clock, the eggs still had not come, and the line had grown longer. The owner said, "There will not be enough for everyone. The Jews can leave." At two in the afternoon, the eggs still had not arrived, and the line was even longer. The store owner said, "Non-party members leave." At midnight the line was still waiting in the freezing cold. No eggs. The owner locked the store and said, "Nothing's changed. The Jews always get the best of everything." '

Mary did not know whether to laugh or cry. *But I'm going to do something about it*, she promised herself.

The folk theatre was on Rapsodia Romana, a bustling street filled with small stands selling flowers and plastic slippers and blouses and pens. The theatre was small and ornate, a relic of more halcyon days. The entertainment itself was boring, the costumes tawdry, and the dancers were awkward. The show seemed interminable, and when it was finally over, Mary was glad to escape into the fresh night air. Florian was standing by the limousine in front of the theatre.

'I'm afraid there will be a delay, Madam Ambassador. A flat tyre. And a thief has stolen the spare. I have sent for one. It should be here in the next hour. Would you like to wait in the car?'

Mary looked up at the full moon shining above. The evening was crisp and clear. She realized she had not walked the streets of Bucharest since she had arrived. She made a sudden decision.

'I think I'll walk back to the Residence.'

He nodded. 'It is a lovely evening for a walk.'

Mary turned and started walking down the street towards the Central Square. Bucharest was a fascinating, exotic city. On the street corners were arcane signs: *Tuten . . . Gospodina . . . Chimice . . .*

She strolled down the Avenue Mosilor and turned into the Piata Rosetti, where there were red and tan trackless trollies, crammed with people. Even at this late hour, most of the shops were open, and there were queues at all of them. Coffee shops were serving *gogoase*, the delicious Romanian doughnuts. The sidewalks were crowded with late night shoppers carrying *pungas*, the string shopping bags. It seemed to Mary that the people were ominously quiet. They seemed to be staring at her, the women avidly eyeing the clothes she was wearing. She began to walk faster.

When she reached the corner of Calea Victoriei, she stopped, unsure of which direction to take. She said to a passer-by, 'Excuse me – could you tell me how to get – ?'

He gave her a quick, frightened look and hurried off.

They're not supposed to talk to foreigners, Mary remembered.

How was she going to get back? She tried to visualize the way she had come with Florian. It seemed to her that the Residence was some-where to the east. She began walking in that direction. Soon she was on a small side street, dimly lit. In the far distance, she could see a broad, well-lighted boulevard. *I can get a taxi there*, Mary thought with relief.

There was the sound of heavy footsteps behind her, and she involun-tarily turned. A large man in an overcoat was coming towards her, moving rapidly. Mary walked faster.

'Excuse me,' the man called out in a heavy Romanian accent. 'Are you lost?'

She was filled with relief. He was probably a policeman of some sort. Perhaps he had been following her to make sure she was safe.

'Yes,' Mary said gratefully. 'I want to go back to –'

There was the sudden roar of a motor, and the sound of a car racing up behind her, and then the squeal of brakes as the car screamed to a stop. The pedestrian in the overcoat grabbed Mary. She could smell his hot, fetid breath and feel his fat fingers bruising her wrist. He started pushing her towards the open door of the car. Mary was fighting to break free . . .

'Get in the car!' the man growled.

'No!' She was yelling, 'Help! Help me!'

There was a shout from across the street, and a figure came racing towards them. The man stopped, unsure of what to do.

The stranger yelled, 'Let go of her!'

He grabbed the man in the overcoat and pulled him away from Mary. She found herself suddenly free. The man behind the wheel started to get out of the car to help his accomplice.

From the far distance came the sound of an approaching siren. The man in the overcoat called out to his companion, and the two men leaped into the car, and it sped away.

A blue and white car with the word 'Militia' on the side, and a flashing blue light on top, pulled to a halt in front of Mary. Two men in uniform hurried out.

In Romanian, one of them asked, 'Are you all right?' And then in halting English, 'What happened?'

Mary was fighting to get herself under control. 'Two men – they – they t-tried to force me into their car. If – if it hadn't been for this gentleman –' She turned.

The stranger was gone.

22

She fought all night long, struggling to escape the men, waking in a panic, falling to sleep and waking again. She kept re-living the scene: The sudden footsteps hurrying towards her, the car pulling up, the man trying to force her into the car. Had they known who she was? Or were they merely trying to rob a tourist dressed in American clothes?

When Mary arrived at her office, Mike Slade was waiting for her. He brought in two cups of coffee and sat down across from her desk. 'How was the theatre?' he asked.

'Fine.' What had happened to her afterwards was none of his business.

'Did you get hurt?'

She looked at him in surprise. 'What?'

He said patiently, 'When they tried to kidnap you. Did they hurt you?'

'I – how do you know about that?'

His voice was filled with irony. 'Madam Ambassador, Romania is one big, open secret. You can't take a bath without everyone knowing about it. It wasn't very clever of you to go for a stroll by yourself.'

'I'm aware of that now,' Mary said coldly. 'It won't happen again.'

'Good.' His tone was brisk. 'Did the man take anything from you?'

'No.'

He frowned. 'It makes no sense. If they had wanted your coat or purse, they could have taken them from you on the street. Trying to force you into a car means it was a kidnapping.'

'Who would want to kidnap me?'

'It wouldn't have been Ionescu's men. He's trying to keep our relations on an even keel. It would have to be some dissident group.'

'Or crooks who planned to hold me for ransom.'

'There are no kidnappings for ransom in this country. If they caught anyone doing that, there wouldn't be a trial – there would be a firing squad.' He took a sip of his coffee. 'May I give you some advice?'

'I'm listening.'

'Go home.'

'What?'

Mike Slade put down the cup. 'All you have to do is send in a letter of resignation, pack up your kids and go back to Kansas, where you'll be safe.'

She could feel her face getting red. 'Mr Slade, I made a mistake. It's not the first one I've made, and it probably won't be the last one. But I was appointed to this post by the President of the United States, and until he fires me, I don't want you or anyone else telling me to go home.' She fought to keep control of her voice. 'I expect the people in this Embassy to work with me, not against me. If that's too much for you to handle, why don't *you* go home?' She was trembling with anger.

Mike Slade stood up. 'I'll see that the morning reports are put on your desk, Madam Ambassador.'

The attempted kidnapping was the sole topic of conversation at the Embassy that morning. *How had everyone found out?* Mary wondered. *And how had Mike Slade found out?* Mary wished she could have learned the name of her rescuer, so that she could have thanked him. In the quick glimpse she had had of him, she had got the impression of an attractive man, probably in his early forties, with prematurely grey hair. He had had a foreign accent – possibly French. If he was a tourist, he could have left Romania by now.

*

An idea kept gnawing at Mary, and it was hard to dismiss. The only person she knew of who wanted to get rid of her was Mike Slade. What if he had set up the attack to frighten her into leaving? He had given her the theatre tickets. He had known where she would be. She could not put it out of her mind.

Mary had debated whether to tell the children about the attempted kidnapping, and decided against it. She did not want to frighten them. She would simply see to it that they were never alone.

There was a cocktail party to attend at the French Embassy that evening in honour of a visiting French concert pianist. Mary was tired and nervous and would have given anything to have avoided it, but she knew she had to go.

She bathed and selected an evening gown, and as she reached for her shoes, she noticed that one shoe had a broken heel. She rang for Carmen.

'Yes, Madam Ambassador?'

'Carmen, would you please take this to a shoemaker and have it repaired?'

'Certainly, Madam. Is there anything else?'

'No, that's all, thank you.'

When Mary arrived at the French Embassy, it was already crowded with guests. She was greeted at the entrance by the French Ambassador's aide, whom Mary had met on a previous visit to the Embassy. He took her hand and kissed it.

'Good evening, Madam Ambassador. It is so kind of you to come.'

'It was so kind of you to invite me,' Mary said.

They both smiled at their empty phrases.

'Permit me to take you to the Ambassador.' He escorted her through the crowded ballroom, where she saw the familiar faces she had been seeing for weeks on end. Mary greeted the French Ambassador, and they exchanged pleasantries.

'You will enjoy Madame Dauphin. She is a remarkable pianist.'

'I'm looking forward to it,' Mary lied.

A servant passed by with a tray of glasses filled with champagne. Mary had learned by now to sip drinks at the various embassies. As she turned to greet the Australian Ambassador, she caught sight of the stranger who had rescued her from the kidnappers. He was standing in a corner talking to the Italian Ambassador and his aide.

'Please excuse me,' Mary said. She moved across the room towards the Frenchman.

He was saying, 'Of course, I miss Paris, but I hope that next year –' He broke off as he saw Mary approaching.

'Ah, the lady in distress.'

'You know each other?' the Italian Ambassador asked.

'We haven't been officially introduced,' Mary replied.

'Madam Ambassador, may I present Dr Louis Desforges.'

The expression on the Frenchman's face changed. '*Madam Ambassador?* I beg your pardon! I had no idea.' His voice was filled with embarrassment. 'I should have recognized you, of course.'

'You did better than that,' Mary smiled. 'You saved me.'

The Italian Ambassador looked at the doctor and said, 'Ah! So *you* were the one.' He turned to Mary. 'I heard about your unfortunate experience.'

'It would have been unfortunate if Dr Desforges hadn't come along. Thank you.'

Louis Desforges smiled. 'I'm happy that I was in the right place at the right time.'

The Ambassador and his aide saw a British contingent enter.

The Ambassador said, 'If you will excuse us, there is someone we have to see.'

The two men hurried off. Mary was alone with the doctor.

'Why did you run away when the police came?'

He studied her a moment. 'It is not good policy to get involved with the Romanian police. They have a way of arresting witnesses, then pumping them for information. I'm a doctor attached to the French Embassy here, and I don't have diplomatic immunity. I do, however, know a great deal about what goes on at our Embassy, and that information could be valuable to the Romanians.' He smiled. 'So forgive me if I seemed to desert you.'

There was a directness about him that was very appealing. In some way that Mary could not define, he reminded her a little bit of Edward. Perhaps because Louis Desforges was a doctor. But, no, it was more than that. He had the same openness that Edward had, almost the same smile.

'If you'll excuse me,' Dr Desforges said, 'I must go and become a social animal.'

'You don't like parties?'

He winced. 'I despise them.'

'Does your wife enjoy them?'

He started to say something, and then hesitated. 'Yes – she did. Very much.'

'Is she here this evening?'

'She and our two children are dead.'

Mary paled. 'Oh, my God. I'm so sorry. How – ?'

His face was rigid. 'I blame myself. We were living in Algeria. I was operating undercover, fighting the terrorists.' His words became slow and halting. 'They found out my identity and blew up the house. I was away at the time.'

'I'm so sorry,' Mary said again. Hopeless, inadequate words.

'Thank you. There is a cliché that time heals everything. I no longer believe it.' His voice was bitter.

Mary thought about Edward and how much she still missed him. But this man had lived with his pain longer.

He looked at her and said, 'If you will excuse me, Madam Ambassador . . .' He turned and walked over to greet a group of arriving guests.

He reminds me a little of you, Edward. You'd like him. He's a very brave man. He's in a lot of pain, and I think that's what draws me to him. I'm in pain, too, darling. Will I ever get over missing you? It's so lonely here. There's no one I can talk to. I desperately want to succeed. Mike Slade is trying to get me to go home. I'm not going. But oh, how I need you. Good night, my darling.

The following morning, Mary telephoned Stanton Rogers. It was wonderful to hear his voice. *It's like a lifeline to home*, she thought.

'I'm getting some excellent reports on you,' Stanton Rogers said. 'The Hannah Murphy story made headlines here. You did an excellent job.'

'Thank you, Stan.'

190

'Mary, tell me about the attempted kidnapping.'

'I've talked to the Prime Minister and the head of *Securitate*, and they have no clues at all.'

'Didn't Mike Slade warn you not to go out alone?'

Mike Slade. 'Yes, he warned me, Stan.' *Shall I tell him that Mike Slade told me to go home?* No, she decided. *I'll handle Mr Slade in my own way.*

'Remember – I'm always here for you. Any time.'

'I know,' Mary said gratefully. 'I can't tell you what it means to me.'

The telephone call made her feel much better.

'We have a problem. There's a leak somewhere in our Embassy.'

Mary and Mike Slade were having a cup of coffee before the daily staff meeting.

'How serious is it?'

'Very. Our Commerce Consular, David Victor, held some meetings with the Romanian Minister of Commerce.'

'I know. We discussed it last week.'

'Right,' Mike said. 'And when David went back for a second meeting, they were ahead of us on every counter-proposal we made. They knew exactly how far we were prepared to go.'

'Isn't it possible that they just figured it out?'

'It's possible, yes. Except that we discussed some new proposals, and they were ahead of us again.'

Mary was thoughtful for a moment. 'You think it's someone on the staff?'

'Not just *someone*. The last executive conference was held in the Bubble Room. Our electronics experts have traced the leak to there.'

Mary looked at him in surprise. There were only eight people allowed at the conferences in the Bubble Room, each an executive member of the Embassy.

'Whoever it is is carrying electronic equipment, probably a tape recorder. I suggest you call a conference meeting this morning in the Bubble Room and have the same group in. Our instruments will be able to pinpoint the guilty person.'

There were eight persons seated around the table in the Bubble Room. Eddie Maltz, the Political Consular and CIA agent, Patricia Hatfield, the Economic Consular, Jerry Davis, Public Affairs, David Victor, Commerce Consular, Lucas Janklow, Administrative Consular, and Colonel William McKinney. Mary was at one end of the table, Mike Slade at the other.

Mary turned to David Victor. 'How are your meetings going with the Romanian Minister of Commerce?'

The Commerce Consular shook his head. 'Frankly, not as well as I had hoped. They seem to know everything I have to say before I say it. I come in with new proposals, and they've already prepared their arguments against them. It's as though they're reading my mind.'

'Maybe they are,' Mike Slade said.

'What do you mean?'

'They're reading somebody's mind in this room.' He picked up a red telephone on the table. 'Send him in.'

A moment later, the huge door was pushed open and a man dressed in civilian clothes entered, carrying a black box with a dial on it.

Eddie Maltz said, 'Wait a minute. No one is allowed in . . .'

'It's all right,' Mary said. 'We have a problem and this man is going to solve it.' She looked up at the newcomer. 'Please go ahead.'

'Right. I'd like everyone to stay just where you are, please.'

As the group watched, he walked over to Mike Slade and held the box close to him. The needle on the dial remained at zero. The man moved on to Patricia Hatfield. The needle remained still. Eddie Maltz was next, then Jerry Davis and Lucas Janklow. The needle remained still. The man moved to David Victor, and finally to Colonel McKinney, but the needle still did not move. The only person left was Mary. When he approached her, the needle began to swing wildly.

Mike Slade said, 'What the hell –' He got to his feet and went over to Mary.

'Are you sure?' Mike demanded of the civilian.

The dial was moving crazily.

'Talk to the machine,' the man said.

Mary rose in confusion.

'Do you mind if we break up this meeting?' Mike asked.

Mary turned to the others. 'That's it for now, thank you.'

Mike Slade said to the technician, 'You stay.'

When the others had left the room, Mike asked, 'Can you pinpoint where the bug is?'

'Sure can.' The man slowly moved the black box down, inches away from Mary's body. As it got closer to her feet, the dial began to move faster.

The civilian straightened up. 'It's your shoes.'

Mary stared at him incredulously. 'You're mistaken. I bought these shoes in Washington.'

Mike said, 'Would you mind taking them off?'

'I –' This whole thing was ridiculous. The machine had to be crazy. Or someone was trying to frame her. This could be Mike Slade's way of getting rid of her. He would report to Washington that she had been caught spying and giving information to the enemy. Well, he was not going to get away with it.

She stepped out of her shoes, picked them up and dropped them into Mike's hands. 'Here,' she said angrily.

He turned them over and examined them. 'Is this a new heel?'

'No, it's –' And then she remembered: *Carmen, would you please take this to a shoemaker and have it repaired?*

Mike was breaking open the heel of the shoe. Inside was a miniature tape recorder.

'We found our spy,' Mike said drily. He looked up. 'Where did you have this heel put on?'

'I – I don't know. I asked one of the maids to take care of it.'

'Wonderful,' he said sardonically. 'In the future, we'd all appreciate it, Madam Ambassador, if you would let your secretary handle things like that.'

There was a telex for Mary.

'Senate Foreign Affairs Committee has agreed to Romanian loan you requested. Announcement to be made tomorrow. Congratulations.

Stanton Rogers.'

Mike read the telex. 'That's good news. Negulesco will be tickled.'

Mary knew that Negulesco, the Romanian Finance Minister, was on shaky ground. This would make him a hero with Ionescu.

'They're not announcing this until tomorrow,' Mary said. She sat there, deep in thought. 'I want you to make an appointment for me with Negulesco this morning.'

'Do you want me to come along?'

'No. I'll do this alone.'

Two hours later, Mary was seated in the office of the Romanian Finance Minister. He was beaming. 'So you have good news for us, yes?'

'I'm afraid not,' Mary said regretfully. She watched his smile fade away.

'*What?* I understood that the loan was – how do you say? – "in the bag"?'

Mary sighed. 'So did I, Minister.'

'What happened? What went wrong?' His face was suddenly grey.

Mary shrugged. 'I don't know.'

'I promised our President –' He stopped, as the full implication of the news hit him. He looked at Mary and said in a hoarse voice, 'President Ionescu is not going to like this. Is there *nothing* you can do?'

Mary said earnestly, 'I'm as disappointed as you, Minister. The vote was going well until one of the Senators learned that a Romanian church group that wanted to visit Utah was refused a visa. The Senator is a Mormon, and he was very upset.'

'A *church group*?' Negulesco's voice had risen an octave. 'You mean the loan was voted down because of a –?'

'That's my understanding.'

'But Madam Ambassador, Romania is *for* the churches. They have a great freedom here!' He was almost babbling now. 'We *love* the churches.'

Negulesco moved over to the chair next to Mary. 'Madam Ambassador – if I could arrange for this group to visit your country, do you think the Senate Finance Committee would approve the loan?'

Mary looked him in the eye and said, 'Minister Negulesco – I can guarantee it. But I would have to know by this afternoon.'

*

Mary sat at her desk, waiting for the phone call, and at 2.30 Negulesco called.

'Madam Ambassador – I have wonderful news! The church group is free to leave at any time! Now do you have any good news for me?'

Mary waited an hour and then called him back. 'I've just received a telex from our State Department. Your loan has been granted.'

23

Mary had been unable to get Dr Louis Desforges out of her mind. He had saved her life, and then disappeared. She was glad she had found him again. On an impulse, Mary went to the American Dollar Shop and bought a beautiful silver bowl for the doctor and had it sent to the French Embassy. It was a small enough gesture after what he had done.

That afternoon, Dorothy Stone said, 'There's a Dr Desforges on the phone. Do you wish to speak to him?'

Mary smiled. 'Yes.' She picked up the telephone. 'Good afternoon.'

'Good afternoon, Madam Ambassador.' The phrase sounded delightful in his French accent. 'I called to thank you for your thoughtful gift. I assure you that it was unnecessary. I was delighted that I was able to be of some service.'

'It was more than just some service,' Mary told him. 'I wish there were some way I could really show my appreciation.'

There was a pause. 'Would you –' He stopped.

'Yes?' Mary prompted.

'Nothing, really.' He sounded suddenly shy.

'Please.'

'Very well.' There was a nervous laugh. 'I was wondering if you might care to have dinner with me one evening, but I know how busy you must be and –'

'I would love to,' Mary said quickly.

'Really?'

She could hear the pleasure in his voice. 'Really.'

'Do you know the Taru Restaurant?'

Mary had been there twice. 'No.'

'Ah, splendid. Then I shall have the pleasure of showing it to you. You probably won't be free Saturday night –?'

'I have to go to a cocktail party at six o'clock, but we could have dinner after that.'

'Wonderful. I understand you have two small children. Would you care to bring them?'

'Thank you, but they're busy on Saturday night.'

She wondered why she had lied.

The cocktail party was at the Swiss Embassy. It was obviously one of the 'A' parties, because President Alexandros Ionescu was there.

When he saw Mary, he walked over to her. 'Good evening, Madam

'Ambassador.' He took her hand and held it longer than necessary. 'I want to tell you how pleased I am that your country has agreed to make us the loan we asked for.'

'And we're very pleased that you allowed the church group to visit the United States, your Excellency.'

He waved a hand carelessly. 'Romanians are not prisoners. Anyone is free to come and go as he pleases. My country is a symbol of social justice and democratic freedom.'

Mary thought of the long queues of people waiting to buy scarce food, and the mob at the airport, and the refugees desperate to leave.

'All power in Romania belongs to the people.'

There are gulags in Romania that we're not allowed to see.

Mary said, 'With all respect, Mr President, there are hundreds, perhaps thousands of Jews who are trying to leave Romania. Your government will not give them visas.'

He scowled. 'Dissidents. Trouble-makers. We are doing the world a favour by keeping them here where we can watch them.'

'Mr President –'

'We have a more lenient policy towards the Jews than any other Iron Curtain country. In 1967, during the Arab–Israeli war, the Soviet Union and every Eastern bloc country except Romania broke off diplomatic relations with Israel.'

'I'm aware of that, Mr President, but there are still –'

'Have you tasted the caviar? It is fresh Beluga.'

*

Dr Louis Desforges had offered to pick Mary up, but she had arranged for Florian to drive her to the Taru Restaurant. She telephoned ahead to inform Dr Desforges that she would be a few minutes late. She had to return to the Embassy to file a report on her conversation with President Ionescu.

Gunny was on duty. The Marine saluted her and unlocked the door. Mary walked into her office and turned on the light. She stood in the doorway, frozen. On the wall, someone had sprayed in red paint, GO HOME BEFORE YOU DIE. She backed out of the room, white-faced, and ran down the hall to the reception desk.

Gunny stood at attention. 'Yes, Madam Ambassador?'

'Gunny – wh – who's been in my office?' Mary demanded.

'Why, no one that I know of, ma'am.'

'Let me see your roster sheet.' She tried to keep her voice from quavering.

'Yes, ma'am.'

Gunny pulled out the Visitors' Access Sheet and handed it to her. Each name had the time of entry listed after it. She started at 5.30, the time she had left the office, and scanned the list. There were a dozen names.

196

Mary looked up at the Marine guard. 'The people on this list – were they all escorted to the offices they visited?'

'Always, Madam Ambassador. No one goes up to the second floor without an escort. Is something wrong?'

Something was very wrong.

Mary said, 'Please send someone to my office to paint out that obscenity on the wall.'

She turned and hurried outside, afraid she was going to be sick. The telex could wait until morning.

Dr Louis Desforges was waiting for Mary when she arrived at the restaurant. He stood up as she approached the table.

'I'm sorry I'm late.' Mary tried to sound normal.

He pulled out her chair. 'That's perfectly all right. I received your message. You were very kind to join me.'

She wished now that she had not agreed to have dinner with him. She was too nervous and upset. She pressed her hands together to keep them from trembling.

He was observing her. 'Are you all right, Madam Ambassador?'

'Yes,' she said. 'I'm fine.' *Go Home Before You Die*. 'I think I'd like a straight Scotch, please.' She hated Scotch, but she hoped it would relax her.

The doctor ordered drinks, then said, 'It can't be easy being an ambassador – especially a woman in this country. Romanians are male chauvinists, you know.'

Mary forced a smile. 'Tell me about yourself.' Anything to take her mind off the threat.

'I am afraid there is not much to tell that is exciting.'

'You mentioned that you fought undercover in Algeria. That sounds exciting.'

He shrugged. 'We live in terrible times. I believe that every man must risk something so that in the end he does not have to risk everything. The terrorist situation is literally that – *terrifying*. We must put an end to it.' His voice was filled with passion.

He's like Edward, Mary thought. *Edward was always passionate about his beliefs*. Dr Desforges was a man who could not be easily swayed. He was willing to risk his life for what he believed in.

He was saying, '. . .If I had known that the price of my fighting would be the lives of my wife and children –' He stopped. His knuckles were white against the table. 'Forgive me. I did not bring you here to talk about my troubles. Let me recommend the lamb. They do it very well here.'

'Fine,' Mary said.

He ordered dinner and a bottle of wine, and they talked. Mary began to relax, to forget the frightening warning painted in red. She was finding it surprisingly easy to talk to this attractive Frenchman. In an odd way, it was like talking to Edward. It was amazing how she and Louis shared so many of the same beliefs and felt the same way about so many things. Louis Desforges was born in a small town in France, and Mary was born in a small town in Kansas, five thousand miles apart, and yet their backgrounds were so similar. His father had been a farmer and had scrimped and saved to send Louis to a medical school in Paris.

'My father was a wonderful man, Madam Ambassador.'

'Madam Ambassador sounds so formal.'

'Mrs Ashley?'

'Mary.'

'Thank you, Mary.'

She smiled. 'You're welcome, Louis.'

Mary wondered what his personal life was like. He was handsome and intelligent. He could surely have all the women he wanted. She wondered if he were living with anyone.

'Have you thought of getting married again?'

He shook his head. 'No. If you had known my wife, you would understand. She was a remarkable woman. No one could ever replace her.'

That's how I feel about Edward, Mary thought. *No one can ever replace him.* He was so special. And yet everyone needed companionship. It was not really a question of replacing a loved one. It was finding someone new to share things with.

Louis was saying, '. . . so when I was offered the opportunity, I thought it would be interesting to visit Romania.' He lowered his voice. 'I confess I feel an evilness about this country.'

'Really?'

'Not the people. They are lovely. The government is everything I despise. There is no freedom here for anyone. The Romanians are virtual slaves. If they want to have decent food and a few luxuries, they are forced to work for the *Securitate*. Foreigners are constantly spied upon.' He glanced around to make sure no one could overhear. 'I shall be glad when my tour of duty is over and I can return to France.'

Without thinking, Mary heard herself saying, 'There are some people who think *I* should go home.'

'I beg your pardon?'

And suddenly Mary found herself pouring out the story of what had happened in her office. She told him about the paint scrawled on her office wall.

'But that is horrible!' Louis exclaimed. 'You have no idea who did this?'

'No.'

Louis said, 'May I make an impertinent confession? Since I found out who you were, I have been asking questions. Everyone who knows you is very impressed with you.'

She was listening to him with intense interest.

'It seems that you have brought here an image of America that is beautiful and intelligent and warm. If you believe in what you are doing, then you must fight for it. You must stay. Do not let anyone frighten you away.'

It was exactly what Edward would have said.

Mary lay in bed, unable to sleep, thinking about what Louis had told her. *He was willing to die for what he believed in. Am I? I don't want to die*, Mary thought. *But no one is going to kill me. And no one is going to scare me.*

She lay awake in the dark. Scared.

The following morning, Mike Slade brought in two cups of coffee. He nodded at the wall where it had been cleaned.

'I hear someone has been spraying graffiti on your walls.'

'Have they found out who did it?'

Mike took a sip of coffee. 'No. I went through the Visitors' List myself. Everyone is accounted for.'

'That means it must have been someone here in the Embassy.'

'Either that, or someone managed to sneak in past the guards.'

'Do you believe that?'

Mike put down his coffee cup. 'Nope.'

'Neither do I.'

'What exactly did it say?'

'Go home before you die.'

He made no comment.

'Who would want to kill me?'

'I don't know.'

'Mr Slade, I would appreciate a straight answer. Do you think I'm in any real danger?'

He studied her thoughtfully. 'Madam Ambassador, they assassinated Abraham Lincoln, John Kennedy, Robert Kennedy, Martin Luther King, and Marin Groza. We're all vulnerable. The answer to your question is "yes".'

If you believe in what you are doing, then you must fight for it. You must stay. Do not let anyone frighten you away.

24

At eight forty-five the following morning, as Mary was in the middle of a conference, Dorothy Stone came rushing into the office and said, 'The children have been kidnapped!'

Mary jumped to her feet. 'Oh, my God!'

'The limousine alarm just went off. They're tracking the car now. They won't get away.'

Mary raced down the corridor to the Communications Room. There were half a dozen men standing around a switchboard. Colonel McKinney was talking into a microphone.

'Roger,' he said. 'I have that. I'll inform the Ambassador.'

'What's happening?' Mary croaked. She could barely get the words out. 'Where are my children?'

The Colonel said, reassuringly, 'They're fine, ma'am. One of them touched the emergency switch in the limousine by accident. The emergency light on top of the limousine flashed on, along with an SOS shortwave signal, and before the driver had gone two blocks, four police cars closed in on them with sirens screaming.'

Mary sagged against the wall with relief. She had not realized how much tension she had been under. *It's easy to understand*, she thought, *why foreigners living here finally turn to drugs or drink . . . or love affairs.*

Mary stayed with the children that evening. She wanted to be as close to them as possible. Looking at them, she wondered: *Are they in danger? Are we all in danger? Who would want to harm us?* She had no answer.

Three nights later Mary had dinner again with Dr Louis Desforges. He seemed more relaxed with her this time, and although the core of sadness she sensed within him was still there, he took pains to be attentive and amusing. Mary wondered if he felt the same attraction towards her that she felt towards him. *It wasn't just a silver bowl I sent him*, she admitted to herself, *it was an invitation.*

Madam Ambassador is so formal. Call me Mary. My God, was she actually pursuing him? And yet: *I owe him a lot – possibly my life. I'm rationalizing*, Mary thought. *That has nothing to do with why I wanted to see him again.*

They had an early dinner at the dining room on the roof of the

Intercontinental Hotel, and when Louis took Mary back to the Residence, she asked, 'Would you like to come in?'

'Thank you,' he said. 'I would.'

The children were downstairs doing their homework. Mary introduced them to Louis.

He bent down before Beth and said, 'May I?' And he put his arms around her and hugged her. He straightened up. 'One of my little girls was three years younger than you. The other one was about your age. I'd like to think they would have grown up to be as pretty as you are, Beth.'

Beth smiled. 'Thank you. Where are –?'

Mary asked hastily, 'Would you all like some hot chocolate?'

They sat in the huge embassy kitchen drinking the hot chocolate and talking.

The children were enchanted with Louis, and Mary thought she had never seen a man with so much hunger in his eyes. He had forgotten about her. He was focused entirely on the children, telling them stories about his daughters and anecdotes and jokes until he had them roaring with laughter.

It was almost midnight when Mary looked at her watch. 'Oh, no! You children should have been in bed hours ago. Scoot.'

Tim went over to Louis. 'Will you come and see us again?'

'I hope so, Tim. It's up to your mother.'

Tim turned to Mary. 'Well, Mom?'

She looked at Louis and said, 'Yes.'

Mary saw Louis to the door. He took her hand in his. 'I won't try to tell you what this evening has meant to me, Mary. There are no words.'

'I'm glad.' She was looking into his eyes, and she felt him moving towards her. She raised her lips.

'Good night, Mary.'

And he was gone.

The following morning when Mary walked into her office, she noticed that another side of the wall had been freshly painted. Mike Slade walked in with two cups of coffee.

'Morning.' He set a cup on her desk.

'Someone wrote on the wall again?'

'Yes.'

'What did it say this time?'

'It doesn't matter.'

'It doesn't matter!' she said furiously. 'It matters to *me*. What kind of security does this Embassy have? I won't have people sneaking into my office and making threats against my life. What did it say?'

'You want it verbatim?'

'Yes.'

'It said, "Leave now or die." '

Mary sank back into her chair, enraged. 'Will you explain to me how someone is able to walk into this Embassy, unseen, and write messages on my wall?'

'I wish I could,' Mike said. 'We're doing everything we can to track it down.'

'Well, "everything you can" is obviously not enough,' she retorted. 'I want a Marine guard posted outside my door at night. Is that understood?'

'Yes, Madam Ambassador. I'll pass the word to Colonel McKinney.'

'Never mind. I'll talk to him myself.'

Mary watched as Mike Slade left her office, and she suddenly wondered if he knew who was behind it.

And she wondered if it could be Mike Slade.

Colonel McKinney was apologetic. 'Believe me, Madam Ambassador, I'm just as upset about this as you are. I'll double the guard in the corridor and see that there's a twenty-four hour watch outside your office door.'

Mary was not mollified. Someone inside the Embassy was responsible for what was happening.

Colonel McKinney was inside the Embassy.

Mary invited Louis Desforges to a small dinner party at the Residence. There were a dozen other guests, and at the end of the evening when the others had departed, Louis said, 'Do you mind if I go up and see the children?'

'I'm afraid they're sleeping by now, Louis.'

'I won't awaken them,' he promised. 'I would just like to look at them.'

Mary walked upstairs with him and watched as he stood in the doorway, silently staring at Tim's sleeping figure.

After a while, Mary whispered, 'Beth's room is this way.'

Mary led him to another bedroom down the hall, and opened the door. Beth was curled up around the pillow, the bed covers twisted around her. Louis walked quietly to the bed and gently straightened out the bedclothes. He stood there for a long moment, his eyes tightly closed. Then he turned and walked out of the room.

'They're beautiful children,' Louis said. His voice was husky.

They stood there, facing each other, and the air between them was charged. He was naked in his need.

It's going to happen, Mary thought. *Neither of us can stop it.*

And their arms were tightly around each other, and his lips were pressed hard against hers.

He pulled away. 'I shouldn't have come. You realize what I'm doing, don't you? I'm re-living my past.' He was quiet for a moment. 'Or perhaps it is my future. Who knows?'

Mary said softly, '*I* know.'

David Victor, the Commerce Consular, hurried into Mary's office. 'I'm afraid I have some very bad news. I just got a tip that President Ionescu is going to approve a contract with Argentina for a million and a half tons of corn and with Brazil for half a million tons of soy beans. We were counting heavily on those deals.'

'How far have the negotiations gone?'

'They're almost concluded. We've been shut out. I was about to send a telex to Washington – with your approval, of course,' he added hastily.

'Hold off a bit,' Mary said. 'I want to think about it.'

'You won't get President Ionescu to change his mind. Believe me, I've tried every argument I could think of.'

'Then we have nothing to lose if I give it a try.' She buzzed her secretary. 'Dorothy, set up an appointment with President Ionescu as quickly as possible.'

Alexandros Ionescu invited Mary to the palace for lunch. As she entered, she was greeted by Nicu, the President's fourteen-year-old son.

'Good afternoon, Madam Ambassador,' he said. 'I am Nicu. Welcome to the palace.'

'Thank you.'

He was a handsome boy, tall for his age, with beautiful black eyes and a flawless complexion. He had the bearing of an adult.

'I have heard very nice things about you,' Nicu said.

'I'm pleased to hear that, Nicu.'

'I will tell my father you have arrived.'

Mary and Ionescu sat across from each other in the formal dining room, just the two of them. Mary wondered where his wife was. She seldom appeared, even at formal functions.

The President had been drinking and was in a mellow mood. He lit a Snagov, the vile-smelling Romanian-made cigarette.

'I understand you have been doing some sightseeing with your children.'

'Yes, your Excellency. Romania is such a beautiful country, and there is so much to see.'

He gave her what he thought was a seductive smile. 'One of these days you must let me show you my country.' His smile became a parody of a leer. 'I am an excellent guide. I could show you many interesting things.'

'I'm sure you could,' Mary said. 'Mr President, I was eager to meet with you today because there is something important I would like to discuss with you.'

Ionescu almost laughed aloud. He knew exactly why she had come. *The Americans wish to sell me corn and soy beans, but they are too late.* The American Ambassador would go away empty-handed this time. Too bad. Such an attractive woman.

'Yes?' he said innocently.

'I want to talk to you about sister cities.'

Ionescu blinked. 'I beg your pardon?'

'Sister cities. You know – like San Francisco and Osaka, Los Angeles and Athens, Washington and Beijing . . .'

'I – I don't understand. What does that have to do with –?'

'Mr President, it occurred to me that you could get headlines all over the world if you made Bucharest a sister city of some American city. Think of the excitement it would create. It would get almost as much attention as President Ellison's people-to-people plan. It would be an important step towards world peace. Talk about a bridge between our countries! I wouldn't be surprised if it got you a Nobel Peace Prize.'

Ionescu sat there, trying to reorient his thinking. He said cautiously, 'A sister city in the United States? It is an interesting idea. What would it involve?'

'Mostly wonderful publicity for you. You would be a hero. It would be your idea. You would pay the city a visit. A delegation from Kansas City would pay *you* a visit.'

'Kansas City?'

'That's just a suggestion, of course. I don't think you'd want a big city like New York or Chicago – too commercial. And Los Angeles is already spoken for. Kansas City is middle-America. There are farmers there, like your farmers. People with down-to-earth values, like your people. It would be the act of a great statesman, Mr President. Your name would be on everyone's lips. No one in Europe has thought of doing this.'

He sat there, silent. 'I – I would naturally have to give this a great deal of thought.'

'Naturally.'

'Kansas City, Kansas, and Bucharest, Romania.' He nodded. 'We are a much larger city, of course.'

'Of course. Bucharest would be the big sister.'

'I must admit it is a very intriguing idea.'

In fact, the more Ionescu thought about it, the more he liked it. *My name will be on everyone's lips. And it will serve to keep the Soviet bear hug from becoming too tight.*

'Is there any chance of a rejection from the American side?' Ionescu asked.

'Absolutely none. I can guarantee it.'

He sat there, reflecting. 'When would this go into effect?'

'Just as soon as you're ready to announce it. I'll handle our end. You're already a great statesman, Mr President, but this would make you even greater.'

Ionescu thought of something else. 'We could set up a trade exchange with our sister city. Romania has many things to sell. Tell me – what crops does Kansas grow?'

'Among other things,' Mary said innocently, 'corn and soy beans.'

'You really made the deal? You actually fooled him?' David Victor asked incredulously.

'Not for a minute,' Mary assured him. 'Ionescu is too smart for that. He knew what I was after. He just liked the package I wrapped it in. You can go in and close the deal. Ionescu's already rehearsing his television speech.'

When Stanton Rogers heard the news, he telephoned Mary. 'You're a miracle worker,' he laughed. 'We thought we'd lost that deal. How in the world did you do it?'

'Ego,' Mary said. 'His.'

'The President asked me to tell you what a really great job you're doing over there, Mary.'

'Thank him for me, Stan.'

'I will. By the way, the President and I are leaving for China in a few weeks. If you need me, you can get in touch with me through my office.'

'Have a wonderful trip.'

Over the swiftly moving weeks, the dancing March winds had given way to spring and then summer, and winter clothes were replaced by light, cool outfits. Trees and flowers blossomed everywhere, and the parks were greening. June was almost over.

*

In Buenos Aires, it was winter. When Neusa Muñez returned to her apartment, it was the middle of the night. The telephone was ringing. She picked it up. '*Si?*'

'Miss Muñez?' It was the gringo from the United States.

'Yeah.'

'May I speak with Angel?'

'Angel no here, *señor*. Wha' you wan'?'

205

The Controller found his irritation mounting. *What kind of man would be involved with a woman like this?* From the description Harry Lantz had given him before Lantz was murdered, she was not only dim-witted, she was very unattractive. 'I want you to give Angel a message for me.'

'Jus' a minute.'

He heard the phone drop, and waited.

Her voice finally came back on. 'Okay.'

'Tell Angel I need him for a contract in Bucharest.'

'Budapes'?'

Jesus! She was beyond anyone's endurance. 'Bucharest, Romania. Tell him it's a five million dollar contract. He has to be in Bucharest by the end of this month. That's three weeks from now. Do you have that?'

'Wait a minute. I'm writin'.'

He waited patiently.

'Okay. How many people Angel gotta kill for five million dollars?'

'A lot . . .'

The queues each day in front of the Embassy continued to disturb Mary. She discussed it again with Mike Slade.

'There must be something we can do to help those people get out of the country.'

'Everything's been tried,' Mike assured her. 'We've applied pressure, we've offered to sweeten the money pot – the answer is "no". Ionescu refuses to cut a deal. The poor bastards are stuck. He has no intention of letting them go. The Iron Curtain isn't just *around* the country – it's *in* the country.'

'I'm going to have a talk with Ionescu again.'

'Good luck.'

Mary asked Dorothy Stone to set up an appointment with the dictator.

A few minutes later, the secretary walked into Mary's office. 'I'm sorry, Madam Ambassador. No appointments.'

Mary looked at her, puzzled. 'What does that mean?'

'I'm not sure. Something weird is going on at the palace. Ionescu isn't seeing anybody. In fact, no one can even get into the palace.'

Mary sat there, trying to figure out what it could be. Was Ionescu preparing to make a major announcement of some kind? Was a coup imminent? Something important must be happening. Whatever it was, Mary knew she had to find out.

'Dorothy,' she said, 'you have contacts over at the Presidential Palace, don't you?'

Dorothy smiled. 'You mean the "old girl network"? Sure. We talk to one another.'

'I'd like you to find out what's going on there , . .'

An hour later, Dorothy reported back. 'I found out what you wanted to know,' she said. 'They're keeping it very hush-hush.'

'Keeping what hush-hush?'

'Ionescu's son is dying.'

Mary was aghast. 'Nicu? What happened?'

'He has botulism poisoning.'

Mary asked quickly, 'You mean there's an epidemic here in Bucharest?'

'No, ma'am. Do you remember the epidemic they had in East Germany recently? Apparently Nicu visited there and someone gave him some canned food as a gift. He ate some of it yesterday.'

'But there's an anti-serum for that!' Mary exclaimed.

'The European countries are out of it. The epidemic last month used it all up.'

'Oh, my God.'

When Dorothy left the office, Mary sat there thinking. It might be too late, but still . . . She remembered how cheerful and happy young Nicu was. He was fourteen years old – only a year older than Beth.

She pressed the intercom button and said, 'Dorothy, get me the Centre for Disease Control in Atlanta, Georgia.'

Five minutes later she was speaking to the director.

'Yes, Madam Ambassador, we have an anti-serum for botulism poisoning, but we haven't had any cases reported in the United States.'

'I'm not in the United States,' Mary told him. 'I'm in Bucharest. I need that serum immediately.'

There was a pause. 'I'll be happy to supply some,' the Director said, 'but botulism poisoning works very rapidly. I'm afraid that by the time it gets there . . .'

'I'll arrange for it to get here,' Mary said. 'Just have it ready. Thank you.'

Ten minutes later, she was speaking to Air Force General Ralph Zukor in Washington.

'Good morning, Madam Ambassador. Well, this is an unexpected pleasure. My wife and I are big fans of yours. How are – ?'

'General, I need a favour.'

'Certainly. Anything you want.'

'I need your fastest jet.'

'I beg your pardon?'

'I need a jet to fly some serum to Bucharest right away.'

'I see.'

'Can you do it?'

'Well, yes. I'll tell you what you have to do. You'll have to get the approval of the Secretary of Defence. There are some requisition forms for you to fill out. One copy should go to me and another copy to the Department of Defence. We'll send those on to –'

Mary listened, seething. 'General – let me tell you what *you* have to do. You have to stop talking and get that damned jet up in the air. If –'

'There's no way that –'

'A boy's life is at stake. And the boy happens to be the son of the President of Romania.'

'I'm sorry, but I can't authorize –'

'General, if that boy dies because some form hasn't been filled out, I promise you that I'm going to call the biggest press conference you've ever seen. I'll let you explain why you let Ionescu's son die.'

'I can't possibly authorize an operation like this without an approval from the White House. If –'

Mary snapped. 'Then get it. The serum will be waiting at Atlanta Airport. And, General – every single minute counts.'

She hung up, and sat there, silently praying.

General Ralph Zukor's aide said, 'What was that all about, sir?'

General Zukor said, 'The Ambassador expects me to send up an SR-71 to fly some serum to Romania.'

The aide smiled. 'I'm sure she has no idea of what's involved, General.'

'Obviously. But we might as well cover ourselves. Get me Stanton Rogers.'

Five minutes later the General was speaking to the President's Foreign Adviser. 'I just wanted to go on record with you that the request was made, and I naturally refused. If –'

Stanton Rogers said, 'General, how soon can you have an SR-71 airborne?'

'In ten minutes, but –'

'Do it.'

Nicu Ionescu's nervous system had been affected. He lay in bed, disoriented, sweating and pale, attached to a respirator. There were three doctors at his bedside.

President Ionescu strode into his son's bedroom. 'What's happening?'

'Your Excellency, we have communicated with our colleagues all over Eastern and Western Europe. There is no anti-serum left.'

'What about the United States?'

The doctor shrugged. 'By the time we could arrange for someone to fly the serum here –' He paused delicately. '. . . I'm afraid it would be too late.'

Ionescu walked over to the bed and picked up his son's hand. It was moist and clammy. 'You're not going to die,' Ionescu wept. 'You're not going to die.'

When the jet touched down at Atlanta International Airport, an Air Force limousine was waiting with the anti-botulism serum, packed in ice. Three minutes later, the jet was back in the air, on a northeast heading.

The SR-71 – the Air Force's fastest supersonic jet, flies at three times the speed of sound. It slowed down once to refuel over the mid-Atlantic. The plane made the four thousand miles flight to Bucharest in a little over two hours.

Colonel McKinney was waiting at the airport. An Army escort cleared the way to the Presidential Palace.

Mary had remained in her office all night, getting up-to-the-minute reports. The last report came in at 6 a.m.

Colonel McKinney telephoned. 'They gave the boy the serum. The doctors say he's going to live.'

'Oh, thank God!'

Two days later, a diamond and emerald necklace was delivered to Mary's office with a note:

'I can never thank you enough.
Alexandros Ionescu.'

'My God!' Dorothy exclaimed when she saw the necklace. 'It must have cost half a million dollars!'

'At least,' Mary said. 'Return it.'

The following morning, President Ionescu sent for Mary.

An aide said, 'The President is waiting for you in his office.'

'May I see Nicu first?'

'Yes, of course.' He led her upstairs.

Nicu was lying in bed, reading. He looked up as Mary entered. 'Good morning, Madam Ambassador.'

'Good morning, Nicu.'

'My father told me what you did. I wish to thank you.'

Mary said, 'I couldn't let you die. I'm saving you for Beth one day.'

Nicu laughed. 'Bring her over and we'll talk about it.'

President Ionescu was waiting for Mary downstairs. He said without preamble, 'You returned my gift.'

'Yes, Your Excellency.'

He indicated a chair. 'Sit down.' He studied her a moment. 'What do you want?'

Mary said, 'I don't make trades for children's lives.'

'You saved my son's life. I must give you something.'

'You don't owe me anything, Your Excellency.'

Ionescu pounded his fist on the desk. 'I will not be indebted to you! Name your price.'

Mary said, 'Your Excellency, there is no price. I have two children of my own. I know how you must feel.'

He closed his eyes for a moment. 'Do you? Nicu is my only son. If anything had happened to him –' He stopped, unable to go on.

'I went upstairs to see him. He looks fine.' She rose. 'If there's nothing else, Your Excellency, I have an appointment back at the Embassy.' She started to leave.

'Wait!'

Mary turned.

'You will not accept a gift?'

'No. I've explained –'

Ionescu held up a hand. 'All right, all right.' He thought for a moment. 'If you were to make a wish, what would you wish for?'

'There is nothing –'

'You must! I insist! One wish. Anything you want.'

Mary stood there, studying his face, thinking. Finally she said, 'I wish that the restriction on the Jews waiting to leave Romania could be lifted.'

Ionescu sat there listening to her words. His fingers drummed on the desk. 'I see.' He was still for a long time. Finally he looked up at Mary. 'It shall be done. They will not all be allowed out, of course, but – I will make it easier.'

When the announcement was made public two days later, Mary received a telephone call from President Ellison himself.

'By God,' he said, 'I thought I was sending over a diplomat, and I got a miracle worker.'

'I was just lucky, Mr President.'

'It's the kind of luck I wish all my diplomats had. I want to congratulate you, Mary, on everything you've been doing over there.'

'Thank you, Mr President.'

210

She hung up, feeling a warm glow.

*

'July is just around the corner,' Harriet Kruger told Mary. 'In the past, the Ambassador always gave a Fourth of July party for the Americans living in Bucharest. If you'd prefer not to –'

'No. I think it's a lovely idea.'

'Fine. I'll take care of all the arrangements. A lot of flags, balloons, an orchestra – the works.'

'Sounds wonderful. Thank you, Harriet.'

It would eat into the Residence expense account, but it would be worth it. *The truth is*, Mary thought, *I miss home.*

Florence and Douglas Schiffer surprised Mary with a visit.

'We're in Rome,' Florence screamed over the telephone. 'Can we come and see you?'

Mary was thrilled. 'How soon can you get here?'

'How does tomorrow grab you?'

When the Schiffers arrived at Otopeni Airport the following day, Mary was there to meet them with the Embassy limousine. There was an excited exchange of hugs and kisses.

'You look fantastic!' Florence said. 'Being an ambassador hasn't changed you a bit.'

You'd be surprised, Mary thought.

On the ride back to the Residence, Mary pointed out the sights, the same sights she had seen for the first time only four months earlier. Had it been only four months? It seemed an eternity.

'This is where you live?' Florence asked, as they drove into the gates of the Residence, guarded by a Marine. 'I'm impressed.'

Mary gave the Schiffers a tour of the Residence.

'My God!' Florence exclaimed. 'A swimming pool, a theatre, a thousand rooms, and your own park.'

They were seated in the large dining room, having lunch and gossiping about their neighbours in Junction City.

'Do you miss the place at all?' Douglas wanted to know.

'Yes.' And even as she said it, Mary realized how far she had come from home. Junction City had meant peace and security, an easy, friendly way of life. Here, there was fear and terror and obscene threats scrawled on her office walls in red paint. *Red, the colour of violence.*

'What are you thinking?' Florence asked.

211

'What? Oh, nothing. I was just daydreaming. What are you two lovely people doing in Europe?'

'I had to attend a medical convention in Rome,' Douglas said.

'Go on – tell her the rest,' Florence prompted.

'Well, the truth is, I wasn't sure I wanted to go, but we were concerned about you and wanted to find out how you were doing. So here we are.'

'I'm so glad.'

'I never thought I'd know such a big star,' Florence sighed.

Mary laughed. 'Florence, being an ambassador doesn't make me a star.'

'Oh, that's not what I'm talking about.'

'What *are* you talking about?'

'Don't you really know?'

'Know what?'

'Mary, there was a big article about you in *Time* last week, with a picture of you and the children. You're being written about in all the magazines and newspapers at home. When Stanton Rogers gives news conferences about foreign affairs, he uses you as a shining example. The President talks about you. Believe me, your name is on everyone's lips.'

'I guess I've been out of touch,' Mary said. She remembered what Stanton had said: *The President ordered the build-up.*

'How long can you stay?' Mary asked.

'I'd love to stay forever, but we planned three days here and then we're on our way back home.'

Douglas asked, 'How *are* you getting along, Mary? I mean about – you know – Edward?'

'I'm getting better,' Mary said slowly. 'I talk to him every night. Does that sound crazy?'

'Not really.'

'It's still hell. But I try. I try.'

'Have you – er – met anyone?' Florence asked delicately.

Mary smiled. 'As a matter of fact, maybe I have. You'll meet him at dinner tonight.'

The Schiffers took to Dr Louis Desforges immediately. They had heard that the French were aloof and snobbish, but Louis proved to be friendly and warm and outgoing. He and Douglas got into long discussions about medicine. It was one of her happiest evenings since she had come to Bucharest. For a brief time, she felt safe and relaxed.

*

At eleven o'clock, the Schiffers retired upstairs to the guest room that had been prepared for them. Mary was downstairs saying good night to Louis.

He said, 'I like your friends very much. I hope I shall see them again.'

'They liked you, too. They're leaving for Kansas in a couple of days,' Mary said.

He studied her. 'Mary – you're not thinking of leaving?'

'No,' Mary said. 'I'm staying.'

He smiled. 'Good.' He hesitated, then said quietly, 'I am going away to the mountains for the weekend. I would like it very much if you came with me.'

'Yes.'

It was as simple as that.

She lay in the dark talking to Edward that night. *Darling, I'll always, always love you, but I mustn't need you any more. It's time I started a new life. You'll always be a part of that life, but there has to be someone else, too. Louis isn't you, but he's Louis. He's strong, and he's good, and he's brave. That's as close as I can come to having you. Please understand, Edward. Please . . .*

She sat up in bed and turned on the bedside light. She stared at her wedding ring for a long time, then she slowly slipped it off her finger.

It was a circle that symbolized an ending, and a beginning.

Mary took the Schiffers on a whirlwind tour of Bucharest, and saw to it that their days were filled. The three days passed too quickly, and when the Schiffers left, Mary felt a sharp pang of loneliness, a sense of being totally isolated from her roots, adrift once again in an alien and dangerous land.

Mary was having her usual morning coffee with Mike Slade, discussing the day's agenda.

When they finished, Mike said, 'I've been hearing rumours.'

Mary had heard them, too. 'About Ionescu and his new mistress? He seems to –'

'About you.'

She felt herself stiffen. 'Really? What kind of rumours?'

'It seems that you're seeing a lot of Dr Louis Desforges.'

Mary felt a flare of anger. 'Whom I see is no one's business.'

'I beg to differ with you, Madam Ambassador. It's the business of everyone in the Embassy. We have a strict rule against getting involved with foreigners, and the doctor is a foreigner. He also happens to be an enemy agent.'

Mary was almost too stunned to speak. 'That's absurd!' she sputtered. 'What do *you* know about Dr Desforges?'

'Think about how you met him,' Mike Slade suggested. 'The damsel in distress and the knight in shining armour. That's the oldest trick in the world. I've used it myself.'

'I don't give a damn what you've done and what you haven't done,' Mary retorted. 'He's worth a dozen of you. He fought against terrorists in Algeria, and they murdered his wife and children.'

Mike said mildly, 'That's interesting. I've been examining his dossier. Your doctor never had a wife or children.'

25

They stopped for lunch at Timisoara, on their way up to the Carpathian Mountains. The inn was called Hunter's Friday, and was decorated in the period atmosphere of a medieval wine cellar.

'The speciality of the house is game,' Louis told Mary. 'I would suggest the venison.'

'Fine.' She had never eaten venison. It was delicious.

Louis ordered a bottle of Zghihara, the local white wine. There was an air of confidence about Louis, a quiet strength that gave Mary a feeling of security.

He had picked her up in town, away from the Embassy. 'It's better not to let anyone know where you are going,' he said, 'or it will be on the tongues of every diplomat in town.'

Too late, Mary thought wryly.

Louis had borrowed the car from a friend at the French Embassy. It had black and white oval CD licence plates.

Mary knew that licence plates were a tool for the police. Foreigners were given licence plates that started with the number twelve. Yellow plates were for officials.

After lunch, they started out again. They passed farmers driving primitive home-made wagons cut from limbs of trees that were twisted together, and caravans of gypsies.

Louis was a skilful driver. Mary studied him as he drove, thinking of Mike Slade's words: *I've been examining his dossier. Your doctor never had a wife or children. He's an enemy agent.*

She did not believe Mike Slade. Every instinct told her he was lying. It was not Louis who had sneaked into her office and scribbled those words on the walls. It was someone else who was threatening her. She trusted Louis. *No one could have faked the emotion I saw on his face when he was playing with the children. No one is that good an actor.*

The air was getting noticeably thinner and cooler, and the vegetation and oak trees had given way to ash trees and spruce and fir.

'There's wonderful hunting here,' Louis said. 'You can find wild boar, roebuck, wolves, and black chamois.'

'I've never hunted.'

'Perhaps one day I can take you.'

The mountains ahead looked like pictures she had seen of the Swiss Alps, their peaks covered by mists and clouds. Along the roadside they passed forests and green meadows dappled with grazing cows. The icy clouds overhead were the colour of steel, and Mary felt that if she reached up and touched them, they would stick to her fingers, like cold metal.

*

It was late afternoon when they reached their destination, Cioplea, a lovely mountain resort that was built like a miniature chalet. Mary waited in the car while Louis registered for both of them.

An elderly porter showed them to their suite. It had a good-sized, comfortable living room, simply furnished, a bedroom, bathroom, and a terrace with a breathtaking view of the mountains.

'For the first time in my life,' Louis sighed, 'I wish I were a painter.'

'It *is* a beautiful view.'

He moved closer to her. 'No. I mean I wish I could paint you.'

She found herself thinking: *I feel like a seventeen-year-old on a first date. I'm nervous.*

He took her in his arms and held her tightly. She buried her head against his chest, and then Louis' lips were on hers, and he was exploring her body, and he moved her hand down to his male hardness, and she forgot everything except what was happening to her.

There was a frantic need in her that went far beyond sex. It was a need for someone to hold her, to reassure her, to protect her, to let her know that she was no longer alone. She needed Louis to be inside her, to be inside him, to be one with him.

They were in the large, double bed, and she felt his tongue feather down her naked body, into the soft depths of her, and then he was inside her, and she screamed aloud with a feral, passionate cry before she exploded into a thousand glorious Marys. And again, and again, until the bliss became almost too much to bear.

Louis was an incredible lover, passionate and demanding, tender and caring. After a long, long time, they lay spent, contented. She nestled in his strong arms, and they talked.

'It's so strange,' Louis said. 'I feel whole again. Since Renée and the children were killed, I've been a ghost, wandering around lost.'

I, too, Mary thought.

'I missed her in all the important ways, and in ways I had never thought of. I felt helpless without her. Silly, trivial things. I did not know how to cook a meal, or do my laundry, or even make my bed properly. We men take so much for granted.'

'Louis, I felt helpless, too. Edward was my umbrella, and when it rained and he wasn't there to protect me, I almost drowned.'

They slept.

They made love again, slowly and tenderly now, the fire banked, the flame slower, more exquisite.

It was almost perfect. *Almost.* Because there was a question Mary wanted to ask, and she knew she dared not: *Did you have a wife and children, Louis?*

The moment she asked that question, she knew everything between them would be over forever. Louis would never forgive her for doubting him. *Damn Mike Slade*, she thought. *Damn him.*

Louis was watching her. 'What were you thinking about?'

'Nothing, darling.'

What were you doing in that dark side street when those men tried to kidnap me, Louis?

*

They dined that evening on the outdoor terrace, and Louis ordered *Cemurata*, the strawberry liqueur made in the nearby mountains.

Saturday they went on a tram to a mountain peak. When they returned, they swam in the indoor pool, made love in the private sauna, and played bridge with a geriatric German couple on their honeymoon.

In the evening, they drove to Eintrul, a rustic restaurant in the mountains, where they had dinner in a large room with an open fireplace with a roaring fire. There were wooden chandeliers hanging from the ceiling, and hunting trophies on the wall over the fireplace. The room was lit by candlelight, and through the windows they could look at the snow-covered hills outside. A perfect setting, with the perfect companion.

And finally, too soon, it was time to leave.

Time to go back to the real world, Mary thought. And what was the real world? A place of threats and kidnapping and horrible graffiti written on her office walls.

The drive back was pleasant and easy. The sexual tension on the drive up had given way to an easy, relaxed feeling of togetherness. Louis was so comfortable to be with.

As they neared the outskirts of Bucharest, they drove by fields of sunflowers, their faces moving towards the sun.

That's me, Mary thought happily. *I'm finally moving into the sunlight.*

*

Beth and Tim were eagerly awaiting their mother's return.

'Are you going to marry Louis?' Beth asked.

Mary was taken aback. They had put into words what she had not dared allow herself to think.

'Well – are you?'

'I don't know,' she said carefully. 'Would you mind if I did?'

'He's not Daddy,' Beth answered slowly, 'but Tim and I took a vote. We like him.'

'So do I,' Mary replied happily. 'So do I.'

There were a dozen red roses with a note: *Thank you for you.*

She read the card. And wondered if he had sent flowers to Renée. And wondered if there had been a Renée and two daughters. And hated herself for it. *Why would Mike Slade make up a terrible lie like that?* There was no way she could ever check it. And at that moment, Eddie Maltz, the Political Consular and CIA agent, walked into her office.

'You're looking fit, Madam Ambassador. Have a good weekend?'

'Yes, thank you.'

They spent some time discussing a colonel who had approached Maltz about defecting.

'He'd be a valuable asset to us. He'll be bringing some useful information with him. I'm sending a black cable out tonight, but I wanted you to be prepared to receive some heat from Ionescu.'

'Thank you, Mr Maltz.'

He rose to leave.

On a sudden impulse, Mary said, 'Wait. I – I wonder if I could ask you for a favour?'

'Certainly.'

She found it unexpectedly awkward to continue. 'It's – personal and confidential.'

'Sounds like our motto,' Maltz smiled.

'I need some information on a Dr Louis Desforges. Have you heard of him?'

'Yes, ma'am. He's attached to the French Embassy. What would you like to know about him?'

This was going to be even more difficult than she had imagined. It was a betrayal. 'I – I'd like to know whether Dr Desforges was once married and had two children. Do you think you could find out?'

'Will twenty-four hours be soon enough?' Maltz asked.

'Yes, thank you.'

Please forgive me, Louis.

A short time later, Mike Slade walked into Mary's office. 'Morning.'

'Good morning.'

He put a cup of coffee on her desk. Something in his attitude seemed subtly changed. Mary was not sure what it was, but she had a feeling that Mike Slade knew all about her weekend. She wondered whether he had spies following her, reporting on her activities.

She took a sip of the coffee. Excellent, as usual. *That's one thing Mike Slade does well*, Mary thought.

'We have some problems,' he said.

And for the rest of the morning, they became involved in a discussion that included more Romanians who wanted to emigrate to America, the Romanian financial crisis, a Marine who had got a Romanian girl pregnant, and a dozen other topics.

At the end of the meeting, Mary was more tired than usual.

Mike Slade said, 'The ballet is opening tonight. Corina Socoli is dancing.'

Mary recognized the name. She was one of the prima ballerinas in the world.

'I have some tickets, if you're interested.'

'No, thanks.' She thought of the last time Mike had given her tickets for the theatre, and what had happened. Besides, she was going to be busy. She was invited to dinner at the Chinese Embassy and was meeting Louis at the Residence afterwards. It would not do for them to be seen too much together in public. She knew that she was breaking the rules by having an affair with a member of another embassy. *But this is not a casual affair.*

As Mary was dressing for dinner, she opened her closet to take out a dinner gown and found that the maid had washed it instead of having it cleaned. It was ruined. *I'm going to fire her*, Mary thought furiously. *Except that I can't. Their damned rules.*

She felt suddenly exhausted. She sank down on the bed. *I wish I didn't have to go out tonight. It would be so nice just to lie here and go to sleep. But you have to, Madam Ambassador. Your country is depending on you.*

She lay there, fantasizing. She would stay in bed instead of going to the dinner party. The Chinese Ambassador would greet his other guests, anxiously waiting for her. Finally, dinner would be announced. The American Ambassador had not arrived. It was a deliberate insult. China had lost face. The Chinese Ambassador would send a black cable, and when his Prime Minister read it, he would be furious. He would telephone the President of the United States to protest. 'Neither you nor anyone else can force my ambassador to go to your dinners,' President Ellison would yell. The Prime Minister would scream, 'No one can talk to me that way. We have our own atomic bombs now, Mr President.' The two leaders would press the nuclear buttons together, and destruction would rain on both countries.

Mary sat up and thought wearily, *I'd better go to the damned dinner.*

The evening was a blur of the same familiar diplomatic corps faces. Mary had only a hazy recollection of the others at her table. She could not wait to get home.

As Florian was driving her back to the Residence, Mary smiled dreamily: *I wonder if President Ellison realizes I prevented an atomic war tonight?*

The following morning when Mary went to the office, she was feeling worse. Her head ached, and she was nauseated. The only thing that made her feel better was the visit from Eddie Maltz.

The CIA agent said, 'I have the information you requested. Dr Louis Desforges was married for thirteen years. Wife's name, Renée. Two daughters, ten and twelve, Phillipa and Geneviève. They were murdered in Algeria by terrorists, probably as an act of vengeance against the doctor, who was fighting them in a covert operation. Do you need any further information?'

'No,' Mary said happily. 'That's fine. Thank you.'

Over morning coffee, Mary and Mike Slade discussed a forthcoming visit from a college group.

'They'd like to meet President Ionescu.'

'I'll see what I can do,' Mary said. Her voice was slurred.

'You okay?'

'I'm just tired.'

'What you need is another cup of coffee. It will perk you up. No pun intended.'

By late afternoon, Mary was feeling worse. She called Louis and cancelled their dinner engagement. She felt too ill to see anybody. She wished that the American doctor were in Bucharest. Perhaps Louis would know what was wrong with her. *If I don't get over this, I'll call him.*

Dorothy Stone had the nurse send up some Tylenol from the pharmacy. It did not help.

Mary's secretary was concerned. 'You really look awful, Madam Ambassador. You should be in bed.'

'I'll be fine,' Mary mumbled.

The day had a thousand hours. Mary met with the students, some Romanian officials, an American banker, an official from the USIS – the United States Information Service – and sat through an endless dinner party at the Dutch Embassy. When she finally arrived home, she fell into bed.

She was unable to sleep. She felt hot and feverish, and she was caught up in a series of nightmares. She was running down a maze of corridors, and every time she turned a corner, she ran into someone writing obscenities in blood. She could only see the back of the man's head. Then Louis appeared, and a dozen men tried to pull him into a car. Mike Slade came running down the street yelling, 'Kill him. He has no family.'

Mary woke up in a cold sweat. The room was unbearably hot. She threw off the covers and was suddenly chilled. Her teeth began to chatter. *My God,* she thought, *what's wrong with me?*

She spent the remainder of the night awake, afraid to go to sleep again, afraid of her dreams.

It took all of Mary's willpower to get up and go to the Embassy the following morning. Mike Slade was waiting for her.

He looked at her critically and said, 'You don't look too well. Why don't you fly to Frankfurt and see our doctor there?'

'I'm fine.' Her lips were dry and cracked, and she felt completely dehydrated.

Mike handed her a cup of coffee. 'I have the new commerce figures here for you. The Romanians are going to need more grain than we thought. Here's how we can capitalize on it . . .'

She tried to pay attention, but Mike's voice kept fading in and out.

*

Somehow she managed to struggle through the day. Louis called twice. Mary told her secretary to tell him she was in meetings. She was trying to conserve every ounce of strength she had left to keep working.

When Mary went to bed that evening, she could feel that her temperature had climbed. Her whole body ached. *I'm really ill*, she thought. *I feel as though I'm dying.* With an enormous effort she reached out and pulled the bellcord. Carmen appeared.

She looked at Mary in alarm. 'Madam Ambassador! What – ?'

Mary's voice was a croak. 'Ask Sabina to call the French Embassy. I need Dr Desforges . . .'

Mary opened her eyes and blinked. There were two blurred Louis figures standing there. He moved to her bedside. He bent down and took a close look at her flushed face. 'My God, what's happening to you?' He felt her forehead. It was hot to the touch. 'Have you taken your temperature?'

'I don't want to know.' It hurt to talk.

Louis sat down on the edge of the bed. 'Darling, how long has this been going on?'

'A few days. It's probably just a virus.'

Louis felt her pulse. It was weak and thready. As he leaned forward, he smelled her breath. 'Have you eaten something today with garlic?'

She shook her head. 'I haven't eaten anything in two days.' Her voice was a whisper.

221

He leaned forward and gently lifted her eyelids. 'Have you been thirsty?'

She nodded.

'Pain, muscle cramps, vomiting, nausea?'

All of the above, she thought wearily. Aloud she said, 'What's the matter with me, Louis?'

'Do you feel like answering some questions?'

She swallowed. 'I'll try.'

He held her hand. 'When did you start feeling this way?'

'The day after we got back from the mountains.' Her voice was a whisper.

'Do you remember having anything to eat or drink that made you feel ill afterwards?'

She shook her head.

'You just kept feeling worse every day?'

She nodded.

'Do you eat breakfast here at the Residence with the children?'

'Usually, yes.'

'And the children are feeling well?'

She nodded.

'What about lunch? Do you eat lunch at the same place every day?'

'No. Sometimes I eat at the Embassy, sometimes I have meetings at restaurants.' Her voice was a whisper.

'Is there any one place you regularly have dinner or anything you regularly eat?'

She felt too tired to carry on this conversation. She wished he would go away. She closed her eyes.

He shook her gently. 'Mary, stay awake. Listen to me.' There was an urgency in his voice. 'Is there any person you eat with constantly?'

She blinked up at him sleepily. 'No.' Why was he asking all these questions. 'It's a virus,' she mumbled. 'Isn't it?'

He took a deep breath. 'No. Someone is poisoning you.'

It sent a bolt of electricity through her body. She opened her eyes wide. 'What? I don't believe it.'

He was frowning. 'I would say it was arsenic poisoning, except that arsenic is not for sale in Romania.'

Mary felt a sudden tremor of fear. 'Who – who would be trying to poison me?'

He squeezed her hand. 'Darling, you've got to think. Are you sure there's no set routine you have, where someone gives you something to eat or drink every day?'

'Of course not,' Mary protested weakly. 'I told you, I –' *Coffee. Mike Slade. My own special brew.* 'Oh, my God!'

'What is it?'

She cleared her throat and managed to say, 'Mike Slade brings me coffee every morning. He's always there waiting for me.'

Louis stared at her. 'No. It couldn't be Mike Slade. What reason would he have for trying to kill you?'

'He – he wants to get rid of me.'

'We'll talk about this later,' Louis said urgently. 'The first thing we have to do is treat you. I'd like to take you to the hospital here, but your Embassy will not permit it. I'm going to get something for you. I'll be back in a few minutes.'

Mary lay there, trying to grasp the meaning of what Louis had told her. *Arsenic. Someone is feeding me arsenic. What you need is another cup of coffee. It will make you feel better. I brew it myself.*

She drifted off into unconsciousness and was awakened by Louis' voice. 'Mary!'

She forced her eyes open. He was at her bedside, taking a syringe out of a small bag.

'Hello, Louis. I'm glad you could come,' Mary mumbled.

Louis felt for a vein in her arm and plunged the hypodermic needle in. 'I'm giving you an injection of Bal. It's an antidote for arsenic. I'm going to alternate it with Penicillamine. I'll give you another one in the morning. Mary?'

She was asleep.

The following morning, Dr Louis Desforges gave Mary an injection, and another one in the evening. The effects of the drugs were miraculous. One by one, the symptoms began to disappear. The following day, Mary's temperature and vital signs were almost completely normal.

Louis was in Mary's bedroom, putting the hypodermic needle in a paper sack, where it would not be seen by a curious staff member. Mary felt drained and weak, as though she had gone through a long illness, but all the pain and discomfort were gone.

'This is twice you've saved my life.'

Louis looked at her soberly. 'I think we'd better find out who's trying to take it.'

'How do we do that?'

'I've been checking around at the various embassies. None of them carries arsenic. I have not been able to find out about the American Embassy. I would like you to do something for me. Do you think you will feel well enough to go to work tomorrow?'

'I think so.'

'I want you to go to the pharmacy in your Embassy. Tell them you need a pesticide. Say that you're having trouble with the insects in your garden. Ask for Antrol. That's loaded with arsenic.'

Mary looked at him, puzzled. 'What's the point?'

'My hunch is that the arsenic had to be flown into Bucharest. If it is

223

anywhere, it will be in the Embassy pharmacy. Anyone who checks out a poison must sign for it. When you sign for the Antrol, see what names are on the sheet . . .'

Gunny escorted Mary through the Embassy door. She walked down the long corridor to the pharmacy, where the nurse was working behind the cage.

She turned as she saw Mary. 'Good morning, Madam Ambassador. Are you feeling better?'

'Yes, thank you.'

'Can I get you something?'

Mary took a nervous breath. 'My – my gardener tells me he's having trouble with insects in the garden. I wondered whether you might have something to help – like Antrol?'

'Why, yes. As a matter of fact, we do have some Antrol,' the nurse said. She reached towards a back shelf and picked up a can with a poison label on it. 'An infestation of ants is very unusual for this time of year.' She put a form in front of Mary. 'You'll have to sign for it, if you don't mind. It has arsenic in it.'

Mary was staring at the form placed in front of her. There was only one name on it.

Mike Slade.

26

When Mary tried to telephone Louis Desforges to tell him what she had learned, his line was busy. He was talking to Mike Slade. Dr Desforges' first instinct had been to report the murder attempt, except that he could not believe Slade was responsible. And so, Louis had decided to telephone Slade himself.

'I have just left your ambassador,' Louis Desforges said. 'She is going to live.'

'Well, that's good news, doctor. Why shouldn't she?'

Louis' tone was cautious. 'Someone has been poisoning her.'

'What are you talking about?' Mike demanded.

'I think perhaps you know what I'm talking about.'

'Hold it! Are you saying that you think *I'm* responsible? You're wrong. You and I had better have a private talk. Some place where we can't be overheard. Can you meet me tonight?'

'At what time?'

'I'm tied up until nine o'clock. Why don't you meet me a few minutes later, at Baneasa Woods? I'll meet you at the fountain and explain everything then.'

Louis Desforges hesitated. 'Very well. I will see you there.' He hung up and thought: *Mike Slade cannot possibly be behind this.*

When Mary tried to telephone Louis again, he had left. No one knew where to reach him.

Mary and the children were having dinner at the Residence.

'You really look a lot better, Mother,' Beth said. 'We were worried.'

'I feel fine,' Mary assured her. And it was the truth. *Thank God for Louis!*

Mary was unable to get Mike Slade out of her mind. She could hear his voice saying: *Here's your coffee. I brewed it myself.* Slowly killing her. She shuddered.

'Are you cold?' Tim asked.

'No, darling.'

She must not involve the children in her nightmares. *Perhaps I should send them back home for a while?* Mary thought. *They could stay with Florence and Doug.* And then she thought: *I could go with them.* But that would be cowardly, a victory for Mike Slade, and whoever he was working with. There was only one person she could think of who could help her. Stanton Rogers. Stanton would know what to do about Mike.

But I can't accuse him without proof, and what proof do I have? That he made coffee for me every morning?

Tim was talking to her. '. . . so we said we'd ask if we could go with them.'

'I'm sorry, darling. What did you say?'

'I said Nikolai asked us if we could go out camping with him and his family next weekend.'

'No!' It came out more harshly than she had intended. 'I want you both to stay close to the Residence.'

'What about school?' Beth asked.

Mary hesitated. She could not keep them prisoners here, and she did not want to alarm them.

'That's fine. As long as Florian takes you there and brings you back. No one else.'

Beth was studying her. 'Mother, is anything wrong?'

'Of course not,' Mary said quickly. 'Why do you ask?'

'I don't know. There's something in the air.'

'Give her a break,' Tim said. 'She had the Romanian flu.'

That's an interesting phrase, Mary thought. *Arsenic poisoning – the Romanian flu.*

'Can we watch a movie tonight?' Tim asked.

'*May* we watch a movie tonight,' Mary corrected him.

'Does that mean "yes"?'

Mary had not planned on running a movie, but she had spent so little time with the children lately that she decided to give them a treat.

'It means "yes".'

'Thank you, Madam Ambassador,' Tim shouted. 'I get to pick the movie.'

'No, you don't. You picked the last one. Can we see *American Graffiti* again?'

American Graffiti. And suddenly Mary knew what proof she might show Stanton Rogers.

At midnight, Mary asked Carmen to call a taxi.

'Don't you want Florian to drive you?' Carmen asked. 'He's –'

'No.'

This was something that had to be done secretly.

When the taxi arrived a few minutes later, Mary got in. 'The American Embassy, please.'

The taxi driver replied, 'It is closed at this hour. There is no one –' He turned around and recognized her. 'Madam Ambassador! This is a great honour.' He began to drive. 'I recognized you from all your pictures in our newspapers and magazines. You are almost as famous as our great leader.'

Others in the Embassy had commented about all the publicity she was receiving in the Romanian press.

The driver was chattering on. 'I like Americans. They are good-hearted people. I hope your President's people-to-people plan works. We Romanians are all for it. It is time the world had peace.'

She was in no mood for a discussion of any kind.

When they arrived at the Embassy, Mary indicated a place marked: *Parcare cu Locuri Rezervate.* 'Pull in there, please, and come back for me in an hour. I'll be returning to the Residence.'

'Certainly, Madam Ambassador.'

A Marine guard was moving towards the taxi. 'You can't park there, it's res –' He recognized Mary, and saluted. 'Sorry. Good evening, Madam Ambassador.'

'Good evening,' Mary said.

The Marine walked her to the entrance and opened the door for her. 'Can I help you?'

'No. I'm going to my office for a few minutes.'

'Yes, ma'am.' He watched her walk down the hall.

Mary turned the lights on in her office and looked at the walls where the obscenities had been washed away. She walked over to the connecting door that led to Mike Slade's office and entered. The room was in darkness. She turned on the lights and looked around.

There were no papers on his desk. She began searching through the drawers. They were empty, except for brochures and bulletins and time-tables. Innocent things that would be of no use to a snooping cleaning woman. Mary's eyes scrutinized the office. It had to be here somewhere. There was no other place he could have kept it, and it was unlikely that he would carry it around with him.

She opened the drawers and started examining their contents again, slowly and carefully. When she came to a bottom drawer, she felt something hard at the back, behind a mass of papers. She pulled it out and held it in her hand, staring at it.

It was a can of red spray paint.

At a few minutes after nine, Dr Louis Desforges was waiting in Baneasa Woods, near the fountain. He wondered if he had done the wrong thing by not reporting Mike Slade. *No*, he thought. *First I must hear what he has to say. If I made a false accusation, it would destroy him.*

Mike Slade suddenly appeared out of the darkness.

'Thanks for coming. We can clear this up very quickly. You said on the telephone you thought someone was poisoning Mary Ashley.'

'I *know* it. Someone was feeding her arsenic.'

'And you think I'm responsible?'

227

'You could have put it in her coffee, a little bit at a time.'

'Have you reported this to anyone?'

'Not yet. I wanted to talk to you first.'

'I'm glad you did,' Mike said. He took his hand out of his pocket. In it was a .475 calibre Magnum pistol.

Louis stared. 'What – what are you doing? Listen to me! You can't –'

Mike Slade pulled the trigger, and watched the Frenchman's chest explode into a red cloud.

27

In the American Embassy, Mary was in the Bubble Room telephoning Stanton Rogers' office on the secure line. It was one o'clock in the morning in Bucharest, and 8 a.m. in Washington, D.C. Mary knew that Stanton Rogers' secretary always arrived at the office early.

'Mr Rogers' office.'

'This is Ambassador Ashley. I know that Mr Rogers is in China with the President, but it's urgent that I speak to him as soon as possible. Is there any way I can reach him there?'

'I'm sorry, Madam Ambassador. His itinerary is very flexible. I have no telephone number for him.'

Mary felt her heart plummet. 'When will you hear from him?'

'It's difficult to say. He and the President have a very busy schedule. Perhaps someone in the State Department could help you?'

'No,' Mary said dully. 'No one else can help me. Thank you.'

She sat in the room alone, staring at nothing, surrounded by the most sophisticated electronic equipment in the world, and none of it of any use to her. Mike Slade was trying to murder her. She *had* to let someone know. But who? Whom could she trust? The only one who knew what Slade was trying to do was Louis Desforges.

Mary tried the number at his residence again, but there was still no answer. She remembered what Stanton Rogers had told her: *If you want to send me any messages you don't want anyone else to read, the code at the top of the cable is three x's.*

Mary hurried back to her office and wrote out an urgent message addressed to Stanton Rogers. She placed three x's at the top. She took out the black code book from a locked drawer in her desk, and carefully encoded what she had written. At least if anything happened to her now, Stanton Rogers would know who was responsible.

Mary walked down the corridor to the Communications Room.

Eddie Maltz, the CIA agent, happened to be behind the cage.

'Good evening, Madam Ambassador. You're working late to-night.'

'Yes,' Mary said. 'There's a message I'd like sent off. I want it to go out right away.'

'I'll take care of it personally.'

'Thank you.' She handed him the message and headed for the front door. She desperately wanted to be close to her children.

In the Communications Room, Eddie Maltz was decoding the message Mary had handed him. When he was finished, he read it through twice, frowning. He walked over to the shredder, threw the message in, and watched it turn into confetti.

Then he placed a call to Floyd Baker, the Secretary of State, in Washington. Code Name: *Thor*.

It took Lev Pasternak two months to follow the circuitous trail that led to Buenos Aires. SIS and half a dozen other security agencies around the world had helped identify Angel as the killer. Mossad had given him the name of Neusa Muñez, Angel's mistress. They all wanted to eliminate Angel. To Lev Pasternak, Angel had become an obsession. Because of Pasternak's failure, Marin Groza had died, and Pasternak could never forgive himself for that. He could, however, make atonement. And he intended to.

He did not get in touch with Neusa Munez directly. He located the apartment building where she lived and kept a watch on it, waiting for Angel to appear. After five days, when there was no sign of him, Pasternak made his move. He waited until the woman left, and after fifteen minutes walked upstairs, picked the lock on her door, and entered the apartment. He searched it swiftly and thoroughly. There were no photographs, memos or addresses that could lead him to Angel. Pasternak discovered the suits in the closet. He examined the Herrera labels, took one of the jackets off the hanger and tucked it under his arm. A minute later, he was gone, as quietly as he had entered.

The following morning Lev Pasternak walked into Herrera's. His hair was dishevelled and his clothes wrinkled, and he smelled of whisky.

The manager of the men's shop came up to him and said disapprovingly, 'May I help you, *señor*?'

Lev Pasternak grinned sheepishly. 'Yeah,' he said. 'Tell you the truth, I got as drunk as a skunk last night. I got inna card game with some South American dudes in my hotel room. I think we all got a little drunk, pal. Anyway, one of the guys – I don't remember his name – left his jacket in my room.' Lev held up the jacket, his hand unsteady. 'It had your label in it, so I figured you could tell me where to return it to him.'

The manager examined the jacket. 'Yes, we tailored this. I would have to look up our records. Where can I reach you?'

'You can't,' Lev Pasternak mumbled. 'I'm on my way to 'nother poker game. Got a card? I'll call you.'

'Yes.' The manager handed him his card.

'You're not gonna steal that jacket, are you?' Lev asked drunkenly.

'Certainly not,' the manager said indignantly.

Lev Pasternak clapped him on the back and said, 'Good. I'll call you later this afternoon.'

That afternoon when Lev called from his hotel room, the manager said, 'The name of the gentleman we made the jacket for is *Señor* H. R. de Mendoza. He has a suite at the Aurora Hotel, Suite Four Seventeen.'

Lev Pasternak checked to make sure that his door was locked. He took a suitcase out of the closet, carried it to the bed and opened it. Inside was a .45 SIG-Saur pistol with a silencer, courtesy of a friend in the Argentinian secret service. Pasternak checked again to make sure the gun was loaded and that the silencer was secure. He put the suitcase back in the closet, and went to sleep.

At 5 a.m., Lev Pasternak was silently moving down the deserted fourth floor corridor of the Aurora Hotel. When he reached 417, he looked around to make sure no one was in sight. He reached down to the lock and quietly inserted a wire. When he heard the door click open, he pulled out the pistol.

He sensed a draught as the door across the hall opened, and before Pasternak could swing around, he felt something hard and cold pressing against the back of his neck.

'I don't like being followed,' Angel said.

Lev Pasternak heard the click of the trigger a second before his brain was torn apart.

*

Angel was not sure whether Pasternak was alone, or working with someone, but it was always nice to take extra precautions. The telephone call had come, and it was time to move. First Angel had some shopping to do. There was a good lingerie shop on Pueyerredón, expensive, but Neusa deserved the best. The inside of the shop was cool and quiet.

'I would like to see a négligé, something very frilly,' Angel said.

The female clerk stared.

'And a pair of panties with a split in the crotch . . .'

Fifteen minutes later, Angel walked into Frenkel's. The shelves were filled with leather purses, gloves and briefcases.

'I would like a briefcase, please. Black.'

The El Aljire in the Sheraton Hotel was one of the finest restaurants in Buenos Aires. Angel sat down at a table in the corner, and placed the new briefcase on the table. The waiter came up to the table.

'Good afternoon.'

231

'I'll start with the *Centolla Pargo*, and after that the *Parrillada* with *Ensalada de Berros*. I'll decide on my dessert later.'

'Certainly.'

'Where are the rest rooms?'

'In the rear, through the far door and to your left.'

Angel got up from the table and walked towards the rear of the restaurant, leaving the briefcase in sight on the table. There was a narrow corridor with two small doors, one marked *Hombres*, and the other marked *Señoras*. At the end of the corridor were double doors leading to the noisy, steamy kitchen. Angel pushed one of the doors open and stepped inside. It was a scene of frantic activity, with chefs and sous-chefs bustling around, trying to keep up with the urgent demands of the lunch hour. Waiters moved in and out of the kitchen with loaded trays. The chefs were screaming at the waiters, and the waiters were screaming at the bus boys.

Angel moved, threading across the room, and stepped out through a back door leading to an alley. A five-minute wait to make sure that no one had followed.

There was a taxi at the corner. Angel gave the driver an address on Humberto 1°, alighted a block away, and hailed another taxi.

'*Donde, por favor?*'

'*Aeropuerto.*'

There would be a ticket for London waiting there. Tourist. First class was too conspicuous.

Two hours later, Angel watched the city of Buenos Aires disappear beneath the clouds, like some celestial magician's trick, and concentrated on the assignment ahead, thinking about the instructions that had been given.

Make sure the children die with her. Their deaths must be spectacular.

Angel did not like to be told how to fulfil a contract. Only amateurs were stupid enough to give advice to professionals. Angel smiled. *They will all die, and it will be more spectacular than anyone bargained for.*

Angel slept, a deep, dreamless sleep.

*

London's Heathrow Airport was crowded with summer tourists, and the taxi ride into Mayfair took more than an hour. The lobby of the Churchill was busy with guests checking in and out.

A bellboy took charge of Angel's three pieces of luggage.

The tip was modest, nothing that the bellboy would remember later. Angel walked over to the bank of hotel elevators, waited until a car was empty, then stepped inside.

When the elevator was on its way, Angel pressed the fifth, seventh, ninth and tenth floors, and got off at the fifth floor. Anyone who might be watching from the lobby would be confused.

A rear service staircase led to an alley, and five minutes after checking into the Churchill, Angel was in a taxi and on the way back to Heathrow.

The passport read H. R. de Mendoza. The ticket was on Tarom Airlines to Bucharest. Angel sent a telegram from the airport:

ARRIVING WEDNESDAY.
H. R. de Mendoza

It was addressed to Eddie Maltz.

*

Early the following morning, Dorothy Stone said, 'Stanton Rogers' office is on the line.'

'I'll take it,' Mary said eagerly. She snatched up the phone. 'Stan?'

She heard his secretary's voice, and wanted to weep in frustration. 'Mr Rogers asked me to call you, Madam Ambassador. He's with the President and unable to get to a telephone, but he asked me to see that you get anything you need. If you'll tell me what the problem is – ?'

'No,' Mary said, trying to keep the disappointment out of her voice. 'I – I have to speak to him myself.'

'I'm afraid that won't be until tomorrow. He said he would call you as soon as he was able to.'

'Thank you. I'll be waiting for his call.' She replaced the receiver. There was nothing to do but wait.

Mary kept trying to telephone Louis at his home. No answer. She tried the French Embassy. They had no idea where he was.

'Please have him call me as soon as you hear from him.'

Dorothy Stone said, 'There's a call for you, but she refuses to give her name.'

'I'll take it.' Mary picked up the phone. 'Hello, this is Ambassador Ashley.'

A soft, female voice with a Romanian accent said, 'This is Corina Socoli.'

The name registered instantly. She was a beautiful young girl in her early twenties, Romania's prima ballerina.

'I need your help,' the girl said. 'I have decided to defect.'

I can't handle this today, Mary thought. *Not now.* She said, 'I – I don't know if I can help you.' Her mind was racing. She tried to remember what she had been told about defectors.

Many of them are Soviet plants. We bring them over, they feed us a

233

few innocuous bits of information or misinformation. Some of them become moles. The real catches are the high-level intelligence officers or scientists. We can always use those. But otherwise, we don't grant political asylum unless there's a damned good reason.

Corina Socoli was sobbing now. 'Please! I am not safe staying where I am. You must send someone to get me.'

Communist governments set some cute traps. Someone posing as a defector asks for help. You bring them into the Embassy, and then they scream that they've been kidnapped. It gives them an excuse to take measures against targets in the United States.

'Where are you?' Mary asked.

There was a pause. Then, 'I suppose I must trust you. I am at the Roscow Inn at Moldavia. Will you come for me?'

'I can't,' Mary said. 'But I'll send someone to get you. Don't call on this phone again. Just wait where you are. I –'

The door opened, and Mike Slade walked in. Mary looked up in shock. He was moving towards her.

The voice at the other end of the phone was saying, 'Hello? Hello?'

'Who are you talking to?' Mike asked.

'To – to Dr Desforges.' It was the first name that came to her mind. She replaced the receiver, terrified.

Don't be ridiculous, she told herself. *You're in the Embassy. He wouldn't dare do anything to you here.*

'Dr Desforges?' Mike repeated slowly.

'Yes. He's – he's on his way over to see me.'

How she wished it were true!

There was a strange look in Mike Slade's eyes. Mary's desk lamp was on, and it threw Mike's shadow against the wall, making him grotesquely large and menacing.

'Are you sure you're well enough to be back at work?'

The cold-blooded nerve of the man. 'Yes. I'm fine.'

She desperately wanted him to leave, so that she could escape. *I must not show him I'm frightened.*

He was moving closer to her. 'You look tense. Maybe you should take the kids and go out to the lake district for a few days.'

Where I'll be an easier target.

Just looking at him filled her with such a fear that she found it hard to breathe. Her intercom phone rang. It was a lifesaver.

'If you'll excuse me . . .'

'Sure.'

Mike Slade stood there a moment, staring at her, then turned and left, taking his shadow with him. Almost sobbing with relief, Mary picked up the telephone. 'Hello?'

It was Jerry Davis, the Public Affairs Consular. 'Madam Ambassador, I'm sorry to disturb you, but I'm afraid I have some terrible news for

234

you. We just received a police report that Dr Louis Desforges has been murdered.'

The room began to swim. 'Are you – are you sure?'

'Yes, ma'am. His wallet was found on his body.'

Sensory memories flooded through her, and a voice over the telephone was saying: *This is Sheriff Munster. Your husband has been killed in a car accident.* And all the old sorrows came rushing back, stabbing at her, tearing her apart.

'How – how did it happen?' Her voice was strangled.

'He was shot to death.'

'Do they – do they know who did it?'

'No, ma'am. The *Securitate* and the French Embassy are investigating.'

She dropped the receiver, her mind and body numb, and leaned back in her chair, studying the ceiling. There was a crack in it. *I must have that repaired,* Mary thought. *We mustn't have cracks in our Embassy. There's another crack. Cracks everywhere. Cracks in our lives, and when there is a crack, evil things get in. Edward is dead. Louis is dead.* She could not bear to think of that. She searched for more cracks. *I can't go through this pain again,* Mary thought. *Who would want to kill Louis?*

The answer immediately followed the question. *Mike Slade.* Louis had discovered that Slade was feeding Mary arsenic. Slade probably thought that with Louis dead, no one could prove anything against him.

A sudden realization struck her and filled her with a new terror. *Who were you talking to? Dr Desforges.* And Mike must have known that Dr Desforges was dead.

She stayed in her office all day, planning her next move. *I'm not going to let him drive me away. I'm not going to let him kill me. I have to stop him.* She was filled with a rage such as she had never known before. She was going to protect herself and her children. And she was going to destroy Mike Slade.

Mary placed another urgent call to Stanton Rogers.

'I gave him your message, Madam Ambassador. He will return your call as soon as possible.'

She could not bring herself to accept Louis' death. He had been so warm, so gentle, and now he was lying in some morgue, lifeless. *If I had gone back to Kansas,* Mary thought dully, *Louis would be alive today.*

'Madam Ambassador . . .'

Mary looked up. Dorothy Stone was holding an envelope out to her.

'The guard at the gate asked me to give you this. He said it was delivered by a young boy.'

The envelope was marked *Personal, for the Ambassador's Eyes Only.*
Mary tore open the envelope. The note was written in a neat, copperplate handwriting. It read:

> Dear Madam Ambassador:
> Enjoy your last day on earth.

It was signed 'Angel'.
Another one of Mike's scare tactics, Mary thought. *It won't work. I'll keep well away from him.*

Colonel McKinney was studying the note. He shook his head. 'There are a lot of sickies out there.' He looked up at Mary. 'You were scheduled to make an appearance this afternoon at the ground-breaking ceremony for the new Library addition. I'll cancel it and –'
'No.'
'Madam Ambassador, it's too dangerous for you to –'
'I'll be safe.' She knew now where the danger lay, and she had a plan to avoid it. 'Where's Mike Slade?' she asked.
'He's in a meeting at the Australian Embassy.'
'Please get word to him that I wish to see him right away.'

'You wanted to talk to me?' Mike Slade's tone was casual.
'Yes. There's something I want you to do.'
'I'm at your command.'
His sarcasm was like a slap.
'I received a telephone call from someone who wants to defect.'
'Who is it?'
She had no intention of telling him. He would betray the girl. 'That's not important. I want you to bring this person in.'
Mike frowned. 'Is this someone the Romanians want to keep?'
'Yes.'
'Well, that could lead to a lot of –'
She cut him short. 'I want you to go to the Roscow Inn at Moldavia and pick her up.'
He started to argue, until he saw the expression on her face. 'If that's what you want, I'll send –'
'No.' Mary's voice was steel. 'I want you to go. I'm sending two men with you.'
With Gunny and another Marine along, Mike would not be able to play any tricks. She had told Gunny not to let Mike Slade out of his sight.
Mike was studying Mary, puzzled. 'I have a heavy schedule. Tomorrow would probably –'

236

'I want you to leave immediately. Gunny is waiting for you in your office. You're to bring the defector back here to me.' Her tone left no room for argument.

Mike nodded slowly. 'All right.'

Mary watched him go, with a feeling of relief so intense that she felt giddy. With Mike out of the way, she would be safe.

She dialled Colonel McKinney's number. 'I'm going ahead with the ceremony this afternoon,' she informed him.

'I strongly advise against it, Madam Ambassador. Why would you want to expose yourself to unnecessary danger when – ?'

'I have no choice. I'm representing our country. How would it look if I hid in a closet every time someone threatened my life? If I do that once, I'll never be able to show my face again. I might as well go home. And Colonel – I have no intention of going home.'

28

The ground-breaking ceremony for the new American Library addition was scheduled to be held at four o'clock in the afternoon at Alexandru Sahia Square, in the large vacant lot next to the main building of the American Library. By 3 p.m., a large crowd had already gathered. Colonel McKinney had had a meeting with Captain Aurel Istrase, head of *Securitate*.

'We shall certainly give your Ambassador maximum protection,' Istrase assured him.

Istrase had been as good as his word. He ordered all automobiles removed from the square, so that there was no danger of a car bomb, police were stationed around the entire area, and a sharpshooter was on the roof of the library building.

At a few minutes before four, everything was in readiness. Electronic experts had swept the entire area and had found no explosives. When all the checks had been completed, Captain Aurel Istrase said to Colonel McKinney, 'We are ready.'

'Very well.' Colonel McKinney turned to an aide. 'Tell the Ambassador to come ahead.'

Mary was escorted to the limousine by four Marines who flanked her as she got into the car.

Florian beamed, 'Good afternoon, Madam Ambassador. It is going to be a big, beautiful new library, no?'

'Yes.'

As he drove, Florian chattered on, but Mary was not listening. She was thinking of the laughter in Louis' eyes, and the tenderness with which he had made love to her. She dug her fingernails into her wrists, trying to make the physical pain replace the anguish inside. *I must not cry*, she told herself. *Whatever I do, I must not cry. There is no more love*, she thought wearily, *only hate. What's happening to the world?*

When the limousine reached the dedication site, two Marines stepped up to the car door, looked around carefully, and opened the door for Mary.

'Good afternoon, Madam Ambassador.'

As Mary walked towards the lot where the ceremony was to take place, two armed members of the *Securitate* walked in front of her, and two behind her, shielding her with their bodies. From the roof top, the sniper alertly scanned the scene below.

The onlookers applauded as the Ambassador stepped into the centre of the small circle that had been cleared for her. The crowd was a mixture of Romanians, Americans and attachés from other embassies in Bucharest. There were a few familiar faces, but most of the people were strangers.

Mary looked over the crowd and thought: *How can I make a speech? Colonel McKinney was right. I should never have come here. I'm miserable and terrified.*

Colonel McKinney was saying, 'Ladies and gentlemen, it is my honour to present the Ambassador from the United States.'

The crowd applauded.

Mary took a deep breath, and began. 'Thank you . . .'

She had been so caught up in the maelstrom of events of the past week that she had not prepared a speech. Some deep wellspring within her gave her the words. She found herself saying, 'What we are doing here today may seem a small thing, but it is important because it is one more bridge between our country and all the countries of Eastern Europe. The new building we are dedicating here today will be filled with information about the United States of America. Here, you will be able to learn about the history of our country, both the good things and the bad things. You will be able to see pictures of our cities and factories and farms . . .'

Colonel McKinney and his men were moving through the crowd slowly. The note had said 'Enjoy your last day on earth.' When did the killer's day end? 6 p.m.? Nine o'clock? Midnight?

'. . . but there is something more important for you to find out than what the United States of America *looks* like. When this new building is finished, you can finally know what America *feels* like. We are going to show you the spirit of the country.'

On the far side of the square, a car suddenly raced past the police barrier and screamed to a stop at the kerb. As a startled policeman moved towards it, the driver jumped out of the car and began running away. As he ran, he pulled a device from his pocket and pressed it. The car exploded, sending out a shower of metal into the crowd. None of it reached the centre where Mary was standing, but the spectators began milling around in panic, trying to flee, to get away from the attack. The sniper on the roof raised his rifle and put a bullet through the fleeing man's heart before he could escape. He shot him twice more to make sure.

It took the Romanian police an hour to clear the crowd away from Alexandru Sahia Square and remove the body of the would-be assassin. The fire department had put out the flames of the burning car. Mary was driven back to the Embassy, shaken.

'Are you sure you wouldn't prefer to go to the Residence and rest?'

Colonel McKinney asked her. 'You've just been through a horrifying experience that –'

'No,' Mary said stubbornly. 'The Embassy.'

That was the only place where she could safely talk to Stanton Rogers. *I must talk to him soon*, Mary thought, *or I'll go to pieces.*

The strain of everything that was happening to her was unbearable. She had made sure that Mike Slade was safely out of the way, yet an attempt had still been made on her life. So he was not working alone.

Mary wished desperately that Stanton Rogers would telephone.

At six o'clock, Mike Slade walked into Mary's office. He was furious.

'I put Corina Socoli in a room upstairs,' he said curtly. 'I wish to hell you'd told me who it was I was picking up. You've made a big mistake. We have to return her. She's a national treasure. There's no way the Romanian government will ever allow her out of the country. If –'

Colonel McKinney hurried into the office. He stopped short as he saw Mike.

'We have an identification on the dead man. He's the Angel, all right. His real name is H. R. de Mendoza.'

Mike was staring at him. 'What are you talking about?'

'I forgot,' Colonel McKinney said. 'You were away during all the excitement. Didn't the Ambassador tell you someone tried to kill her today?'

Mike turned to look at Mary. 'No.'

'She received a death warning from Angel. He tried to assassinate her at the ground-breaking ceremony this afternoon. One of Istrase's snipers got him.'

Mike stood there, silently, his eyes fixed on Mary.

Colonel McKinney said, 'Angel seems to have been on everybody's "Most Wanted List".'

'Where's his body?' Mike asked.

'In the morgue at police headquarters.'

The body was lying on a stone slab, naked. He had been an ordinary looking man, medium height, with unremarkable features, a naval tattoo on one arm, a small, thin nose that went with his tight mouth, very small feet, and thinning hair. His clothes and belongings were piled on a table.

'Mind if I have a look?'

The police sergeant shrugged. 'Go ahead. I'm sure he won't mind.' He snickered at his joke.

Mike picked up the jacket and examined the label. It was from a shop in Buenos Aires. The leather shoes also had an Argentinian label. There were piles of money next to the clothing, some Romanian lei, a few French francs, some English pounds, and at least ten thousand dollars in Republic of Argentina pesos – some in the new ten peso notes, and the rest in the devalued Un Million de Peso notes.

Mike turned to the sergeant. 'What do you have on him?'

'He flew in from London on Tarom Airlines two days ago. He checked into the Intercontinental Hotel under the name of de Mendoza. His passport shows his home address as Buenos Aires. It is forged.'

The policeman moved in to take a closer look at the body. 'He does not look like an international killer, does he?'

'No,' Mike agreed. 'He doesn't.'

Two dozen blocks away, Angel was walking past the Residence, fast enough so as not to attract the attention of the four armed Marines guarding the front entrance, and slowly enough to absorb every detail of the front of the building. The photographs that had been sent were excellent, but Angel believed in personally checking out every detail. Near the front door was a fifth guard in civilian clothes, holding two Doberman pinschers on leashes.

Angel grinned at the thought of the charade that had been played out in the town square. It had been child's play to hire a junkie for the price of a noseful of cocaine. *Throw everyone off guard. Let them sweat.* The big event was yet to come. *For five million dollars, I will give them a show they will never forget. What do the television networks call them? Spectaculars. They will get a spectacular in living colour.*

There will be a Fourth of July celebration at the Residence, the voice had said. *There will be balloons, a Marine band, entertainers.* Angel smiled and thought: *A five million dollar spectacular.*

Dorothy Stone hurried into Mary's office. 'Madam Ambassador – you're wanted right away in the Bubble Room. Mr Stanton Rogers is calling from Washington.'

'Mary – I can't understand a word you're saying. Slow down. Take a deep breath and start again.'

My God, Mary thought. *I'm babbling like a hysterical ninny.* There was such a mixture of violent emotions churning in her that she could barely get the words out. She was terrified and relieved and angry, all at the same time, and her voice came out in a series of choked words.

She took a deep, shuddering breath. 'I'm sorry, Stan – didn't you get my cable?'

'No. I've just returned. There was no cable from you. What's wrong back there?'

Mary fought to control her hysteria. *Where should I begin?* She took a deep breath. 'Mike Slade is trying to murder me.'

There was a shocked silence. 'Mary – you really can't believe –'

'It's true. I know it is. I met a doctor from the French Embassy – Louis Desforges. I became ill, and he found out I was being poisoned with arsenic. Mike was doing it.'

This time Stanton Rogers' voice was sharper. 'What makes you think that?'

'Louis – Dr Desforges – figured it out. Mike Slade made coffee for me every morning with arsenic in it. I have proof that he got hold of the arsenic. Last night, Louis was murdered, and this afternoon someone working with Slade tried to assassinate me.'

This time the silence was even longer.

When Stanton Rogers spoke again, his tone was urgent. 'What I'm going to ask you is very important, Mary. Think carefully. Could it have been anyone besides Mike Slade?'

'No. He's been trying to get me out of Romania from the very beginning.'

Stanton Rogers said crisply, 'All right. I'm going to inform the President. We'll handle Slade. In the meantime, I'll arrange extra protection for you there.'

'Stan – Sunday night I'm giving a Fourth of July party at the Residence. The guests have already been invited. Do you think I should cancel it?'

There was a thoughtful silence. 'As a matter of fact, the party might be a good idea. Keep a lot of people around you. Mary – I don't want to frighten you any more than you already are, but I would suggest that you do not let the children out of your sight. Not for a minute. Slade might try to get at you through them.'

She felt a shudder go through her. 'What's behind all this? Why is he doing this?'

'I wish I knew. It makes no sense. But I'm damned well going to find out. In the meantime, keep as far away from him as you possibly can.'

Mary said grimly, 'Don't worry. I will.'

'I'll be in touch with you.'

When Mary hung up, it was as though an enormous burden had been lifted from her shoulders. *Everything's going to be all right*, she told herself. *The children and I are going to be fine.*

Eddie Maltz answered on the first ring.

The conversation lasted for ten minutes.

'I'll make sure everything is there,' Eddie Maltz promised.

Angel hung up.

Eddie Maltz thought: *I wonder what the hell Angel needs all that stuff for*. He looked at his watch. *Forty-eight hours to go.*

The moment Stanton Rogers finished talking to Mary, he placed an emergency call to Colonel McKinney.

'Bill, Stanton Rogers.'

'Yes, sir. What can I do for you?'

'I want you to pick up Mike Slade. Hold him in close custody until you hear from me.'

When the Colonel spoke, there was an incredulous note in his voice. 'Mike Slade?'

'I want him held and isolated. He's probably armed and dangerous. Don't let him talk to anyone.'

'Yes, sir.'

'I want you to call me back at the White House as soon as you have him.'

'Yes, sir.'

                                    *

Stanton Rogers' phone rang two hours later. He snatched up the receiver. 'Hello?'

'It's Colonel McKinney, Mr Rogers.'

'Do you have Slade?'

'No, sir. There's a problem.'

'What problem?'

'Mike Slade has disappeared.'

29

Sofia, Bulgaria
Saturday, July 3rd

In a small, nondescript building on Prezviter Kozma 32, a group of Eastern Committee members was meeting. Seated around the table were powerful representatives from Russia, China, Czechoslovakia, Pakistan, India and Malaysia.

The chairman was speaking: 'We welcome our brothers and sisters on the Eastern Committee who have joined us today. I am happy to tell you that we have excellent news from the Committee. Everything is now in place. The final phase of our plan is about to be successfully concluded. It will happen tomorrow night at the American Ambassador's Residence in Bucharest. Arrangements have been made for international press and television coverage.'

Code name Kali spoke. 'The American Ambassador and her two children –?'

'Will be assassinated, along with a hundred or so other Americans. We are all aware of the grave risks, and the holocaust that may follow. It is time to put the motion to a vote.' He started at the far end of the table. 'Brahma?'

'Yes.'

'Vishnu?'

'Yes.'

'Ganesha?'

'Yes.'

'Yama?'

'Yes.'

'Indra?'

'Yes.'

'Krishna?'

'Yes.'

'Rama?'

'Yes.'

'Kali?'

'Yes.'

'It is unanimous,' the chairman declared. 'We owe a particular vote

of thanks to the person who has helped so much to bring this about.'
He turned to the American.

'My pleasure,' Mike Slade said.

The decorations for the Fourth of July party were flown into Bucharest on a C-120 Hercules, late Saturday afternoon, and were trucked directly to a United States government warehouse. The cargo consisted of one thousand red, white and blue balloons, packed in flat boxes, three steel cylinders of helium to blow up the balloons, two hundred and fifty rolls of confetti, party favours, noisemakers, a dozen banners, and six dozen miniature American flags. The cargo was unloaded in the warehouse at 8 p.m. Two hours later, a jeep arrived with two oxygen cylinders stamped with US Army markings. The driver placed them inside.

At 1 a.m., when the warehouse was deserted, Angel appeared. The warehouse door had been left unlocked. Angel walked over to the cylinders, examined them carefully, and went to work. The first task was to empty the three helium tanks until each was only one third full. After that, the rest was simple.

On the morning of the Fourth of July, the Residence was in a state of chaos. Floors were being scrubbed, chandeliers dusted, rugs cleaned. Every room contained its own series of distinctive noises. There was hammering, as a podium at one end of the ballroom was being built for the band, the whir of vacuum cleaners in the hallways, sounds of cooking from the kitchen.

At four o'clock that afternoon, a United States Army truck pulled up at the service entrance of the Residence and was stopped. The guard on duty said to the driver, 'What have you got in there?'

'Goodies for the party.'

'Let's take a look.'

The guard inspected the inside of the truck. 'What's in the boxes?'

'Some helium and balloons and flags and stuff.'

'Open them.'

Fifteen minutes later, the truck was passed through. Inside the compound a corporal and two Marines began to unload the equipment and carry it into a large storage room off the main ballroom.

As they began to unpack, one of the Marines said, 'Look at all these balloons? Who the hell is going to blow them up?'

At that moment, Eddie Maltz walked in, accompanied by a stranger wearing army fatigues.

'Don't worry,' Eddie Maltz said. 'This is the age of technocracy.' He nodded towards the stranger. 'Here's the one that's in charge of the balloons. Colonel McKinney's orders.'

One of the Marine guards grinned at the stranger. 'Better you than me.'

The two Marines left.

'You have an hour,' Eddie Maltz told the stranger. 'Better get to work. You've got a lot of balloons to blow up.'

Maltz nodded to the corporal and walked out.

The corporal walked over to one of the cylinders. 'What's in these babies?'

'Helium,' the stranger said curtly.

As the corporal stood watching, the stranger picked up a balloon, put the tip to the nozzle of a cylinder for an instant, and as the balloon filled, tied off the tip. The balloon floated to the ceiling. The whole operation took no more than a second.

'Hey, that's great,' the corporal smiled.

In her office at the Embassy, Mary Ashley was finishing up some action telexes that had to be sent out immediately. She desperately wished the party could have been called off. There were going to be more than two hundred guests. She hoped Mike Slade was caught before the party began.

Tim and Beth were under constant supervision at the Residence. *How could Mike Slade bear to harm them?* Mary remembered how much he had seemed to enjoy playing with them. *He's not sane.*

Mary rose to put some papers in the shredder – and froze. Mike Slade was walking into her office through the connecting door. Mary opened her mouth to scream.

'Don't!'

She was terrified. There was no one near enough to save her. He could kill her before she could call for help. He could escape the same way he had come in. How had he got past the guards? *I must not show him how frightened I am.*

'Colonel McKinney's men are looking for you. You can kill me,' Mary said defiantly, 'but you'll never escape.'

'You've been listening to too many fairy tales. Angel's the one who's trying to kill you.'

'You're a liar. Angel is dead. I saw him shot.'

'Angel is a professional from Argentina. The last thing he would do is walk around with Argentinian labels in his clothes, and Argentinian pesos in his pocket. The slob the police killed was an amateur who was set up.'

Keep him talking. 'I don't believe a word you're saying. *You* killed Louis Desforges. You tried to poison me. Do you deny that?'

Mike studied her for a long moment. 'No, I don't deny it. You'd better hear the story from a friend of mine.' He turned towards the door to his office. 'Come in, Bill.'

Colonel McKinney walked into the room. 'I think it's time we all had a chat, Madam Ambassador . . .'

In the Residence storage room, the stranger in Army fatigues was filling the balloons under the watchful eye of the Marine corporal.

Boy, that's one ugly customer, the corporal thought to himself. *Whew!*

The corporal could not understand why the white balloons were being filled from one cylinder, the red balloons from a second cylinder, and the blue ones from a third. *Why not use each cylinder until it's empty?* the corporal wondered. He was tempted to ask, but he did not want to start a conversation. *Not with this one.*

Through the open door that led to the ballroom, the corporal could see trays of hors d'oeuvres being carried out of the kitchen into the ballroom and set on tables along the sides of the room. *It's going to be a great party*, the corporal thought.

Mary was seated in her office, facing Mike Slade and Colonel McKinney.

'Let's start at the beginning,' Colonel McKinney said. 'On inauguration day when the President announced that he wanted to open relations with every Iron Curtain country, he exploded a bombshell. There's a faction in our government that's convinced that if we get involved with Romania, Russia, Bulgaria, Albania, Czechoslovakia, etc., that the communists will destroy us. On the other side of the Iron Curtain, there are communists who believe that our President's plan is a trick – a Trojan Horse to bring our capitalist spies into their countries. A group of powerful men on both sides had formed a super-secret alliance called Patriots for Freedom. They decided the only way to destroy the President's plan was to let him start it, and then sabotage it in such a dramatic way that it would never be tried again. That's where you came into the picture.'

'But – why me? Why was I chosen?'

'Because the packaging was important,' Mike said. 'You were perfect. Adorable you, from middle-America, with two adorable kids – all that was missing was an adorable dog and an adorable cat. You were exactly the image they needed – the Ambassador with sizzle – Mrs America with two squeaky clean kids. They were determined to have you. When your husband got in the way, they murdered him and made it look like an accident so you wouldn't have any suspicions and refuse the post.'

'Oh, my God!' The horror of what he was saying was appalling.

'Their next step was your build-up. Through the "old-boy" network, they used their press connections around the world and saw to it that you became everyone's darling. Everybody was rooting for you. You were the beautiful lady who was going to lead the world down the road to peace.'

'And – and now?'

Mike's voice gentled. 'Their plan is to assassinate you and the children as publicly and as shockingly as possible – to sicken the world so much that it would put an end to any further ideas of détente.'

Mary sat there in stunned silence.

'That states it bluntly,' Colonel McKinney said quietly, 'but accurately. Mike is with the CIA. After your husband and Marin Groza were murdered, Mike started to get on the trail of the Patriots for Freedom. They thought he was on their side, and they invited him to join. We talked the idea over with President Ellison, and he gave his approval. The President has been kept abreast of every development. His overriding concern has been that you and your children be protected. He didn't dare discuss what he knew with you or anyone else, because Ned Tillingast, the head of the CIA, had warned him there were high-level leaks.'

Mary's head was spinning. She said to Mike, 'But – you tried to kill me.'

He sighed. 'Lady, I've been trying to save your life. I tried every way I knew to get you to take the kids and go home where you'd be safe.'

'But – you poisoned me.'

'Not fatally. I wanted to get you just sick enough so that you'd have to leave Romania. Our doctors were waiting for you. I couldn't tell you the truth because it would have blown the whole operation, and we would have lost our one chance to catch them. Even now, we don't know who put the organization together. He never attends meetings. He's known only as the Controller.'

'And Louis?'

'The doctor was one of them. He was Angel's back-up. He was an expert with explosives. They assigned him here so he could stay close to you. A phoney kidnapping was set up and you were rescued by Mr Charm.' He saw the expression on Mary's face. 'You were lonely and vulnerable, and they worked on that. You weren't the first one to fall for the good doctor.'

Mary remembered something. *The smiling chauffeur. No Romanian is happy, only foreigners. I would hate to have my wife become a widow.*

She said slowly, 'Florian was in on it. He used the flat tyre as an excuse to get me out of the car.'

'We'll have him picked up.'

Something was bothering Mary. 'Mike – why did you kill Louis?'

'I had no choice. The whole point of their plan was to murder you and the children as spectacularly as possible in full public view. Louis knew I was a member of the Committee. When he figured out that I was the one poisoning you, he became suspicious of me. That wasn't the way you were supposed to die. I had to kill him before he exposed me.'

Mary sat there, listening as the pieces of the puzzle fell into place. The man she had distrusted had poisoned her to keep her alive, and the man she thought she loved had saved her for a more dramatic death. She and her children had been used. *I was the Judas goat*, Mary thought. *All the warmth that everyone showed me was phoney. The only one who was real was Stanton Rogers. Or was he –?*

'Stanton –' Mary began. 'Is he –?'

'He's been protective of you all the way,' Colonel McKinney assured her. 'When he thought Mike was the one trying to kill you, he ordered me to arrest him.'

Mary turned to look at Mike. He had been sent over here to protect her, and all the time she had looked on him as the enemy. Her thoughts were in a turmoil.

'Louis never had a wife or children?'

'No.'

Mary remembered something. 'But – I asked Eddie Maltz to check, and he told me that Louis was married and had two daughters.'

Mike and Colonel McKinney exchanged a look.

'He'll be taken care of,' McKinney said. 'I sent him to Frankfurt. I'll have him picked up.'

'Who is Angel?' Mary asked.

Mike answered. 'He's an assassin from South America. He's probably the best in the world. The Committee agreed to pay him five million dollars to kill you.'

Mary listened to the words in disbelief.

Mike went on. 'We know he's in Bucharest. Ordinarily, we'd have everything covered – airports, roads, railway stations – but we don't have a single description of Angel. He uses a dozen different passports. No one has ever talked directly to him. They deal through his mistress, Neusa Muñez. The different groups in the Committee are so compartmentalized that I haven't been able to learn who's been assigned to help him here, or what Angel's plan is.'

'What's to stop him from killing me?'

'Us.' It was Colonel mcKinney talking. 'With the help of the Romanian government, we've taken extraordinary precautions for the party tonight. We've covered every possible contingency.'

'What happens now?' Mary asked.

Mike said carefully, 'That's up to you. Angel was ordered to carry out the contract at your party tonight. We're sure we can catch him, but if you and the children aren't at the party . . .' His voice trailed off.

'Then he won't try anything.'

'Not today. Sooner or later, he'll try again.'

'You're asking me to set myself up as a target.'

Colonel McKinney said, 'You don't have to agree, Madam Ambassador.'

I could end this now. I could go back to Kansas with the children and leave this nightmare behind. I could pick up my life again, go back to teaching, live like a normal human being. No one wants to assassinate school teachers. Angel would forget about me.

She looked up at Mike and Colonel McKinney and said, 'I won't expose my children to danger.'

Colonel McKinney said, 'I can arrange for Beth and Tim to be spirited out of the Residence and taken back here under escort.'

Mary looked at Mike for a long time. Finally she spoke. 'How does a Judas goat dress?'

30

At the Embassy, in Colonel McKinney's office, two dozen Marines were being given their orders.

'I want the Residence guarded like Fort Knox,' Colonel McKinney snapped. 'The Romanians are being cooperative. Ionescu is having his soldiers cordon off the square. No one gets through the line without a pass. We'll have our own checkpoints at every entrance to the Residence. Everyone going in or out will have to pass through a metal detector. The building and grounds will be completely surrounded. We'll have snipers on the roof. Any questions?'

'No, sir.'

'Dismissed.'

There was a tremendous feeling of excitement in the air. Huge spotlights ringed the Residence, lighting up the sky. The crowd was kept moving by a detachment of American MPs and Romanian police. Plainclothesmen mingled with the multitude, looking for anything suspicious. Some of them moved around with trained police dogs sniffing for explosives.

The press coverage was enormous. There were photographers and reporters from a dozen countries. They had all been carefully checked, and their equipment searched before they were allowed to enter the Residence.

'A cockroach couldn't sneak into this place tonight,' the Marine officer in charge of security boasted.

*

In the storage room, the Marine corporal was getting bored watching the person in army fatigues filling up the balloons. He pulled out a cigarette and started to light it.

Angel yelled, 'Put that out!'

The Marine looked up, startled. 'What's the problem? You're filling those with helium, aren't you? Helium doesn't burn.'

'Put it out! Colonel McKinney said no smoking here.'

The Marine grumbled, 'Shit.' He dropped the cigarette and put it out with the sole of his shoe.

Angel watched to make sure there were no sparks left, then turned back to the task of filling each balloon from a different cylinder.

It was true that helium did not burn, but none of the cylinders was filled with helium. The first tank was filled with propane, the second

251

tank with white phosphorus, and the third with an oxygen-acetylene mix. Angel had left just enough helium in each tank the night before to make the balloons rise.

Angel was filling the white balloons with propane, the red balloons with oxygen-acetylene, and the blue balloons with white phosphorus. When the balloons were exploded, the white phosphorus would act as an incendiary for the initial gas discharge, drawing in oxygen so that all breath would be sucked out of the body of everybody within fifty yards. The phosphorus would instantly turn to a hot, searing, molten liquid, falling on everyone in the room. The thermal effect would destroy the lungs and throat, and the blast would flatten an area of a square block. *It's going to be beautiful.*

Angel straightened up and looked at the colourful balloons floating against the ceiling of the storage room. 'I am finished.'

'Okay,' the corporal said. 'Now all we have to do is push these babies out into the ballroom and let the guests have some fun.' The corporal called over four guards. 'Help me get these balloons out there.'

One of the guards opened wide the doors to the ballroom. The room had been decorated with American flags and red, white and blue bunting. At the far end was the raised stand for the band. The ballroom was already crowded with guests helping themselves at the buffet tables set up along both sides of the room.

'It's a lovely room,' Angel said. *In one hour, it will be filled with burnt corpses.* 'Could I take a picture of it?'

The corporal shrugged. 'Why not? Let's go, fellas.'

The Marines pushed past Angel and started shoving the inflated balloons into the ballroom, watching as they floated to the ceiling high above.

'Easy,' Angel warned. 'Easy.'

'Don't worry,' a Marine called. 'We won't break your precious balloons.'

Angel stood in the doorway, staring at the riot of colours ascending in a rising rainbow, and smiled. One thousand of the lethal little beauties nestled against the ceiling. Angel took a camera from a pocket and stepped into the ballroom.

'Hey! You're not allowed in here,' the corporal said.

'I just want to take a picture to show my daughter.'

I'll bet that's some looking daughter, the corporal thought sardonically. 'All right. But make it quick.'

Angel glanced across the room at the entrance. Ambassador Mary Ashley was entering with her two children. Angel grinned. Perfect timing.

When the corporal turned his back, Angel quickly set the camera down under a cloth-covered table, where it could not be seen. The motor-driven automatic timing device was set for a one-hour delay. Everything was ready.

The Marine was approaching.

'I'm finished,' Angel said.

'I'll have you escorted out.'

'Thank you.'

Five minutes later, Angel was outside the Residence, strolling down Alexandru Sahia Street.

In spite of the fact that it was a hot and humid night, the area outside the American embassy Residence had become a madhouse. Police were fighting to keep back the hundreds of curious Romanians who kept arriving. Every light in the Residence had been turned on, and the building blazed against the black night sky.

Before the party began, Mary had taken the children upstairs.

'We have to have a family conference,' she said. She felt she owed them the truth.

They sat listening, wide-eyed, as their mother explained what had been happening, and what might be about to happen.

'I'll see to it that you're in no danger,' Mary said. 'You'll be taken out of here, where you'll be safe.'

'But what about you?' Beth asked. 'Someone is trying to kill you. Can't you come with us?'

'No, darling. Not if we want to catch this man.'

Tim was trying not to cry. 'How do you know they'll catch him?'

Mary thought about that for a moment, and said, 'Because Mike Slade said so. Okay, fellas?'

Beth and Tim looked at each other. They were both white-faced, terrified. Mary's heart went out to them. *They're too young to have to go through this*, she thought. *Anyone is too young to have to go through this.*

She dressed carefully, wondering if she was dressing for her death. She chose a full-length, formal red silk chiffon gown and red silk high-heel sandals. She studied her reflection in the mirror. Her face was pale. *Mirror, mirror, on the wall – am I going to live or die tonight?*

Fifteen minutes later, Mary, Beth and Tim entered the ballroom. They walked across the floor, greeting guests, trying to conceal their nervousness. When they reached the other side of the room, Mary turned to the children. 'You have homework to do,' she said loudly. 'Back to your rooms.'

253

She watched them leave, a lump in her throat, thinking: *I hope to God Mike Slade knows what he's doing.*

There was a loud crash, and Mary jumped. She spun round to see what was happening, her pulse racing. A waiter had dropped a tray and was picking up the broken plates. Mary tried to stop the pounding of her heart. How was Angel planning to assassinate her? She looked around the festive ballroom, but there was no clue.

The moment the children left the ballroom, they were escorted to a service entrance by Colonel McKinney.

He said to the two armed Marines waiting at the door, 'Take them to the Ambassador's office. Don't let them out of your sight.'

Beth held back. 'Is mother really going to be all right?'

'She's going to be just fine,' McKinney promised. And he prayed that he was right.

Mike Slade watched Beth and Tim leave, then went to find Mary.

'The children are on their way. I have to do some checking. I'll be back.'

'Don't leave me.' The words came out before she could stop herself. 'I want to go with you.'

'Why?'

She looked at him and said honestly, 'I feel safer with you.'

Mike grinned. 'Now that's a switch. Come on.'

Mary followed him, staying close behind him. The orchestra had begun playing, and people were dancing. The repertoire was American songs, mostly from Broadway musicals. They played the score from *Oklahoma* and *South Pacific, Annie Get Your Gun*, and *My Fair Lady*. The guests were enjoying themselves tremendously. Those who were not dancing were helping themselves from the silver trays of champagne being offered or from the buffet tables.

The room looked spectacular. Mary raised her head, and there were the balloons, a thousand of them – red, white and blue – floating against the pink ceiling. It was a festive occasion. *If only death were not a part of it*, she thought.

Her nerves were so taut that she was ready to scream. A guest brushed against her, and she braced herself for the prick of a deadly needle. Or was Angel going to shoot her in front of all these people? Or stab her? The suspense of what was about to happen was unbearable. In the midst of the laughing, chattering guests, she felt naked and vulnerable. Angel could be anywhere. He could be watching her this minute.

'Do you think Angel is here now?' Mary asked.

'I don't know,' Mike said. And that was the most frightening thing of all. He saw the expression on her face. 'Look, if you want to leave –'

'No. You said I'm the bait. Without the bait, he won't spring the trap.'

He nodded and squeezed her arm. 'Right.'

Colonel McKinney was approaching. 'We've done a thorough search, Mike. We haven't been able to find a thing. I don't like it.'

'Let's take another look around.' Mike signalled to four armed Marines standing by, and they moved up next to Mary. 'Be right back,' Mike said.

Mary swallowed nervously. 'Please.'

Mike and Colonel McKinney, accompanied by two guards with sniffer dogs, searched every upstairs room in the embassy Residence.

'Nothing,' Mike said.

They talked to a Marine guarding the back staircase.

'Did any strangers come up here?'

'No, sir. It's your average quiet Sunday night.'

Not quite, Mike thought bitterly.

They moved towards a guest room down the hall. An armed Marine was standing guard. He saluted the Colonel and stood aside to let them enter. Corina Socoli was lying on the bed, reading a book in Romanian. Young and beautiful and talented; the Romanian national treasure. Could she be a plant? Could she be helping Angel?

Corina looked up. 'I am sorry I am going to miss the party. It sounds like such fun. Ah, well. I will stay here and finish my book.'

'Do that,' Mike said. He closed the door. 'Let's try the downstairs again.'

They returned to the kitchen.

'What about poison?' Colonel McKinney asked. 'Would he use that?'

Mike shook his head. 'Not photogenic enough. Angel's going for the big bang.'

'Mike, there's no way anyone could get explosives into this place. Our experts have gone over it, the dogs have gone over it – the place is clean. He can't hit us through the roof, because we have fire power up there. It's impossible.'

'There's one way.'

Colonel McKinney looked at Mike. 'How?'

'I don't know. But Angel does.'

They searched the library and the offices again. Nothing. They passed the storage room where the corporal and his men were shoving out the last of the balloons, watching them as they floated to the ceiling.

'Pretty, huh?' the corporal said.

'Yeah.'

They started to walk on. Mike stopped. 'Corporal, where did these balloons come from?'

'From the US air base in Frankfurt, sir.'

Mike indicated the helium cylinders. 'And these?'

'Same place. They were escorted to our warehouse per your instructions, sir.'

Mike said to Colonel McKinney, 'Let's start upstairs again.'

They turned to leave. The corporal said, 'Oh, Colonel – the person you sent forgot to leave a time slip. Is that going to be handled by military payroll or civilian?'

Colonel McKinney frowned. 'What person?'

'The one you authorized to fill the balloons.'

Colonel McKinney shook his head. 'I never – who said I authorized it?'

'Eddie Maltz. He said you –'

Colonel McKinney said, '*Eddie Maltz?* I ordered him to Frankfurt.'

Mike turned to the corporal, his voice urgent. 'What did this man look like?'

'Oh, it wasn't a man, sir. It was a woman. To tell you the truth, I thought she looked weird. Fat and ugly. She had a funny accent. She was pockmarked and had kind of a puffy face.'

Mike said to McKinney, excitedly, 'That sounds like Harry Lantz's description of Neusa Muñez that he gave the Committee.'

The revelation hit them both at the same time.

Mike said slowly, 'Oh, my God! Neusa Muñez is Angel!' He pointed to the cylinders. 'She filled the balloons from these?'

'Yes, sir. It was funny. I lit a cigarette, and she screamed at me to put it out. I said, "Helium doesn't burn," and she said –'

Mike looked up. 'The balloons! The explosives are in the balloons!'

The two men stared at the high ceiling, covered with the spectacular red, white and blue balloons.

'She's using some kind of a remote control device to explode them.' He turned to the corporal. 'How long ago did she leave?'

'I guess about an hour ago.'

Under the table, unseen, the timing device had six minutes left on the dial.

Mike was frantically scanning the huge room. 'She could have put it anywhere. It could go off at any second. We could never find it in time.'

Mary was approaching. Mike turned to her. 'You've got to clear the room. Fast! Make an announcement. It will sound better coming from you. Get everybody outside.'

She was looking at him, bewildered. 'But – why? What's happened?'

'We found our playmate's toy,' Mike said grimly. He pointed. 'Those balloons. They're lethal.'

Mary was looking up at them, horror on her face. 'Can't we take them down?'

Mike snapped, 'There must be a thousand of them. By the time you start pulling them down, one by one –'

Her throat was so dry she could hardly get the words out. 'Mike – I know a way.'

The two men were staring at her.

'The Ambassador's folly. The roof. It slides open.'

Mike tried to control his excitement. 'How does it work?'

'There's a switch that –'

'No,' Mike said. 'Nothing electrical. A spark could set them all off. Can it be done manually?'

'Yes.' The words were tumbling out. 'The roof is divided in half. There's a crank on each side that –' She was talking to herself.

The two men were frantically racing upstairs. When they reached the top floor, they found the door opening onto a loft, and hurried inside. A wooden ladder led to a catwalk above that was used by workmen to clean the ceiling of the ballroom. A crank was fastened to the wall.

'There must be another one on the other side,' Mike said.

He started across the narrow catwalk, pushing his way through the sea of deadly balloons, struggling to keep his balance, trying not to look down at the mob of people far below. A current of air pushed a mass of balloons against him, and he slipped. One foot went off the catwalk. He began to fall. He grabbed the boards as he fell, hanging on. Slowly, he managed to pull himself up. He was soaked in perspiration. He inched his way along the rest of the way. Fastened to the wall was the crank.

'I'm ready,' Mike called to the Colonel. 'Careful. No sudden moves.'

'Right.'

Mike began turning the crank very slowly.

Under the table, the timer was down to two minutes.

Mike could not see Colonel McKinney because of the balloons, but he could hear the sound of the other crank being turned. Slowly, very slowly, the roof started to slide open. A few balloons lifted by the helium drifted into the night air, and as the roof opened farther, more balloons began to escape. Hundreds of them poured through the opening, dancing into the star-filled night, drawing oohs and ahs from the unsuspecting guests below, and the people out in the street.

On the ground floor there were 45 seconds left on the remote control timer. A cluster of balloons caught on the edge of the ceiling, just out of Mike's reach. He strained forward, trying to free them. They swayed, just beyond his fingertips. Carefully, he moved out on the catwalk with nothing to hold onto, and strained to push them free. *Now!*

Mike stood there, watching the last of the balloons escape. They soared higher and higher, painting the velvet night with their vivid colours, and suddenly the sky exploded.

There was a tremendous roar, and the tongues of red and white flames shot high into the air. It was a Fourth of July celebration such as had never been seen before. Below, everyone applauded.

Mike watched, drained, too tired to move. It was over.

The round-up was timed to take place simultaneously, in far-flung corners of the world.

Floyd Baker, the Secretary of State, was in bed with his mistress when the door burst open. Four men came into the room.

'What the hell do you mean by – ?'

One of the men pulled out an identification card. 'FBI, Mr Secretary. You're under arrest.'

Floyd Baker stared at them unbelievingly. 'You must be mad. What's the charge?'

'Treason, Thor.'

General Oliver Brooks, Odin, was having breakfast at his club when two FBI agents walked up to his table and arrested him.

Sir Alex Hyde-White, KBE, MP, Freyr, was being toasted at a parliamentary dinner when the club steward approached him. 'Excuse me, Sir Alex. There are some gentlemen outside who would like a word with you . . .'

*

In Paris, in the Chambre des Députés de la République Française, a deputy, Balder, was called off the floor and arrested by the DGSE.

In the parliament building in New Delhi, the speaker of the Lok Sabha, Vishnu, was bundled into a limousine and taken to jail.

In Rome, the Deputy of the Camera dei Deputati, Tyr, was in a Turkish bath when he was arrested.

The sweep went on:

In Mexico and Albania and Japan, high officials were arrested and

258

held in jails. A member of the Bundestag in West Germany; a deputy in the Nationalrat in Austria; the Vice Chairman of the Presidium of the Soviet Union.

The arrests included the president of a large shipping company, and a powerful union leader. A television evangelist and the head of an oil cartel.

Eddie Maltz was shot while trying to escape.

Pete Connors committed suicide while FBI agents were trying to break down the door to his office.

Mary and Mike Slade were seated in the Bubble Room, receiving reports from around the world.

Mike was on the telephone. 'Vreeland,' he said. 'He's an MP in the South African government.' He replaced the receiver and turned to Mary. 'They've got most of them. Except for the Controller and Neusa Muñez – Angel.'

'No one knew that Angel was a woman?' Mary marvelled.

'No. She had all of us fooled. Lantz described her to the Patriots for Freedom Committee as a fat, ugly moron.'

'What about the Controller?' Mary asked.

'No one ever saw him. He gave orders by telephone. He was a brilliant organizer. The Committee was broken up into small cells, so that one group never knew what the other was doing.'

Angel was furious. In fact, she was more than furious. She was like an enraged animal. The contract had gone wrong somehow, but she had been prepared to make up for it.

She had called the private number in Washington, and using her dull, listless voice, had said, 'Angel say to tell you not to worry. There was som' mistake, but he weel take care of it, meester. They will all die nex' time, and –'

'There won't be a next time,' the voice had exploded. 'Angel bungled it. He's worse than an amateur.'

'Angel tol' me –'

'I don't give a damn what he told you. He's finished. He won't get a cent. Just tell the son-of-a-bitch to keep away. I'll find someone else who knows how to do the job.'

And he had slammed the phone down.

The gringo bastard. No one had ever treated Angel like that and lived to talk about it. Pride was at stake. The man was going to pay. Oh, how he would pay!

*

The private phone in the Bubble Room rang. Mary picked it up. It was Stanton Rogers.

'Mary! You're safe! Are the children all right?'

'We're all fine, Stan.'

'Thank God it's over. Tell me exactly what happened.'

'It was Angel. She tried to blow up the Residence and –'

'You mean *he*.'

'No. Angel is a woman. Her name is Neusa Muñez.'

There was a long, stunned silence. '*Neusa Muñez?* That fat, ugly moron was *Angel?*'

Mary felt a sudden chill go through her. She said slowly, 'That's right, Stan.'

'Is there anything I can do for you, Mary?'

'No. I'm on my way to see the children. I'll talk to you later.'

She replaced the receiver and sat there, dazed.

Mike looked at her. 'What's the matter?'

She turned to him. 'You said that Harry Lantz told only some Committee members what Neusa Muñez looked like?'

'Yes.'

'Stanton Rogers just described her.'

When Angel's plane landed at Dulles Airport, she went to a telephone booth and dialled the Controller's private number.

The familiar voice said, 'Stanton Rogers.'

Two days later, Mike, Colonel McKinney and Mary were seated in the Embassy conference room. An electronics expert had just finished de-bugging it.

'It all fits together now,' Mike said. 'The Controller *had* to be Stanton Rogers, but none of us could see it.'

'But why would he want to kill me?' Mary asked. 'In the beginning, he was *against* my being appointed ambassador. He told me so himself.'

Mike explained. 'Once he realized what you and the children symbolized, everything clicked. After that, he *fought* for you to get the nomination. That's what threw us off the track. He was behind you all the way, seeing to it that you got a build-up in the press, making sure you were seen in all the right places by the right people.'

Mary shuddered. 'Why would he want to get involved with – ?'

'Stanton Rogers never forgave Paul Ellison for being President. He

260

felt cheated. He started out as a liberal, and he married a right-wing reactionary. My guess is that his wife turned him around.'

'Have they found him yet?'

'No. He's disappeared. But he can't hide for very long.'

Stanton Rogers' head was found in a Washington garbage dump two days later. His eyes had been torn out.

31

President Paul Ellison was calling from the White House. 'I'm refusing to accept your resignation.'

'I'm sorry, Mr President, but I can't –'

'Mary, I know how much you've been through, but I'm asking you to remain in your post in Romania.'

I know how much you've been through. Did anyone have any idea? She had been so unbelievably naïve when she arrived, filled with such ideals and high hopes. She was going to be the symbol and spirit of her country. She was going to show the world how wonderful Americans really were; and all the time she had been a cat's-paw. She had been used by her President, her government, by everyone around her. She and her children had been placed in mortal danger. She thought of Edward, and of how he had been murdered, and of Louis and his lies and his death. She thought of the destruction Angel had sown.

I'm not the same person I was when I came here, Mary thought. *I was an innocent. I've grown up the hard way, but I've grown up. I've managed to accomplish something here. I got Hannah Murphy out of prison, and I made our grain deal. I saved the life of Ionescu's son, and I got the Romanians their bank loan. I rescued some Jews.*

'Hello. Are you there?'

'Yes, sir.' She looked across her desk at Mike Slade, who was slouched back in his chair, studying her.

'You've done a truly remarkable job,' the President said. 'We're all terribly proud of you. Have you seen the newspapers?'

She did not give a damn about the newspapers.

'You're the person we need over there. You'll be doing our country a great service, my dear.'

The President was waiting for an answer. Mary was thinking, weighing her decision. *I've become a damned good ambassador, and there's so much more that still has to be done here.*

She said, finally, 'Mr President, if I did agree to stay, I would insist that our country give sanctuary to Corina Socoli.'

'I'm sorry, Mary. I've already explained why we can't do that. It would offend Ionescu and –'

'He'll get over it. I know Ionescu, Mr President. He's using her as a bargaining chip.'

There was a long, thoughtful silence. 'How would you get her out of Romania?'

'An Army cargo plane is due to arrive in the morning. I'll send her out in that.'

There was a pause. 'I see. Very well. I'll square it with State. If that's all – ?'

Mary looked over at Mike Slade again. 'No, sir. There's one thing more. I want Mike Slade to stay here with me. I need him. We make a good team.'

Mike was watching her, a private smile on his lips.

'I'm afraid that's impossible,' the President said firmly. 'I need Slade back here. He already has another assignment.'

Mary sat there, holding the phone, saying nothing.

The President went on. 'We'll send you someone else. You can have your choice. Anyone you want.'

Silence.

'We really do need Mike here, Mary.'

Mary glanced over at Mike again.

The President said, 'Mary? Hello? What is this – some kind of blackmail?'

Mary sat, silently waiting.

Finally, the President said grudgingly, 'Well, I suppose if you really need him, we might spare him for a little while.'

Mary felt her heart lighten. 'Thank you, Mr President. I'll be happy to stay on as Ambassador.'

The President had a final parting shot. 'You're a hell of a negotiator, Madam Ambassador. I have some interesting plans in mind for you when you're finished there. Good luck. And stay out of trouble.'

The line went dead.

Mary slowly replaced the receiver. She looked across at Mike. 'You're going to be staying here. He told me to stay out of trouble.'

Mike Slade grinned. 'He has a nice sense of humour.' He rose and moved towards her. 'Do you remember the day I met you and called you a perfect ten?'

How well she remembered. 'Yes.'

'I was wrong. *Now* you're a perfect ten.'

She felt a warm glow. 'Oh, Mike . . .'

'Since I'm staying on, Madam Ambassador, we'd better talk about the problem we're having with the Romanian Commerce Minister.' He looked into her eyes and said softly, 'Coffee?'

EPILOGUE

Alice Springs, Australia

The chairman was addressing the Committee. 'We have suffered a set-back, but because of the lessons we have learned, our organization will become even stronger. Now it is time to take a vote. Aphrodite?'
'Yes.'
'Athene?'
'Yes.'
'Cybele?'
'Yes.'
'Selene?'
'Considering the horrible murder of our former Controller, shouldn't we wait until – ?'
'Yes, or no, please?'
'No.'
'Nike?'
'Yes.'
'Nemesis?'
'Yes.'
'The motion is carried. Please observe the usual precautions, ladies . . .'

The Sands of Time

To Frances Gordon,
with love.

My special thanks go to Alice Fisher,
whose assistance in helping me research this
novel was invaluable

Grateful acknowledgement is made to Marcelle Bernstein
for use of material from *Nuns*.

Grateful acknowledgement is made for use of
'Gacela of Desperate Love' by Frederico Garcia Lorca
from *Selected Poems of Frederico Garcia Lorca*,
copyright © 1952 by New Directions
Publishing Corporation. Translated by W. S. Merwin.
Reprinted by permission of New Directions
Publishing Corporation.

Grateful acknowledgement is made for use of
the Ernest Hemmingway epigraph to the
New Masses Magazine

Lives of great men all remind us
We can make our lives sublime,
And, departing, leave behind us
Footprints on the Sands of Time.

HENRY WADSWORTH
LONGFELLOW

The dead do not need to rise.

They are a part of the earth now and the earth can never be conquered for the earth endures forever, it will outlive all systems of tyranny. Those who have entered it honourably, and no men entered earth more honourably than those who died in Spain, have already achieved immortality.

ERNEST HEMINGWAY

AUTHOR'S NOTE

This is a work of fiction. And yet . . .

The romantic land of flamenco and Don Quixote and exotic-looking señoritas with tortoise-shell combs in their hair is also the land of Torquemada, the Spanish Inquisition and one of the bloodiest civil wars in history. More than half a million people lost their lives in the battles for power between the Republicans and the rebel Nationalists in Spain. In 1936, between February and June, 269 political murders were committed, and the Nationalists executed Republicans at the rate of a thousand a month, with no mourning permitted. One hundred and sixty churches were burned to the ground, and nuns were removed forcibly from convents, 'as though,' wrote the Duc de Saint-Simon, of an earlier conflict between the Spanish government and the church, 'they were whores in a bawdy house'. Newspaper offices were sacked and strikes and riots were endemic throughout the land. The Civil War ended in a victory for the Nationalists under Franco and, following his death, Spain became a monarchy.

The Civil War, which lasted from 1936 to 1939, may be officially over, but the two Spains that fought it have never been reconciled. Today another war continues to rage in Spain, the guerrilla war fought by the Basques to regain the autonomy they had won under the Republic and lost under the Franco regime. The war is being fought with bombs, bank robberies to finance the bombs, assassinations and riots.

When a member of ETA, a Basque guerrilla underground group, died in a Madrid hospital after being tortured by the police, the nationwide riots that followed led to the resignation of the Director General of Spain's police force, five security chiefs and two hundred senior police officers.

In 1986, in Barcelona, the Basques publicly burned the Spanish flag, and in Pamplona thousands fled in fear when Basque nationalists clashed with police in a series of mutinies that eventually spread across Spain and threatened the stability of the government. The para-military police retaliated by going on a rampage, firing at random at Basques' homes and shops. The terrorism that goes on is more violent than ever.

Dealing with two turbulent weeks in 1976, this is a work of fiction. And yet . . .

271

1

Pamplona, Spain 1976

If the plan goes wrong, we will all die. He went over it again in his mind for the last time, probing, testing, searching for flaws. He could find none. The plan was daring, and it called for careful, split-second timing. If it worked, it would be a spectacular feat, worthy of the great El Cid. If it failed . . .

Well, the time for worrying is past, Jaime Miró thought philosophically. *It's time for action.*

Jaime Miró was a legend, a hero to the Basque people and anathema to the Spanish government. He was six feet tall, with a strong, intelligent face, a muscular body, and brooding dark eyes. Witnesses tended to describe him as taller than he was, darker than he was, fiercer than he was. He was a complex man, a realist who understood the enormous odds against him, a romantic ready to die for what he believed.

Pamplona was a town gone mad. It was the final morning of the running of the bulls, the Fiesta de San Fermín, the annual celebration held from 7 July to the 14th. Thirty thousand visitors had swarmed into the city from all over the world. Some had come merely to watch the dangerous bull-running spectacle, others to prove their manhood by taking part in it, running in front of the charging beasts. All the hotel rooms had long since been taken, and university students from Navarra had bedded down in doorways, bank entrances, cars, the public square, and even the streets and pavements of the town.

The tourists packed the cafés and hotels, watching the noisy, colourful parades of *papier mâché gigantes*, and listening to the music of the marching bands. Members of the parade wore violet cloaks, some with hoods of green, others garnet, and still others wearing golden hoods. Flowing through the streets, the processions looked like rivers of rainbows. Exploding firecrackers running along poles and wires of the tramways added to the noise and general confusion.

The crowd had come to attend the evening bullfights, but the most spectacular event was the *Encierro* – the early morning running of the bulls that would fight later in the day.

Ten minutes before midnight in the darkened streets of the lower part of town, the bulls had been driven from the *corrales de gas*, the reception pens, to run across the river on a bridge to the corral at the

273

bottom of Calle Santo Domingo, where they would be kept for the night. In the morning they would be turned loose to run along the narrow Calle Santo Domingo, penned in the street by wooden barricades at each corner until at the end they would run into the corrals at the Plaza de Hemingway, where they would be held until the afternoon bullfight.

From midnight until 6.00 a.m., the visitors stayed awake, drinking and singing and making love, too excited to sleep. Those who would participate in the running of the bulls wore the red scarves of San Fermin around their throats.

At a quarter to six in the morning, bands started circulating through the streets, playing the stirring music of Navarre. At seven o'clock sharp, a rocket flew into the air to signal that the gates of the corral had been opened. The crowd was filled with feverish anticipation. Moments later a second rocket went up to warn the town that the bulls were running.

What followed was an unforgettable spectacle. First came the sound. It started as a faint, distant ripple on the wind, almost imperceptible, and then it grew louder and louder until it became an explosion of pounding hoofs, and suddenly bursting into view appeared six oxen and six enormous bulls. Each weighing 1,500 pounds, they charged down the Calle Santo Domingo like deadly express trains. Inside the wooden barricades that had been placed at each intersecting street corner to keep the bulls confined to the one street, were hundreds of eager, nervous young men who intended to prove their bravery by facing the maddened animals.

The bulls raced down from the far end of the street, past the Calle Laestrafeta and the Calle de Javier, past *farmacias* and clothing stores and fruit markets, towards the Plaza de Hemingway, and there were cries of '*¡Olé!*' from the frenzied crowd. As the animals charged nearer, a mad scramble began to escape the sharp horns and lethal hoofs. The sudden reality of approaching death made some of the participants run for the safety of doorways and fire escapes. They were followed by taunts of '*cobardón*' – coward. A few in the path of the bulls stumbled and fell and were quickly hauled to safety.

A small boy and his grandfather were standing behind the barricades, both breathless with the excitement of the spectacle taking place only a few feet from them.

'Look at them!' the old man exclaimed. '*¡Magnífico!*'

The little boy shuddered. '*Tengo miedo, abuelo.* I'm afraid.'

The old man put his arm around him. '*Sí*, Manuelo. It is frightening. But wonderful, too. I once ran with the bulls. There's nothing like it. You test yourself against death, and it makes you feel like a man.'

As a rule, it took two minutes for the animals to gallop the 900 yards along the Calle Santo Domingo to the arena, and the moment the bulls were safely in the corral, a third rocket would be sent into the air. On this day, the third rocket did not go off, for an incident occurred that had never happened in Pamplona's 400-year history of the running of the bulls.

As the animals raced down the narrow street, half a dozen men dressed in the colourful costumes of the *feria* shifted the wooden barricades and the bulls found themselves forced off the restricted street and turned loose into the heart of the city. What had a moment before been a happy celebration instantly turned into a nightmare. The frenzied beasts charged into the stunned onlookers. The young boy and his grandfather were among the first to die, knocked down and trampled by the charging bulls. Vicious horns sliced into a baby's pram, killing an infant and sending its mother down to the ground to be crushed. Death was in the air everywhere. The animals crashed into helpless bystanders, knocking down women and children, plunging their long, deadly horns into pedestrians, food stands, statues, sweeping aside everything unlucky enough to be in their path. People were screaming in terror, desperately fighting to get out of the way of the lethal behemoths.

A bright red truck suddenly appeared in the path of the bulls and they turned and charged towards it, down the Calle de Estrella, the street that led to the *cárcel*, Pamplona's prison.

The *cárcel* is a forbidding-looking two-storey stone building with heavily barred windows. There are turrets at each of its four corners, and the red and yellow Spanish flag flies over the door. A stone gate leads to a small courtyard. The second floor of the building consists of a row of cells that holds prisoners condemned to die.

Inside the prison, a heavyset guard in the uniform of the *policía armada* was leading a priest garbed in plain black robes along the second floor corridor. The policeman carried a sub-machine-gun.

Noting the questioning look in the priest's eye at the sight of the weapon, the guard said, 'One can't be too careful here, Father. We have the scum of the earth on this floor.'

The guard directed the priest to walk through a metal detector very much like those used at airports.

'I'm sorry, Father, but the rules –'

'Of course, my son.'

As the priest passed through the security portal, a shrieking siren cut through the corridor. The guard instinctively tightened his grip on his weapon.

The priest turned and smiled back at the guard.

'My mistake,' he said as he removed a heavy metal cross that hung from his neck on a silver chain and handed it to the guard. This time as he passed through, the machine was silent. The guard handed the cross back to the priest and the two continued their journey deeper into the bowels of the prison.

The stench in the corridor near the cells was overpowering.

The guard was in a philosophical mood. 'You know, you're wasting your time here, Father. These animals have no souls to save.'

'Still, we must try, my son.'

The guard shook his head. 'I tell you the gates of hell are waiting to welcome both of them.'

The priest looked at the guard in surprise. 'Both of them? I was told there were three who needed confession.'

The guard shrugged. 'We saved you some time. Zamora died in the infirmary this morning. Heart attack.'

The men had reached the two farthest cells.

'Here we are, Father.'

The guard unlocked a cell door, then stepped cautiously back as the priest entered the cell. The guard locked the door again, and stood in the corridor, alert for any sign of trouble.

The priest went to the figure lying on the dirty prison cot. 'Your name, my son?'

'Ricardo Mellado.'

The priest stared down at him. It was difficult to tell what the man looked like. His face was swollen and raw. His eyes were almost shut. Through thick lips, he said, 'I'm glad you were able to come, Father.'

The priest replied, 'Your salvation is the church's duty, my son.'

'They are going to hang me this morning?'

The priest patted his shoulder gently. 'You have been sentenced to die by the garrotte.'

Ricardo Mellado stared up at him. 'No!'

'I'm sorry. The orders were given by the Prime Minister himself.'

The priest placed his hand on the prisoner's head and intoned: '*Dime tus pecados . . .*'

Ricardo Mellado said, 'I have sinned greatly in thought, word and deed, and I repent all my sins with all my heart.'

'*Ruego a nuestro Padre celestial por la salvación de tu alma. In el nombre del Padre, del Hijo y del Espiritu Santo . . .*'

The guard listening outside the cell thought to himself: *What a stupid waste of time. God will spit in that one's eye.*

The priest was finished. '*Adiós*, my son. May God receive your soul in peace.'

The priest moved to the cell door and the guard unlocked it, then stepped back, keeping his gun aimed at the prisoner. When the door was locked again, the guard moved to the adjoining cell and opened the door.

'He's all yours, Father.'

The priest stepped into the second cell. The man inside had also been badly beaten. The priest looked at him a long moment. 'What is your name, my son?'

'Felix Carpio.' He was a husky, bearded man with a fresh, livid scar on his cheek that the beard failed to conceal. 'I'm not afraid to die, Father.'

'That is well, my son. In the end none of us is spared.'

As the priest began to hear Carpio's confession, waves of distant sound, at first muffled, then growing louder, began to reverberate through the building. It was the thunder of pounding hoofs and the screams of the running mob. The guard listened, startled. The sounds were rapidly moving closer.

'You'd better hurry, Father. Something peculiar is happening outside.'

'I'm finished.'

The guard quickly unlocked the cell door. The priest stepped out into the corridor and the guard locked the door behind him. There was the sound of a loud crash from the front of the prison. The guard turned to peer out the narrow, barred window.

'What the hell was that noise?'

The priest said, 'It sounded as though someone wishes an audience with us. May I borrow that?'

'Borrow what?'

'Your weapon, *por favor*.'

As the priest spoke, he stepped close to the guard. He silently removed the top of the large cross that hung around his neck, revealing a long, wicked-looking stiletto. In one lightning move he plunged the knife into the guard's chest.

'You see, my son,' Jaime Miró said, as he pulled the sub-machine-gun from the dying guard's hands, 'God and I decided that you no longer have need of this weapon.'

The guard slumped to the cement floor. Jaime Miró took the keys from the body and swiftly opened the two cell doors. The sounds from the street were getting louder.

'Let's move,' Jaime commanded.

Ricardo Mellado picked up the machine gun. 'You make a damned good priest. You almost convinced me.' He tried to smile with his swollen mouth.

'They really worked you two over, didn't they? Don't worry. They'll pay for it.'

Jaime Miró put his arms around the two men and helped them down the corridor.

'What happened to Zamora?'

'The guards beat him to death. We could hear his screams. They took him off to the infirmary and said he died of a heart attack.'

Ahead of them was a locked iron door.

'Wait here,' Jaime Miró said.

He approached the door and said to the guard on the other side, 'I'm finished here.'

The guard unlocked the door. 'You'd better hurry, Father. There's some kind of disturbance going on out –' He never finished his sentence. As Jaime's knife went into him, blood welled out of the guard's mouth.

Jaime motioned to the two men. 'Come on.'

Felix Carpio picked up the guard's gun, and they started downstairs. The scene outside was chaos. The police were running around frantically trying to see what was happening and to deal with the crowds of screaming people in the courtyard who were scrambling to escape the maddened bulls. One of the bulls had charged into the front of the building, smashing the stone entrance. Another was tearing into the body of a uniformed guard on the ground. The red truck was in the courtyard, its motor running. In the confusion, the three men went almost unnoticed. Those who did see them were too busy saving themselves to do anything about them.

Without a word, Jaime and his men jumped into the back of the truck and it sped off, scattering frantic pedestrians through the crowded streets. The *guardia civil*, the paramilitary rural police decked out in green uniforms and black patent leather hats, were trying in vain to control the hysterical mob. The *policia armada*, stationed in provincial capitals, were also helpless in the face of the mad spectacle. People were struggling to flee in every direction, desperately trying to avoid the enraged bulls. The danger lay less with the bulls and more with the people themselves as they trampled one another in their eagerness to escape, and old men and women were pushed aside under the feet of the running mob.

Jaime stared in dismay at the stunning spectacle. 'It wasn't planned for it to happen this way!' he exclaimed. He stared helplessly at the carnage that was being wreaked, but there was nothing he could do to stop it. He closed his eyes to shut out the sight.

The truck reached the outskirts of Pamplona and headed south, leaving behind the noise and confusion of the rioting.

'Where are we going, Jaime?' Ricardo Mellado asked.

'There's a safe house outside Torré. We'll stay there until dark and then move on.'

Felix Carpio was wincing with pain.

Jaime Miró watched him, his face filled with compassion. 'We'll be there soon, my friend,' he said gently.

He was unable to get the terrible scene at Pamplona out of his mind.

Thirty minutes later they approached the little village of Torré, and skirted it to drive to an isolated house in the mountains above the village. Jaime Miró helped the two men out of the back of the red truck.

'You'll be picked up at midnight,' the driver said.

'Have them bring a doctor,' Jaime replied. 'And get rid of the truck.'

The three of them entered the house. It was a farmhouse, simple and comfortable, with a fireplace in the living room and a beamed ceiling. There was a note on the table. Jaime Miró read it and smiled at the welcoming phrase: *Mi casa es su casa*. On the bar were bottles of wine. Jaime Miró poured drinks.

Ricardo Mellado said, 'There are no words to thank you, my friend. Here's to you.'

Jaime raised his glass. 'Here's to freedom.'

There was the sudden chirp of a canary in a cage. Jaime Miró walked over to it, and he watched its wild fluttering for a moment. Then he opened the cage, gently lifted the bird out and carried it to an open window.

'Fly away, *pajarito*,' he said softly. 'All living creatures should be free.'

2

Madrid

Prime Minister Leopoldo Martinez was in a rage. He was a small, bespectacled man, and his whole body shook as he talked. 'Jaime Miró must be stopped,' he cried. His voice was high and shrill. 'Do you understand me?' He glared at the half dozen men gathered in the room. 'We're looking for one terrorist, and the whole army and police force are unable to find him.'

The meeting was taking place at Moncloa Palace, where the Prime Minister lived and worked, five kilometres from the centre of Madrid, on the Carretera de Galicia, a highway with no identifying signs. The building itself was green brick, with wrought iron balconies, green window shades, and guard towers at each corner.

It was a hot, dry day, and through the windows, as far as the eye could see, columns of heat waves rose like battalions of ghostly soldiers.

'Yesterday Miró turned Pamplona into a battleground.' Martinez slammed a fist down on his desk. 'He murdered two prison guards and smuggled two of his terrorists out of prison. Many innocent people were killed by the bulls he let loose.'

For a moment no one said anything.

When the Prime Minister had taken office, he had declared, smugly, 'My first act will be to put a stop to these separatist groups. Madrid is the great unifier. It transforms Andalusians, Basques, Catalans and Galicians into Spaniards.'

He had been unduly optimistic. The fiercely independent Basques had other ideas, and the wave of bombings, bank robberies and demonstrations by terrorists of the ETA organization, Euzkadi ta Azkatasuna, had continued unabated.

The man at Martinez's right said quietly, 'I'll find him.'

The speaker was Colonel Ramón Acoca, head of the GOE, the *Grupo de Operaciones Especiales*, formed to pursue Basque terrorists. Acoca was a giant, in his middle sixties, with a scarred face and cold, obsidian eyes. He had been a young officer under Francisco Franco during the Civil War, and he was still fanatically devoted to Franco's philosophy, 'We are responsible only to God and to history.'

Acoca was a brilliant officer, and he had been one of Franco's must trusted aides. The Colonel missed the iron-fisted discipline, the swift punishment of those who questioned or disobeyed the law. He had gone through the turmoil of the Civil War, with its Nationalist alliance of Monarchists, rebel generals, landowners, church hierarchy and the fascist Falangists on one side, and the Republican government forces, including Socialists, Communists, liberals and Basque and Catalan separatists on the other. It had been a terrible time of destruction and killing in a madness that pulled in men and war matériel from a dozen countries and left a horrifying death toll. And now the Basques were fighting and killing again.

Colonel Acoca headed an efficient, ruthless cadre of anti-terrorists. His men worked underground, wore disguises and were neither publicized nor photographed for fear of retaliation.

If anyone can stop Jaime Miró, Colonel Acoca can, the Prime Minister thought. But there was a catch: *Who's going to be the one to stop Colonel Acoca?*

Putting the Colonel in charge had not been the Prime Minister's idea. He had received a phone call in the middle of the night on his private line. He recognized the voice immediately.

'We are greatly disturbed by the activities of Jaime Miró and his terrorists. We suggest that you put Colonel Ramón Acoca in charge of the GOE. Is that clear?'

'Yes, sir. It will be taken care of immediately.'

The line went dead.

The voice belonged to a member of the OPUS MUNDO. The organization was a secret cabal that included bankers, lawyers, heads of powerful corporations and government ministers. It was rumoured to have enormous funds at its disposal, but where the money came from or how it was used or manipulated was a mystery. It was not considered healthy to ask too many questions about it.

The Prime Minister had placed Colonel Acoca in charge, as he had been instructed to, but the giant had turned out to be an uncontrollable fanatic. His GOE had created a reign of terror. The Prime Minister thought of the Basque rebels Acoca's men had caught near Pamplona. They had been convicted and sentenced to hang. It was Colonel Acoca who had insisted that they be executed by the barbaric *garrotte vil*, the iron collar fitted with a spike which gradually tightened, eventually cracked the vertebra and severed the victim's spinal cord.

Jaime Miró had become an obsession with Colonel Acoca.

'I want his head,' Colonel Acoca said. 'Cut off his head and the Basque movement dies.'

An exaggeration, the Prime Minister felt, although he had to admit that there was a core of truth in it. Jaime Miró was a charismatic leader, fanatical about his cause, and therefore dangerous.

But in his own way, the Prime Minister thought, *Colonel Acoca is just as dangerous.*

Primo Casado, the Director General de Seguridad, was speaking.

'Your Excellency, no one could have foreseen what happened in Pamplona. Jaime Miró is –'

'I *know* what he is,' the Prime Minister snapped. 'I want to know *where* he is.' He turned to Colonel Acoca.

'I'm on his trail,' the Colonel said. His voice chilled the room. 'I would like to remind Your Excellency that we are not fighting just one man. We are fighting the Basque people. They give Jaime Miró and his terrorists food and weapons and shelter. The man is a hero to them. But do not worry. Soon he will be a hanging hero. After I give him a fair trial, of course.'

Not we. I. The Prime Minister wondered whether the others had noticed. *Yes*, he thought nervously. *Something will have to be done about the Colonel soon.*

The Prime Minister got to his feet. 'That will be all for now, gentlemen.'

The men rose to leave. All except Colonel Acoca. He stayed.

Leopoldo Martinez began to pace. 'Damn the Basques. Why can't they be satisfied just to be Spaniards? What more do they want?'

'They're greedy for power,' Acoca said. 'They want autonomy, their own language and their flag –'

'No. Not as long as I hold this office. I'm not going to permit them to tear pieces out of Spain. The government will tell them what they can have and what they can't have. They're nothing but rabble who . . .'

An aide came into the room. 'Excuse me, Your Excellency,' he said apologetically. 'Bishop Ibanez has arrived.'

'Send him in.'

The Colonel's eyes narrowed. 'You can be sure the church is behind all this. It's time we taught them a lesson.'

The Church is one of the great ironies of our history, Colonel Acoca thought bitterly.

In the beginning of the Civil War, the Catholic Church had been on the side of the Nationalist forces. The Pope backed Generalissimo Franco, and in so doing allowed him to proclaim that he was fighting on the side of God. But when the Basque churches and monasteries and priests were attacked, the Church withdrew its support.

'You must give the Basques and the Catalans more freedom,' the Church had demanded. 'And you must stop executing Basque priests.'

Generalissimo Franco had been furious. How dare the Church try to dictate to the government?

A war of attrition began. More churches and monasteries were attacked by Franco's forces. Nuns and priests were murdered. Bishops were placed under house arrest, and priests all over Spain were fined for giving sermons that the government considered seditious. It was only when the Church threatened Franco with excommunication that he stopped his attacks.

282

The goddamned Church! Acoca thought. With Franco dead it was interfering again.

He turned to the Prime Minister. 'It's time the bishop is told who's running Spain.'

Bishop Calvo Ibanez was a thin, frail-looking man with a cloud of white hair swirling around his head. He peered at the two men through his pince-nez spectacles.

'*Buenas tardes.*'

Colonel Acoca felt the bile rise in his throat. The very sight of clergymen made him ill. They were Judas goats leading their stupid lambs to slaughter.

The bishop stood there, waiting for an invitation to sit down. It did not come. Nor was he introduced to the Colonel. It was a deliberate slight.

The Prime Minister looked to Acoca for direction.

Acoca said curtly, 'Some disturbing news has been brought to our attention. Basque rebels are reported to be holding meetings in Catholic monasteries. It has also been reported that the Church is allowing monasteries and convents to store arms for the rebels.' There was steel in his voice. 'When you help the enemies of Spain, you *become* an enemy of Spain.'

Bishop Ibanez stared at him for a moment, then turned to Leopoldo Martinez. 'Your Excellency, with due respect, we are all children of Spain. The Basques are not your enemy. All they ask is the freedom to –'

'They don't ask,' Acoca roared. 'They demand! They go around the country pillaging, robbing banks and killing policemen, and you dare to say they are not our enemies?'

'I admit that there have been inexcusable excesses. But sometimes in fighting for what one believes –'

'They don't believe in anything but themselves. They care nothing about Spain. It is as one of our great writers said, "No one in Spain is concerned about the common good. Each group is concerned only with itself. The Church, the Basques, the Catalans. Each one says fuck the others."'

The bishop was aware that Colonel Acoca had misquoted Ortega y Gasset. The full quote had included the army and the government; but he wisely said nothing. He turned to the Prime Minister again, hoping for a more rational discussion.

'Your Excellency, the Catholic Church –'

The Prime Minister felt that Acoca had pushed far enough. 'Don't misunderstand us, Bishop. In principle, of course, this government is behind the Catholic Church one hundred per cent.'

Colonel Acoca spoke up again. 'But we cannot permit your churches and monasteries and convents to be used against us. If you continue to

283

allow the Basques to store arms in them and to hold meetings, you will have to take the consequences.'

'I am sure that the reports that you have received are erroneous,' the bishop said smoothly. 'However, I shall certainly investigate at once.'

The Prime Minister murmured, 'Thank you, Bishop. That will be all.'

Prime Minister Martinez and Colonel Acoca watched him depart.

'What do you think?' Martinez asked.

'He knows what's going on.'

The Prime Minister sighed. *I have enough problems right now without stirring up trouble with the Church.*

'If the Church is for the Basques, then it is against us.' Colonel Acoca's voice hardened. 'I would like your permission to teach the bishop a lesson.'

The Prime Minister was stopped by the look of fanaticism in the man's eyes. He became cautious. 'Have you really had reports that the churches are aiding the rebels?'

'Of course, Excellency.'

There was no way of determining if the man was telling the truth. The Prime Minister knew how much Acoca hated the Church. But it might be good to let the Church have a taste of the whip, providing Colonel Acoca did not go too far. Prime Minister Martinez stood there thoughtfully.

It was Acoca who broke the silence. 'If the churches are sheltering terrorists, then the churches must be punished.'

Reluctantly, the Prime Minister nodded. 'Where will you start?'

'Jaime Miró and his men were seen in Ávila yesterday. They are probably hiding at the convent there.'

The Prime Minister made up his mind. 'Search it,' he said.

That decision set off a chain of events that was to rock all of Spain and shock the world.

3

Ávila

The silence was like a gentle snowfall, soft and hushed, as soothing as the whisper of a summer wind, as quiet as the passage of stars. The Cistercian Convent of the Strict Observance lay outside the walled town of Ávila, the highest city in Spain, 112 kilometres north-west of Madrid. The convent had been built for silence. The rules had been adopted in 1601 and remained unchanged through the centuries: liturgy, spiritual exercise, strict enclosure, penance and silence. Always the silence.

The convent was a simple, four-sided group of rough stone buildings around a cloister dominated by the church. Around the central court the open arches allowed the light to pour in on the broad flagstones of the floor where the nuns glided noiselessly by. There were forty nuns at the convent, praying in the church and living in the cloister. The convent at Ávila was one of seven left in Spain, a survivor out of hundreds that had been destroyed by the Civil War in one of the periodic anti-Church movements that took place in Spain over the centuries.

The Cistercian Convent of the Strict Observance was devoted solely to a life of prayer. It was a place without seasons or time and those who entered were forever removed from the outside world. The Cistercian life was contemplative and penitential; the divine office was recited daily and enclosure was complete and permanent.

All the sisters dressed identically, and their clothing, like everything else in the convent, was touched by the symbolism of centuries. The *capucha*, the cloak and hood, symbolized innocence and simplicity, the linen tunic the renouncement of the works of the world, and mortification, the scapular, the small squares of woollen cloth worn over the shoulders, the willingness to labour. A wimple, a covering of linen laid in plaits over the head and around the chin, sides of the face and neck, completed the habit.

Inside the walls of the convent was a system of internal passageways and staircases linking the dining room, community room, the cells and the chapel, and everywhere there was an atmosphere of cold, clean spaciousness. Thick-paned latticed windows overlooked a high-walled garden. Every window was covered with iron bars and was above the line of vision, so that there would be no outside distractions. The refectory, the dining hall, was long and austere, its windows shuttered and curtained. The candles in the ancient candlesticks cast evocative shadows on the ceilings and walls.

In four hundred years nothing inside the walls of the convent had changed, except the faces. The sisters had no personal possessions, for they desired to be poor, emulating the poverty of Christ. The church itself was bare of ornaments, save for a priceless solid gold cross that had been a long-ago gift from a wealthy postulant. Because it was so out of keeping with the austerity of the order, it was kept hidden away in a cabinet in the refectory. A plain, wooden cross hung at the altar of the church.

The women who shared their lives with the Lord lived together, worked together, ate together and prayed together, yet they never touched and never spoke. The only exception permitted was when they heard mass or when the Reverend Mother Prioress Betina addressed them in the privacy of her office. Even then, an ancient sign language was used as much as possible.

The Reverend Mother was a *religeuse* in her seventies, a bright-faced robin of a woman, cheerful and energetic, who gloried in the peace and joy of convent life, and of a life devoted to God. Fiercely protective of her nuns, she felt more pain when it was necessary to enforce discipline, than did the one being punished.

The nuns walked through the cloisters and corridors with downcast eyes, hands folded in their sleeves at breast level, passing and re-passing their sisters without a word or sign of recognition. The only voice of the convent was its bells – the bells that Victor Hugo called 'the Opera of the Steeples'.

The sisters came from disparate backgrounds and from many different countries. Their families were aristocrats, farmers, soldiers . . . They had come to the convent as rich and poor, educated and ignorant, miserable and exalted, but now they were one in the eyes of God, united in their desire for eternal marriage to Jesus.

The living conditions in the convent were spartan. In winter the cold was knifing, and a chill, pale light filtered in through leaded windows. The nuns slept fully dressed on pallets of straw, covered with rough woollen sheets, each in her tiny cell, furnished only with a straight-backed wooden chair. There was no washstand. A small earthenware jug and basin stood in a corner on the floor. No nun was ever permitted to enter the cell of another, except for the Reverend Mother Betina. There was no recreation of any kind, only work and prayers. There were work areas for knitting, book binding, weaving and making bread.

There were eight hours of prayer each day: Matins, Lauds, Prime, Terce, Sext, None, Vespers and Compline. Besides these there were other devotions: benedictions, hymns and litanies.

Matins were said when half the world was asleep and the other half was absorbed in sin.

Lauds, the office of daybreak, followed Matins, and the rising sun was hailed as the figure of Christ triumphant and glorified.

Prime was the church's morning prayer, asking for the blessings on the work of the day.

Terce was at nine o'clock in the morning, consecrated by St Augustine to the Holy Spirit.

Sext was at 11.30 a.m., evoked to quench the heat of human passions.

None was silently recited at three in the afternoon, the hour of Christ's death.

Vespers was the evening service of the church, as Lauds was her daybreak prayer.

Compline was the completion of the Little Hours of the day. A form of night prayers, a preparation for death as well as sleep, ending the day on a note of loving submission: *Manus tuas, domine, commendo spiritum meum. Redemisti nos, domine, deus, veritatis.*

In some of the other orders, flagellation had been stopped, but in the cloistered Cistercian convents and monasteries it survived. At least once a week, and sometimes every day, the nuns punished their bodies with the Discipline, a twelve-inch long whip of thin waxed cord with six knotted tails that brought agonizing pain, and was used to lash the back, legs and buttocks. Bernard of Clairvaux, the ascetic abbot of the Cistercians, had admonished: 'The body of Christ is crushed . . . our bodies must be conformed to the likeness of our Lord's wounded body.'

It was a life more austere than in any prison, yet the inmates lived in an ecstasy such as they had never known in the outside world. They had renounced physical love, possessions and freedom of choice, but in giving up those things they had also renounced greed and competition, hatred and envy, and all the pressures and temptations that the outside world imposed. Inside the convent reigned an all-pervading peace and the ineffable sense of joy at being one with God. There was an indescribable serenity within the walls of the convent and in the hearts of those who lived there. If the convent was a prison, it was a prison in God's Eden, with the knowledge of a happy eternity for those who had freely chosen to be there and to remain there.

Sister Lucia was awakened by the tolling of the convent bell. She opened her eyes, startled and disoriented for an instant. The little cell she slept in was dismally black. The sound of the bell told her that it was 3.00 a.m., when the office of vigils began, while the world was still in darkness.

Shit! This routine is going to kill me, Sister Lucia thought.

She lay back on her tiny, uncomfortable cot, desperate for a cigarette. Reluctantly, she dragged herself out of bed. The heavy habit she wore and slept in rubbed against her sensitive skin like sandpaper. She thought of all the beautiful designer gowns hanging in her apartment in Rome and at her chalet in Gstaad. The Valentinos and Armanis and Giannis.

From outside her cell Sister Lucia could hear the soft, swishing movement of the nuns as they gathered in the passage. Carelessly, she made up her bed and stepped out into the long corridor, where the nuns were lining up, eyes downcast. Slowly, they all began to move towards the chapel.

They look like a bunch of penguins, Sister Lucia thought. It was beyond her comprehension why these women had deliberately thrown away their lives, giving up sex, pretty clothes and gourmet food. *Without those things, what reason is there to go on living? And the goddamned rules!*

When Sister Lucia had first entered the convent, the Reverend Mother had said to her, 'You must walk with your head bowed. Keep your hands folded under your habit. Take short steps. Walk slowly. You must never make eye contact with any of the other sisters, or even glance at them. You may not speak. Your ears are to hear only God's words.'

'Yes, Reverend Mother.'

For the next month Lucia took instruction.

'Those who come here come not to join others, but to dwell alone with God, *solitariamente*. Solitude of spirit is essential to a union with God. It is safeguarded by the rules of silence.'

'Yes, Reverend Mother.'

'You must always obey the silence of the eyes. Looking into the eyes of others would distract you with useless images.'

'Yes, Reverend Mother.'

'The first lesson you will learn here will be to rectify the past, to purge out old habits and worldly inclinations, to blot out every image of the past. You will do purifying penance and mortification to strip yourself of self-will and self-love. It is not enough for us to be sorry for our past offences. Once we discover the infinite beauty and holiness of God, we want to make up not only for our own sins, but for every sin that has ever been committed.

'Yes, Reverend Mother.'

'You must struggle with sensuality, what John of the Cross called, "the night of the senses".'

'Yes, Reverend Mother.'

'Each nun lives in silence and in solitude, as though she were already in heaven. In this pure, precious silence for which she hungers, she is able to listen to the infinite silence and possess God.'

At the end of the first month, Lucia took her initial vows. On the day of the ceremony she had her hair shorn. It was a traumatic experience. The Reverend Mother Prioress performed the act herself. She summoned Lucia into her office and motioned for her to sit down. She stepped behind her, and before Lucia knew what was happening, she heard the snip of scissors and felt something tugging at her hair. She started to protest, but she suddenly realized that what was happening could only improve her disguise. *I can always let it grow back later*, Lucia thought. *Meanwhile, I'm going to look like a plucked chicken.*

When Lucia returned to the grim cubicle she had been assigned, she thought: *This place is a snake pit.* The floor consisted of bare boards. The pallet and the hard-backed chair took up most of the room. She was desperate to get hold of a newspaper. *Fat chance*, she thought. In this place they had never heard of newspapers, let alone radio or television. There were no links to the outside world at all.

But what got on Lucia's nerves most of all was the unnatural silence. The only communication was through hand signals, and learning those drove her crazy. When she needed a broom, she was taught to move her outstretched right hand from right to left, as though sweeping. When the Reverend Mother was displeased, she brought together the tips of her little fingers three times in front of her body, the other fingers pressing into her palm. When Lucia was slow in doing her work, the Reverend Mother pressed the palm of her right hand against her left shoulder. To reprimand Lucia, she scratched her own cheek near her right ear with all the fingers of her right hand in a downward motion.

For Christ's sake, Lucia thought, *it looks like she's scratching a flea bite.*

They had reached the chapel. The nuns said a silent mass, the sequence from the age-old Sanctus to the Pater Noster, but Sister Lucia's thoughts were on more important things than God.

In another month or two, when the police stop looking for me, I'll be out of this madhouse.

After morning prayers, Sister Lucia marched with the others to the dining room, surreptitiously breaking the rule, as she did every day, by studying their faces. It was her only entertainment. It was incredible to think that none of them knew what the other sisters looked like.

She was fascinated by the faces of the nuns. Some were old, some were young, some pretty, some ugly. She could not understand why they all seemed so happy. There were three faces that Lucia found particularly interesting. One was Sister Teresa, a woman who appeared to be in her sixties. She was far from beautiful, and yet there was a spirituality about her that gave her an almost unearthly loveliness. She seemed always to be smiling inwardly, as though she carried some wonderful secret within herself.

Another nun that Lucia found fascinating was Sister Graciela. She was a stunningly beautiful woman in her early thirties. She had olive skin, exquisite features, and eyes that were luminous black pools.

She could have been a film star, Lucia thought. *What's her story? Why would she bury herself in a place like this?*

The third nun who captured Lucia's interest was Sister Megan. Blue-eyed, blonde eyebrows and lashes. She was in her late twenties and had a fresh, open faced look.

What is she doing here? What are any of these women doing here? They're locked up behind these walls, given a tiny cell to sleep in, rotten food, eight hours of prayers, hard work and too little sleep. They must be pazzo – all of them.

She was better off than they were, because they were stuck here for the rest of their lives, while she would be out of here in a month or two. *Maybe three*, Lucia thought. *This is a perfect hiding place. I'd be a fool to rush away. In a few months, the police will decide that I'm dead. When I leave here and get my money out of Switzerland, maybe I'll write a book about this crazy place.*

A few days earlier Sister Lucia had been sent by the Reverend Mother to the office to retrieve a paper and while there she had taken the opportunity to start looking through the files. Unfortunately she had been caught in the act of snooping.

'You will do penance by using the Discipline,' the Mother Prioress Betina signalled her.

Sister Lucia bowed her head meekly and signalled, 'Yes, Reverend Mother.'

Lucia returned to her cell, and minutes later the nuns walking through the corridor heard the awful sound of the whip as it whistled through the air and fell again and again. What they could not know was that Sister Lucia was whipping the bed.

These freaks may be into S & M, but not yours truly.

Now they were seated in the refectory, forty nuns at two long tables. The Cistercian diet was strictly vegetarian. Because the body craved meat, it was forbidden. Long before dawn, a cup of tea or coffee and a few ounces of dry bread were served. The principal meal was taken at 11.00 a.m., and consisted of a thin soup, a few vegetables and occasionally a piece of fruit.

We are not here to please our bodies, but to please God.

I wouldn't feed this breakfast to my cat, Sister Lucia thought. *I've been here two months, and I'll bet I've lost ten pounds. It's God's version of a health farm.*

When breakfast was ended, two nuns brought washing-up bowls to each end of the table and set them down. The sisters seated about the table sent their plates to the sister who had the bowl. She washed each plate, dried it on a towel and returned it to its owner. The water got darker and greasier.

And they're going to live like this for the rest of their lives, Sister Lucia thought disgustedly. *Oh, well. I can't complain. At least it's better than a life sentence in prison . . .*

She would have given her immortal soul for a cigarette.

Five hundred yards down the road, Colonel Ramón Acoca and two dozen carefully selected men from the GOE, the *Grupo de Operaciones Especiales*, were preparing to attack the convent.

4

Colonel Ramón Acoca had the instincts of a hunter. He loved the chase, but it was the kill that gave him a deep visceral satisfaction. He had once confided to a friend, 'I have an orgasm when I kill. It doesn't matter whether it's a deer or a rabbit or a man – there's something about taking a life that makes you feel like God.'

Acoca had been in military intelligence, and he had quickly achieved a reputation for being brilliant. He was fearless, ruthless and intelligent, and the combination brought him to the attention of one of General Franco's aides.

Acoca had joined Franco's staff as a lieutenant, and in less than three years he had risen to the rank of colonel, an almost unheard-of feat. He was put in charge of the Falangists, the special group used to terrorize those who opposed Franco.

It was during the war that Acoca had been sent for by a member of the OPUS MUNDO.

'I want you to understand that we're speaking to you with the permission of General Franco.'

'Yes, sir.'

'We've been watching you, Colonel. We are pleased with what we see.'

'Thank you, sir.'

'From time to time we have certain assignments that are – shall we say – very confidential. And very dangerous.'

'I understand, sir.'

'We have many enemies. People who don't understand the importance of the work we're doing.'

'Yes, sir.'

'Sometimes they interfere with us. We can't permit that to happen.'

'No, sir.'

'I believe we could use a man like you, Colonel. I think we understand each other.'

'Yes, sir. I'd be honoured to be of service.'

'We would like you to remain in the army. That will be valuable to us. But from time to time, we will have you assigned to these special projects.'

'Thank you, sir.'

'You are never to speak of this.'

'No, sir.'

The man behind the desk had made Acoca nervous. There was something overpoweringly frightening about him.

In time, Colonel Acoca was called upon to handle half a dozen assignments for the OPUS MUNDO. As he had been told, they were all dangerous. And very confidential.

On one of the missions Acoca had met a lovely young girl from a fine family. Up to then, all of his women had been whores or camp followers, and Acoca had treated them with savage contempt. Some of the women had genuinely fallen in love with him, attracted by his strength. He reserved the worst treatment for them.

But Susana Cerredilla belonged to a different world. Her father was a professor at Madrid University, and Susana's mother was a lawyer. Susana was seventeen years old, and she had the body of a woman and the angelic face of a Madonna. Ramón Acoca had never met anyone like this woman-child. Her gentle vulnerability brought out in him a tenderness he had not known he was capable of. He fell madly in love with her, and for reasons which neither her parents nor Acoca understood, she fell in love with him.

On their honeymoon, it was as though Acoca had never known another woman. He had known lust, but the combination of love and passion was something he had never previously experienced.

Three months after they were married, Susana informed him that she was pregnant. Acoca was wildly excited. To add to their joy, he was assigned to the beautiful little village of Castilbanca, in the Basque country. It was in the autumn of 1936 when the fighting between the Republicans and Nationalists was at its fiercest.

On a peaceful Sunday morning, Ramón Acoca and his bride were having coffee in the village plaza when the square suddenly filled with Basque demonstrators.

'I want you to go home,' Acoca said. 'There's going to be trouble.'

'But you – ?'

'Please. I'll be all right.'

The demonstrators were beginning to get out of hand.

With relief, Ramón Acoca watched his bride walk away from the crowd towards a convent at the far end of the square. And as she reached it, the door to the convent suddenly swung open and armed Basques who had been hiding inside, swarmed out with blazing guns. Acoca had watched helplessly as his wife went down in a hail of bullets, and it was on that day that he had sworn vengeance on the Basques. The Church had also been responsible.

And now he was in Ávila, outside another convent. *This time they'll die.*

Inside the convent, in the dark before dawn, Sister Teresa held the Discipline tightly in her right hand and whipped it hard across her body, feeling the knotted tails slashing into her as she silently recited the *Miserere*. She almost screamed aloud, but noise was not permitted, and she kept the screams inside her. *Forgive me, Jesus, for my sins. Bear witness that I punish myself, as you were punished, and I inflict wounds upon myself, as wounds were inflicted upon you. Let me suffer, as you suffered.*

She was near fainting from the pain. Three more times she flagellated herself and then sank, agonized, upon her cot. She had not drawn blood. That was forbidden. Wincing against the agony that each movement brought, Sister Teresa returned the whip to its black case and rested it in a corner. It was always there, a constant reminder that the slightest sin had to be paid for with pain.

Sister Teresa's transgression had happened that morning as she was rounding the corner of a corridor, eyes down, and bumped into Sister Graciela. Startled, Sister Teresa had looked into Sister Graciela's face. Sister Teresa had immediately reported her infraction and the Reverend Mother Betina had frowned disapprovingly and made the sign of discipline, moving her right hand three times from shoulder to shoulder, her hand closed as though holding a whip, the tip of her thumb held against the inside of her forefinger.

Lying on her cot that night, Sister Teresa had been unable to get out of her mind the extraordinarily beautiful face of the young girl she had gazed at. Sister Teresa knew that as long as she lived she would never speak to her and would never even look at her again, for the slightest sign of intimacy between nuns was severely punished. In an atmosphere of rigid moral and physical austerity, no relationships of any kind were allowed to develop. If two sisters worked side by side and seemed to enjoy each other's silent company, the Reverend Mother would immediately have them separated. Nor were the sisters permitted to sit next to the same person at table twice in a row. The church delicately called the attraction of one nun to another 'a particular friendship', and the penalty was swift and severe. Sister Teresa had served her punishment for breaking the rule.

Now the tolling bell came to Sister Teresa as though from a great distance. It was the voice of God, reproving her.

In the next cell, the sound of the bell rang through the corridors of Sister Graciela's dreams, and the pealing of the bell was mingled with the lubricious creak of bedsprings. The Moor was moving towards her, naked, his manhood tumescent, his hands reaching out to grab her. Sister Graciela opened her eyes, instantly awake, her heart pounding frantically. She looked around, terrified, but she was alone in her tiny cell and the only sound was the reassuring tolling of the bell.

Sister Graciela knelt at the side of her cot. *Jesus, thank You for delivering me from the past. Thank You for the joy I have in being here in Your light. Let me glory only in the happiness of Your being. Help me, my Beloved, to be true to the call You have given me. Help me to ease the sorrow of Your sacred heart.*

Sister Graciela rose and carefully made her bed, then joined the procession of her sisters as they moved silently towards the chapel for Matins. She could smell the familiar scent of burning candles and feel the worn stones beneath her sandalled feet.

In the beginning when Sister Graciela had first entered the convent, she had not understood it when the Mother Prioress had told her that a nun was a woman who gave up everything in order to possess everything. Sister Graciela had been fourteen years old then. Now, seventeen years later, it was clear to her. In contemplation she possessed everything, for contemplation was the mind replying to the soul, the waters of Siloh that flowed in silence. Her days were filled with a wonderful peace.

Thank You for letting me forget the terrible past, Father. Thank You for standing beside me. I couldn't face my terrible past without you . . . Thank You . . . Thank You . . .

When Matins were over, the nuns returned to their cells to sleep until Lauds, the rising of the sun.

Outside, Colonel Ramón Acoca and his men moved swiftly in the darkness. When they reached the convent, Colonel Acoca said, 'Jaime Miró and his men will be armed. Take no chances.'

He looked at the front of the convent, and for an instant, he saw that other convent with Basque partisans rushing out of it, and Susana going down in a hail of bullets.

'Don't bother taking Jaime Miró alive,' he said.

Sister Megan was awakened by the silence. It was a different silence, a moving silence, a hurried rush of air, a whisper of bodies. There were sounds she had never heard in her fifteen years in the convent. She was suddenly filled with a premonition that something was terribly wrong.

She rose quietly in the darkness and opened the door to her cell. Unbelievably, the long stone corridor was filled with men. A giant with a scarred face was coming out of the Reverend Mother's cell, pulling her by the arm. Megan stared in shock. *I'm having a nightmare*, Megan thought. *These men can't be here.*

'Where are you hiding him?' Colonel Acoca demanded.

The Reverend Mother Betina had a look of stunned horror on her face. 'Ssh! This is God's temple. You are desecrating it.' Her voice was trembling. 'You must leave at once.'

The Colonel's grip tightened on her arm and he shook her. 'I want Miró, Sister.'

The nightmare was real.

Other cell doors were beginning to open, and nuns were appearing, looks of total confusion on their faces. There had never been anything in their experience to prepare them for this extraordinary happening.

Colonel Acoca pushed Sister Betina away and turned to Patricio Arrieta, one of his lieutenants. 'Search the place. Top to bottom.'

Acoca's men began to spread out, invading the chapel, the refectory and the cells, waking those nuns who were still asleep, and forcing them roughly to their feet through the corridors and into the chapel. The nuns obeyed wordlessly, keeping even now their vows of silence. To Megan the scene was like a film with the sound turned off.

Acoca's men were filled with a sense of vengeance. They were all Falangists, and they remembered only too well how the Church had turned against them during the Civil War and supported the Loyalists against their beloved leader, Generalissimo Franco. This was their chance to get their own back. The nuns' strength and silence made the men more furious than ever.

As Acoca passed one of the cells, a scream echoed from it. Acoca looked in and saw one of his men ripping the habit from a nun. Acoca moved on.

Sister Lucia was awakened by the sounds of men's voices yelling. She sat up in a panic. *The police have found me*, was her first thought. *I've got to get out of here*. There was no way out of the convent except through the front door.

She hurriedly rose and peered out into the corridor. The sight that met her eyes was astonishing. The corridor was filled not with policemen, but with men in civilian clothes, carrying weapons, smashing lamps and tables. There was confusion everywhere as they raced around.

The Reverend Mother Betina was standing in the centre of the chaos, praying silently, watching them desecrate her beloved convent. Sister Megan moved to her side, and Lucia joined them.

'What the h – what's happening? Who are they?' Lucia asked. They were the first words she had spoken aloud since entering the convent.

The Reverend Mother put her right hand under her left armpit three times, the sign for *hide*.

Lucia stared at her unbelievingly. 'You can talk now. Let's get out of here, for Christ's sake. And I mean for Christ's sake.'

Patricio Arrieta, the Colonel's key aide, hurried up to Acoca. 'We've searched everywhere, Colonel. There's no sign of Jaime Miró or his men.'

'Search again,' Acoca said stubbornly.

It was then that the Reverend Mother remembered the one treasure that the convent had. She hurried over to Sister Teresa and whispered, 'I have a task for you. Remove the gold cross from the chapel and take it to the convent at Mendavia. You must get it away from here. Hurry!'

Sister Teresa was shaking so hard that her wimple fluttered in waves. She stared at the Reverend Mother, paralyzed. Sister Teresa had spent the last thirty years of her life in the convent. The thought of leaving it was beyond imagining. She raised her hand and signed, *I can't.*

The Reverend Mother was frantic. 'The cross must not fall into the hands of these men of Satan. Now do this for Jesus.'

A light came into Sister Teresa's eyes. She stood very tall. She signed, *for Jesus.* She turned and hurried towards the chapel.

Sister Graciela approached the group, staring in wonder at the wild confusion around her.

The men were getting more and more violent, smashing everything in sight. Colonal Acoca watched them, approvingly.

Lucia turned to Megan and Graciela. 'I don't know about you two, but I'm getting out of here. Are you coming?'

They stared at her, too dazed to respond.

Sister Teresa was hurrying towards them, carrying something wrapped in a piece of canvas. Some of the men were herding more nuns into the refectory.

'Come on,' Lucia said.

Sisters Teresa, Megan and Graciela hesitated for a moment, then followed Lucia towards the front door. As they turned at the end of the long corridor, they could see that the huge door had been smashed in.

A man suddenly appeared in front of them. 'Going somewhere, ladies? Get back. My friends have plans for you.'

Lucia said, 'We have a gift for you.' She picked up one of the heavy metal candlesticks that lined the hallway tables and smiled.

The man was looking at it, puzzled. 'What can you do with that?'

'This.' Lucia swung the candelabra against his head, and he fell to the ground, unconscious.

The three nuns stared in horror.

'Move!' Lucia said.

A moment later Lucia, Megan, Graciela and Teresa were outside in the front courtyard, hurrying through the gate into the starry night.

Lucia stopped. 'I'm leaving you. They're going to be searching for you, so you'd better get away from here.'

She turned and started towards the mountains that rose in the distance, high above the convent. *I'll hide out up there until the search cools off and then I'll head for Switzerland. Of all the rotten luck. Those bastards blew a perfect cover.*

As Lucia made her way towards higher ground, she glanced down. From her vantage point she could see the three sisters. Incredibly, they were still standing in front of the convent gate, like three black-clad statues. *For God's sake*, she thought. *Get going before they catch you. Move!*

They could not move. It was as though all their senses had been paralyzed for so long that they were unable to take in what was happening to them. The nuns stared down at their feet. They were so dazed they could not think. They had been cloistered for so long behind the gates of God, secluded from the world, that now that they were outside the protective gates, they were filled with feelings of confusion and panic. They had no idea where to go or what to do. Inside, their lives had been organized for them. They had been fed, clothed, told what to do and when to do it. They had lived by the Rule. Suddenly there was no Rule. What did God want from them? What was His plan? They stood huddled together, afraid to speak, afraid to look at one another.

Hesitantly, Sister Teresa pointed to the lights of Ávila in the distance and signed, *that way*. Uncertainly, they began to move towards the town.

Watching them from the hills above, Lucia thought: *No, you idiots! That's the first place they'll look for you. Well, that's your problem. I have my own problems.* She stood there for a moment, watching them walk towards their doom, going to their slaughter. *Shit.*

Lucia scrambled down the hill, stumbling over the loose scree, and ran after them, her cumbersome habit slowing her down.

'Wait a minute,' she called. 'Stop!'

The sisters stopped and turned.

Lucia hurried up to them, out of breath. 'You're going the wrong way. The first place they'll search for you is in town. You've got to hide out somewhere.'

The three sisters stared at her in silence.

Lucia said impatiently, 'The mountains. Get up to the mountains. Follow me.'

She turned and started back towards the mountains. The others watched, and after a moment, they began to trail after her, one by one.

From time to time Lucia looked back to make sure they were following. *Why can't I mind my own business?* she thought. *They're not my responsibility. It's more dangerous if we're all together.* She kept climbing, making sure they stayed in sight.

The others were having a difficult time of it, and every time they slowed down, Lucia stopped to let them catch up with her. *I'll get rid of them in the morning.*

'Let's move faster,' Lucia called.

At the Abbey, the raid had come to an end. The dazed nuns, their habits wrinkled and bloodstained, were being rounded up and put into unmarked, closed trucks.

'Take them back to my headquarters in Madrid,' Colonel Acoca ordered. 'Keep them in isolation.'

'What charge –?'

'Harbouring terrorists.'

'Yes, Colonel,' Patricio Arrieta said. He hesitated. 'Four of the nuns are missing.'

Colonel Acoca's eyes turned cold. 'Find them.'

Colonel Acoca flew back to Madrid to report to the Prime Minister. 'Jaime Miró escaped before we reached the convent.'

Prime Minister Martinez nodded. 'Yes, I heard.' And he wondered whether Jaime Miró had ever been in the convent to begin with. There was no doubt about it. Colonel Acoca was getting dangerously out of control. There had been angry protests about the brutal attack on the convent. The Prime Minister chose his words carefully, 'The newspapers have been hounding me about what happened.'

'The newspapers are making a hero of this terrorist,' Acoca said, stone faced. 'We must not let them pressure us.'

'He's causing the government a great deal of embarrassment, Colonel. And those four nuns – if they talk –'

'Don't worry. They can't get far. I'll catch them and I'll find Miró.'

The Prime Minister had already decided that he could not afford to take any more chances. 'Colonel, I want you to be sure the thirty-six nuns you have are well-treated, and I'm ordering the army to join the search for Miró and the others. You'll work with Colonel Sostelo.'

There was a long, dangerous pause. 'Which one of us will be in charge of the operation?' Acoca's eyes were icy.

The Prime Minister swallowed. 'You will be, of course.'

Lucia and the three sisters travelled through the early dawn, moving north-east into the mountains, heading away from Ávila and the convent. The nuns, used to moving in silence, made little noise. The only sounds were the rustle of their robes, the clicking of their rosaries, an occasional snapping twig, and their gasps for breath as they climbed higher and higher.

They reached a plateau of the Guardarrama mountains and walked along a rutted road bordered by stone walls. They passed fields with sheep and goats. By sunrise they had covered several miles and found themselves in a wooded area outside the small village of Villacastin.

I'll leave them here, Lucia decided. *Their God can take care of them now. He certainly took great care of me*, she thought bitterly. *Switzerland is farther away than ever. I have no money and no passport, and I'm dressed like an undertaker. By now those men know we've escaped. They'll keep looking until they find us. The sooner I get away by myself, the better.*

But at that instant, something happened that made her change her plans.

Sister Teresa was moving through the trees when she stumbled and the package she had been so carefully guarding fell to the ground. It spilled out of its canvas wrapping and Lucia found herself staring at a large, exquisitely wrought gold cross glowing in the rays of the rising sun.

That's real gold, Lucia thought. *Someone up there is looking after me. That cross is manna. Sheer manna. It's my ticket to Switzerland.*

Lucia watched as Sister Teresa picked up the cross and carefully put it back in its wrapping. Lucia smiled to herself. It was going to be easy to take it. These nuns would do anything she told them.

The town of Ávila was in an uproar. News of the attack on the convent had spread quickly, and Father Berrendo was elected to confront Colonel Acoca. The priest was in his seventies, with an outward frailty that belied his inner strength. He was a warm and understanding shepherd to his parishioners. But at the moment he was filled with a cold fury.

Colonel Acoca kept him waiting for an hour, then allowed the priest to be shown into his office.

Father Berrendo said without preamble, 'You and your men attacked a convent without provocation. It was an act of madness.'

'We were simply doing our duty,' the Colonel said curtly. 'The Abbey was sheltering Jaime Miró and his band of murderers, so the sisters brought this on themselves. We're holding them for questioning.'

'Did you find Jaime Miró in the Abbey?' the priest demanded angrily.

Colonel Acoca said smoothly, 'No. He and his men escaped before we got there. But we'll find them, and justice will be done.'

My justice, Colonel Acoca thought savagely.

5

The nuns travelled slowly. Their garb was ill-designed for the rugged terrain. Their sandals were too thin to protect their feet against the stony ground, and their habits caught on everything. Sister Teresa found she could not even say her rosary. She needed both hands to keep the branches from snapping in her face.

In the light of day, freedom seemed even more terrifying than before. God had cast the sisters out of Eden into a strange, frightening world, and His guidance that they had leaned on for so long was gone. They found themselves in an uncharted country with no map and no compass. The walls that had protected them from harm for so long had vanished and they felt naked and exposed. Danger was everywhere, and they no longer had a place of refuge. They were aliens. The unaccustomed sights and sounds of the country were dazzling. There were insects and bird songs and hot, blue skies assaulting the senses. And there was something else that was disturbing.

When they first fled the convent, Teresa, Graciela and Megan had carefully avoided looking at one another, instinctively keeping to the rules. But now, each found herself avidly studying the faces of the others. Also, after all the years of silence, they found it difficult to speak, and when they did speak, their words were halting, as though they were learning a strange new skill. Their voices sounded strange in their ears. Only Lucia seemed uninhibited and sure of herself, and the others automatically turned to her for leadership.

'We might as well introduce ourselves,' Lucia said. 'I'm Sister Lucia.'

There was an awkward pause, and Graciela said shyly, 'I'm Sister Graciela.'

The dark-haired, arrestingly beautiful one.

'I'm Sister Megan.'

The young blonde with the striking blue eyes.

'I'm Sister Teresa.'

The eldest of the group. Fifty? Sixty?

As they lay in the woods resting outside of the village, Lucia thought: *They're like newborn birds fallen out of their nests. They won't last five minutes on their own. Well, too bad for them. I'll be on my way to Switzerland with the cross.*

Lucia walked to the edge of the clearing they were in and peered through the trees towards the little village below. A few people were walking along the street, but there was no sign of the men who had raided the convent. *Now*, Lucia thought. *Here's my chance.*

301

She turned to the others. 'I'm going down to the village to try to get us some food. You wait here.' She nodded towards Sister Teresa. 'You come with me.'

Sister Teresa was confused. For thirty years she had obeyed only the orders of Reverend Mother Betina and now suddenly this sister had taken charge. *But what is happening is God's will*, Sister Teresa thought. *He has appointed her to help us, so she speaks with His voice.* 'I must get this cross to the convent at Mendavia as soon as possible.'

'Right. When we get down there, we'll ask for directions.'

The two of them started down the hill towards the town, Lucia keeping a careful lookout for trouble. There was none.

This is going to be easy, Lucia thought.

They reached the outskirts of the little town. A sign said, 'Villacastin'. Ahead of them was the main street. To the left was a small, deserted street.

Good, Lucia thought. There would be no one to witness what was about to happen.

Lucia turned into the side street. 'Let's go this way. There's less chance of being seen.'

Sister Teresa nodded and obediently followed Lucia. The question now was how to get the cross away from her.

I could grab it and run, Lucia thought, *but she'd probably scream and attract a lot of attention. No, I'll have to make sure she stays quiet.*

The small limb of a tree had fallen to the ground in front of her, and Lucia paused, then stooped to pick it up. It was heavy. *Perfect.* She waited for Sister Teresa to catch up to her.

'Sister Teresa . . .'

The nun turned to look at her, and as Lucia started to raise the club, a male voice from out of nowhere said, 'God be with you, Sisters.'

Lucia spun around, ready to run. A man was standing there, dressed in the long brown robe and cowl of a friar. He was tall and thin, with an aquiline face and the saintliest expression Lucia had ever seen. His eyes seemed to glow with a warm inner light, and his voice was soft and gentle.

'I'm Friar Miguel Carrillo.'

Lucia's mind was racing. Her first plan had been interrupted. But now, suddenly, she had a better one. 'Thank God you found us,' Lucia said.

This man was going to be her escape. He would know the easiest way for her to get out of Spain.

'We come from the Cistercian convent near Ávila,' Lucia explained. 'Last night some men raided it. All the nuns were taken. Four of us managed to escape.'

When the friar replied, his voice was filled with anger. 'I come from the monastery at Saint Generro, where I have been for the past twenty years. We were attacked the night before last.' He sighed. 'I know that

God has some plan for all His children, but I must confess that at this moment I don't understand what it might be.'

'These men are searching for us,' Lucia said. 'It is important that we get out of Spain as fast as possible. Do you know how that can be done?'

Friar Carrillo smiled gently. 'I think I can help you, Sister. God has brought us together. Take me to the others.'

Lucia brought the friar to the group.

'This is Friar Carrillo,' she said. 'He's been in a monastery for the last twenty years. He's come to help us.'

Their reactions to the friar were mixed. Graciela dared not look directly at him. Megan studied him with quick, interested glances, and Sister Teresa regarded him as a messenger sent by God, who would lead them to the convent at Mendavia.

Friar Carrillo said, 'The men who attacked the convent will undoubtedly keep searching for you. But they will be looking for four nuns. The first thing we must do is get you a change of clothing.'

Megan reminded him, 'We have no clothes to change into.'

Friar Carrillo gave her a beatific smile. 'Our Lord has a very large wardrobe. Do not worry, my child. He will provide. Let us go into town.'

It was two o'clock in the afternoon, siesta time, and Friar Carrillo and the four sisters walked down the main street of the village, alert for any signs of their pursuers. The shops were closed, but the restaurants and bars were open and from them they could hear strange music issuing, hard, dissonant and raucous sounding.

Friar Carrillo saw the look on Sister Teresa's face. 'That's rock and roll,' he said. 'Very popular with the young these days.'

A pair of young women standing in front of one of the bars stared at the nuns as they passed. The nuns stared back, wide-eyed, at the strange clothing the pair wore. One wore a skirt so short it barely covered her thighs, the other wore a longer skirt that was split up to the sides of her thighs. Both wore tight knitted bodices with no sleeves.

They might as well be naked, Sister Teresa thought, horrified.

In the doorway stood a man who wore a turtleneck sweater, a strange-looking jacket without a collar, and a jewelled pendant.

Unfamiliar odours greeted the nuns as they passed a bodega. Nicotine and whisky.

Megan was staring at something across the street. She stopped.

Friar Carrillo said, 'What is it? What's the matter?' He turned to look.

Megan was watching a woman carrying a baby. How many years had it been since she had seen a baby, or even a small child? Not since the orphanage, fourteen years ago. The sudden shock made Megan realize how far her life had been removed from the outside world.

Sister Teresa was staring at the baby, too, but she was thinking of something else. *It's Monique's baby.* The baby across the street was screaming. *It's screaming because I deserted it. But no, that's impossible. That was thirty years ago.* Sister Teresa turned away, the baby's cries ringing in her ears. They moved on.

They passed a cinema. The poster read, *Three Lovers*, and the photographs displayed showed skimpily-clad women embracing a bare-chested man.

'Why, they're – they're almost naked!' Sister Teresa exclaimed.

Friar Carrillo frowned. 'Yes. It's disgraceful what the cinema is permitted to show these days. That film is pure pornography. The most personal and private acts are there for everyone to see. They turn God's children into animals.'

They passed a hardware store, a hairdressing salon, a flower shop, a sweet shop, all closed for the siesta, and at each shop the sisters stopped and stared at the windows, filled with once familiar, faintly remembered goods.

When they came to a women's dress shop, Friar Carrillo said, 'Stop.'

The blinds were pulled down over the front windows and a sign on the front door said, 'Closed'.

'Wait here for me, please.'

The four women watched as he walked to the corner and turned out of sight. They looked at one another blankly. Where was he going, and what if he did not return?

A few minutes later, they heard the sound of the front door of the shop opening, and Friar Carrillo stood in the doorway, beaming. He motioned them inside. 'Hurry.'

When they were all in the shop and the friar had locked the door, Lucia asked, 'How did you –?'

'God provides a back door as well as a front door,' the friar said gravely. But there was an impish edge to his voice that made Megan smile.

The sisters looked around the shop in awe. The store was a multi-coloured cornucopia of dresses and sweaters and bras and stockings, high-heeled shoes and boleros. Objects they had not seen in years. And the styles seemed so strange. There were handbags and scarves and compacts and blouses. It was all too much to absorb. The women stood there, gaping.

'We must move quickly,' Friar Carrillo warned them, 'and leave before siesta is over and the shop reopens. Help yourselves. Choose whatever fits you.'

Lucia thought: *Thank God I can finally dress like a woman again.* She walked over to a rack of dresses and began to sort through them. She found a beige skirt and tan silk blouse to go with it. *It's not Balenciaga, but it will do for now.* She picked out panties and a bra and a pair of soft boots. She stepped behind a clothes rack, stripped and in a matter of minutes was dressed and ready to go.

The others were slowly selecting their outfits.

Graciela chose a white cotton dress that set off her black hair and dark complexion, and a pair of sandals.

Megan chose a patterned blue cotton dress that fell below the knees and low-heeled shoes.

Sister Teresa had the most difficult time choosing something to wear. The array of choices was too dazzling. There were silks and flannels and tweeds and leather. There were cottons and twills and corduroys, and there were plaids and checks and stripes of every colour. And they all seemed – *skimpy*, was the word that came to Sister Teresa's mind. For the past thirty years she had been decently covered by the heavy robes of her calling. And now she was being asked to shed them and put on these indecent creations. She finally selected the longest skirt she could find, and a long-sleeved, high-collared cotton blouse.

Friar Carrillo urged, 'Hurry, Sisters. Get undressed and change.'

They looked at one another in embarrassment.

He smiled. 'I'll wait in the office, of course.'

He walked to the back of the shop and entered the office.

The sisters began to undress, painfully self-conscious in front of one another.

In the office, Friar Carrillo had pulled a chair up to the transom and was looking out through it, watching the sisters strip. He was thinking: *Which one am I going to screw first?*

Miguel Carrillo had begun his career as a thief when he was only ten years old. He was born with curly blond hair and an angelic face, and they had proved to be of inestimable value in his chosen profession. He started at the bottom, snatching handbags and shoplifting, and as he got older, his career expanded and he began robbing drunks and preying on wealthy women. Because of his enormous appeal, he was very successful. He devised several original swindles, each more ingenious than the last. Unfortunately, his latest swindle had proved to be his undoing.

Posing as a friar from a distant monastery, Carrillo travelled from church to church begging sanctuary for the night. It was always granted, and in the morning when the priest came to open the church doors, all the valuable artefacts would be missing, along with the good friar. Unfortunately, fate had double-crossed him and two nights earlier in Benjar, a small town near Ávila, the priest had returned unexpectedly and Miguel Carrillo had been caught in the act of pilfering the church treasury. The priest was a beefy, heavyset man, and he had wrestled Carrillo to the floor and announced that he was going to turn him over to the police. A heavy silver chalice had fallen to the floor, and Carrillo had picked it up and hit the priest with it. Either the chalice was too heavy, or the priest's skull was too thin, but in any case the priest lay dead on the floor. Miguel Carrillo had fled, panicky, anxious to put

305

himself as far away from the scene of the crime as possible. He had passed through Ávila and heard the story of the attack on the convent by Colonel Acoca and the secret GOE. It was fate that Carrillo had chanced upon the four escaped nuns.

Now, eager with anticipation, he studied their naked bodies, and thought: *There's another interesting possibility. Since Colonel Acoca and his men are looking for the sisters, there is probably a nice, fat reward on their heads. I'll lay them first, and then turn them over to Acoca.*

The women, except for Lucia, who was already dressed, were totally naked. Carrillo watched as they awkwardly put on the new underclothes. Then they finished dressing, clumsily buttoning unaccustomed buttons and fastening zips, hurrying to get away before they were caught.

Time to get to work, Carrillo thought happily. He got down from the chair and walked out into the shop. He approached the women, studied them approvingly, and said, 'Excellent. No one in the world would ever take you for nuns. I might suggest scarves for your heads.' He selected one for each of them and watched them put them on.

Miguel Carrillo had made his decision. Graciela was going to be the first. She was undoubtedly one of the most beautiful women he had ever seen. And that body! *How could she have wasted it on God? I'll show her what to do with it.*

He said to Lucia, Teresa and Megan, 'You must all be hungry. I want you to go to the café we passed and wait for us there. I'll go to the church and borrow some money from the priest so we can eat.' He turned to Graciela. 'I want you to come with me, Sister, to explain to the priest what happened at the convent.'

'I – very well.'

Carrillo said to the others, 'We'll be along in a little while. I would suggest you use the back door.'

He watched as Lucia, Teresa and Megan left. When he heard the door close behind them, he turned to Graciela. *She's fantastic*, he thought. *Maybe I'll keep her with me, break her in to some cons. She could be a big help.*

Graciela was watching him. 'I'm ready.'

'Not yet.' Carrillo pretended to study her for a moment. 'No, I'm afraid it won't do. That dress is all wrong for you. Take it off.'

'But – why?'

'It doesn't fit properly,' Carrillo said glibly. 'People will notice, and you don't want to attract attention.'

She hesitated, then moved behind a rack.

'Hurry, now. We have very little time.'

Awkwardly, Graciela slipped the dress over her head. She was in her panties and brassiere when Carrillo suddenly appeared.

'Take everything off.' His voice was husky.

Graciela stared at him. 'What? No!' she cried. 'I – I can't. Please –
I –'

Carrillo moved closer to her. 'I'll help you, Sister.'

His hands reached out and he ripped off her brassiere and tore at her
panties.

'No!' she screamed. 'You mustn't! Stop it!'

Carrillo grinned. '*Carita*, we're just getting started. You're going to
love this.'

His strong arms were around her. He forced her to the floor and
lifted his robe.

It was as though a curtain in Graciela's mind suddenly descended. It
was the Moor trying to thrust himself inside her, tearing into the depths
of her, and her mother's shrill voice was screaming.

And Graciela thought, terrified, *No, not again. No, please – not
again* . . .

She was struggling fiercely now, fighting Carrillo off, trying to get up.

'Goddamn you,' he cried.

He slammed his fist into her face, and Graciela fell back, stunned
and dizzy.

She found herself spinning back in time.

Back . . . Back . . .

6

Las Navas del Marqués,
Spain 1950

She was five years old. Her earliest memories were of a procession of naked strangers climbing in and out of her mother's bed.

Her mother explained, 'They are your uncles. You must show them respect.'

The men were gross and crude and lacked affection. They stayed for a night, a week, a month, and then vanished. When they left, Dolores Pinero would immediately look for a new man.

In her youth, Dolores Pinero had been a beauty, and Graciela had inherited her mother's looks. Even as a child, Graciela was stunning to look at, with high cheekbones, an olive complexion, shiny black hair and thick, long eyelashes. Her young body was nubile with promise. With the passage of years, Dolores Pinero's body had turned to fat and her wonderfully boned face had become bruised with the bitter blows of time.

Although Dolores Pinero was no longer beautiful, she was accessible, and she had the reputation of being a passionate bed partner. Making love was her one talent, and she employed it to try to please men into bondage, hoping to keep them by buying their love with her body. She made a meagre living as a seamstress because she was an indifferent one, and was hired only by the women of the village who could not afford the better ones.

Graciela's mother despised her daughter, for she was a constant reminder of the one man whom Dolores Pinero had ever loved. Graciela's father was a handsome young mechanic who had proposed to the beautiful young Dolores, and she had eagerly let him seduce her. When she had broken the news that she was pregnant, he had disappeared, leaving Dolores with the curse of his seed.

Dolores Pinero had a vicious temper, and she took her vengeance out on the child. Any time Graciela did something to displease her, her mother would hit her and scream, 'You're as stupid as your father!'

There was no way for the child to escape the rain of blows or the constant screaming. Graciela would wake up every morning and pray: 'Please, God, don't let Mama beat me today.

'Please, God, make Mama happy today.
'Please, God, let Mama say she loves me today.'

When she was not attacking Graciela, her mother ignored her. Graciela prepared her own meals and took care of her clothes. She made her lunch to take to school, and she would say to her teacher, 'My mother made me *empanadas* today. She knows how much I like *empanadas*.'

Or: 'I tore my dress, but my mother sewed it up for me. She loves doing things for me.'

Or: 'My mother and I are going to the pictures tomorrow.'

And it would break her teacher's heart. Las Navas del Marqués is a small village an hour from Ávila, and like all villages everywhere, everyone knew everyone else's business. The lifestyle of Dolores Pinero was a disgrace, and it reflected on Graciela. Mothers refused to let their children play with the little girl, lest their morals be contaminated. Graciela went to the school on Plazoleta del Cristo, but she had no friends and no playmates. She was one of the brightest students in the school, but her exam results were poor. It was difficult for her to concentrate, for she was always tired.

Her teacher would admonish her, 'You must get to bed earlier, Graciela, so that you are rested enough to do your work properly.'

But her exhaustion had nothing to do with getting to bed late. Graciela and her mother shared a small, two-room *casa*. The girl slept on a couch in the tiny room, with only a thin, worn curtain separating it from the bedroom. How could Graciela tell her teacher about the obscene sounds in the night that awakened her and kept her awake, as she listened to her mother making love to whichever stranger happened to be in her bed?

When Graciela brought home her report card, her mother would scream, 'These are the cursed marks I expected you to get, and do you know why you got these terrible marks? Because you're stupid. Stupid!'

And Graciela would believe it and try hard not to cry.

In the afternoons when school was over, Graciela would wander around by herself, walking through the narrow, winding streets lined with acacia and sycamore trees, past the whitewashed stone houses, where loving fathers lived with their families. Graciela had many playmates, but they were all in her mind. There were beautiful girls and handsome boys, and they invited her to all their parties, where they served wonderful cakes and ice cream. Her imaginary friends were kind and loving, and they all thought she was very smart. When her mother was not around, Graciela would carry on long conversations with them.

Would you help me with my homework, Graciela? I don't know how to do sums, and you're so good at them.

309

What shall we do tonight, Graciela? We could go to the pictures, or walk into town and have a lemonade.

Will your mother let you come to dinner tonight, Graciela? We're having paella.

No, I'm afraid not. Mother gets lonely if I'm not with her. I'm all she has, you know.

On Sundays, Graciela rose early and dressed quietly, careful not to awaken her mother and whichever uncle was in her bed, and walked to the San Juan Bautista Church, where Father Perez talked of the joys of life after death, a fairytale life with Jesus; and Graciela could not wait to die and meet Jesus.

Father Perez was an attractive priest in his early forties. He had ministered to the rich and the poor, and the sick and the vital, since he had come to Las Navas del Marqués several years earlier, and there were no secrets in the little village to which he was not privy. Father Perez knew Graciela as a regular church-goer, and he, too, was aware of the stories of the constant stream of strangers who shared Dolores Pinero's bed. It was not a fit home for a young girl, but there was nothing anyone could do about it. It amazed the priest that Graciela had turned out as well as she had. She was kind and gentle and never complained or talked about her home life.

Graciela would appear at church every Sunday morning wearing a clean, neat outfit that he was sure she had washed herself. Father Perez knew she was shunned by the other children in town, and his heart went out to her. He made it a point to spend a few moments with her after mass each Sunday, and when he had time, he would take her to a little café for a treat of *helado*.

In the winter Graciela's life was a dreary landscape, monotonous and gloomy. Las Navas del Marqués was in a valley surrounded by the Cruz Verde mountains and, because of that, the winters were six months long. The summers were easier to bear, for then the tourists arrived and filled the town with laughter and dancing and the streets came alive. The tourists would gather at the Plaza de Manuel Delgado Barredo, with its little bandstand built on stone, and listen to the orchestra and watch the natives dance the Sardana, the centuries-old traditional folk dance, barefoot, their hands linked, as they moved gracefully around in a colourful circle. Graciela watched the visitors as they sat at the pavement cafés drinking *aperitivos* or shopping at the *pescadería* – the fish market, or the *farmacia*. At one o'clock in the afternoon the *bodega* was always filled with tourists drinking *chateo* and picking at *tapas*, seafood and olives and chips.

The most exciting thing for Graciela was to watch the *paseo* each evening. Boys and girls would walk up and down the Plaza Mayor in segregated groups, the boys eyeing the girls, while parents and grandparents and friends watched, hawk-eyed, from sidewalk cafés. It was the traditional mating ritual, observed for centuries. Graciela longed to join in it, but her mother forbade her.

'Do you want to be a *puta*?' she would scream at Graciela. 'Stay away from boys. They want only one thing from you. I know from experience,' she added bitterly.

If the days were bearable, the nights were an agony. Through the thin curtain that separated their beds, Graciela could hear the sounds of savage moaning and writhings and heavy breathing, and always the obscenities.

'Faster . . . harder!'

'*¡Cógeme!*'

'*¡Mámame la verga!*'

'*¡Métela en el culo!*'

Before she was ten years old, Graciela had heard every obscene word in the Spanish vocabulary. They were whispered and shouted and shuddered and moaned. The cries of passion repelled Graciela, and at the same time awakened strange longings in her.

When Graciela was fourteen years old, the Moor moved in. He was the biggest man Graciela had ever seen. His skin was shiny black, and his head was shaved. He had enormous shoulders, a barrel chest and huge arms. The Moor had arrived in the middle of the night when Graciela was asleep, and she got her first sight of him in the morning when he pushed the curtain aside and walked stark naked past Graciela's bed to go outside to the outhouse in the yard. Graciela looked at him and almost gasped aloud. He was enormous, in every part. *That will kill my mother*, Graciela thought.

The Moor was staring at her. 'Well, well. And who do we have here?'

Dolores Pinero hurried out of her bed and moved to his side. 'My daughter,' she said curtly.

A wave of embarrassment swept over Graciela, as she saw her mother's naked body next to the man.

The Moor smiled, showing beautiful white, even teeth. 'What's your name, *guapa*?'

Graciela was too shamed by his nakedness to speak.

'Her name's Graciela. She's retarded.'

'She's beautiful. I'll bet you looked like that when you were young.'

'I'm still young,' Dolores Pinero snapped. She turned to her daughter. 'Get dressed. You'll be late for school.'

'Yes, Mama.'

The Moor stood there, eyeing her.

311

The older woman took his arm and said cajolingly, 'Come back to bed, *querida*. We're not finished yet.'

'Later,' the Moor said. He was still looking at Graciela.

The Moor stayed. Every day when Graciela came home from school she prayed that he would be gone. For reasons she did not understand, he terrified her. He was always polite to her and never made any advances, yet the mere thought of him sent shivers through her body.

His treatment of her mother was something different. The Moor stayed in the small house most of the day, drinking heavily. He took whatever money Dolores Pinero earned. Sometimes at night in the middle of lovemaking, Graciela would hear him beating her mother, and in the morning Dolores Pinero would appear with a blackened eye or split lip.

'Mama, why do you put up with him?' Graciela asked.

'You wouldn't understand,' she said sullenly. 'He's a real man, not a midget like the others. He knows how to satisfy a woman.' She ran her hand through her hair coquettishly. 'Besides, he's madly in love with me.'

Graciela did not believe it. She knew that the Moor was using her mother, but she did not dare protest again. She was too terrified of her mother's temper, for when Dolores Pinero was really angry, a kind of insanity took possession of her. She had once chased Graciela with a kitchen knife because she had dared make a pot of tea for one of the 'uncles'.

Early one Sunday morning Graciela rose to get ready for church. Her mother had left early to deliver some dresses. As Graciela pulled off her nightgown, the curtain was pushed aside and the Moor appeared. He was naked.

'Where's your mother, *guapa*?'

'Mama went out early. She had some errands to do.'

The Moor was studying Graciela's nude body. 'You really are a beauty,' he said softly.

Graciela felt her face flush. She knew what she should do. She should cover her nakedness, put on her skirt and blouse and leave. Instead, she stood there, unable to move. She watched his manhood begin to swell and grow before her eyes. She could hear the voices ringing in her ears:

'Faster . . . Harder!'

She felt faint.

The Moor said huskily, 'You're a child. Get your clothes on and get out of here.'

And Graciela found herself moving. Moving towards him. She

reached up and slid her arms around his waist and felt his male hardness against her body.

'No,' she moaned. 'I'm not a child.'

The pain that followed was like nothing Graciela had ever known. It was excruciating, unbearable. It was wonderful, exhilarating, beautiful. She held the Moor tightly in her arms, screaming with ecstasy. He brought her to orgasm after orgasm, and Graciela thought: *So this is what the mystery is all about.* And it was so wonderful to finally know the secret of all creation, to be a part of life at last, to know what joy was for now and for ever.

'*What the fuck are you doing?*'

It was Dolores Pinero's voice screaming, and for an instant everything stopped, frozen in time. Dolores Pinero was standing at the side of the bed, staring down at her daughter and the Moor.

Graciela looked up at her mother, too terrified to speak. Dolores Pinero's eyes were filled with an insane rage.

'You bitch!' she yelled. 'You rotten bitch.'

'Mama – please –'

Dolores Pinero picked up a heavy iron ashtray at the bedside and slammed it against her daughter's head.

That was the last thing Graciela remembered.

She awoke in a large, white hospital ward with two dozen beds in it, all of them occupied. Harried nurses scurried back and forth, trying to attend to the needs of the patients.

Graciela's head was racked with excruciating pain. Each time she moved, rivers of fire flowed through her. She lay there, listening to the cries and moans of the other patients.

Late in the afternoon, a young doctor stopped by the side of her bed. He was in his early thirties, but he looked old and tired.

'Well,' he said. 'You're finally awake.'

'Where am I?' It hurt her to speak.

'You're in the charity ward of the Hospital Provincial in Ávila. You were brought in yesterday. You were in terrible shape. We had to stitch up your forehead.' The doctor went on: 'Our chief surgeon decided to sew you up himself. He said you were too beautiful to have scars.'

He's wrong, Graciela thought. *I'll be scarred for the rest of my life.*

On the second day Father Perez came to see Graciela. A nurse moved a chair to the bedside. The priest looked at the beautiful, pale young girl lying there and his heart melted. The terrible thing that had happened to her was the scandal of Las Navas del Marqués, but there was nothing anyone could do about it. Dolores Pinero had told the *policia* that her daughter had injured her head in a fall.

313

Now, Father Perez asked, 'Are you feeling better, child?'

Graciela nodded, and the movement made her head pound.

'The *policia* have been asking questions. Is there anything you would like me to tell them?'

There was a long silence. Finally she said, 'It was an accident.'

He could not bear the look in her eyes. 'I see.'

What he had to say was painful beyond words. 'Graciela, I spoke with your mother . . .'

And Graciela knew. 'I – I can't go home again, can I?'

'No, I'm afraid not. We'll talk about it.' Father Perez took Graciela's hand. 'I'll come back to see you tomorrow.'

'Thank you, Father.'

When he left, Graciela lay there, and she prayed: *Dear God, please let me die. I don't want to live.*

She had nowhere to go and no one to go to. Never again would she see her home. She would never see her school again, or the familiar faces of her teachers. There was nothing in the world left for her.

A nurse stopped at her bedside. 'You need anything?'

Graciela looked up at her in despair. What was there to say?

The following day the doctor appeared again.

'I have good news,' he said awkwardly. 'You're well enough to leave now.' That was a lie, but the rest of his speech was true. 'We need the bed.'

She was free to go – but go where?

When Father Perez arrived an hour later, he was accompanied by another priest.

'This is Father Berrendo, an old friend of mine.'

Graciela glanced up at the frail-looking priest. 'Father.'

He was right, Father Berrendo thought. *She is beautiful.*

Father Perez had told him the story of what had happened to Graciela. The priest had expected to see some visible signs of the kind of environment the child had lived in, a hardness, a defiance, or self-pity. There were none of those things in the young girl's face.

'I'm sorry you've had such a bad time,' Father Berrendo told her. The sentence carried a deeper meaning.

Father Perez said, 'Graciela, I must return to Las Navas del Marqués. I am leaving you in Father Berrendo's hands.'

Graciela was filled with a sudden sense of panic. She felt as though her last link with home was being cut. 'Don't go,' she pleaded.

Father Perez took her hand in his. 'I know you feel alone,' he said warmly, 'but you're not. Believe me, child, you're not.'

A nurse approached the bed carrying a bundle. She handed it to

314

Graciela. 'Here are your clothes. I'm afraid you're going to have to leave now.'

An even greater panic seized her. '*Now?*'

The two priests exchanged a look.

'Why don't you get dressed and come with me?' Father Berrendo suggested. 'We can talk.'

Fifteen minutes later Father Berrendo was helping Graciela out of the hospital door into the warm sunlight. There was a garden in front of the hospital with brightly coloured flowers, but Graciela was too dazed even to notice them.

When they were seated in his office, Father Berrendo said, 'Father Perez told me that you have no place to go.'

Graciela nodded.

'No relatives?'

'Only –' It was difficult to say it. 'Only – my mother.'

'Father Perez said that you were a regular churchgoer in your village.'

A village she would never see again. 'Yes.'

Graciela thought of those Sunday mornings, and the beauty of the church services and how she had longed to be with Jesus and escape from the pain of the life she lived.

'Graciela, have you ever thought of entering a convent?'

'No.' She was startled by the idea.

'There is a convent here in Ávila – the Cistercian convent. They would take care of you there.'

'I – I don't know.' The idea was frightening.

'It is not for everyone,' Father Berrendo told her. 'And I must warn you, it is the strictest order of them all. Once you walk through the gates and take the vows, you have made a promise to God never to leave.'

Graciela sat there, her mind filled with conflicting thoughts, staring out the window. The idea of shutting herself away from the world was terrifying. *It would be like going to prison.* But on the other hand, what did the world have to offer her? Pain and despair beyond bearing. She had often thought of suicide. This might offer a way out of her misery.

Father Berrendo said, 'It's up to you, my child. If you like, I will take you to meet the Reverend Mother Prioress.'

Graciela nodded. 'All right.'

The Reverend Mother studied the face of the young girl before her. Last night for the first time in many, many years she had heard the voice. *A young child will come to you. Protect her.* 'How old are you, my dear?'

'Fourteen.'

She's old enough. In the fourth century the Pope decreed that girls could be permitted to become nuns at the age of twelve.

'I'm afraid,' Graciela said to the Reverend Mother Betina.

I'm afraid. The words rang in Betina's mind: *I'm afraid . . .*

That had been so many long years ago. She was speaking to her priest. 'I don't know if I have a calling for this, Father. I'm afraid.'

'Betina, the first contact with God can be very disturbing, and the decision to dedicate your life to Him is a difficult one.'

How did I find my calling? Betina had wondered.

She had never been even faintly interested in religion. As a young girl she had avoided church and Sunday school. In her teens she was more interested in parties and clothes and boys. If her friends in Madrid had been asked to select possible candidates to become a nun, Betina would have been at the bottom of the list. More accurately, she would not even have been on their list. But when she was nineteen, events started to happen that changed her life.

She was in her bed, asleep, when a voice said, 'Betina, get up and go outside.'

She opened her eyes and sat up, frightened. She turned on the bedside lamp. She was alone. *What a strange dream.*

But the voice had been so real. She lay down again, but it was impossible to go back to sleep.

Betina, get up and go outside.

It's my subconscious, she thought. *Why would I want to go outside in the middle of the night?*

She turned out the light and a moment later turned it on again. *This is crazy.*

But she put on a dressing-gown and slippers and went downstairs. The household was asleep.

She opened the kitchen door, and as she did a wave of fear swept over her, because somehow she knew that she was supposed to go out the back into the yard. She looked around in the darkness, and her eye caught a glint of moonlight shining on an old refrigerator that had been abandoned and was used to store tools.

Betina suddenly knew why she was there. She walked over to the refrigerator as though hypnotized, and opened it. Her three-year-old brother was inside, unconscious.

That was the first incident. In time, Betina rationalized it as a perfectly normal experience. *I must have heard my brother get up and go out into the yard, and I knew the refrigerator was there, and I was worried about him so I went outside to check.*

The next experience was not so easy to explain. It happened a month later.

In her sleep, Betina heard a voice say, 'You must put out the fire.'

She sat up, wide awake, her pulse racing. Again, it was impossible to go back to sleep. She put on a dressing-gown and slippers and went into the landing. No smoke. No fire. She opened her parents' bedroom door. Everything was normal there. There was no fire in her brother's bedroom. She went downstairs and looked through every room. There was no sign of a fire.

I'm an idiot, Betina thought. *It was only a dream.*

She went back to bed, just as the house was rocked by an explosion. She and her family escaped, and the firemen managed to put out the fire.

'It started in the basement,' a fireman explained. 'And a boiler exploded.'

The next incident happened three weeks later. This time it was no dream.

Betina was on the patio, reading, when she saw a stranger walking across the yard. He looked at her and in that instant she felt a malevolence coming from him that was almost palpable. He turned away and was gone.

Betina was unable to get him out of her mind.

Three days later, she was in an office building, waiting for the lift. The lift door opened, and she was about to step into it when she looked at the lift operator. It was the man she had seen in her garden. Betina backed away, frightened. The lift door closed and the lift went up. Moments later, it crashed, killing everyone in it.

The following Sunday, Betina went to church.

Dear Lord, I don't know what's happening to me, and I'm scared. Please guide me and tell me what you want me to do.

The answer came that night as Betina slept. The voice said one word. *Devotion.*

She thought about it all night, and in the morning she went to talk to the priest.

He listened intently to what she had to say.

'Ah. You are one of the fortunate ones. You have been chosen.'

'Chosen for what?'

'Are you willing to devote your life to God, my child?'

'I – I don't know. I'm afraid.'

But in the end, she had joined the convent.

I chose the right path, the Reverend Mother Betina thought, *because I have never known so much happiness . . .*

And now there was this battered child saying, 'I'm afraid.'

The Reverend Mother took Graciela's hand. 'Take your time, Graciela. God won't go away. Think about it and come back and we can discuss it.'

But what was there to think about? *I've got nowhere else in the world to go*, Graciela thought. And the silence would be welcome. *I have heard too many terrible sounds.* She looked at the Reverend Mother and said, 'I will welcome the silence.'

That had been seventeen years earlier, and in that time Graciela had found peace for the first time in her life. Her life was dedicated to God. The past no longer belonged to her. She was forgiven the horrors she had grown up with. She was Christ's bride, and at the end of her life, she would join Him.

As the years passed in deep silence, despite the occasional nightmares, the terrible sounds in her mind gradually faded away.

Sister Graciela was assigned to work in the garden, tending the tiny rainbows of God's miracle, never tiring of their splendour. The walls of the convent rose high above her on all sides like a stone mountain, but Graciela never felt that they were shutting her in; they were shutting the terrible world out, a world she never wanted to see again.

Life in the convent was serene and peaceful. But now, suddenly her terrible nightmares had turned into a reality. Her world had been invaded by barbarians. They had forced her out of her sanctuary, into the world she had renounced for ever. And her sins came flooding back, filling her with horror. The Moor had returned. She could feel his hot breath on her face. As she fought him, Graciela opened her eyes, and it was the friar on top of her trying to penetrate her. He was saying, 'Stop fighting me, Sister. You're going to enjoy this!'

'Mama,' Graciela cried aloud. 'Mama! Help me!'

7

Lucia Carmine felt wonderful as she walked down the street with Megan and Teresa. It was marvellous to wear feminine clothes again and hear the whisper of silk against her skin. She glanced at the others. They were walking nervously, unaccustomed to their new clothes, looking self-conscious and embarrassed in their skirts and stockings. *They look as though they've been dropped from another planet. They certainly don't belong on this one*, Lucia thought. *They might as well be wearing signs that say: 'Catch Me.'*

Sister Teresa was the most uncomfortable of the women. Thirty years in the convent had deeply ingrained a sense of modesty in her, and it was being violated by the events that had been thrust upon her. This world to which she had once belonged now seemed unreal. It was the convent that was real, and she longed to hurry back to the sanctuary of its protective walls.

Megan was aware that men were eyeing her as she walked down the street, and she blushed. She had lived in a world of women for so long that she had forgotten what it was like to see a man, let alone have one smile at her. It was embarrassing, indecent . . . exciting. The men aroused feelings in Megan that had been long since buried. For the first time in years, she was conscious of her femaleness.

They were passing the bar they had gone by before and the music was blaring out into the street. What had Friar Carrillo called it? *Rock and roll. Very popular with the young.* Something bothered her. And suddenly Megan realized what it was. When they had passed the cinema, the friar had said: *It's disgraceful what the cinema is permitted to show these days. That film is pure pornography. The most personal and private acts are there for everyone to see.*

Megan's heart began to beat faster. If Friar Carrillo had been locked up in a monastery for the past twenty years, how could he possibly have known about rock music or what was in the film? Something was terribly wrong.

She turned to Lucia and Teresa and said urgently, 'We've got to return to the shop.'

They watched as Megan turned and ran back, and they quickly began to follow her.

Graciela was on the floor, desperately fighting to get free, scratching and clawing at Carrillo.

'God damn you! Hold still!' He was getting winded.

He heard a sound and glanced up. He saw the heel of a shoe swinging towards his head, and that was the last thing he remembered.

Megan picked up the trembling Graciela and held her in her arms. 'Shh. It's all right. He won't bother you any more.'

It was several minutes before Graciela could speak. 'He – he – it wasn't my fault this time,' she said pleadingly.

Lucia and Teresa had come into the shop. Lucia sized up the situation at a glance.

'The bastard!'

She looked down at the unconscious, half-naked figure on the floor. As the others watched, Lucia grabbed some belts from a counter and tied Miguel Carrillo's hands tightly behind his back. 'Tie his feet,' she told Megan.

Megan went to work.

Finally, Lucia stood up, satisfied. 'There. When they open up the shop this afternoon, he can explain to them what he was doing here.' She looked at Graciela closely. 'Are you all right?'

'I – I – yes.' She tried to smile.

'We'd better get out of here,' Megan said. 'Get dressed. Quickly.'

When they were ready to leave, Lucia said, 'Wait a minute.'

She went over to the cash register and pressed a key. There were a few hundred peseta notes inside. She scooped them up, picked up a purse from a counter and put the money inside. She saw the disapproving expression on Teresa's face.

Lucia said, 'Look at it this way, Sister. If God didn't want us to have this money, He wouldn't have put it there for us.'

They were seated in the café, having a conference. Sister Teresa was speaking. 'We must get the cross to the convent at Mendavia as quickly as possible. There will be safety there for all of us.'

Not for me, Lucia thought. *My safety is that Swiss bank. But first things first. I've got to get hold of that cross.*

'The convent at Mendavia is north of here, isn't it?'

'Yes.'

'The men will be looking for us in every town. So we'll sleep in the hills tonight.'

Nobody will hear her even if she does scream.

A waitress brought menus to the table and handed them out. The sisters examined them, their expressions confused. Suddenly Lucia understood. It had been so many years since they had been given choices of any kind. At the convent they had automatically eaten the simple food placed before them. Now they were confronted with a cornucopia of unfamiliar delicacies.

Sister Teresa was the first to speak. 'I – I will have some coffee and bread, please.'

Sister Graciela said, 'I, too.'

Megan said, 'We have a long, hard journey ahead of us. I suggest that we order something more nourishing, like eggs.'

Lucia looked at her with new eyes. *She's the one to keep an eye on*, Lucia thought. Aloud she said, 'Sister Megan is right. Let me order for you, Sisters.'

She ordered sliced oranges, *Tortillas de Patatas*, bacon, hot rolls, jam and coffee.

'We're in a hurry,' she told the waitress.

Siesta ended at 4.30, and the town would be waking up. She wanted to be out of there before that happened, before they discovered Miguel Carrillo in the dress shop.

When the food arrived, the sisters sat there staring at it.

'Help yourselves,' Lucia urged them.

They began to eat, hesitatingly at first, and then with gusto, overcoming their feelings of guilt.

Sister Teresa was the only one having a problem. She took one bite of food and said, 'I – I can't. It's – it's surrendering.'

Megan said, 'Sister, you want to get to the convent, don't you? Then you must eat to keep up your strength.'

Sister Teresa said primly, 'Very well. I'll eat. But I promise you, I won't enjoy it.'

It was all Lucia could do to keep a straight face. 'Good, Sister. Eat.'

When they had finished, Lucia paid the bill with some of the money she had taken from the cash register and they walked out into the hot sunshine. The streets were beginning to come alive, and the shops were starting to open. *By now they have probably caught Miguel Carrillo*, Lucia thought.

Lucia and Teresa were impatient to get out of town, but Graciela and Megan were walking slowly, fascinated by the sights and sounds and the smells of the town.

Not until they had reached the outskirts and headed towards the mountains did Lucia begin to relax. They moved steadily north, climbing upwards, making slow progress in the hilly terrain. Lucia was tempted to ask Sister Teresa if she would like her to carry the package, but she did not want to say anything that might make the older woman suspicious.

When they reached a small glade in the highland, surrounded by trees, Lucia said, 'We can spend the night here. In the morning we'll head for the convent at Mendavia.'

The others nodded, believing her.

The sun moved slowly across the blue sky, and the glade was silent, except for the soothing sounds of summer. Finally, night fell.

One by one the women stretched out on the green grass.

Lucia lay there, breathing lightly, listening for a deeper silence, waiting for them to fall asleep so that she could make her move.

Sister Teresa was finding it difficult to sleep. It was a strange experience sleeping out under the stars, surrounded by her sisters. They had names now, and faces and voices, and she was afraid that God was going to punish her for this forbidden knowledge. She felt terribly lost.

Sister Megan, too, was having difficulty getting to sleep. She was filled with the excitement of the day's events. *How did I know that the friar was a fraud?* she wondered. *And where did I get the courage to save Sister Graciela?* She smiled, unable to keep from being a tiny bit pleased with herself, even though she knew such a feeling was a sin.

Graciela was asleep, emotionally drained by what she had gone through. She tossed and turned in her sleep, haunted by dreams of being chased down dark, long, endless corridors.

Lucia Carmine lay still, waiting. She lay there for almost two hours and then quietly sat up and moved through the darkness towards Sister Teresa. She would take the package and disappear.

As she neared Sister Teresa, Lucia saw that the nun was awake on her knees, praying. Damn! Lucia hurriedly retreated.

Lucia lay down again, forcing herself to be patient. Sister Teresa could not pray all night. She had to get some sleep.

Lucia planned. The money taken from the cash register would be enough for her to take a bus or a train to Madrid. Once there, it would be simple to find a pawnbroker. She saw herself walking in and handing him the golden cross. The pawnbroker would suspect that it was stolen, but that would not matter. He would have plenty of customers eager to buy it.

I will give you one hundred thousand pesetas for it.

She would pick it up from the counter. *I would rather sell my body first.*

One hundred and fifty thousand pesetas.

I would prefer to melt it down and let the gold run in the gutter.

Two hundred thousand pesetas. That is my last offer.

You are robbing me blind, but I will accept it.

The pawnbroker would eagerly reach for it.

On one condition.

A condition?

Yes. I misplaced my passport. Do you know someone who can arrange a passport for me? Her hands would still be on the golden cross.

He would hesitate, then say, *I happen to have a friend who does things like that.*

And the deal would be done. She would be on her way to Switzerland

322

and freedom. She remembered her father's words: *There is more money there than you could spend in ten lifetimes.*

Her eyes began to close. It had been a long day.

In her half-sleep, Lucia heard the sound of a church bell from the distant village. It sent memories flooding through her, of another place, another time . . .

8

Taormina, Sicily 1968

She was awakened every morning by the distant sound of the bells of the Church of San Domenico, high in the Peloritani mountains surrounding Taormina. She enjoyed waking up slowly, languorously stretching like a cat. She kept her eyes closed, knowing that there was something wonderful to remember. *What was it?* The question teased at her mind, and she pushed it back, not wanting to know just yet, wanting to savour the surprise. And suddenly her mind was joyously flooded with it. She was Lucia Maria Carmine, the daughter of Angelo Carmine, and that was enough to make anyone in the world happy.

They lived in a large, storybook villa filled with more servants than the fifteen-year-old Lucia could count. A bodyguard drove her to school each morning in an armoured limousine. She grew up with the prettiest dresses and the most expensive toys in all of Sicily, and was the envy of her schoolmates.

But it was her father around whom Lucia's life centred. In her eyes, he was the most handsome man in the world. He was short and heavyset, with a strong face and stormy brown eyes that radiated power. He had two sons, Arnaldo and Victor, but it was his daughter whom Angelo Carmine adored. And Lucia worshipped him. In church when the priest spoke of God, Lucia always thought of her father.

He would come to her bedside in the morning and say, 'Time to get up for school, *faccia del angelo*.' Angel face.

It was not true, of course. Lucia knew she was not really beautiful. *I'm attractive*, she thought, studying herself objectively in the mirror. Yes. Striking, rather than beautiful. Her reflection showed a young girl with an oval face, creamy skin, even, white teeth, a strong chin – too strong? – voluptuous, full lips – too full? – and dark, knowing eyes. But if her face fell just short of being beautiful, her body more than made up for it. At fifteen, Lucia had the body of a woman, with round, firm breasts, a narrow waist and hips that moved with sensuous promise.

'We're going to have to marry you off early,' her father would tease her. 'Soon you will drive the young men *pazzi*, my little virgin.'

'I want to marry someone like you, Papa, but there is no one like you.'

He laughed. 'Never mind. We'll find you a prince. You were born under a lucky star, and one day you will know what it is like to have a man hold you in his arms and make love to you.'

Lucia blushed. 'Yes, Papa.'

It was true that no one had made love to her – not for the past twelve hours. Benito Patas, one of her bodyguards, always came to her bed when her father was out of town. Having Benito make love to her in her house added to the thrill because Lucia knew that her father would kill them both if he ever discovered what was going on.

Benito was in his thirties, and it flattered him that the beautiful young virgin daughter of the great Angelo Carmine had chosen him to deflower her.

'Was it as you expected?' he asked the first time he bedded her.

'Oh, yes,' Lucia breathed. 'Better.'

She thought: *While he's not as good as Mario, Tony or Enrico, he's certainly better than Roberto and Leo.* She could not remember the names of all the others.

At thirteen, Lucia had felt that she had been a virgin long enough. She had looked around and decided that the lucky boy would be Paolo Costello, the son of Angelo Carmine's doctor. Paolo was seventeen, tall and husky, and the star soccer player at his school. Lucia had fallen madly in love with Paolo the first time she had seen him. She managed to run into him as often as possible. It never occurred to Paolo that their constant meetings had been carefully contrived. He regarded the attractive young daughter of Angelo Carmine as a child. But on a hot summer day in August, Lucia decided she could wait no longer. She telephone Paolo.

'Paolo – this is Lucia Carmine. My father has something he would like to discuss with you, and he wondered whether you could meet him this afternoon at our pool house?'

Paolo was both surprised and flattered. He was in awe of Angelo Carmine, but he had not known that the powerful Mafioso was even aware of his existence. 'I would be delighted,' Paolo said. 'What time would he like me to be there?'

'Three o'clock.'

Siesta time, when the world would be asleep. The pool house was isolated, at the far end of their widespread property, and her father was out of town. There would be no chance of their being interrupted.

Paolo arrived promptly at the appointed hour. The gate leading to the garden was open, and he walked directly to the pool house. He stopped at the closed door and knocked. 'Signore Carmine? *Pronto* . . . ?'

There was no response. Paolo checked his watch. Cautiously, he opened the door and stepped inside. The room was dark.

'Signore Carmine?'

A figure moved towards him. 'Paolo . . .'

He recognized Lucia's voice. 'Lucia, I'm looking for your father. Is he here?'

She was closer to him now, close enough for Paolo to see that she was stark naked.

'My God!' Paolo gasped. 'What –?'

'I want you to make love to me.'

'You're *pazza*! You're only a child. I'm getting out of here.' He started towards the door.

'Go ahead. I'll tell my father you raped me.'

'No, you wouldn't.'

'Leave, and you'll find out.'

He stopped. If Lucia carried out her threat, there was not the slightest doubt in Paolo's mind as to what his fate would be. Castration would be only the beginning.

He walked back to Lucia to reason with her. 'Lucia, dear –'

'I like it when you call me dear.'

'No – listen to me, Lucia. This is very serious. Your father will kill me if you tell him I raped you.'

'I know.'

He made another stab at it. 'My father would be disgraced. My whole family would be disgraced.'

'I know.'

It was hopeless. 'What do you want from me?'

'I want you to do it to me.'

'No. It is impossible. If your father found out, he would kill me.'

'And if you leave here, he will kill you. You haven't got much choice, have you?'

He stared at her, panicky. 'Why me, Lucia?'

'Because I'm in love with you, Paolo!' She took his hands and pressed them gently between her legs. 'I'm a woman. Make me feel like one.'

In the dim light Paolo could see the twin mounds of her breasts, her hard nipples, and the soft, dark hair between her legs.

Jesus, Paolo thought. *What can a man do?*

She was leading him to a couch, helping him out of his trousers and his shorts. She knelt and put his male hardness in her mouth, sucking it gently, and Paolo thought: *She's done this before*. And when he was on top of her, plunging deep inside her, and she had her hands tightly wrapped around his backside, her hips thrusting hungrily against his, Paolo thought: *My God, she's marvellous*.

Lucia was in heaven. It was as though she had been born for this. Instinctively she knew exactly what to do to please him and to please herself. Her whole body was on fire. She felt herself building to a climax, higher and higher, and when it finally happened, she screamed aloud in sheer joy. They both lay there, spent, breathing hard.

Lucia finally spoke. She said, 'Same time tomorrow.'

When Lucia was sixteen, Angelo Carmine decided that it was time for his daughter to see something of the world. With an elderly Aunt Rosa as chaperone, Lucia spent her school holidays in Capri and Ischia, Venice and Rome, and a dozen other places.

'You must be cultured – not a peasant, like your Papa. Travel will round out your education. In Capri Aunt Rosa will take you to see the Carthusian Monastery of St James and the Chapel of San Michele and the Palazzo a Mare . . .'

'Yes, Papa.'

'In Venice there is St Mark's Basilica, the Doges' Palace, the church of San Gregorio, and the Accademia Museum.'

'Yes, Papa.'

'Rome is the treasure house of the world. There you must visit the Citta Vaticano, and the Basilica of Santa Maria Maggiore, and the Galleria Borghese, of course.'

'Of course.'

'And Milano! You must go to the Conservatorio for a concert recital. I will arrange tickets for La Scala for you and Aunt Rosa. You will see the Municipal Museum of Art, and there are dozens of churches and museums.'

'Yes, Papa.'

With very careful planning, Lucia managed to see none of those places. Aunt Rosa insisted on taking a siesta every afternoon and retiring early each evening.

'You must get your rest too, child.'

'Certainly, Aunt Rosa.'

And so while Aunt Rosa slept, Lucia danced at the Quisisana in Capri, rode in a *carrozza* with a beplumed and behatted horse pulling it, joined a group of college boys at the Marina Piccola, went on picnics at Bagni di Tiberio, and took the *Funicolare* up to Anacapri, where she joined a group of French students for drinks at the Piazza Umertol.

In Venice a handsome gondolier took her to a disco, and a fisherman took her fishing at Chioggia. And Aunt Rosa slept.

In Rome Lucia drank wine from Apulia and discovered all the off-beat fun restaurants like Marte and Ranieri and Giggi Fazi.

Wherever she went, Lucia found hidden little bars and nightclubs and romantic, good-looking men, and she thought: *Dear Papa was so right. Travel has rounded out my education.*

In bed, she learned to speak several different languages, and she thought: *This is so much more fun than my language classes at school.*

When Lucia returned home to Taormina, she confided to her closest girl-friends: 'I was naked in Naples, stoned in Salermo, felt up in Florence, and laid in Lucca.'

Sicily itself was a wonder to explore, an island of Grecian temples, Roman Byzantine amphitheatres, chapels, Arab baths and Swabian castles.

Lucia found Palermo raucous and lively, and she enjoyed wandering around the Kalsa, the old Arab quarter, and visiting the Opera dei Pupi, the puppet theatre. But Taormina, where she was born, was her favourite. It was a picture postcard of a city on the Ionian Sea on a mountain overlooking the world. It was a city of dress shops and jewellery stores, bars and beautiful old squares, *trattorias* and colourful hotels like the Excelsior Palace and the San Domenico.

The winding road leading up from the seaport of Nachos is steep and narrow and dangerous, and when Lucia Carmine was given a car on her fifteenth birthday, she broke every traffic law in the book but was never once stopped by the *Carabiniere*. After all, she was the daughter of Angelo Carmine.

To those who were brave enough or stupid enough to inquire, Angelo Carmine was in the property business. And it was partially true, for the Carmine family owned the villa at Taormina, a house on Lake Como at Cernobbio, a lodge at Gstaad, an apartment in Rome, and a large farm outside Rome. But it happened that Angelo Carmine was also in more colourful businesses. He owned a dozen whorehouses, two gambling casinos, six ships that brought in cocaine from his plantations in Colombia, and an assortment of other very lucrative enterprises, including loan sharking. Angelo Carmine was the Capo of the Sicilian Mafiosi, so it was only appropriate that he lived well. His life was an inspiration to others, heartwarming proof that a poor Sicilian peasant who was ambitious and worked hard could become rich and successful.

Angelo Carmine had started out as an errand boy for the Mafiosi when he was twelve. By fifteen he had become an enforcer for the loan sharks, and at sixteen he had killed his first man and made his bones. Shortly after that, he married Lucia's mother, Anna. In the years that followed, Angelo Carmine had climbed the treacherous corporate ladder to the top, leaving a string of dead enemies behind him. He had grown, but Anna had remained the simple peasant girl he married. She bore him three fine children, but after that her contribution to Angelo's life came to a halt. As though knowing she no longer had a place in her family's life, she obligingly died and was considerate enough to manage it with a minimum of fuss.

Arnaldo and Victor were in business with their father, and from the time Lucia was a small girl, she eavesdropped on the exciting conversations between her father and her brothers, and listened to the tales of how they had outwitted or overpowered their enemies. To Lucia, her father was a knight in shining armour. She saw nothing wrong in what her father and brothers were doing. On the contrary, they were helping people. If people wanted to gamble, why let stupid laws stand in their way? If men took pleasure in buying sex, why not assist them? And how generous of her father and brothers to loan money to people who were turned away by the hard-hearted bankers. To Lucia, her father and brothers were model citizens. The proof of it lay in her father's friends. Once a week Angelo Carmine gave an enormous dinner party at the villa, and oh, the people who would be seated at the Carmine table! The mayor would be there, and a few aldermen, and judges, and seated next to them were film stars and opera singers and often the chief of police and a monsignor. Several times a year the governor himself would appear.

Lucia lived an idyllic life, filled with parties and beautiful clothes and jewels, cars and servants, and powerful friends. And then one February, on her twenty-third birthday, it all came to an abrupt end.

It began innocuously enough. Two men came to the villa to see her father. One of the men was their friend, the chief of police, and the other was his lieutenant.

'Forgive me, *Padrone*,' the police chief apologized, 'but this is a stupid formality which the Commissioner is forcing me to go through with. A thousand pardons, *Padrone*, but if you will be kind enough to accompany me to the police station, I will see to it that you are home in time to enjoy your daughter's birthday party.'

'No problem,' Angelo Carmine said genially. 'A man must do his duty.' He grinned. 'This new Commissioner who's been appointed by the President is – in the American phrase – "an eager beaver", eh?'

'I'm afraid that is so,' the police chief sighed. 'But don't worry. You and I have seen these pains-in-the-asses come and go very quickly, eh, *Padrone*?'

They laughed and left.

Angelo Carmine was not home for the party that day, nor the next. In fact, he never saw any of his homes again. The State entered a one-hundred-count indictment against him that included murder, drug trafficking, prostitution, arson, and scores of other crimes. Bail was denied. A police dragnet went out that swept up Carmine's crime organization. He had counted on his powerful connections in Sicily to have the charges against him dismissed, but instead he was taken to Rome in the middle of the night and held at the Regina Coeli, the notorious Queen of Heaven prison. He was put in a small cell that contained barred windows, a radiator, a narrow bed and a toilet with no seat. It was outrageous! It was an indignity beyond imagining.

In the beginning Angelo Carmine was sure that Tommaso Contorno, his lawyer, would have him released immediately.

When Contorno came to the visiting room of the prison, Carmine stormed at him, 'They've closed down my whorehouses and drug operation and they know everything about my money laundering operation. Somebody is talking. Find out who it is and bring me his tongue.'

'Do not worry, *Padrone*,' Contorno assured him. 'We will find him.'

His optimism turned out to be unfounded. In order to protect their witnesses, the State adamantly refused to reveal their names until the trial began.

Two days before the trial, Angelo Carmine and the other members of the Mafia were transferred to Rebibbia Prigione, a top-security prison twelve miles outside of Rome. A nearby courtroom had been fortified like a bunker. A hundred and sixty accused Mafia members were brought in through an underground tunnel wearing handcuffs and chains and put in thirty cages made of steel and bullet-proof glass. Armed guards surrounded the inside and outside of the courtroom and spectators were searched before they were allowed to enter.

When Angelo Carmine was marched into the courtroom, his heart leaped for joy, for the judge on the bench was Giovanni Buscetta, a man who had been on the Carmine payroll for the last fifteen years and who was a frequent guest at the Carmine house. Angelo Carmine knew at last that justice was going to be served.

The trial began. Angelo Carmine looked to *Omerta*, the Sicilian code of silence, to protect him. But to his astonishment, the chief witness for the State turned out to be none other than Benito Patas, the bodyguard. Benito Patas had been with the Carmine family so long and had been so trusted that he had been allowed to be in the room at meetings where confidential matters of business were discussed, and since that business consisted of every illegal activity on the police statutes, Patas was privy to a great deal of information. When the police had apprehended Patas minutes after he had cold-bloodedly murdered and mutilated the new boyfriend of his mistress, they had threatened him with life imprisonment, and Patas had reluctantly agreed to help the police build their case against Carmine in exchange for a lighter sentence. Now, to Angelo Carmine's horrified disbelief, he sat in the courtroom and listened to Patas reveal the innermost secrets of the Carmine fiefdom.

Lucia was also in the courtroom every day listening to the man who had been her lover destroying her father and her brothers.

Benito Patas' testimony opened the floodgates. Once the Commissioner's investigation began, dozens of victims came forward to tell their stories of what Angelo Carmine and his hoodlums had done to them. The Mafia had muscled into their businesses, blackmailed them, forced them into prostitution, murdered or crippled their loved ones, sold drugs to their children. The list of horrors was endless.

Even more damaging was the testimony of the *Pentiti*, the repentant members of the Mafia who decided to talk.

Lucia was allowed to visit her father in prison.

He greeted her cheerfully. He hugged her and whispered, 'Do not worry, *faccia del angelo*. Judge Giovanni Buscetta is my secret ace in the hole. He knows all the tricks of the law. He will use them to see that your brothers and I are acquitted.'

Angelo Carmine proved to be a poor prophet.

The public had been outraged by the excesses of the Mafia, and when the trial finally ended, Judge Giovanni Buscetta, an astute political animal, sentenced the Mafia members to long prison terms and sentenced Angelo Carmine and his two sons to the maximum permitted by Italian law, life imprisonment, a mandatory sentence of twenty-eight years.

For Angelo Carmine it was a death sentence.

All of Italy cheered. Justice had finally triumphed. But to Lucia, it was a nightmare beyond imagining. The three men she loved most in the world were being sent to hell.

Once again, Lucia was allowed to visit her father in his cell. The overnight change in him was heartbreaking. In the space of a few days, he had become an old man. His figure had shrunk and his healthy, ruddy complexion had turned sallow.

'They have betrayed me,' he moaned. 'They have all betrayed me. Judge Giovanni Buscetta – I owned him, Lucia! I made him a wealthy man, and he did this terrible thing to me. And Patas. I was like a father to him. What has the world come to? Whatever happened to honour? They are Sicilians, like me.'

Lucia took her father's hand in hers and said in a low voice, 'I am Sicilian, too, Papa. You shall have your vengeance. I swear it to you, on my life.'

'My life is over,' her father told her. 'But yours is still ahead of you. I have a numbered account in Zurich. The Bank Leu. There is more money there than you could spend in ten lifetimes.' He whispered a number in her ear. 'Leave cursed Italy. Take the money and enjoy yourself.'

Lucia held him close. 'Papa –'

'If you ever need a friend, you can trust Dominic Durell. We are like brothers. He has a home in France at Béziers, near the Spanish border.'

'I'll remember.'

'Promise me you'll leave Italy.'

'Yes, Papa. But there is something I have to do first.'

Having a burning desire for revenge was one thing. Figuring out a way to get it was another. She was alone, and it was not going to be easy.

Lucia thought of the Italian expression, '*Rubare il mestiere.*' *You steal their profession. I must think the way they do.*

A few weeks after her father and brothers had started serving their prison sentences, Lucia Carmine appeared at the home of Judge Giovanni Buscetta. The judge himself opened the door.

He stared at Lucia in surprise. He had seen her often when he was a guest at the Carmine home, but they had never had much to say to each other.

'Lucia Carmine? What are you doing here? You shouldn't have –'

'I have come to thank you, Your Honour.'

He studied her suspiciously. 'Thank me for what?'

Lucia looked deep into his eyes. 'For exposing my father and brothers for what they were. I was an innocent, living in that house of horrors. I had no idea what monsters –' She broke down and began to sob.

The judge stood there uncertainly, then patted her shoulder. 'There, there. Come in and have some tea.'

'Th – thank you.'

When they were seated in the living room, Judge Buscetta said, 'I had no idea that you felt that way about your father. I had the impression that you were very close.'

'Only because I had no idea what he and my brothers were really like. When I found out –' She shuddered. 'You don't know what it was like,' Lucia said. 'I wanted to get away, but there was no escape for me.'

'I didn't understand.' He patted her hand. 'I'm afraid I misjudged you, my dear.'

'I was terrified of him.' Her voice was filled with passion.

Judge Buscetta noticed, not for the first time, what a beautiful young girl Lucia was. She was wearing a simple black dress that revealed the outlines of her lush body. He looked at her rounded breasts and could not help observing how grown up she had become.

It would be amusing, Buscetta thought, *to sleep with the daughter of Angelo Carmine. He's powerless to hurt me now. The old bastard thought he owned me, but I was too smart for him. Lucia is probably a virgin. I could teach her a few things in bed.*

An elderly housekeeper brought in a tray of tea and a plate of biscuits. She put them on a table. 'Shall I pour?'

'Let me,' Lucia said. Her voice was warm and filled with promise.

Judge Buscetta smiled at Lucia. 'You can go,' he told the housekeeper.

'Yes, sir.'

The judge watched as Lucia walked over to the small table where the tray had been set down and carefully poured out tea for the judge and herself.

'I have a feeling you and I could become very good friends, Lucia,' Giovanni Buscetta said, probing.

Lucia gave him a seductive smile. 'I would like that very much, Your Honour.'

'Please – Giovanni.'

'Giovanni.' Lucia handed him his cup. She raised her cup in a toast. 'To the death of villains.'

Smiling, Buscetta lifted his cup. 'To the death of villains.' He took a swallow and grimaced. The tea tasted bitter.

'Is it too – ?'

'No, no. It is fine, my dear.'

Lucia raised her cup again. 'To our friendship.'

She took another sip, and he joined her.

'To –'

Buscetta never finished his toast. He was seized by a sudden spasm, and he felt a red-hot poker stabbing at his heart. He grabbed his chest. 'Oh, my God! Call a doctor . . .'

Lucia sat there, calmly sipping her tea, watching him stumble to his feet and fall to the floor. He lay there, his body twitching, and then he was still.

'That's one, Papa,' Lucia said.

Benito Patas was in his cell playing solitaire when the jailer announced, 'You have a conjugal visitor.'

Benito beamed. He had been given special status as an informer, with many privileges, and conjugal visits was one of them. Patas had half a dozen girl-friends, and they alternated their visits. He wondered which one had come today.

He studied himself in the little mirror hanging on the wall of his cell, put some pomade on his hair, slicked it back, then followed the guard through the prison corridor to the section where there were private rooms.

The guard motioned him inside. Patas strutted into the room, filled with anticipation. He stopped and stared in surprise.

'Lucia! My God, what the hell are you doing here? How did you get in?'

Lucia said softly, 'I told them we were engaged, Benito.'

She was wearing a stunning red, low-cut silk dress that clung to the curves of her body.

Benito Patas backed away from her. 'Get out.'

'If you wish. But there is something you should hear first. When I saw you get up on the stand and testify against my father and brothers, I hated you. I wanted to kill you.' She moved closer to him. 'But then I realized that what you were doing was an act of bravery. You dared to stand up and tell the truth. My father and my brothers were not evil

333

men, but they did evil things, and you were the only one strong enough to stand up against them.'

'Believe me, Lucia,' he said, 'the police forced me to –'

'You don't have to explain,' she said softly. 'Not to me. Remember the first time we made love? I knew then that I was in love with you and that I always would be.'

'Lucia, I would never have done what I –'

'*Caro*, I want us to forget what happened. It's done. What's important now is you and me.'

She was close to him now, and he could smell her heady perfume. His mind was in a state of confusion. 'Do – do you mean that?'

'More than I've ever meant anything in my life. That's why I came here today, to prove it to you. To show you that I'm yours. And not with just words.'

Her fingers went to her shoulder straps, and an instant later her dress shimmered to the floor. She was naked. 'Do you believe me now?'

By God, she was beautiful. 'Yes, I believe you.' His voice was husky.

Lucia moved close to him, and her body brushed against his. 'Get undressed,' she whispered. 'Hurry!'

She watched Patas as he undressed. When he was naked, he took her hand and led her to the little bed in the corner of the room. He did not bother with foreplay. In a moment he was on top of her, spreading her legs, plunging deep inside her, an arrogant smile on his face.

'It's like old times,' he said smugly. 'You couldn't forget me, could you?'

'No,' Lucia whispered in his ear. 'And do you know why I couldn't forget you?'

'No, *mi amore*. Tell me.'

'Because I'm Sicilian, like my father.'

She reached behind her head and removed the long, ornate pin that held her hair in place.

Benito Patas felt something stab him under his rib cage, and the sudden pain made him open his mouth to scream, but Lucia's mouth was on his, kissing him, and as Benito's body bucked and writhed on top of her, Lucia had an orgasm.

A few minutes later she was clothed again, and the pin had been replaced in her hair. Benito was under the blanket, his eyes closed. Lucia knocked at the cell door and smiled at the guard who opened it to let her out. 'He's asleep,' she whispered.

The guard looked at the beautiful young woman and smiled. 'You probably wore him out.'

'I hope so,' Lucia said.

The sheer daring of the two murders took Italy by storm. The beautiful young daughter of a Mafioso had avenged her father and brothers, and the excitable Italian public cheered her, rooting for her to escape. The police, quite naturally, took a rather different point of view. Lucia Carmine had murdered a respected judge and had then committed a second murder within the very walls of a prison. In their eyes, equal to her crimes was the fact that she had made fools of them. The newspapers were having a wonderful time at their expense.

'I want her neck,' the police commissioner roared to the deputy commissioner. 'And I want it *today*.'

The manhunt intensified. The object of all this attention was hiding in the home of Salvatore Giuseppe, one of her father's men who had managed to escape the firestorm.

In the beginning, Lucia's only thought had been to avenge the honour of her father and brothers. She had fully expected to be caught and was prepared to sacrifice herself. When she had managed to walk out of the prison and make her escape, however, her thoughts changed from vengeance to survival. Now that she had accomplished what she had set out to do, life suddenly became precious again. *I'm not going to let them capture me*, she vowed to herself. *Never.*

Salvatore Giuseppe and his wife had done what they could to disguise Lucia. They had lightened her hair, stained her teeth, and bought her glasses and some ill-fitting clothes. Salvatore examined their handiwork critically.

'It is not bad,' he said. 'But it is not enough. We must get you out of Italy. You have to go somewhere where your picture is not on the front page of every newspaper. Somewhere you can hide out for a few months.'

And Lucia remembered:

If you ever need a friend, you can trust Dominic Durell. We are like brothers. He has a home in France at Béziers, near the Spanish border.

'I know where I can go,' Lucia said. 'I'll need a passport.'

'I will arrange it.'

Twenty-four hours later Lucia was looking at a passport in the name of Lucia Roma, with a photograph taken in her new persona.

'Where will you go?'

'My father has a friend in France who will help me.'

Salvatore said, 'If you wish me to accompany you to the border –?'

Both of them knew how dangerous that could be.

'No, Salvatore,' Lucia said. 'You have done enough for me. I must do this alone.'

The following morning Salvatore Giuseppe rented a Fiat in the name of Lucia Roma and handed her the keys.

'Be careful,' he pleaded.

'Don't worry. I was born under a lucky star.'

Had not her father told her so?

At the Italian–French border the cars waiting to get into France were advancing slowly in a long line. As Lucia moved closer to the immigration booth, she became more and more nervous. They would be looking for her at all exit points. If they caught her, she knew she would be sentenced to prison for life. *I'll kill myself first*, Lucia thought.

She had reached the immigration officer.

'Passport, signorina.'

Lucia handed him her black passport through the car window. As the officer took it, he glanced at Lucia, and she saw a puzzled look come into his eyes. He looked from the passport to her face and back again, this time more carefully. Lucia felt her body tense.

'You're Lucia Carmine,' he said.

9

'Lucia Carmine.'

'No!' Lucia cried. The blood drained from her face. She looked around for a way to escape. There was none. And suddenly, to her disbelief, the guard was smiling. He leaned towards her and whispered, 'Your father was good to my family, signorina. You may pass through. Good luck.'

Lucia felt dizzy with relief. '*Grazie.*'

She stepped on the accelerator and drove the twenty-five yards towards the French border. The French immigration officer prided himself on being a connoisseur of beautiful women, and the woman who pulled up before him was certainly no beauty. She had mousy hair, thick glasses, stained teeth and was dowdily dressed.

Why can't Italian women look as beautiful as French women? he thought disgustedly. He stamped Lucia's passport and waved her through.

She arrived in Béziers many hours later.

The phone was answered on the first ring, and a smooth male voice said, 'Hello.'

'Dominic Durell, please.'

'This is Dominic Durell. Who is this speaking?'

'Lucia Carmine. My father told me –'

'Lucia!' His voice was warm with welcome. 'I was hoping to hear from you.'

'I need help.'

'You can count on me.'

Lucia's heart lightened. It was the first good news she had heard in a long time. She suddenly realized how drained she was.

'I need a place where I can hide out from the police.'

'No problem. My wife and I have a perfect place for you to use for as long as you like.'

It was almost too good to be true.

'Thank you.'

'Where are you, Lucia?'

'I'm –'

At that moment the blare of a police shortwave radio crackled over the phone. It was instantly shut off.

'Lucia –'

A loud alarm rang in her head.

'Lucia – where are you? I'll come and get you.'

Why would he have a police radio in his house? And he had answered the telephone on the first ring. Almost as though he had been expecting her call.

'Lucia – can you hear me?'

She knew, with an absolute certainty, that the man on the other end of the line was a policeman. So the dragnet was out for her. This call was being traced.

'Lucia –'

She replaced the receiver and walked quickly away from the telephone booth.

I've got to get out of France, she thought.

She returned to her car and took a map from the glove compartment. The Spanish border was only a short distance away. She replaced the map and started off. She turned a corner and headed south towards San Sebastian.

It was at the Spanish border that things started to go wrong.

'Passport, please.'

Lucia handed the Spanish immigration officer her passport. He gave it a cursory glance and started to hand it back, but something made him hesitate. He took a closer look at Lucia, and his expression changed.

'Just a moment, please. I will have to have this stamped inside.'

He recognized me, Lucia thought desperately. She watched him walk into the little office kiosk and show the passport to another officer. The two of them were talking excitedly. She had to escape. She opened the door on the driver's side and stepped out. A group of German tourists who had just cleared customs was noisily boarding an excursion coach next to Lucia's car. The sign on the front of the coach read 'Madrid'.

'*Achtung!*' their guide was calling out. '*Schnell.*'

Lucia glanced towards the hut. The guard who had taken her passport was yelling into the telephone.

'All aboard, *bitte.*'

Without a second thought, Lucia moved towards the laughing, chattering tour group and stepped on to the coach, averting her face from the guide. She took a seat in the rear of the coach, keeping her head down. *Move!* she prayed. *Now.*

Through the window Lucia saw that another guard had joined the first two and the three of them were examining her passport. As though in answer to Lucia's prayer, the coach door closed and the engine sprang into life. A short time later the coach was rolling out of San Sebastian towards Madrid. What would happen when the border guards found that she had left her car? Their first thought would be that she had gone to the ladies' room. They would wait and finally send someone in to get her. Their next step would be to search the area to see if she had hidden somewhere. By then dozens of cars and buses would have passed through. The police would have no idea where she had gone, nor in which direction she was travelling.

The tour group on the coach was obviously having a happy holiday. *Why not?* Lucia thought bitterly. *They haven't got the police snapping at their heels. Was it worth risking the rest of my life for?* She thought about it, reliving the scenes with Judge Buscetta and Benito in her mind.

I have a feeling you and I could become very good friends, Lucia . . . To the death of villains.

And Benito Patas: *It's like old times. You couldn't forget me, could you?*

And she had made the two traitors pay for their sins against her family. *Was it worth it?* They were dead, but her father and brothers would suffer for the rest of their lives. *Oh, yes*, Lucia thought. *It was worth it.*

Someone on the coach started a German song, and the others joined in:

'*In München ist ein Hofbrau Haus, ein, zwei, drei . . .*'

I'll be safe with this group for a while, Lucia thought. *I'll decide what to do next when I get to Madrid.*

She never reached Madrid.

At the walled city of Ávila, the tour coach made a scheduled stop for refreshments and what the guide delicately referred to as a 'comfort station'.

'*Alle raus aus dem Bus*,' he called.

Lucia stayed in her seat, watching the passengers rise and scramble for the front door of the coach. *I'll be safer if I stay here.* But the guide noticed her.

'Out, *Fräulein*,' he said. 'We have only fifteen minutes.'

Lucia hesitated, then reluctantly rose and moved towards the door.

As she passed the guide, he said, '*Warten Sie, bitte!* You are not of this tour.'

Lucia gave him a warm smile. 'No,' she said. 'You see, my car broke down in San Sebastian and it is very important that I get to Madrid, so I –'

'*Nein!*' the guide bellowed. 'This is not possible. This is a private tour.'

'I know,' Lucia told him, 'but you see, I need –'

'You must arrange this with the company headquarters in Munich.'

'I can't. I'm in a terrible hurry and –'

'*Nein, nein.* You will get me in trouble. Go away or I will call the police.'

'But –'

Nothing she said could sway him. Twenty minutes later Lucia watched the coach pull away and roar down the highway towards Madrid. She was stranded with no passport and almost no money, and by now the police of half a dozen countries would be looking for her to arrest her for murder.

She turned to examine her surroundings. The coach had stopped in front of a circular building with a sign in front that read '*Estación de Autobuses*'.

I can get another bus here, Lucia thought.

She walked into the station. It was a large building with marble walls, and scattered around the room were a dozen ticket windows with a sign over each one: *Segovia . . . Muñogalindo . . . Valladolid . . . Salamanca . . . Madrid*. Stairs and an escalator led to the downstairs level where the buses departed. There was a *pastelería* where they sold doughnuts and sweets and sandwiches wrapped in wax paper, and Lucia suddenly realized that she was starved.

I'd better not buy anything, she thought, *until I find out how much a bus ticket costs*.

As she started towards the window marked Madrid, two uniformed policemen hurried into the station. One of them was carrying a photograph. They moved from window to window showing the picture to the clerks.

They're looking for me. That damned bus driver reported me.

A family of newly arrived passengers was coming up the escalator. As they moved towards the door, Lucia stepped up beside them, mingling with them, and went outside.

She walked down the cobblestoned streets of Ávila, trying not to rush, afraid of drawing attention to herself. She turned into the Calle de la Madre Soledad, with its granite buildings and black wrought-iron balconies, and when she reached the Plaza de la Santa, she sat down on a park bench to try to figure out her next move. A hundred yards away, several women and some couples were seated in the park, enjoying the afternoon sunshine.

As Lucia sat there, a police car appeared. It pulled up at the far end of the square and two policemen got out. They moved over to one of the women seated alone and began questioning her. Lucia's heart began to beat faster.

She forced herself to get to her feet slowly, her heart pounding, and turned away from the policemen and kept walking. The next street was called, unbelievably, 'The Street of Life and Death'. *I wonder if it's an omen.*

There were realistic-looking stone lions in the plaza, their tongues out, and in Lucia's fevered imagination, they seemed to be snapping at her. Ahead of her was a large cathedral, and on its façade was a carved medallion of a young girl and a grinning skull. The very air seemed to be filled with death.

Lucia heard the sound of a church bell and looked up through the open city gate. In the distance, high on a hill, rose the walls of an abbey. She stood there, staring at it.

'Why have you come to us, my daughter?' the Reverend Mother Betina asked softly.

'I need a place of refuge.'

'And you have decided to seek the refuge of God?'

Exactly. 'Yes.' Lucia began to improvise. 'This is what I have always wanted – to devote myself to the life of the spirit.'

'In our souls it is what we all wish for, is it not, daughter?'

Jesus, she's really falling for it, Lucia thought happily.

The Reverend Mother went on: 'You must understand that the Cistercian Order is the strictest of all the orders, my child. We are completely isolated from the outside world.'

Her words were music to Lucia's ears.

'Those who enter these walls have vowed never to leave.'

'I never want to leave,' Lucia assured her. *Not for the next few months, anyway.*

The Reverend Mother rose. 'It is an important decision. I suggest that you go and think about it carefully before you make up your mind.'

Lucia felt the situation slipping away from her and she began to panic. She had nowhere to go. Her only hope was to stay behind these walls.

'I have thought about it,' Lucia said quickly. 'Believe me, Reverend Mother, I've thought about nothing else. I want to renounce the world.' She looked the Mother Prioress in the eye. 'I want to be here more than I want to be anywhere else in the world.' Lucia's voice rang with truth.

The Reverend Mother was puzzled. There was something unsettled and frantic about this woman that was disturbing. And yet what better reason for anyone to come to this place where their spirit would be calmed by meditation and prayer?

'Are you Catholic?'

'Yes.'

The Reverend Mother picked up an old-fashioned quill pen. 'Tell me your name, child.'

'My name is Lucia Car – *Roma*.'

'Are your parents alive?'

'My father is.'

'What does he do?'

'He was a businessman. He's retired.' She thought of how pale and wasted he looked the last time she had seen him, and a pang went through her.

'Do you have any brothers or sisters?'

'Two brothers.'

'And what do they do?'

Lucia decided she needed all the help she could get. 'They're priests.'

'Lovely.'

The catechism went on for three hours. At the end of that time, the Reverend Mother Betina said, 'I will find you a bed for the night. In the morning you will begin instructions and when they are finished, if you still feel the same, you may join the order. But I warn you, it is a very difficult path you have chosen.'

'Believe me,' Lucia said earnestly. 'I have no choice.'

The night wind was soft and warm, whispering its way across the wooded glade, and Lucia slept. She was at a party in a beautiful villa, and her father and brothers were there, and everyone was having a wonderful time, and a stranger walked into the room and said, 'Who the hell are these people?' And the lights went out and a bright flashlight shone in her face and she came awake and sat up, the light blinding her.

There were half a dozen men surrounding the nuns in the clearing. With the light in her eyes, Lucia could only dimly make out their shapes.

'Who are you?' the man demanded again. His voice was deep and rough.

Lucia was instantly awake, her mind alert. She was trapped. But if these men were from the police, they would have known who the nuns were. And what were they doing in the woods at night?

Lucia took a chance. 'We are sisters from the convent at Ávila,' she said. 'Some government men came and –'

'We heard about it,' the man interrupted.

The other sisters were all sitting up now, awake and terrified.

'Who – who are you?' Megan asked.

'My name is Jaime Miró.'

There were six of them, dressed in rough trousers, leather jackets, turtleneck sweaters and canvas rope-soled shoes, and the traditional Basque berets. They were heavily armed, and in the dim moonlight they had a demonic look. Two of the men looked as though they had been badly beaten.

The man who called himself Jaime Miró was tall and lean, with fierce black eyes. 'They could have been followed here.' He turned to one of the members of his band. 'Have a look around.'

'Si.'

Lucia realized that it was a woman who answered. Lucia watched her move silently into the trees.

'What are we going to do with them?' Ricardo Mellado asked.

Jaime Miró said, '*Nada*. We leave them and move on.'

One of the men protested, 'Jaime – these are little sisters of Jesus.'

'Then let Jesus take care of them,' Jaime Miró said curtly. 'We have work to do.'

The nuns were all standing now, waiting. The men were gathered around Jaime, arguing with him.

'We can't let them get caught. Acoca and his men are searching for them.'

'They're searching for us, too, *amigo*.'

'The sisters will never make it without our help.'

Jaime Miró said firmly, 'No. We're not risking our lives for them. We have problems of our own.'

Felix Carpio, one of his lieutenants, said, 'We could escort them part of the way, Jaime. Just until they get away from here.' He turned to the nuns. 'Where are you sisters headed?'

Teresa spoke up, the light of God in her eyes. 'I have a holy mission. There is a convent at Mendavia that will shelter us.'

Felix Carpio said to Jaime Miró, 'We could escort them there. Mendavia's on our way to San Sebastian.'

Jaime Miró turned on him, furious. 'You damned fool! Why don't you put up a signpost telling everyone where we're going?'

'I only meant –'

'*Mierda!*' His voice was filled with disgust. 'Now we have no choice. We'll have to take them with us. If Acoca finds them, he'll make them talk. They're going to slow us down and make it that much easier for Acoca and his butchers to track us.'

Lucia was only half listening. The gold cross lay within tempting reach. *But these damned men! You have lousy timing, God, and a weird sense of humour.*

'All right,' Jaime Miró was saying. 'We'll have to make the best of it. We'll take them as far as the convent and drop them, but we can't all travel together like some bloody circus.' He turned to the nuns. He could not keep the anger out of his voice. 'Do any of you even know where Mendavia is?'

The sisters looked at one another.

Graciela said, 'Not exactly.'

'Then how the hell did you ever expect to get there?'

'God will lead us,' Sister Teresa said firmly.

Another one of the men, Rubio Arzano, grinned. 'You're in luck.' He nodded towards Jaime. 'He came down to guide you in person, sister.'

Jaime silenced him with a look. 'We'll split up. We'll take three different routes.'

He pulled a map out of a backpack and the men squatted down on the ground, shining flashlights on the map.

'The convent at Mendavia is here, south-east of Logroño. I'll head north through Valladolid, then up to Burgos.' He ran his fingers along the map and turned to Rubio; a tall, pleasant-looking man. 'You take the route to Olmedo up to Peñafiel and Aranda de Duero.'

'Right, *amigo*.'

Jaime Miró was concentrating on the map again. He looked up at Ricardo Mellado, one of the men whose face was bruised. 'Ricardo, head for Segovia, then take the mountain route to Cerezo de Abajo, then to Soria. We'll all meet at Logroño.' He put the map away. 'Logroño is two hundred and ten kilometres from here.' He calculated silently. 'We'll meet there in seven days. Keep away from the main roads.'

Felix asked, 'Where in Logroño shall we meet?'

Ricardo said, 'The Cirque Japon will be playing in Logroño next week.'

'Good. We'll meet there. The matinee performance.'

Felix Carpio, the bearded one, spoke up. 'Who are the nuns going to travel with?'

'We'll split them up.'

It was time to put a stop to this, Lucia decided. 'If the soldiers are searching for you, signore, then we'd be safer travelling on our own.'

'But *we* wouldn't be, Sister,' Jaime said. 'You know too much about our plans now.'

'Besides,' the man called Rubio added, 'you wouldn't have a chance. We know the country. We're Basques, and the people up north are our friends. They'll help us and hide us from the nationalist soldiers. You'd never get to Mendavia by yourselves.'

I don't want to get to Mendavia, you idiot.

Jaime Miró was saying, grudgingly, 'All right, then, let's get moving. I want us far away from here by dawn.'

Sister Megan stood quietly listening to the man who was giving orders. He was rude and arrogant, but somehow he seemed to radiate a reassuring sense of power.

Jaime Miró looked over at Teresa and pointed to Tomas Sanjuro and Rubio Arzano. 'They will be responsible for you.'

Sister Teresa said, 'God is responsible for me.'

'Sure,' Jaime replied drily. 'I suppose that's how you got here in the first place.'

Rubio walked over to Teresa. 'Rubio Arzano at your service, Sister. How are you called?'

'I am Sister Teresa.'

Lucia spoke up quickly. 'I will travel with Sister Teresa.' There was no way she was going to let them separate her from the gold cross.

344

Jaime Miró nodded. 'All right.' He pointed to Graciela. 'Ricardo, you'll take this one.'

Ricardo Mellado nodded. '*Bueno.*'

The woman, whom Jaime had sent to reconnoitre, had returned to the group. 'It's all clear,' she said.

'Good.' Jaime Miró looked at Megan. 'You come with us, Sister.'

Megan nodded. Jaime Miró fascinated her. And there was something intriguing about the woman. She was dark and fierce-looking, with the hawk-like features of a predator. Her mouth was a red wound. There was something intensely sexual about her.

The woman walked up to Megan. 'I'm Amparo Jiron. Keep your mouth shut, Sister, and there will be no trouble.'

Jaime said to the others, 'Let's get moving. We'll meet in Logroño in seven days. Don't let the sisters out of your sight.'

Sister Teresa and the man called Rubio Arzano had already started to move down the path. Lucia hurried after them. She had seen the map that Rubio Arzano had put in his backpack. *I'll take it*, Lucia decided, *when he's asleep*.

Their flight across Spain began.

10

Miguel Carrillo was nervous. In fact, Miguel Carrillo was *very* nervous. It had not been a wonderful day for him. What had started so well in the morning when he had encountered the four nuns and convinced them that he was a friar, had ended up with him being knocked unconscious and tied hand and foot and left on the floor of the dress shop.

It was the owner's wife who had discovered him. She was a heavyset, elderly woman with a moustache and a foul temper. She had looked down at him, trussed up on the floor and said, '*¡Madre de Dios!* Who are you? What are you doing here?'

Carrillo had turned on all his charm. 'Thank heavens you've come, *señorita*.' He had never met anyone who was more obviously a *señora*. 'I've been trying to get out of these straps so I could use your phone to call the police.'

'You haven't answered my question.'

He tried to struggle into a more comfortable position. 'The explanation is simple, *señorita*. I am Friar Gonzales. I come from a monastery near Madrid. I was passing by your beautiful shop when I saw two young men breaking into it. I felt it was my duty as a man of God to stop them. I followed them inside hoping to persuade them of the errors of their ways, but they overpowered me and tied me up. Now, if you would be good enough to untie me –'

'*¡Mierda!*'

He stared at her. 'I beg your pardon?'

'Who are you?'

'I told you, I'm –'

'What you are is the worst liar I've ever heard.'

She walked over to the robes that the nuns had discarded.

'What are those?'

'Ah. Those, yes. The two young men were wearing them as disguises, you see, and –'

'There are four outfits here. You said there were two men.'

'Right. The other two joined them later, and –'

She walked over to the phone.

'What are you doing?'

'Calling the police.'

'That's not necessary, I assure you. As soon as you release me, I'm going right to the police station to make a full report.'

The woman looked down at him.

'Your robe is open, Friar.'

346

The police were even less sympathetic than the woman had been. Carrillo was being questioned by four members of the *guardia civil*. Their green uniforms and eighteenth-century black patent leather hats were enough to inspire fear throughout Spain, and they certainly worked their magic on Carrillo.

'Are you aware that you answer to the exact description of a man who murdered a priest up north?'

Carrillo sighed. 'I am not surprised. I have a twin brother, may heaven punish him. It is because of him that I joined the monastery. Our poor mother –'

'Spare us.'

A giant with a scarred face walked into the room.

'Good afternoon, Colonel Acoca.'

'Is this the man?'

'Yes, Colonel. Because of the nuns' robes that we found with him in the shop, we thought you might be interested in questioning him yourself.'

Colonel Ramón Acoca walked up to the hapless Carrillo. 'Yes. I'm very interested.'

Carrillo gave the Colonel his most ingratiating smile. 'I'm glad you're here, Colonel. I'm on a mission for my church, and it's very important that I get to Barcelona as quickly as possible. As I tried to explain to these nice gentlemen, I am a victim of circumstances simply because I tried to be a good samaritan.'

Colonel Acoca nodded pleasantly. 'Since you are in a hurry, I will try not to waste your time.'

Carrillo beamed at him. 'Thank you, Colonel.'

'I'm going to ask you a few simple questions. If you answer truthfully, everything will be fine. If you lie to me, it will be very painful for you.' He slipped something into his hand.

Carrillo said righteously, 'Men of God do not lie.'

'I'm very happy to hear that. Tell me about the four nuns.'

'I don't know anything about four nuns, Col –'

The fist that hit him in the mouth had brass knuckles on it, and blood spurted across the room.

'My God! What are you doing?' Carrillo gasped.

Colonel Acoca repeated his question. 'Tell me about the four nuns.'

'I don't –'

The fist slammed into Carrillo's mouth again, breaking teeth.

Carrillo was choking on his blood. 'Don't. I –'

'Tell me about the four nuns.' Acoca's voice was soft and reasonable.

'I –' He saw the fist being raised. 'Yes! I – I –'

The words came tumbling out. 'They were in Villacastin, running away from their convent. Please don't hit me again.'

'Go on.'

'I – I told them I would help them. They needed to change clothes.'

347

'So you broke into the shop . . .'

'No. I – yes. I – they stole some clothes and then they knocked me out and left me.'

'Did they say where they were headed?'

A peculiar sense of dignity suddenly took possession of Carrillo. 'No.' His not mentioning Mendavia had nothing to do with protecting the nuns. Carrillo did not give a damn about them. It was because the Colonel had ruined his face. It was going to be very difficult to make a living after he was released from prison.

Colonel Acoca turned to the members of the *guardia civil*.

'See what a little friendly persuasion can do? Send him to Madrid and hold him for murder.'

Lucia, Sister Teresa, Rubio Arzano and Tomas Sanjuro walked northeast, heading towards Olmeda, staying away from the main roads and walking through fields of grain. They passed flocks of sheep and goats, and the innocence of the pastoral countryside was in ironic contrast to the grave danger they were all in. They walked through the night, and at dawn they headed for a secluded spot in the hills.

Rubio Arzano said, 'The town of Olmeda is just ahead. We'll stop here until nightfall. You both look as though you could do with some sleep.'

Sister Teresa was physically exhausted. But something was happening to her emotionally that was far more disturbing. She felt she was losing touch with reality. It had begun with the disappearance of her precious rosary. Had she lost it – or had someone stolen it? She was not sure. It had been her solace for more years than she could remember. How many thousands of Hail Marys and how many Our Fathers and how many Hail, Holy Queens? It had become a part of her, her security, and now it was missing.

Had she lost it in the convent during the attack? And had there really been an attack? It seemed so unreal now. She was no longer sure what was real and what was imaginary. The baby she had seen. Was it Monique's baby? Or was God playing tricks on her? It was all so confusing. When she was young, everything had been so simple. When she was young . . .

11

Èze, France 1924

When she was only eight years old, most of the happiness in Teresa DeFosse's life came from the church. It was like a sacred flame drawing her to its warmth. She visited the Chapelle des Penitents Blancs, and prayed at the cathedral in Monaco and Notre Dame Bon Voyage in Cannes, but most frequently she attended services at the church in Èze.

Teresa lived in a château on a mountain above the medieval village of Èze, near Monte Carlo, overlooking the Côte d'Azur. The village was perched high on a rock and it seemed to Teresa that she could look down upon the whole world. There was a monastery at the top, with rows of houses cascading down the side of the mountain to the blue Mediterranean below.

Monique, a year younger than Teresa, was the beauty in the family. Even when she was a child, one could see that she would grow up to be an exquisite woman. She had fine-boned features, sparkling blue eyes, and an easy self-assurance that suited her looks.

Teresa was the ugly duckling. The truth was that the DeFosses were embarrassed by their elder daughter. If Teresa had been conventionally ugly, they might have sent her to a plastic surgeon and had her nose shortened, or her chin brought forward, or her eyes fixed. But the problem was that all Teresa's features were just slightly askew. Everything seemed out of place, as though she were a comedienne who had donned her face for laughter.

But if God had cheated her in the matter of looks, He had compensated for it by blessing her with a remarkable gift. Teresa had the voice of an angel. It had been noticed the first time she sang in the church choir. The parishioners listened in astonishment to the pure, clear tones that came from the young child. And as Teresa grew older, her voice grew even more beautiful. She was given all the solos to sing in church. There, she felt as though she belonged. But away from church, Teresa was inordinately shy, painfully aware of her appearance.

At school it was Monique who had all the friends. Boys and girls alike flocked to her side. They wanted to play with her, be seen with her. Monique was invited to all the parties. Teresa was invited also, but it was an after-thought, the fulfilling of a social obligation, and Teresa was painfully aware of it.

'Now, Renée. You can't invite one of the DeFosse children without the other. It would be bad manners.'

Monique was ashamed to have an ugly sister. She felt that it was somehow a reflection on her.

Teresa's parents behaved properly towards their elder daughter. They fulfilled their parental duty punctiliously, but it was obvious that it was Monique they adored. The one ingredient that Teresa longed for was missing: love.

She was an obedient child, willing and eager to please, a good student who loved music, history and foreign languages and worked hard in school. Her teachers and the servants and the townspeople felt sorry for her. As a tradesman said one day when Teresa left his shop, 'God wasn't paying attention when he made her.'

Where Teresa found love was in the church. The priest loved her, and Jesus loved her. She went to mass every morning and made the fourteen stations of the cross. Kneeling in the cool, vaulted church, she felt God's presence. When she sang there, Teresa was filled with a sense of hope, of expectation. She felt as though something wonderful were about to happen to her. It was the only thing that made her life bearable.

Teresa never confided her unhappiness to her parents or to her sister, for she did not want to burden them, and she hugged to herself the secret of how much God loved her and how much she loved God.

Teresa adored her sister. They played together in the estate grounds surrounding their château, and she let Monique win the games they played. They went exploring together, down the steep stone steps cut into the mountain to Èze Village below, and wandered down the narrow streets of artists' shops to watch the artists in front selling their wares.

As the girls grew into their teens, the predictions of the villagers came true. Monique grew more beautiful. The boys came flocking around Monique, while Teresa stayed in her room sewing or reading or went shopping in the village.

As Teresa passed the drawing room one day, she heard her mother and father in a discussion.

'She's going to be an old maid. We're going to have her on our hands all our lives.'

'Teresa will find someone. She has a very sweet disposition.'

'That's not what the young men of today are after. They want someone they can enjoy having in their bed.'

Teresa fled.

Teresa still sang in church on Sundays, and because of that an event occurred that almost changed her life. In the congregation was a Madame Neff, the aunt of a radio station director in Nice.

She stopped to speak to Teresa one Sunday morning. 'You're wasting

350

your life here, my dear. You have an extraordinary voice. You should be using it.'

'I am using it. I –'

'I'm not talking about –' She looked around the church. '– *this*. I'm talking about your using your voice professionally. I pride myself on knowing talent when I hear it. I want you to sing for my nephew. He can put you on the radio. Are you interested?'

'I – I don't know.' The very thought of it terrified Teresa.

'Talk it over with your family.'

'I think it's a wonderful idea,' Teresa's mother said.

'It could be a good thing for you,' her father agreed.

It was Monique who had reservations about it. 'You're not a professional,' she said. 'You could make a fool of yourself.' Which had nothing to do with Monique's reasons for trying to discourage her sister. What Monique was afraid of was that Teresa would *succeed*. Monique was the one who had always been in the limelight. *It's not fair*, she thought, *that God should have given Teresa a voice like that. What if she should become famous? I would be left out, ignored.*

And so Monique tried to persuade her sister not to audition.

But the following Sunday at church, Madame Neff stopped Teresa and said, 'I've talked to my nephew. He is willing to give you an audition. He's expecting you on Wednesday at three o'clock.'

And so it was that the following Wednesday a very nervous Teresa appeared at the radio station in Nice and met the director.

'I'm Louis Bonnet,' he said curtly. 'I can give you five minutes.'

Teresa's physical appearance only confirmed his worst fears. His aunt had sent him talent before.

I should tell her to stick to her kitchen. But he knew that he would not. The problem was that his aunt was very rich, and he was her only heir.

Teresa followed Louis Bonnet down a narrow corridor into a small broadcasting studio.

'Have you ever sung professionally?'

'No, sir.' Her blouse was soaked with perspiration. *Why did I ever let myself get talked into this?* Teresa wondered. She was in a panic, ready to flee.

Bonnet placed her in front of a microphone. 'I don't have a piano player around today, so you're going to have to sing *a capella*. Do you know what *a capella* means?'

'Yes, sir.'

'Wonderful.' He wondered, not for the first time, if his aunt was rich enough to make all these stupid auditions worthwhile.

'I'll be in the control booth. You'll have time for one song.'

'Sir – what shall I –?'

He was gone. Teresa was alone in the room staring at the microphone in front of her. She had no idea what she was going to sing. 'Just go and meet him,' his aunt had said. 'The station has a musical programme every Saturday evening, and . . .'

I've got to get out of here.

Louis' voice came out of nowhere. 'I haven't got all day.'

'I'm sorry. I can't –'

But the director was determined to punish her for wasting his time.

'Just a few notes,' he insisted. Enough so he could report to his aunt what a fool the girl had made of herself. Perhaps that would persuade her to stop sending him her protégées.

'I'm waiting,' he said.

He leaned back in his chair and lit a Gitane. Four more hours to go. Yvette would be waiting for him. He would have time to call at her apartment before he went home to his wife. Maybe there would even be time to –

He heard it then, and he could not believe it. It was a voice so pure and so sweet that it sent chills down his spine. It was a voice filled with longing and desire, a voice that sang of loneliness and despair, of lost loves and dead dreams, and it brought tears to his eyes. It stirred emotions in him that he had thought long since dead. All he could say to himself was, 'Jesus Christ! Where has she been?'

An engineer had wandered into the control booth, and he stood there listening, mesmerized. The door was open and others began to come in, drawn by the voice. They stood there silently listening to the poignant sound of a heart desperately crying out for love, and there was not another sound in the room.

When the song ended, there was a long silence, and one of the women said, 'Whoever she is, don't let her get away.'

Louis Bonnet hurried out of the room into the broadcasting studio. Teresa was getting ready to leave.

'I'm sorry I took too long. You see, I've never –'

'Sit down, Maria.'

'Teresa.'

'Sorry.' He took a deep breath. 'We do a musical radio broadcast every Saturday night.'

'I know. I listen to it.'

'How would you like to be on it?'

She stared at him, unable to believe what she was hearing. 'You mean – you want to *employ* me?'

'Beginning this week. We'll start you at the minimum. It will be a great showcase for you.'

It was almost too good to be true. *They're* going to pay me to sing.

'Pay you? How much?' Monique asked.

'I don't know. I don't care.' *The important thing is that somebody wants me*, she almost said, but she stopped herself.

'That's wonderful news. So you're going to be on the radio!' her father said.

Her mother was already making plans.

'We'll see that all our friends listen, and we'll have them send in letters saying how good you are.'

Teresa looked at Monique, waiting for her to say, *You don't have to do that. Teresa is good.*

But Monique said nothing. *It will blow over quickly*, she thought.

She was wrong.

That Saturday night at the broadcasting station, Teresa was in a panic.

'Believe me,' Louis Bonnet assured her, 'it's perfectly natural. All artists go through this.'

They were seated in the small green-room used by performers.

'You're going to be a sensation.'

'I'm going to be sick.'

'There's no time. You're on in two minutes.'

Teresa had rehearsed that afternoon with the small orchestra that was going to accompany her. The rehearsal had been extraordinary. The stage from which they broadcast was crowded with station personnel who had heard about the young girl with the incredible voice. They listened in awed silence as Teresa rehearsed the songs she was going to sing. There was no question in any of their minds but that they were witnessing the birth of an important star.

'It's too bad she's not better looking,' a stage manager commented, 'but in radio who can tell the difference?'

Teresa's performance that evening was superb. She was aware that she had never sung better. And who knew where this could lead? She might become famous and have men at her feet, begging her to marry them. As they begged Monique.

As though reading her thoughts, Monique said, 'I'm really happy for you, Sis, but don't let yourself get carried away by all this. These things never last.'

This will, Teresa thought happily. *I'm finally a person. I'm somebody.*

On Monday morning, there was a long-distance telephone call for Teresa.

'It's probably somebody's idea of a joke,' her father warned her. 'He says he's Jacques Raimu.' *The most important stage director in France.*

Teresa picked up the telephone, wary. 'Hello?'

353

'Miss DeFosse?'

'Yes.'

'Teresa DeFosse?'

'Yes.'

'This is Jacques Raimu. I heard your radio programme on Saturday night. You're exactly what I'm looking for.'

'I – I don't understand.'

'I'm staging a play at the Comédie Française, a musical. I start rehearsals next week. I've been searching for someone with a voice like yours. To tell you the truth, there *is* no one with a voice like yours. Who is your agent?'

'Agent? I – I have no agent.'

'Then I'll come up there and we'll work out a deal between us.'

'Monsieur Raimu – I – I'm not very pretty.' It was painful for her to say the words, but she knew that it was necessary. *He mustn't have any false expectations.*

He laughed. 'You will be when I get through with you. Theatre is make-believe. Stage makeup can do all kinds of incredible magic.'

'But –'

'I'll drive up to see you tomorrow.'

It was a dream on top of a fantasy. To be starring in a play by Raimu!

'I'll work out the contract with him,' Teresa's father said. 'You must be careful when you deal with theatre people.'

'We must get you a new dress,' her mother said. 'And I'll invite him to dinner.'

Monique said nothing. What was happening was unbearable. It was unthinkable that her sister was going to become a star. Perhaps there was a way . . .

Monique saw to it that she was the first one downstairs when Jacques Raimu arrived at the DeFosse château that afternoon. He was greeted by a young girl so beautiful that his heart jumped. She was dressed in a simple white afternoon frock that set off her figure to perfection.

My God, he thought. *Those looks and that voice! She's perfect. She's going to be an enormous star.*

'I can't tell you how happy I am to meet you,' Raimu said.

Monique smiled warmly. 'I'm very happy to meet you. I'm a big admirer of yours, Monsieur Raimu.'

'Good. Then we'll work well together. I brought a script with me. It's a beautiful love story, and I think –'

Teresa came into the room. She was wearing a new dress, but she looked awkward in it. She stopped as she saw Jacques Raimu.

'Oh – hello. I didn't know you were here. I mean – you're early.'

He looked at Monique inquiringly.

'This is my sister,' Monique said. 'Teresa.'

They both watched the expression on his face change. It went from shock to disappointment to disgust.

'You're the singer?'

'Yes.'

He turned to Monique. 'And you're –'

Monique smiled innocently. 'I'm Teresa's sister.'

Raimu turned to examine Teresa again, then shook his head. 'I'm sorry,' he said to Teresa. 'You're too –' he fumbled for a word. '– You're too young. If you'll excuse me, I must get back to Paris.'

And they stood there watching him walk out the door.

It worked, Monique thought jubilantly. *It worked.*

That was the last broadcast Teresa ever made. Louis Bonnet pleaded with her to come back, but the hurt was too deep.

After looking at my sister, Teresa thought, *how could anyone want me? I'm so ugly.*

As long as she lived, she would never forget the look on Jacques Raimu's face.

It's my fault for having silly dreams, Teresa told herself. *It's God's way of punishing me.*

After that, Teresa would only sing in church, and she became more of a recluse than ever.

During the next ten years the beautiful Monique turned down more than a dozen marriage proposals. She was proposed to by the sons of the mayor, the banker, the doctor, the merchants in the village. Her suitors ranged from young men fresh out of school to established and successful men in their forties and fifties. They were rich and poor, handsome and ugly, educated and uneducated. And to all of them Monique said *non*.

'What are you looking for?' her father asked, baffled.

'Papa, everyone here is boring. Èze is such an unsophisticated place. My dream prince is in Paris.'

And so her father dutifully sent her to Paris. As an afterthought, he sent Teresa with her. The two girls stayed at a small hotel near the Bois de Boulogne.

Each sister saw a different Paris. Monique attended charity balls and glamorous dinner parties and had tea with titled young men. Teresa visited Les Invalides and the Louvre. Monique went to the races at Longchamps and to galas at Malmaison. Teresa went to the Cathedral of Notre Dame to pray, and walked along the tree-shaded path of the Canal St Martin. Monique went to Maxim's and the Moulin Rouge, while Teresa strolled along the Quays, browsing at the book stalls and the flower vendors and stopping at the Basilica St Denis. Teresa enjoyed Paris, but as far as Monique was concerned, the trip was a failure.

When she returned home, she said, 'I can't find any man I want to marry.'

'You met no one who interested you?' her father asked.

'Not really. There was a young man who took me to dinner at Maxim's. His father owns coal mines.'

'What was he like?' her mother asked eagerly.

'Oh, he was rich, handsome, polite, and he adored me.'

'Did he ask you to marry him?'

'Every ten minutes. Finally I simply refused to see him again.'

Her mother stared at Monique in amazement. 'Why?'

'Because all he could talk about was coal: bituminous coal, lump coal, black coal, grey coal. Boring, boring, boring.'

The following year Monique decided she wanted to return to Paris again.

'I'll pack my things,' Teresa said.

Monique shook her head. 'No. This time I think I'll go alone.'

So while Monique went to Paris, Teresa stayed at home and went to church every morning and prayed that her sister would find a handsome prince. And one day the miracle occurred. A miracle because it was to Teresa that it happened. His name was Raoul Giradot.

He had gone to church on Sunday and heard Teresa sing. He had never heard anything like it. *I must meet her*, he vowed.

Early on Monday morning, Teresa called at the village general store to buy fabric for a dress she was making. Raoul Giradot was working behind the counter.

He looked up as Teresa walked in, and his face lit up. 'The voice!'

She stared at him, flustered. 'I – I beg your pardon?'

'I heard you sing in church yesterday. You are magnificent.'

He was handsome and tall, with intelligent, flashing dark eyes and lovely, sensual lips. He was in his early thirties, a year or two older than Teresa.

Teresa was so taken aback by his appearance that she could only stammer. She stared at him, her heart pounding. 'T – thank you,' Teresa said. 'I – I – I would like three yards of muslin, please.'

Raoul smiled. 'It will be my pleasure. This way.'

It was suddenly difficult for Teresa to concentrate on her errand. She was overpoweringly aware of the young man's presence, his good looks and charm, the masculine aura surrounding him.

When Teresa had decided on her purchase and Raoul was wrapping it for her, she dared to say, 'You're – you're new here, aren't you?'

He looked at her and smiled, and it sent shivers through Teresa.

'*Oui*. I arrived in Èze a few days ago. My aunt owns this shop and she needed help, so I thought I would work here for a while.'

How long is a while? Teresa found herself wondering.

'You should be singing professionally,' Raoul told her.

She remembered the expression on Raimu's face when he had seen her. No, she would never risk exposing herself publicly again. 'Thank you,' Teresa mumbled.

He was touched by her embarrassment and shyness. He tried to draw her into conversation.

'I haven't been to Èze before. It's a beautiful little town.'

'Yes,' Teresa mumbled.

'Were you born here?'

'Yes.'

'Do you like it?'

'Yes.'

Teresa picked up her parcel and fled.

The following day Teresa found an excuse to go back to the shop again. She had stayed up half the night preparing what she was going to say to Raoul.

I'm glad you like Èze . . .

The monastery was built in the fourteenth century, you know . . .

Have you ever visited Saint-Paul-de-Vence? There's a lovely chapel there . . .

I enjoy Monte Carlo, don't you? It's wonderful to have it so close to here. Sometimes my sister and I drive down the Grand Corniche and go to the Fort Antoine Theatre. Do you know it? It's the big, open-air theatre . . .

Did you know that Nice was once called Nkaia? Oh, you didn't? Yes, it was. The Greeks were there a long time ago. There's a museum in Nice with the remains of cavemen who lived there thousands of years ago. Isn't that interesting?

Teresa was prepared with dozens of such verbal gambits. Unfortunately, the moment she walked into the shop and saw Raoul everything flew out of her head. She simply stared at him, unable to speak.

'*Bonjour*,' Raoul said cheerfully. 'It's nice to see you again, Mademoiselle DeFosse.'

'M – merci.' She felt like an idiot. *I'm thirty years old*, she told herself, *and I'm acting like a silly schoolgirl. Stop it.*

But she could not stop it.

'And what may I do for you today?'

'I – I need more muslin.'

Which was the last thing she needed.

Teresa watched Raoul as he went to get the bolt of fabric. He set it on the counter and started to measure it out.

'How many yards would you like?'

She started to say two, but what came out was, 'Are you married?'

357

He looked up at her with a warm smile on his face. 'No,' he said. 'I haven't been that fortunate yet.'

You are going to be, Teresa thought. *As soon as Monique returns from Paris.*

Monique was going to adore this man. They were perfect for each other. The thought of Monique's reaction when she met Raoul filled Teresa with happiness. It would be lovely to have Raoul Giradot as her brother-in-law.

The following day as Teresa was passing the shop, Raoul caught sight of her and hurried outside.

'Good afternoon, Mademoiselle. I was about to take a break. If you're free, would you care to join me for tea?'

'I – I – yes, thank you.'

She was tongue-tied in his presence, and yet Raoul could not have been more pleasant. He did everything he could to put her at ease, and soon Teresa found herself telling this stranger things she had never told anyone before. They talked of loneliness.

'Crowds can make one lonely,' Teresa said. 'I always feel like an island in a sea of people.'

He smiled. 'I understand.'

'Oh, but you must have so many friends.'

'Acquaintances. In the end, does anyone really have many friends?'

It was as though she were speaking to a mirror image. The hour melted away so quickly, and soon it was time for him to go back to work.

As they rose, Raoul asked, 'Will you join me for lunch tomorrow?'

He was being kind, of course. Teresa knew that no man could ever be attracted to her. Especially someone as wonderful as Raoul Giradot. She was sure that he was kind to everyone.

'I would enjoy that,' Teresa said.

When she went to meet Raoul the following day, he said boyishly, 'I've been given the afternoon off. If you're not too busy, why don't we drive down to Nice?'

They drove along the Moyen Corniche, with his car top down, and the city was spread out like a magic carpet below. Teresa leaned back in her seat and thought: *I've never been so happy.* And then, filled with guilt: *I'm being happy for Monique.*

Monique was returning from Paris the following day. Raoul would be Teresa's gift to her sister. Teresa was realistic enough to know that the Raouls of the world were not for her. She had had enough pain in her life. She had long since learned what was real and what was imposs-ible. The handsome man seated beside her driving the car was an impossible dream she dared not even let herself think about.

They had lunch at Le Chantecler in the Negrecso Hotel in Nice. It was a superb meal, but afterwards Teresa had no recollection of what she had eaten. It seemed to her that she and Raoul had not stopped talking. They had so much to say to each other. He was witty and charming, and he appeared to find Teresa interesting – really interesting. He asked her opinion about many things and listened attentively to her answers. They agreed on almost everything. It was as though they were soul mates. If Teresa had any regrets about what was about to happen, she resolutely forced them out of her mind.

'Would you like to come to dinner at the château tomorrow night? My sister is returning from Paris. I would like you to meet her.'

'I'd be delighted, Teresa.'

When Monique returned home the following day, Teresa hurried to greet her at the door.

In spite of her resolve, Teresa could not help asking, 'Did you meet anyone interesting in Paris?' And she held her breath, waiting for her sister's answer.

'The same boring men,' Monique replied.

So God had made the final decision.

'I've invited someone to dinner tonight,' Teresa said. 'I think you're going to like him.'

I must never let anyone know how much I care for him, Teresa thought.

That evening at half seven promptly, the butler ushered Raoul Giradot into the drawing room where Teresa, Monique and their parents were waiting.

'This is my mother and father. Monsieur Raoul Giradot.'

'How do you do?'

Teresa took a deep breath. 'And my sister, Monique.'

'How do you do?' Monique's expression was polite, nothing more.

Teresa looked at Raoul, expecting him to be stunned by Monique's beauty.

'Enchanted.' Merely courteous.

Teresa stood there, holding her breath, waiting for the sparks that she knew would start flying between them. But Raoul was looking at Teresa.

'You look lovely tonight, Teresa.'

She blushed and stammered, 'Th – thank you.'

Everything about that evening was topsy-turvy. Teresa's plan to bring Monique and Raoul together, to watch them get married, to have Raoul as a brother-in-law – none of it even began to happen. Incredibly, Raoul's attention was focused entirely on Teresa. It was like some impossible dream come true. She felt like Cinderella, only she was the ugly sister and the prince had chosen her. It was unreal, but it was happening, and Teresa found herself struggling to resist Raoul and his charm because she knew that it was too good to be true, and she dreaded being hurt again. All these years she had hidden her emotions, guarding against the pain that came with rejection. Now, instinctively, she tried to do the same. But Raoul was irresistible.

'I heard your daughter sing,' Raoul said. 'She is a miracle!'

Teresa found herself blushing.

'Everyone loves Teresa's voice,' Monique said sweetly.

It was a heady evening. But the best was yet to come.

When dinner was finished, Raoul said, 'Your grounds look lovely.' He turned to Teresa. 'Would you show me the gardens?'

Teresa looked over at Monique, trying to read her sister's emotions, but Monique seemed completely indifferent.

She must be deaf, dumb and blind, Teresa thought.

And then she recalled all the times Monique had gone to Paris and Cannes and St Tropez looking for her perfect prince but had never found him.

So it's not the fault of the men. It's the fault of my sister. She has no idea what she wants.

Teresa turned to Raoul. 'I would love to.'

Outside, Teresa could not let the subject drop.

'How did you like Monique?'

'She seems very nice,' Raoul replied. 'Ask me how I like her sister.'

And he took Teresa in his arms and kissed her.

It was like nothing Teresa had ever experienced before. She trembled in his arms, and she thought: *Thank you, God. Oh, thank you.*

'Will you have dinner with me tomorrow night?' Raoul asked.

'Yes,' Teresa breathed. 'Oh, yes.'

When the two sisters were alone, Monique said, 'He really seems to like you.'

'I think so,' Teresa said shyly.

'Do you like him?'

'Yes.'

'Well, be careful, big sister,' Monique laughed. 'Don't get in over your head.'

Too late, Teresa thought helplessly. *Too late*.

Teresa and Raoul were together every day after that. Monique usually chaperoned them. The three of them walked along the promenades and beaches at Nice and laughed at the wedding-cake hotels. They lunched at a charming bistro at Cap d'Antibes, and visited the Matisse Chapel in Vence. They dined at the Château de la Chèvre d'Or, and at the fabulous La Ferme St Michel. One morning at 5.00 a.m. the three of them went to the open farmers' market that filled the streets of Monte Carlo and bought fresh breads and vegetables and fruit.

On Sundays, when Teresa sang in church, Raoul and Monique were there to listen, and afterwards Raoul would hug Teresa and say, 'You really are a miracle. I could listen to you sing for the rest of my life.'

Four weeks after Teresa met him, Raoul proposed.

'I'm sure you could have any man you want, Teresa,' Raoul said, 'but I would be honoured if you chose me.'

For one terrible moment Teresa thought he was ridiculing her, but before she could speak, he went on.

'My darling, I must tell you that I have known many women, but you are the most sensitive, the most talented, the warmest –'

Each word was music to Teresa's ears. She wanted to laugh; she wanted to cry. *How blessed I am*, she thought, *to love and be loved.*

'Will you marry me?'

And her look was answer enough.

When Raoul left, Teresa went flying into the library where her sister, mother and father were having coffee.

'Raoul asked me to marry him.' Her face was glowing, and there was almost a beauty about her.

Her parents stared at her, stunned. It was Monique who spoke.

'Teresa, are you sure he's not after the family money?'

It was like a slap in the face.

'I don't mean that unkindly,' Monique went on, 'but it all seems to be happening so fast.'

Teresa was determined not to let anything spoil her happiness. 'I know you want to protect me,' she told her sister, 'but Raoul has money. His father left him a small inheritance, and he's not afraid to work for a living.' She took her sister's hand in hers and begged, 'Please be glad for me, Monique. I never thought I'd know this feeling. I'm so happy I could die.'

And then the three of them embraced her and told her how pleased they were for her and they began to talk excitedly about plans for the wedding.

Very early the next morning Teresa went to church and knelt to pray.

'Thank you, Father. Thank You for giving me such happiness. I will do everything to make myself worthy of your love and of Raoul's. Amen.'

Teresa walked into the general store, her feet above the ground, and said, 'If you please, sir, I would like to order some material for a wedding gown.'

361

Raoul laughed and took her in his arms. 'You're going to make a beautiful bride.'

And Teresa knew he meant it. That was the miracle.

The wedding was set to take place a month later in the village church. Monique, of course, was to be the maid of honour.

At five o'clock on Friday afternoon, Teresa spoke to Raoul for the last time. At 12.30 on Saturday, standing in the church vestry waiting for Raoul, who was thirty minutes late, Teresa was approached by the priest. He took her arm and led her aside, and she wondered at his agitation. Her heart began to pound.

'What is it? Is something wrong? Has anything happened to Raoul?'

'Oh, my dear,' her father said. 'My poor, dear Teresa.'

She was beginning to panic. 'What is it, Father? Tell me!'

'We – we just received word a moment ago. Raoul –'

'Is it an accident? Was he hurt?'

'Giradot left town a half an hour ago.'

'*He what?* Then some emergency must have come up to make him –'

'He left with your sister. They were seen taking the train to Paris.'

The room began to whirl. *No*, Teresa thought. *I mustn't faint. I mustn't embarrass God.*

She had only a hazy memory of the events that followed. Teresa's mother put her arms around her daughter and said, 'My poor Teresa. That your own sister could be so cruel. I'm so sorry.'

But Teresa was suddenly calm. She knew how to make everything all right.

'Don't worry, Mama. I don't blame Raoul for falling in love with Monique. Any man would. I should have known that no man could ever love me.'

'You're wrong,' her father cried. 'You're worth ten of Monique.'

But his compassion came years too late.

'I would like to go home now, please.'

They made their way through the crowd. The guests at the church moved aside to let them pass, staring silently after them.

When they returned to the château, Teresa said again, 'Please don't worry about me. I promise you that everything is going to be fine.'

Then she went up to her father's room, took out his razor and slashed her wrists.

12

When Teresa opened her eyes, the family doctor and the village priest were standing beside her bed.

'No!' she screamed. 'I don't want to come back. Let me die. Let me die!'

The priest said, 'Suicide is a mortal sin. God gave you life, Teresa. Only He may decide when it is finished. You are young. You have a whole lifetime ahead of you.'

'To do what?' Teresa sobbed. 'Suffer more? I can't stand the pain I'm in. I can't stand it!'

He said gently, 'Jesus stood the pain and died for the rest of us. Don't turn your back on Him.'

The doctor finished examining Teresa. 'You need to rest. I've told your mother to put you on a light diet for a while.' He wagged a finger at her. 'That does not include razor blades.'

The following morning Teresa dragged herself out of bed. When she walked into the drawing room, her mother said in alarm, 'What are you doing up? The doctor told you –'

Teresa said hoarsely, 'I have to go to church. I have to talk to God.'

Her mother hesitated. 'I'll go with you.'

'No. I must go alone.'

'But –'

Her father nodded. 'Let her go.'

They watched the dispirited figure walk out of the house.

'What's going to happen to her?' Teresa's mother moaned.

'God only knows.'

She entered the familiar church, walked up to the altar and knelt.

'I've come to Your house to tell You something, God. I despise You. I despise You for letting me be born ugly. I despise You for letting my sister be born beautiful. I despise You for letting her take away the only man I ever loved. I spit on You.'

Her last words were so loud that the people inside turned to stare at her as she rose and stumbled out of the church.

Teresa had never believed there could be such pain. It was unbearable. It was impossible to think of anything else. She was unable to eat or sleep. The world seemed muffled and far away. Memories kept flashing into her mind, like scenes from a film.

She remembered the day she and Raoul and Monique had walked along the beach at Nice.

'It's a beautiful day for a swim,' Raoul said.

'I'd love to go, but we can't. Teresa doesn't swim.'

'I don't mind if you two go ahead. I'll wait for you at the hotel.'

And she had been so pleased that Raoul and Monique were getting along so well together.

They were lunching at a small inn near Cagnes. The maître d' said, 'The lobster is particularly good today.'

'I'll have it,' Monique said. 'Poor Teresa can't. Shellfish makes her break out in hives.'

St Tropez. 'I miss horseback riding. I used to ride every morning at home. Do you want to ride with me, Teresa?'

'I – I'm afraid I don't ride, Raoul.'

'I wouldn't mind going with you,' Monique said. 'I love to ride.'

And they had been gone all morning.

There were a hundred clues, and she had missed all of them. She had been blind because she wanted to be blind. The looks that Raoul and Monique had exchanged, the innocent touching of hands, the whispers and the laughter.

How could I have been so stupid?

At night when Teresa finally managed to doze off, she had dreams. It was always a different dream. It was always the same dream.

Raoul and Monique were on a train, naked, making love and the train was crossing a trestle high over a canyon, and the trestle collapsed and everyone on the train plunged to their deaths.

Raoul and Monique were in a hotel room, naked in bed, and Raoul laid down a cigarette and the room exploded in flames and the two of them were burned to death, and their screams awakened Teresa.

Raoul and Monique fell from a mountain, drowned in a river, died in an airplane crash.

It was always a different dream.

It was always the same dream.

Teresa's mother and father were frantic. They watched their daughter wasting away, and there was nothing they could do to help her. And then suddenly Teresa began to eat. She ate constantly. She could not seem to get enough food. She gained her weight back, and then kept gaining and gaining until her body was gross.

When her mother and father tried to talk to her about her pain, Teresa said, 'I'm fine now. Don't worry about me.'

Teresa carried on her life as though nothing were wrong. She continued to go into town and shop and do all the errands she had always done. She joined her mother and father for dinner each evening and read or sewed. She had built an emotional fortress around herself, and she was determined that no one would ever breach it. *No man will ever want to look at me. Never again.*

Outwardly, Teresa seemed fine. Inside, she was sunk in an abyss of deep, desperate loneliness. Even when she was surrounded by people, she sat in a lonely chair in a lonely room, in a lonely house, in a lonely world.

A little over a year after Raoul had left Teresa, her father was packing to leave for Ávila.

'I have some business to transact there,' he told Teresa. 'But after that, I'll be free. Why don't you come with me? Ávila is a fascinating town. It will do you good to get away from here for a while.'

'No, thank you, Father.'

He looked at his wife and sighed. 'Very well.'

The butler walked into the drawing room.

'Excuse me, Miss DeFosse. This letter just arrived for you.'

Even before Teresa opened it, she was filled with a prescience of something terrible looming before her.

The letter read:

> Teresa, my darling Teresa:
>
> God knows I do not have a right to call you darling, after the terrible thing I have done, but I promise to make it up to you if it takes me a lifetime. I don't know where to begin.
>
> Monique has run off and left me with our two-month-old daughter. Frankly, I am relieved. I must confess that I have been in hell ever since the day I left you. I will never understand why I did what I did. I seem to have been caught up in some kind of magic spell of Monique's, but I knew from the beginning that my marriage to her was a terrible mistake. It was you I always loved. I know now that the only place I can find my happiness is at your side. By the time you receive this letter, I will be on my way back to you.
>
> I love you, and I have always loved you, Teresa. For the sake of the rest of our lives together, I beg your forgiveness. I want . . .

She could not finish reading the letter. The thought of seeing Raoul again and his and Monique's baby was unthinkable, obscene.

She threw the letter down, hysterical.

'I must get out of here,' Teresa screamed. 'Tonight. Now. Please . . . please!'

It was impossible for them to calm her.

'If Raoul is coming here,' her father said, 'you should at least talk to him.'

'No! If I see him, I'll kill him.' She grabbed her father's arms, tears streaming down her face. 'Take me with you,' Teresa pleaded.

She would go anywhere, as long as she escaped from this place.

And so that evening Teresa and her father set out for Ávila.

Teresa's father was distraught over his daughter's unhappiness. He was not by nature a compassionate man, but in the last year Teresa had won his admiration by her courageous behaviour. She had faced the townspeople with her head held high and had never complained. He felt helpless, unable to console her.

He remembered how much solace she had once found in the church, and when they arrived in Ávila he said to Teresa, 'Father Berrendo, the priest here, is an old friend of mine. Perhaps he can help you. Will you speak to him?'

'No.' She would have nothing to do with God.

Teresa stayed in the hotel room alone while her father conducted his business. When he returned, Teresa was seated in the same chair, staring at the walls.

'Teresa, please see Father Berrendo.'

'No.'

He was at a loss. Teresa refused to leave the hotel room and she refused to return to Èze.

In the end, the priest came to see Teresa.

'Your father tells me that you once attended church regularly.'

Teresa looked into the eyes of the frail-looking priest and said coldly, 'I'm no longer interested. The Church has nothing to offer me.'

Father Berrendo smiled. 'The Church has something to offer everyone, my child. The Church gives us hope and dreams . . .'

'I've had my fill of dreams. Never again.'

He took her hands in his thin hands and saw the white scars of razor slashes on her wrists, as faint as a long ago memory.

'God doesn't believe that. Talk to Him and He will tell you.'

Teresa sat there, staring at the wall, and when the priest finally made his way out, she was not even aware of it.

The following morning Teresa walked into the cool, vaulted church, and almost immediately the old, familiar feeling of peace stole over her. The last time she had been in a church was to curse God. A feeling of deep shame filled her. It was her own weakness that had betrayed her, not God.

'Forgive me,' she whispered. 'I have sinned. I have lived in hate. Help me. Please help me.'

She looked up, and Father Berrendo was standing there. When she finished, he led her into his office behind the vestry.

'I don't know what to do, Father. I don't believe in anything any more. I've lost faith.' Her voice was filled with despair.

'Did you have faith when you were a young girl?'

'Yes. Very much.'

'Then you still have it, my child. Faith is real and permanent. It is everything else that is transient.'

They talked that day for hours.

When Teresa returned to the hotel late in the afternoon, her father said, 'I must get back to Èze. Are you ready to leave?'

'No, Papa. Let me stay here for a while.'

He hesitated. 'Will you be all right?'

'Yes, Father. I promise.'

Teresa and Father Berrendo met every day after that. Father Berrendo's heart went out to Teresa. He saw in her not a fat, unattractive woman, but a beautiful, unhappy spirit. They spoke of God and creation and the meaning of life, and slowly, almost in spite of herself, Teresa began to find comfort again. Something that Father Berrendo said one day triggered a deep response.

'My child, if you do not believe in this world, then believe in the next world. Believe in the world where Jesus is waiting to receive you.'

And for the first time since the terrible thing that had happened to her, Teresa began to feel at peace again. The church had become her haven, just as it had once been. But there was her future to think about.

'I have no place to go.'

'You could return home.'

'No. I could never go back there. I could never face Raoul again. I don't know what to do. I want to hide, and there is no place to hide.'

Father Berrendo was silent for a long time. Finally he spoke. 'You could stay here.'

She looked around the office, puzzled. 'Here?'

'The Cistercian convent is nearby.' He leaned forward. 'Let me tell you about it. It is a world inside a world, where everyone is dedicated to God. It is a place of peace and serenity.'

And Teresa's heart began to lift. 'It sounds wonderful.'

'I must caution you. It is one of the strictest orders in the world. Those who are admitted take a vow of chastity, silence and obedience. No one who enters there ever leaves.'

The words sent a thrill through Teresa. 'I will never want to leave. It is what I have been searching for, Father. I despise the world I live in.'

But Father Berrendo was still concerned. He knew that Teresa would be facing a life totally different from anything she had ever experienced.

'There can be no turning back.'

'I won't turn back.'

367

Early the next day, Father Berrendo took Teresa to the convent to meet the Reverend Mother Betina. He left the two of them there to talk.

The moment Teresa entered the convent, she knew. *At last*, she thought exultantly. *At last.*

Teresa telephoned her mother and father.

'I've been so worried,' her mother said. 'When are you coming home?'

'I am home.'

The Bishop of Ávila performed the rite:

'Creator, Lord, send thy benediction upon thy handmaid that she shall be fortified with celestial virtue, that she may maintain complete faith and unbroken fidelity.'

Teresa responded, 'The kingdom of this world and all secular adornings, I have despised for the love of our Lord, Jesus Christ.'

The bishop made the sign of the cross over her.

'*De largitatis tuae fonte defluxit ut cum honorem nupiarum nulla interdicta minuissent ac super sanctum conjugium nuptialis benedictio permaneret existerent connubium, concupiscerent sacramentum, nec imitarentur quod nuptiis agitur, sed diligerent quod nuptiis prae notatur.* Amen.'

'Amen.'

'I espouse thee to Jesus Christ, the son of the Supreme Father. Therefore receive the seal of the Holy Ghost, so that thou be called the spouse of God, and if thou serve him faithfully, be crowned everlastingly.' The bishop rose. 'God, the Father Almighty, Creator of heaven and earth, who hath vouchsafed to choose you to an espousalship like that of the blessed Mary, mother of our Lord, Jesus Christ – *ad beatae Mariae matris Domini nostri* Jesus Christ consortium – hallow you, that in the presence of God and of His angels, you may persevere, untouched and undefiled, and hold to your purpose, love, chastity, and keep patience that you may merit to receive the crown of His blessing, through the same Christ our Lord. God make you strong when frail, strengthen you when weak, relieve and govern your mind with piety and direct your ways. Amen.'

Now, thirty years later, lying in the woods watching the sun come up over the horizon, Sister Teresa thought: *I came to the convent for all the wrong reasons. I was not running to God. I was running away from the world. But God read my heart.*

She was sixty years old, and the last thirty years of her life had been the happiest she had ever known. And now she had suddenly been flung back into the world she had run away from. And her mind was playing strange tricks on her.

She was no longer sure what was real and what was unreal. The past and the present seemed to be blending together in a strange dizzying blur. *Why is this happening to me? What does God have planned for me?*

13

For Sister Megan, the journey was an adventure. She had become used to the new sights and sounds that surrounded her, and the speed with which she had adapted surprised her.

She found her companions fascinating. Amparo Jiron was a powerful woman, easily able to keep up with the two men, and yet at the same time she was very feminine.

Felix Carpio, the husky man with a reddish beard and a scar, seemed amiable and pleasant.

But to Megan, the most compelling of the group was Jaime Miró. There was a relentless strength about him, an unshakable faith in his beliefs that reminded Megan of the nuns in the convent.

When they began the journey, Jaime and Amparo and Felix were carrying sleeping-bags and rifles on their shoulders.

'Let me carry one of the sleeping-bags,' Megan suggested.

Jaime Miró had looked at her in surprise, then shrugged. 'All right, Sister.'

He handed her the bag. It was heavier than Megan had expected, but she did not complain. *As long as I'm with them, I'm going to do my share.*

It seemed to Megan that they had been walking for ever, stumbling through the darkness, hit by branches, scratched by underbrush, attacked by insects, guided only by the light of the moon.

Who are these people? Megan wondered. *And why are they being hunted?* Because Megan and the other nuns were also being pursued, Megan felt a strong rapport with her new companions.

There was little talking, but from time to time they held cryptic conversations.

'Is everything set at Valladolid?'

'Right, Jaime. Rubio and Tomas will meet us at the bank during the bullfight.'

'Good. Send word to Largo Cortez to expect us. But don't give him a date.'

'*Comprendo.*'

Who are Largo Cortez and Rubio and Tomas? Megan wondered. And what was going to happen at the bullfight and the bank? She almost started to ask, but thought better of it. *I have the feeling they wouldn't welcome a lot of questions.*

Near dawn they smelled smoke from the valley below them.

'Wait here,' Jaime whispered. 'Be quiet.'

They watched as Jaime made his way towards the edge of the forest and disappeared from sight.

Megan said, 'What is it – ?'

'Shut up!' Amparo Jiron hissed.

Fifteen minutes later Jaime Miró returned.

'Soldiers. We'll circle around them.'

They back-tracked for half a mile, then moved cautiously through the woods until they reached a side road. The countryside stretched out ahead of them, redolent with the odours of mown hay and ripe fruit.

Megan's curiosity got the better of her. 'Why are the soldiers looking for you?' she asked.

Jaime Miró said, 'Let's say we don't see eye to eye.'

And she had to be satisfied with that. *For now*, she thought. She was determined to know more about this man.

Half an hour later when they reached a sheltered clearing, Jaime said, 'The sun's up. We'll stay here until nightfall.' He looked at Megan. 'Tonight we're going to have to travel faster.'

She nodded. 'Very well.'

Jaime took the sleeping-bags and rolled them out.

Felix Carpio said to Megan, 'You take mine, Sister. I'm used to sleeping on the ground.'

'It's yours,' Megan said. 'I couldn't – '

'For Christ's sake,' Amparo snapped. 'Get into the bag. We don't want you to keep us awake screaming about goddamned spiders.' There was an animosity in her tone that Megan did not understand.

Without another word, Megan climbed into the sleeping-bag. *What's bothering her?* Megan wondered.

Megan watched as Jaime unrolled his sleeping-bag a few feet away from where she lay. He crawled into the bag. Amparo Jiron crawled in beside him. *I see*, Megan thought.

Jaime looked over at Megan. 'You'd better get some sleep,' he said. 'We have a long way ahead of us.'

Megan was awakened by a moaning. It sounded as though someone were in terrible pain. Megan sat up, concerned. The sounds were coming from Jaime's sleeping-bag. *He must be terribly ill*, was her first thought.

The moaning was getting louder, and then Megan heard Amparo Jiron's voice saying, 'Oh, yes, yes. Give it to me, *Querida*. Harder! Yes! Now! Now!'

And Megan's face flushed. She tried to close her ears to the sounds she was hearing, but it was impossible. And she wondered what it would be like to have Jaime Miró make love to her.

Instantly Megan crossed herself and began to pray: *Forgive me,*

Father. Let my thoughts be filled only with You. Let my spirit seek You that it may find its source and good in You.

And the sounds went on. Finally, when Megan thought she would be unable to bear it an instant longer, they stopped. But there were other noises to keep her awake. The sounds of the forest ricocheted around her. There was a cacophony of mating birds and crickets and the chattering of small animals and the guttural growlings of larger ones. Megan had forgotten how noisy the outside world could be. She missed the wonderful silence of the convent. To her own astonishment, she even missed the orphanage. The terrible, wonderful orphanage . . .

14

Ávila 1957

They called her 'Megan the Terror'.

They called her 'Megan the Blue-eyed Devil'.

They called her 'Megan the Impossible'.

She was ten years old.

She had been brought to the orphanage when she was an infant, left on the doorstep of a farmer and his wife who were unable to care for her.

The orphanage was an austere, two-storey, white-washed building on the outskirts of Ávila, in the poorer section of the city, off the Plaza de Saint Vicente, run by Mercedes Angeles, an Amazon of a woman with a fierce manner that belied the warmth she felt for her wards.

Megan was different from the other children, an alien with blonde hair and bright blue eyes, standing out in stark contrast to the dark-eyed, dark-haired children. But from the beginning, Megan was different in other ways. She was a fiercely independent child, a leader, a mischief-maker. Whenever there was trouble at the orphanage, Mercedes Angeles could be certain that Megan was at the bottom of it.

Over the years, Megan led riots protesting about the food, she tried to form the children into a union, and she found inventive ways of tormenting the supervisors, including half a dozen escape attempts. Needless to say, Megan was immensely popular with the other children. She was younger than many of them, but they all turned to her for guidance. She was a natural leader. And the younger children loved to have Megan tell them stories. She had a wild imagination.

'Who were my parents, Megan?'

'Ah. Your father was a clever jewel thief. He climbed over the roof of a hotel in the middle of the night to steal a diamond belonging to a famous actress. Well, just as he was putting the diamond in his pocket, the actress woke up. She turned on the light and saw him.'

'Did she have him arrested?'

'No. He was very handsome.'

'What happened then?'

'They fell in love and got married. Then you were born.'

'But why did they send me to an orphanage? Didn't they love me?'

That was always the difficult part. 'Of course they loved you. But –

well – they were skiing in Switzerland and they were killed in a terrible avalanche –'

'What's a terrible avalanche?'

'That's when a bunch of snow comes down all at once and buries you.'

'And my mother and father both died?'

'Yes. And their last words were that they loved you. But there was no one to take care of you, so you were sent here.'

Megan was as anxious as the others to know who her parents were, and at night she would put herself to sleep by making up stories to herself: 'My father was a soldier in the Civil War,' she would think. 'He was a captain and very brave. He was wounded in battle, and my mother was the nurse who took care of him. They married, and he went back to the front and was killed. My mother was too poor to keep me, so she had to leave me at the farmhouse, and it broke her heart.' And she would weep with pity for her courageous, dead father and her bereaved mother.

Or: 'My father was a bullfighter. He was one of the great Matadors. He was the toast of Spain. Everyone adored him. My mother was a beautiful flamenco dancer. They were married, but he was killed one day by a huge, dangerous bull. My mother was forced to give me up.'

Or: 'My father was a clever spy from another country . . .'

The fantasies were endless.

There were thirty children in the orphanage, ranging from abandoned newborn infants to fourteen-year-olds. Most of them were Spanish, but there were children there from half a dozen countries, and Megan became fluent in several languages. She slept in a dormitory with a dozen other girls. There were late-night whispered conversations about dolls and clothes, and as the girls grew older, about sex. It soon became the primary topic of conversation.

'I hear it hurts a lot.'

'I don't care. I can't wait to do it.'

'I'm going to get married, but I'm never going to let my husband do it to me. I think it's dirty.'

One night, when everyone was asleep, Primo Conde, one of the young boys at the orphanage, crept into the girls' dormitory. He moved to the side of Megan's bed.

'Megan . . .' His voice was a whisper.

She was instantly awake. 'Primo? What's the matter?'

He was sobbing, frightened. 'Can I get into bed with you?'

'Yes. Be quiet.'

Primo was thirteen, the same age as Megan, but he was small for his age, and had been an abused child. He suffered from terrible nightmares and would wake up in the middle of the night screaming. The other

374

children tormented him, and Megan was the one who always protected him.

Primo climbed into bed beside her, and Megan felt the tears running down his cheeks. She held him close in her arms.

'It's all right,' Megan whispered. 'It's all right.'

She rocked him gently and his sobs subsided. His body was pressed against hers, and she could feel his growing excitement.

'Primo . . .'

'I'm sorry. I – I can't help it.'

His erection was pressing into her.

'I love you, Megan. You're the only one I care about in the whole world.'

'You haven't been out in the world yet.'

'Please don't laugh at me.'

'I'm not.'

'I have no one but you.'

'I know.'

'I love you.'

'I love you, too, Primo.'

'Megan – would you – let me make love to you? Please.'

'No.'

There was silence. 'I'm sorry I bothered you. I'll go back to my bed.' His voice was filled with pain. He started to move away.

'Wait.' Megan held him close to her, wanting to ease his suffering, feeling aroused herself. 'Primo, I – I can't let you make love to me, but I can do something to make you feel better. Will that be all right?'

'Yes.' His voice was a murmur.

He was wearing pyjamas. Megan pulled the cord that held his pyjama bottom up and reached inside. *He's a man*, Megan thought. She held him gently in her hand and began to stroke him. Primo groaned and said, 'Oh, that feels wonderful,' and a moment later, 'God, I love you, Megan.'

Her body was on fire, and if at that moment he had said, 'I want to make love to you,' she would have said yes.

But he lay there, silent, and in a few minutes he returned to his own bed.

There was no sleep for Megan that night. And she had never allowed him to come into her bed again.

The temptation was too great.

From time to time the children would be called into the supervisor's office to meet a prospective foster parent. It was always a moment of great excitement for the children, for it would mean a chance to escape from the dreary routine of the orphanage, a chance to have a real home, to belong to someone.

Over the years Megan watched as other orphans were chosen. They went to the homes of merchants, farmers, bankers, shopkeepers. But it was always the other children, never Megan. Her reputation proceeded her. She would hear the prospective parents talk among themselves.

'She's a very pretty child, but I hear she's difficult.'

'Isn't she the one who smuggled twelve dogs into the orphanage last month?'

'They say she's a ringleader. I'm afraid she wouldn't get along with our children.'

They had no idea how much the other children adored Megan.

Father Berrendo came to the orphanage once a week to visit the wards, and Megan looked forward to his visits. Megan was an omnivorous reader, and the priest and Mercedes Angeles saw to it that she was well supplied with books. She could discuss things with the priest that she dared not talk about with anyone else. It was Father Berrendo to whom the farm couple had turned over the infant Megan.

'Why didn't they want to keep me?' Megan asked.

The old priest said gently, 'They wanted to very much, Megan, but they were old and ill.'

'Why do you suppose my real parents left me at that farm?'

'I'm sure it was because they were poor and couldn't afford to keep you.'

As Megan grew up, she became more and more devout. She was stirred by the intellectual aspects of the Catholic Church. She read St Augustine's Confessions, the writings of St Francis of Assisi, Thomas Merton, Thomas More, and a dozen others. Megan went to church regularly, and she enjoyed the solemn rituals, the Gloria Patri, receiving the Eucharist, the doxology, the benediction. Perhaps most of all, she loved the wonderful feeling of serenity that always stole over her in church.

'I want to become a Catholic,' Megan told Father Berrendo one day.

He took her hand in his and said with a twinkle, 'Perhaps you are already, Megan, but we'll hedge our bets.' He gave her the Catholic cathechism:

'Quid petis ab Ecclesia dei?'

'Fidem!'

'Fides quid tibi praestat?'

'Vitam Aeternam.'

'Abrenuntias Satanae?'

'Sic.'

'Dost thou believe in God the Father Almighty, creator of heaven and earth?'

'Credo!'

'Dost thou believe in Jesus Christ, His only son, who was born and suffered?'

'*Credo!*'

'Dost thou believe in the Holy Spirit in the Holy Catholic Church, the communion of saints, the remission of sins, the resurrection of the body and eternal life?'

'*Credo!*'

The priest blew gently into her face. '*Exi ab eo spiritus immunde.* Depart from her, thou impure spirit and give place to the Holy Spirit, the paraclete.' He breathed again into her face. 'Megan, receive the good Spirit through this breathing and receive the blessing of God. Peace be with thee.'

At fifteen Megan had become a beautiful young woman, with long blonde hair and a milky complexion that set her off even more from most of her companions.

One day she was summoned to the office of Mercedes Angeles. Father Berrendo was there.

'Hello, Father.'

'Hello, my dear Megan.'

Mercedes Angeles said, 'I'm afraid we have a problem, Megan.'

'Oh?' She wracked her brain, trying to remember her latest misdeed.

The head mistress went on: 'There is an age limit here of fifteen, and you've reached your fifteenth birthday.'

Megan had long known of the rule, of course. But she had put it in the back of her mind, because she did not want to face the fact that she had nowhere in the world to go, that no one wanted her, and that she was going to be abandoned once again.

'Do I – do I have to leave?'

The kindly Amazon was upset, but she had no choice. 'I'm afraid we must abide by the rules. We can find a position for you as a maid.'

Megan had no words.

Father Berrendo spoke. 'Where would you like to go?'

As she thought about it, an idea came to Megan. There *was* somewhere for her to go.

From the time Megan was twelve years old, she had helped earn her keep at the orphanage by making outside deliveries in town, and many of them were made to the Cistercian convent. They were always delivered to the Reverend Mother Betina. Megan had sneaked glimpses of the nuns praying, or walking through the corridors, and she had sensed an almost overpowering feeling of serenity. She envied the joy that the nuns seemed to radiate. To Megan, the convent seemed a house of love.

The Reverend Mother had taken a liking to the bright young girl, and they had had long talks over the years.

'Why do people join convents?' Megan had asked.

'People come to us for many reasons. Most come to dedicate themselves to God. But some come because they have no hope. We give them hope. Some come because they feel they have no reason to live. We show them that God is the reason. Some come because they are running away. Others come here because they are alienated and they want to belong.'

That was what had struck a responsive chord in the young girl. *I've never really belonged to anyone*, Megan thought. *This is my chance.*

'I think I would like to join the convent.'

Six weeks later, Megan took her vows.

And finally Megan had found what she had been searching for so long. She belonged. These were her sisters, the family she had never had, and they were all one under their Father.

Megan worked in the convent as a bookkeeper, keeping the records. She was fascinated by the ancient sign language that the sisters used when they needed to communicate with the Reverend Mother. There were 472 signs, enough to convey among themselves everything they needed to express.

When it was a sister's turn to dust the long corridors, Prioress Betina held out her right hand with the heel forward and blew on the back of it. If a nun had a fever, she went to the Reverend Mother and pressed the tip of her right forefinger and middle finger on the outside of her left wrist. If a request was to be delayed, Prioress Betina held her right fist before her right shoulder and pushed it slightly forward and down. *Tomorrow.*

One November morning Megan was introduced to the rites of death. A nun was dying, and a wooden rattle was rung in the cloister, the signal for the beginning of a ritual unchanged since the year 1030. All those who could answer the call hurried to kneel in the infirmary for the anointing and the psalms. They silently prayed for the saints to intercede for the departing sister's soul. To signify that it was time for the last sacraments to be given, the Mother Prioress held out her left hand with the palm up and drew a cross on it with the tip of her right thumb.

And finally, there was the sign of death itself, a sister placing the tip of her right thumb under her chin and raising it slightly.

When the last prayers had been said, the body was left alone for an hour so that the soul could go in peace. At the foot of the bed the great Paschal candle, the Christian symbol of eternal light, burned in its wooden holder.

The infirmarian washed the body and clothed the dead nun in her habit, black scapular over white cowl, rough stockings and handmade sandals. From the garden one of the nuns brought fresh flowers, woven into a crown. When the dead woman was dressed, six of the nuns in a procession carried her to the church and placed her on the white-sheeted bier facing the altar. She would not be left alone before her God, and in their stalls by her side, two nuns stayed through the rest of the day and on through the night praying, while the Paschal candle flickered at her side.

The next afternoon, after the requiem mass, she was carried through the cloister by the nuns to the private, walled cemetery where even in death the nuns kept their enclosure. The sisters, three and three, lowered her carefully into the grave, supported on white bands of linen. It was the Cistercian custom for their dead to lie uncovered in the earth, buried without a coffin. And the last service they performed for their sister was for two nuns to start to drop soil softly on to her still body before they all returned to the church to say the psalms of penance. Three times they begged that God have mercy on her soul:

Domine miserere super peccatrice
Domine miserere super peccatrice
Domine miserere super peccatrice

There were often times when young Megan was filled with melancholy. The convent gave her serenity, and yet she was not completely at peace. It was as though a part of her was missing. She felt longings that she should have long ago forgotten. She found herself thinking about the friends she had left behind in the orphanage, and wondering what had happened to them. And she wondered what was happening in the outside world, the world that she had renounced, a world where there was music and dancing and laughter.

Megan went to Reverend Mother Betina.

'It happens to all of us from time to time,' she assured Megan. 'The church calls it "acedia". It is a spiritual malaise, an instrument of Satan. Do not worry about it, child. It will pass.'

And it did.

But what did not pass was the bone-deep longing to know who her parents were. *I'll never know*, Megan thought despairingly. *Not as long as I live.*

15

New York City 1976

The reporters gathered outside the grey façade of New York's Waldorf Astoria Hotel watched the parade of celebrities in evening dress alight from their limousines, enter the revolving doors and head for the Grand Ballroom on the third floor. The guests had come from around the world.

Cameras flashed as reporters called out, 'Mr Vice President, would you look this way, please?'

'Governor Adams, could I have one more picture, please?'

There were senators and representatives from several foreign countries, business tycoons and celebrities. And they were all there to celebrate Ellen Scott's sixtieth birthday. In truth, it was not so much Ellen Scott that they were honouring as the philanthropy of Scott Industries, one of the most powerful conglomerates in the world. The huge, sprawling empire included oil companies and steel mills, communications systems and banks. All the money raised this evening would go to international charities.

Scott Industries had interests in every part of the world. Twenty-five years earlier, its President, Milo Scott, had died unexpectedly of a heart attack, and his wife, Ellen, had taken over the management of the huge conglomerate and in the ensuing years had proved to be a brilliant executive, more than tripling the assets of the company.

The Grand Ballroom of the Waldorf Astoria is an enormous room, decorated in beige and gold, with a red-carpeted stage at one end and a balcony curving around the entire room, holding thirty-three boxes with a chandelier over each one. In the centre balcony sat the guest of honour. There were at least 600 men and women present, dining at tables gleaming with silver.

When dinner was finished, the Governor of New York strode on to the stage.

'Mr Vice President, ladies and gentlemen, honoured guests, we are all here tonight for one purpose: to pay tribute to a remarkable woman and to her unselfish generosity over the years. Ellen Scott is the kind of person who could have made a success in any field. She would have been a great scientist or doctor. She would also have made a great politician, and I must tell you that if Ellen Scott decides to run for

380

President of the United States, I'll be the first one to vote for her. Not in the next election, of course, but the one after that.'

There was laughter and applause.

'But Ellen Scott is much more than just a brilliant woman. She is a charitable, compassionate human being who never hesitates to get involved in the problems that face the world today –'

The speech went on for ten more minutes, but Ellen Scott was no longer listening. *How wrong he is*, she thought wryly. *How wrong they all are. Scott Industries isn't even my company. Milo and I stole it. And I'm guilty of a far greater crime than that. It doesn't matter any longer. Not now. Because I'll be dead soon.*

She remembered the doctor's exact words as he read the lab report that was her death sentence.

'I'm dreadfully sorry, Mrs Scott, but I'm afraid there's no way to break this to you gently. The cancer has spread throughout your lymphatic system. It's inoperable.'

She had felt the sudden leaden weight in her stomach.

'How . . . how long do I have?'

He hesitated. 'A year – maybe.'

Not enough time. Not with so much still to do. 'You will say nothing of this, of course.' Her voice was steady.

'Certainly not.'

'Thank you, doctor.'

She had no recollection of leaving the Presbyterian Medical Center or of the drive downtown. Her only thought was: *I must find her before I die.*

Now the Governor's speech was over.

'Ladies and gentlemen, it is my honour and privilege to introduce Mrs Ellen Scott.'

Ellen Scott rose to a standing ovation. She walked towards the stage, a thin, grey-haired, straight-backed woman, smartly dressed and projecting a vitality she no longer felt.

Looking at me is like seeing the distant light of a long dead star, she thought bitterly. *I'm not really here any more.*

On the stage she waited for the applause to die down. *They're applauding a monster. What would they do if they knew?* When she spoke, her voice was firm.

'Mr Vice President, Senators, Governor Adams . . .'

A year, she was thinking. *I wonder where she is and if she is still alive. I must find out.*

She talked on, automatically saying all the things her audience expected to hear. 'I gladly accept this tribute not for myself, but for all those who have worked so hard to lighten the burden of those who are less fortunate than we are . . .'

Her mind was drifting back forty-two years to Gary, Indiana . . .

At eighteen, Ellen Dudash was employed at the Scott Industries automotive parts plant in Gary, Indiana. She was an attractive, outgoing girl, popular with her fellow workers. On the day Milo Scott came to inspect the plant, Ellen was selected to escort him around.

'Hey! How about you, Ellie? Maybe you'll marry the boss's brother and we'll all be working for you.'

Ellen Dudash laughed. 'Right. And that's when pigs will grow wings.'

Milo Scott was not at all what Ellen had expected. He was in his early thirties, tall and slim. *Not bad looking*, Ellen thought. He was shy and almost deferential.

'It's very kind of you to take the time to show me around, Miss Dudash. I hope I'm not taking you away from your work.'

She grinned. 'I hope you are.'

He was so easy to talk to.

I can't believe I'm kidding around with the big boss's brother. Wait till I tell Mom and Pop about this.

Milo Scott seemed genuinely interested in the workers and their problems. Ellen took him through the department where the round drive gears and the long driven gears were made. She showed him through the annealing room, where the soft gears were put through a hardening process, and the packing section and the shipping department, and he seemed properly impressed.

'It's certainly a large operation, isn't it, Miss Dudash?'

He owns all of this, and he acts like an awed kid. I guess it takes all kinds.

It was in the assembly section where the accident happened. An overhead cable car carrying metal bars to the machine shop snapped and a load of iron came tumbling down. Milo Scott was directly beneath it. Ellen saw it coming a fraction of a second before it hit, and without thinking, shoved Milo Scott out of harm's way. Two of the heavy iron bars hit her before she could escape, and she was knocked unconscious.

She awakened in a private suite in a hospital. The room was literally filled with flowers. When Ellen opened her eyes and looked around, she thought: *I've died and gone to heaven.*

There were orchids and roses and lilies and chrysanthemums and rare blooms she could not even begin to identify.

Her right arm was in a cast and her ribs were taped and felt bruised.

A nurse came in. 'Ah, you're awake, Miss Dudash. I'll inform the doctor.'

'Where – where am I?'

'Blake Center – it's a private hospital.'

Ellen looked around the large suite. *I can never afford to pay for all this.*

'We've been screening your calls.'

'What calls?'

'The press has been trying to get in to interview you. Your friends have been calling. Mr Scott has telephoned several times . . .'

Milo Scott! 'Is he all right?'

'I beg your pardon?'

'Was he hurt in the accident?'

'No. He was here again early this morning, but you were asleep.'

'He came to see *me*?'

'Yes.' She looked around the room. 'Most of these flowers are from him.'

Unbelievable.

'Your mother and father are in the waiting room. Do you feel up to seeing them now?'

'Of course.'

'Thank you. I'll send them in.'

Boy, I've never been treated like this in a hospital before, Ellen thought.

Her mother and father walked in and came up to the bed. Ellen's parents had been born in Poland and their English was tentative. Ellen's father was a mechanic, a burly, rough-hewn man in his fifties, and Ellen's mother was a bluff, northern European peasant.

'I brought you some soup, Ellen.'

'Mom – they feed people in hospitals.'

'Not my soup, they don't feed you in the hospital. Eat it and you'll get well faster.'

Her father said, 'Have you see the papers? I brung you copy.' He handed the newspaper to her. The headline read:

FACTORY WORKER RISKS LIFE TO SAVE BOSS.

She read the story twice.

'That was brave thing you done to save him.'

Brave? It was stupid. If I had had time to think, I would have saved myself. That was the dumbest thing I ever did. Why, I could have been killed!

Milo Scott came to see Ellen later that morning. He was carrying another bouquet of flowers.

'These are for you,' he said awkwardly. 'The doctor tells me you're going to be fine. I – I can't tell you how grateful I am to you.'

'It was nothing.'

'It was the most courageous act I've ever seen. You saved my life.'

She tried to move, but it sent a sharp pain through her arm.

'Are you all right?'

'Sure.' Her side was beginning to throb. 'What did the doc say was wrong with me?'

'You have a broken arm and three broken ribs.'

He couldn't have given her worse news. Her eyes filled with tears.

'What's the matter?'

How could she tell him? He would only laugh at her. She had been saving up for a long-awaited vacation to New York, on a tour with some of the girls from the factory. It had been her dream. *Now I'll be out of work for a month or more. There goes Manhattan.*

Ellen had worked since she was fifteen. She had always been fiercely independent and self-sufficient, but now she thought: *Maybe if he's so grateful he'll pay part of my hospital bills. But I'll be damned if I'll ask him.* She was beginning to feel drowsy. *It must be the medication.*

She said sleepily, 'Thank you for all the flowers, Mr Scott. And it was nice meeting you.' *I'll worry about the hospital bills later.*

Ellen Dudash slept.

The following morning, a tall, distinguished-looking man came into Ellen's suite.

'Good morning, Miss Dudash. How are you feeling this morning?'

'Better, thank you.'

'I'm Sam Norton. I'm chief public relations officer for Scott Industries.'

'Oh.' She had never seen him before. 'Do you live here?'

'No. I flew in from Washington.'

'To see me?'

'To assist you.'

'To assist me *what*?'

'The press is outside, Miss Dudash. Since I don't believe you've ever held a press conference, I thought perhaps you could use some help.'

'What do they want?'

'Mainly, they're going to ask you to tell them about how and why you saved Mr Scott.'

'Oh. That's easy. If I had stopped to think, I'd have run like hell.'

Norton stared at her. 'Miss Dudash – I don't think I would say that, if I were you.'

'Why not? It's the truth.'

This was not at all what he had expected. The girl seemed to have no idea of her situation.

There was something worrying Ellen, and she decided to get it out in the open. 'Are you going to see Mr Scott?'

'Yes.'

'Would you do me a favour?'

'If I can, certainly.'

'I know the accident's not his fault, and he didn't ask me to push him out of the way, but –' The strong, independent streak in her made her hesitate. 'Oh, never mind.'

Ah, here it comes, Norton thought. How much reward was she going to try to extort? Would it be cash? A better job? What? 'Please, go on, Miss Dudash.'

She blurted it out. 'The truth is, I don't have a lot of money, and I'm going to lose some pay because of this, and I don't think I can afford all these hospital bills. I don't want to bother Mr Scott, but if he could arrange a loan for me, I'd pay it back.' She saw the expression on Norton's face, and misread it. 'I'm sorry. I guess I sound mercenary. It's just that I've been saving up for a trip, and – well, this screws everything up.' She took a deep breath. 'It's not his problem. I'll manage.'

He almost kissed her. *How long has it been since I've come across real innocence? It's enough to restore my faith in womankind.*

He sat down at the side of her bed, and his professional manner disappeared. He took her hand. 'Ellen, I have a feeling you and I are going to be great friends. I promise you, you're not going to have to worry about money. The first thing we have to do is get you through this press conference. We want you to come out of this looking good, so that –' He stopped himself. 'I'm going to be honest. My job is to see that Scott Industries comes out of this looking good. Do you understand?'

'I guess so. You mean it wouldn't sound so good if I said I wasn't really interested in saving Milo Scott? It would sound better if I said something like, "I like working for Scott Industries so much that when I saw Milo Scott was in danger, I knew I had to try to save him, even at the risk of my own life?"'

'Yes.'

She laughed. 'Okay. If it'll help you. But I don't want to kid you, Mr Norton. I don't know what made me do it.'

He smiled. 'That will be our secret. I'll let the lions in.'

There were more than two dozen reporters and photographers from radio, newspapers and magazines. It was a man-bites-dog story, and the press intended to make the most of it. It was not every day that a pretty young employee risked her life to save her boss. And the fact that her employer happened to be Milo Scott did not hurt the story one bit.

'Miss Dudash – when you saw all that iron hurtling down at you, what was your first thought?'

Ellen looked over at Sam Norton with a straight face and said, 'I thought, "I must save Mr Scott. I'd never forgive myself if I let him be killed."'

The press conference proceeded smoothly, and when Sam Norton saw that Ellen was beginning to tire, he said, 'That's it, ladies and gentlemen. Thank you very much.'

'Did I do all right?'

'You were great. Now get some sleep.'

She slept fitfully. She dreamed that she was in the lobby of the Empire State Building, and they would not let her in because she did not have enough money to buy a ticket.

Milo Scott came to visit Ellen Dudash that afternoon. She was surprised to see him. She had heard that his home was in New York.

'I heard the press conference went very well. You're quite a heroine.'

'Mr Scott – I have to tell you something. I'm not a heroine. I didn't stop to think about saving you. I – I just did it.'

'I know. Sam Norton told me.'

'Well, then –'

'Ellen, there are all kinds of heroism. You didn't think about saving me, but you did it instinctively, instead of saving yourself.'

'I – I just wanted you to know.'

'Sam also told me that you're worried about the hospital bills.'

'Well –'

'They're all taken care of. And as for your losing some wages –' He smiled. 'Miss Dudash, I – I don't think you know how much I owe you.'

'You don't owe me anything.'

'The doctor told me that you'll be leaving the hospital tomorrow. Will you let me buy you dinner?'

He doesn't understand, Ellen thought. *I don't want his charity. Or his pity*. 'I meant it when I said you don't owe me anything. Thanks for taking care of the hospital bills. We're even.'

'Good. Now may I buy you dinner?'

That was how it began. Milo Scott stayed in Gary for a week, and he saw Ellen every night.

Ellen's mother and father warned, 'Be careful. Big bosses don't go out with factory girls unless they want something.'

That had been Ellen Dudash's attitude at the beginning. Milo Scott changed her mind. He was a perfect gentleman at all times, and the truth finally dawned on Ellen: *He really enjoys being with me*. Where Milo was shy and reserved, Ellen was forthright and open. All his life, Milo had been surrounded by women whose burning ambition was to become a part of the powerful Scott dynasty. They had played their calculating games. Ellen Dudash was the first totally honest woman Milo had ever met. She said exactly what was on her mind. She was bright, she was attractive, and most of all, she was fun to be with. By the end of the week, they were both falling in love.

'I want to marry you,' Milo Scott said. 'I can't think about anything else. Will you marry me?'

'No.'

Nor had Ellen been able to think about anything else. The truth was that she was terrified. The Scotts were as close as America could come to royalty. They were famous, rich and powerful. *I don't belong in their circle. I would only make a fool of myself. And of Milo*. But she knew she was fighting a losing battle.

They were married by a justice of the peace in Greenwich, and returned to Manhattan so that Ellen Dudash could meet her in-laws.

Byron Scott greeted his brother with, 'What the fuck have you done – marry a Polish hooker? Are you out of your mind?'

Susan Scott was just as ungiving. 'Of course she married Milo for his money. When she finds out he doesn't have any, we'll arrange an annulment. This marriage will never last.'

They badly underestimated Ellen Dudash.

'Your brother and sister-in-law hate me, but I didn't marry them. I married you. I don't want to come between you and Byron. If this is making you too unhappy, Milo, say so, and I'll leave.'

He took his bride in his arms and whispered, 'I adore you, and when Byron and Susan really get to know you, they'll adore you.'

She held him closely and thought: *How naïve he is. And how I love him.*

Byron and Susan were not unpleasant to their new sister-in-law. They were patronizing. To them, she would always be the little Polish girl who worked in one of the Scott factories.

Ellen studied, and read, and learned. She watched how the wives of Milo's friends dressed and copied them. She was determined to become a fit wife to Milo Scott, and in time she succeeded. But not in the eyes of her in-laws. And slowly her naïveté turned to cynicism. *The rich and powerful aren't all that wonderful,* she thought. *All they want is to be richer and more powerful.*

Ellen was fiercely protective of Milo, but there was little she could do to help him. Scott Industries was one of the few privately held conglomerates in the world, and all the stock belonged to Byron. Byron's younger brother was a salaried employee, and he never let him forget it. Byron treated his brother shabbily. Milo was given all the dirty jobs to do, and never given credit.

'Why do you put up with it, Milo? You don't need him. We could move away from here. You could start your own business.'

'I couldn't leave Scott Industries. Byron needs me.'

But in time, Ellen came to understand the real reason. Milo was weak. He needed someone strong to lean on. Ellen knew then that he would never have the courage to leave the company.

All right, she thought fiercely. *One day the company will be his. Byron can't live for ever. Milo is his only heir.*

When Susan Scott announced that she was pregnant, it was a blow to Ellen. *The baby's going to inherit everything.*

When the baby was born, Byron Scott said, 'It's a girl, but I'll teach her how to run the company.'

The bastard, Ellen Scott thought. Her heart ached for Milo.

All Milo said was, 'Isn't she a beautiful baby?'

16

The pilot of the Lockheed Lodestar was worried.

'A front is closing in. I don't like the look of it.' He nodded to the co-pilot. 'Take over.' He left the cockpit to go back to the cabin.

There were five passengers on board besides the pilot and co-pilot: Byron Scott, the brilliant, dynamic founder and chief executive officer of Scott Industries, his attractive wife, Susan; their year-old daughter, Patricia; Milo Scott, Byron Scott's younger brother; and Milo's wife, Ellen Scott. They were flying in one of the company planes from Paris to Madrid. Bringing the baby had been a last-minute impulse on Susan Scott's part.

'I hate to be away from her for so long,' she told her husband.

'Afraid she'll forget us?' he teased. 'All right. We'll take her with us.'

Now that World War II was over, Scott Industries was rapidly expanding into the European market. In Madrid, Byron Scott would investigate the possibilities of opening a new steel mill.

The pilot approached him.

'Excuse me, sir. We're heading into some thunder clouds. It doesn't look very good ahead. Do you want to turn back?'

Byron Scott looked out of the small window. They were flying through a grey mass of cumulus clouds, and every few seconds distant lightning illuminated them. 'I have a meeting in Madrid tonight. Can you go around the storm?'

'I'll try. If I can't, then I'm going to have to turn us around.'

Byron Scott nodded. 'All right.'

'Would you all fasten your seat belts, please?'

The pilot hurried back to the cockpit.

Susan Scott had heard the conversation. She picked up the baby and held her in her arms, suddenly wishing she had not brought her along. *I've got to tell Byron to have the pilot turn back*, she thought.

'Byron –'

They were suddenly caught in the eye of the storm, and the plane began bucking up and down, caught in the gusting winds. The motion began to grow more violent. Rain was smashing against the windows. The storm had closed off all visibility. The passengers felt as though they were riding on a rolling cotton sea.

Byron Scott flicked down the intercom switch. 'Where are we, Blake?'

'We're a hundred kilometres northwest of Madrid, over the town of Ávila.'

Byron Scott looked out of the window again. 'We'll forget Madrid tonight. Let's turn around and get the hell out of here.'

'Roger.'

He was a fraction too late. As the pilot started to bank the plane, a mountain peak looked suddenly in front of him. There was no time to avoid the crash. There was a rending tear, and the sky exploded as the plane tore into the side of the mountain, ripping apart, scattering chunks of fuselage and wings along a high plateau.

There was an unnatural silence that lasted for what seemed an eternity. It was broken by the crackle of flames starting to lick at the undercarriage.

'Ellen –'

Ellen Scott opened her eyes. She was lying under a tree. Her husband was bending over her, lightly slapping her face. When he saw that she was alive, he said, 'Thank God.'

Ellen Scott sat up, dizzy, her head throbbing, every muscle in her body aching. She looked around at the obscene pieces of wreckage that had once been an airplane filled with human bodies, and shuddered.

'The others?' she asked hoarsely.

'They're dead.'

She stared at her husband. 'Oh, my God! No!'

He nodded, his face tight with grief. 'Byron, Susan, the baby, the pilots, everyone.'

Ellen Scott closed her eyes again and said a silent prayer. *Why were Milo and I spared?* she wondered. It was hard to think clearly. *We have to go down and get help. But it's too late. They're all dead.* It was impossible to believe. They had been so full of life just a few minutes before.

'Can you stand up?'

'I – I think so.'

Milo Scott helped his wife to her feet. There was a surge of sickening dizziness, and she stood there, waiting for it to pass.

Milo turned to look at the plane. Flames were beginning to get higher. 'Let's get out of here,' he said. 'The damned thing is going to blow up any second.'

They quietly moved away and watched it burn. A moment later, there was an explosion as the gas tanks blew apart and the plane was engulfed in flames.

'It's a miracle we're alive,' Milo Scott said.

It was a miracle. But not for the others.

Ellen Scott looked at the burning plane. Something was nagging at the edges of her mind, but she was having trouble thinking clearly. Something about Scott Industries. And then suddenly she knew.

'Milo?'

'Yes?' He was not really listening.

'It's fate.'

The fervour in her voice made him turn. 'What?'

'Scott Industries – it belongs to you, now.'

'I don't –'

'Milo, God left it to you.' Her voice was filled with a burning intensity. 'All your life you've lived in the shadow of your big brother.' She was thinking clearly now, coherently, and she forgot her headache and the pain. The words came tumbling out now in a spate that shook her whole body. 'You worked for Byron for twenty years building up the company. You're as responsible for its success as he is, but did he – did he ever give you credit for it? No. It was always *his* company, his success, his profits. Well now you – you finally have a chance to come into your own.'

He looked at her, horrified. 'Ellen – their bodies are – how can you even think about –?'

'I know. But we didn't kill them. It's our turn, Milo. We've finally come into our own. There's no one alive to claim the company but us. It's ours! Yours!'

And at that moment they heard the cry of a baby. Ellen and Milo Scott stared at each other unbelievingly.

'It's Patricia! She's *alive*. Oh, my God!'

They found the baby near a clump of bushes. By some miracle she was unhurt.

Milo Scott picked her up gently and held her close. 'Ssh! It's all right, darling,' he whispered. 'Everything's going to be all right.'

Ellen was standing at his side, a look of shock on her face. 'You – you said she was dead.'

'She must have been knocked unconscious.'

Ellen Scott stared at the baby for a long time. 'She should have been killed with the others,' she said in a strangled voice.

He looked up at her, shocked. 'What are you saying?'

'Byron's will leaves everything to Patricia. You can look forward to spending the next twenty years being her guardian so that when she grows up she can treat you as shabbily as her father did. Is that what you want?'

He was silent.

'We'll never have a chance like this again.' She was staring at the baby, and there was a wild look in her eyes that Milo had never seen before. It was almost as though she wanted to –

She's not herself. She's suffering from a concussion. 'For God's sake, Ellen, what are you thinking?'

She looked at her husband for a long moment, and the wild light faded from her eyes. 'I don't know,' she said calmly. After a pause she said, 'There's something we can do. We can leave her somewhere, Milo. The pilot said we were near Ávila. There should be plenty of tourists there. There's no reason for anyone to connect the baby with the plane crash.'

He shook his head. 'Their friends know that Byron and Susan took Patricia with them.'

Ellen Scott looked at the burning plane. 'That's no problem. They all burned up in the crash. We'll have a private memorial service here.'

'Ellen,' he protested. 'We can't do this. We'd never get away with it.'

'God did it for us. We *have* gotten away with it.'

Milo Scott looked at the baby. 'But she's so –'

'She'll be fine,' Ellen said soothingly. 'We'll drop her off at a nice farmhouse outside of town. They'll adopt her and she'll grow up to have a lovely life here.'

He shook his head. 'I can't do it. No.'

'If you love me you'll do this for us. You have to choose, Milo. You can either have me, or you can spend the rest of your life working for your brother's child.'

'Please, I –'

'Do you love me?'

'More than my life,' he said simply.

'Then prove it.'

They made their way carefully down the mountainside in the dark, whipped by the wind. Because the plane had crashed in a high wooded area, the sound was muffled, so the townspeople would be unaware of what had happened.

Three hours later, on the outskirts of Ávila, Ellen and Milo reached a small farmhouse. It was not yet dawn.

'We'll leave her here,' Ellen whispered.

He made one last try. 'Ellen, couldn't we –?'

'Do it!' she said fiercely.

Without another word, he turned and carried the baby to the door of the farmhouse. She was wearing only a torn pink nightgown and had a blanket wrapped around her.

Milo Scott looked at Patricia for a long moment, his eyes filled with tears, then laid her gently down.

He whispered, 'Have a good life, darling.'

The crying awakened Anunción Moras. For a sleepy moment, she thought it was the bleating of a goat or a lamb. How had it got out of its pen?

Grumbling, she rose from her warm bed, put on an old faded dressing-gown, and walked to the door.

When she saw the infant lying on the ground screaming and kicking, she said, '¡*Madre de Dios!*' and yelled for her husband.

They brought the child inside and stared at it. It would not stop crying, and it seemed to be turning blue.

'We've got to get her to the hospital.'

They hurriedly wrapped another blanket around the baby, carried her to their pick-up truck and drove her to the hospital. They sat on a bench in the long corridor waiting for someone to attend to them, and thirty minutes later a doctor came and took the baby away to examine her.

When he returned, he said, 'She's got pneumonia.'

'Is she going to live?'

The doctor shrugged.

Milo and Ellen Scott stumbled into the police station at Ávila.

The desk sergeant looked up at the two bedraggled tourists. '*Buenos días*. Can I help you?'

'There's been a terrible accident,' Milo Scott said. 'Our plane crashed up in the mountains and . . .'

One hour later a rescue party was on its way to the mountainside. When they arrived, there was nothing to see but the smouldering, charred remains of an aircraft and its passengers.

The investigation of the airplane accident conducted by the Spanish authorities was cursory.

'The pilot should not have attempted to fly into such a bad storm. We must attribute the accident to pilot error.'

There was no reason for anyone in Ávila to associate the airplane crash with a small child left on the doorstep of a farmhouse.

It was over.

It was just beginning.

Milo and Ellen Scott held a private memorial service for Byron Scott, his wife Susan, and their daughter, Patricia. When they returned to New York, they held a second memorial service, attended by the shocked friends of the Scotts.

'What a terrible tragedy. And poor little Patricia.'

'Yes,' Ellen Scott said sadly. 'The only blessing is that it happened so quickly that none of them suffered.'

The financial community was shaken by the news. It was almost unanimously agreed that with Byron Scott's death, Scott Industries had suf-

393

fered an irreparable loss. 'Don't listen to what any of them say,' Ellen Scott told her husband, 'you're better than Byron ever was. The company is going to be bigger than ever.'

Milo took her in his arms. 'I don't know what I'd do without you.'

She smiled. 'You'll never have to. From now on we're going to have everything in the world we've ever dreamed of.'

She held him close and thought: *Who would have believed that Ellen Dudash, from a poor Polish family in Gary, Indiana, would have one day said, 'From now on, we're going to have everything in the world we ever dreamed of?'*

And meant it.

For ten days the baby remained in the hospital, fighting for her life, and when the crisis was past, Father Berrendo went to see the farmer and his wife.

'I have joyous news for you,' he said happily. 'The child is going to be all right.'

The Morases exchanged an uncomfortable look.

'I'm glad for her sake,' the farmer said evasively.

Father Berrendo beamed. 'She is a gift from God.'

'Certainly, Father. But my wife and I have talked it over and decided that God is too generous to us. His gift requires feeding. We can't afford to keep it.'

'But she's such a beautiful baby,' Father Berrendo pointed out. 'And –'

'Agreed. But my wife and I are old and sick, and we can't take on the responsibility of bringing up a baby. God will have to take back his gift.'

And so it was that with nowhere else to go the baby was sent to the orphanage in Ávila.

They were seated in the law offices of Byron Scott's attorney for the reading of the will. Besides the lawyer, only Milo and Ellen Scott were present. Ellen Scott was filled with a sense of almost unbearable excitement. A few words on a piece of paper were going to make her and Milo rich beyond imagining.

We'll buy old masters and a place in Southampton, and a castle in France. And that's only the beginning.

The lawyer started to speak, and Ellen turned her attention to him. Months before she had seen a copy of Byron Scott's will and knew exactly what it said:

In the event that my wife and I should both be deceased, I bequeath all my stock in Scott Industries to my only child, Patricia, and I appoint

*my brother, Milo, as executor of my estate until she reaches the legal age
and is able to take over, etc., etc.*

Well, all that is changed now, Ellen thought excitedly.

The lawyer, Lawrence Gray, said solemnly, 'This has been a terrible
shock to all of us. I know how much you loved your brother, Milo, and
as for that darling little baby . . .' He shook his head. 'Well, life must
go on. You may not be aware that your brother had changed his will.
I won't bother you with the legalese. I will just read you the gist of it.'
He thumbed through the will and came to the paragraph he was looking
for. 'I amend this will so that my daughter, Patricia, will receive the
sum of five million dollars plus a distribution of one million dollars a
year for the rest of her life. All the stock in Scott Industries held in my
name will go to my brother, Milo, as a reward for the faithful and
valuable services he has provided the company through the years.'

Milo Scott felt the room begin to sway.

Mr Gray looked up. 'Are you all right?'

Milo was finding it difficult to breathe. *Good God, what have we
done? We've taken away her birthright, and it wasn't necessary at all.
Now we can give it back to her.*

He turned to say something to Ellen, but the look in her eyes stopped
him.

'There has to be *something* we can do, Ellen. We can't just leave Patricia
there. Not now.'

They were in their Fifth Avenue apartment getting dressed to go to
a charity dinner.

'That's exactly what we're going to do,' Ellen told him. 'Unless you'd
like to bring her back here and try to explain why we said she was
burned to death in the airplane crash.'

He had no answer to that. He thought for a moment. 'All right, then.
We'll send her money every month so she –'

'Don't be a fool, Milo.' Her voice was curt. 'Send her money? And
have the police start checking on why someone is sending her money
and trace it back to us? No. If your conscience bothers you, we'll have
the company give money to charity. Forget about the child, Milo. She's
dead. Remember?'

Remember . . . remember . . . remember . . .

The words echoed in Ellen Scott's mind as she looked out at the
audience in the Waldorf Astoria ballroom and finished her speech.
There was another standing ovation.

You're standing up for a dead woman, she thought.

That night the ghosts came again. She had thought she had exorcised
them long ago. In the beginning, after the memorial services for her

brother-in-law and sister-in-law, and Patricia, the night visitors had come frequently. Pale mists had hovered over her bed and voices had whispered in her ear. She would awaken, her pulse racing, but there was nothing to see. She told none of this to Milo. He was weak, and it might have terrified him into doing something foolish, something that would jeopardize the company. If the truth got out, the scandal would destroy Scott Industries, and Ellen Scott was determined that that must never happen. And so she suffered the ghosts in silence, until finally they went away and left her in peace.

Now, the night of the banquet, they returned. She awakened and sat up in her bed and looked around. The room was empty and quiet, but she knew they had been there. What were they trying to tell her? Did they know she would be joining them soon?

Ellen Scott rose and walked into the spacious, antique-filled drawing room of the beautiful townhouse she had bought after Milo had passed away. She looked around the lovely room and thought: *Poor Milo.* He had had so little time to enjoy any of the benefits of his brother's death. He had died of a heart attack a few years after the plane crash, and Ellen Scott had taken over the company, running it with an efficiency and expertise that had catapulted Scott Industries into greater international prominence.

The company belongs to the Scott family, she thought. *I'm not going to turn it over to faceless strangers.*

And that led her thoughts to Byron's and Susan's daughter. The rightful heiress to the throne that had been stolen from her. Was there fear in her thoughts? Was it a wish to make an atonement before her own death?

Ellen Scott sat in her drawing room all night staring into nothingness, thinking and planning. How long ago had it been? Twenty-eight years. Patricia would be a grown woman now, assuming that she was still alive. What had her life become? Had she married a farmer or a merchant in the village? Did she have children? Was she still living in Ávila, or had she gone away to some other place?

I must find her, Ellen Scott thought. *And quickly. If Patricia is still alive, I've got to see her, talk to her. I have to finally set the account straight. Money can turn lies into truth. I'll find a way to solve the situation without ever letting her know what really happened.*

The following morning Ellen Scott sent for Alan Tucker, chief of security for Scott Industries. He was a former detective, in his forties, a thin, balding, sallow-looking man, hard-working and brilliant.

'I want you to go on a mission for me.'

'Yes, Mrs Scott.'

She studied him for a moment, wondering how much she could tell him. *I can tell him nothing*, she decided. *As long as I am alive, I refuse to put myself or the company in jeopardy. Let him find Patricia first, and then I'll decide how to handle her.*

She leaned forward. 'Twenty-eight years ago, an orphan was left on the doorstep of a farmhouse outside of Ávila, Spain. I want you to find out where she is today and bring her back here to me as quickly as possible.'

Alan Tucker's face remained impassive. Mrs Scott did not like her employees to show emotion.

'Yes, ma'am. I'll leave tomorrow.'

17

Colonel Ramón Acoca was in an expansive mood. All the pieces were finally falling into place.

An orderly came into the office. 'Colonel Sostelo has arrived.'

'Show him in.'

I won't be needing him any more, Acoca thought. *He can go back to his tin soldiers.*

Colonel Fal Sostelo walked in. 'Colonel.'

'Colonel.'

It's ironic, Sostelo thought. *We hold the same rank, but the scarred giant has the power to break me. Because he's connected to the OPUS MUNDO.*

It was an indignity for Sostelo to have to answer Acoca's summons, as though he were some unimportant subordinate. But he managed to show none of his feelings. 'You wanted to see me?'

'Yes.' Acoca waved him to a chair. 'Sit down. I have some news for you. Jaime Miró has the nuns.'

'*What?*'

'Yes. They're travelling with Miró and his men. He's split them up into three groups.'

'How – how do you know that?'

Ramón Acoca leaned back in his chair. 'Do you play chess?'

'No.'

'Pity. It's a very educational game. In order to be a good player, it's necessary to get into the mind of your opponent. Jaime Miró and I play chess with each other.'

Fal Sostelo was staring at him. 'I don't understand how –'

'Not literally, Colonel. We don't use a chess board. We use our minds. I probably understand Jaime Miró better than anyone in the world. I know how his mind works. I knew that he would try to blow up the dam at Puenta la Reina. We captured two of his lieutenants there, and it was only by luck that Miró himself got away. I knew that he would try to rescue them, and Miró knew that I knew it.' Ramón Acoca shrugged. 'I didn't anticipate that he would use the bulls to effect their escape.' There was a note of admiration in his voice.

'You sound as though you –'

'Admire him? I admire his mind. I despise the man.'

'Do you know where Miró is headed?'

'He is travelling north. I will catch him within the next three days.'

Colonel Sostelo was gaping at him, stunned.

'It will finally be checkmate.'

It was true that Colonel Acoca understood Jaime Miró, and the way his mind worked, but it was not enough for him. The Colonel wanted an edge, to ensure victory, and he had found it.

'How – ?'

'One of Miró's terrorists,' Colonel Acoca said, 'is an informer.'

Rubio, Tomas and the two sisters avoided the large cities and took side roads, passing old stone villages with grazing sheep and goats, and shepherds listening to music and soccer games on their transistor radios. It was a colourful juxtaposition of the past and the present, but Lucia had other things on her mind.

She stayed close to Sister Teresa, watching for the first opportunity to get the cross and leave. The two men were always at their side. Rubio Arzano was the more considerate of the two, a tall, pleasant-looking, cheerful man. *A simple-minded peasant*, Lucia decided.

Tomas Sanjuro was slight and balding. *He looks more like a shop assistant than a terrorist. It will be easy to outwit them both.*

They walked across the plains north of Ávila by night, cooled by the winds blowing down from the Guadarrama Steppe. There was a haunting emptiness about the plains by moonlight. They passed *granjas* of wheat and olive trees and vines and maize, and they foraged for potatoes and lettuce, fruit from the trees and eggs and chickens from the hen coops.

'The whole countryside of Spain is a huge market,' said Rubio Arzano.

Tomas Sanjuro grinned. 'And it's all for free.'

Sister Teresa was totally oblivious to her surroundings. Her only thought was to reach the convent at Mendavia. The cross was getting heavy, but she was determined not to let it out of her hands. *Soon*, she thought. *We'll be there soon. We're fleeing from Gethsemane and our enemies to the new mansion He has prepared for us.*

Lucia said, 'What?'

Sister Teresa was unaware that she had spoken aloud.

'I – nothing,' she mumbled.

Lucia took a closer look at her. The older woman seemed distracted and vaguely disoriented, unaware of what was happening around her.

Lucia nodded towards the canvas package that Sister Teresa carried. 'That must be heavy,' Lucia said sympathetically. 'Wouldn't you like me to carry it for a while?'

Sister Teresa clutched it to her body more tightly. 'Jesus carried a heavier burden. I can carry this for Him.' Did it not say in Luke: *If any man would come after me, let him deny himself and take up his cross daily and follow me.*

'I'll carry it,' Teresa said stubbornly.

There was something odd in her tone.

'Are you all right, Sister?'

'Of course.'

Sister Teresa was far from all right. She had not been able to sleep. She felt dizzy and feverish. Her mind was playing tricks again. *I mustn't let myself become ill*, she thought. *Sister Betina will scold me.* But Sister Betina was not there. It was so confusing. And who were these men? *I don't trust them. What do they want with me?*

Rubio Arzano had attempted to strike up a conversation with Sister Teresa, trying to make her feel at ease.

'It must seem strange to you, being out in the world again, Sister. How long were you in the convent?'

Why did he want to know? 'Thirty years.'

'My, that's a long time. Where are you from?'

It was painful for her even to say the word. 'Èze.'

His face brightened. 'Èze? I spent a summer there once on holiday. It's a lovely town. I know it well. I remember –'

I know it well. How well? Did he know Raoul? Had Raoul sent him? And the truth hit her like a bolt of lightning. These strangers had been sent to bring her back to Èze, to Raoul Giradot. They were kidnapping her. God was punishing her for deserting Monique's baby. She was certain now that the baby she had seen in the village square in Villacastin was her sister Monique's. *But it couldn't have been, could it? That was thirty years ago*, Teresa muttered to herself. *They're lying to me.*

Rubio Arzano was watching her, listening to her mumbling.

'Is something wrong, Sister?'

Sister Teresa shrank away from him. 'No.'

She was on to them now. She was not going to let them take her back to Raoul and the baby. She had to get to the convent at Mendavia and hand over the gold crucifix, and then God would forgive her for the terrible sin she had committed. *I must be clever. I must not let them know I am on to their secret.*

She looked up at Rubio Arzano. 'I am fine,' Sister Teresa said.

They moved on across the dry, sunbaked plains. They came to a small village where peasant women dressed in black were doing their wash at a spring covered by a roof resting on four ancient beams. The water poured into a long wooden trough and out again, so that it was always fresh, and the women scrubbed their wash on stone slabs and rinsed it clean in the running water.

It's such a peaceful scene, Rubio thought. It reminded him of the farm he had left behind. *It's what Spain used to be like. No bombs, no killing. Will we ever know peace again?*

'Buenos días.'

'Buenos días.'

'I wonder if we might have a drink? Travelling is thirsty work.'

400

'Certainly. Please help yourselves.'
The water was cold and refreshing.
'*Gracias. Adiós.*'
'*Adiós.*'
Rubio hated to leave.

The two women and their escorts moved on, past cork and olive trees, the summer air filled with the smell of ripe grapes and oranges. They went by orchards of apples and cherry and plum trees, and farms noisy with the sound of chickens and pigs and goats.

Rubio and Tomas walked ahead, talking quietly together.

They are talking about me. They think I do not know their plan. Sister Teresa moved nearer to them so she could hear what they were saying.

'. . . A reward of five hundred thousand pesetas on our heads. Of course Colonel Acoca would pay more for Jaime, but he doesn't want his head. He wants his *cojones.*'

The men laughed.

As Sister Teresa listened to them talk, her conviction grew stronger. *These men are killers doing Satan's work, messengers of the devil sent to damn me to everlasting hell. But God is stronger than they are. He will not let them take me back home.*

Raoul Giradot was at her side, smiling the smile that she knew so well.

The voice!

I beg your pardon?

I heard you sing yesterday. You are magnificent.

May I help you?

I would like three yards of muslin, please.

Certainly. This way . . . My aunt owns this shop and she needed help, so I thought I'd work for her for a while.

I'm sure you could have any man you want, Teresa, but I hope you will choose me.

He looked so handsome.

I have never known anyone like you, my darling.

Raoul was taking her in his arms and kissing her.

You're going to make a beautiful bride.

But now I'm Christ's bride. I can't return to Raoul.

Lucia was watching her closely. Sister Teresa was talking to herself, but Lucia could not make out the words.

She's cracking up, Lucia thought. *She's not going to make it. I've got to get hold of that cross soon.*

It was dusk when they saw the town of Olmedo in the distance.

Rubio stopped. 'There will be soldiers there. Let's move up to the hills and skirt the city.'

They moved off the road and left the plains, headed for the hills above Olmedo. The sun was skipping across the mountain tops and the sky was beginning to darken.

'We've only a few more miles to go,' Rubio Arzano said reassuringly. 'Then we can rest.'

They had reached the top of a high ridge when Tomas Sanjuro suddenly held up a hand. 'Hold it,' he whispered.

Rubio Arzano walked to his side and they moved to the edge of the ridge and looked down into the valley below. There was an encampment of soldiers there.

'*¡Mierda!*' Rubio whispered. 'There must be a whole platoon. We'll stay up here for the rest of the night. They'll probably pull out in the morning and we can move on.' He turned to Lucia and Sister Teresa, trying not to show how worried he was. 'We'll spend the night here, Sisters. We must be very quiet. There are soldiers down there and we don't want them to find us.'

It was the best news Lucia could have heard. *It's perfect*, she thought. *I'll disappear with the cross during the night. They won't dare try to follow me because of the soldiers.*

To Sister Teresa, the news had a different meaning. She had heard the men say that someone named Colonel Acoca was searching for them. *They called Colonel Acoca the enemy. But these men are the enemy, so Colonel Acoca must be my friend. Thank you, dear God, for sending me Colonel Acoca.*

The tall man called Rubio was speaking to her.

'Do you understand, Sister? We must all be very, very quiet.'

'Yes, I understand.' *I understand more than you think.* They had no idea that God permitted her to see into their evil hearts.

Tomas Sanjuro said kindly, 'I know how difficult this must be for both of you, but don't worry. We'll see that you get safely to the convent.'

To Èze, he means. Oh, but he is cunning. He speaks the honeyed words of the devil. But God is within me, and He is guiding me. She knew what she must do. But she had to be careful.

The two men arranged the sleeping-bags for the women, next to each other.

'Both of you get some sleep now.'

The women got into the unfamiliar sleeping-bags. The night was incredibly clear and the sky was spangled with glimmering stars. Lucia looked up at them and thought happily: *In just a few hours now, I'll be on my way to freedom. As soon as they're all asleep.*

She yawned. She had not realized how tired she was. The long, hard journey and the emotional strain had taken their toll. Her eyes felt heavy. *I'll just rest for a little while*, Lucia thought.

She slept.

Sister Teresa lay near Lucia, wide awake, fighting the demons trying to possess her, trying to send her soul to hell. *I must be strong. The*

Lord is testing me. I have been exiled, so that I can find my way back to Him. And these men are trying to stop me. I must not let them.

At four o'clock in the morning, Sister Teresa silently sat up and looked around. Tomas Sanjuro was asleep only a few feet from her. The tall, dark man called Rubio was keeping watch at the edge of the clearing, his back to her. She could see his silhouette against the trees.

Very quietly, Sister Teresa rose. She hesitated, thinking about the cross. *Should I carry it with me? But I'll be coming back here very soon. I must find a place where it will be safe until I return.* She looked over to where Sister Lucia lay sleeping. *Yes. It will be safe with my sister in God*, Sister Teresa decided.

Silently she moved over to the sleeping-bag and gently slipped the wrapped cross inside. Lucia did not stir. Sister Teresa turned and moved into the woods, out of Rubio Arzano's sight, and carefully began to make her way downhill towards the soldiers' camp. The hill was steep and slippery with dew, but God gave her wings and she sped downhill without stumbling or falling, hurrying towards her salvation.

In the darkness ahead the figure of a man suddenly materialized.

A voice called out, 'Who goes there?'

'Sister Teresa.'

She approached the sentry. He wore an army uniform and was carrying a rifle, pointed at her.

'Where did you come from, old woman?' he demanded.

She looked at him with golden eyes. 'God sent me.'

The sentry stared at her. 'Did He, now?'

'Yes. He sent me to see Colonel Acoca.'

The guard shook his head. 'You'd better tell Him you're not the Colonel's type. *Adiós, señora.*'

'You don't understand. I am Sister Teresa from the Abbey Cistercian. I have been taken prisoner by Jaime Miró and his men.' She watched the stunned expression that came over his face.

'You're — you're from the convent?'

'Yes.'

'The one at Ávila?'

'Yes,' Teresa said impatiently. What was the matter with the man? Didn't he realize how important it was that she be rescued from those evil men?

The soldier said carefully, 'The Colonel isn't here just now, Sister —'

It was an unexpected blow.

'— But Colonel Sostelo is in charge. I can take you to him.'

'Will he be able to help me?'

'Oh, I'm sure he will. Follow me, please.'

The sentry was scarcely able to believe his good fortune. Colonel Fal Sostelo had sent squadrons of soldiers scouring the entire countryside searching for the four nuns, and they had had no success. Now one of the sisters had stumbled into the camp and given herself up to him. The Colonel was going to be pleased. The Colonel was going to be very pleased.

They reached the tent where Colonel Fal Sostelo and his second in command were poring over a map. The men looked up as the sentry and a woman entered.

'Excuse me, Colonel. This is Sister Teresa from the Cistercian convent.'

Colonel Sostelo stared at her, unbelievingly. All of his energies for the last three days had been focused on finding Jaime Miró and the nuns, and now, here in front of him was one of them. There *was* a God.

'Sit down, Sister.'

There is no time for that, Sister Teresa thought. She had to make him realize how urgent this was. 'We must hurry. They are trying to take me back to Èze.'

The Colonel was puzzled. 'Who's trying to take you back to Èze?'

'The men of Jaime Miró.'

He got to his feet. 'Sister – do you by any chance happen to know where these men are?'

Sister Teresa said impatiently, 'Of course.' She turned and pointed. 'They're up in those hills hiding from you.'

18

Alan Tucker arrived in Ávila the day after his conversation with Ellen Scott. It had been a long flight, and Tucker should have been exhausted, but he was exhilarated. Ellen Scott was not a woman given to whims. *There's something strange going on behind all this*, Alan Tucker thought, *and if I play my cards right, I have a hunch it could be very profitable for me.*

He checked into the Cuatro Postes Hotel and said to the clerk behind the desk, 'Is there a newspaper office around here?'

'Down the street, *señor*. To your left, two blocks. You can't miss it.'

'Thank you.'

'*De nada*.'

Walking down the main street, watching the town come alive after its afternoon siesta, Tucker thought about the mysterious girl he had been sent to bring back. This had to be something important. But important *why*? He could hear Ellen Scott's voice.

If she's alive, bring her back to me. You are not to discuss this with anyone.

No, ma'am. What shall I tell her?

Simply tell her that a friend of her father's wishes to meet her. She'll come.

Tucker found the newspaper office. Inside, he approached one of the half a dozen people working behind desks. '*Perdón*, I would like to see the managing editor.'

The man pointed to an office. 'In there, *señor*.'

'*Gracias*.'

Tucker walked over to the open door and looked inside. A man in his mid-thirties was seated behind a desk, busily editing copy.

'Excuse me,' Tucker said. 'Could I speak to you for a moment?'

The man looked up. 'What can I do for you?'

'I'm looking for a *señorita*.'

The editor smiled. 'Aren't we all, *señor*?'

'She was left at a farmhouse around here when she was an infant.'

The smile faded. 'Oh. She was abandoned?'

'Yes.'

'And you are trying to find her?'

'Yes.'

'How many years ago would that be, *señor*?'

'Twenty-eight.'

The young man shrugged. 'It was before my time.'

Perhaps it's not going to be so easy. 'Would you happen to know anything about the woman or could you suggest someone who might be able to help me?'

The editor leaned back in his chair, thinking. 'As a matter of fact, I can. I would suggest you speak with Father Berrendo.'

Father Berrendo sat in his study, a rug over his thin legs, listening to the stranger.

When Alan Tucker had finished talking, Father Berrendo said, 'Why do you wish to know about this matter, *señor*? It happened so long ago. What is your interest in it?'

Tucker hesitated, choosing his words carefully. 'I am not at liberty to say. I can only assure you that I mean the woman no harm. If you could just tell me where the farmhouse is where she was left – ?'

The farmhouse. Memories came flooding back of the day the Morases had come to him after they had taken the little girl to hospital.

I think she's dying, Father. What shall we do?

Father Berrendo had talked to his friend, Don Morago, the chief of police.

'I think the baby was abandoned by tourists visiting Ávila. Could you check the hotels and inns and see if anyone arrived with a baby and left without one?'

The police had gone through the registration cards that all hotels were required to fill out, but they were of no help.

'It is as if the baby just dropped out of the sky,' Don Morago said.

And he had no idea of how close he had come to solving the mystery.

When Father Berrendo had taken the infant to the orphanage, Mercedes Angeles had asked, 'Has the baby got a name?'

'I don't know.'

'Wasn't there a blanket or something with the name on it?'

'No.'

Mercedes Angeles looked at the infant in the priest's arms. 'Well, we'll just have to give her a name, won't we?'

She had recently finished reading a romantic novel, and she liked the name of the heroine in it.

'Megan,' she said. 'We'll call her Megan.'

And fourteen years later, Father Berrendo had taken Megan to the Abbey Cistercian.

So many years after that, this stranger was looking for her. *Life always comes full circle*, Father Berrendo thought. *In some mysterious way, it has come full circle for Megan.* No, not Megan. That was the name given her by the orphanage.

'Sit down, *señor*,' Father Berrendo said. 'There is much to tell you.' And he told him.

When the priest had finished, Alan Tucker sat there quietly, his mind racing. There had to be a strong reason for Ellen Scott's interest in a baby abandoned at a farmhouse in Spain twenty-eight years earlier. A woman now called Megan, according to the priest.

Tell her that a friend of her father's wishes to meet her.

If he remembered correctly, Byron Scott and his wife and daughter had died in an airplane crash many years ago somewhere in Spain. Could there be a connection? Alan Tucker felt a growing sense of excitement.

'Father – I'd like to get into the convent to see her. It's very important.'

The priest shook his head. 'I'm afraid you are too late. The convent was attacked two days ago by agents of the government.'

Alan Tucker stared at him. 'Attacked? What happened to the nuns?'

'They were arrested and taken to Madrid.'

Alan Tucker got to his feet. 'Thank you, Father.' He would catch the first plane to Madrid.

Father Berrendo went on: 'Four of the nuns escaped. Sister Megan was one of them.'

Things were becoming complicated. 'Where is she now?'

'No one knows. The police and the army are searching for her and the other sisters.'

'I see.' Under ordinary circumstances, Alan Tucker would have telephoned Ellen Scott and informed her that he had reached a dead end. But all his instincts as a detective told him that there was something here that warranted further investigation.

He placed a call to Ellen Scott.

'There's a complication, Mrs Scott.' He repeated his conversation with the priest.

There was a long silence. 'No one knows where she is?'

'She and the others are on the run, but they can't hide out much longer. The police and half the Spanish army are looking for them. When they surface, I'll be there.'

Another silence. 'This is very important to me, Tucker.'

'Yes, Mrs Scott.'

Alan Tucker returned to the newspaper office. He was in luck. It was still open.

He said to the editor, 'I would like to look through your files, if I may.'

'Are you looking for something in particular?'

'Yes. There was an airplane crash here.'

'How long ago, *señor*?'

If I'm right – 'Twenty-eight years ago. Nineteen forty-eight.'

It took Alan Tucker fifteen minutes to find the item he was looking for. The headline leaped out at him.

PLANE CRASH KILLS EXECUTIVE FAMILY

1 October 1948. Byron Scott, President of Scott Industries, his wife, Susan, and their one-year-old daughter, Patricia, were burned to death in an airplane crash . . .

I've hit the jackpot! He could feel his pulse begin to race. *If this is what I think it is, I'm going to be a rich man . . . a very rich man.*

19

She was naked in her bed, and she could feel the male hardness of Benito Patas pressing into her groin. His body felt wonderful, and she moved closer to him, grinding her hips against him, feeling the heat growing in her loins. She started to stroke him, to excite him. But something was wrong. *I killed Patas*, she thought. *He's dead.*

Lucia opened her eyes and sat up, trembling, looking around wildly. Benito was not there. She was in the forest, in a sleeping-bag. Something was pressing against her thigh. Lucia reached down inside the sleeping-bag and pulled out the canvas-wrapped cross. She stared at it, unbelievingly. *God has just performed a miracle for me*, Lucia thought.

She had no idea how the cross had got there, nor did she care. She had it in her hands at last. All she had to do now was to slip away from the others.

She crept out of the sleeping-bag and looked over to where Sister Teresa had slept. She was gone. Lucia looked around in the darkness, and she could barely make out the figure of Tomas Sanjuro at the edge of the clearing, facing away from her. She was not sure where Rubio was. *It doesn't matter. It's time to get out of here*, Lucia thought.

She started to move to the edge of the clearing, away from Sanjuro, bending low so she would not be seen.

At that instant all hell broke loose.

Colonel Fal Sostelo had had a command decision to make. He had been given orders by the Prime Minister himself to work closely with Colonel Ramón Acoca to help capture Jaime Miró and the nuns. But fate had blessed him by delivering one of the nuns into his hands. Why share the credit with Colonel Acoca when he could catch the terrorists and keep all the glory? *Fuck Colonel Acoca*, Fal Sostelo thought. *This one is mine. Maybe the OPUS MUNDO will use me instead of Acoca, with all his bullshit about chess games and getting into the minds of people. No, it's time to teach the scarred giant a lesson.*

Colonel Sostelo gave specific orders to his men.

'Don't take any prisoners. You're dealing with terrorists. Shoot to kill.'

Major Ponte hesitated. 'Colonel, there are nuns up there with Miró's men. Shouldn't we – ?'

'Let the terrorists hide behind the nuns? No. We'll take no chances.'

Fal Sostelo selected a dozen men to accompany him on the raid and he saw to it that they were heavily armed. They moved noiselessly in the dark, up the slope of the mountain. The moon had disappeared behind clouds. There was almost no visibility. *Good. They won't be able to see us coming.*

When his men were in position, Colonel Sostelo shouted, for the sake of the record, 'Put down your arms. You're surrounded.' And in the same breath he called out the command, 'Fire! Keep firing!'

A dozen automatic weapons began spraying the clearing.

Tomas Sanjuro never had a chance. A hail of machine gun bullets caught him in the chest and he was dead before he hit the ground. Rubio Arzano was at the far edge of the clearing when the firing started. He saw Sanjuro fall, and he whirled and started to raise his gun to return the fire but stopped. It was pitch black in the clearing and the soldiers were firing blindly. If he returned their fire, he would give his position away.

To his amazement, he saw Lucia crouched two feet away from him.

'Where's Sister Teresa?' he whispered.

'She's – she's gone.'

'Stay low,' Rubio told her.

He grabbed Lucia's hand and zigzagged towards the forest, away from the enemy fire. Shots whizzed dangerously close as they ran, but moments later, Lucia and Rubio were among the trees. They continued running.

'Hold on to me, Sister,' he said.

They heard the sound of their attackers behind them, but gradually it died away. It was impossible to pursue anyone through the inky blackness of the woods.

Rubio stopped to let Lucia catch her breath.

'We've lost them for now,' Rubio told her. 'But we have to keep moving.'

Lucia was breathing hard.

'If you want to rest for a minute – ?'

'No,' she said. She was exhausted, but she had no intention of letting them catch her. Not now when she had the cross. 'I'm fine,' she said. 'Let's get out of here.'

Colonel Fal Sostelo was facing disaster. One terrorist dead, but God alone knew how many had escaped. He did not have Jaime Miró and he had only one of the nuns. He knew he would have to inform Colonel Acoca of what had happened. He was not looking forward to it.

The second call from Alan Tucker to Ellen Scott was even more disturbing than the previous call.

'I've come across some rather interesting information, Mrs Scott,' he said cautiously.

'Yes?'

'I went through some old newspaper files here, hoping to get more information on the girl.'

'And?' She braced herself for what she knew was coming.

Tucker kept his voice casual. 'It seems that the girl was abandoned about the time of your plane crash.'

Silence.

He went on: 'The one that killed your brother-in-law and his wife and their daughter, Patricia.'

Blackmail. There was no other explanation. So he had found out.

'That's right,' Ellen Scott said casually. 'I should have mentioned that. I'll explain everything when you get back. Have you any more news of the girl?'

'No, but she can't hide out for very long. The whole country's looking for her.'

'Let me hear from you as soon as she's found.'

The line went dead.

Alan Tucker sat there, staring at the dead telephone in his hand. *She's a cool lady*, he thought admiringly. *I wonder how she's going to feel about having a partner?*

I made a mistake in sending him, Ellen Scott thought. *Now I'll have to stop him.* And what was she going to do about the girl? *A nun! I won't judge her until I see her.*

Her secretary buzzed her on the intercom.

'They're ready for you in the board room, Mrs Scott.'

'I'm coming.'

Lucia and Rubio Arzano kept moving through the woods, stumbling and slipping, attacked by tree limbs and bushes and insects, but each step took them farther away from their pursuers.

Finally, Rubio Arzano said, 'We can stop here. They won't find us.'

They were high in the mountains in the middle of a dense forest.

Lucia lay down on the ground, fighting to catch her breath. In her mind, she replayed the terrible scene she had witnessed earlier. Tomas shot down without warning. *And the bastards intended to murder us all*, Lucia thought. The only reason she was still alive was because of the man sitting beside her.

Lucia watched Rubio as he got to his feet and scouted the area around them.

'We can spend the rest of the night here, Sister.'

'All right.' She was impatient to get moving, but she knew she needed to rest.

As though reading her mind, Rubio Arzano said, 'We'll move on again at dawn.'

Lucia felt a gnawing in her stomach. Even as she was thinking about it, Rubio Arzano said, 'You must be hungry. I'll go and find some food for us. Will you be all right here by yourself?'

'Yes. I'll be fine.'

The big man crouched down beside her.

'Please try not to be frightened. I know how difficult it must be for you to be out in the world again after all those years in the convent. Everything must seem very strange to you.'

Lucia looked up at him and said tonelessly, 'I'll try to get used to it.'

'You're very brave, Sister.' Rubio rose. 'I'll be back soon.'

She watched Rubio disappear into the trees. It was time to make a decision, and she had two choices: she could escape now, try to reach a nearby town and trade the gold cross for a passport and enough money to get to Switzerland, or she could stay with this man until they got farther away from the soldiers. *That will be safer*, Lucia decided.

Lucia heard a noise in the woods and swung around. It was Rubio Arzano. He moved towards her, smiling. In his hand he held his beret, bulging with tomatoes, grapes and apples.

He sat down on the ground next to her. 'Supper. A nice, plump poulet was available but the fire we would have needed to cook it would have given us away.'

Lucia stared at the contents of the beret. 'It looks like manna from heaven. I'm starving.'

They had finished eating and were sitting against a tree. Rubio Arzano was talking, but Lucia was paying no attention, absorbed in her own thoughts.

'Ten years, you said you were in the convent, Sister?'

Lucia was startled out of her reverie. 'What?'

'You've been in the convent for ten years?'

'Oh. Yes.'

He shook his head. 'Then you have no idea what's been happening in all that time.'

'Uh – no.'

'In the last ten years the world has changed a great deal, Sister.'

'Has it?'

'*Sí.*' Rubio said earnestly, 'Franco has died.'

'No!'

'Oh, yes. Last year.'

And named Don Juan Carlos, his heir.

'You may find this very hard to believe, but a man has walked on the moon. That is the truth.'

'Really?' *Actually, two men*, Lucia thought. *What were their names? Neil Armstrong and Buzz Something.*

'Oh, yes. North Americans. And there is now a plane for passengers that travels faster than sound.'

'Incredible.' *I can't wait to travel in Concorde*, Lucia thought.

Rubio was childlike, so pleased to be bringing her up to date on world events.

'There has been a revolution in Portugal, and in the United States of America, their President Nixon was involved in a big scandal and had to resign.'

Rubio is really sweet, Lucia decided.

He took out a pack of Ducados cigarettes, the heavy black tobacco of Spain. 'I hope it won't offend you if I smoke, Sister?'

'No,' Lucia said. 'Please go ahead.'

She watched him light up, and the moment the smoke reached her nostrils she was desperate to have a cigarette.

'Do you mind if I try one?'

He looked at her in surprise. 'You wish to try a cigarette?'

'Just to see what it's like,' Lucia said quickly.

'Oh. Of course.'

He held the pack towards her. She took out a cigarette, put it between her lips and he lit the end of it for her. Lucia inhaled deeply, and as the smoke filled her lungs, she felt wonderful.

Rubio was watching her, puzzled.

Lucia coughed. 'So that's what a cigarette tastes like.'

'Do you like it?'

'Not really, but –'

She took another deep, satisfying puff. God, how she had missed this. But she knew she had to be careful. She did not want to make him suspicious. She put out the cigarette she had held clumsily in her fingers. She had been in the convent for only a few months, and yet Rubio was right. It did seem strange to be out in the world again. She wondered how Megan and Graciela were doing. And what had happened to Sister Teresa? Had she been captured by the soldiers?

Lucia's eyes were beginning to sting. It had been a long, tension-filled night. 'I think I may take a little nap.'

'Don't worry. I will watch over you, Sister.'

'Thank you,' she smiled. Within moments, she was asleep.

Rubio Arzano looked down at her and thought: *I have never seen a woman like this one.* She was so spiritual that she had dedicated her life to God, and yet at the same time there was an earthiness about her.

And she had behaved this night as bravely as any man. *You are a very special woman*, Rubio Arzano thought as he watched her sleep. *Little sister of Jesus.*

20

Colonel Fal Sostelo was on his tenth cigarette. *I can't put it off any longer*, he decided. *Bad news is best got out of the way quickly.*

He took several deep breaths to calm himself and then he dialled a number. When he had Ramón Acoca on the telephone, he said, 'Colonel, we raided a terrorist camp last night, where I was informed Jaime Miró was, and I thought you should know about it.'

There was a dangerous silence.

'Did you catch him?'

'No.'

'You undertook this operation without consulting me?'

'There was no time to –'

'But there was time to let Miró escape.' Ramón Acoca's voice was filled with fury. 'What led you to undertake this magnificently executed operation?'

Colonel Sostelo swallowed. 'We caught one of the nuns from the convent. She led us to Miró and his men. We killed one of them in the attack.'

'But the others all escaped?'

'Yes, Colonel.'

'Where is the nun now? Or did you let her get away, too?' His tone was scathing.

'No, Colonel,' Sostelo said quickly. 'She is here at the camp. We have been questioning her and –'

'Don't. I'll question her myself. I'll be there in one hour. See if you can manage to hang on to her until I get there.' He slammed down the receiver.

Exactly one hour later, Colonel Ramón Acoca arrived at the camp where they were holding Sister Teresa. With him were a dozen of his men from the GOE.

'Bring the nun to me,' Colonel Acoca ordered.

Sister Teresa was brought to the headquarters tent where Colonel Acoca was waiting for her. He stood up politely when she entered the tent and smiled.

'I am Colonel Acoca.'

At last! 'I knew you would come. God told me.'

He nodded pleasantly. 'Did he? Good. Please sit down, Sister.'

415

Sister Teresa was too nervous to sit. 'You must help me.'

'We're going to help each other,' the Colonel assured her. 'You escaped from the Abbey Cistercian at Ávila, is that correct?'

'Yes. It was terrible. All those men. They did godless things and –'

And stupid things. We let you and the others escape. 'How did you get here, Sister?'

'God brought me here. He's testing me as He once tested –'

Colonel Acoca said patiently, 'As well as God, did some men also bring you here, Sister?'

'Yes. They kidnapped me. I had to escape from them.'

'You told Colonel Sostelo where he could find those men?'

'Yes. The evil ones. Raoul is behind it all, you see. He sent me a letter and said –'

'Sister, the man we're looking for in particular is Jaime Miró. Have you seen him?'

She shivered. 'Yes. Oh, yes. He –'

The Colonel leaned forward. 'Excellent. Now you must tell me where I can find him.'

'He and the others are on their way to Èze.'

He frowned, puzzled. 'To Èze? To France?'

Her words were a wild babble. 'Yes. Monique deserted Raoul, and he sent the men to kidnap me because of the baby so –'

He tried to control his growing impatience. 'Miró and his men are headed north. Èze is to the east.'

'– You must not let them take me back to Raoul. I don't want to see him ever again. You can understand that. I couldn't face him –'

Colonel Acoca said curtly, 'I don't give a damn about this Raoul. I want to know where I can find Jaime Miró.'

'I told you. He is in Èze waiting for me. He wants to –'

'You're lying. I think you're trying to protect Miró. Now I don't want to hurt you, so I'm going to ask you once more. Where is Jaime Miró?'

Sister Teresa stared at him helplessly. 'I don't know,' she whispered. She looked around wildly. 'I don't know.'

'A moment ago you said he was in Èze.' His voice was like a whiplash.

'Yes. God told me.'

Colonel Acoca had had enough. The woman was either demented or a brilliant actress. Either way, she sickened him with all her talk of God.

He turned to Patricio Arrieta, his lieutenant. 'The sister's memory needs prodding. Take her to the quartermaster's tent. Perhaps you and your men can help her remember where Jaime Miró is.'

'Yes, Colonel.'

Patricio Arrieta and the men with him had been part of the group that had attacked the convent at Ávila. They felt responsible for letting the four nuns escape. *Well, we can make up for that now,* Arrieta thought.

416

Arrieta turned to Sister Teresa. 'Come along with me, Sister.'

'Yes.' *Dear blessed Jesus, thank You.* She babbled on. 'Are we leaving now? You won't let them take me to Èze, will you?'

'No,' Arrieta assured her. 'You're not going to Èze.'

The Colonel is right, he thought. *She is playing games with us. Well, we'll show her some new games. I wonder if she'll lie quietly, or if she'll scream?*

When they reached the quartermaster's tent, Arrieta said, 'Sister, we've going to give you one last chance. Where is Jaime Miró?'

Haven't they asked me that before? Or was that someone else? Was it here or – it's all terribly confusing. 'He kidnapped me for Raoul because Monique deserted him and he thought –'

'*Bueno.* If that's the way you want it,' Arrieta said, 'we'll see if we can't refresh your memory for you.'

'Yes. Please. Everything is so puzzling.'

Half a dozen of Acoca's men had entered the tent, along with some of Sostelo's uniformed soldiers.

Sister Teresa looked up. She blinked dazedly. 'Are these men going to take me to the convent now?'

'They're going to do better than that,' Patricio Arrieta grinned. 'They're going to take you to heaven, Sister.'

The men moved closer to her, surrounding her.

'That's a pretty dress you're wearing,' a soldier said. 'Are you sure you're a nun, darling?'

'Oh, yes,' she said. Raoul had called her darling. Was this Raoul? 'You see, we had to change clothes to escape from the soldiers.' But these were soldiers. Everything was muddled.

One of the men pushed Teresa down on the cot. 'You're no beauty, but let's see what you look like underneath all those clothes.'

'What are you doing?'

He reached down and ripped off the top of her dress while another man tore at her skirt.

'That's not a bad body for an old lady, is it, fellows?'

Teresa screamed.

She looked up at the circle of men surrounding her. *God will strike them all dead. He will not let them touch me, for I am His vessel. I am one with the Lord, drinking from His fountain of purity.*

One of the soldiers unfastened his belt. An instant later she felt rough hands pushing her legs apart, and as the soldier sprawled on top of her, she felt his hard flesh penetrate her and again she screamed.

'Now, God! Punish them now.'

She waited for the clap of thunder, the bright flash of lightning that would destroy them all.

Nothing happened.

Another soldier climbed on top of her. A red haze came over her eyes. Teresa lay there waiting for God to strike, almost unaware of the men who were ravaging her. She no longer felt the pain.

Lieutenant Arrieta was standing next to the cot. After each man finished with Teresa, he said, 'Have you had enough, Sister? You can stop this at any time. All you have to do is tell me where Jaime Miró is.'

Sister Teresa did not hear him. She screamed in her mind: *Smite them down with Your power, Lord. Wipe them out as You wiped out the other wicked ones at Sodom and Gomorrah.*

Incredibly, He did not answer. It was not possible, for God was everywhere. And then she knew. As the sixth man entered her body, the epiphany suddenly came to her.

God was not listening to her because there was no God. All these years she had deceived herself into worshipping a Supreme power and had served Him faithfully. But there was no Supreme Power. *If God exists, He would have saved me.*

The red haze lifted from Sister Teresa's eyes and she got a clear look at her surroundings for the first time. There were at least a dozen soldiers in the tent waiting their turn to rape her. Lieutenant Arrieta was standing at one side of the bed watching. The soldiers in line were in full uniform, not bothering to undress.

As one soldier lifted himself from Teresa, the next soldier opened his fly and took out his penis. He squatted down over her and a moment later penetrated her.

There is no God, but there is a Satan, and these are his helpers, Sister Teresa thought. *And they must die. All of them.*

As the soldier plunged into her, Sister Teresa grabbed the pistol from his holster and before anyone could react, she turned the pistol on Arrieta. The bullet hit him in the throat.

Sister Teresa pointed the gun at the other soldiers and kept firing. Four of them fell to the floor dead before the others came to their senses and began shooting at her. Because of the soldier on top of her, they had difficulty aiming.

Sister Teresa and her last ravisher died at the same moment.

21

Jaime Miró came awake instantly, aroused by a movement at the edge of the clearing. He slipped out of the sleeping-bag and rose, gun in hand. He saw Megan on her knees, praying. He stood there, studying her. There was an unearthly beauty about the image of this lovely woman praying in the forest in the middle of the night, and Jaime found himself resenting it. *If Felix Carpio hadn't blurted out that we were headed for San Sebastian, I wouldn't have been burdened with the sister in the first place.*

It was imperative that he get to San Sebastian as quickly as possible. Colonel Acoca and his men and the army were all around them, and it would have been difficult enough slipping through their net alone. With the added burden of this woman to slow him down, the danger was increased tenfold.

He walked over to Megan, angry, and his voice was harsher than he had intended.

'I told you to get some sleep. I don't want you slowing us down tomorrow.'

Megan looked up and said quietly, 'I'm sorry if I've angered you.'

'Sister, I save my anger for more important things. Your kind just bore me. You spend your lives hiding behind stone walls waiting for a free trip to the next world. You make me sick, all of you.'

'Because we believe in the next world?'

'No, Sister. Because you don't believe in this one. You ran away from it.'

'To pray for you. We spend our lives praying for you.'

'And you think that will solve the problems of the world?'

'In time, yes.'

'There is no time. Your God can't hear your prayers because of the noise of the cannons and the screams of children being torn apart by bombs.'

'When you have faith –'

'Oh, I have lots of faith, Sister. I have faith in what I'm fighting for. I have faith in my men, and in my guns. What I don't have faith in are people who walk on water. If you think your God is listening now, tell him to get us to the convent at Mendavia so I can be rid of you.'

He was angry with himself for losing his temper. It wasn't her fault that the church had stood idly by while Franco's Falangists tortured and raped and murdered Basques and Catalans. *It wasn't her fault*, Jaime told himself, *that my family was among the victims.*

Jaime had been a young boy then, but it was a memory that would be etched for ever in his brain . . .

He had been awakened in the middle of the night by the noise of bombs falling. They fell from the sky like deadly flowers of sound planting their seeds of destruction everywhere.

'Get up, Jaime. Hurry!'

The fear in his father's voice was more frightening to the boy than the terrible roar of the aerial bombardment.

Guernica was a stronghold of the Basques and General Franco had decided to make it an object lesson.

'Destroy it.'

The dreaded Nazi Condor Legion and half a dozen Italian planes had mounted a concentrated attack, and they showed no mercy. The townspeople tried to flee from the rain of death pouring down from the skies, but there was no escape.

Jaime, his mother and father and two older sisters fled with the others.

'To the church,' Jaime's father said. 'They won't bomb the church.'

He was right. Everyone knew that the church was on the side of the Caudillo, turning a blind eye to the savage treatment of his enemies.

The Miró family headed for the church, fighting their way through the panicky crowds trying to flee.

The young boy held his father's hand in a fierce grip and tried not to hear the terrible noises around him. He remembered a time when his father was not frightened, was not running away.

'Are we going to have a war, Papa?'

'No, Jaime. That's just newspaper talk. All we're asking is that the government give us a reasonable amount of independence. The Basques and the Catalans are entitled to have their own language and flag and holidays. We're still one nation. And Spaniards will never fight against Spaniards.'

Jaime was too young then to understand it, but of course it was more than the issue of the Catalans and Basques that was at stake. It was a deep ideological conflict between the Republican government and the right-wing Nationalists, and what started out as a spark of dissension quickly became an uncontrollable conflagration that drew in a dozen foreign powers.

When Franco's superior forces had defeated the Republicans and the Nationalists were firmly in control of Spain, Franco turned his attention to the intransigent Basques.

'Punish them.'

And the blood continued to flow.

A hard core of Basque leaders had formed ETA, a movement for a Basque Free State, and Jaime's father was asked to join.

420

'No. It is wrong. We must gain what is rightfully ours by peaceful means. War accomplishes nothing.'

But the hawks proved stronger than the doves, and ETA quickly became a prime target.

Jaime had friends whose fathers were members of ETA, and he listened to the stories of their heroic exploits.

'My father and a group of his friends bombed the headquarters of the *guardia civil*,' they would say.

Or, 'Did you hear about the bank robbery in Barcelona? My father did that. Now they can buy weapons to fight the fascists.'

And Jaime's father was saying, 'Violence is wrong. We must negotiate.'

'We blew up one of their factories in Madrid. Why isn't your father on our side? Is he a coward?'

'Don't listen to your friends, Jaime,' his father told him. 'What they are doing is criminal.'

'Franco ordered a dozen Basques executed without even a trial. We're staging a nationwide strike. Is your father going to join us?'

'Papa – ?'

'We are all Spaniards, Jaime. We must not let anyone divide us.'

And the boy was torn. *Are my friends right? Is my father a coward?* Jaime believed his father.

And now – armageddon. The world was collapsing around him. The streets of Guernica were crowded with a screaming mob trying to escape from the falling bombs. All around them buildings and statues and pavements were exploding in showers of concrete and blood.

Jaime and his mother and father and sisters had reached the large church, the only building in the square still standing. A dozen people were pounding at the door.

'Let us in! In the name of Jesus, open up!'

'What's going on?' cried Jaime's father.

'The priests have locked the church. They won't let us in.'

'Let's break the door in!'

'No!'

Jaime looked at his father in surprise.

'We don't break into God's house,' his father said. 'He will protect us wherever we are.'

Too late, they saw the squad of Falangists that appeared from around the corner and opened machine-gun fire on them, mowing down the unarmed crowd of men, women and children in the square. Even as Jaime's father felt the bullets tearing into him, he grabbed his son and pushed him down to safety, his own body shielding Jaime from the deadly hail of bullets.

An eerie silence seemed to blanket the world. The sounds of guns and running feet and screams vanished, a trick of magic. Jaime opened his eyes and lay there for a long time, feeling the weight of his father's body on him, like a loving blanket. His father and mother and sisters were dead, along with hundreds of others. And in front of their bodies were the locked doors of the church.

Late that night, Jaime made his way out of the city and two days later when he reached Bilbao, he joined ETA.

The recruiting officer had looked at him and said, 'You're too young to join, son. You should be in school.'

'You're going to be my school,' Jaime Miró said quietly. 'You're going to teach me how to fight to avenge the murder of my family.'

He never looked back. He was battling for himself and for his family, and his exploits became legendary. Jaime planned and executed daring raids against factories and banks and carried out the executions of the oppressors. When any of Jaime's men were captured, he conducted daredevil missions to rescue them.

When Jaime heard about the GOE being formed to pursue Basques, he smiled and said, 'Good. They've noticed.'

Jaime never asked himself if the risks he took had anything to do with the cries of, 'Your father is a coward,' or if he was trying to prove anything to himself and to others. It was enough that he proved his bravery again and again, that he was not afraid to risk his life for what he believed in.

Now, because one of his men had talked too freely, Jaime found himself saddled with a nun.

It's ironic that her Church is on our side now. But it's much too late, unless they can arrange a Second Coming and include my mother and father and sisters, he thought bitterly.

They walked through the woods at night, the white moonlight dappling the forest around them. They avoided the towns and main roads, alert for any sign of danger. Jaime ignored Megan. He walked with Felix, talking about past adventures, and Megan found herself intrigued. She had never known anyone like Jaime Miró. He was filled with such self-assurance.

If anyone can get me to Mendavia, Megan thought, *this man can.*

There had been moments when Jaime had felt pity for the sister, and even a reluctant admiration for the way she coped on the arduous journey. He wondered how his other men were getting along with their charges from God.

At least he had Amparo Jiron. At night Jaime found her a great comfort.

She's as dedicated as I am, Jaime thought. *She has even more reason than I do to hate the government.*

Amparo's entire family had been wiped out by the Nationalist army. She was fiercely independent, and filled with a deep passion.

At dawn they were nearing Salamanca, on the banks of the Rio Tormes.

'Students come here from all over Spain,' Felix explained to Megan, 'to attend the university here. It's probably the best in all of Spain.'

Jaime was not listening. He was concentrating on his next move. *If I were the hunter, where would I set my trap?*

He turned to Felix. 'We'll skip Salamanca. There's a *parador* just outside town. We will stop there.'

The *parador* was a small inn away from the mainstream of tourist traffic. Stone steps led to the lobby, which was guarded by an ancient knight in armour.

As the group approached the entrance, Jaime said to the two women, 'Wait here.'

He nodded to Felix Carpio and the two men disappeared.

'Where are they going?' Megan asked.

Amparo Jiron gave her a contemptuous look. 'Maybe they went looking for your God.'

'I hope they find him,' Megan said evenly.

Ten minutes later the men were back.

'All clear,' Jaime told Amparo. 'You and the sister will share a room. Felix will stay with me.' He handed her a key.

Amparo said petulantly, '*Querido*, I want to stay with you, not –'

'Do as I say. Keep an eye on her.'

Amparo turned to Megan. '*Bueno*. Come along, Sister.'

Megan followed Amparo up the stairs.

The room was one of a dozen set in a row along the grey, bare corridor. Amparo unlocked the door and the two women entered. The room was small and drab and sparsely furnished, with wooden floors, stucco walls, a bed, a small cot, a battered dressing-table and two chairs.

Megan looked around the room and exclaimed, 'It's lovely.'

Amparo Jiron swung around in anger, thinking that Megan was being sarcastic. 'Who the hell are you to complain about –?'

'It's so large,' Megan went on.

Amparo looked at her for a moment, then laughed. Of course it would seem large compared to the cells that the sisters lived in.

Amparo started to get undressed.

Megan could not help staring at her. It was the first time she had really

423

looked at Amparo Jiron in the daylight. The woman was beautiful, in an earthy way. She had red hair, white skin, and was full-breasted, with a small waist and hips that swayed as she moved.

Amparo saw her watching. 'Sister – would you tell me something? Why would anyone join a convent?'

It was a simple question to answer. 'What could be more wonderful than to devote oneself to the glory of God?'

'Offhand, I could think of a thousand things.' Amparo walked over to the bed and sat down. 'You can sleep on the cot. From what I've heard about convents, your God doesn't want you to be too comfortable.'

Megan smiled. 'It doesn't matter. I'm comfortable inside.'

In their room across the corridor, Jaime Miró was stretching out on the bed. Felix Carpio was trying to get settled on the small cot. Both men were fully dressed. Jaime's gun was under his pillow. Felix's gun was on the small, battered table next to him.

'What do you think makes them do it?' Felix wondered aloud.

'Do what, *amigo*?'

'Lock themselves up in a convent all their lives like prisoners.'

Jaime Miró shrugged. 'Ask the sister. I wish to hell we were travelling alone. I have a bad feeling about this.'

'Jaime, God will thank us for this good deed.'

'Do you really believe that? Don't make me laugh.'

Felix did not pursue the subject. It was not tactful to discuss the Catholic Church with Jaime. The two men were silent, each preoccupied with his own thoughts.

Felix Carpio was thinking: *God put the sisters in our hands. We must get them to a convent safely.*

Jaime was thinking about Amparo. He wanted her badly now. *That damned nun.* He started to pull up the covers when he realized there was something he still had to do.

In the small, dark lobby downstairs, the manager sat quietly, waiting until he was sure that the new guests were asleep. His heart was pounding as he picked up the telephone and dialled a number.

A lazy voice answered, 'Police Headquarters.'

The manager whispered into the telephone to his nephew, 'Florian, I have Jaime Miró and three of his people here. How would you like the honour of capturing them?'

22

Many miles to the east, in a wooded area along the way to Peñafiel, Lucia Carmine was asleep.

Rubio Arzano sat watching her, reluctant to awaken her. *She sleeps like an angel*, he thought.

But it was almost dawn, time to be moving on.

Rubio leaned over and whispered gently in her ear, 'Sister Lucia . . .'

Lucia opened her eyes.

'It is time for us to go.'

She yawned and stretched lazily. The blouse she was wearing had become unbuttoned and part of her breast was showing. Rubio hastily looked away.

I must guard my thoughts. She is the bride of Jesus.

'Sister . . .'

'Yes?'

'I – I wonder if I could ask a favour of you.' He was almost blushing.

'Yes?'

'I – it's been a long time since I prayed. But I was brought up a Catholic. Would you mind saying a prayer?'

That was the last thing Lucia had expected.

How long has it been since I said a prayer? she wondered.

The convent did not count. While the others were praying, her mind had been busy with plans to escape.

'I – I don't –'

'I'm sure it would make us both feel better.'

How could she explain that she did not remember any prayers? 'I – er –' *Yes.* There was one she remembered. She had been a little girl kneeling at her bedside and her father had stood beside her, ready to tuck her into bed. Slowly, the words of the twenty-third Psalm started coming.

'The Lord is my shepherd. I shall not want. He maketh me to lie down in green pastures. He leadeth me beside the still waters. He restoreth my soul. He leadeth me in the paths of righteousness, for His name's sake . . .'

Memories came flooding back.

She and her father had owned the world. And he had been so proud of her.

You were born under a lucky star, faccia del angelo.

And hearing that, Lucia had felt lucky and beautiful. Nothing could

425

ever hurt her. Was she not the beautiful daughter of the great Angelo Carmine?

'. . . Yea, though I walk through the valley of the shadow of death, I will fear no evil . . .'

The evil ones were the enemies of her father and brothers. And she had made them pay.

'. . . For Thou art with me; Thy rod and Thy staff they comfort me . . .'

Where was God when I needed comforting?

'Thou preparest a table before me in the presence of mine enemies; Thou anointest my head with oil, my cup runneth over. . .'

She was speaking more slowly now, her voice a whisper. What had happened, she wondered, to the little girl in the white communion dress? The future had been so golden. Somehow it had all gone wrong. Everything. *I've lost my father and my brothers and myself.*

In the convent she had not thought about God. But now, out here with this simple peasant . . .

Would you mind saying a prayer for us?

Lucia went on. 'Surely goodness and mercy shall follow me all the days of my life; And I will dwell in the house of the Lord for ever.'

Rubio was watching her, moved.

'Thank you, Sister.'

Lucia nodded, unable to speak. *What's the matter with me?* Lucia asked herself.

'Are you ready, Sister?'

She looked at Rubio Arzano and said, 'Yes. I'm ready.'

Five minutes later they were on their way.

They were caught in a sudden downpour and took shelter in a deserted cabin. The rain beat against the roof and sides of the cabin like angry fists.

'Do you think the storm will ever let up?'

Rubio smiled. 'It's not a real storm, Sister. It's what we Basques call a *sirimiri*. It will stop as quickly as it started. The earth is dry right now. It needs this rain.'

'Really?'

'Yes. I'm a farmer.'

It shows, Lucia thought.

'Forgive me for saying this, Sister, but you and I have a lot in common.'

Lucia looked over at the country bumpkin and thought: *That will be the day.* 'We do?'

'Yes. I truly believe that in many ways being on a farm must be much like being in a convent.'

The connection eluded her. 'I don't understand.'

'Well, Sister, in a convent you think a lot about God and His miracles. Is that not true?'

'Yes.'

'In a sense a farm is God. One is surrounded by creation – all the things that grow from God's earth, whether it's wheat or olives or grapes – everything comes from God, does it not? These are all miracles, and you watch them happen every day, and because you help them grow, you are part of the miracle.'

Lucia had to smile at the enthusiasm in his voice.

Suddenly the rain stopped.

'We can move on now, Sister.'

'We will be coming to Rio Duero soon,' Rubio said. 'The Peñafiel Falls is just ahead of us. We will go on to Aranda de Duero and then Logroño, where we will meet the others.'

You'll be going to those places, Lucia thought. *And good luck to you. I'll be in Switzerland, my friend.*

They heard the sound of the Falls half an hour before they reached them. The Peñafiel Falls was a beautiful sight cascading down into the swift-moving river. The roar of it was almost deafening.

'I want to bathe,' Lucia said. It seemed years since she had last had a bath.

Rubio Arzano stared at her. 'Here?'

No, you idiot, in Rome. 'Yes.'

'Be careful. The river is swollen because of the rain.'

'Don't worry.' She stood there, patiently waiting.

'Oh. I will go away while you undress.'

'Stay nearby,' Lucia said quickly. There were probably wild animals in the woods.

As Lucia started to undress, Rubio hastily walked a few yards away and turned his back.

'Don't go in too far, Sister,' he called. 'The river is treacherous.'

Lucia put down the wrapped cross where she could keep an eye on it. The cool morning air felt wonderful on her naked body. When she had stripped completely, she stepped into the water. It was cold and invigorating. She turned and saw that Rubio was steadfastly looking in the other direction, his back turned to her. She smiled to herself. All the other men she had known would be feasting their eyes.

She stepped in deeper, avoiding the rocks that were all around, and splashed the water over herself, feeling the rushing river tugging hard at her legs.

A few feet away a small tree was being swept downstream. As Lucia

427

turned to watch it, she suddenly lost her balance and slipped, screaming. She fell hard, slamming her head against a boulder.

Rubio turned and watched in horror as Lucia disappeared downstream in the raging waters.

23

At the police station in Salamanca, when Sergeant Florian Santiago replaced the receiver, his hands were trembling.

I have Jaime Miró and three of his people here. How would you like the honour of capturing them?

The government had offered a large reward for the head of Jaime Miró, and now the Basque outlaw was in his hands. The reward money would change his whole life. He could afford to send his children to a better school, he could buy a washing machine for his wife and jewellery for his mistress. Of course he would have to share some of the reward money with his uncle. *I'll give him twenty per cent*, Santiago thought. *Or maybe ten per cent.*

He was well aware of Jaime Miró's reputation, and he had no intention of risking his life trying to capture the terrorist. *Let others face the danger and give me the reward.*

He sat at his desk deciding the best way to handle the situation. Colonel Acoca's name immediately sprang to his mind. Everybody knew there was a blood vendetta between the Colonel and the outlaw. Besides, the Colonel had the whole GOE at his command. Yes, that was definitely the way to proceed.

He picked up a telephone, and ten minutes later he was speaking to the Colonel himself.

'This is Sergeant Florian Santiago calling from the police station at Salamanca. I have tracked down Jaime Miró.'

Colonel Ramón Acoca fought to keep his voice even. 'Are you certain of this?'

'Yes, Colonel. He is at the Parador Nacional Raimundo de Borgón, just outside of town. He is spending the night. My uncle is the manager. He telephoned me himself. There is another man and two women with Miró.'

'Your uncle is positive it is Miró?'

'Yes, Colonel. He and the others are sleeping in the two back rooms on the second floor of the inn.'

Colonel Acoca said, 'Listen to me very carefully, Sergeant. I want you to go to the *parador* immediately and stand watch outside to make certain none of them leaves. I should be able to reach there in an hour. You are not to go inside. And stay out of sight. Is that clear?'

'Yes, sir. I will leave immediately.' He hesitated. 'Colonel, about the reward money –'

'When we catch Miró, it's yours.'

429

'Thank you, Colonel. I am most –'

'Go.'

'Yes, sir.'

Florian Santiago replaced the receiver. He was tempted to call his mistress to tell her the exciting news, but that could wait. He would surprise her later. Meanwhile, he had a job to do.

He summoned one of the policemen on duty upstairs.

'Take over the desk. I have an errand to do. I'll be back in a few hours.' *And I'll come back a rich man*, he thought. *The first thing I'll buy will be a new car – a Seat. A blue one. No, maybe it will be white.*

Colonel Ramón Acoca replaced the receiver and sat still, letting his brain go to work. This time there would be no slip-up. It was the final move in the chess game between them. He would have to proceed very carefully. Miró would have sentries alert for trouble.

Acoca called in his aide-de-camp.

'Yes, Colonel?'

'Pick out two dozen of your best marksmen. See that they're armed with automatic weapons. We're leaving for Salamanca in fifteen minutes.'

'Yes, sir.'

There would be no escape for Miró. The Colonel was already planning the raid in his mind. The *parador* would be completely surrounded by a cordon that would move in quickly and quietly. *A sneak attack before the butcher has a chance to murder any more of my men. We'll kill them all in their sleep.*

Fifteen minutes later, his aide returned.

'We're ready to move, Colonel.'

Sergeant Santiago lost no time in getting to the *parador*. Even without the Colonel's warning, he would have had no intention of going after the terrorists. But now, in obedience to Acoca's orders, he stood in the shadows, twenty yards away from the inn, where he had a good view of the front door. There was a chill in the night air, but the thought of the reward money kept Santiago warm. He wondered whether the two women inside were pretty and whether they were in bed with the men. Of one thing Santiago was certain: in a few hours, they would all be dead.

The army truck moved into town quietly and drove towards the *parador*. Colonel Acoca flicked on a flashlight and looked at his map, and

430

when they were a mile from the inn, he said, 'Stop here. We'll walk the rest of the way. Maintain silence.'

Florian Santiago was unaware of their approach until a voice in his ear startled him with, 'Who are you?'

He turned and found himself facing Colonel Ramón Acoca. *My God, he's frightening-looking*, Santiago thought.

'I am Sergeant Santiago, sir.'

'Has anyone left the inn?'

'No, sir. They're all inside, probably asleep by now.'

The Colonel turned to his aide. 'I want half our men to form a perimeter around the hotel. If anyone tries to escape, they are to shoot to kill. The others will come with me. The fugitives are in the two back bedrooms upstairs. Let's go.'

Santiago watched as the Colonel and his men entered the front door of the *parador*, moving quietly. Santiago wondered if there would be a lot of shooting. And if there was, he wondered if his uncle might be killed in the cross-fire. That would be a pity. But on the other hand, there would be no one he would have to share the reward money with.

When Colonel Acoca and his men reached the top of the stairs, he whispered, 'Take no chances. Open fire as soon as you see them.'

His aide asked, 'Colonel, would you like me to go ahead of you?'

'No.' He intended to have the pleasure of killing Jaime Miró himself.

At the end of the corridor were the two rooms where Miró and his group were staying. Colonel Acoca silently motioned six of his men to cover one door and the other six to cover the other door.

'Now!' he screamed.

It was the moment he had been burning for. At his signal, the soldiers kicked in both doors simultaneously and rushed into the rooms, weapons ready. They stood there in the middle of the empty rooms staring at the rumpled beds.

'Spread out. Hurry! Downstairs!' Acoca shrieked.

The soldiers raced through every room in the hotel, smashing doors open, waking up startled guests. Jaime Miró and the others were nowhere to be found. The Colonel stormed downstairs to confront the hotel manager. There was no one in the lobby.

'Hello,' he called out. 'Hello.' There was no response. The coward was hiding.

One of the soldiers was staring at the floor behind the desk. 'Colonel . . .'

Acoca strode over to his side and stared down at the floor. The bound and gagged body of the manager was slumped against the wall. A sign had been hung around his neck. It read:

PLEASE DO NOT DISTURB.

24

Rubio Arzano watched in horror as Lucia disappeared under the rushing waters and was swept downstream. In a split second, he turned to race along the river bank, leaping over small logs and bushes. At the first bend of the river, he caught a glimpse of Lucia's body coming towards him. Diving in, he swam frantically to reach her, struggling against the powerful current. It was almost impossible. He felt himself being pulled away. Lucia was ten feet from him, but it seemed like miles. He made one last heroic effort and grabbed her arm, his fingers almost slipping away. He held her in a death grip, as he began grappling his way to the safety of the shore.

When Rubio finally reached the river bank, he pulled Lucia up on to the grass and he lay there, fighting for breath. Lucia was unconscious and not breathing. Rubio turned her over on her stomach, straddled her and began applying pressure against her lungs. A minute went by, then two, and just as he was beginning to despair, a stream of water gushed out of her mouth and she groaned. Rubio uttered a prayer of thanks.

He kept up the pressure, gentler now, until her heartbeat was steady. She began to shiver from the cold. Rubio hurried over to a clump of trees and pulled down handfuls of leaves. He carried them over to her and started to dry her body with them. He was wet and cold, and his clothes were soaked, but he paid no attention. He had been panicky with fear that Sister Lucia would die. Now, as he gently rubbed her naked body with the dry leaves, unworthy thoughts came into his mind.

She has the body of a goddess. Forgive me, Lord, she belongs to You, and I must not think these wicked thoughts . . .

Lucia was gradually awakened by the gentle stroking of her body. She was on the beach with Ivo, and his soft tongue was moving down her body. *Oh, yes,* she thought. *Oh, yes. Don't stop, caro.* She was aroused before she even opened her eyes.

When Lucia had fallen into the river, her last thought had been that she was going to die. But she was alive, and she found herself looking up at the man who had saved her. Without even thinking, Lucia reached up and pulled Rubio down to her. There was a look of shocked surprise on his face.

'Sister –' he protested. 'We can't –'

'Sh!'

Her lips were on his, fierce and hungry and demanding, and her tongue was exploring his mouth. It was too much for Rubio.

'Hurry,' Lucia whispered. 'Hurry.'

She watched as Rubio nervously stripped off his wet clothes. *He deserves a reward*, she thought. *So do I.*

As Rubio moved hesitantly towards her, he said, 'Sister, we shouldn't –'

Lucia was in no mood for conversation. She felt him joining his body to hers in a timeless, mindless ritual, and she gave herself up to the glorious sensations that flooded her. It was all the sweeter because of her close brush with death.

Rubio was a surprisingly good lover, both gentle and fierce at the same time. He had a vulnerability that took Lucia completely by surprise. And there was a look of such tenderness in his eyes that Lucia felt a sudden lump in her throat.

I hope the big oaf isn't falling in love with me. He's so eager to please me. When was the last time a man cared about pleasing me? Lucia wondered. And she thought of her father. And she wondered how he would have liked Rubio Arzano. And then she wondered why she wondered whether her father would have liked Rubio Arzano. *I must be crazy. This man is a farmer. I'm Lucia Carmine, the daughter of Angelo Carmine. Rubio's life has nothing to do with my life. We were thrown together by a stupid accident of fate.*

Rubio was holding her and saying over and over, 'Lucia. My Lucia.'

And the shining in his eyes told her everything he felt. *He's so dear,* she thought. And then: *What is the matter with me? Why am I even thinking about him like this? I'm running away from the police and –*
She suddenly remembered the gold cross and gasped. *Oh, my God! How could I have forgotten it even for a moment?*

She sat up quickly. 'Rubio, I left a – a package on the bank of the river back there. Would you bring it to me, please? And my clothes?'

'Of course. I'll be right back.'

Lucia sat there waiting, frantic that something might have happened to the cross. What if it was gone? What if someone had come along and picked it up?

It was with an enormous feeling of relief that Lucia saw Rubio returning with the wrapped cross under his arm. *I mustn't let it out of my sight again,* she thought. 'Thank you.'

Rubio handed Lucia her clothes. She looked up at him and said softly, 'I won't need these right away.'

The sun on her naked skin made her feel lazy and warm, and there was a wonderful comfort in Rubio's arms. It was as though they had found a peaceful oasis and the dangers they had been running away from seemed light years away.

'Tell me about your farm,' Lucia said idly.

His face lit up, and there was pride in his voice. 'It was a small farm outside a little village near Bilbao. It was in my family for generations.'

'What happened to it?'

His expression darkened. 'Because I am Basque, the government in Madrid punished me with extra taxes. When I refused to pay, they confiscated the farm. That was when I met Jaime Miró. I joined him to fight against the government for what is right. I have a mother and two sisters, and one day we will have our farm back, and I will run it again.'

Lucia thought of her father and two brothers locked away in a prison for ever. 'Are you close to your family?'

Rubio smiled warmly. 'Of course. Families are our first love, are they not?'

Yes, Lucia thought. *But I will never see mine again.*

'Tell me about your family, Lucia,' Rubio said. 'Before you joined the convent, were you close to them?'

The conversation was taking a dangerous turn. *What can I tell him? My father is a mafioso. He and my two brothers are in prison for murder.* 'Yes – we are very close.'

'What does your father do?'

'He – he's a businessman.'

'Have you got brothers and sisters?'

'I have two brothers. They work for him.'

'Lucia, why did you enter the convent?'

Because the police are looking for me for murdering two men. I've got to stop this conversation, Lucia thought. Aloud, she said, 'I needed to get away.' *That's close enough to the truth.*

'You felt the world was – was too much for you?'

'Something like that.'

'I have no right to say this, Lucia, but I am in love with you.'

'Rubio –'

'I want to marry you. In all my life, I have never said that to another woman.'

There was something so touching and earnest about him. *He doesn't know how to play games*, she thought. *I must be careful not to hurt him. But the idea of Angelo Carmine's daughter being a farmer's wife!* Lucia almost laughed aloud.

Rubio misunderstood the smile on Lucia's face. 'I will not live in hiding for ever. The government will have to make peace with us. Then I will return to my farm. *Querida* – I want to spend the rest of my life making you happy. We will have many children and the girls will all look like you . . .'

I can't let him go on like this, Lucia decided. *I should stop him now.* But somehow she could not bring herself to do it. She listened to Rubio paint romantic pictures of their life together, and she found herself almost wishing it could happen. She was so tired of running away. It would be wonderful to find a haven where she could be safe, taken care of by someone who loved her . . . *I must be losing my mind.*

'Let's not talk about it now,' Lucia said. 'We should be moving on.'

They travelled northeast, following the winding banks of the Duero River, with its hilly countryside and lush green trees. They stopped at the picturesque village of Villalba de Duero at the foot of the mountains, and stopped to buy bread and cheese and wine and had an idyllic picnic in a grassy meadow.

Lucia felt content at Rubio's side. There was a quiet strength about him that seemed to give her strength. *He's not for me, but he's going to make some lucky woman very happy*, she thought.

When they had finished eating, Rubio said, 'The next town is Aranda de Duero. It's a fairly large town. It would be best if we skirted around it to avoid the GOE and the soldiers.'

It was the moment of truth, time to leave him. She had been waiting for them to reach a large town. Rubio Arzano and his farm were a dream, escaping to Switzerland was the reality. Lucia knew how much she was going to hurt him, and she could not bear to look into his eyes when she said, 'Rubio – I'd like us to go into town.'

He frowned. 'That could be dangerous, *querida*. The soldiers –'

'They won't be looking for us there.' She thought quickly. 'Besides, I – I need a change of clothes. I can't keep going on in this.'

The idea of entering the town disturbed Rubio, but all he said was, 'If that is what you wish.'

In the distance the walls and buildings of Aranda de Duero loomed before them, like a man-made mountain hewn out of the earth.

Rubio tried one more time. 'Lucia – you're sure you must go into the town?'

'Yes. I'm sure.'

The two of them crossed the long bridge that led to the main street, Avenida Castilla, and headed for the centre of town. They passed a sugar factory and churches and poultry shops, and the air was thick with their smells. Shops and blocks of flats lined the avenue. They walked slowly, careful not to draw attention to themselves. Finally, to her relief, Lucia saw what she had been looking for – a sign that read: '*Casa de Empeños*' – a pawnshop. She said nothing.

They reached the village square, with its shops and markets and bars, and they passed the *Taverna Cueva*, with its long bar and wooden tables. There was a juke box inside, and hanging from the oak beam ceiling were hams and strings of garlic.

Lucia saw her opportunity. 'I'm thirsty, Rubio,' she said. 'Can we go in there?'

'Of course.'

Rubio took Lucia's arm and led her inside.

There were half a dozen men crowded around the bar. Lucia and Rubio took a table in the corner.

'What would you like, *querida*?'

'Order a glass of wine for me, please. I'll be right back. There's something I have to do.'

She rose and walked out into the street, leaving Rubio staring after her, puzzled.

Outside, Lucia turned and hurried back to the *Casa de Empeños*, clutching her tightly wrapped package. Across the street she saw a door with a black sign in white lettering that read, '*Policía*'. She stared at it a moment, her heart skipping a beat, then skirted it and entered the pawnshop.

A shrunken man with a large head stood behind the counter, barely visible.

'*Buenos días, señorita.*'

'*Buenos días, señor.* I have something I would like to sell.' She was so nervous that she had to press her knees together to keep them from shaking.

'*Sí?*'

Lucia unwrapped the gold cross and held it out. 'Would – would you be interested in buying this?'

The pawnbroker took it in his hands, and Lucia watched the light that came into his eyes.

'May I ask where you acquired this?'

'It was left to me by an uncle who has just died.' Her throat was so dry she could hardly speak.

The man fingered the cross, turning it over in his hands slowly. 'How much are you asking for it?'

Her dream was coming to life. 'I want two hundred and fifty thousand pesetas.'

He frowned and shook his head. 'No. It is worth only a hundred thousand pesetas.'

'I would sell my body first.'

'Perhaps I could go as high as one hundred and fifty thousand pesetas.'

'I would rather melt it down and let the gold run in the streets.'

'Two hundred thousand pesetas. That is my last offer.'

Lucia took the gold cross from him. 'You are robbing me blind, but I will accept it.'

She could see the excitement in his face. '*Bueno, señorita.*' He reached for the cross.

Lucia pulled it back. 'There is a condition.'

'What condition would that be, *señorita*?'

'My passport was stolen. I need a new one in order to get out of the country to visit my stricken aunt.'

He was studying her now, his eyes wise. He nodded. 'I see.'

'If you can help me with my problem, then the cross is yours.'

He sighed. 'Passports are difficult to come by, *señorita*. The authorities are very strict.'

Lucia watched him, saying nothing.

'I don't see how I can help you.'

'Thank you, anyway, *señor*.' She started towards the door.

He let her reach it before he said, '*Momentito*.'

Lucia stopped.

'Something has just occurred to me. I have a cousin who is sometimes involved in delicate matters like this. He is a *distant* cousin, you understand.'

'I understand.'

'I could speak to him. When do you require this passport?'

'Today.'

The large head nodded slowly. 'And if I can do this thing, we have a deal?'

'When I get my passport.'

'Agreed. Come back after eight o'clock and my cousin will be here. He will arrange to take the necessary photograph and insert it in the passport.'

Lucia could feel her heart pounding. 'Thank you, *señor*.'

'Would you like to leave the cross here for safekeeping?'

'It will be safe with me.'

'Eight o'clock, then. *Hasta luego*.'

She left the shop. Outside she carefully avoided the police station and headed back to the *taverna*, where Rubio was waiting. Her footsteps slowed. She had finally succeeded. With the money from the cross, she would be able to get to Switzerland and freedom. She should have been happy. Instead she felt strangely depressed.

What's wrong with me? I'm on my way. Rubio will get over me soon enough. He'll find someone else.

She remembered the look in his eyes when he said, *I want to marry you. In all my life, I have never said that to another woman.*

Damn the man, she thought. *Well, he's not my problem.*

Outside the *taverna* she paused and took a deep breath. She forced a smile and walked inside to join him.

25

The news media were in a feeding frenzy. The headlines tumbled over one another. There was the attack on the convent; the wholesale arrest of the nuns for sheltering terrorists; the escape of four nuns; the murder of half a dozen soldiers by one of the nuns before she was shot and killed. The international news wires were on fire.

Reporters had arrived in Madrid from all parts of the world and Prime Minister Martinez, in an effort to cool things down, had agreed to a press conference. They were gathered in his office, almost four dozen reporters, from all over the world. Colonel Ramón Acoca and Colonel Fal Sostelo were at the Prime Minister's side. The Prime Minister had seen that afternoon's headline in the London *Times*: TERRORISTS AND NUNS EVADE SPAIN'S ARMY AND POLICE.

A reporter from *Paris Match* was asking, 'Mr Prime Minister, do you have any idea where the missing nuns are now?'

Prime Minister Leopoldo Martinez replied, 'Colonel Acoca is in charge of the search operation. I will let him answer that.'

Colonel Acoca said, 'We have reason to believe that they are in the hands of the Basque terrorists. I'm also sorry to say there is evidence to indicate that the nuns are collaborating with the terrorists.'

The reporters were scribbling feverishly.

'What about the shooting of Sister Teresa and the soldiers?'

'We have information that Sister Teresa was working with Jaime Miró. Under the pretext of helping us find Miró, she went into an army camp and murdered half a dozen soldiers before she could be stopped. I can assure you that the army and the GOE are bending every effort to bring the criminals to justice.'

'And the nuns who were arrested and taken to Madrid?'

'They are being interrogated,' Colonel Acoca said.

The Prime Minister was anxious to end the meeting. It was difficult for him to keep his temper in check. The failure to locate the nuns or capture the terrorists made his government – and himself – look inept and foolish, and the press was taking full advantage of the situation.

'Can you tell us anything about the backgrounds of the four nuns who escaped, Prime Minister?' asked a reporter from OGGI.

'I'm sorry. I can give you no further information. I repeat, ladies and gentlemen, the government is doing everything in its power to find the nuns.'

'Prime Minister, there have been reports about the brutality of the attack on the convent at Ávila. Would you respond to that?'

It was a sore point with Martinez because it was true. Colonel Acoca had grossly exceeded his authority. But he would deal with the Colonel later. This was the time for a show of unity.

He turned to the Colonel and said smoothly, 'Colonel Acoca can respond to that.'

Colonel Acoca said, 'I, too, have heard those unfounded reports. The facts are simple. We received reliable information that the terrorist Jaime Miró and a dozen of his men were hiding in the Abbey Cistercian and that they were heavily armed. By the time we raided the abbey, they had fled.'

'Colonel, we heard that some of your men molested –'

'That is an outrageous accusation.'

Prime Minister Martinez said, 'Thank you, ladies and gentlemen. That will be all. You will be informed of any further developments.'

The press conference was over. When the reporters left, the Prime Minister turned to Colonel Acoca and Colonel Sostelo. 'They're making us look like savages in the eyes of the world.'

Colonel Acoca had not the slightest interest in the Prime Minister's opinion. What concerned him was a telephone call he had received in the middle of the night.

'Colonel Acoca?'

It was a voice he was all too familiar with. He was instantly wide awake.

'Yes, sir.'

'We're disappointed in you. We had hoped to see some results before this.'

'Sir, I'm closing in on them.' He found that he was perspiring heavily. 'I ask that you be a little more patient. I won't disappoint you.'

He held his breath, waiting for a response.

'You're running out of time.'

The line went dead.

Colonel Acoca replaced the receiver and sat there, frustrated. *Where is that bastard Miró?*

26

I'm going to kill her, Ricardo Mellado thought. *I could strangle her with my bare hands, throw her off the mountain, or simply shoot her. No, I think strangling her would give me the greatest pleasure.*

Sister Graciela was the most exasperating human being he had ever encountered. She was impossible. In the beginning when Jaime Miró had assigned him to escort her, Ricardo Mellado had been pleased. True, she was a nun, but she was also the most ravishing beauty he had ever laid eyes on. He was determined to get to know her, to find out why she had decided to lock up all that exquisite beauty behind convent walls for the rest of her life. Under the skirt and blouse she was wearing, he could discern the rich, nubile curves of a woman. *It's going to be a very interesting trip*, Ricardo decided.

But things had taken a totally unexpected turn. The problem was that Sister Graciela refused to speak to him. She had not said one word since their journey began, and what completely baffled Ricardo was that she did not appear to be angry or frightened or upset. Not at all. She simply retreated into some remote part of herself and appeared totally uninterested in him and in what was going on around her. They had travelled at a good pace, walking along hot, dusty side roads, past fields of wheat, rippling golden in the sunlight, and fields of barley, oats and grapevines. They skirted the little villages along the way and went by fields of sunflowers with their wide yellow faces following the sun.

When they crossed the Moros River, Ricardo asked, 'Would you like to rest awhile, Sister?'

Silence.

They were approaching Segovia before heading north-east to the snow-capped Guadarrama mountains. Ricardo kept trying to make polite conversation, but it was completely hopeless.

'We will be at Segovia soon, Sister.'

No reaction.

What could I have done to offend her? 'Are you hungry, Sister?'

Nothing.

It was as though he were not there. He had never felt so frustrated in his life. *Perhaps the woman is retarded*, he thought. *That must be the answer. God gave her an unearthly beauty and then cursed her with a feeble mind.* But he did not believe it.

When they reached the outskirts of Segovia, Ricardo noted that the town was crowded, which meant that the *guardia civil* would be even more alert than usual.

As they approached the Plaza del Conde de Cheste, Ricardo saw soldiers of the *guardia civil* strolling in their direction. He whispered, 'Hold my hand, Sister. We must look like two lovers out for a stroll.'

She ignored him.

Jesus, Ricardo thought. *Maybe she's deaf and dumb.*

He reached over and took her hand in his, and her sudden fierce resistance surprised him. She pulled away as if she had been stung.

The guards were getting closer.

Ricardo leaned towards Graciela. 'You mustn't be angry,' he said loudly. 'My sister feels the same way. After dinner last night when she put the children to bed she was saying that it would be much better if we men didn't sit around together smoking smelly cigars and telling stories while you women went off by yourselves. I'll bet –'

The guards had passed. Ricardo turned to look at Graciela. Her face was expressionless. Mentally, Ricardo began to curse Jaime, wishing he had given him one of the other nuns. This one was made of stone, with no chisel hard enough to penetrate that cold exterior.

In all modesty, Ricardo Mellado knew that he was attractive to women. Enough of them had told him so. He was light complexioned, tall and well-built, with a patrician nose, an intelligent face and perfect white teeth. He came from one of the most prominent Basque families. His father was a banker from the Basque country in the north and had seen to it that Ricardo was well educated. He had gone to the University of Salamanca, and his father had looked forward to his son joining him in the family business.

When Ricardo returned home, he dutifully went to work at the bank, but within a short period of time he became involved with the problems of his people. He began attending meetings and rallies and protests against the government and he soon became one of the leaders of ETA. His father learned about his son's activities and called him into his huge, panelled office and lectured him.

'I am a Basque, too, Ricardo, but I am also a businessman. We cannot foul our own nest by encouraging a revolution in the country where we make our living.'

'None of us is trying to overthrow the government, Father. All we're demanding is freedom. The government's oppression of the Basques and the Catalans is intolerable.'

The senior Mellado leaned back in his chair and studied his son. 'My good friend the Mayor had a quiet word with me yesterday. He suggested it would be to your benefit not to attend any more rallies. It would be better if you expended your energy on bank business.'

'Father –'

'Listen to me, Ricardo. When I was young, my blood ran hot, too.

441

But there are other ways to cool it off. You're engaged to a lovely girl. I hope you will have many children.' He waved his hand at their surroundings. 'And you have much to look forward to in your future.'

'But don't you see – ?'

'I see more clearly than you, my son. Your prospective father-in-law is also unhappy with your activities. I would not want anything to happen that would prevent the wedding. Do I make myself clear?'

'Yes, Father.'

The following Saturday Ricardo Mellado was arrested leading a Basque rally in an auditorium in Barcelona. He refused to let his father bail him out unless he would also bail out the other demonstrators who had been arrested. His father refused. Ricardo's career was ended and so was his engagement. That had been five years earlier. Five years of danger and narrow escapes. Five years filled with the excitement of fighting for a cause he passionately believed in. Now he was on the run, a fugitive from the police, escorting a retarded and mute nun across Spain.

'We'll go this way,' he said to Sister Graciela. He was careful not to touch her arm.

They turned off the main street on to St Valentin. On the corner was a shop that sold musical instruments.

Ricardo said, 'I have an idea. Wait here, Sister. I'll be right back.'

He entered the shop and walked up to a young clerk standing behind the counter.

'*Buenos días.* May I help you?'

'Yes. I would like to buy two guitars.'

The clerk smiled. 'Ah, you are in luck. We've just got in some Ramir-ezes. They are the best.'

'Perhaps something of not such a high quality. My friend and I are only amateurs.'

'As you wish, *señor.* What about these?' The clerk walked over to a section of the store where a dozen guitars were on display. 'I can let you have two Konos for five thousand pesetas apiece.'

'I think not.' Ricardo selected two inexpensive guitars. 'These will do nicely,' he said.

A few moments later Ricardo walked back out to the street, carrying the two guitars. He had half hoped Sister Graciela would be gone. She was standing there, patiently waiting.

Ricardo opened the strap on one of the guitars and held out the instrument to her. 'Here, Sister. Put this over your shoulder.'

She stared at him.

'It isn't necessary for you to play it,' Ricardo said patiently. 'It is only for effect.'

He shoved the guitar at her, and she reluctantly took it. They walked along the winding streets of Segovia under the enormous viaduct built by the Romans centuries ago.

Ricardo decided to try again. 'You see this viaduct, Sister? There is no cement between the stones. Legend has it that it was built by the devil two thousand years ago, stone piled on stone, with nothing but the devil's magic to hold it together.' He looked at her for some reaction.

Nothing.

To hell with her, Ricardo Mellado thought. *I give up.*

The members of the *guardia civil* were everywhere, and whenever they passed them, Ricardo would pretend to be in earnest conversation with Graciela, always careful to avoid body contact.

The numbers of police and soldiers seemed to be increasing, but Ricardo felt reasonably safe. They would be looking for a nun in robes and a group of Jaime Miró's men, but they would have no reason to suspect two young tourists alone, carrying guitars.

Ricardo was feeling hungry, and even though Sister Graciela had said nothing, he was sure that she must be hungry also. They passed a small *bodega*.

'We'll stop in here and have a bite to eat, Sister.'

She stood there, watching him.

He sighed. 'Right. Suit yourself.'

He walked inside the small café. A moment later Graciela followed him.

When they were seated, Ricardo asked, 'What would you like to order, Sister?'

There was no response. She was infuriating.

Ricardo said to the waitress, 'Two *gazpachos* and two helpings of *chorizos*.'

When the soup and sausages came, Graciela ate what was put in front of her. He noticed that she ate automatically, without enjoyment, as though fulfilling some duty. The men seated at other tables were staring at her, and Ricardo could not blame them. *It would take the young Goya to capture her beauty*, he thought.

In spite of Graciela's sullen behaviour, Ricardo felt a lump in his throat every time he looked at her, and he cursed himself for a romantic fool. She was an enigma, buried behind some kind of impenetrable wall. Ricardo Mellado had known dozens of beautiful women, but none of them had ever affected him this way. There was something almost mystical about her beauty. The irony was that he had absolutely no idea what lay behind the breath-taking façade. Was she intelligent or stupid? Interesting or dull? Cold-blooded or passionate? *I hope she's stupid, dull, and cold-blooded*, Ricardo thought, *or I won't be able to stand losing her. As though I could ever have her. She belongs to God*. He looked away, afraid that she might sense what he was thinking.

When it was time to leave, Ricardo paid the bill and they rose. During the journey he had noticed that Sister Graciela was limping slightly. *I'll have to get us some kind of transportation*, he thought. *We still have a long way to go.*

443

They started down the street, and at the far end of town, in the Manzanares el Real, they came upon a gypsy caravan. There were four colourfully decorated wagons in the caravan, pulled by horses. In the back of the wagons were women and children, all dressed in gypsy costumes.

Ricardo said, 'Wait here, Sister. I'm going to try to get us a lift.'

He approached the driver of the front wagon, a burly man in full gypsy regalia, including wearing earrings.

'*Buenos tardes*, señor. I would consider it a great kindness if you could give my fiancée and me a lift.'

The gypsy looked over to where Graciela was standing. 'It is possible. Where are you headed?'

'To the Guadarrama mountains.'

'I can take you as far as Cerezo.'

'That would be of great value. Thank you.'

He shook the gypsy's hand and put money in it.

'Get in the last wagon.'

'*Gracias*.'

Ricardo returned to where Graciela was waiting. 'The gypsies are going to take us as far as Cerezo de Abajo,' he told her. 'We'll go in the last wagon.'

For an instant, he was sure she was going to refuse. She hesitated, then started towards the wagon.

There were half a dozen gypsies inside the wagon and they made room for Ricardo and Graciela. As they climbed aboard, Ricardo started to help the sister up, but the moment he touched her arm, she pushed him away with a fierceness that took him by surprise. *All right, to hell with you*. He caught a glimpse of Graciela's bare leg as she lifted herself on to the wagon, and he could not help thinking: *She has the most beautiful legs I've ever seen*.

They made themselves as comfortable as possible on the hard wooden floor of the wagon and the long journey began. Graciela sat in a corner, her eyes closed and her lips moving in prayer. Ricardo could not take his eyes off her.

As the day wore on, the sun became a hot furnace, beating down on them, baking the earth, and the sky was a deep, cloudless blue. From time to time as the wagon crossed the plains, huge birds soared overhead. *Buitre leonado*, Ricardo thought. The lion-coloured griffon vultures.

Late in the afternoon the gypsy caravan came to a stop. The leader approached their wagon.

'This is as far as we can take you. We're headed for Vinuelas.'

Wrong direction. 'This is fine,' Ricardo assured him. 'Thank you.'

He started to reach out a hand for Graciela and quickly thought better of it.

Ricardo turned to the leader of the gypsies. 'I would consider it a kindness if you would sell some food to my fiancée and me.'

The chief turned to one of the women and said something in a foreign tongue, and a few moments later two packages of food were handed to Ricardo.

'*Muchas gracias*.' He pulled out some money.

The gypsy chief studied him for a moment. 'You and the sister have already paid for the food.'

You and the sister. So he knew. Yet Ricardo felt no sense of danger. The gypsies were as oppressed by the government as were the Basques and Catalans.

'*Vayan con Dios*.'

Ricardo stood there watching the caravan move out of sight. He turned to Graciela. She was watching him, silent, impassive.

'You won't have to put up with my company much longer,' Ricardo assured her. 'In two days we will be in Logroño. You'll meet your friends there and you'll be on your way to the convent at Mendavia.'

No reaction. He could have been talking to a stone wall. *I am talking to a stone wall.*

They had been dropped off in a peaceful valley rich with orchards of apple, pear and fig trees. A few feet away from them was the Tormes River, filled with fat trout. In the past, Ricardo had fished there often. It would have been an ideal place to stay and rest, but there was a long road to travel.

He turned to study the Guadarrama mountains, the range that lay ahead of them. Ricardo knew the area well. There were several trails that wound through the length of the mountains. *Cabras*, wild mountain goats, and wolves roamed the passes, and Ricardo would have chosen that if he had been travelling alone. But with Sister Graciela at his side, he decided on the safest.

'Well, we'd better get started,' Ricardo said. 'We have a long climb ahead of us.'

He had no intention of missing the rendezvous with the others in Logroño. Let the silent sister become someone else's headache.

Sister Graciela stood there waiting for Ricardo to lead the way. He turned and began to climb. As they started up the steep mountain path, Graciela slipped on some loose pebbles and Ricardo instinctively reached out to help her. She jerked away from his hand and righted herself. *Fine*, he thought angrily. *Break your neck.*

They kept moving upwards, heading towards the majestic peak high above. The trail started to get steeper and narrower and the chilled air became thinner. They were heading east, passing through a forest of pine trees. Ahead of them lay a village that was a haven for skiers and mountain climbers. There would be hot food and warmth and rest there,

445

Ricardo knew. It was tempting. *Too dangerous*, he decided. It would be a perfect place for Acoca to set a trap.

He turned to Sister Graciela. 'We'll skirt the village. Can you go on a little farther before we rest?'

She looked at him and, as her answer turned and began to walk.

The unnecessary rudeness offended him, and he thought: *Thank heavens at Logroño I will be rid of her. Why in the name of God do I have mixed feelings about that?*

They skirted the village, walking along the edge of the forest, and soon they were on the path again, climbing upwards. It was getting more difficult to breathe, and the path grew steeper. As they rounded a bend, they came upon an empty eagle's nest. They skirted another mountain village, quiet and peaceful in the afternoon sun, and rested outside it, stopping at a mountain stream where they drank the icy water.

By dusk they had reached a rugged area that was famous for its caves. After that the trail would start downwards.

From now on, Ricardo thought, *it will be easy. The worst is over.*

He heard a faint buzzing sound overhead. He looked up, searching for the source of it. An army plane appeared suddenly over the top of the mountain, flying towards them.

'Down!' Ricardo shouted. 'Down!'

Graciela kept walking. The plane circled and began to swoop lower.

'Get down!' Ricardo yelled again.

He jumped on her and pushed her down to the ground, his body on top of hers. What happened next took him completely by surprise. Without any warning, Graciela began yelling hysterically, fighting him. She was kicking him in the groin, clawing at his face, trying to rip at his eyes. But the most astonishing thing was what she was saying. She was screaming out a string of obscenities that sent Ricardo into shock, a verbal torrent of filth that assailed him. He could not believe that these words were coming from that beautiful, innocent mouth.

He tried to grab her hands to protect himself from her raking nails. She was like a wildcat under him.

'Stop it!' he shouted. 'I'm not going to hurt you. It's an army scout plane. They've seen us. We've got to get out of here.'

He held her down until her frantic struggling finally ceased. Strange, strangled sounds were coming from her, and he realized that she was sobbing. Ricardo, with all his experience with women, was completely baffled. He was straddled atop a hysterical nun who had the vocabulary of a truck driver, and he had no notion of what to do next.

He made his voice as calm and as reasonable as possible. 'Sister, we have to find a place to hide quickly. The plane will have reported us and in a few hours there'll be soldiers swarming all over the place. If you ever want to reach the convent, you'll get up and come with me.'

He waited a moment, then carefully raised himself off her and sat alongside her until the sobs subsided. Finally Graciela sat up. Her face was smudged from the dirt, her hair was tousled, her eyes were red from crying, and yet her beauty made Ricardo ache.

He said quietly, 'I'm sorry I frightened you. I don't seem to know how to behave with you. I promise to try to be more careful in the future.'

She looked up at him with her luminous black eyes filled with tears, and Ricardo had no idea what she was thinking. He sighed and rose. She followed suit.

'There are dozens of caves around here,' Ricardo told her. 'We'll hide in one of them for the night. By dawn we can be on our way again.'

His face was raw and bleeding where she had clawed at him, but in spite of what had happened, he felt a defencelessness about her, a fragility that touched him, that made him want to say something to reassure her. But now he was the one who was silent.

He could not think of a single thing to say.

The Cuevas del Aguila have been carved out by aeons of winds and floods and earthquakes, and they come in an infinite variety. Some of the caves are mere indentations in the mountain rocks, others are endless tunnels never explored by man.

A mile from where they had spotted the plane, Ricardo found a cave that was to his satisfaction. The low entrance was almost covered by underbrush.

'Stay here,' he said.

He ducked into the entrance and walked into the cave. It was dark inside, with only faint light spilling through the opening. There was no telling what the length of the cave was, but it did not matter, for there was no reason to explore it.

He went back outside to Graciela.

'It looks safe,' Ricardo said. 'Wait inside, please. I'll gather some branches to cover up the mouth of the cave. I'll be back in a few minutes.'

He watched Graciela as she went silently into the cave, and Ricardo wondered whether she would be there when he returned. He realized that he desperately wanted her to be.

Inside the cave, Graciela watched him leave. She sank to the cold ground in despair.

I can't stand any more, she thought. *Where are you, Jesus? Please release me from this hell.*

And it had been hell. From the beginning Graciela had been fighting the attraction she felt towards Ricardo. She thought of the Moor. *I'm afraid of myself. Of the evil in me. I want this man, and I must not.*

And so she had built a barrier of silence between them, the silence she had lived with in the convent. But now, without the discipline of the convent, without the Instrument and prayers, without the crutch of the rigid routine, Graciela found herself unable to banish her inner darkness. She had spent years fighting the satanic urges of her body, fighting the remembered sounds, the moans and sighs that came from her mother's bed.

The Moor was looking at her naked body.

You're just a child. Get your clothes on and get out of here . . .

I'm a woman.

She had spent so many years trying to forget the feel of the Moor inside her, trying to push out of her mind the rhythm of their bodies moving together, filling her, giving her a feeling of being alive at last.

Her mother screaming, *You bitch!*

And the doctor saying: *Our chief surgeon decided to sew you up himself. He said you were too beautiful to have scars.*

All the years of praying had been to purge herself of guilt. And they had failed.

The first time Graciela looked at Ricardo Mellado, the past had come flooding back. He was handsome and gentle and kind. When Graciela was a little girl, she had dreamed of someone like Ricardo. And when he was near her, when he touched her, her body was instantly aflame and she was filled with a deep shame. *I am the bride of Christ, and my thoughts are a betrayal of God. I belong to You, Jesus. Please help me now. Cleanse my mind of impure thoughts.*

Graciela had tried desperately to keep the wall of silence between them, a wall that no one but God could penetrate, a wall to keep out the devil. But did she want to keep the devil out? When Ricardo had jumped on her and pushed her to the ground, it was the Moor making love to her, and the friar trying to rape her, and in her surging panic, it was them she was fighting off. *No*, she admitted to herself, *that's not the truth*. It was her own deep desire she was fighting. She was torn between her spirit and the cravings of her flesh. *I must not give in. I must get back to the convent. He'll be back any minute. What should I do?*

Graciela heard a low mewing from the back of the cave and quickly turned. There were four green eyes staring at her in the dark, moving towards her. Graciela's heart began to beat faster.

Two baby wolf cubs trotted up to her on soft, padded feet, rubbing their heads against her. She smiled and began to stroke them gently. There was a sudden rustle from the entrance of the cave. *Ricardo is back*, she thought.

The next instant, an enormous grey wolf was flying at her throat.

27

Lucia Carmine paused outside the *taverna* in Aranda de Duero and took a deep breath. Through the window she could see Rubio Arzano seated inside, waiting for her.

I must not let him suspect, she thought. *At eight o'clock I'll have a new passport and be on my way to Switzerland.*

She forced a smile and entered the *taverna*. Rubio grinned in relief when he saw her, and as he rose, the look in his eyes gave Lucia a pang.

'I was very worried, *querida*. When you were gone for so long, I was afraid something terrible had happened to you.'

Lucia put her hand over his. 'Nothing happened.' *Except that I've bought my way to freedom. I'll be out of the country tomorrow.*

Rubio sat there looking into her eyes, holding her hand, and there was such an intense feeling of love coming from him that Lucia felt uneasy. *Doesn't he know it could never work? No. Because I haven't the courage to tell him. He's not in love with me. He's in love with the woman he thinks I am. He'll be much better off without me.*

She turned away and looked around the room for the first time. It was filled with locals. Most of them seemed to be staring at the two strangers.

One of the young men in the café started to sing and others joined in. A man walked over to the table where Lucia and Rubio were sitting.

'You're not singing, *señor*. Join us.'

Rubio shook his head. 'No.'

'What's the problem, *amigo*?'

'It's your song.' Rubio saw the puzzled expression on Lucia's face, and explained. 'It is one of the old songs praising Franco.'

Other men began to gather around the table. It was obvious that they had been drinking.

'You were against Franco, *señor*?'

Lucia saw Rubio's fists clench. *Oh, God, not now. He mustn't start anything that will attract attention.*

She said to him warningly, 'Rubio . . .'

And, thank God, he understood.

He looked up at the young men and said pleasantly, 'I have nothing against Franco. I just don't know the words.'

'Ah. Then we'll all hum the song together.'

They stood there waiting for Rubio to refuse.

Rubio glanced at Lucia. '*Bueno*.'

The men began to sing again, and Rubio hummed loudly. Lucia could feel the tension in him as he held himself under control. *He's doing this for me.*

When the song ended, a man slapped Rubio on the back. 'Not bad, old man. Not bad at all.'

Rubio sat there silently willing them to go away.

One of the men saw the package in Lucia's lap.

'What are you hiding there, *querida*?'

His companion said, 'I'll bet she's got something better than that up her skirt.'

The men laughed.

'Why don't you pull your panties down and show us what you've got there?'

Rubio sprang to his feet and grabbed one of the men by the throat. He punched him so hard that he flew across the room, breaking a table.

'No!' Lucia screamed. 'Don't!'

But it was too late. In an instant it became a free-for-all, with everybody eagerly joining in. A wine bottle shattered the glass behind the bar. Chairs and tables were knocked over as men went flying through the air, screaming curses. Rubio knocked down two men and a third ran towards him and hit him in the stomach. He gave a grunt of pain.

'Rubio! Let's get out of here!' Lucia screamed.

He nodded. He was clutching his stomach. They pushed their way through the mêlée and found themselves outside on the street.

'We've got to get away,' Lucia said.

You will have your passport tonight. Come back after eight o'clock.

She had to find a place to hide until then. *Damn him! Why couldn't he have controlled himself?*

They turned down Calle Santa Maria, and the noises of the fight behind them gradually diminished. Two streets away they came to a large church, the Iglesia Santa Maria. Lucia ran up the steps, opened the door and peered inside. The church was deserted.

'We'll be safe in here,' she said.

They walked into the dimness of the church. Rubio was still holding his stomach.

'We can rest for a while.'

'Yes.'

Rubio let his hand fall away from his stomach, and blood came gushing out.

Lucia felt sick. 'My God! What happened?'

'A knife,' Rubio whispered. 'He used a knife.' He slumped to the floor.

Lucia knelt at his side, panicky. 'Don't move.'

She removed his shirt and pressed it against his stomach, trying to stem the flow of blood. Rubio's face was chalk white.

'You shouldn't have fought them, you idiot,' Lucia said angrily.

His voice was a slurred whisper. 'I could not let them speak to you that way.'

I could not let them speak to you that way.

Lucia was touched as she had never been touched before. She stood there staring at him and thought: *How many times has this man risked his life for me?*

'I won't let you die,' she said fiercely. 'I'm not going to let you die.' She stood up abruptly. 'I'll be right back.'

She found water and towels in the priest's changing room in the rear of the church and she bathed Rubio's wound. His face was hot to the touch, and his body was soaked in perspiration. Lucia put cold towels on his forehead. Rubio's eyes were closed and he seemed to be asleep. Lucia cradled his head in her arms and talked to him. It did not matter what she said. She was talking to keep him alive, forcing him to hold on to the thin thread of his existence. She babbled on, afraid to stop for even a second.

'We'll work your farm together, Rubio. I want to meet your mother and sisters. Do you think they'll like me? I want them to, so much. And I'm a good worker, *caro*. You'll see. I've never worked on a farm, but I'll learn. We'll make it the best farm in all of Spain.'

She spent the afternoon talking to him, bathing his fevered body, changing the dressing. The bleeding had almost stopped.

'You see, *caro*? You're getting better. You're going to be well. I told you. You and I will have such a wonderful life together, Rubio. Only please don't die. Please!'

She found that she was weeping.

She watched the afternoon shadows paint the church walls through the stained-glass windows and slowly fade away. The setting sun dimmed the sky and finally it was dark. Lucia changed Rubio's bandage again, and so close that it startled her, the church bell began to ring. She held her breath and counted. One . . . three . . . five . . . seven . . . eight. Eight o'clock. It was calling her, telling her it was time to return to the *Casa de Empeños*. Time to escape from this nightmare and save herself.

She knelt down beside Rubio and felt his forehead again. He was burning with fever. His body was soaked with perspiration and his breathing was shallow and rasping. She could see no sign of bleeding, but that could mean that he was bleeding internally. *God damn it. Save yourself, Lucia.*

'Rubio . . . darling . . .'

He opened his eyes, only half conscious.

'I have to leave for a little while,' Lucia said.

He gripped her hand. 'Please . . .'

'It's all right,' she whispered. 'I'll be back.'

451

She rose and took a long last look at him. *I can't help him*, she thought.

Lucia picked up the gold cross and turned and hurried out the church door, her eyes filled with tears. She stumbled out on to the street and began to walk rapidly, heading towards the pawnshop. The man and his cousin would be there waiting for her with her passport to freedom. *In the morning when church services begin, they'll find Rubio and get him to a doctor. They'll treat him and he'll get well. Except that he will not live through the night*, Lucia thought. *Well, that's not my problem.*

The *Casa de Empeños* was just ahead. She was only a few minutes late. She could see that the lights were on in the shop. The men were waiting for her.

She began walking faster, then running. She crossed the street and burst through the open door.

Inside the police station, a uniformed officer was behind the desk. He looked up as Lucia appeared.

'I need you,' Lucia cried. 'A man has been stabbed. He may be dying.'

The policeman did not ask questions. He picked up a telephone and spoke into it. When he put the phone down, he said, 'Someone will be with you in a moment.'

Two detectives appeared almost immediately.

'Someone has been stabbed, *señorita*?'

'Yes. Please follow me. Hurry!'

'We'll pick up the doctor on the way,' one of the detectives said. 'Then you can take us to your friend.'

They picked up the doctor at his home and Lucia hurried the group to the church.

When they entered the church the doctor walked over to the still figure on the floor and knelt beside him.

A moment later he looked up. 'He's alive, but barely. I'll call for an ambulance.'

Lucia sank to her knees and said silently, *Thank you, God. I've done all I can. Now let me get away safely and I'll never bother you again.*

One of the detectives had been staring at Lucia all the way to the church. She looked so familiar. And then he suddenly realized why. She bore an uncanny resemblance to the picture in the Red, Top Priority Circulation from Interpol.

The detective whispered something to his companion and now they both turned to study her. The two of them walked over to Lucia.

'Excuse me, *señorita*. Would you be good enough to come back to the station with us? We have a few questions we wish to ask you.'

28

Ricardo Mellado was a short distance away from the mountain cave when suddenly he saw a large grey wolf trotting towards the entrance. He froze for a single instant, then moved as he had never moved in his life. He raced towards the mouth of the cave, and burst through the entrance.

'Sister!'

In the dim light he saw the huge, grey shape leaping towards Graciela. Instinctively, he reached for his pistol and fired. The wolf let out a yelp of pain and turned towards Ricardo. He felt the sharp fangs of the wounded beast tearing at his clothing and smelled the animal's fetid breath. The wolf was stronger than he had expected, heavily muscled and powerful. Ricardo tried to fight free, but it was impossible.

He felt himself beginning to lose consciousness. He was only dimly aware of Graciela coming towards him and he called, 'Get away!'

He saw Graciela's hand raised above his head, and as it started to descend towards him, he glimpsed a huge rock in it and he thought: *She's going to kill me.*

An instant later the rock swept past him and smashed into the wolf's skull. There was a last savage gasp and the animal lay still on the ground. Ricardo was huddled on the floor, fighting for breath. Graciela knelt at his side.

'Are you all right?' Her voice was trembling with concern.

He managed to nod. He heard a whimpering sound behind him and turned to see the cubs huddled in a corner.

He lay there, gathering his strength. Then he rose with difficulty.

They staggered out into the clean mountain air, shaken. Ricardo stood there, taking deep, lung-filling breaths until his head cleared. The physical and emotional shock of their close brush with death had taken a severe toll on both of them.

'Let's get away from this place. They may come looking for us here.'

Graciela shuddered at the reminder of how much danger they were still in.

They travelled along the steep mountain path for the next hour, and when they finally reached a small stream, Ricardo said, 'Let's stop here.'

With no bandages or antiseptic, they cleaned the scratches as best they could, bathing them in the clean, cold spring water. Ricardo's arm was so stiff that he had trouble moving it. To his surprise, Graciela said, 'Let me do it.'

He was even more surprised by the gentleness with which she did the task.

Without warning, Graciela began trembling violently in an aftermath of shock.

'It's all right,' Ricardo said. 'It's all over.'

She could not stop shaking.

Ricardo took her in his arms and said soothingly, 'Ssh. It's dead. There's nothing more to fear.'

He was holding her closely, and he could feel her thighs pressing against his body and her soft lips were on his and she was holding him close, whispering things he could not understand.

It was as though he had known Graciela always. And yet he knew nothing about her. *Except that she's God's miracle*, he thought.

Graciela was also thinking of God. *Thank you, God, for this joy. Thank you for finally letting me feel what love is.*

It had been an experience for which she had no words, beyond anything she had ever imagined.

Ricardo was watching her, and her beauty still took his breath away. *She belongs to me now*, Ricardo thought. *She doesn't have to go back to a convent. We'll get married and have beautiful children – strong sons.*

'I love you,' he said. 'I'll never let you go, Graciela.'

'Ricardo –'

'Darling, I want to marry you. Will you marry me?'

And without even thinking, Graciela said, 'Yes. Oh, yes.'

And she was in his arms again, and she thought: *This is what I wanted and thought I would never have.*

Ricardo was saying, 'We'll live in France for a while, where we'll be safe. This fight will be over soon, and we'll return to Spain.'

She knew that she would go anywhere with this man, and that if there was danger, she wanted to share it with him.

They talked of so many things. Ricardo told her how he had first become involved with Jaime Miró, and of the broken engagement and of his father's displeasure. But when Ricardo waited for Graciela to speak about her past, she was silent.

She looked at him and thought: *I can't tell him. He'll hate me.* 'Hold me,' Graciela begged.

They slept and woke up at dawn to watch the sun creeping over the ridge of the mountain, bathing the hills in a warm red glow.

Ricardo said, 'We'll be safer hiding out here today. We'll start travelling when it gets dark.'

They ate from the sack of food that the gypsies had given them, and planned their future.

'There are wonderful opportunities here in Spain,' Ricardo said. 'Or there will be when we have peace. I have dozens of ideas. We'll own our own business. We'll buy a beautiful home and raise handsome sons.'

'And beautiful daughters.'

'And beautiful daughters.' He smiled. 'I never knew I could be so happy.'

'Nor I, Ricardo.'

'We'll be in Logroño in two days and meet the others,' Ricardo said. He took her hand. 'We'll tell them you won't be returning to the convent.'

'I wonder if they'll understand.' Then she laughed. 'I don't really care. God understands. I loved my life in the convent,' she said softly, 'but –' She leaned over and kissed him.

Ricardo said, 'I have so much to make up to you.'

She was puzzled. 'I don't understand.'

'Those years you were in the convent, shut away from the world. Tell me, darling – does it bother you that you've lost all those years?'

How could she make him see? 'Ricardo – I didn't lose anything. Have I really missed so much?'

He thought about it, not knowing where to begin. He realized that events he thought of as important would not really have mattered to the nuns in their isolation. Wars, like the Arab–Israeli War? Assassinations of political leaders such as the American President John Kennedy and his brother Robert Kennedy? And of Martin Luther King, Jr., the great black leader of the non-violence movement for black equality? The Berlin Wall? Famines? Floods? Earthquakes? Strikes and demonstrations protesting at man's inhumanity to man?

In the end, how deeply would any of these things have affected her personal life? Or the personal lives of the majority of people on this earth?

Finally, Ricardo said, 'In one sense, you haven't missed much. But in another sense, yes. Something important has been going on. Life. While you were shut away all those years, babies have been born and have grown up; lovers have married; people have suffered and been happy; people have died, and all of us out here were a part of that, a part of the living.'

'And you think I never was?' Graciela asked. And the words came tumbling out before she could stop them. 'I was once a part of that life you are talking about, and it was a living hell. My mother was a whore, and every night I had a different uncle. When I was fourteen years old I gave my body to a man because I was attracted to him and jealous of my mother and what she was doing.' The words were coming in a torrent now. 'I would have become a whore, too, if I had stayed there to be part of the life you think is so precious. No, I don't believe I ran away from anything. I ran *to* something. I found a safe world that is peaceful and good.'

Ricardo was staring at her, horrified. 'I – I'm sorry,' he said. 'I didn't mean to –'

She was sobbing now, and he took her in his arms and said, 'Sh! It's all right. That's over. You were a child. I love you.'

And it was as though Ricardo had given her absolution. She had told him about the awful things she had done in the past, and still he forgave her. And – wonder of wonders – loved her.

He held her very close. 'There is a poem by Federico García Lorca:

> The night does not wish to come
> so that you cannot come
> and I cannot go.
> But you will come
> with your tongue burned by the salt rain.
> The day does not wish to come
> so that you cannot come
> and I cannot come
> and I cannot go.
> But I will come
> through the muddy waters of darkness.
> Neither night nor day wishes to come
> so that I may die for you and you die
> for me.'

And suddenly she thought of the soldiers who were hunting them and she wondered if she and her beloved Ricardo were going to live long enough to have a future together.

29

There was a link missing, a clue to the past, and Alan Tucker was determined to find it. There had been no mention in the newspaper of a baby being abandoned, but it should be easy enough to find out the date it was brought to the orphanage. If the date coincided with the time of the plane crash, Ellen Scott would have some interesting explaining to do. *She couldn't be that stupid*, Alan Tucker thought. *To risk pretending that the Scott heiress was dead, and then leave her on the doorstep of a farmhouse. Risky. Very risky. On the other hand, look at the reward: Scott Industries. Yes, she could have pulled it off. If it is a skeleton in her closet, it's a live one, and it's going to cost her plenty.*

Tucker knew that he had to be very careful. He had no illusion about whom he was dealing with. He was confronting raw power. He knew he had to have all the evidence in hand before he made his move.

His first stop was to return to Father Berrendo.

'Father – I would like to speak to the farmer and his wife, where Patricia – Megan was dropped off.'

The old priest smiled. 'I hope your conversation with them will not take place for a long time.'

Tucker stared at him. 'You mean – ?'

'They died many years ago.'

Damn. But there had to be other avenues to explore. 'You said the baby was taken to a hospital with pneumonia?'

'Yes.'

There would be records there. 'Which hospital was it?'

'It burned down in nineteen sixty-one. There is a new hospital now.' He saw the look of dismay on his visitor's face. 'You must remember, *señor*, that the information you are seeking goes back twenty-eight years. Many things have changed.'

Nothing's going to stop me, Alan Tucker thought. *Not when I've come this close. There must be a file on her somewhere.*

There was still one place left to investigate. The orphanage.

He was reporting daily now to Ellen Scott.

'Keep me informed of every development. I want to know the moment the girl is found.'

And Alan Tucker wondered about the urgency in her voice.

She seems in an awful big rush over something that happened all those years ago. Why? Well, that can wait. First I have to get the proof I'm looking for.

That morning Alan Tucker visited the orphanage. He looked around the dreary community room where a noisy, chattering group of children were playing, and he thought: *This is where the heiress to the Scott dynasty grew up, while that bitch in New York kept all the money and all the power. Well, she's going to share some of that with yours truly. Yes, sir, we'll make a great team, Ellen Scott and me.*

A young woman came up to him and said, 'May I help you, *señor?*'

He smiled. *Yeah. You can help me to about a billion dollars.* 'I'd like to talk to whoever's in charge here.'

'That would be Señora Angeles.'

'Is she here?'

'*Sí, señor*. I will take you to her.'

He followed the woman through the main hall to a small office at the rear of the building.

'Go in, please.'

Alan Tucker entered the office. The woman seated at the desk was in her eighties. She had once been a very large woman, but her frame had shrunk, so she looked as though her body had at one time belonged to someone else. Her hair was grey and thin, but her eyes were bright and clear.

'Good morning, *señor*. May I help you? You have come to adopt one of our lovely children? We have so many delightful ones to choose from.'

'No, *señora*. I have come to inquire about a child who was left here many years ago.'

Mercedes Angeles frowned. 'I do not understand.'

'A baby girl was brought in here –' He pretended to consult a piece of paper – 'in October of nineteen forty-eight.'

'That is so long ago. She would not be here now. You see, we have a rule, *señor*, that at the age of fifteen –'

'No, *señora*. I know she's not here. What I wish to know is the exact date she was brought here.'

'I'm afraid I cannot help you, *señor*.'

His heart sank.

'You see, so many children are brought in here. Unless you know her name –'

Patricia Scott, he thought. Aloud, he said, 'Megan. Her name is Megan.'

Mercedes Angeles' face lit up. 'No one could forget that child. She was a devil, and everyone adored her. Do you know that one day she –'

Alan Tucker had no time for anecdotes. His instincts told him how close he was to getting hold of a piece of the Scott fortune. And this gabby old woman was the key to it. *I must be patient with her.* 'Señora Angeles – I don't have much time. Would you have that date in your files?'

'Of course, *señor*. We are commanded by the state to keep very accurate records.'

Tucker's heart lifted. *I should have brought a camera to take a picture of the file. Never mind. I'll have it photocopied.* 'Could I see that file, *señora*?'

She frowned. 'I don't know. Our records are confidential and –'

'Of course,' Tucker said smoothly, 'and I certainly respect that. You said you were fond of little Megan, and I know you'd want to do anything you could to help her. Well, that's why I'm here. I have some good news for her.'

'And for this you need the date she was brought in here?'

He said glibly, 'That's just so I'll have the proof that she's the person I think she is. Her father died and left her a small inheritance, and I want to make sure she gets it.'

The woman nodded wisely. 'I see.'

Tucker pulled a roll of bills from his pocket. 'And to show my appreciation for the trouble I've put you to, I'd like to contribute a hundred dollars to your orphanage.'

She was looking at the roll of bills, an uncertain expression on her face.

He peeled off another bill. 'Two hundred.'

She frowned.

'All right. Five hundred.'

Mercedes Angeles beamed. 'That is very generous of you, *señor*. I will go and get the file.'

I've done it, he thought jubilantly. *Jesus Christ, I've done it! She stole Scott Industries for herself. If it hadn't been for me, she would have gotten away with it.*

When he confronted Ellen Scott with his evidence there was no way she could deny it. The plane crash happened on 1 October. Megan was in the hospital for ten days. So she would have been brought into the orphanage around 11 October.

Mercedes Angeles returned to the office, holding a file in her hands. 'I found it,' she said proudly.

It was all Alan Tucker could do to keep from grabbing it out of her hands. 'May I look at it?' he asked politely.

'Certainly. You have been so generous.' She frowned. 'I hope you will not mention this to anyone. I should not be doing this at all.'

'It will be our secret, *señora*.'

She handed him the file.

He took a deep breath and opened it. At the top it said: 'Megan. Baby Girl. Parents unknown.' And then the date. But there was some mistake.

'It says here that Megan was brought in here on 14 June 1948.'

'*Si*, señor.'

'That's impossible!' He was almost screaming. *The plane crash happened on 1 October.*

There was a puzzled expression on her face. 'Impossible, *señor*? I do not understand.'

'Who – who keeps these records?'

'I do. When a child is left here, I put down the date and whatever information is given to me.'

His dream was collapsing. 'Couldn't you have made a mistake? About the date, I mean – couldn't it have been October the eleventh?'

'*Señor*,' she said indignantly. 'I know the difference between June the fourteenth and October the eleventh.'

It was over. He had built a dream on too flimsy a foundation. So Patricia Scott had really died in the plane crash. It was a coincidence that Ellen Scott was searching for a girl who had been born around the same time.

Alan Tucker rose heavily and said, 'Thank you, *señora*.'

'*De nada*, *señor*.'

She watched him leave. He was such a nice man. And so generous. His five hundred dollars would buy many things for the orphanage. So would the hundred thousand dollar cheque sent by the kind lady who had telephoned from New York. *October the eleventh was certainly a lucky day for our orphanage. Thank you, Lord.*

Alan Tucker was reporting.

'Still no hard news, Mrs Scott. They're rumoured to be heading north. As far as I know, the girl is safe.'

The tone of his voice has completely changed, Ellen Scott thought. *The threat is gone. So he's visited the orphanage. He's back to being an employee. Well, after he finds Patricia, that will change, too.*

'Report in tomorrow.'

'Yes, Mrs Scott.'

30

'Preserve me, Oh God, for in Thee I take refuge. Thou art my Lord; I have no good apart from Thee. I love Thee, O Lord, my strength. The Lord is my rock and my fortress and my deliverer . . .'

Sister Megan glanced up to see Felix Carpio watching her, a concerned expression on his face.

She's really frightened, he thought.

Ever since they had started on their journey, he had seen Sister Megan's deep anxiety. *Of course. It's only natural. She's been locked up in a convent for God only knows how many years, and now she's suddenly thrown out into a strange, terrifying world. We'll have to be very gentle with the poor girl.*

Sister Megan was indeed frightened. She had been praying hard ever since leaving the convent.

Forgive me, Lord, for I love the excitement of what is happening to me, and I know that is wicked of me.

But no matter how hard Sister Megan prayed, she could not help thinking. *I don't remember when I've had such a good time.* It was the most amazing adventure she had ever had. In the orphanage she had often planned daring escapes, but that was child's play. This was the real thing. She was in the hands of terrorists, and they were being pursued by the police and the army. But instead of being terrified, Sister Megan felt strangely exhilarated.

After travelling all night they stopped at dawn. Megan and Amparo Jiron stood by as Jaime Miró and Felix Carpio huddled over a map.

'It's four miles to Medina del Campo,' Jaime said. 'Let's avoid it. There's a permanent army garrison stationed there. We'll keep heading north-east to Valladolid. We should reach it by early afternoon.'

Easily, Sister Megan thought happily.

It had been a long and gruelling night without rest, but Megan felt wonderful. Jaime was deliberately pushing the group, but Megan understood what he was doing. He was testing her, waiting for her to crack. *Well, he's in for a surprise*, she thought.

As a matter of fact, Jaime Miró found himself intrigued by Sister Megan. Her behaviour was not at all what he would have expected of a nun. She was miles away from her convent, travelling through strange territory, being hunted, and she seemed to be actually enjoying it. *What kind of nun is she?* Jaime Miró wondered.

Amparo Jiron was less impressed. *I'll be glad to be rid of her*, she

461

thought. She stayed close to Jaime, letting the nun walk with Felix Carpio.

The countryside was wild and beautiful, caressed by the soft fragrance of the summer wind. They passed old villages, some of them deserted and forlorn, and saw an ancient abandoned castle high on a hill.

Amparo seemed to Megan like a wild animal – gliding effortlessly over hills and valleys, never seeming to tire.

When finally hours later Valladolid loomed up in the distance, Jaime called a halt.

Jaime turned to Felix. 'Everything is arranged?'

'Yes.'

Megan wondered exactly what had been arranged. She found out very quickly.

'Tomas is instructed to contact us at the bullring.'

'What time does the bank close?'

'Five o'clock. There will be plenty of time.'

Jaime nodded. 'And today there should be a fat pay-roll.'

Good Lord, they're going to rob a bank, Megan thought. It was a little more excitement than she had bargained for.

'What about a car?' Amparo was asking.

'No problem,' Jaime assured her.

They're going to steal one, Megan thought. *God isn't going to like this.*

When the group reached the outskirts of Valladolid, Jaime warned, 'Stay with the crowds. Today is bullfight day and there will be thousands of people. Let's not get separated.'

Jaime Miró had been right about the crowds. Megan had never seen so many people. The streets were swarming with pedestrians and cars and motorcycles, for the bullfight had drawn not only tourists, but citizens from all the neighbouring towns. Even the children on the street were playing at bullfighting.

Megan was fascinated by the crowds and the noise and the bustle around her. She looked into the faces of passers-by and wondered what their lives were like. *Soon enough I'll be back in the convent where I won't be allowed to look at anyone's face again. I might as well take advantage of this while I can.*

The pavements were filled with vendors displaying trinkets, religious medals and crosses, and everywhere was the pungent smell of fritters frying in boiling oil.

Megan suddenly realized how hungry she was.

It was Felix who said, 'Jaime, we're all hungry. Let's try some of those fritters.'

Felix bought four of them and handed one to Megan. 'Try this, Sister. You'll like it.'

It was delicious. For so many of her years, food was not meant to be enjoyed, but to sustain the body for the glory of the Lord. *This one's for me*, Megan thought irreverently.

'The arena is this way,' Jaime said.

They followed the crowds past the park in the middle of town to the Plaza Poinente, which flowed into the Plaza de Toros. The arena itself was inside an enormous adobe structure, three storeys high. There were four ticket windows at the entrance. Signs on the left said, '*Sol*', and on the right, '*Sombra*'. Sun or shade. There were hundreds of people standing in queues waiting to purchase tickets.

'Wait here,' Jaime ordered.

They watched him as he walked over to where half a dozen touts were hawking tickets.

Megan turned to Felix. 'Are we going to watch a bullfight?'

'Yes, but don't worry, Sister,' Felix reassured her. 'You will find it exciting.'

Worry? Megan was thrilled by the idea. At the orphanage, one of her fantasies had been that her father had been a great torero, and Megan had read every book on bullfighting that she could get her hands on.

Felix was saying, 'The real bullfights are held in Madrid and Barcelona. The bullfight here will be by *novilleros*, instead of professionals. They are amateurs. They have not been granted the *alternativa*.

Megan knew that the *alternativa* was the accolade given only to the top-ranked matadors.

'The ones we will see today fight in rented costumes instead of the gold-encrusted suit of lights, against bulls with filed, dangerous horns that the professionals refuse to fight.'

'Why do they do it?'

Felix Carpio shrugged. '*Mas cornadas da el hambre*. Hunger is more painful than horns.'

Jaime returned, holding four tickets. 'We're all set,' Jaime said. 'Let's go in.'

Megan felt a growing sense of excitement.

As they approached the entrance to the huge arena, they passed a poster plastered to the wall. Megan stopped and stared at it.

'Look!'

There was a picture of Jaime Miró, and under it:

WANTED FOR MURDER
JAIME MIRÓ
ONE MILLION PESETAS REWARD
FOR HIS CAPTURE
DEAD OR ALIVE

And suddenly it brought back to Megan the sober realization of the

463

kind of man she was travelling with, the terrorist who held her life in his hands.

Jaime was studying the picture. 'Not a bad likeness.' He ripped off the poster, folded it and put it in his pocket.

What good will that do? Amparo wondered. *They must have posted hundreds of them*.

Jaime grinned. 'This particular one is going to bring us a fortune, *querida*.'

What a strange remark, Megan thought. She could not help admiring his coolness. There was an air of solid competence about Jaime Miró that Megan found reassuring. *The soldiers will never catch him*, she thought.

'Let's go inside.'

There were twelve widely spaced entrances to the building. The red iron doors had been flung open, each one numbered. Inside the entrance there were *puestos* selling cola and beer, and next to them small toilet cubicles. In the stands, each section and seat were numbered. The tiers of stone benches made a complete circle, and in the centre was the large arena covered with sand. There were commercial signs everywhere: BANCO CENTRAL . . . BOUTIQUE CALZADOS . . . SCHWEPPES . . . RADIO POPULAR . . .

Jaime had purchased tickets on the shady side and as they sat down on the stone benches, Megan looked around in wonder. It was not at all as she had imagined it. When she was a young girl, she had seen romantic colour photographs of the bullring in Madrid, huge and elaborate. This was a makeshift ring. The *tribunàs* were rapidly filling up with spectators.

A trumpet sounded. The bullfight began.

Megan leaned forward in her seat, her eyes wide. A huge bull charged into the ring and a matador stepped out from behind a small wooden barrier at the side of the ring and began teasing the animal.

'The picadors will be next,' Megan said excitedly.

Jaime Miró looked at her in wonder. He had been concerned that the bullfight would make her ill and that she would attract attention to them. Instead, she seemed to be having a wonderful time. *Strange*.

A picador was approaching the bull, riding a horse covered with a heavy blanket. The bull lowered its head and charged at the horse, and as it buried its horns in the blanket, the picador drove an eight foot *pica* into the bull's shoulder.

Megan was watching, fascinated. 'He's doing that to weaken the bull's neck muscles,' she explained, remembering the well-loved books she had read all those years ago.

Felix Carpio blinked in surprise. 'That's right, Sister.'

Megan watched as the pairs of colourfully decorated *banderillas* were slammed into the bull's shoulders.

Now it was the matador's turn. He stepped into the ring holding at his side a red cape with a sword inside it. The bull turned and began to charge.

Megan was getting more excited. 'He will make his passes now,' she said. 'First the *pase verónica*, then the *media verónica*, and last the *rebolera*.'

Jaime could contain his curiosity no longer. 'Sister – where did you learn all this?'

Without thinking, Megan said, 'My father was a bullfighter. Watch!'

The action was so swift that Megan could barely follow it. The maddened bull kept charging at the matador, and each time he neared him, the matador swung his red cape to the side and the bull followed the cape. Megan was concerned.

'What happens if the bullfighter gets hurt?'

Jaime shrugged. 'In a place like this, the town barber will take him over to the barn and sew him up.'

The bull charged again, and this time the matador leapt out of the way. The crowd booed.

Felix Carpio said apologetically, 'I am sorry this is not a better fight, Sister. You should see the great ones. I have seen Manolete and el Cordobés and Ordonez. They made bullfighting a spectacle never to be forgotten.'

'I have read about them,' Megan said.

Felix asked, 'Have you ever heard the wonderful story about Manolete?'

'Which story?'

'At one time, the story goes, Manolete was just another bullfighter, no better and no worse than a hundred others. He was engaged to a beautiful young girl, but one day when Manolete was in the ring a bull gored him in the groin and the doctor patched him up and told him that he would no longer be able to have children. Manolete loved his fiancée so much that he didn't tell her, because he was afraid she wouldn't marry him. They married and a few months later she proudly told Manolete that she was going to have a baby. Well, of course he knew that it wasn't his baby, and he left her. The heartbroken girl killed herself. Manolete reacted like a madman. He had no more desire to live, so he went into the bullring and did things that no matador had ever done before. He kept risking his life, hoping to be killed, and he became the greatest matador in the world. Two years later he fell in love again and married the young lady. A few months after the wedding she came to him and proudly announced that she was going to have his baby. And that's when Manolete discovered that the doctor had been wrong.'

Megan said, 'How awful.'

Jaime laughed aloud. 'That's an interesting story. I wonder if there is any truth to it.'

'I would like to think so,' Felix said.

Amparo was listening, her face impassive. She had watched Jaime's growing interest in the nun with resentment. *The sister had better watch her step.*

Aproned food vendors were moving up and down the aisles calling out their wares. One of them approached the row where Jaime and the others were seated.

'*Empanadas*,' he called out. '*Empanadas calientes*.'

Jaime raised a hand. '*Aquí*.'

The vendor skilfully tossed a wrapped package across the crowd into Jaime's hands. Jaime handed ten pesetas to the man next to him to be passed to the vendor. Megan watched as Jaime lowered the wrapped *empanada* to his lap and carefully opened it. Inside the wrapping was a piece of paper. Jaime read it, then read it again, and Megan saw his jaw tighten.

Jaime slipped the paper into his pocket. 'We're leaving,' he said curtly. 'One at a time.' He turned to Amparo. 'You first. We'll meet at the gate.'

Wordlessly, Amparo got up and made her way across to the aisle.

Jaime nodded to Felix, and Felix rose and followed Amparo.

'What is happening?' Megan asked. 'Is something wrong?'

'We're leaving for Logroño.' He rose. 'Watch me, Sister. If I'm not stopped, go to the gate.'

Megan watched, tense, as Jaime made his way to the aisle and started towards the exit. No one seemed to pay any attention to him. When Jaime had disappeared from sight, Megan rose and started to leave. There was a roar from the crowd and she turned to look back at the bullring. A young matador was lying on the ground being gored by the savage bull. Blood was pouring on to the sand. Megan closed her eyes and offered up a silent prayer: *Oh, blessed Jesus, have mercy on this man. He shall not die, but he shall live. The Lord has chastened him sorely, but he has not given him over to death. Amen.* She opened her eyes, turned and hurried out.

Jaime, Amparo and Felix were waiting for her at the entrance.

'Let's move,' Jaime said.

They started walking.

'What's wrong?' Felix asked Jaime.

'The soldiers shot Tomas,' Jaime said tersely. 'He's dead. And the police have Rubio. He was stabbed in a bar fight.'

Megan crossed herself. 'What's happened to Sister Teresa and Sister Lucia?' she asked anxiously.

'I don't know.' Jaime turned to the others. 'We must hurry.' He looked at his watch. 'The bank should be busy.'

'Jaime, maybe we should wait,' Felix suggested. 'It's going to be dangerous for just the two of us to hold up the bank now.'

Megan listened to what he was saying and thought: *That won't stop him*. She was right.

The three of them were headed for the huge car-park behind the arena. When Megan caught up with them, Felix was examining a blue Seat sedan.

'This should do,' Felix said.

He fumbled with the lock on the door for a moment, opened it and put his head inside. He crouched down under the wheel, and a moment later the engine started.

'Get in,' Jaime told them.

Megan stood there, uncertainly. 'You're stealing a car?'

'For Christ's sake,' Amparo hissed. 'Stop acting like a nun and get into the car.'

The two men were in the front seat, with Jaime at the wheel. Amparo scrambled into the back.

'Are you coming or not?' Jaime demanded.

Megan took a deep breath and got into the car next to Amparo. They started off. Megan closed her eyes. *Dear Lord, where are You leading me?*

'If it makes you feel any better, Sister,' Jaime said, 'we're not stealing this car. We're confiscating it in the name of the Basque army.'

Megan started to say something, then stopped. There was nothing she could say that would make him change his mind. She sat there in silence as Jaime drove towards the centre of town.

He's going to rob a bank, Megan thought, *and in the eyes of God, I'll be as guilty as he is*. She crossed herself and began silently to pray.

The Banco de Bilbao is on the ground floor of a nine-storey apartment building on the Calle de Cervantes at the Plaza de Circular.

When the car pulled up in front of the building, Jaime said to Felix, 'Keep the engine running. If there's any trouble, take off and meet the others in Logroño.'

Felix stared at him in surprise. 'What are you talking about? You're not going in there *alone*? You can't. The odds are too great, Jaime. It's too dangerous.'

Jaime slapped him on the shoulder. 'If they get hurt, they get hurt,' he said with a grin. He stepped out of the car.

They watched as Jaime walked into a leather goods shop next door to the bank. A few minutes later he emerged carrying an attaché case. He nodded to the group in the car and entered the bank.

Megan could hardly breathe. She began to pray:

> *Prayer is a calling.*
> *Prayer is a listening.*
> *Prayer is a dwelling.*

> *Prayer is a presence.*
> *Prayer is a lamp*
> *aflame with Jesus.*
> *I am calm and filled with peace.*

She was not calm and filled with peace.

Jaime Miró walked through two sets of doors that led to the marble lobby of the bank. Inside the entrance, mounted high on the wall, he noted a security camera. He gave it a casual glance, then looked the room over. Behind the counters a staircase led to a second floor, where bank officers were working at desks. It was near closing time and the bank was filled with customers eager to finish transacting their business. There were queues of people in front of the three tellers' cages, and Jaime noticed that several of the customers were carrying packages.

Jaime stepped into a queue and patiently waited his turn.

When he reached the teller's cage, he smiled pleasantly and said, '*Buenos tardes.*'

'*Buenos tardes, señor.* What can we do for you today?'

Jaime leaned against the window and pulled out the folded wanted poster. He handed it to the teller. 'Would you take a look at this, please?'

The teller smiled. 'Certainly, *señor.*'

He unfolded it, and as he saw what it was, his eyes widened. He looked up at Jaime, and panic was in his eyes.

'It's a nice likeness, isn't it?' Jaime said softly. 'As you can tell from that, I have killed many people, so one more really won't make a difference to me. Do I make myself understood?'

'P-perfectly, *señor.* P-perfectly. I have a family. I beg of you –'

'I respect families, so I will tell you what I want you to do to save your children's father.' Jaime pushed the attaché case towards the teller. 'I want you to fill this for me. I want you to do it quickly and quietly. If you truly believe that the money is more important than your life, then go ahead and raise the alarm.'

The teller shook his head. 'No, no, no.'

He began to pull money out of the cash drawer and stuff it into the attaché case. His hands were trembling.

When the attaché case was full, the cashier said, 'There you are, *señor.* I – I promise you I won't raise any alarm.'

'That's very wise of you,' Jaime said. 'I'll tell you why, *amigo.*' He turned around and pointed to a middle-aged woman standing near the end of the line, carrying a package wrapped in brown paper. 'Do you see that woman? She is one of us. There is a bomb in that package. If the alarm should sound, she will set off the bomb instantly.'

The cashier turned even paler. 'No, please!'

'You will wait until ten minutes after she leaves the bank before you make a move,' Jaime warned.

'On my children's life,' the teller whispered.

'*Buenos tardes.*'

Jaime took the attaché case and moved towards the door. He felt the cashier's eyes riveted on him.

Jaime stopped at the side of the woman with the package.

'I must compliment you,' Jaime said. 'That is a most becoming dress you are wearing.'

She blushed. 'Why thank you, *señor – gracias.*'

'*De nada.*'

Jaime turned to nod to the cashier, then strolled out of the bank. It would be at least fifteen minutes before the woman finished her business and left. By that time, he and the others would be long gone.

As Jaime came out of the bank and walked towards the car, Megan almost fainted with relief.

Felix Carpio grinned. 'The bastard got away with it.' He turned to Megan. 'I beg your pardon, Sister.'

Megan had never been so glad to see anyone in her life. *He did it*, she thought. *And all by himself. Wait until I tell the sisters what happened.* And then she remembered. She could never tell this to anyone. When she went back to the convent, there would be only silence for the rest of her life. It gave her an odd feeling.

Jaime said to Felix, 'Move over, *amigo*. I'll drive.' He tossed the briefcase into the back seat.

'Everything went well?' Amparo asked.

Jaime laughed. 'Couldn't have gone better. I must remember to thank Colonel Acoca for his calling card.'

The car started down the street. At the first corner, Calle de Tudela, Jaime made a left turn. Suddenly, appearing out of nowhere, a policeman moved in front of the car and held out a hand signalling him to stop. Jaime stepped on the brake. Megan's heart began to pound.

The policeman walked over to the car.

Jaime asked calmly, 'What's the problem, officer?'

'The problem, *señor*, is that you are driving the wrong way down a one-way street. Unless you can prove you are legally blind, you are in trouble.' He pointed to the sign at the entrance. 'The street is clearly marked. Motorists are expected to respect a sign like that. That is the reason it has been placed there.'

Jaime said apologetically, 'A thousand pardons. My friends and I were in such a serious discussion that I did not see the sign.'

The policeman was leaning into the driver's window. He was studying Jaime, a puzzled expression on his face.

'You will be so good as to let me see your registration, please.'

'Of course,' Jaime said.

He reached down for the revolver which was under his jacket. Felix was ready to spring into action. Megan held her breath.

Jaime pretended to be searching his pockets. 'I know I have it here somewhere.'

At that moment from across the Plaza came a loud scream and the policeman turned to look. A man on the street corner was beating a woman, hitting her about the head and shoulders with his fists.

'Help!' she cried. 'Help me! He's killing me!'

The policeman hesitated for only an instant. 'Wait here,' he commanded.

He raced back down the street towards the man and woman.

Jaime put the car into gear and slammed down on the accelerator. The car shot down the one-way street, scattering traffic headed towards them, horns angrily blaring at them. When they reached the corner, Jaime made another turn towards the bridge that led out of town on the Avenida Sanchez Arjona.

Megan looked at Jaime and crossed herself. She could hardly breathe.

'Would you – would you have killed the policeman if that man had not attacked the woman?'

Jaime did not bother to answer.

'The woman wasn't being attacked, Sister,' Felix explained. 'Those were our people. We are not alone. We have many friends.'

Jaime's face was grim. 'We're going to have to get rid of this car.'

They were leaving the outskirts of Valladolid. Jaime turned on to N620, the highway to Burgos, on the way to Logroño. He was careful to stay within the speed limit.

'We'll get rid of the car as soon as we get past Burgos,' he announced.

I can't believe this is happening to me, Megan thought. *I escaped from the convent, I'm running away from the army, and I'm travelling in a stolen car with terrorists who have just robbed a bank. Lord, what else do You have in mind for me?*

31

Colonel Ramón Acoca and half a dozen members of the GOE were in the middle of a strategy meeting. They were studying a large map of the countryside.

The scarred giant said, 'It's obvious that Miró is heading north towards Basque country.'

'That could mean Burgos, Vitoria, Logroño, Pamplona or San Sebastian.'

San Sebastian, Acoca thought. *But I've got to catch him before he reaches there.*

He could hear the voice on the phone: *You're running out of time.*

He could not afford to fail.

They were driving through the rolling hills that heralded the approach to Burgos.

Jaime was quiet behind the wheel. When he finally spoke, he said, 'Felix, when we get to San Sebastian, I want to make arrangements to get Rubio away from the police.'

Felix nodded. 'It will be a pleasure. It will drive them crazy.'

Megan said, 'What about Sister Lucia?'

'What?'

'Didn't you say that she had been captured, too?'

Jaime said wryly, 'Yes, but your Sister Lucia turned out to be a criminal wanted by the police for murder.'

The news shook Megan. She remembered how Lucia had taken charge and had persuaded them to hide in the hills. She liked Sister Lucia.

She said stubbornly, 'Since you're going to rescue Rubio, you should save them both.'

What the devil kind of nun is this? Jaime wondered.

But she was right. Smuggling Rubio and Lucia out from under the noses of the police would be wonderful propaganda and would make headlines.

Amparo had sunk into a sullen silence.

Suddenly, in the distance, on the road ahead of them were three army trucks filled with soldiers.

'We'd better get off this road,' Jaime decided.

At the next intersection he turned on to Highway N120 and headed east.

'Santo Domingo de la Calzada is up ahead. There's an old deserted castle there. We can spend the night in it.'

They could see its outline from the distance, high on a hill. Jaime took a side road, avoiding the town, and the castle loomed larger and larger as they approached it. A few hundred yards from it was a lake.

Jaime stopped the car. 'Everybody out, please.'

When they were all out of the car, Jaime pointed the steering wheel down the hill towards the lake, jammed the accelerator down, released the handbrake and jumped clear. They stood there watching as the car disappeared into the water.

Megan was about to ask him how they were going to get to Logroño. She stopped herself. *Foolish question. He will steal another car, of course.*

The group turned to examine the abandoned castle. There was a huge stone wall circling it, with crumbling turrets on each corner.

'In the old days,' Felix told Megan, 'princes used these castles as prisons for their enemies.'

And Jaime is an enemy of the state, and if he is caught, there will be no prison for him. Only death, Megan thought. *He has no fear.* She remembered his words:

I have faith in what I'm fighting for. I have faith in my men, and in my guns.

They walked up the stone steps that led to the front gate. The gates were iron and had rusted away so badly that they were able to push them open and squeeze through into a courtyard paved in stone.

The inside of the castle seemed enormous to Megan. There were narrow passageways and rooms everywhere, and facing the outside were gun ports, where the defenders of the castle could repel attackers.

Stone steps led to a second floor and there was another *claustro*, an inner patio. The stone steps narrowed as they walked up to a third floor, and then a fourth. The castle was deserted.

'Well at least there are plenty of places to sleep here,' Jaime said. 'Felix and I will go forage for food. Pick out your rooms.'

The two men started downstairs again.

Amparo turned to Megan. 'Come on, Sister.'

They walked down the corridor and the rooms all looked alike to Megan. They were empty stone cubicles, cold and austere, some larger than others.

Amparo picked out the largest. 'Jaime and I will sleep here.' She looked at Megan and asked slyly, 'Would you like to sleep with Felix?'

Megan looked at her and said nothing.

'Or perhaps you'd rather sleep with Jaime.' Amparo stepped closer to Megan. 'Don't get any ideas, Sister. He's much too much man for you.'

'You don't have to concern yourself. I'm not interested.' And even as she said it, Megan wondered whether Jaime Miró was much too much man for her.

When Jaime and Felix returned to the castle an hour later, Jaime was clutching two rabbits and Felix was carrying firewood. Felix bolted the front door behind them. Megan watched as the men made a fire in the large fireplace. Jaime skinned and cooked the rabbits on a spit over the fire.

'Sorry we can't offer you ladies a real feast,' Felix said, 'but we'll eat well in Logroño. Meanwhile – enjoy.'

When they had finished their meagre meal, Jaime said, 'Let's get to sleep. I want to make an early start in the morning.'

Amparo said to Jaime, 'Come, *querido*. I have our bedroom picked out.'

'*Bueno*. Let's go.'

Megan watched them go upstairs, hand in hand.

Felix turned to Megan. 'Have you chosen your bedroom, Sister?'

'Yes, thank you.'

'All right, then.'

Megan and Felix walked up the stairs together.

'Good night,' Megan said.

He handed Megan a sleeping-bag. 'Good night, Sister.'

Megan wanted to ask Felix about Jaime, but she hesitated. Jaime might think she was prying, and for some reason, Megan wanted very much for Jaime to have a good opinion of her. *That's really odd*, Megan thought. *He's a terrorist, a murderer, a bank robber, and heaven only knows what else, and I'm worried about whether the man thinks well of me.*

But even as Megan thought it, she knew that there was another side to it. *He's a freedom fighter. He robs banks to finance his cause. He risks his life for what he believes in. He's a brave man.*

As Megan passed their bedroom, she heard Jaime and Amparo inside laughing. She walked into the small, bare room where she was to sleep and knelt on the cold stone floor. 'Dear God, forgive me for –' *Forgive me for what? What have I done?*

For the first time in her life, Megan was unable to pray. Was God up there listening?

Megan crawled into the sleeping-bag Felix had given her, but sleep was as remote as the cold stars she could see through the narrow window.

What am I doing here? Megan wondered. Her thoughts drifted back to the convent . . . the orphanage. And before the orphanage? *Why was I left there? I don't really believe that my father was a brave soldier or a great bullfighter. But wouldn't it be wonderful to know?*

It was almost dawn before Megan drifted off to sleep.

At the prison in Aranda de Duero, Lucia Carmine was a celebrity.

'You're a big fish in our little pond,' the guard told her. 'The Italian government is sending someone to escort you home. I'd like to escort you to my house, *bonita puta*. What bad thing did you do?'

'I cut off a man's balls for calling me *bonita puta*. Tell me – how is my friend?'

'He's going to live.'

Lucia said a silent prayer of gratitude. She looked around the stone walls of her grim, grey cell and thought: *How the hell do I get out of here?*

32

The report of the bank robbery was handled through regular police channels, and it was not until two hours after the robbery occurred that a police lieutenant notified Colonel Acoca about it.

An hour later, Colonel Acoca was in Valladolid. He was furious at the delay.

'Why wasn't I informed immediately?'

'I'm sorry, Colonel, but it never occurred to us that –'

'You had him in your hands and you let him get away!'

'It wasn't our –'

'Send in the bank teller.'

The bank teller was filled with a sense of self-importance. 'It was my window he came to. I could tell he was a killer by the look in his eye. He –'

'There is no doubt in your mind that the man who held you up was Jaime Miró?'

'None. He even showed me a wanted poster of himself. It was –'

'Did he come into the bank alone?'

'Yes. He pointed to a woman in the queue and he said she was a member of his gang, but after Miró left I recognized her. She's a secretary who's a regular customer and –'

Colonel Acoca said impatiently, 'When Miró left, did you see in which direction he went?'

'Out the front door.'

The interview with the traffic policeman was no more helpful.

'There were four of them in the car, Colonel. Jaime Miró and another man and two women in the back.'

'In what direction were they headed?'

The policeman hesitated. 'They could have gone in any direction, sir, once they got off the one-way street.' His face brightened. 'I can describe the car, though.'

Colonel Acoca shook his head in disgust. 'Don't bother.'

She was dreaming, and in her dream there were the voices of a mob and they were coming for her to burn her at the stake for robbing a bank. *It wasn't for me. It was for the cause.* The voices grew louder.

Megan opened her eyes and sat up, staring at the unfamiliar castle walls. The sound of voices was real. They were coming from outside.

Megan rose and hurried over to the narrow window. Directly below, in front of the castle, was an encampment of soldiers. Megan was filled with a sudden panic. *They've caught us. I've got to find Jaime.*

She hurried to the room where he and Amparo had slept and looked inside. It was empty. She ran down the steps to the reception hall on the main floor. Jaime and Amparo were standing near the bolted front door, whispering.

Felix ran up to them. 'I checked the back. There's no other way out of here.'

'What about the back windows?'

'Too small. The only way out is through the front door.'

Where the soldiers are, Megan thought. *We're trapped.*

Jaime was saying, 'It's just our damned bad luck that they picked this place to camp.'

'What are we going to do?' Amparo whispered.

'There's nothing we can do. We'll have to stay here until they leave. If –'

And at that moment there was a loud knock at the front door. An authoritative voice called out, 'Open up in there.'

Jaime and Felix exchanged a quick look, and without a word drew their guns.

The voice called out again, 'We know there's someone in there. Open up.'

Jaime said to Amparo and Megan, 'Get out of the way.'

It's hopeless, Megan thought, as Amparo moved behind Jaime and Felix. *There must be two dozen armed soldiers out there. We haven't got a chance.*

Before the others could stop her, Megan moved swiftly to the front door and opened it.

'Thank the Lord you've come!' Megan exclaimed. 'You must help me.'

33

The army officer stared at Megan. 'Who are you? What are you doing in there? I'm Captain Rodriguez, and we're looking for –'

'You're just in time, Captain.' She grabbed his arm. 'My two little sons have typhoid fever, and I've got to get them to a doctor. You must come in and help me with them.'

'Typhoid fever?'

'Yes.' Megan was pulling on his arm. 'It is terrible. They are burning up. They are covered with sores and are very sick. Bring your men in and help me carry them out to –'

'*Señora*! You must be mad. That is highly contagious.'

'Never mind that. They need your help. They may be dying.' She was pulling on his arm.

'Let go of me.'

'You can't leave me. What will I do?'

'Get back inside and stay there until we can notify the police to send an ambulance or a doctor.'

'But –'

'That's an order, *señora*. Get inside.'

He called out, 'Sergeant, we're moving out of here.'

Megan closed the front door, leaning against it, drained.

Jaime was staring at her in stunned amazement. 'My God, that was brilliant. Where did you learn to lie like that?'

Megan turned to him and sighed. 'When I was in the orphanage, we had to learn to defend ourselves. I hope God will forgive me.'

'I wish I could have seen the look on that Captain's face.' Jaime burst into laughter. 'Typhoid fever! Jesus Christ!' He saw the look on Megan's face. 'I beg your pardon, Sister.'

From outside they could hear the sounds of the soldiers packing their tents and moving out.

When the troops had departed, Jaime said, 'The police will be here soon. Anyway, we have an appointment in Logroño.'

Fifteen minutes after the soldiers had departed, Jaime said, 'It should be safe to leave now.' He turned to Felix. 'See what you can pick up in town. Preferably a sedan.'

Felix grinned. 'No problem.'

Half an hour later they were in a beat-up grey sedan heading east.

To Megan's surprise, she was seated next to Jaime. Felix and Amparo were in the back seat. Jaime glanced at Megan, a grin on his face.

'Typhoid fever,' he said. And burst out laughing.

Megan smiled. 'He *did* seem eager to get away, didn't he?'

'Did you say you were in an orphanage, Sister?'

'Yes.'

'Where?'

'In Ávila.'

'You don't look Spanish.'

'So I've been told.'

'It must have been hell for you in the orphanage.'

She was startled by the unexpected concern. 'It could have been,' she said. 'But it wasn't.' *I wouldn't let it be*, she thought.

'Have you any idea who your parents were?'

Megan recalled her fantasies. 'Oh, yes. My father was a brave Englishman who drove an ambulance for the loyalists in the Spanish Civil War. My mother was killed in the fighting and I was left on the doorstep of a farmhouse.' Megan shrugged. 'Or my father was a foreign prince who had an affair with a peasant girl and abandoned me to avoid a scandal.'

Jaime glanced at her, saying nothing.

'I –' she stopped abruptly. 'I don't know who my parents were.'

They drove on in silence for a while.

'How long were you behind the walls of the convent?'

'About fifteen years.'

Jaime was astonished. 'Jesus!' Hastily, he added, 'I beg your pardon, Sister. But it's like talking to someone from another planet. You have no idea what's happened in the world in the past fifteen years.'

'I'm sure that whatever changed is only temporary. It will change again.'

'Do you still want to go back to a convent?'

The question took Megan by surprise.

'Of course.'

'*Why?*' Jaime made a sweeping gesture. 'I mean – there is so much that you must miss behind the walls. Here we have music and poetry. Spain gave the world Cervantes and Picasso, Lorca, Pizarro, DeSoto, Cortez. This is a magical country.'

There was a surprising mellowness about this man, a soft fire.

Unexpectedly Jaime said, 'I'm sorry for wanting to desert you earlier, Sister. It was nothing personal. I have had bad experiences with your Church.'

'That is difficult to believe.'

'Believe it.' His voice was bitter.

In his mind's eye he could see the buildings and statues and streets of Guernica exploding in showers of death. He could still hear the screams of the bombs mingling with the screams of the helpless victims being torn apart. The only place of sanctuary was the church.

The priests have locked the church. They won't let us in.

And the deadly hail of bullets that had murdered his mother and father and sisters. *No. Not the bullets*, Jaime thought. *The Church.*

'Your Church stood behind Franco and allowed unspeakable things to be done to innocent civilians.'

'I'm sure the Church protested,' Megan said.

'No. It wasn't until nuns were being raped by his Falangists and priests were being murdered and churches were being burned that finally the Pope broke with Franco. But that didn't bring my mother or father or sisters back to life.'

The passion in his voice was frightening.

'I'm sorry. But that was long ago. The war is over.'

'No. Not for us it isn't. The government will still not permit us to fly the Basque flag or celebrate our national holidays or speak our own language. No, Sister. We're still being oppressed. We'll keep on fighting until we gain our independence. There are half a million Basques in Spain and a hundred and fifty thousand more in France. We want our independence – but your God is too busy to help us.'

Megan said earnestly, 'God cannot take sides, for He is in all of us. We are all a part of Him, and when we try to destroy Him, we destroy ourselves.'

To Megan's surprise, Jaime smiled. 'We are a lot alike, you and I, Sister.'

'We are?'

'We may believe in different things, but we believe with a passion. Most people go through life without caring deeply about anything. You devote your life to God; I devote my life to a cause. We care.'

And Megan thought: *Do I care enough? And if I do, why am I enjoying being with this man? I should be thinking only of returning to a convent.* There was a power in Jaime Miró that was like a magnet. *Is he like Manolete? Risking his life taking daring chances because he has nothing to lose?*

'What will they do to you if the soldiers catch you?' Megan asked.

'Execute me.' He said it so matter-of-factly that for a moment Megan thought she had misunderstood.

'Aren't you afraid?'

'Of course I'm afraid. We're all afraid. None of us wants to die, Sister. We'll meet your God soon enough. We don't want to rush it.'

'Have you done such terrible things?'

'That depends on your point of view. The difference between a patriot and a rebel depends on who is in power at the moment. The government calls us terrorists. We call ourselves freedom fighters. Jean Jacques Rousseau said that freedom is the power to choose our own chains. I want that freedom.' He studied her a moment. 'But you don't have to concern yourself with any of these things, do you? Once you're back in the convent, you'll no longer be interested in the world outside.'

Was that true? Being out in the world again had turned her life upside down. Had she given up her freedom? There was so much she wanted to know, so much she had to learn. She felt like an artist with a blank canvas about to start sketching a new life. *If I go back to a convent*, she thought, *I will be shut away from life again.* And even as she thought it, Megan was appalled by the word *if. When I go back*, she corrected herself hastily. *Of course I'm going back. I have nowhere else to go.*

They camped that night in the woods.

Jaime said, 'We're about thirty miles from Logroño and we aren't supposed to meet the others for two days. It will be safer for us to stay on the move until then. So tomorrow we will head toward Vitoria. The next day we'll go into Logroño and just a few hours after that, Sister, you'll be at the convent in Mendavia.'

For ever. 'Will you be all right?' Megan asked.

'Are you worried about my soul, Sister, or my body?'

Megan found herself blushing.

'Nothing will happen to me. I'll cross the border into France for a while.'

'I will pray for you,' Megan told him.

'Thank you,' he said gravely. 'I will think of you praying for me and it will make me feel safer. Get some sleep now. We'll make Leon tomorrow.'

As Megan turned to lie down, she saw Amparo staring at her from the far end of the clearing. There was a look of naked hatred on Amparo's face.

No one takes my man from me. No one.

480

34

Early the following morning, they reached the outskirts of Nanclares, a small village west of Vitoria. They came to a filling station with a garage, where a mechanic was working on a car. Jaime pulled into the garage.

'*Buenos días*,' the mechanic said. 'What is the problem?'

'If I knew,' Jaime replied, 'I would fix it myself and charge for it. This car is as useless as a mule. It sputters like an old woman and has no energy.'

'It sounds like my wife,' the mechanic grinned. 'I think you may have a carburettor problem, *señor*.'

Jaime shrugged. 'I know nothing about cars. All I know is that I have a very important appointment in Madrid tomorrow. Can you have it fixed by this afternoon?'

The mechanic said, 'I have two jobs ahead of you, *señor*, but –' He let the rest of the sentence hang in the air.

'I will be glad to pay you double.'

The mechanic's face brightened. 'Will two o'clock be all right?'

'Wonderful. We'll get something to eat and come back at two.'

Jaime turned to the others, who had been listening to the conversation in amazement. 'We're in luck,' Jaime said. 'This man is going to fix the car for us. Let's go eat.'

They got out of the car and followed Jaime down the street.

'Two o'clock,' the mechanic said.

'Two o'clock.'

When they were out of earshot, Felix said, 'What are you doing? There's nothing wrong with the car.'

Except that by now the police will be looking for it, Megan thought. *But they'll be looking on the road, not in a garage. It's a clever way to get rid of it.*

'By two o'clock we'll be gone, won't we?' Megan asked.

Jaime looked at her and grinned. 'I have to make a phone call. Wait here.'

Amparo took Jaime's arm. 'I'll go with you.'

Megan and Felix watched them walk off.

Felix looked at Megan and said, 'You and Jaime are getting along well, yes?'

'Yes.' She felt suddenly shy.

'He is not an easy man to know. But he is a man of great honour and great bravery. He is a very caring man. There is no one like him. Did I tell you how he saved my life, Sister?'

'No. I would like to hear.'

'A few months ago the government executed six freedom fighters. In revenge, Jaime decided to blow up the dam at Puente la Reina, south of Pamplona. The town below was headquarters for the army. We moved in at night, but someone tipped off the GOE, and Acoca's men caught three of us. We were sentenced to die. It would have taken an army to storm our prison, but Jaime figured out a way. He set the bulls loose in Pamplona, and in the confusion got two of us away. The third one was beaten to death by Acoca's men. Yes, Sister, Jaime Miró is very special.'

When Jaime and Amparo returned, Felix asked, 'What is happening?'

'Friends are picking us up. We'll have a lift into Vitoria.'

Half an hour later, a truck appeared. The back of it was covered by canvas.

'Welcome,' the driver said cheerfully. 'Hop in.'

'Thank you, *amigo*.'

'It's a pleasure to be of assistance to you, *señor*. It's good that you called. The damned soldiers are swarming around like fleas. It is not safe for you and your friends to be out in the open.'

They climbed into the back of the truck, and the huge vehicle headed northeast.

'Where will you be staying?' the driver asked.

'With friends,' Jaime said.

And Megan thought: *He doesn't trust anyone. Not even someone who is helping him. But how can he? His life is in danger.* And she thought of how terrible it must be for Jaime to be living under that shadow, running from the police and the army. And all because he believed in an ideal so much that he was willing to die for it. What was it he had said? *The difference between a patriot and a rebel depended on who was in power at the moment.*

The drive was a pleasant one. The thin canvas cover offered security, and Megan realized how much tension she had felt when they were out in the open fields, knowing that they were all being hunted. *And Jaime lives under that tension constantly. How strong he is.*

She and Jaime talked, and the conversation flowed easily as though they had known each other for ever. Amparo Jiron sat listening to them, saying nothing, her face impassive.

'When I was a boy,' Jaime told Megan, 'I wanted to be an astronomer.'

Megan was curious. 'What made you – ?'

'I had seen my mother and father and sisters shot down, and friends murdered, and I couldn't face what was happening here on this bloody earth. The stars were an escape. They were millions of light years away, and I used to dream of going to them one day and getting away from this awful planet.'

She was watching him, silent.

'But there is no escape, is there? In the end, we all have to face up to our responsibilities. So I came back down to earth. I used to believe that one person could not make a difference. But I know now that that is not true. Jesus made a difference, Muhammad and Gandhi and Einstein and Churchill.' He smiled wryly. 'Don't misunderstand, Sister. I'm not comparing myself to any of them. But in my small way, I do what I can. I think we must all do what we can.'

And Megan wondered whether his words were meant to have a special meaning for her.

'When I got the stars out of my eyes, I studied to be an engineer. I learned to build buildings. Now I blow them up. And the irony is that some of the buildings I've blown up are ones that I've built.'

They reached Vitoria at dusk.

'Where shall I take you?' the truck driver asked.

'You can drop us off here, at the corner, *amigo*.'

The truck driver nodded. 'Right. Keep up the good fight.'

Jaime helped Megan down from the truck. Amparo watched, her eyes blazing. She allowed her man to touch no other woman. *She's a whore*, Amparo thought. *And Jaime is horny for that bitch of a nun. Well, that won't last. He will soon find that her milk is thin. He needs a real woman.*

The group took to the side streets, keeping a wary eye out for trouble. Twenty minutes later, they arrived at a one-storey stone house nestled in a narrow street and surrounded by a high fence.

'This is it,' Jaime said. 'We will stay here tonight and leave tomorrow when it is dark.'

They entered through the front gate and went to the door. It took Jaime but a moment to slip the lock and they all went inside.

'Whose house is this?' Megan asked.

'You ask too many questions,' Amparo said. 'Just be grateful we've kept you alive.'

Jaime looked at Amparo a moment. 'She's proved her right to ask questions.' He turned to Megan. 'It's the house of a friend. You're in Basque country now. From here on our journey will be easier. There will be comrades everywhere, watching and protecting us. You'll be at the convent the day after tomorrow.'

And Megan felt a small chill that was almost a sorrow. *What is the matter with me?* she wondered. *Of course I want to go back. Forgive me, Lord. I asked that You bring me home to Your safety, and You are.*

'I'm starved,' Felix said. 'Let's see what's in the kitchen.'

It was completely stocked.

483

Jaime said, 'He left plenty of food for us. I will make us a wonderful dinner.' He smiled at Megan. 'I think we deserve it, don't you?'

Megan said, 'I didn't know men cooked.'

Felix laughed. 'Basque men take pride in their cooking. You are in for a treat. You will see.'

Handing Jaime the ingredients he asked for, they watched as he prepared a piperade of fresh roasted, peeled green peppers, sliced white onions, tomatoes, eggs and ham sautéed together. As it started to cook, Megan said, 'It smells delicious.'

'Ah, that's just the appetizer. I'm going to make a famous Basque dish for you, *pollo al chilindrón*.'

He didn't say 'for us', Amparo noted. *He said, 'for you'. For the bitch.*

Jaime cut up slices of chicken, sprinkled salt and pepper over them and browned the chicken in hot oil while in a separate pan he started cooking onions, garlic and tomatoes. 'We'll let it simmer for half an hour.'

Felix had found a bottle of red wine. He passed out glasses. 'The red wine of Rioja. You will like this.' He offered a glass to Megan. 'Sister?'

The last time Megan tasted wine had been at communion. 'Thank you,' she said.

Slowly Megan raised the glass to her lips and took a sip. It was delicious. She took another sip and she could feel a warmth moving down her body. It felt wonderful. *I must enjoy all this while I can*, Megan thought. *It will be over soon.*

During dinner, Jaime seemed unusually preoccupied.

'What's troubling you, *amigo*?' Felix asked.

Jaime hesitated. 'We have a traitor in the movement.'

There was a shocked silence.

'What – what makes you think that?' Felix demanded.

'Acoca. He keeps getting too close to us.'

Felix shrugged. 'He's the fox and we're the rabbits.'

'It's something more than that.'

'What do you mean?' Amparo asked.

'When we were going to blow up the dam at Puenta la Reina, Acoca was tipped off.' He looked at Felix. 'He set a trap and caught you and Ricardo and Zamora. If I hadn't been delayed, I would have been captured with you. And look what happened at the *parador*.'

'You heard the manager telephoning the police,' Amparo pointed out.

Jaime nodded. 'Right. Because I had a feeling that something was wrong.'

Amparo's face was sombre. 'Who do you think it is?'

Jaime shook his head. 'I'm not sure. Someone who knows all our plans.'

'Then let's change our plans,' Amparo said. 'We'll meet the others at Logroño and skip Mendavia.'

Jaime glanced at Megan. 'We can't do that. We have to get the sisters to their convent.'

Megan looked at him and thought: *He's already done enough for me. I mustn't put him in greater danger than he's already in.*

'Jaime, I can –'

But he knew what she was going to say. 'Don't worry, Megan. We're all going to get there safely.'

He's changed, Amparo thought. *In the beginning he wanted nothing to do with any of them. Now he's willing to risk his life for her. And he calls her Megan. It's no longer Sister.*

Jaime was going on. 'There are at least fifteen people who know our plans.'

'We have to find out which one it is,' Amparo insisted.

'How do we do that?' Felix asked. He was nervously picking at the edges of the tablecloth.

Jaime said, 'Paco is in Madrid doing some checking for me. I've arranged for him to telephone me here.' He looked at Felix for a moment, then looked away.

What he had not said was that no more than half a dozen people knew the exact route that the three groups were taking. It was true that Felix Carpio had been imprisoned by Acoca. It was also true that that would have provided a perfect alibi for Felix. At the propitious moment, an escape could have been planned for him. *Except that I got him out first*, Jaime thought. *Paco is checking on him. I hope he calls soon.*

Amparo rose and turned to Megan. 'Help me with the dishes.'

The two women began clearing the table and the men went into the living room.

'The nun – she's holding up well,' Felix said.

'Yes.'

'You like her, don't you?'

Jaime found it difficult to look at Felix. 'Yes. I like her.' *And you would betray her along with the rest of us.*

'What about you and Amparo?'

'We're cut from the same cloth. She believes in the cause as much as I do. Her entire family was killed by Franco's Falangists.' Jaime rose and stretched. 'Time to turn in.'

'I don't think I'm going to be able to sleep tonight. Are you certain there's a spy?'

Jaime looked at him and said, 'I'm certain.'

When Jaime came downstairs for breakfast in the morning, Megan did not recognize him. His face had been darkened and he was wearing a wig and a moustache. He was dressed in scruffy clothes. He looked ten years older.

'Good morning,' he said. And his voice coming out of that body startled her.

'Where did you – ?'

'This is a house I use from time to time. I keep an assortment of things here that I need.'

He said it casually, but it gave Megan a sudden insight into the kind of life he led. How many other houses and disguises did he need to stay alive? How many other close calls had he had that she knew nothing about? She remembered the ruthlessness of the men who had attacked the convent and she thought: *If they catch Jaime, they'll show him no mercy. I wish I knew how to protect him.*

And Megan's mind was filled with thoughts she had no right to be thinking.

Amparo prepared breakfast. *Bacalao* – steamed, salted codfish – goat's milk, cheese and thick, hot chocolate with *churros*.

As they were eating, Felix asked, 'How long are we going to stay here?'

Jaime replied casually, 'We'll leave when it gets dark.'

But he had no intention of letting Felix use that information.

'I have some errands to do,' he told Felix. 'I'll need your help.'

'Right.'

Jaime called Amparo aside. 'When Paco calls, tell him I'll be back shortly. Take a message.'

She nodded. 'Be careful.'

'Don't worry.' He turned to Megan. 'Your last day. Tomorrow you'll be at the convent. You must be eager to get there.'

She looked at him a long moment. 'Yes.' *Not eager*, Megan thought. *Anxious. I wish I weren't anxious. I'm going to shut myself away from this, but for the rest of my life, I'm going to wonder what happened to Jaime and Felix and the others.*

Megan stood there watching as Jaime and Felix left. She sensed a tension between the two men that she did not understand.

Amparo was studying her, and Megan remembered her words: *Jaime is too much man for you.*

Amparo said curtly, 'Make up the beds. I'll prepare lunch.'

'All right.'

Megan went into the bedroom. Amparo stood there watching her, then walked into the kitchen.

For the next hour, Megan worked, busily concentrating on cleaning and dusting and polishing, trying not to think, trying to keep her mind off what was bothering her.

I must put him out of my mind, she thought.

It was impossible. He was like a force of nature, taking over everything in his path.

She polished harder.

When Jaime and Felix returned, Amparo was waiting for them at the door. Felix looked pale.

'I'm not feeling too well. I think I'll lie down for a bit.'

They watched him disappear into a bedroom.

'Paco called,' Amparo said excitedly.

'What did he say?'

'He has some information for you, but he didn't want to discuss it on the phone. He's sending someone to meet you. This person will be at the town square at noon.'

Jaime frowned, thoughtful. 'He didn't say who it is?'

'No. Just that it was urgent.'

'Damn it. I – never mind. All right. I'll go and meet him. I want you to keep an eye on Felix.'

She looked at him, puzzled. 'I don't un–?'

'I don't want him using the telephone.'

A flash of understanding crossed her face. 'You think that Felix is – ?'

'Please. Just do as I ask.' He looked at his watch. 'It's almost noon. I'll leave now. I should be back in an hour. Take care, *querida*.'

'Don't worry.'

Megan heard their voices.

I don't want him using the telephone.

You think that Felix is –?

Please. Just do as I ask.

So Felix is the traitor, Megan thought. She had seen him go into his bedroom and close the door. She heard Jaime leave.

Megan walked into the living room.

Amparo turned. 'Have you finished?'

'Not quite, I –' She wanted to ask where Jaime had gone, what they were going to do with Felix, what was going to happen next, but she did not want to discuss that with this woman. *I'll wait until Jaime returns.*

'Finish up,' Amparo said.

Megan turned and went back into the bedroom. She thought about Felix. He had seemed so friendly, so warm. He had asked her many questions, but now that seeming act of friendliness took on a different meaning. The bearded man was looking for information that he could pass on to Colonel Acoca. All their lives were in danger.

Amparo may need help, Megan thought. She started towards the living room, then stopped.

A voice was saying, 'Jaime just left. He will be alone on a bench in the main plaza. Your men should have no trouble picking him up.'

Megan stood there, frozen.

'He's walking, so it should take him about fifteen minutes to get there.'

Megan listened with growing horror.

'Remember our deal, Colonel,' Amparo said into the telephone. 'You promised not to kill him.'

Megan backed into the hallway. Her mind was in a turmoil. So Amparo was the traitor. And she had sent Jaime into a trap.

Backing away quietly, so Amparo would not hear her, Megan turned and ran out the back door. She had no idea how she was going to help Jaime. She knew only that she had to do something. She stepped outside the gate and started down the street, moving as fast as she could without attracting attention, heading towards the centre of the town.

'Please, God. Let me be on time,' Megan prayed.

The walk to the town square was a pleasant one, with side streets shaded by towering trees, but Jaime was unaware of his surroundings. He was thinking about Felix. He had been like a brother to Felix, had given him his full trust. What had turned Felix into a traitor willing to put all their lives in jeopardy? Perhaps Paco's messenger would have the answer. *Why couldn't Paco have discussed it on the telephone?* Jaime wondered.

Jaime was approaching the town square. In the middle of the plaza was a fountain and shady trees with benches scattered around. Children were playing games. A couple of old men were playing *boule*. Half a dozen men were seated on park benches, enjoying the sunshine, reading, dozing, or feeding the pigeons. Jaime crossed the street, slowly moving along the path, and took a seat on one of the benches. He looked at his watch just as the tower clock began chiming noon. Paco's man should be coming.

Out of the corner of his eye, Jaime saw a police car pull up at the far end of the square. He looked in the other direction. A second police car arrived. Officers were getting out, moving towards the park. His heart began to beat faster. It was a trap. But who had set it? Was it Paco, who sent the message, or Amparo who delivered it? She had sent him to the park. But why? Why?

There was no time to worry about that now. He had to escape. But Jaime knew that the moment he tried to make a run for it, they would shoot him down. He could try to bluff it out, but they knew he was there.

Think of something. Fast!

A street away, Megan was hurrying towards the park. As it came into view, she took in the scene at a glance. She saw Jaime seated on a bench, and the policemen closing in on the park from both sides.

Megan's mind was racing. There was no way for Jaime to escape.

Megan was walking past a *tienda*. Ahead of her, blocking her path, a mother was pushing a pram. The woman stopped, set the pram against the wall of the shop and went inside to make a purchase. Without a moment's hesitation, Megan grabbed the handle of the pram and moved across the street into the park.

The police were walking along the benches now, questioning the men seated there. Megan elbowed her way past a policeman and went up to Jaime, pushing the pram ahead of her.

She yelled, '¡*Madre de Dios!* There you are, Manuel! I've been looking everywhere for you. I've had enough! You promised to paint the house this morning, and here you are sitting in the park like some millionaire. Mother was right. You're a good-for-nothing bum. I never should have married you in the first place!'

It took Jaime less than a fraction of a second. He got to his feet. 'Your mother is an expert on bums. She married one. If she –'

'Who are you to talk? If it wasn't for my mother, our baby would starve to death. You certainly don't bring any bread into the house . . .'

The policemen had stopped, taking in the argument.

'If that one was my wife,' one of them muttered, 'I'd send her back to her mother.'

'I'm damned tired of your nagging, woman,' Jaime roared. 'I've warned you before. When we get home, I'm going to teach you a lesson.'

'Good for him,' one of the policemen said.

Jaime and Megan noisily quarrelled their way out of the park, pushing the pram before them. The policemen turned their attention back to the men seated on the benches.

'Identification, please?'

'What's the problem, officer?'

'Never mind. Just show me your papers.'

All over the park, men were pulling out wallets and extracting bits of paper to prove who they were. In the midst of this, a baby began to cry. One of the policemen looked up. The pram had been abandoned at the corner. The quarrelling couple had vanished.

Thirty minutes later, Megan walked in at the front door of the house. Amparo was nervously pacing up and down.

'Where have you been?' Amparo demanded. 'You shouldn't have left the house without telling me.'

'I had to go out to take care of something.'

'What?' Amparo asked suspiciously. 'You don't know anyone here. If you –'

Jaime walked in through the door. The blood drained from her face. She quickly regained her composure.

'What – what happened?' Amparo asked. 'Didn't you go to the park?'

Jaime said quietly, 'Why, Amparo?'

And she looked into his eyes and she knew it was over.

'What made you change?'

She shook her head. 'I haven't changed. You have. I've lost everyone I loved in this stupid war you're fighting. I'm sick of all the bloodshed. Can you stand hearing the truth about yourself, Jaime? You're as bad as the government you're fighting. Worse, because they're willing to make peace, and you're not. You think you're helping our country? You're destroying it. You rob banks and blow up cars and murder innocent people, and you think you're a hero. I loved you, and I believed in you once, but –' Her voice broke. 'This bloodshed has to end.'

Jaime walked up to her, and his eyes were ice. 'I should kill you.'

'No,' Megan gasped. 'Please! You can't.'

Felix had come into the room and was listening to the conversation. 'Jesus Christ! So she's the one. What do we do with the bitch?'

Jaime said, 'We'll have to take her with us and keep an eye on her.' He took Amparo by the shoulders and said softly, 'If you try one more trick, I promise you you'll die.' He shoved her away and turned to Megan and Felix. 'Let's get out of here before her friends arrive.'

490

35

'You had Miró in your hands and you let him escape?'

'Colonel – with all due respect – my men –'

'Your men are assholes. You call yourselves policemen? You're a disgrace to your uniforms.'

The chief of police stood there, cringing under the withering scorn of Colonel Acoca. There was nothing else he could do, for the Colonel was powerful enough to have his head. And Acoca was not yet through with him.

'I hold you personally responsible. I'll see that you're relieved from duty.'

'Colonel –'

'Get out. You make me sick to my stomach.'

Colonel Acoca was boiling with frustration. There had not been enough time for him to reach Vitoria and catch Jaime Miró. He had had to entrust that to the local police. And they had bungled it. God alone knew where Miró had gone to now.

Colonel Acoca went to the map spread out on a table in front of him. *They will be staying in Basque country, of course. That could be Burgos or Logroño or Bilbao or San Sebastian. I'll concentrate on the north-east. They'll have to surface somewhere.*

He recalled his conversation with the Prime Minister that morning.

'Your time is running out, Colonel. Have you read the morning papers? The world press is making us look like clowns. Miró and those nuns have made us a laughingstock.'

'Prime Minister, you have my assurance –'

'King Juan Carlos has ordered me to set up an official inquiry board into the whole matter. I can't hold it off any longer.'

'Delay the inquiry for just a few more days. I'll have Miró and the nuns by then.'

There was a pause. 'Forty-eight hours.'

It was not the Prime Minister whom Colonel Acoca was afraid of disappointing, nor was it the King. It was the OPUS MUNDO. When he had been summoned to the panelled office of one of Spain's leading industrialists, his orders had been explicit: 'Jaime Miró is creating an atmosphere harmful to our organization. Stop him. You will be well rewarded.'

And Colonel Acoca knew what the unspoken part of the conversation was: *Fail and you will be punished.* Now his career was in jeopardy. And all because some stupid policemen had let Miró walk away under

491

their noses. Jaime Miró might hide anywhere. But the nuns . . . A wave of excitement coursed through Colonel Acoca. The nuns! They were the key. Jaime Miró might hide anywhere, but the sisters could find sanctuary only in another convent. And it would almost certainly be in a convent of the same order.

Colonel Acoca turned to study the map again. And there it was: *Mendavia*. There was a convent of the Cistercian order at Mendavia. *That's where they're headed*, Acoca thought triumphantly. *Well, so am I.*

Only I'll be there first, waiting for them.

The journey for Ricardo and Graciela was coming to an end.

The last few days had been the happiest that Ricardo had ever known. He was being hunted by the military and the police, his capture meant certain death, and yet none of that seemed to matter. It was as though he and Graciela had carved out an island in time, a paradise where nothing could touch them. They had turned their desperate journey into a wonderful adventure that they shared together.

They talked endlessly, exploring and explaining, and their words were tendrils that drew them even closer together. They spoke of the past, the present, and the future. Particularly the future.

'We'll be married in church,' Ricardo said. 'You'll be the most beautiful bride in the world . . .'

And Graciela could visualize the scene and was thrilled by it.

'And we'll live in the most beautiful house . . .'

And she thought: *I've never had a house of my own, or a real room of my own.*

There was the little casa she shared with her mother and all the uncles, and then the convent cell, living with the sisters.

'And we'll have handsome sons and beautiful daughters . . .'

And I will give them all the things I never had. They will be so loved.

And Graciela's heart soared.

There was one thing troubling her. Ricardo was a soldier fighting for a cause he passionately believed in. Would he be contented living in France, withdrawing from the battle? She knew she had to discuss it with him.

Ricardo – how much longer do you think this revolution is going to go on?

It was a question she had not asked.

It's already gone on too long, Ricardo thought. The government had made peace overtures, but ETA had rejected them. It had done worse than reject them. It had responded to the offers with a series of increased terrorist attacks. Ricardo had tried to discuss it with Jaime.

'They're willing to compromise, Jaime. Shouldn't we meet them half way?'

'Their offer is a trick – they want to destroy us. They're forcing us to go on fighting.'

And because Ricardo loved Jaime and believed in him, he continued to support him. But the doubts refused to die. And as the bloodshed increased, so did his uncertainty. And now Graciela was asking, *How much longer do you think this revolution is going to go on?*

'I don't know,' Ricardo told her. 'I wish it were over. But I will tell you this, my darling. Nothing will ever come between us – not even a war. There will never be words enough to tell you how much I love you.'

And they went on dreaming.

They travelled during the night, making their way through the fertile, green countryside, past El Burgo and Soria. At dawn, from the top of a hill, they saw Logroño in the far distance. To the left of the road was a stand of pine trees and beyond that a forest of electric power lines. Graciela and Ricardo followed the winding road down to the outskirts of the bustling city.

'Where are we going to meet the others?' Graciela asked.

Ricardo pointed to a poster on a building they were passing. It read:

CIRQUE JAPON!
THE WORLD'S MOST SENSATIONAL CIRCUS FRESH FROM JAPAN!
24 JULY FOR ONE WEEK
AVENIDA CLUB DEPORTIVO

'There,' Ricardo told her. 'We'll meet them there this afternoon.'

In another part of the city, Megan, Jaime, Amparo and Felix were also looking at a circus poster. There was a feeling of enormous tension in the group. Amparo was never out of their sight. Ever since the incident at Vitoria, the men treated Amparo as an outcast, ignoring her most of the time and speaking to her only when necessary.

Jaime looked at his watch. 'The circus should be starting,' he said. 'Let's go.'

At police headquarters in Logroño, Colonel Ramón Acoca was finalizing his plans.

'Are the men deployed around the convent?'

'Yes, Colonel. Everything is in place.'

'Excellent.'

Acoca was in an expansive mood. The trap he had set was foolproof, and there would be no bungling policemen to spoil his plans this time.

493

He was personally conducting the operation. The OPUS MUNDO was going to be proud of him. He went over the details with his officers once again.

'The nuns are travelling with Miró and his men. It's important that we catch them *before* they walk into the convent. We'll be spread out in the woods around it. Don't move until I give the signal to close in.'

'What are our orders if Jaime Miró resists?'

Acoca said softly, 'I hope he does try to resist.'

An orderly came into the room. 'Excuse me, Colonel. There is an American here who would like to speak to you.'

'I have no time now.'

'Yes, sir.' The orderly hesitated. 'He says it's about one of the nuns.'

'Oh? An American, did you say?'

'Yes, Colonel.'

'Send him in.'

A moment later, Alan Tucker was ushered in.

'I'm sorry to disturb you, Colonel. I'm Alan Tucker. I'm hoping you can help me.'

'Yes? How, Mr Tucker?'

'I understand that you're looking for one of the nuns from the Abbey Cistercian – a Sister Megan.'

The Colonel sat back in his chair, studying the American. 'How does that concern you?'

'I'm looking for her too. It's very important that I find her.'

Interesting, Colonel Acoca thought. *Why is it so important for this American to find a nun?* 'You have no idea where she is?'

'No. The newspapers –'

The goddamn press again. 'Perhaps you could tell me why you are looking for her.'

'I'm afraid I can't discuss that.'

'Then I'm afraid I can't help you.'

'Colonel – could you let me know if you find her?'

Acoca gave him a thin smile. 'You'll know.'

The whole country was following the hegira of the nuns. The press had reported the narrow escape of Jaime Miró and one of the nuns in Vitoria.

So they're heading north, Alan Tucker thought. *Their best bet to get out of the country is probably San Sebastian. I've got to get hold of her.* He sensed that he was in trouble with Ellen Scott. *I handled that badly*, he thought. *I can make up for it by bringing her Megan.*

He placed a call to Ellen Scott.

The Cirque Japon was held in Logroño's outlying district of Guanos, in a huge tent, and ten minutes before the circus was due to begin, the tent was filled to capacity. Megan, Jaime, Amparo and Felix made their way down the crowded aisle to their reserved seats. There were two empty seats next to Jaime.

He stared at them and said, 'Something's wrong. Ricardo and Sister Graciela were supposed to be here.' He turned to Amparo. 'Did you –?'

'No. I swear it. I know nothing about it.'

The lights dimmed and the show began. There was a roar from the crowd, and they turned to look at the arena. A bicycle rider was circling the ring, and as he pedalled an acrobat leaped onto his shoulder. Then, one by one, a swarm of other performers jumped on, clinging to the front and back and sides of the bicycle until it was invisible. The audience cheered.

A trained bear act was on next, and then a tightrope walker. The audience was enjoying the show tremendously, but Jaime and the others were too nervous to pay any attention. Time was running out.

'We'll wait another fifteen minutes,' Jaime decided. 'If they're not here by then –'

A voice said, 'Excuse me – are these seats taken?'

Jaime looked up to see Ricardo and Graciela, and grinned. 'No. Please sit down.' And then, in a relieved whisper, 'I'm damned glad to see you.'

Ricardo nodded at Megan and Amparo and Felix. He looked around. 'Where are the others?'

'Haven't you seen the newspapers?'

'Newspapers? No. We've been in the mountains.'

'I have bad news,' Jaime said. 'Rubio is in a prison hospital.'

Ricardo stared at him. 'How –?'

'He was stabbed in a bar fight. The police picked him up.'

'*Mierda!*' Ricardo was silent a moment, then sighed. 'We'll just have to get him out, won't we?'

'That's my plan,' Jaime agreed.

'Where's Sister Lucia?' Graciela asked. 'And Sister Teresa?'

It was Megan who answered. 'Sister Lucia has been arrested. She was – she was wanted for murder. Sister Teresa is dead.'

Graciela crossed herself. 'Oh, my Lord.'

In the arena a clown was walking a tightrope, carrying a poodle under each arm, and two Siamese cats in his capacious pockets. As the dogs tried to reach the cats, the wire swayed wildly and the clown pretended to be fighting to keep his balance. The audience was roaring. It was difficult to hear anything over the noise of the crowd. Megan and Graciela had so much to tell each other. Almost simultaneously, they began to talk in the sign language of the convent. The two men looked on in astonishment.

Ricardo and I are going to marry . . .

That's wonderful . . .

What has been happening to you?

Megan started to reply and realized there were no signs to convey the things she wanted to say. It would have to wait.

'Let's move,' Jaime said. 'There's a van outside waiting to take us to Mendavia. We'll drop the sisters off there and be on our way.'

They started up the aisle, Jaime holding Amparo's arm.

When they were outside in the car-park, Ricardo said, 'Jaime, Graciela and I are getting married.'

A grin lit up Jaime's face. 'That's wonderful! Congratulations.' He turned to Graciela. 'You couldn't have picked a better man.'

Megan put her arms around Graciela. 'I'm very happy for you both.'

And she thought: *Was it easy for her to make the decision to leave the convent? Am I wondering about Graciela? Or am I wondering about myself?*

Colonel Acoca was receiving an excited report from an aide.

'They were seen at the circus less than an hour ago. By the time we could bring up reinforcements, they had gone. They left in a blue and white van. You were right, Colonel. They are headed for Mendavia.'

So it's finally over, Colonel Acoca thought. The chase had been an exciting one, and he had to admit that Jaime Miró had been a worthy opponent. *The OPUS MUNDO will have even bigger plans for me now.*

Through a pair of high-powered Zeiss binoculars, Colonel Acoca watched the blue and white van appear over the crest of a hill and head for the convent below. Heavily armed troops were hidden among the trees along both sides of the road and around the convent itself. There was no way that anyone could escape.

As the van approached the entrance to the convent and braked to a stop, Colonel Acoca barked into his walkie-talkie, 'Close in! Now!'

The manoeuvre was executed perfectly. Two squads of soldiers armed with automatic weapons swung into position, blocking the road and surrounding the van. Colonel Acoca stood watching the scene for an instant, savouring his moment of glory. Then he slowly approached the van, gun in hand.

'You're surrounded,' he called out. 'You haven't got a chance. Come out with your hands up. One at a time. If you try to resist, you'll all die.'

There was a long moment of silence, and then the van door slowly opened and three men and three women emerged, trembling, their hands raised high above their heads.

They were strangers.

36

High on a hill above the convent, Jaime and the others observed Acoca and his men move in on the van. They saw the terrified passengers get out, hands raised, and watched the scene played out in pantomime.

Jaime Miró could almost hear the dialogue:

Who are you?

We work at a hotel outside Logroño.

What are you doing here?

A man gave us five thousand pesetas to deliver this van to the convent.

What man?

I don't know. I never saw him before.

Is this his picture?

Yes. That's him.

'Let's get out of here,' Jaime said.

They were in a white station wagon, heading back to Logroño. Megan was looking at Jaime in wonder.

'How did you know?'

'That Colonel Acoca would be waiting for us at the convent? He told me.'

'*What?*'

'The fox has to think like the hunter, Megan. I put myself in Acoca's place. Where would he set a trap for me? He did exactly what I would have done.'

'And if he had not shown up?'

'Then it would have been safe to take you into the convent.'

'What happens now?' Felix asked.

It was the question uppermost in all their minds.

'Spain isn't safe for any of us for a while,' Jaime decided. 'We'll head directly for San Sebastian and into France.' He looked at Megan. 'There are Cistercian convents there.'

It was more than Amparo could bear.

'Why don't you give yourself up? If you keep on this way, there will be more blood spilled and more lives taken –'

'You've lost the right to speak,' Jaime said curtly. 'Just be grateful you're still alive.' He turned to Megan. 'There are ten mountain passes across the Pyrenees leading from San Sebastian to France. We'll cross there.'

'It's too dangerous,' Felix objected. 'Acoca's going to be looking for us in San Sebastian. He'll be expecting us to cross the border into France.'

'If it's that dangerous –' Graciela began.

'Don't worry,' Jaime assured her. 'San Sebastian is Basque country.'

The station wagon was approaching the outskirts of Logroño again.

'All the roads to San Sebastian will be watched,' Felix warned. 'How do you plan for us to get there?'

Jaime had already decided. 'We'll take the train.'

'The soldiers will be searching the trains,' Ricardo objected.

Jaime gave Amparo a thoughtful look. 'No. I don't think so. Our friend here is going to help us. Do you know how to reach Colonel Acoca?'

She hesitated. 'Yes.'

'Good. You're going to call him.'

They stopped at one of the telephone booths along the highway. Jaime followed Amparo into the booth and closed the door. He was holding a pistol to her side.

'You know what to say?'

'Yes.'

He watched her dial a number, and when a voice answered, she said, 'This is Amparo Jiron. Colonel Acoca is expecting my call . . . Thank you.' She looked up at Jaime. 'They're putting me through.' The gun was pressing against her. 'Do you have to –?'

'Just do as you were told.' His voice was ice.

A moment later, Jaime heard Acoca's voice come over the phone. 'Where are you?'

The gun pressed against her harder. 'I – I'm – we're just leaving Logroño.'

'Do you know where our friends are going?'

'Yes.'

Jaime's face was inches from her, his eyes hard.

'They've decided to reverse themselves to throw you off. They're on their way to Barcelona. He's driving a white Seat. He'll be taking the main highway.'

Jaime nodded at her.

'I – I have to go now. The car is here.'

Jaime pressed down the receiver. 'Very good. Let's go. We'll give him half an hour to call off his men here.'

Thirty minutes later they were at the railway station.

There were three classes of trains from Logroño to San Sebastian: the *Talgo* was the luxury train; the second classtrain was the *Ter;* and the worst and cheapest trains, uncomfortable and dirty, were misnamed

498

the *expresos*, which stopped at every little station from Logroño to San Sebastian.

Jaime said, 'We'll take the *expreso*. By now all of Acoca's men will be busy stopping every white Seat on the road to Barcelona. We'll buy our tickets separately and meet in the last compartment of the train.' Jaime turned to Amparo. 'You go first. I'll be right behind you.'

And she knew why, and hated him for it. If Colonel Acoca had set a trap, she would be the bait. Well, she was Amparo Jiron. She would not flinch.

She walked into the station while Jaime and the others watched. There were no soldiers.

They're all out covering the highway to Barcelona. It's going to be a madhouse, Jaime thought wryly. *Every other car is a white Seat.*

One by one the group purchased their tickets and headed for the train. They boarded without incident. Jaime took the seat next to Megan. Amparo sat in front of them, next to Felix. Across the way Ricardo and Graciela sat together.

Jaime said to Megan, 'We'll reach San Sebastian in three hours. We'll spend the night there and in the early morning we'll cross over into France.'

'And after we get to France?'

She was thinking of what would happen to Jaime, but when he replied, he said, 'Don't worry. There's a Cistercian convent just a few hours across the border.' He hesitated. 'If that's what you still want.'

So he had understood her doubts. *Is that what I want?* They were coming to more than a border that divided two countries. This border would divide her old life from her future life . . . which would be . . . what? She had been desperate to return to a convent, but now she was filled with doubts. She had forgotten how exciting the world outside the walls could be. *I've never felt so alive.* Megan looked over at Jaime and admitted to herself: *And Jaime Miró is a part of it.*

He caught her glance and looked into her eyes, and Megan thought: *He knows it.*

The *expreso* stopped at every hamlet and village along the track. The train was packed with farmers and their wives, merchants and salesmen, and at each stop passengers noisily embarked and disembarked.

The *expreso* made its way slowly through the mountains, fighting the steep gradients.

When the train finally pulled into the station in San Sebastian, Jaime said to Megan, 'The danger is over. This is our city. I've arranged for a car to be here for us.'

A large sedan was waiting in front of the station. A driver wearing a *boina vasca*, the big, wide-brimmed beret of the Basques, greeted Jaime with warm hugs, and the group got into the car.

Megan noticed that Jaime stayed close to Amparo, ready to grab her if she tried to make a move. *What's he going to do with her?* Megan wondered.

'We were worried about you, Jaime,' the driver said. 'According to the press, Colonel Acoca is conducting a big hunt for you.'

Jaime laughed. 'Let him keep hunting, Gil. I am out of season.'

They drove down the Avenida Sancho el Savio, towards the beach. It was a cloudless summer day and the streets were crowded with strolling couples bent on pleasure, and the harbour was alive with yachts and smaller craft. The distant mountains formed a picturesque backdrop for the city. Everything seemed so peaceful.

'What are the arrangements?' Jaime asked the driver.

'The Hotel Niza. Largo Cortez is waiting for you.'

'It will be good to see the old pirate again.'

The Niza was a medium class hotel in the Plaza Juan de Olezabal, off San Martin Street on the corner of a busy square. It was a white building with brown shutters and a big blue sign on the top of the roof. The rear of the hotel backed on to a beach.

When the car pulled up in front of the hotel, the group got out and followed Jaime into the lobby.

Largo Cortez, the hotel owner, ran up to greet them. He was a large man. He had only one arm as the result of a daring exploit, and he moved awkwardly, as though off-balance.

'Welcome,' he beamed. 'I have been expecting you for a week now.'

Jaime shrugged. 'We had a few delays, *amigo*.'

Largo Cortez grinned. 'I read about them. The papers are full of nothing else.' He turned to look at Megan and Graciela. 'Everyone is supporting you, Sisters. I have your rooms all prepared.'

'We'll be staying overnight,' Jaime told him. 'We'll leave first thing in the morning and cross into France. I want a good guide who knows all the passes – either Cabrera Infante or José Cebrian.'

'I will arrange it,' the hotel owner assured him. 'There will be six of you?'

Jaime glanced at Amparo. 'Five.'

Amparo looked away.

'I suggest that none of you registers,' Cortez said. 'What the police don't know won't hurt them. Why don't you let me take you to your rooms, where you can refresh yourselves? Then we'll have a magnificent supper.'

'Amparo and I are going to the bar to have a drink,' Jaime said. 'We'll join you later.'

Largo Cortez nodded. 'As you wish, Jaime.'

Megan was watching Jaime, puzzled. She wondered what he planned to do with Amparo. Was he going to cold-bloodedly –? She could not bear even to think about it.

Amparo was wondering, too, but she was too proud to ask.

Jaime led her into the bar at the far end of the lobby and took a table in the corner.

When the waiter approached them, Jaime said, 'A glass of wine, *por favor*.'

'One?'

'One.'

Amparo watched as Jaime took out a small packet and opened it. It contained a fine, powdery substance.

'Jaime –' There was desperation in Amparo's voice. 'Please listen to me! Try to understand why I did what I did. You're tearing the country apart. Your cause is hopeless. You must stop this insanity.'

The waiter reappeared and set a glass of wine on the table. When he walked away, Jaime carefully poured the contents of the packet into the glass and stirred it. He pushed the glass in front of Amparo.

'Drink it.'

'No!'

'Not many of us are privileged to choose the way we die,' Jaime said quietly. 'This way will be quick and painless. If I turn you over to my people, I can't make any such promise.'

'Jaime – I loved you once. You must believe me. Please –'

'Drink it.' His voice was implacable.

Amparo looked at him for a long moment, then picked up the glass. 'I'll drink to your death.'

He watched as Amparo put the glass to her lips and swallowed the wine in one gulp.

She shuddered. 'What happens now?'

'I'll help you upstairs. I'll put you to bed. You'll sleep.'

Amparo's eyes filled with tears. 'You're a fool,' she whispered. 'Jaime – I'm dying, and I tell you that I loved you so –' Her words were beginning to slur.

Jaime rose and helped Amparo to her feet. She stood up, unsteady. The room seemed to be rocking.

'Jaime –'

He guided her out of the door and into the lobby, holding her up. Largo Cortez was waiting for him with a key.

'I'll take her to her room,' Jaime said. 'See that she's not disturbed.'

'Right.'

Cortez watched as Jaime half-carried Amparo up the stairs.

In her room, Megan was thinking how strange it felt to be by herself in a hotel in a resort town. San Sebastian was filled with people on holiday, honeymooners, lovers enjoying themselves in a hundred other hotel rooms.

501

But what had Jaime done to Amparo? Could he possibly have . . . but no, he could never have done that. Or could he?

And suddenly Megan wished Jaime were there with her, and wondered what it would be like to have him making love to her. All the feelings that she had been suppressing for so long came flooding into her mind in a wild torrent of emotions. *I want him*, she thought. *Oh, Lord, what's happening to me? What can I do?*

Ricardo was whistling as he dressed. He was in a wonderful mood. *I'm the luckiest man in the world*, he thought. *We'll be married in France. There's a beautiful church across the border in Bayonne. Tomorrow . . .*

In her room, Graciela was taking a bath, luxuriating in the warm water, thinking of Ricardo. She smiled to herself and thought: *I'm going to make him so happy. Thank you, God.*

Felix Carpio was thinking about Jaime and Megan. *A blind man can see the electricity between them*, he thought. *It is going to bring bad luck. Nuns belong to God. It's bad enough that Ricardo has taken Sister Graciela from her calling.* But Jaime had always been reckless. What was he going to do about this one?

The five of them met for supper in the hotel dining room. No one mentioned Amparo.

Looking at Jaime, Megan felt suddenly embarrassed, as though he could read her mind. *It's better not to ask questions*, she decided. I know he could never do anything brutal.

They found that Largo Cortez had not exaggerated about the supper. The meal began with *gazpacho*, the thick, cold soup made from tomatoes, cucumbers and water-soaked bread, followed by a salad of fresh greens, a huge dish of *paella* – rice, shrimp, chicken and beef in a wonderful sauce, and ended with a delicious flan. It was the first hot meal Ricardo and Graciela had had in a long time.

When the meal was over, Megan rose. 'I should be getting to bed.'

'Wait,' Jaime said. 'I've got to talk to you.' He escorted her to a deserted corner of the lobby. 'About tomorrow . . .'

'Yes?'

And she knew what he was going to ask. What she did not know was what *she* was going to answer. *I've changed*, Megan thought. *I was so sure about my life before. I believed I had everything I wanted.*

And Jaime was saying, 'You don't really want to go back to a convent, do you?'

Do I?

He was waiting for an answer.

I have to be honest with him, Megan thought. She looked into his eyes and said, 'I don't know what I want, Jaime. I'm confused.'

Jaime smiled. He hesitated, choosing his words carefully. 'Megan – this fight will be over soon. We'll get what we want because the people are behind us. I can't ask you to share the danger with me now, but I would like you to wait for me. I have many Basque friends living in France. You would be safe with them.'

Megan looked at him a long time before she answered. 'Jaime – give me time to think about it.'

'Then you're not saying no?'

Megan said quietly, 'I'm not saying no.'

None of the group slept that night. They had too much to think about, too many conflicts to resolve. Megan stayed awake, reliving the past. The years in the orphanage, and the sanctuary of the convent . . . The sudden expulsion into a world she had given up for ever. Jaime Miró was risking his life fighting for what he believed in. *And what do I believe in?* Megan asked herself. *How do I want to spend the rest of my life?*

She had made a choice once. Now she was forced to choose again. She would have to have an answer by morning.

Graciela was thinking about the convent, too. *They were such happy, peaceful years. I felt so close to God. Will I miss that?*

Jaime was thinking about Megan. *She mustn't go back. I want her at my side. What will her answer be?*

Ricardo was too excited to sleep, busily making plans for the wedding. The church at Bayonne . . .

Felix was wondering how to dispose of Amparo's body. *Let Largo Cortez take care of it.*

Early the following morning, the group met in the lobby. Jaime approached Megan.

'Good morning.'

'Good morning.'

'Have you thought about our conversation?'

She had thought of nothing else all night. 'Yes, Jaime.'

He looked into her eyes, trying to read the answer there. 'Will you wait for me?'

'Jaime –'

At that moment Largo Cortez hurried up to them. With him was a leathery-looking man in his fifties.

'I'm afraid there won't be any time for breakfast,' Cortez said. 'You should be leaving. This is José Cebrian, your guide. He will take you across the mountains into France. He's the best guide in San Sebastian.'

'I'm glad to see you, José,' Jaime said. 'What's your plan?'

'We're going to take the first part of the journey by foot,' José Cebrian told the group. 'On the other side of the border, I've arranged for cars to be waiting for us. We should hurry. Come along, please.'

The group moved out into the street, painted yellow by the rays of the bright sun.

Largo Cortez came out of the hotel to see them off. 'Safe journey,' he said.

'Thank you for everything,' Jaime replied. 'We'll be back, *amigo*. Sooner than you think.'

'We go this way,' José Cebrian ordered.

The group started to turn towards the square. And at that moment, soldiers and members of the GOE suddenly materialized at both ends of the street, sealing it off. There were at least a dozen of them, all heavily armed. Colonel Ramón Acoca and Colonel Fal Sostelo were leading them.

Jaime glanced quickly towards the beach, looking for an escape route. Another dozen soldiers were approaching from there. There was no escape. They would have to fight. Jaime instinctively reached for his gun.

Colonel Acoca called out, 'Don't even think about it, Miró, or we'll shoot all of you down where you're standing.'

Jaime's mind was racing furiously, looking for a way out. How had Acoca known where to find him? Jaime turned and saw Amparo standing in the doorway, a look of profound sorrow on her face.

Felix said, 'What the bloody hell! I thought you –'

'I gave her sleeping pills. They should have knocked her out until we got across the border.'

'The bitch!'

Colonel Acoca walked towards Jaime. 'It's over.' He turned to one of his men. 'Disarm them.'

Felix and Ricardo were looking towards Jaime for guidance, ready to follow his lead. Jaime shook his head. Reluctantly, he handed over his gun, and Felix and Ricardo followed suit.

'What are you going to do with us?' Jaime asked.

Several passersby stopped to watch the proceedings.

Colonel Acoca's voice was curt. 'I'm taking you and your gang of murderers back to Madrid. We'll give you a fair military trial and then hang you. If I had my way, I'd hang you here, now.'

'Let the sisters go,' Jaime said. 'They had nothing to do with this.'

'They're accomplices. They're as guilty as you are.'

Colonel Acoca turned and gave a signal. The soldiers motioned to the onlookers to move aside to let three army trucks drive up.

'You and your assassins will travel in the middle truck,' the Colonel informed Jaime. 'My men will be in front of you and at the back of you. If any of you makes one false move, they have orders to kill all of you. Do you understand?'

Jaime nodded.

Colonel Acoca spat into Jaime's face. 'Good. Into the truck.'

There was an angry murmur from the growing crowd.

Amparo watched impassively from the doorway as Jaime and Megan, Graciela and Ricardo and Felix climbed into the truck, surrounded by soldiers with automatic weapons.

Colonel Fal Sostelo walked up to the driver of the first truck. 'We'll head straight for Madrid. No stops along the way.'

'Yes, Colonel.'

By now, many people had gathered in the street to watch what was happening. Colonel Acoca started to climb into the first truck. He called out to those in front of the truck, 'Clear the way.'

From the side streets more people began to emerge.

'Move along,' Colonel Acoca called. 'Out of the way.'

And still they came, the men wearing the wide Basque *boinas*. It was as though they were responding to some invisible signal. *Jaime Miró is in trouble*. They came from shops and homes. Housewives dropped what they were doing and moved out into the street. Shopkeepers about to open for business heard the news and hurried on to the hotel. And still they came. Artists and plumbers and doctors, mechanics and salesmen and students, many carrying shotguns and rifles. They were Basques, and this was their homeland. It started with a few, and then a hundred, and within minutes it had swollen to more than a thousand, filling the pavements and streets, completely surrounding the army trucks. They were ominously silent.

Colonel Acoca observed the huge crowd in desperation. He screamed, 'Everybody get out of the way or we'll start shooting.'

Jaime called out, 'I wouldn't advise it. These people hate you for what you're trying to do to them. A word from me and they'll tear you and your men to pieces. There's one thing you forgot, Colonel. San Sebastian is a Basque town. It's my town.' He turned to his group. 'Let's get out of here.'

Jaime helped Megan down from the truck, and the others followed. Colonel Acoca watched helplessly, his face tight with fury.

The crowd was waiting, hostile and silent. Jaime walked up to the Colonel. 'Take your trucks and get back to Madrid.'

Acoca looked around at the still growing mob. 'I – you won't get away with this, Miró.'

'I have got away with it. Now get out of here.' He spat in Acoca's face.

The Colonel stared at him for a long, murderous moment. *It can't end this way*, he thought desperately. *I was so close. It was checkmate.* But he knew that it was worse than a defeat for him. It was a death sentence. The OPUS MUNDO would be waiting for him in Madrid. He looked at the sea of people surrounding him. He had no choice.

He turned to his driver, and his voice was choked with fury. 'We're moving out.'

The crowd stepped back, watching as the soldiers climbed into the trucks. A moment later, the trucks began rolling down the street, and the crowd began to cheer wildly. It started out as a cheer for Jaime Miró, and it grew louder and louder, and they were cheering for their freedom and their fight against tyranny, and their coming victory, and the streets reverberated with the noise of their celebration.

Two teenagers were screaming themselves hoarse. One turned to the other. 'Let's join ETA.'

An elderly couple held each other, and the woman said, 'Now maybe they'll give us back our farm.'

An old man stood alone in the crowd, silently watching the army trucks leave. When he spoke, he said, 'They'll be back one day.'

Jaime took Megan's hand and said, 'It's over. We're free. We'll be across the border in an hour. I'll take you to my aunt.'

She looked into his eyes. 'Jaime –'

A man pushed his way towards them through the crowd and hurried up to Megan.

'Excuse me,' he said breathlessly. 'Are you Sister Megan?'

She turned to him, puzzled. 'Yes.'

He breathed a sigh of relief. 'I've had quite a time finding you. My name is Alan Tucker. I wonder if I could speak to you for a moment?'

'Yes.'

'Alone.'

'I'm sorry. I'm just leaving for –'

'Please. This is very important. I've come all the way from New York to find you.'

She looked at him, puzzled. 'To find me? I don't understand. Why –?'

'I'll explain it to you, if you'll give me a moment.'

The stranger took her arm and walked her down the street, talking rapidly. Megan glanced back once at where Jaime Miró was standing, waiting for her.

Megan's conversation with Alan Tucker turned her world upside down.

'The woman I represent would like to see you.'

506

'I don't understand. What woman? What does she want with me?'

I wish I knew the answer to that, Alan Tucker thought. 'I'm not at liberty to discuss that. She's waiting for you in New York.'

It made no sense. There must be some mistake. 'Are you sure you have the right person – Sister Megan?'

'Yes. But your name isn't Megan. It's Patricia.'

And in a sudden, blinding flash, Megan knew. After all these years, her fantasy was about to come true. She was finally going to learn who she was. The very idea of it was thrilling . . . and terrifying.

'When – when would I have to leave?' Her throat was suddenly so dry that she could barely speak the words.

I want you to find out where she is and bring her back as quickly as possible.

'Right away. I'll arrange a passport for you.'

She turned and saw Jaime standing in front of the hotel, waiting.

'Excuse me a moment.'

Megan walked back to him in a daze, and she felt as though she were living a dream.

'Are you all right?' Jaime asked. 'Is that man bothering you?'

'No. He's – no.'

Jaime took Megan's hand. 'I want you to come with me now. We belong together, Megan.'

Your name isn't Megan. It's Patricia.

And she looked at Jaime's strong, handsome face, and she thought: *I want us to be together. But we'll have to wait. First I have to find out who I am.*

'Jaime – I want to be with you. But there is something I have to do first.'

He studied her, his face troubled. 'You're going to leave?'

'For a little while. But I'll be back.'

He looked at her for a long time, then slowly nodded. 'All right. You can reach me through Largo Cortez.'

'I'll come back to you. I promise.'

And she meant it. But that was before the meeting with Ellen Scott.

37

'Deus Israel vos; et ipse sit vobiscum, qui, misertus est duobus unicis
plenius benedis cere . . . The God of Israel joins you together, and He
be with you and now, Lord, make them bless Thee more fully. Blessed
are all they that love the Lord, that walk in His ways. Glory . . .'

Ricardo looked away from the priest and glanced at Graciela standing
at his side. *I was right. She is the most beautiful bride in the world.*

Graciela was still, listening to the words of the priest echoing through
the cavernous, vaulted church. There was such a sense of peace in the
church. It seemed to Graciela to be filled with the ghosts of the past,
all the thousands of people who had come here generation after generation, to find forgiveness and fulfilment and joy. It reminded her so much
of the convent. *I feel as though I've come home again*, Graciela thought.
As though I belong.

'Exaudi nos, omni potens et misericors deus; ut quod nostro ministra-
tur officio tua benedictione potius impleatua per dominum . . . Hear
us, Almighty and merciful God, that what is done by our ministry may
be abundantly fulfilled with Thy blessing . . .'

He has blessed me, more than I deserve. Let me be worthy of Him.

'In te sperav, domine: Dixi: Tues deus meus: in manibus tuis tempora
mea . . .'

'In Thee, O Lord, have I hoped; I said: Thou art my God; my times
are in Thy hands . . .'

*My times are in Thy hands. I took a solemn vow to devote the rest of
my life to Him.*

'Suscipe quaesumus domine, pro sacra connubii lege munus
oblatum . . .'

'Receive, we beseech Thee, O Lord, the offering we make to Thee
on behalf of the holy hands of wedlock . . .'

The words seemed to reverberate in Graciela's head. She felt as
though time had stopped.

'Deus qui potestate virtutis tuae de nihilo cuneta fecisti . . .'

'Oh, God, who has hallowed wedlock to foreshadow the union of
Christ with the church . . . look in Thy mercy upon this, Thy handmaid,
who is to be joined in wedlock and entreats protection and strength
from Thee . . .'

But how can He show me mercy when I am betraying Him?

Graciela was suddenly finding it difficult to breathe. The walls seemed
to be closing in on her.

'Nihil in ea ex actibus suis ille auctor praevaricationis usurpet . . .'

'Let the father of sin work none of his evil deeds in her . . .'

That was the moment when Graciela knew. And she felt as though a great burden had been lifted from her. She was filled with an exalted, ineffable joy.

The priest was saying, 'May she win the peace of the kingdom of heaven. We ask Thee to bless this marriage, and –'

'I'm already married,' Graciela said aloud.

There was a moment of shocked silence. Ricardo and the priest were staring at her. Ricardo's face was pale.

'Graciela, what are you –?'

She took his arm and said gently, 'I'm sorry, Ricardo.'

'I – I don't understand. Have – have you stopped loving me?'

She shook her head. 'I love you more than my life. But my life doesn't belong to me any more. I gave it to God a long time ago.'

'No! I can't let you sacrifice your –'

'Darling Ricardo . . . It is not a sacrifice. It's a blessing. In the convent I found the first peace I had ever known. You're a part of the world I gave up – the best part. But I did give it up. I must return to my world.'

The priest was standing there, listening, silent.

'Please forgive me for the pain I am causing you, but I can't go back on my vows. I would be betraying everything I believe in. I know that now. I could never make you happy, because I could never be happy. Please understand.'

Ricardo stared at her, shaken, and no words would come. It was as though something in him had died.

Graciela looked at his stricken face, and her heart went out to him. She kissed him on the cheek. 'I love you,' she said softly. Her eyes filled with tears. 'I will pray for you. I will pray for us both.'

38

On a late Friday afternoon, a military ambulance drove up to the emergency entrance to the hospital at Aranda de Duero. An ambulance attendant accompanied by two uniformed policemen went through the swing doors and approached the supervisor behind the desk.

'We have an order here to pick up a Rubio Arzano,' one of the policemen said. He handed over the document.

The supervisor looked at it and frowned. 'I don't think I have the authority to release him. It should be handled by the administrator.'

'Fine. Get him.'

The supervisor hesitated. 'There's a problem. He's away for the weekend.'

'It's not our problem. There's our release order, signed by Colonel Acoca. Do you want to call him and tell him you won't honour it?'

'No,' he said hastily. 'That won't be necessary. I'll have them get the prisoner ready.'

Half a mile away, in front of the city jail, two detectives emerged from a police car and entered the building. They approached the desk sergeant.

One of the men showed his badge. 'We're here to pick up Lucia Carmine.'

The sergeant looked at the two detectives in front of him and said, 'No one told me anything about this.'

One of the detectives sighed. 'Goddamned bureaucracy. The left hand never tells the right hand what it's doing.'

'Let me see that release order.'

The detectives handed it to him.

'Colonel Acoca signed it, huh?'

'That's right.'

'Where are you taking her?'

'Madrid. The Colonel is going to question her himself.'

'Is he? Well, I think I'd better check it out with him.'

'There's no need to do that,' the detective protested.

'Mister, we've got orders to keep a tight grip on this lady. The Italian government is having an orgasm over getting her back. If Colonel Acoca wants her, he's going to have to tell me himself.'

'You're wasting time, and –'

'I have a lot of time, *amigo*. What I don't have is another ass if I lose

510

mine over this.' He picked up the phone and said, 'Get me Colonel Acoca in Madrid.'

'Jesus Christ!' the detective said. 'My wife is going to kill me if I'm late for dinner again. Besides, the Colonel's probably not even in, and –'

The phone on the desk rang. The sergeant reached for it.

'I have the Colonel's office on the line.'

The sergeant gave the detectives a triumphant look. 'Hello. This is the desk sergeant at the police station in Aranda de Duero. It is important that I speak to Colonel Acoca.'

One of the detectives looked at his watch impatiently. '*Mierda!* I have better things to do than stand around and –'

'Hello. Colonel Acoca?'

The voice boomed out over the phone. 'Yes. What is it?'

'I have two detectives here, Colonel, who want me to release a prisoner into your custody.'

'Lucia Carmine?'

'Yes, sir.'

'Did they show you an order signed by me?'

'Yes, sir. They –'

'Then what the fuck are you bothering me for? Release her.'

'I just thought –'

'Don't think. Follow orders.'

The line went dead.

The sergeant swallowed. 'He – er –'

'He has a short fuse, hasn't he?' the detective grinned.

The sergeant rose, trying to retain his dignity. 'I'll have her brought out.'

In the alley at the back of the police station, a small boy was watching a man on the telephone pole disconnect a clamp from a wire and climb down.

'What are you doing?' the boy asked.

The man ruffled his hand through the boy's hair. 'Helping out a friend, *muchacho*. Helping out a friend.'

Three hours later, at an isolated farmhouse to the north, Lucia and Rubio Arzano were reunited.

He was awakened by the telephone at 3.00 a.m. The familiar voice said, 'The Committee would like to meet with you.'

'Yes, sir. When?'

'Now, Colonel. A limousine will pick you up in one hour. Be ready, please.'

'Yes, sir.'

511

He replaced the receiver and sat on the edge of the bed. He lit a cigarette and let the smoke bite deep into his lungs.

A limousine will pick you up in one hour. Be ready, please.

He would be ready.

He went into the bathroom and examined his image in the mirror. He was looking into the eyes of a defeated man.

I was so close, he thought bitterly. *So close.*

Colonel Acoca began to shave, very carefully, and when he was finished, he took a long, hot shower, then selected the clothes he was going to wear.

Exactly one hour later, he walked to the front door and took a last look at the home he knew he would never see again. There would be no meeting, of course. They would have nothing further to discuss with him.

There was a long, black limousine waiting in front of the house. A door opened as he approached the car. There were two men in the front and two in the back.

'Get in, Colonel.'

He took a deep breath and entered the car. A moment later, it sped away into the black night.

It's like a dream, Lucia thought. *I'm looking out the window at the Swiss Alps. I'm actually here.*

Jaime Miró had arranged for a guide to see that she reached Zurich safely. She had arrived late at night.

In the morning, I'll go to the Leu Bank.

The thought made her nervous. What if something had gone wrong? What if the money was no longer there? What if . . . ?

As the first light of dawn inched over the mountains, Lucia was still awake.

A few minutes before nine, she left the Baur au Lac Hotel and stood in front of the bank, waiting for it to open.

A kindly-looking, middle-aged man unlocked the door. 'Come in, please. I hope you haven't been waiting long?'

Only a few months, Lucia thought. 'No. Not at all.'

He ushered her inside. 'What can we do for you?'

Make me rich. 'My father has an account here. He asked me to come in and – and take it over.'

'Is it a numbered account?'

'Yes.'

'May I have the number, please?'

'B2A149207.'

He nodded. 'One moment, please.'

She watched him disappear towards a vault at the back. The bank was beginning to fill with customers. *It must be there*, Lucia thought. *Nothing must go –*

The man was approaching her. She could read nothing in his face.

'This account – you say it was in your father's name?'

Her heart sank. 'Yes. Angelo Carmine.'

He studied her for a moment. 'The account carries two names.'

Did that mean she would not be able to touch it? 'What –' She could scarcely get the words out. '– What's the other name?'

'Lucia Carmine.'

And in that instant, she owned the world.

The account amounted to a little over thirteen million dollars.

'How would you like it handled?' the banker asked.

'Could you transfer it to a bank in Brazil? Rio?'

'Certainly. It will be there this afternoon.'

It was that simple.

Lucia's next stop was at a travel agency near the hotel. There was a large poster in the window advertising Brazil.

It's an omen, Lucia thought happily. She went inside.

'May I help you?'

'Yes. I would like two tickets to Brazil.'

There are no extradition laws there.

She could not wait to tell Rubio how well everything was going. He was in Biarritz waiting for her call. They would be going to Brazil together.

'We can live in peace there for the rest of our lives,' she had told him.

Now, everything was finally set. After all the adventure and the dangers . . . the arrest of her father and brothers and her vengeance against Benito Patas and Judge Buscetta . . . the police looking for her and her escape to the convent . . . Acoca's men and the phony friar . . . Jaime Miró and Teresa and the gold cross . . . and Rubio Arzano. Most of all, dear Rubio. How many times had he risked his life for her? He had saved her from the soldiers in the woods . . . from the raging waters at the waterfall . . . from the men in the bar at Aranda de Duero. The very thought of Rubio warmed Lucia.

She returned to her hotel room and picked up the telephone, waiting for the operator to answer.

There will be something for him to do in Rio. What? What can he do? He'll probably want to buy a farm somewhere out in the country. But then what would I do?

An operator's voice said, 'Number, please.'

Lucia sat there staring out of the window at the snow-covered Alps. *We have two different lives, Rubio and I. We live in different worlds. I'm the daughter of Angelo Carmine.*

'Number, please?'

He's a farmer. That's what he loves. How can I take him away from that? I can't do that to him.

The operator was getting impatient. 'Can I help you?'

Lucia said slowly, 'No. Thank you.' She replaced the receiver.

Early the following morning, she boarded a Swissair flight to Rio. She was alone.

39

The meeting had taken place in the luxurious drawing room of Ellen Scott's townhouse. She paced back and forth, waiting for Alan Tucker to arrive with the girl. No. Not a girl. A woman. A nun. What would she be like? What had life done to her? *What have I done to her?*

The butler walked into the room. 'Your guests have arrived, Madam.'

She took a deep breath. 'Show them in.'

A moment later, Megan and Alan Tucker entered.

She's beautiful, Ellen Scott thought.

Tucker smiled. 'Mrs Scott, this is Megan.'

Ellen Scott looked at him and said quietly, 'I won't need you any more.' And her words had a finality to them.

His smile faded.

'Goodbye, Tucker.'

He stood there a moment, uncertain, then nodded and left. He could not get over his feeling that he had missed something. Something important. *Too late*, he thought. *Too bloody late.*

Ellen Scott was studying Megan. 'Sit down, please.'

Megan took a chair, and the two women sat there inspecting each other.

She looks like her mother, Ellen Scott thought. *She's grown up to be a beautiful woman.* She recalled the terrible night of the accident, the storm and the burning plane.

You said she was dead . . . There's another way . . . The pilot said we were near Ávila. There should be plenty of tourists there. There's no reason for anyone to connect the baby with the plane crash . . . We'll drop her off at a nice farmhouse outside of town. They'll adopt her and she'll grow up to have a lovely life here . . . You have to choose, Milo. You can either have me, or you can spend the rest of your life working for your brother's child.

And now here was the past confronting her. Where to begin?

'I'm Ellen Scott, President of Scott Industries. Have you heard of it?'

'No.'

Of course she would not have heard of it, Ellen Scott chided herself.

This was going to be more difficult than she had anticipated. She had concocted a story about an old friend of the family who had died, and a promise to take care of his daughter, and – but the moment she had looked at Megan, Ellen Scott knew that it would not work. She had no choice. She had to trust Patricia – Megan – not to destroy them all. Ellen Scott thought of what she had done to the woman seated before her, and her eyes filled with tears. *But it's too late for tears. It's time to make amends. It's time to tell the truth.*

Ellen Scott leaned across to Megan and took her hand. 'I have a story to tell you,' she said quietly.

That had been three years earlier. For the first year, until she became too ill to continue, Ellen Scott had taken Megan under her wing. Megan had gone to work for Scott Industries, and her aptitude and intelligence had delighted the older woman.

'You'll have to work hard,' Ellen Scott said. 'You'll learn, as I had to learn. In the beginning, it will be difficult, but in the end, it will become your life.'

And it had.

Megan worked hours that none of her employees could even begin to emulate.

'You get to your office at four o'clock in the morning and work all day. How do you do it?'

Megan smiled and thought: *If I slept until four o'clock in the morning at the convent, Sister Betina would scold me.*

Ellen Scott was gone, but Megan had kept learning, and kept watching the company grow. *Her* company. Ellen Scott had adopted her. 'So we won't have to explain why you're a Scott,' she said. But there was a note of pride in her voice.

It's ironic, Megan thought. *All those years at the orphanage when no one would adopt me. And now I'm being adopted by my own family.*

He has a wonderful sense of humour.

40

A new man was behind the wheel of the getaway car, and it made Jaime Miró nervous.

'I'm not sure of him,' he told Felix Carpio. 'What if he drives off and leaves us?'

'Relax. He's my cousin's brother-in-law. He'll be fine. He's been begging for a chance to go out with us.'

'I have a bad feeling,' Jaime said.

They had arrived in Seville early that afternoon, and had examined half a dozen banks before choosing their target. The bank was on a side street, small, not too much traffic, close to a factory which would be making deposits there. Everything seemed perfect. Except for the man in the getaway car.

'Is he all that's worrying you?' Felix asked.

'No.'

'What, then?'

It was a difficult one to answer. 'Call it a premonition.' He tried to say it lightly, mocking himself.

Felix took it seriously. 'Do you want to call it off?'

'Because I have the nerves of an old washerman today? No, *amigo*. It will all go as smooth as silk.'

In the beginning, it had.

There were half a dozen customers in the bank, and Felix held them at bay with an automatic weapon while Jaime cleared out the cash drawers. Smooth as silk.

As the two men were leaving, heading for the getaway car, Jaime called out, 'Remember, *amigos*, the money is for a good cause.'

It was out in the street that it began to fall apart. There were police everywhere. The driver of the getaway car was on his knees on the pavement, a police pistol at his head.

As Jaime and Felix came into view, a detective called out, 'Drop your weapons.'

Jaime hesitated for one split second. Then he raised his gun.

517

41

The converted 727 was flying at 35,000 feet, over the Grand Canyon. It had been a long, hard day. *And it's not over yet*, Megan thought.

She was on her way to California to sign the papers that would give Scott Industries one million acres of timberland north of San Francisco. She had struck a hard bargain.

It's their fault, Megan thought. *They shouldn't have tried to cheat me. I'll bet I'm the first bookkeeper they've ever come up against from a Cistercian convent.* She laughed aloud.

The steward approached her. 'Can I get you anything, Miss Scott?'

'No, thank you.'

She saw a stack of newspapers and magazines in the rack. She had been so busy with the deal that she had had no time to read anything. 'Let me see the *New York Times*, please.'

The story was on the front page and it leaped out at her. There was a photograph of Jaime Miró. Below it the communique read: 'Jaime Miró, leader of ETA, the radical Basque separatist movement in Spain, was wounded and captured by police during a bank hold-up yesterday afternoon in Seville. Killed in the attack was Felix Carpio, another of the alleged terrorists. The authorities had been conducting a search for Miró since . . .'

Megan read the rest of the article and sat there for a long time, frozen, remembering the past. It was like a distant dream, photographed through a gauze curtain, hazy and unreal.

This fight will be over soon. We'll get what we want because the people are behind us . . . I would like you to wait for me . . .

Long ago she had read of a civilization that believed if you saved a person's life, that you were responsible for him. Well, she had saved Jaime twice – once at the castle, and again at the park. *I'll be damned if I'm going to let them kill him now.*

She reached for the telephone next to her seat and said to the pilot, 'Turn the plane around. We're going back to New York.'

A limousine was there for her at La Guardia, and by the time she arrived in her office it was 2.00 a.m. Lawrence Gray Jr. was waiting for her. His father had been the company's attorney for years and had retired. The son was bright and ambitious.

Without preamble, Megan said, 'Jaime Miró. What do you know about him?'

The reply was immediate. 'He's a Basque terrorist, head of ETA. I think I just read that he was captured a day or so ago.'

'Right. The government is going to have to put him on trial. I want to have someone there. Who's the best trial lawyer in the country?'

'I'd say Curtis Hayman.'

'No. Too much of a gentleman. We need a killer.' She thought for a moment. 'Get Mike Rosen.'

'He's booked for the next hundred years, Megan.'

'Unbook him. I want him in Madrid for the trial.'

He frowned. 'We can't get involved in a public trial in Spain.'

'Sure we can. *Amicus curae*. We're friends of the defendant.'

He studied her a moment. 'Do you mind if I ask you a personal question?'

'Yes. Get on this.'

'I'll do my best.'

'Larry . . .'

'Yes?'

'And then some.' There was steel in her voice.

Twenty minutes later, Lawrence Gray walked into Megan's office. 'Mike Rosen is on the phone. I think I woke him up. He wants to talk to you.'

Megan picked up the telephone. 'Mr Rosen? What a pleasure this is. We've never met, but I have a feeling you and I are going to become very good friends. A lot of people sue Scott Industries just for the target practice, and I've been looking around for someone to take charge of all our litigation. Yours is the one name that keeps coming up. Naturally, I'm prepared to pay you a large retainer for –'

'Miss Scott –?'

'Yes.'

'I don't mind a little snow job, but you're giving me frostbite.'

'I don't understand.'

'Then let me put it in legal parlance for you. Cut out the bullshit. It's two o'clock in the morning. You don't hire people at two o'clock in the morning.'

'Mr Rosen –'

'Mike. We're going to be good friends, remember? But friends have to trust one another. Larry tells me you want me to go to Spain to try to save some Basque terrorist who's in the hands of the police.'

She started to say, 'He's not a terrorist –' but stopped herself. 'Yes.'

'What's your problem? Is he suing Scott Industries because his gun jammed?'

'He –'

'I'm sorry, friend. I can't help you. My schedule is so tight that I gave up going to the bathroom six months ago. I can recommend a few lawyers . . .'

No, Megan thought. *Jaime Miró needs you.* And she was suddenly seized by a sense of hopelessness. Spain was another world, another time. When she spoke, her voice sounded weary. 'Never mind,' she said. 'It's a personal matter. I'm sorry for coming on so strongly.'

'Hey! That's what CEOs are supposed to do. Personal is different, Megan. To tell you the truth, I'm dying to hear what interest the head of Scott Industries has in saving a Spanish terrorist. Are you free for lunch tomorrow?'

She was going to let nothing stand in her way. 'Yes.'

'Le Cirque at one o'clock?'

Megan felt her spirits lifting. 'Fine.'

'You make the reservation. But I have to warn you about something.'

'Yes?'

'I have a very nosy wife.'

They met at Le Cirque, and when Sirio had seated them, Mike Rosen said, 'You're better looking than your picture. I'll bet everybody tells you that.'

He was very short, and he dressed carelessly. But there was nothing careless about his mind. His eyes radiated a blazing intelligence.

'You've aroused my curiosity,' Mike Rosen said. 'What's your interest in Jaime Miró?'

There was so much to tell. Too much to tell. All Megan said was, 'He's a friend. I don't want him to die.'

Rosen leaned forward in his seat, his legs swinging in the air. 'I went through the newspaper files on him this morning. If Don Juan Carlos' government executes Miró only once, he'll be way ahead of the game. They're going to get hoarse just reading the charges against your friend.' He saw the expression on Megan's face. 'I'm sorry, but I have to be honest. Miró has been a very busy man. He holds up banks, blows up cars, murders people –'

'He's not a murderer. He's a patriot. He's fighting for his rights.'

'Okay, okay. He's my hero too. What do you want me to do?'

'Save him.'

'Megan, we're such good friends that I'm going to tell you the absolute truth. Jesus Christ himself couldn't save him. You're looking for a miracle that –'

'I believe in miracles. Will you help me?'

He studied her a moment. 'What the hell. What are friends for? Have you tried the paté? I hear they make it kosher.'

The Fax from Madrid read: 'Have spoken to half a dozen top European lawyers. They refuse to represent Miró. Tried to have myself admitted to trial as *amicus curae*. Court ruled against me. Wish I could pull off

520

that miracle for you, friend, but Jesus hasn't risen yet. Am on my way home. You owe me a lunch. Mike.'

The trial was set to begin on 17 September.

'Cancel my appointments,' Megan told her assistant. 'I have some business to take care of in Madrid.'

'How long will you be gone?'

'I don't know.'

She planned her strategy on the plane flying over the Atlantic. *There has to be a way*, Megan thought. *I have money and I have power. The Prime Minister is the key. I have to get to him before the trial starts. After that, it will be too late.*

Megan had an appointment with Prime Minister Leopoldo Martinez twenty-four hours after she arrived in Madrid. He invited her to Moncloa Palace for lunch.

'Thank you for seeing me so promptly,' Megan said. 'I know what a busy man you are.'

He raised a hand in deprecation. 'My dear Miss Scott, when the head of an organization as important as Scott Industries flies to my country to see me, I can only be honoured. Please tell me how I can assist you.'

'I really came here to assist you,' Megan said. 'It occurred to me that while we have a few factories in Spain, we're not using nearly enough of the potential that your country has to offer.'

He was listening closely now, his eyes shining. 'Yes?'

'Scott Industries is about to open a huge electronics plant. It should employ somewhere between a thousand and fifteen hundred people. If it is as successful as we think it will be, we'll open satellite factories.'

'And you have not decided in which country you wish to open this plant?'

'That's right. I'm personally in favour of Spain, but quite frankly, Your Excellency, some of my executives are not too happy with your civil rights record.'

'Really?'

'Yes. They felt that those who object to some of the policies of the state are treated too harshly.'

'Do you have anyone in particular in mind?'

'As a matter of fact, I do. Jaime Miró.'

He sat there staring at her. 'I see. And if we were to be lenient with Jaime Miró, we would get the electronics factory and –'

'And a lot more,' Megan assured him. 'Our factories will raise the standard of living in every community they're in.'

521

The Prime Minister frowned. 'I'm afraid there is one small problem.'

'What? We can negotiate further.'

'This is something that cannot be negotiated, Miss Scott. Spain's honour is not for sale. You cannot bribe us or buy us or threaten us.'

'Believe me, I'm not –'

'You came here with your handouts and expect us to run our courts to please you? Think again, Miss Scott. We don't need your factories.'

I've made it worse, Megan thought, despairingly.

The trial lasted six weeks in a heavily guarded courtroom that was closed to the public.

Megan remained in Madrid, following the news reports of the trial each day. From time to time, Mike Rosen telephoned her.

'I know what you're going through, friend. I think you should come home.'

'I can't, Mike.'

She tried to see Jaime.

'Absolutely no visitors.'

On the last day of the trial, Megan stood outside the courtroom, lost in a crowd of people. Reporters came streaming out of the building, and Megan stopped one of them.

'What happened?'

'They found him guilty on all counts. He's going to get the garrotte.'

42

At five a.m. on the morning scheduled for the execution of Jaime Miró, crowds began to gather outside the central prison in Madrid. Barricades set up by the *guardia civil* kept the swelling mob of onlookers across the wide street, away from the front entrance to the prison. Armed troops and tanks blocked the iron prison gates.

Inside the prison, in the office of Warden Gomez de la Fuente, an extraordinary meeting was taking place. In the room were Prime Minister Leopoldo Martinez, Alonzo Sebastian, the new head of GOE, and the warden's executive deputies, Juanito Molinas and Pedros Arrango.

Warden de la Fuente was a heavyset, middle-aged, grim-faced man who had passionately devoted his life to disciplining the miscreants that the government had placed in his charge. Molinas and Arrango, his hard-bitten assistants, had served with de la Fuente for the past twenty years.

Prime Minister Martinez was speaking. 'I would like to know what arrangements you have made to ensure that there will be no trouble in carrying out Miró's execution.'

Warden de la Fuente replied, 'We have prepared for every possible contingency, Your Excellency. As Your Excellency observed when you arrived, a full company of armed soldiers is stationed around the prison. It would take an army to break in.'

'And inside the prison itself?'

'The precautions are even more stringent. Jaime Miró is locked in a double security cell on the second floor. The other prisoners on that floor have been temporarily transferred. Two guards are stationed at each end of the cell block. I have ordered a general lock-down, so that all prisoners will remain in their cells until after the execution.'

'What time will that take place?'

'At noon, Your Excellency. I have postponed mess hall until one o'clock. That will give us enough time to get Miró's body out of here.'

'What plans have you made for disposing of it?'

'I am following your suggestion, Excellency. His burial in Spain would cause the government embarrassment if the Basques should turn his grave into some kind of shrine. We have been in touch with his aunt in France. She lives in a small village outside Bayonne. She has agreed to bury him there.'

The Prime Minister rose. 'Excellent.' He sighed. 'I still think a hanging in the public square would have been more appropriate.'

'Yes, Your Excellency. But in that case, I could no longer have been responsible for controlling the mob outside.'

'I suppose you're right. There's no point in stirring up any more excitement than is necessary. The garrotte is more painful and slower. And if any man deserves the garrotte, it is Jaime Miró.'

Warden de la Fuente said, 'Excuse me, Your Excellency, but I understand that a commission of judges is meeting to consider a last minute appeal from Miró's attorneys. If it should come through, what should I —?'

The Prime Minister interrupted. 'It won't. The execution will proceed as scheduled.'

The meeting was over.

At 7.30 a.m., a bread truck arrived in front of the prison gate.

'Delivery.'

One of the prison guards stationed at the entrance looked in at the driver. 'You're new, aren't you?'

'Yeah.'

'Where's Julio?'

'He's sick in bed today.'

'Why don't you go join him, *amigo*?'

'What?'

'No deliveries this morning. Come back this afternoon.'

'But every morning —'

'Nothing goes in, and only one thing is going out. Now back up, turn around and get your ass out of here before my pals get nervous.'

The driver looked around at the armed soldiers staring at him. 'Sure. Okay.'

They watched as he turned the truck around and disappeared down the street. The commander of the post reported the incident to the warden. When the story was checked out, it was learned that the regular employee was in the hospital, a victim of a hit and run driver.

At eight a.m., a car bomb exploded across the street from the prison, wounding half a dozen bystanders. Under ordinary circumstances, the guards would have left their posts to investigate and assist the wounded. But they had strict orders. They remained at their stations and the *guardia civil* was summoned to take charge.

The incident was promptly reported to Warden de la Fuente.

'They're getting desperate,' he said. 'Be prepared for anything.'

At 9.15 a.m., a helicopter appeared over the prison grounds. Painted on its sides were the words: LA PRENSA, Spain's prominent daily newspaper.

Two anti-aircraft guns had been set up on the prison roof. The lieutenant in charge waved a flag to warn off the plane. It continued to hover. The officer picked up a field telephone.

'Warden, we have a copter overhead.'

'Any identification?'

'It says *La Prensa*, but the sign looks freshly painted.'

'Give it one warning shot. If it doesn't move, blow it out of the sky.'

'Yes, sir.' He nodded to his gunner. 'Put a close one in.'

The shot landed five yards to the side of the helicopter. They could see the pilot's startled face. The gunner loaded again. The helicopter swooped up and disappeared across the skies of Madrid.

What the hell is next? the lieutenant wondered.

At 11.00 a.m. Megan Scott appeared at the reception office of the prison. She looked drawn and pale. 'I want to see Warden de la Fuente.'

'Do you have an appointment?'

'No, but –'

'I'm sorry. The Warden isn't seeing anyone this morning. If you telephone this afternoon –'

'Tell him it's Megan Scott.'

He took a closer look at her. *So this is the rich American who's trying to get Jaime Miró released. I wouldn't mind having her work on me for a few nights.* 'I'll tell the Warden you're here.'

Five minutes later Megan was seated in Warden de la Fuente's office. With him were half a dozen members of the prison board.

'What can I do for you, Miss Scott?'

'I would like to see Jaime Miró.'

The warden sighed. 'I'm afraid that is not possible.'

'But I'm –'

'Miss Scott – we are all aware of who you are. If we could accommodate you, I assure you that we would be more than happy to do so,' he smiled. 'We Spaniards are really an understanding people. We are also sentimental, and from time to time we are not averse to turning a blind eye to certain rules and regulations.' His smile disappeared. 'But not today, Miss Scott. No. Today is a very special day. It has taken us years to catch the man you wish to see. So this is a day of rules and regulations. The next one to see Jaime Miró will be his God – if he has one.'

Megan stared at him, miserable. 'Could – could I just look at him for a moment?'

One of the members of the prison board, touched by the anguish in Megan's face, was tempted to intervene. He stopped himself.

'I'm sorry,' Warden de la Fuente said. 'No.'

'Could I send him a message?' Her voice was choked.

'You would be sending a message to a dead man.' He looked at his watch. 'He has less than an hour to live.'

'But he's appealing his sentence. Isn't a panel of judges meeting to decide if – ?'

'They've voted against it. I received word from them fifteen minutes ago. Miró's appeal has been denied. The execution will take place. Now, if you'll excuse me –'

He rose, and the others followed suit. Megan looked around the room at their cold faces and shuddered.

'May God have mercy on all of you,' she said.

They watched, silent, as she fled from the room.

At ten minutes before the noon hour, the door to Jaime Miró's cell was opened. Warden Gomez de la Fuente was accompanied by his two assistants, Molinas and Arrango, and Dr Miguel Anunción. Four armed guards stood watch in the corridor.

The warden entered the cell. 'It's time.'

Jaime rose from his cot. He was handcuffed and shackled. 'I was hoping you'd be late.' There was an air of dignity about him that Warden de la Fuente could not help but admire.

At another time, under other circumstances, we might have been friends.

Jaime stepped out into the deserted corridor, his movements clumsy because of the shackles. He was flanked by the guards and Molinas and Arrango. 'The garrotte?' Jaime asked.

The warden nodded. 'The garrotte.' Excruciatingly painful, inhuman. It was a good thing, the warden thought, that the execution would take place in a private room, away from the eyes of the public and the press.

The procession made its way down the corridor. From outside, in the street, they could hear the chant of the crowd: 'Jaime . . . Jaime . . . Jaime . . .' It was a swelling, bursting from a thousand throats growing louder and louder.

'They're calling for you,' Pedros Arrango said.

'No. They're calling for themselves. They're calling for freedom. Tomorrow they'll have another name. I may die – but there will always be another name.'

They passed through two security gates to a small chamber at the end of the corridor, with an iron green door. From around the corner a black-robed priest appeared.

'Thank heavens I'm in time. I've come to give the condemned man the last rites.'

As he moved towards Miró, two guards blocked his way.

'Sorry, Father,' Warden de la Fuente said. 'Nobody goes near him.'

'But I'm –'

526

'If you want to give him his last rites, you'll have to do it through closed doors. Out of the way, please.'

A guard opened the green door. Standing inside, next to a chair bolted to the floor, with heavy armstraps, was a huge man wearing a half mask. In his hands he held the garrotte.

The warden nodded towards Molinas and Arrango and the doctor, and they entered the room after Jaime. The guards remained outside. The green door was locked and bolted.

Inside the room, assistants Molinas and Arrango led Jaime to the chair. They unlocked his handcuffs, then strapped him in, pulling the heavy straps against his arms, while Dr Anunción and Warden de la Fuente watched. Through the thick closed door, they could barely hear the chanting of the priest.

De la Fuente looked at Jaime and shrugged. 'It doesn't matter. God will understand what he is saying.'

The giant holding the garrotte moved to the back of Jaime. Warden Gomez de la Fuente asked, 'Do you want a cloth over your face?'

'No.'

The warden looked at the giant and nodded. The giant lifted the garrotte in his hand and reached forward.

Outside the guards at the door could hear the chanting of the mob in the street.

'You know something?' one of the guards grumbled. 'I wish I was out there with them.'

Five minutes later, the green door opened.

Dr Anunción said, 'Bring in the body bag.'

Following instructions, Jaime Miró's body was smuggled out through a back door of the prison. The body bag was thrown into the back of an unmarked van. But the moment the vehicle pulled out of the prison grounds, the crowd in the street pressed forward, as though drawn to it by some mystic magnet.

'Jaime . . . Jaime . . .'

But the cries were softer now. Men and women wept, and their children looked on in wonder, not understanding what was happening. The van made its way through the crowd and finally turned on to a highway.

'Jesus,' the driver said. 'That was spooky. The guy must have had something.'

'Yeah. And thousands of people knew it too!'

At two o'clock that afternoon, Warden Gomez de la Fuente and his two assistants, Juanito Molinas and Pedros Arrango appeared at the office of Prime Minister Martinez.

'I want to congratulate you,' the Prime Minister said. 'It was executed perfectly.'

The warden spoke. 'Mr Prime Minister, we're not here to receive your congratulations. We're here to resign.'

Martinez stared at them, baffled. 'I – I don't understand. What – ?'

'It's a matter of humanity, Your Excellency. We just watched a man die. Perhaps he deserved to die. But not like that. It – it was barbaric. I want no more part of this or anything like it, and my colleagues feel the same way.'

'Perhaps you should give this more thought. Your pensions –'

'We have to live with our consciences.' Warden de la Fuente handed the Prime Minister three pieces of paper. 'Here are our resignations.'

Late that night, the van crossed the French border and headed for the village of Bidache, near Bayonne. They pulled up before a neat farmhouse.

'This is the place. Let's get rid of the body before it starts to smell.'

The door to the farmhouse was opened by a woman in her middle fifties. 'You brought him?'

'Yes, ma'am. Where would you like it – er – him?'

'In the parlour, please.'

'Yes, ma'am. I – I wouldn't wait too long to bury him. You know what I mean?'

She watched the two men carry in the body bag and set it on the floor.

'Thank you.'

'*De nada.*'

She stood there watching as they drove away.

Another woman walked in from the other room and ran towards the body bag. She hastily unzipped it.

Jaime Miró was lying there smiling up at them. 'Do you know something? That garrotte could be a real pain in the neck.'

'White wine or red?' Megan asked.

528

43

At Barajas Airport in Madrid, former Warden Gomez de la Fuente and his former assistants, Molinas and Arrango, and Dr Anunción and the giant in the mask were in the departure lounge.

'I still think you're making a mistake not coming with me to Costa Rica,' de la Fuente said. 'With your five million dollars, you can buy the whole fucking island.'

Molinas shook his head. 'Arrango and I are going to Switzerland. I'm tired of the sun. We're going to buy ourselves a few dozen snow bunnies.'

'Me, too,' the giant said.

They turned to Miguel Anunción.

'What about you, doctor?'

'I'm going to Bangladesh.'

'*What?*'

'That's right. I'm going to use the money to open a hospital there. You know, I thought about it a long time before I accepted Megan Scott's offer. But I figured that if I can save a lot of innocent lives by letting one terrorist live, it's a good trade-off. Besides, I must tell you, I liked Jaime Miró.'

44

It had been a good season in the French countryside, with fine weather, showering farmers with an abundance of crops. *I wish that every year could be as wonderful as this*, Rubio Arzano thought. *It has been a good year in more ways than one.*

First his marriage and then, a year ago, the birth of the twins. *Whoever dreamed a man could be this happy?*

It was starting to rain. Rubio turned the tractor around and headed for the barn. He thought about the twins. The boy was going to be big and strapping. But his sister! She was going to be a handful. *She's going to give her man a lot of trouble*, Rubio grinned to himself. *She takes after her mother.*

He drove the tractor into the barn and headed for the house, feeling the cool rain against his face. He opened the door and stepped inside.

'You're just in time,' Lucia smiled. 'Dinner's ready.'

The Reverend Mother Prioress Betina awakened with a premonition that something wonderful was about to happen.

Of course, she thought, *enough good things have already happened.*

The Cistercian convent had long since been reopened, under the protection of King Don Juan Carlos. Sister Graciela and the nuns who had been taken to Madrid were safely returned to the convent, where they were allowed to retreat once again into the blessed solitude and silence.

Shortly after breakfast, the Mother Prioress walked into her office and stopped, staring. On her desk, shining with a dazzling brightness, lay the gold cross.

It was accepted as a miracle.

AFTERWORD

Madrid has tried to buy peace by offering the Basques limited autonomy, allowing them to have their own flag, their own language, and a
Basque police department. ETA replied by assassinating Constantin
Ortin Gil, Madrid's military governor, and later Luis Carrero Blanco,
the man chosen by Franco to be his successor.

The violence keeps escalating.

In a three-year period, ETA terrorists have killed more than 600
victims. The slaughter continues and the retaliation by the police has
been equally ruthless.

Not so many years ago, ETA had the sympathy of the two and a
half million Basque people, but continued terrorism has eroded their
support. In Bilbao, the very heart of the Basque homeland, 100,000
people took to the streets to demonstrate *against* ETA. The Spanish
people feel it is time for peace, time to heal the wounds.

The OPUS MUNDO is more powerful than ever, but few people are
willing to discuss it.

As for the Cistercian convents of the Strict Observance, there are in
existence today fifty-four convents, worldwide, seven of them in Spain.

Their timeless ritual of eternal silence and seclusion remains
unchanged.

The Doomsday Conspiracy

This is for Jerry Davis

ACKNOWLEDGEMENT

I wish to express my appreciation to James J. Hurtak, Ph.D., and his wife Desirée, for making available to me their invaluable technical expertise.

May you live in interesting times

Ancient Chinese curse

PROLOGUE

Uetendorf, Switzerland

SUNDAY, OCTOBER 14TH, 1550 HOURS

The witnesses standing at the edge of the field were staring in horrified silence, too stunned to speak. The scene that lay before them was grotesque, a primeval nightmare dredged up from some deep, dark depths of primitive man's collective unconscious. Each witness had a different reaction. One fainted. A second one vomited. A woman was shaking uncontrollably. Another one thought: *I'm going to have a heart attack!* The elderly priest clutched his beads and crossed himself. *Help me, Father. Help us all. Protect us against this evil incarnate. We have finally seen the face of Satan. It is the end of the world. Judgement Day has come.*

Armageddon is here . . . Armageddon . . . Armageddon . . .

SUNDAY, OCTOBER 14TH, 2100 HOURS

FLASH MESSAGE
TOP SECRET ULTRA
NSA TO DEPUTY DIRECTOR COMSEC
EYES ONLY
SUBJECT: OPERATION DOOMSDAY
MESSAGE: ACTIVATE
NOTIFY NORAD, CIRVIS, GEPAN, DIS,
GHG, VSAF, INS
END OF MESSAGE

SUNDAY, OCTOBER 14TH, 2115 HOURS

FLASH MESSAGE
TOP SECRET ULTRA
NSA TO DEPUTY DIRECTOR –
NAVAL INTELLIGENCE 17TH DISTRICT
EYES ONLY
SUBJECT: COMMANDER ROBERT
BELLAMY
ARRANGE TEMPORARY TRANSFER THIS
AGENCY,
EFFECTIVE IMMEDIATELY.
YOUR CONCURRENCE IN THE ABOVE IS
ASSUMED
END OF MESSAGE

BOOK ONE
The Hunter

1

DAY ONE

Monday, October 15th

He was back in the crowded hospital ward at Cu Chi Base in Vietnam, and Susan was leaning over his bed, lovely in her crisp, white nurse's uniform, whispering, 'Wake up, sailor. You don't want to die.'

And when he heard the magic of her voice, he could almost forget his pain. She was murmuring something else in his ear, but a loud bell was ringing and he could not hear her clearly. He reached up to pull her closer and his hands clutched empty air.

It was the sound of the telephone that brought Robert Bellamy fully awake. He opened his eyes reluctantly, not wanting to let go of the dream. The telephone at his bedside was insistent. He looked at the clock. Four a.m. He snatched up the telephone, angry at having his dream interrupted. 'Do you know what the hell time it is?'

'Commander Bellamy?' A deep, male voice.

'Yes . . .'

'I have a message for you, Commander. You are ordered to report to General Hilliard at National Security Agency Headquarters at Fort Meade at 0600 this morning. Is the message understood, Commander?'

'Yes.' *And no. Mostly no.*

Commander Robert Bellamy slowly replaced the receiver, puzzled. What the devil could NSA want with him? He was assigned to ONI, Office of Naval Intelligence. And what could be urgent enough to call for a meeting at six o'clock in the morning? He lay down again and closed his eyes, trying to recapture the dream. It had been so real. He knew, of course, what had triggered it. Susan had telephoned the evening before.

'Robert . . .'

The sound of her voice did to him what it always did. He took a shaky breath. 'Hello, Susan.'

'Are you all right, Robert?'

'Sure. Fantastic. How's Moneybags?'

'Please, don't.'

'All right. How's Monte Banks?'

545

He could not bring himself to say 'your husband'. *He* was her husband.

'He's fine. I just wanted to tell you that we're going to be away for a little while. I didn't want you to worry.'

That was so like her, so Susan. He fought to keep his voice steady. 'Where are you going this time?'

'We're flying to Brazil.'

On Moneybags' private 727.

'Monte has some business interests there.'

'Really? I thought he owned the country.'

'Stop it, Robert. Please.'

'Sorry.'

There was a pause. 'I wish you sounded better.'

'If you were here, I would.'

'I want you to find someone wonderful and be happy.'

'I did find someone wonderful, Susan.' The damned lump in his throat made it difficult for him to speak. 'And do you know what happened? I lost her.'

'If you're going to do this, I won't call you again.'

He was filled with sudden panic. 'Don't say that. Please.' She was his lifeline. He could not bear the thought of never speaking to her again. He tried to sound cheerful. 'I'm going to go out and find some luscious blonde and screw us both to death.'

'I want you to find someone.'

'I promise.'

'I'm concerned about you, darling.'

'No need. I'm really fine.' He almost gagged on his lie. If she only knew the truth. But it was nothing he could bring himself to discuss with anyone. Especially Susan. He could not bear the thought of her pity.

'I'll telephone you from Brazil,' Susan said.

There was a long silence. They could not let go of each other, because there was too much to say, too many things that were better left unsaid, that had to be left unsaid.

'I have to go now, Robert.'

'Susan?'

'Yes?'

'I love you, baby. I always will.'

'I know. I love you too, Robert.'

And that was the bittersweet irony of it. They still loved each other so much.

You two have the perfect marriage, all their friends used to say. What had gone wrong?

Commander Robert Bellamy got out of bed, and walked through the silent living room in his bare feet. The room screamed out Susan's absence. There were dozens of photographs of Susan and himself scattered around, frozen moments in time. The two of them fishing in the Highlands of Scotland, standing in front of a Buddha near a Thai klong, riding a carriage in the rain through the Borghese gardens in Rome. And in each picture they were smiling and hugging, two people wildly in love.

He went into the kitchen and put on a pot of coffee. The kitchen clock read 4:15. He hesitated a moment, then dialled a number. There were six rings, and finally he heard Admiral Whittaker's voice at the other end of the line. 'Hello.'

'Admiral . . .'

'Yes?'

'It's Robert. I'm terribly sorry to wake you, sir. I just had a rather strange phone call from the National Security Agency.'

'NSA? What did they want?'

'I don't know. I've been ordered to report to General Hilliard at 0600.'

There was a thoughtful silence. 'Perhaps you're being transferred there.'

'I can't be. It doesn't make sense. Why would they . . . ?'

'It's obviously something urgent, Robert. Why don't you give me a call after the meeting?'

'I will. Thank you.'

The connection was broken. *I shouldn't have bothered the old man*, Robert thought. The Admiral had retired as head of Naval Intelligence two years earlier. *Forced* to retire, was more like it. The rumour was that, as a sop, the Navy had given him a little office somewhere and put him to work counting barnacles on the mothball fleet, or some such shit. The Admiral would have no idea about current intelligence activities. But he was Robert's mentor. He was closer to Robert than anyone in the world, except, of course, Susan. And Robert had needed to talk to someone. With Susan gone, he felt as though he were living in a time warp. He fantasized that somewhere, in another dimension of time and space, he and Susan were still happily married, laughing and carefree and loving. *Or maybe not*, Robert thought, wearily. *Maybe I just don't know when to let go*.

The coffee was ready. It tasted bitter. He wondered whether the beans came from Brazil.

He carried the coffee cup into the bathroom and studied his image in the mirror. He was looking at a man in his early forties, tall and lean and physically fit, with a craggy face, a strong chin, black hair and intelligent, probing dark eyes. There was a long, deep scar on his chest, a souvenir from the plane crash. But that was yesterday. That was Susan. This was today. Without Susan. He shaved and showered and walked over to his clothes closet. *What do I wear*, he wondered, *Navy uniform or civilian clothes? And, on the other hand, who gives a damn?* He put on a charcoal-grey suit, a white shirt and a grey silk tie. He knew very little about the National Security Agency, only that the 'puzzle palace', as it was nicknamed, superseded all other American intelligence agencies and was the most secretive of them all. *What do they want with me? I'll soon find out.*

2

The National Security Agency is hidden discreetly away on eighty-two rambling acres at Fort Meade, Maryland, in two buildings that together are twice the size of the CIA complex in Langley, Virginia. The Agency, created to give technical support to protect United States communications and acquire worldwide intelligence data, employs thousands of people, and so much information is generated by its operations that it shreds more than forty tons of documents every day.

It was still dark when Commander Robert Bellamy arrived at the first gate. He drove up to an eight-foot-high cyclone fence with a topping of barbed wire. There was a sentry booth there, manned by two armed guards. One of them stayed in the booth, watching, as the other approached the car. 'Can I help you?'

'Commander Bellamy to see General Hilliard.'

'May I see your identification, Commander?'

Robert Bellamy pulled out his wallet and removed his 17th District Naval Intelligence ID card. The guard studied it carefully and returned it. 'Thank you, Commander.'

He nodded to the guard in the booth and the gate swung open. The guard inside picked up a telephone. 'Commander Bellamy is on his way.'

A minute later Robert Bellamy drove up to a closed, electrified gate. An armed guard approached the car. 'Commander Bellamy?'

'Yes.'

'May I see your identification, please?'

He started to protest and then he thought, *What the hell? It's their zoo*. He took out his wallet again and showed his identification to the guard.

'Thank you, Commander.' The guard gave some invisible sign and the gate opened.

As Robert Bellamy drove ahead, he saw a third cyclone fence ahead of him. *My God*, he thought, *I'm in the Land of Oz*.

Another uniformed guard walked up to the car. As Robert Bellamy reached for his wallet the guard looked at the licence plate and said, 'Please drive straight ahead to the administration building, Commander. There will be someone there to meet you.'

'Thank you.'

The gate swung open and Robert followed the driveway up to an enormous white building. A man in civilian clothes was standing outside, waiting, shivering in the chill October air. 'You can leave your car right there, Commander,' he called out. 'We'll take care of it.'

Robert Bellamy left the keys in his car and stepped out. The man greeting him appeared to be in his thirties, tall, thin and sallow. He looked as though he had not seen the sun in years.

'I'm Harrison Keller. I'll escort you to General Hilliard's office.'

They walked into a large high-ceilinged entrance hall. A man in civilian clothes was seated behind a desk. 'Commander Bellamy . . .'

Robert Bellamy swung around. He heard the click of a camera.

'Thank you, sir.'

Robert Bellamy turned to Keller. 'What . . . ?'

'This will take only a minute,' Harrison Keller assured him.

Sixty seconds later, Robert Bellamy was handed a blue and white identification badge with his photograph on it.

'Please wear this at all times while you're in the building, Commander.'

'Right.'

They started walking down a long, white corridor. Robert Bellamy noticed security cameras mounted at twenty-foot intervals on both sides of the hall.

'How big is this building?'

'Just over two million square feet, Commander.'

'*What?*'

'Yes. This corridor is the longest corridor in the world, nine hundred and eighty feet. We're completely self-contained here. We have a shopping centre, cafeteria, post exchange, eight snack bars, a hospital complete with operating room, a dentist's office, a branch of the State Bank of Laurel, a dry-cleaning shop, a shoe shop, a barber shop, and a few other odds and ends.'

It's a home away from home, Robert thought. He found it oddly depressing.

They passed an enormous open area filled with a vast sea of computers. Robert stopped in amazement.

'Impressive, isn't it? That's just one of our computer rooms. The complex contains three billion dollars' worth of decoding machines and computers.'

'How many people work in this place?'

'About sixteen thousand.'

So what the hell do they need me for? Robert Bellamy wondered.

He was led into a private elevator that Keller operated with a key. They went up one floor and started on another trek down a long corridor until they reached a suite of offices at the end of the hall.

'Right in here, Commander.' They entered a large reception office with four secretaries' desks. Two of the secretaries had already arrived for work. Harrison Keller nodded to one of them. She pressed a button and a door to the inner office clicked open.

'Go right in, please, gentlemen. The General is expecting you.'
Harrison Keller said, 'This way.'

Robert Bellamy followed him into the inner sanctum. He found himself in a spacious office, the ceilings and walls heavily soundproofed. The room was comfortably furnished, filled with photographs and personal artifacts. It was obvious that the man behind the desk spent a lot of time there.

General Mark Hilliard, Deputy Director of NSA, appeared to be in his middle fifties, very tall, with a face carved in flint, icy, steely eyes, and a ramrod-straight posture. The General was dressed in a grey suit, white shirt and grey tie. *I guessed right*, Robert thought.

Harrison Keller said, 'General Hilliard, this is Commander Bellamy.'
'Thank you for dropping by, Commander.'
As though it had been an invitation to some tea party.
The two men shook hands.
'Sit down. I'll bet you could do with a cup of coffee.'
The man was a mind-reader. 'Yes, sir.'
'Harrison?'
'No, thank you.' He took a chair in the corner.

A buzzer was pressed, the door opened and an oriental in a mess jacket entered with a tray of coffee and Danish pastry. Robert noted that he was not wearing an identification badge. *Shame.* The coffee was poured. It smelled wonderful.

'How do you take yours?' General Hilliard asked.
'Black, please.' The coffee tasted great.
The two men were seated in soft leather chairs facing each other.
'The Director asked that I meet with you.'

The Director. Edward Sanderson. A legend in espionage circles. A brilliant, ruthless puppet-master, credited with masterminding dozens of daring coups all over the world. A man seldom seen in public and whispered about in private.

'How long have you been with the 17th District Naval Intelligence Group, Commander?' General Hilliard asked.

Robert played it straight. 'Fifteen years.' He would have bet a month's pay that the General could have told him the time of day when he had joined ONI.

'Before that, I believe you commanded a naval air squadron in Vietnam.'
'Yes, sir.'
'You were shot down. They didn't expect you to pull through.'

The doctor was saying, 'Forget about him. He won't make it.' He had wanted to die. The pain was unbearable. And then Susan was leaning over him. *Open your eyes, sailor, you don't want to die.* He had forced his eyes open and through the haze of pain was staring at the most beautiful woman he had ever seen. She had a soft oval face and thick black hair, sparkling brown eyes and a smile like a blessing. He had tried to speak, but it was too much of an effort.

General Hilliard was saying something.

Robert Bellamy brought his mind back to the present. 'I beg your pardon, General?'

'We have a problem, Commander. We need your help.'

'Yes, sir?'

The General stood up and began to pace. 'What I'm about to tell you is extremely sensitive. It's above Top Secret.'

'Yes, sir.'

'Yesterday, in the Swiss Alps, a NATO weather balloon crashed. There were some experimental military objects aboard the balloon that are highly secret.'

Robert found himself wondering where all this was leading.

'The Swiss government has removed those objects from the balloon, but, unfortunately, it seems that there were some witnesses to the crash. It is of vital importance that none of them talk to anyone about what they saw. It could provide valuable information to certain other countries. Do you follow me?'

'I think so, sir. You want me to speak to the witnesses and warn them not to discuss what they saw.'

'Not exactly, Commander.'

'Then I don't under . . .'

'What I want you to do is simply track down those witnesses. Others will talk to them about the necessity for silence.'

'I see. Are the witnesses all in Switzerland?'

General Hilliard stopped in front of Robert. 'That's our problem, Commander. You see, we have no idea where they are. Or who they are.'

Robert thought he had missed something. 'I beg your pardon?'

'The only information we have is that the witnesses were on a tour bus. They happened to be passing the scene when the weather balloon crashed near a little village called . . .' He turned to Harrison Keller.

'Uetendorf.'

The General turned back to Robert. 'The passengers got off the bus for a few minutes to look at the crash and then continued on. When the tour ended, the passengers dispersed.'

Robert said slowly, 'General Hilliard, are you saying that there is *no* record of who these people are or where they went?'

'That is correct.'

'And you want me to go over and find them?'

'Exactly. You've been very highly recommended. I'm told that you speak half a dozen languages fluently and you have an excellent field record. The Director arranged to have you temporarily transferred to NSA.'

Terrific. 'I assume I'll be working with the Swiss government on this?'

552

'No, you'll be working alone.'

'Alone? But . . .'

'We must not involve anyone else in this mission. I can't stress enough the importance of what was in that balloon, Commander. Time is of the essence. I want you to report your progress to me every day.'

The General wrote a number on a card and handed it to Robert. 'I can be reached through this number day or night. There's a plane waiting to fly you to Zürich. You'll be escorted to your apartment, so you can pack what you need, and then you'll be taken to the airport.'

So much for 'Thank you for dropping by'. Robert was tempted to say, 'Will someone feed my goldfish while I'm gone?' but he had a feeling the answer would be, 'You have no goldfish.'

'In your work with ONI, Commander, I assume you've acquired intelligence contacts abroad?'

'Yes, sir. I have quite a few friends who could be use . . .'

'You're not to get in touch with any of them. You are not authorized to make any contacts at all. The witnesses you're looking for are undoubtedly nationals of various countries.' The General turned to Keller. 'Harrison . . .'

Keller walked over to a filing cabinet in the corner and unlocked it. He removed a large manila envelope and passed it to Robert.

'There's fifty thousand dollars in here in different European currencies, and another twenty thousand in US dollars. You will also find several sets of false identifications that may come in handy.'

General Hilliard held out a thick, shiny black plastic card with a white stripe on it. 'Here's a credit card that . . .'

'I doubt if I'll need that, General. The cash will be enough, and I have an ONI credit card.'

'Take it.'

'Very well.' Robert examined the card. It was drawn on a bank he had never heard of. At the bottom of the card was a telephone number. 'There's no name on the card,' Robert said.

'It's the equivalent of a blank cheque. It requires no identification. Just have them call the telephone number on the card. It's very important that you keep it with you at all times.'

'Right.'

'And Commander?'

'Sir?'

'You must find those witnesses. Every one of them. I'll inform the Director that you have started the assignment.'

The meeting was over.

Harrison Keller walked Robert to the outer office. A uniformed marine was seated there. He rose as the two men came in.

'This is Captain Dougherty. He'll take you to the airport. Good luck.'

'Thanks.'

553

The two men shook hands. Keller turned and walked back into General Hilliard's office.

'Are you ready, Commander?' Captain Dougherty asked.

'Yes.' *But ready for what?* He had handled difficult intelligence assignments in the past, but never anything as crazy as this. He was expected to track down an unknown number of unknown witnesses from unknown countries. *What are the odds against that?* Robert wondered. *I feel like the White Queen in* Through the Looking-glass. *'Why sometimes I've believed as many as six impossible things before breakfast.'* Well, this was all six of them.

'I have orders to take you directly to your apartment and then to Andrews Air Force Base,' Captain Dougherty said. 'There's a plane waiting to . . .'

Robert shook his head. 'I have to make a stop at my office first.'

Dougherty hesitated. 'Very well. I'll go there with you and wait for you.'

It was as though they didn't trust him out of their sight. Because he knew that a weather balloon had crashed? It made no sense. He surrendered his badge at the reception desk, and walked outside, into the chill breaking dawn. His car was gone. In its place was a stretch limousine.

'Your car will be taken care of, Commander,' Captain Dougherty informed him. 'We'll ride in this.'

There was a high-handedness about all this that Robert found vaguely disturbing.

'Fine,' he said.

And they were on their way to the offices of Naval Intelligence. The pale morning sun was disappearing behind rain clouds. It was going to be a miserable day. *In more ways than one*, Robert thought.

3

Ottawa, Canada, 2400 Hours

His code name was Janus. He was addressing the twelve men in the heavily guarded room of a military compound.

'As you have all been informed, Operation Doomsday has been activated. There are a number of witnesses who must be found as quickly and as quietly as possible. We are not able to attempt to track them down through regular security channels because of the danger of a leak.'

'Who are we using?' The Russian. *Huge. Short-tempered.*

'His name is Commander Robert Bellamy.'

'How was he selected?' The German. *Aristocratic. Ruthless.*

'The Commander was chosen after a thorough computer search of the files of the CIA, FBI, and a half dozen other security agencies.'

'Please, may I inquire what are his qualifications?' The Japanese. *Polite. Sly.*

'Commander Bellamy is an experienced field officer who speaks six languages fluently and has an exemplary record. Again and again he has proved himself to be very resourceful. He has no living relatives.'

'Is he aware of the urgency of this?' The Englishman. *Snobbish. Dangerous.*

'He is. We have every expectation that he will be able to locate all the witnesses very quickly.'

'Does he understand the purpose of his mission?' The Frenchman. *Argumentative. Stubborn.*

'No.'

'And when he has found the witnesses?' The Chinese. *Clever. Patient.*

'He will be suitably rewarded.'

4

The headquarters of the Office of Naval Intelligence occupies the entire fifth floor of the sprawling Pentagon, an enclave in the middle of the largest office building in the world, with seventeen miles of corridors, and twenty-nine thousand military and civilian employees.

The interior of the Office of Naval Intelligence reflects its sea-going inheritance. The desks and file cabinets are either olive green, from the World War II era, or battleship grey, from the Vietnam era. The walls and ceilings are painted a buff or cream colour. In the beginning, Robert had been put off by the spartan decor, but he had long since grown accustomed to it.

Now, as he walked into the building and approached the reception desk, the familiar guard at the desk said, 'Good morning, Commander. May I see your pass?'

Robert had been working here for seven years, but the ritual never changed. He dutifully displayed his pass.

'Thank you, Commander.'

On his way to his office, Robert thought about Captain Dougherty, waiting for him in the parking lot at the River Entrance. Waiting to escort him to the plane that would fly him to Switzerland to begin an impossible hunt.

When Robert reached his office, his secretary, Barbara, was already there.

'Good morning, Commander. The Acting Director would like to see you in his office.'

'He can wait. Get me Admiral Whittaker, please.'

'Yes, sir.'

A minute later Robert was speaking with the Admiral.

'I presume you have finished your meeting, Robert?'

'A few minutes ago.'

'How did it go?'

'It was . . . interesting. Are you free to join me for breakfast, Admiral?' He tried to keep his voice casual.

There was no hesitation. 'Yes. Shall we meet there?'

'Fine. I'll leave a visitor's pass for you.'

'Very well. I'll see you in an hour.'

Robert replaced the receiver and thought, *It's ironic that I have to leave a visitor's pass for the Admiral. A few years ago he was the fair-haired boy here, in charge of Naval Intelligence. How must he feel?*

Robert buzzed his secretary on the intercom.

'Yes, Commander?'
'I'm expecting Admiral Whittaker. Arrange a pass for him.'
'I'll take care of it right away.'
It was time to report to the Acting Director. Dustin fucking Thornton.

5

Dustin (Dusty) Thornton, Acting Director of the Office of Naval Intelligence, had won his fame as one of the greatest athletes ever to come out of Annapolis. Thornton owed his present exalted position to a football game. An Army-Navy game, to be precise. Thornton, a towering monolith of a man, had played fullback as a senior at Annapolis, in the Navy's most important game of the year. At the beginning of the fourth quarter, with Army leading 13–0, two touchdowns and a conversion ahead, destiny stepped in and changed Dustin Thornton's life. Thornton intercepted an Army pass, pivoted around and charged through the Army phalanx for a touchdown. Navy missed on the extra point but soon scored a field goal. After the ensuing kick-off Army failed to make a first down and punted into Navy territory. The score stood at Army 13, Navy 9, and the clock was running.

When play resumed, the ball was passed to Thornton, and he went down under a heap of Army uniforms. It took him a long time to get to his feet. A doctor came running out onto the field. Thornton angrily waved him away.

With seconds left to play, signals were called for a lateral pass. Thornton caught it on his own ten-yard line, and took off. He was unstoppable. He charged through the opposition like a tank, knocking down everyone unlucky enough to get in his way. With two seconds to go, Thornton crossed the goal line for the winning touchdown and Navy scored its first victory against Army in four years. That, in itself, would have had little effect on Thornton's life. What made the event significant was that seated in a box reserved for VIPs were Willard Stone and his daughter, Eleanor. As the crowd rose to their feet, wildly cheering the Navy hero, Eleanor turned to her father and said quietly, 'I want to meet him.'

Eleanor Stone was a woman of large appetites. Plain-faced, she had a voluptuous body and an insatiable libido. Watching Dustin Thornton savagely plough his way down the football field, she fantasized what he would be like in bed. If his manhood was as big as the rest of his body . . . She was not disappointed.

Six months later, Eleanor and Dustin Thornton were married. That was the beginning. Dustin Thornton went to work for his father-in-law and was inducted into an arcane world he had not dreamed existed.

Willard Stone, Thornton's new father-in-law, was a man of mystery. A billionaire with powerful political connections, and a past shrouded in secrecy, he was a shadowy figure who pulled strings in a dozen capitals of the world. He was in his late sixties, a meticulous man whose every movement was precise and methodical. He had razor-sharp features, with hooded eyes that revealed nothing. Willard Stone believed in wasting neither words nor emotions, and he was ruthless in obtaining what he wanted.

The rumours about him were fascinating. He was reported to have murdered a competitor in Malaysia, and to have had a torrid affair with the favourite wife of an emir. He was said to have backed a successful revolution in Nigeria. The government had brought half a dozen indictments against him, but they were always mysteriously dropped. There were tales of bribes, and senators suborned, business secrets stolen, and witnesses who disappeared. Stone was an advisor to presidents and kings. He was raw, naked power. Among Stone's many properties was a large, isolated estate in the Colorado mountains, where every year scientists, captains of industry and world leaders gathered for seminars. Armed guards kept out unwanted visitors.

Willard Stone had not only approved his daughter's marriage, he had encouraged it. His new son-in-law was brilliant, ambitious, and most important, malleable.

Twelve years after the marriage, Stone arranged for Dustin to be appointed Ambassador to South Korea. Several years later, the President appointed him Ambassador to the United Nations. When Admiral Ralph Whittaker was suddenly ousted as Acting Director of ONI, Thornton took his place.

That day, Willard Stone sent for his son-in-law.

'This is merely the beginning,' Stone promised. 'I have bigger plans for you, Dustin. Great plans.' And he had proceeded to outline them.

Two years earlier, Robert had had his first meeting with the new Acting Director of ONI.

'Sit down, Commander.' There was no cordiality in Dustin Thornton's voice. 'I see by your record that you're something of a maverick.'

What the hell does he mean? Robert wondered. He decided to keep his mouth shut.

Thornton looked up. 'I don't know how Admiral Whittaker ran this office when he was in charge, but from now on we're doing everything by the book. I expect my orders to be carried out to the letter. Do I make myself clear?'

Jesus, Robert thought, *what the hell are we in for here?*

'Do I make myself clear, Commander?'

'Yes. You expect your orders to be carried out to the letter.' He wondered whether he was expected to salute.

'That's all.'

But it was not all.

A month later, Robert was sent to East Germany to bring in a scientist who wanted to defect. It was a dangerous assignment because the Stasi,

East Germany's Central Security Secret Police, had learned about the proposed defection and was watching the scientist closely. In spite of that, Robert had managed to smuggle the man across the border, to a safe house. He was making arrangements to bring him to Washington, when he received a call from Dustin Thornton, telling him that the situation had changed, and that he was to drop the assignment.

'We can't just dump him here,' Robert had protested. 'They'll kill him.'

'That's his problem,' Thornton had replied. 'Your orders are to come back home.'

Screw you, Robert thought. *I'm not going to abandon him*. He had called a friend of his in MI6, British Intelligence, and explained the situation.

'If he goes back to East Germany,' Robert said, 'they'll chop him. Will you take him?'

'I'll see what can be done, old chap. Bring him along.'

And the scientist had been given haven in England.

Dustin Thornton never forgave Robert for disobeying his instructions. From that point on, there was open animosity between the two men. Thornton had discussed the incident with his father-in-law.

'Loose cannons like Bellamy are dangerous,' Willard Stone warned. 'They're a security hazard. Men like that are expendable. Remember that.'

And Thornton had remembered.

Now, walking down the corridor toward Dustin Thornton's office, Robert could not help thinking about the difference between Thornton and Whittaker. In a job like this, trust was the *sine qua non*. He did not trust Dustin Thornton.

Thornton was seated behind his desk when Robert walked into his office.

'You wanted to see me?'

'Yes. Sit down, Commander.' Their relationship had never reached the 'Robert' phase.

'I've been told you've been temporarily transferred to the National Security Agency. When you come back, I have a . . .'

'I'm not coming back. This is my last assignment.'

'What?'

'I'm quitting.'

Thinking about it later, Robert was not sure exactly what reaction he had expected. Some kind of scene. Dustin Thornton could have shown surprise, or he could have argued, or been angry, or relieved. Instead, he had merely looked at Robert and nodded. 'That's it then, isn't it?'

When Robert returned to his own office, he said to his secretary,

'Barbara, I'm going to be away for a while. I'll be leaving in about an hour.'

'Is there some place where you can be reached?'

Robert remembered General Hilliard's orders. 'No.'

'There are some meetings you . . .'

'Cancel them.' He looked at his watch. It was time to meet Admiral Whittaker.

They had breakfast in the centre yard of the Pentagon at the Ground Zero Café, so named because it was once thought that the Pentagon was where the first nuclear bomb attack against the United States would take place. Robert had arranged for a corner table where they would have a degree of privacy. Admiral Whittaker was punctual, and as Robert watched him approach the table, it seemed to him that the Admiral looked older and smaller, as though semi-retirement had somehow aged and shrunk him. He was still a striking-looking man with strong features, a Roman nose, good cheekbones, and a crown of silvered hair. Robert had served under the Admiral in Vietnam and later in the Office of Naval Intelligence, and he had a high regard for him. *More than a high regard*, Robert admitted to himself. Admiral Whittaker was his surrogate father.

The Admiral sat down. 'Good morning, Robert. Well, did they transfer you to NSA?'

Robert nodded. 'Temporarily.'

The waitress arrived and the two men studied the menu.

'I had forgotten how bad the food here was.' Admiral Whittaker smiled. He looked around the room, his face filled with an unspoken nostalgia.

He wishes he were back here, Robert thought. *Amen*.

They ordered. When the waitress was out of earshot, Robert said, 'Admiral, General Hilliard is sending me on an urgent three-thousand-mile trip to locate some witnesses who saw a weather balloon crash. I find that strange. And there's something else that's even stranger. "Time is of the essence," to quote the General, but I've been ordered not to use any of my intelligence contacts abroad to help me.'

Admiral Whittaker looked puzzled. 'I suppose the General must have his reasons.'

Robert said, 'I can't imagine what they are.'

Admiral Whittaker studied Robert. Commander Bellamy had served under him in Vietnam and had been the best pilot in the squadron. The Admiral's son, Edward, had been Robert's bombardier, and on the terrible day their plane had been shot down, Edward had been killed. Robert had barely survived. The Admiral had gone to the hospital to visit him.

'He's not going to make it,' the doctors had told him. Robert, lying

561

there in agonizing pain, had whispered, 'I'm sorry about Edward . . .
I'm so sorry.'

Admiral Whittaker had squeezed Robert's hand. 'I know you did
everything you could. You've got to get well, now. You're going to be
fine.' He wanted desperately for Robert to live. In the Admiral's mind,
Robert was his son now, the son who would take Edward's place.

And Robert had pulled through.

'Robert . . .'

'Yes, Admiral?'

'I hope your mission is successful.'

'So do I. It's my last one.'

'You're still determined to quit?'

The Admiral was the only one Robert had confided in. 'I've had
enough.'

'Thornton?'

'It's not just him. It's me. I'm tired of interfering with other people's
lives.' *I'm tired of the lies and the cheating, and the broken promises that
were never meant to be kept. I'm tired of manipulating people, and of
being manipulated. I'm tired of the games and the danger and the
betrayals. It's cost me everything I ever gave a damn about.*

'Do you have any idea what you're going to do?'

'I'll try to find something useful to do with my life, something
positive.'

'What if they won't let you go?'

Robert said, 'They have no choice, have they?'

6

The limousine was waiting at the River Entrance parking lot.

'Are you ready, Commander?' Captain Dougherty asked.

As ready as I'll ever be, Robert thought. 'Yes.'

Captain Dougherty accompanied Robert to his apartment so he could pack. Robert had no idea how many days he would be gone. *How long does an impossible assignment take?* He packed enough clothes for a week and, at the last minute, put in a framed photograph of Susan. He stared at it for a long time and wondered if she was enjoying herself in Brazil. He thought, *I hope not. I hope she's having a lousy time*. And was immediately ashamed of himself.

When the limousine arrived at Andrews Air Force Base, the plane was waiting. It was a C20A, an Air Force jet.

Captain Dougherty held out his hand. 'Good luck, Commander.'

'Thanks.' *I'll need it.* Robert walked up the steps to the cabin. The crew was inside, finishing the pre-flight check. There was a pilot, a co-pilot, a navigator and a steward, all in Air Force uniforms. Robert was familiar with the plane. It was loaded with electronic equipment. On the outside, near the tail, was a high-frequency antenna that looked like an enormous fishing pole. Inside the cabin were twelve red telephones on the walls and a white, unsecured, phone. Radio transmissions were in code, and the plane's radar was on a military frequency. The primary colour inside was Air Force blue, and the cabin was furnished with comfortable club chairs.

Robert found that he was the only passenger. The pilot greeted him. 'Welcome aboard, Commander. If you'll put on your seat belt, we have clearance to take off.'

Robert strapped himself in and leaned back in his seat as the plane taxied down the runway. A minute later, he felt the familiar pull of gravity as the jet screamed into the air. He had not piloted a plane since his crash, when he had been told he would never be able to fly again. *Fly again, hell*, Robert thought, *they said I wouldn't live. It was a miracle . . . No, it was Susan . . .*

Vietnam. He had been sent there with the rank of Lieutenant Commander, stationed on the aircraft carrier *Ranger* as a tactics officer, responsible for training fighter pilots and planning attack strategy. He had led a bomber squadron of A-6A Intruders, and there was very little time away from the pressures of battle. One of the few leaves he had was in Bangkok for a week of R and R, and during that time he never bothered to sleep. The city was a Disneyland designed for the pleasure of the male animal. He had met an exquisite Thai girl his first hour in town, and she had stayed at his side the whole time and taught him a few Thai phrases. He had found the language soft and mellifluous.

Good morning: *Arun sawasdi*

Where are you from?: *Khun ma chak nai?*

Where are you going now?: *Khun kamrant chain pai?*

She taught him other phrases too, but she would not tell him what they meant, and when he said them, she giggled.

When Robert returned to the *Ranger*, Bangkok seemed like a faraway dream. The war was the reality, and it was a horror. Someone showed him one of the leaflets the marines dropped over Vietnam. It read:

'DEAR CITIZENS:

'The US Marines are fighting alongside the Government of Vietnam forces in Duc Pho in order to give the Vietnamese people a chance to live a free, happy life, without fear of hunger and suffering. But many Vietnamese have paid with their lives, and their homes have been destroyed because they helped the Vietcong.

'The hamlets of Hai Mon, Hai Tan, Sa Binh, Ta Binh, and many others have been destroyed because of this. We will not hesitate to destroy every hamlet that helps the Vietcong, who are powerless to stop the combined might of GVN and its allies. The choice is yours. If you refuse to let the Vietcong use your villages and hamlets as their battle-field, your homes and your lives will be saved.'

We're saving the poor bastards, all right, Robert thought grimly. *And all we're destroying is their country.*

The aircraft carrier *Ranger* was equipped with all the state-of-the-art technology that could be crammed into it. The ship was home base for sixteen aircraft, forty officers and three hundred and fifty enlisted men. Flight schedules were handed out three or four hours before the first launch of the day.

In the Mission Planning section of the ship's Intelligence Centre, the latest information and reconnaissance photos were given to the bombardiers, who then planned their flight patterns.

'Jesus, they gave us a beauty this morning,' Edward Whittaker, Robert's bombardier, said.

Edward Whittaker looked like a younger version of his father, but he had a completely different personality. Where the Admiral was a formidable figure, dignified and austere, his son was down-to-earth, warm and friendly. He had earned his place as 'just one of the boys'. The other airmen forgave him for being the son of their commander. He was the best bombardier in the squadron, and he and Robert had become fast friends.

'Where are we heading?' Robert asked.

'For our sins, we've drawn Package Six.'

It was the most dangerous mission of all. It meant flying north to Hanoi, Haiphong, and up the Red River delta, where the flak was heaviest. There was a catch-22: they were not permitted to bomb any strategic targets if there were civilians nearby, and the North Vietnamese, not being stupid, immediately placed civilians around all their military installations. There was a lot of grumbling in the allied military, but President Lyndon Johnson, safely back in Washington, was giving the orders.

The twelve years that United States troops fought in Vietnam was the longest period it has ever been at war. Robert Bellamy had come into it late in 1972, when the Navy were having major problems. Their F-4 squadrons were being destroyed. In spite of the fact that their planes were superior to the Russian MiGs, the American Navy were losing one F-4 for every two MiGs shot down. It was an unacceptable ratio.

Robert was summoned to the headquarters of Admiral Ralph Whittaker.

'You sent for me, Admiral?'

'You have the reputation of being a hotshot pilot, Commander. I need your help.'

'Yes, sir?'

'We're getting murdered by the goddamned enemy. I have had a thorough analysis made. There's nothing wrong with our planes – it's the training of the men who are flying them. Do you understand?'

'Yes, sir.'

'I want you to pick a group and retrain it in manoeuvres and weapons employment . . .'

The new group was called Top Gun, and before they were through, the ratio changed from two to one to twelve to one. For every two F-4s lost, twenty-four MiGs were shot down. The assignment had taken eight weeks of intensive training, and Commander Bellamy had finally returned to his ship. Admiral Whittaker was there to greet him. 'That was a damned fine job, Commander.'

'Thank you, Admiral.'

'Now, let's get back to work.'

'I'm ready, sir.'

Robert had flown thirty-four bombing missions from the *Ranger* without incident.

His thirty-fifth mission was Package Six.

They had passed Hanoi and were heading northwest toward Phu Tho and Yen Bay, and the flak was getting increasingly heavy. Edward

Whittaker was seated on Robert's right, staring at the radar screen, listening to the ominous bass tones of enemy search radars sweeping the sky.

The sky directly ahead of them looked like the Fourth of July, streaked with white smoke from the light guns below, dark grey bursts from the fifty-five-millimetre shells, black clouds from the hundred-millimetre shells, and coloured tracer bullets from heavy machine-gun fire.

'We're approaching target,' Edward said. His voice through the head-phones sounded eerily faraway.

'Roger.'

The A-6A Intruder was flying at 450 knots, and at that speed, even with the drag and weight of the bomb load, it handled remarkably well, moving too fast for enemies to track it.

Robert reached out and turned on the master armament switch. The dozen 500-pound bombs were now ready to be released. He was headed straight for the target.

A voice on his radio said, 'Romeo . . . you have a bogey at four o'clock high.'

Robert turned to look. A MiG was hurtling toward him, coming out of the sun. Robert banked and sent the plane into a steep dive. The MiG was on his tail. It loosed a missile. Robert checked his instrument panel. The missile was closing in rapidly. A thousand feet away . . . Six hundred . . . Four hundred . . .

'Holy shit!' Edward yelled. 'What are we waiting for?'

Robert waited until the last second, then released a stream of metal chaff, and went into a steep climbing turn, leaving the missile to follow the chaff and crash harmlessly into the ground below.

'Thank you, God,' Edward said. 'And you, pal.'

Robert continued the climb and swung behind the MiG. The pilot started to take evasive action, but it was too late. Robert loosed a Sidewinder missile and watched it crawl up the tail pipe of the MiG and explode. An instant later the sky was showered with pieces of metal.

A voice came over the intercom. 'Nice work, Romeo.'

The plane was over the target now. 'Here we go,' Edward said. He pressed the red button that released the bombs and watched them tumble down toward their target. Mission accomplished. Robert headed the plane back toward the carrier.

At that instant, they felt a heavy thud. The swift and graceful bomber suddenly became sluggish.

'We've been hit!' Edward called.

Both fire warning lights were flashing red. The plane was moving erratically, out of control.

A voice came over the radio. 'Romeo, this is Tiger. Do you want us to cover you?'

Robert made a split-second decision. 'No, go on to your targets. I'm going to try to make it back to base.'

The plane had slowed down, and was becoming more difficult to handle.

'Faster,' Edward said nervously, 'or we're going to be late for lunch.'

Robert looked at the altimeter. The needle was dropping rapidly. He activated his radio mike. 'Romeo to home base. We've taken a hit.'

'Home base to Romeo. How bad is it?'

'I'm not sure. I think I can bring it home.'

'Hold on.' A moment later the voice returned. 'Your signal is "Charlie on arrival".'

That meant they were cleared to land on the carrier immediately.

'Roger.'

'Good luck.'

The plane was starting to roll. Robert fought to correct it, trying to gain altitude. 'Come on, baby, you can make it.' Robert's face was tight. They were losing too much altitude. 'What's our ETA?'

Edward looked at his chart. 'Seven minutes.'

'I'm going to get you that hot lunch.' Robert was nursing the plane along with all the skill at his command, using the throttle and rudder to try to keep it on a straight course. The altitude was still dropping alarmingly. Finally, ahead of him, Robert saw the sparkling blue waters of the Tonkin Gulf.

'We're home free, buddy,' Robert said. 'Just a few more miles.'

'Terrific. I never doubted . . .'

And out of nowhere, two MiGs descended on the plane with a thunderous roar. Bullets began thudding against the fuselage.

'Eddie! Bail out!' He turned to look. Edward was slumped against his seat belt, his right side torn open, blood spattering the cockpit.

'No!' It was a scream.

A second later, Robert felt a sudden, agonizing blow to his chest. His flight suit was instantly soaked in blood. The plane started to spiral downward. He felt himself losing consciousness. With his last ounce of strength, he unfastened his seat belt. He turned to take a final look at Edward. 'I'm sorry,' he whispered. He blacked out and later had no recollection of how he ejected out of the plane and parachuted into the water below. A May Day call had been sent out, and a Sikorsky SH-3A Sea King helicopter from the USS *Yorktown* was circling, waiting to pick him up. In the distance, the crew could see Chinese junks rapidly closing in for the kill, but they were too late.

When they loaded Robert into the helicopter, a medical corpsman took one look at his torn body and said, 'Jesus Christ, he'll never even make it to the hospital.'

They gave Robert a shot of morphine, wrapped pressure bandages tightly around his chest, and flew him to the 12th Evacuation Hospital at Cu Chi Base.

The '12th Evac' that served Cu Chi, Tay Ninh, and Dau Tieng bases had four hundred beds in a dozen wards, housed in Quonset huts arranged around a U-shaped compound connected by covered walkways. The hospital had two intensive care units, one for surgery cases, the other for burns, and each unit was seriously overcrowded. When Robert was brought in, he left a bright red trail of blood across the hospital floor.

A harried surgeon cut the bandages from Robert's chest, took one look and said wearily, 'He's not going to make it. Take him in back to cold storage.'

And the doctor moved on.

Robert, fading in and out of consciousness, heard the doctor's voice from a far distance. *So, this is it*, he thought. *What a lousy way to die.*

'You don't want to die, do you, sailor? Open your eyes. Come on.'

He opened his eyes and saw a blurred image of a white uniform and a woman's face. She was saying something more, but he could not make out the words. The ward was too noisy, filled with a cacophony of screams and moans of patients, and doctors yelling out orders, and nurses frantically running around ministering to the savaged bodies that lay there.

Robert's memory of the next forty-eight hours was a haze of pain and delirium. It was only later that he learned that the nurse, Susan Ward, had persuaded a doctor to operate on him and had donated her own blood for a transfusion. They had put three IVs into Robert's ravaged body, and pumped blood through them simultaneously, fighting to keep him alive.

When the operation was over, the surgeon in charge sighed. 'We've wasted our time. He's got no more than a ten per cent chance of pulling through.'

But the doctor did not know Robert Bellamy. And he did not know Susan Ward. It seemed to Robert that whenever he opened his eyes, Susan was there, holding his hand, stroking his forehead, ministering to him, willing him to live. He was delirious most of the time. Susan sat quietly next to him in the dark ward in the middle of the lonely nights, and listened to his ravings.

'. . . the DOD is wrong, you can't head in perpendicular to the target or you'll hit the river . . . tell them to angle the dives a few degrees off target-heading . . . tell them . . .' he mumbled.

Susan said soothingly, 'I will.'

Robert's body was soaked in perspiration. She sponged him off.

'. . . you have to remove all five of the safety pins or the seat won't eject. Check them . . .'

'All right. Go back to sleep now.'

'. . . the shackles on the multiple ejector racks malfunctioned. God only knows where the bombs landed . . .'

Half the time Susan could not understand what her patient was talking about.

Susan Ward was the head emergency operating-room nurse and the best. She had come from a small town in Idaho, and had grown up with the boy next door, Frank Prescott, the son of the Mayor. Everyone in town assumed they would be married one day.

Susan had a younger brother, Michael, whom she adored. On his eighteenth birthday he was sent to Vietnam, and Susan wrote to him every day. Three months after he had enlisted, Susan's family received a telegram, and she knew what it contained before they opened it.

When Frank Prescott heard the news, he rushed over. 'I'm really sorry, Susan. I liked Michael a lot.' And then he made the mistake of saying, 'Let's get married right away.'

And Susan had looked at him and made a decision. 'No. I have to do something important with my life.'

'For God's sake! What's more important than marrying me?'

The answer was Vietnam.

Susan Ward went to nursing school.

She had been in Vietnam for eleven months, working tirelessly, when Commander Robert Bellamy was wheeled in and sentenced to die. Triage was a common practice in emergency evacuation hospitals. The doctors would examine two or three patients and make summary judgements as to which one they would try to save. For reasons which were never truly clear to her, Susan had taken one look at the torn body of Robert Bellamy and had known that she could not let him die. Was it her brother she was trying to save? Or was it something else? She was exhausted and overworked, but instead of taking her time off, she spent every spare moment tending to him.

Susan had looked up her patient's record. An ace Navy pilot and instructor, he had earned the Naval Cross. His birthplace was Harvey, Illinois, a small industrial city south of Chicago. He had enlisted in the Navy from college, and had trained at Pensacola. He was unmarried.

Each day, as Robert Bellamy was recuperating, walking the thin line between death and life, Susan whispered to him, 'Come on, sailor. I'm waiting for you.'

One night, six days after he had been brought into the hospital, Robert was rambling on in his delirium, when suddenly he sat straight up in bed, looked at Susan, and said clearly, 'It's not a dream. You're real.'

Susan felt her heart give a little jump. 'Yes,' she said softly, 'I'm real.'

'I thought I was dreaming. I thought I had gone to heaven and God assigned you to me.'

She looked into Robert's eyes and said seriously, 'I would have killed you if you had died.'

His eyes swept the crowded ward. 'Where . . . where am I?'

'The 12th Evacuation Hospital at Cu Chi.'

'How long have I been here?'

'Six days.'

'Eddie . . . he . . .'

'I'm sorry.'

'I have to tell the Admiral.'

She took Robert's hand and said, gently, 'He knows. He's been here to visit you.'

Robert's eyes filled with tears. 'I hate this goddamn war. I can't tell you how much I hate it.'

From that moment on, Robert's progress astonished the doctors. All his vital signs stabilized.

'We'll be shipping him out of here soon,' they told Susan. And she felt a sharp pang.

Robert was not sure exactly when he fell in love with Susan Ward. Perhaps it was the moment when she was dressing his wounds, and nearby they heard the sounds of bombs dropping and she murmured, 'They're playing our song.'

Or perhaps it was when they told Robert he was well enough to be transferred to Walter Reed Hospital in Washington to finish his convalescence, and Susan said, 'Do you think I'm going to stay here and let some other nurse have that great body? Oh, no. I'm going to pull every string I can to go with you.'

They were married two weeks later. It took Robert a year to heal completely, and Susan tended to his every need, night and day. He had never met anyone like her, nor had he dreamed that he could ever love anyone so much. He loved her compassion and sensitivity, her passion and vitality. He loved her beauty and her sense of humour.

On their first anniversary he said to her, 'You're the most beautiful, the most wonderful, the most caring human being in the world. There is no one on this earth with your warmth and wit and intelligence.'

And Susan had held him tightly and whispered in a nasal, chorus-girl voice, 'Likewise, I'm sure.'

They shared more than love. They genuinely liked and respected each other. All their friends envied them, and with good reason. Whenever they talked about a perfect marriage, it was always Robert and Susan they held up as an example. They were compatible in every way, complete soulmates. Susan was the most sensual woman Robert had ever known, and they were able to set each other on fire with a touch, a word. One evening, when they were scheduled to go to a formal dinner party, Robert was running late. He was in the shower when Susan came into the bathroom, carefully made up and dressed in a lovely strapless evening gown.

'My God, you look sexy,' Robert said. 'It's too bad we don't have more time.'

'Oh, don't worry about that,' Susan murmured. And a moment later she had stripped off her clothes and joined Robert in the shower.

They never got to the party.

Susan sensed Robert's needs almost before he knew them, and she saw to it that they were attended to. And Robert was equally attentive to her. Susan would find love notes on her dressing-room table, or in her shoes when she started to get dressed. Flowers and little gifts would be delivered to her on Ground Hog Day and President Polk's birthday and in celebration of the Lewis and Clark Expedition.

And the laughter that they shared. The wonderful laughter . . .

The pilot's voice crackled over the intercom. 'We'll be landing in Zürich in ten minutes, Commander.'

Robert Bellamy's thoughts snapped back to the present, to his assignment. In his fifteen years with Naval Intelligence, he had been involved in dozens of challenging cases, but this one promised to be the most bizarre of them all. He was on his way to Switzerland to find a busload of anonymous witnesses who had disappeared into thin air. *Talk about looking for a needle in a haystack. I don't even know where the haystack is. Where is Sherlock Holmes when I need him?*

'Will you fasten your seat belt, please?'

The C20A was flying over dark forests, and a moment later, skimming over the runway etched by the landing lights of the Zürich International Airport. The plane taxied to the east side of the airport, and headed for the small General Aviation Building, away from the main terminal. There were still puddles on the tarmac from the earlier rainstorms, but the night sky was clear.

'Crazy weather,' the pilot commented. 'Sunny here Sunday, rainy all day today, and clearing tonight. You don't need a watch here, what you really need is a barometer. Can I arrange a car for you, Commander?'

'No, thanks.' From this moment on, he was completely on his own. Robert waited until the plane taxied away, then he boarded a minibus to the airport hotel where he collapsed into a dreamless sleep.

7

DAY TWO

0800 Hours

The next morning Robert approached a clerk behind the Europcar desk.
'*Guten Tag.*'

It was a reminder that he was in the German-speaking part of Switzerland. '*Guten Tag.* Do you have a car available?'

'Yes, sir, we do. How long will you be needing it?'

Good question. An hour? A month? Maybe a year or two? 'I'm not
sure.'

'Do you plan to return the car to this airport?'

'Possibly.'

The clerk looked at him strangely. 'Very well. Will you fill out these
papers, please?'

Robert paid for the car with the special black credit card General
Hilliard had given him. The clerk examined it, perplexed, then said,
'Excuse me.' He disappeared into an office and when he returned,
Robert said, 'Any problem?'

'No, sir. None at all.'

The car was a grey Opel Omega. Robert got onto the Airport Highway and headed for downtown Zürich. He enjoyed Switzerland. It was
one of the most beautiful countries in the world. Years earlier, he had
skied there. In more recent times, he had carried out assignments there,
liaising with Espionage Abteilung, the Swiss intelligence agency. During
World War II, the agency had been organized into three bureaux; D,
P and I, covering Germany, France and Italy, respectively. Now its
main purpose was related to espionage operations conducted under
cover of United Nations diplomacy, from the various UN organizations
in Geneva. Robert had friends in Espionage Abteilung, but he
remembered General Hilliard's words: *You're not to get in touch with
any of them.*

The drive into the city took twenty-five minutes. Robert reached the
Dübendorf downtown off-ramp and headed for the Dolder Grand
Hotel. It was exactly as he remembered it: an overgrown Swiss château
with turrets, stately and imposing, surrounded by greenery and overlooking Lake Zürich. He parked the car and walked into the lobby. On
the left was the reception desk.

'*Guten Tag.*'

'*Guten Tag. Haben sie ein Zimmer für eine Nacht?*'

'*Ja. Wie möchten Sie bezahlen?*'

'*Mit Kreditkarte.*' The black and white credit card that General Hilliard had given him. Robert asked for a map of Switzerland, and was escorted to a comfortable room in the new wing of the hotel. It had a small balcony that overlooked the lake. Robert stood there, breathing in the crisp, autumn air, thinking about the task that lay ahead of him.

He had nothing to go on. Not one damned thing. All the factors in the equation of his assignment were completely unknown. The name of the tour bus company. The number of passengers. Their names and whereabouts. *Are the witnesses all in Switzerland? That's our problem. We have no idea where they are or who they are.* And it wasn't enough to find some of the witnesses. *You must find every one of them.* The only information he had was the date: Sunday, October 14th, and the place: Uetendorf.

He needed a handle, something to grab onto.

If he remembered correctly, all-day tour buses left from only two major cities. Zürich and Geneva. Robert opened a desk drawer and took out the bulky *Telefonbuch. I should look under M, for miracle,* Robert thought. There were more than half a dozen tour companies listed. SUNSHINE TOURS, SWISSTOUR, TOUR SERVICE, TOURALPINO, TOURISMA REISEN . . . He would have to check each of them. He copied down the addresses of all the companies and drove to the offices of the nearest one listed: Tour Service.

There were two clerks behind the counter, taking care of tourists. When one of them was free, Robert said, 'Excuse me. My wife was on one of your tours last Sunday and she left her purse on the bus. I think she got excited because of seeing that weather balloon that crashed near Uetendorf.'

The clerk frowned, '*Es tut mir sehr leid*. You must be mistaken. Our tours do not go near Uetendorf.'

'Oh. Sorry.' *Strike one.*

The next stop promised to be more fruitful.

'Do your tours go to Uetendorf?'

'Oh, *ja*.' The clerk smiled. 'Our tours go everywhere in Switzerland. They are the most scenic. We have a tour to Zermatt, the Tell Special. There is also the Glacier Express and the Palm Express. The Great Circle Tour leaves in fifteen . . .'

'Did you have a tour Sunday that stopped to watch that weather balloon that crashed? I know my wife was late getting back to the hotel and . . .'

The clerk behind the counter said, indignantly, 'We take great pride in the fact that our tours are *never* late. We make no unscheduled stops.'

'Then one of your buses didn't stop to look at that weather balloon?'

'Absolutely not.'

'Thank you.' *Strike two.*

The third office Robert visited was located at Bahnhofplatz, and the sign outside said SUNSHINE TOURS. Robert walked up to the counter. 'Good afternoon. I wanted to ask you about one of your tour buses. I heard that a weather balloon crashed near Uetendorf and that your driver stopped for half an hour so the passengers could look at it.'

'No, no. He only stopped for fifteen minutes. We have very strict schedules.

Home run!

'What was your interest in this, did you say?'

Robert pulled out one of the identification cards that had been given him. 'I'm a reporter,' Robert said earnestly, 'and I'm doing a story for *Travel & Leisure* magazine on how efficient the buses in Switzerland are, compared with other countries. I wonder if I might interview your driver?'

'That would make a very interesting article. Very interesting, indeed. We Swiss pride ourselves on our efficiency.'

'And that pride is well deserved,' Robert assured him.

'Would the name of our company be mentioned?'

'Prominently.'

The clerk smiled. 'Well, then I see no harm.'

'Could I speak with him now?'

'This is his day off.' He wrote a name on a piece of paper. Robert Bellamy read it upside down. *Hans Beckerman.*

The clerk added an address. 'He lives in Kappel. That's a small village about forty kilometres from Zürich. You should be able to find him at home now.'

Robert Bellamy took the paper. 'Thank you very much. By the way,' Robert said, 'just so we have all the facts for the story, do you have a record of how many tickets you sold for that particular tour?'

'Of course. We keep records of all our tours. Just a moment.' He picked up a ledger underneath the counter and flipped a page. 'Ah, here we are. Sunday. Hans Beckerman. There were seven passengers. He drove the Iveco that day, the small bus.'

Seven unknown passengers and the driver. Robert took a stab in the dark. 'Would you happen to have the names of those passengers?'

'Sir, people come in off the street, buy their ticket and take the tour. We don't ask for identification.'

Wonderful. 'Thank you again.' Robert started toward the door.

The clerk called out, 'I hope you will send us a copy of the article.'

'Absolutely,' Robert said.

The first piece of the puzzle lay in the tour bus, and Robert drove to

Talstrasse where the buses departed, as though it might reveal some hidden clue. The Iveco bus was brown and silver, small enough to traverse the steep Alpine roads, with seats for fourteen passengers. *Who were the seven, and where had they disappeared to?* Robert got back in his car. He consulted his map and marked it. He took Lavessneralle out of the city, into the Albis, the start of the Alps, toward the village of Kappel. He headed south, driving past the small hills that surround Zürich, and began the climb into the magnificent mountain chain of the Alps. He drove through Adliswil and Langnau and Hausen, and nameless hamlets with chalets and colourful picture-postcard scenery, until almost an hour later, he came to Kappel. The little village consisted of a restaurant, a church, a post office, and a dozen houses scattered around the hills. Robert parked the car and walked into the restaurant. A waitress was clearing a table near the door.

'*Entschuldigen Sie bitte, Fraulein. Welche Richtung ist das Haus von Herrn Beckerman?*'

'*Ja.*' She pointed down the road. '*An der Kirche rechts.*'

'*Danke.*'

Robert turned right at the church and drove up to a modest two-storey stone house with a ceramic tiled roof. He got out of the car and walked up to the door. He could see no bell, and knocked.

A heavyset woman with a faint moustache answered the door. '*Ja?*'

'I'm sorry to bother you. Is Mr Beckerman in?'

She eyed him suspiciously. 'What do you want with him?'

Robert gave her a winning smile. 'You must be Mrs Beckerman.' He pulled out his reporter's identification card. 'I'm doing a magazine article on Swiss bus drivers, and your husband was recommended to my magazine as having one of the finest safety records in the country.'

She brightened and said proudly, 'My Hans is an excellent driver.'

'That's what everyone tells me, Mrs Beckerman. I would like to do an interview with him.'

'An interview with my Hans for a magazine?' She was flustered. 'That is very exciting. Come in, please.'

She led Robert into a small, meticulously neat living room. 'Wait here, *bitte*. I will get Hans.'

The house had a low, beamed ceiling, dark wooden floors and plain wooden furniture. There was a small stone fireplace and lace curtains at the windows.

Robert stood there, thinking. This was not only his best lead, it was his *only* lead. *People come in off the street, buy their ticket and take the tour. We don't ask for identification . . . There's no place to go from here*, Robert thought grimly. *If this doesn't work out, I can always place an ad: Will the seven bus passengers who saw a weather balloon crash Sunday please assemble in my hotel room at 1200 tomorrow morning? Breakfast will be served.*

A thin, bald man appeared. His complexion was pale, and he wore a thick, black moustache that was startlingly out of keeping with the rest of his appearance. 'Good afternoon, *Herr* . . . ?'

'Smith. Good afternoon.' Robert's voice was hearty. 'I've certainly been looking forward to meeting you, Mr Beckerman.'

'My wife tells me you are writing a story about bus drivers.' He spoke with a heavy German accent.

Robert smiled ingratiatingly. 'That's right. My magazine is interested in your wonderful safety record and . . .'

'*Scheissdreck!*' Beckerman said rudely. 'You are interested in the thing that crashed Sunday afternoon, no?'

Robert managed to look abashed. 'As a matter of fact, yes, I am interested in discussing that, too.'

'Then why do you not come out and say so? Sit down.'

'Thank you.' Robert took a seat on the couch.

Beckerman said, 'I am sorry I cannot offer you a drink, but we do not keep *schnapps* in the house anymore.' He tapped his stomach. 'Ulcers. The doctors cannot even give me drugs to relieve the pain. I am allergic to all of them.' He sat down opposite Robert. 'But you did not come here to talk about my health, eh? What is it you wish to know?'

'I want to talk to you about the passengers who were on your bus Sunday when you stopped near Uetendorf where the weather balloon crashed.'

Hans Beckerman was staring at him. 'Weather balloon? What weather balloon? What are you talking about?'

'The balloon that . . .'

'You mean the spaceship.'

It was Robert's turn to stare. 'The . . . *spaceship*?'

'*Ja*, the flying saucer.'

It took a moment for the words to sink in. Robert felt a sudden chill. 'Are you telling me that you saw a flying saucer?'

'*Ja*. With dead bodies in it.'

Yesterday, in the Swiss Alps, a NATO weather balloon crashed. There were some experimental military objects aboard the balloon that are highly secret.

Robert tried hard to sound calm. 'Mr Beckerman, are you certain that what you saw was a flying saucer?'

'Of course. What they call a UFO.'

'And there were dead people inside?'

'Not people, no. *Creatures*. It is hard to describe them.' He gave a little shiver. 'They were very small with big, strange eyes. They were dressed in suits of a silver metallic colour. It was very frightening.'

Robert listened, his mind in a turmoil. 'Did your passengers see this?'

'Oh, *ja*. We all saw it. I stopped there for maybe fifteen minutes. They wanted me to stay longer, but the company is very strict about schedules.'

Robert knew the question was futile before he even asked it. 'Mr Beckerman, would you happen to know the names of any of your passengers?'

'Mister, I drive a bus. The passengers buy a ticket in Zürich and we take a tour southwest to Interlaken and then northwest to Bern. They can either get off at Bern or return to Zürich. Nobody gives their names.'

Robert said, desperately, 'There's *no* way you can identify any of them?'

The bus driver thought for a moment. 'Well, I can tell you there were no children on that trip. Just men.'

'Only men?'

Beckerman thought for a moment. 'No. That's not right. There was one woman, too.'

Terrific. That really narrows it down, Robert thought. *Next question: Why the hell did I ever agree to this assignment?* 'What you're saying, Mr Beckerman, is that a group of tourists boarded your bus at Zürich, and then when the tour was over, they simply scattered?'

'That's right, Mr Smith.'

So there was not even a haystack. 'Do you remember *anything* at all about the passengers? Anything they said or did?'

Beckerman shook his head. 'Mister, you get so you don't pay no attention to them. Unless they cause some trouble. Like that German.'

Robert sat very still. He asked softly, 'What German?'

'*Affenarsch!* All the other passengers were excited about seeing the UFO and those dead creatures in it, but this old man kept complaining about how we had to hurry up to get to Bern because he had to prepare some lecture for the University in the morning . . .'

A beginning. 'Do you remember anything else about him?'

'No.'

'Nothing at all?'

'He was wearing a black overcoat.'

Great. 'Mr Beckerman, I want to ask you for a favour. Would you mind driving out with me to Uetendorf?'

'It's my day off. I am busy with . . .'

'I'll be glad to pay you.'

'*Ja?*'

'Two hundred marks.'

'I don't . . .'

'I'll make it four hundred marks.'

Beckerman thought for a moment. 'Why not? It's a nice day for a drive, *nicht?*'

They headed south, past the picturesque villages of Immensee and Meggen and through Luzern. The scenery was breathtakingly beautiful, but Robert had other things on his mind.

They passed through Sarnen, and Brünig, the pass leading to

577

Interlaken. They sped past Leissigen and Faulensee with its lovely blue lake dotted with white sailboats.

'How much further is it?' Robert asked.

'Soon,' Hans Beckerman promised.

They had been driving for almost an hour when they came to Spiez. Hans Beckerman said, 'It is not far now. Just past the next town, Thun.'

Robert felt his heart beginning to beat faster. He was about to witness something that was far beyond imagination, alien visitors from the stars. They drove through Thun, and a few minutes later, as they neared a grove of trees across the highway, Hans Beckerman pointed and said, 'There!'

Robert braked to a stop and pulled over to the side of the road.

'Across the highway. Behind those trees.'

Robert felt a growing sense of excitement. 'Right. Let's have a look.'

A truck was speeding by. When it had passed, Robert and Hans Beckerman crossed the road. Robert followed the bus driver up a small incline, into the stand of trees.

The highway was completely hidden from sight. As they stepped into a clearing, Beckerman announced, 'It is right there.'

Lying on the ground in front of them were the torn remains of a weather balloon.

8

I'm getting too old for this, Robert thought, wearily. *I was really beginning to fall for his flying saucer fairy tale.*

Hans Beckerman was staring at the metallic object on the ground, a confused expression on his face. '*Verfälschung!* That is not it.'

Robert sighed. 'No, it isn't, is it?'

Beckerman shook his head. 'It was here yesterday.'

'Your little green men probably flew it away.'

Beckerman was stubborn. 'No, no. They were both *tot* – dead.'

Tot – dead. That sums up my mission pretty well. My only lead is a crazy old man who sees spaceships.

Robert walked over to the balloon to examine it more closely. It was a large aluminium envelope, fourteen feet in diameter, with serrated edges where it had ripped open when it crashed to earth. All the instruments had been removed, just as General Hilliard had told him. *I can't stress enough the importance of what was in that balloon.*

Robert circled the deflated balloon, his shoes squishing in the wet grass, looking for anything that might give him the slightest clue. Nothing. It was identical to a dozen other weather balloons he had seen over the years.

The old man still would not give up, filled with Germanic stubbornness. 'Those alien things . . . They made it look like this. They can do anything, you know.'

There's nothing more to be done here, Robert decided. His socks had got wet walking through the tall grass. He started to turn away, then hesitated, struck by a thought. He walked back to the balloon. 'Lift up a corner of this, will you?'

Beckerman looked at him a moment, surprised. 'You wish me to raise it up?'

'*Bitte.*'

Beckerman shrugged. He picked up a corner of the lightweight material and lifted it, while Robert raised another corner. Robert held the piece of aluminium over his head while he walked underneath the balloon toward the centre. His feet sank into the grass. 'It's wet under here,' Robert called out.

'Of course.' The *Dummkopf* was left unsaid. 'It rained all yesterday. The whole ground is wet.'

Robert crawled out from under the balloon. 'It should be dry.' *Crazy weather, the pilot said. Sunny here Sunday. The day the balloon crashed.*

Rainy all day today, and clearing tonight. You don't need a watch here, what you really need is a barometer.

'What?'

'What was the weather like when you saw the UFO?'

Beckerman thought for a moment. 'It was a nice afternoon.'

'Sunny?'

'*Ja*. Sunny.'

'But it rained all day yesterday?'

Beckerman was looking at him, puzzled. 'So?'

'So if the balloon was here all night, the ground under it should be dry – or damp, at the most, through osmosis. But it's soaking wet, like the rest of this area.'

Beckerman was staring. 'I don't understand. What does that mean?'

'It could mean,' Robert said carefully, 'that someone placed this balloon here yesterday, after the rain started, and took away what you saw.' Or was there some saner explanation he had not thought of?

'Who would do such a crazy thing?'

Not so crazy, Robert thought. *The Swiss government could have planted this to deceive any curious visitors. The first stratagem of a cover-up is disinformation.* Robert walked through the wet grass, scanning the ground, cursing himself for being a gullible idiot.

Hans Beckerman was watching Robert suspiciously. 'What magazine did you say you write for, mister?'

'*Travel & Leisure*.'

Hans Beckerman brightened. 'Oh. Then I suppose you will want to take a picture of me, like the other fellow did.'

'What?'

'That photographer who took pictures of us.'

Robert froze. 'Who are you talking about?'

'That photographer fellow. The one who took pictures of us at the wreck. He said he would send us each a print. Some of the passengers had cameras, too.'

Robert said slowly, 'Just a moment. Are you saying that someone took a picture of the passengers here in front of the UFO?'

'That's what I am trying to tell you.'

'And he promised to send you each a print?'

'That's right.'

'Then he must have taken your names and addresses.'

'Well, sure. Otherwise, how would he know where to send them?'

Robert stood still, a feeling of euphoria sweeping over him. *Serendipity, Robert, you lucky sonofabitch*! An impossible mission had suddenly become a piece of cake. He was no longer looking for seven unknown passengers. All he had to do was find one photographer. 'Why didn't you mention him before, Mr Beckerman?'

'You asked me about passengers.'

'You mean, he wasn't a passenger?'

Hans Beckerman shook his head. '*Nein*.' He pointed. 'His car was stalled across the highway. A tow truck was starting to haul it away, and then there was this loud crash, and he ran across the road to see what was happening. When he saw what it was, the fellow ran back to his car, grabbed his cameras and came back. Then he asked us all to pose in front of the saucer thing.'

'Did this photographer give you his name?'

'No.'

'Do you remember anything about him?'

Hans Beckerman concentrated. 'Well, he was a foreigner. American or English.'

'You said a tow truck was getting ready to haul his car away?'

'That's right.'

'Do you remember which way the truck was headed?'

'North. I figured he was towing it into Bern. Thun is closer, but on Sunday all the garages in Thun are closed.'

Robert grinned. 'Thank you. You've been very helpful.'

'You won't forget to send me your article when it's finished?'

'No. Here's your money and an extra hundred marks for your great help. I'll drive you home.' They walked over to the car. As Beckerman opened the door, he stopped and turned toward Robert. 'That was very generous of you.' He took from his pocket a small rectangular piece of metal, the size of a cigarette lighter, containing a tiny white crystal.

'What's this?'

'I found it on the ground Sunday before we got back on the bus.'

Robert examined the strange object. It was as light as paper and was the colour of sand. A rough edge at one end indicated that it might be part of another piece. *Part of the equipment that had been in the weather balloon? Or part of a UFO?*

'Maybe it will bring you luck,' said Beckerman, as he placed the bills Robert had given him in his wallet. 'It certainly worked for me.' He smiled broadly and got into the car.

It was time to ask himself the hard question: *Do I really believe in UFOs?* He had read dozens of wild newspaper stories about people who said they had been beamed up into UFOs and had had all kinds of weird experiences, and he had always attributed those reports to people who were either looking for publicity or who should have thrown themselves on the mercy of a good psychiatrist. But in the past few years there had been reports that were less easy to dismiss. Reports of UFO sightings by astronauts, Air Force pilots and police officials, people with credibility, who shunned publicity. In addition, there had been the disturbing report of the UFO crash at Roswell, New Mexico, where the bodies of aliens had purportedly been discovered. The government was supposed to have hushed that up and removed all the evidence. In

581

World War II, pilots had reported strange sightings of what they called 'Foo fighters', unidentified objects that buzzed them and then disappeared. There were stories of whole towns that had been visited by unexplainable objects speeding through the sky. *What if there really were aliens in UFOs from another galaxy?* Robert wondered. *How would it affect our world? Would it mean peace? War? The end of civilization as we know it?* He found himself half hoping that Hans Beckerman was a raving lunatic, and that what had crashed was really a weather balloon. He would have to find another witness either to verify Beckerman's story or refute it. On the surface, the story seemed incredible, and, yet, there was something nagging at Robert. *If it were only a weather balloon that had crashed, even if it did carry special equipment, why had he been called into a meeting at the National Security Agency at six o'clock in the morning and told that it was urgent that all the witnesses be found quickly? Was there a cover-up? And if so . . . why?*

9

Later that day a press conference was held in Geneva, in the austere offices of the Bundesgasse, the Swiss Ministry of Internal Affairs. There were more than fifty reporters in the room, and an overflow crowd outside in the corridor. There were representatives from television, radio and the press from more than a dozen countries, many loaded with microphones and television gear. They all seemed to be speaking at once.

'We've heard reports that it was not a weather balloon . . .'

'Is it true that it was a flying saucer?'

'There are rumours that there were alien bodies aboard the ship . . .'

'Was one of the aliens alive?'

'Is the government trying to hide the truth from the people . . . ?'

The press officer raised his voice to regain control. 'Ladies and gentlemen, there has been a simple misunderstanding. We get calls all the time. People see satellites, shooting stars . . . Isn't it interesting that reports of UFOs are always made anonymous? Perhaps this caller really believed it was a UFO, but in actuality, it was a weather balloon that fell to the ground. We have arranged transportation to take you to it. If you will follow me, please . . .'

Fifteen minutes later, two busloads of reporters and television cameras were on their way to Uetendorf to see the remains of a crashed weather balloon. When they arrived, they stood in the wet grass, surveying the torn metallic envelope. The press officer said, 'This is your mysterious flying saucer. It was sent aloft from our air base in Vevey. To the best of our knowledge, ladies and gentlemen, there are no unidentified flying objects that our government has not been satisfactorily able to explain, nor to our knowledge are there any extraterrestrials visiting us. It is our government's firm policy that if we should come across any such evidence, we would immediately make that information available to the public. If there are no further questions . . .'

10

Hangar 17 at Langley Air Force Base in Virginia was locked in complete and rigid security. Outside, four armed marines guarded the perimeters of the building, and inside, three high-ranking Army officers stayed on alternate watches of eight hours each, guarding a sealed room inside the hangar. None of the officers knew what he was guarding. Besides the scientists and doctors who were working inside, there had been only three visitors permitted in the sealed chamber.

The fourth visitor was just arriving. He was greeted by Brigadier General Paxton, the officer in charge of security. 'Welcome to our menagerie.'

'I've been looking forward to this.'

'You won't be disappointed. Come this way, please.'

Outside the door of the sealed room was a rack containing four white, sterile suits that completely covered the body.

'Would you please put one on?' the General asked.

'Certainly.' Janus slipped into the suit. Only his face was visible through the glass mask. He put large white slippers over his shoes, and the General led him to the entrance of the sealed room. The marine guard stepped aside, and the General opened the door. 'In here.'

Janus entered the chamber and looked around. In the centre of the room was the spaceship. On white autopsy tables at the other side lay the bodies of the two aliens. A pathologist was performing an autopsy on one of them.

General Paxton directed the visitor's attention to the spaceship.

'We're dealing here with what we believe to be a scout ship,' General Paxton explained. 'We're sure it has some way of communicating directly with the mothership.'

The two men moved closer to examine the spacecraft. It was approximately thirty-five feet in diameter. The interior was shaped like a pearl, with an expandable ceiling, and contained three couches, resembling recliner chairs. The walls were covered with panels containing vibrating metal discs.

'There's a lot here we haven't been able to figure out yet,' General Paxton admitted. 'But what we've already learned is amazing.' He pointed to an array of equipment in small panels. 'There's an integrated wide-field-of-view optical system, what appears to be a life-scan system, a communication system with voice-synthesis capability, and a navigational system that, frankly, has us stumped. We think it works on some kind of electromagnetic pulse.'

'Any weapons aboard?' Janus asked.

General Paxton spread out his hands in a gesture of defeat. 'We're not sure. There's a lot of hardware here we don't begin to understand.'

'What is its source of energy?'

'Our best guess is that it uses monoatomic hydrogen in a closed loop so its waste product is water that can be continually recycled into hydrogen for power. With all that perpetual energy, it has a free ride in interplanetary space. It may be years before we solve all the secrets here. And there's something else that's puzzling. The bodies of the two aliens were strapped into their couches. But the indentations in the third couch indicate that it was occupied.'

'Are you saying,' Janus asked slowly, 'that one may be missing?'

'It certainly looks that way.'

Janus stood there a moment frowning. 'Let's have a look at our trespassers.'

The two men walked over to the tables where the two aliens lay. Janus stood there, staring at the strange figures. It was incredible that things so foreign to humanity could exist as sentient beings. The foreheads of the aliens were larger than he had expected. The creatures were completely bald, with no eyelids or eyebrows. The eyes resembled ping-pong balls.

The doctor performing the autopsy looked up as the men approached. 'It's fascinating,' he said. 'A hand has been severed from one of the aliens. There's no sign of blood, but there are what appear to be veins that contain a green liquid. Most of it has drained out.'

'A green liquid?' Janus asked.

'Yes.' The doctor hesitated. 'We believe these creatures are a form of vegetable life.'

'A thinking vegetable? Are you serious?'

'Watch this.' The doctor picked up a watering can and sprinkled water over the arm of the alien with a missing hand. For a moment, nothing happened. And then suddenly at the end of the arm, green matter oozed out and slowly began to form a hand.

The two men stared, shocked. 'Jesus! Are these things dead or not?'

'That's an interesting question. These two figures are not alive in the human sense, but neither do they fit our definition of death. I would say they're dormant.'

Janus was still staring at the newly formed hand.

'Many plants show various forms of intelligence.'

'Intelligence?'

'Oh, yes. There are plants that disguise themselves, protect themselves. At this moment, we're doing some amazing experiments on plant life.'

Janus said, 'I would like to see those experiments.'

'Certainly. I'll be happy to arrange it.'

The huge greenhouse laboratory was in a complex of government buildings thirty miles outside of Washington, DC. Hanging on the wall was an inscription that read:

> THE MAPLES AND FERNS ARE STILL
> UNCORRUPT,
> YET, NO DOUBT, WHEN THEY COME TO
> CONSCIOUSNESS,
> THEY, TOO, WILL CURSE AND SWEAR.
> RALPH WALDO EMERSON
> *Nature*, 1836

Professor Rachman, who was in charge of the complex, was an earnest gnome of a man, filled with enthusiasm for his profession. 'It was Charles Darwin who was the first to perceive the ability of plants to think. Luther Burbank followed up by communicating with them.'

'You really believe that is possible?'

'We know it is. George Washington Carver communed with plants and they gave him hundreds of new products. Carver said, "When I touch a flower, I am touching Infinity. Flowers existed long before there were human beings on this earth, and they will continue to exist for millions of years after. Through the flower, I talk to Infinity . . ."'

Janus looked around the enormous greenhouse they were standing in. It was filled with plants and exotic flowers that rainbowed the room. The mixture of perfumes was overpowering.

'Everything in this room is alive,' Professor Rachman said. 'These plants can feel love, hate, pain, excitement . . . just as animals do. Sir Jagadis Chandra Bose proved that they respond to a tone of voice.'

'How does one prove something like that?' Janus asked.

'I will be happy to demonstrate.' Rachman walked over to a table covered with plants. Beside the table was a polygraph machine. Rachman lifted one of the electrodes and attached it to a plant. The needle on the face of the polygraph was at rest. 'Watch,' he said.

He leaned closer to the plant and whispered, 'I think you are very beautiful. You are more beautiful than all the other plants here . . .'

Janus watched the needle move ever so slightly.

Suddenly Professor Rachman screamed at the plant, 'You are ugly! You are going to die! Do you hear me? You are going to die!'

The needle began to quiver, then it moved sharply upward.

'My God,' Janus said. 'I can't believe it.'

'What you see,' Rachman said, 'is the equivalent of a human being screaming. National magazines have published articles about these experiments. One of the most interesting was a blind experiment conducted by six students. One of them, unknown to the others, was chosen to walk into a room with two plants, one of them wired to a polygraph. He completely destroyed the other plant. Later, one by one, the stu-

586

dents were sent into the room to pass by the plants. When the innocent students walked in, the polygraph registered nothing. But the moment the guilty one appeared, the needle on the polygraph shot up.'

'That's incredible.'

'But true. We've also learned that plants respond to different kinds of music.'

'*Different* kinds?'

'Yes. They did an experiment at Temple Buell College in Denver where healthy flowers were put in three separate glass cases. Acid rock music was piped into one case, soft East Indian sitar music was piped into the second case, and the third had no music. A CBS camera crew recorded the experiment, using time-lapse photography. At the end of two weeks, the flowers exposed to the rock music were dead, the group with no music was growing normally, and the ones that heard the sitar music had turned into beautiful blooms, with stems and flowers reaching toward the source of the sound. Walter Cronkite ran the film on his news show. If you wish to check it, it was on October 26, 1970.'

'Are you saying plants have an intelligence?'

'They breathe, and eat, and reproduce. They can feel pain, and they can utilize defences against their enemies. For example, terpenes are used by certain plants to poison the soil around them and to discourage competitors. Other plants exude alkaloids to make them unpalatable to insects. We've proved that plants communicate with one another by pheromones.'

'Yes, I've heard of that,' Janus said.

'Some plants are meat eaters. The Venus flytrap, for example. Certain orchids look and smell like female bees, to decoy male bees. Others resemble female wasps to attract the males to visit them and pick up pollen. Another type of orchid has an aroma like rotting meat to coax carrion flies in the neighbourhood to come to them.'

Janus was listening to every word.

'The Pink Lady's-Slipper has a hinged upper lip that closes when a bee lands, and traps it. The only escape is through a narrow passageway out the rear, and as the bee fights its way to freedom, it picks up a cap of pollen. There are five thousand flowering plants that grow in the northeast, and each species has its own characteristics. There is no doubt about it. It's been proven over and over that living plants have an intelligence.'

Janus was thinking: *And the missing alien is at large somewhere.*

11

DAY THREE

Bern, Wednesday, October 17th

Bern was one of Robert's favourite cities. It was an elegant town, filled
with lovely monuments and beautiful old stone buildings dating back
to the eighteenth century. It was the capital of Switzerland and one of
its most prosperous cities, and Robert wondered whether the fact that
the street cars were green had anything to do with the colour of money.
He had found that the Berners were more easy-going than the citizens
from other parts of Switzerland. They moved more deliberately, spoke
more slowly, and were generally calmer. He had worked in Bern several
times in the past with the Swiss Secret Service, operating out of their
headquarters at Waisenhausplatz. He had friends there who could have
been helpful, but his instructions were clear. Puzzling, but clear.

It took fifteen phone calls for Robert to locate the garage that towed
the photographer's car. It was a small garage located on Fribourgstrasse,
and the mechanic, Fritz Mandel, was also the owner. Mandel appeared
to be in his late forties, with a gaunt, acne-pitted face, a thin body, and
an enormous beer belly. He was working down in the pit of the grease
rack when Robert arrived.

'Good afternoon,' Robert called.

Mandel looked up. '*Guten Tag*. What can I do for you?'

'I'm interested in a car you towed in Sunday.'

'Just a minute till I finish this up.'

Ten minutes later, Mandel climbed out of the pit and wiped his oily
hands on a filthy cloth.

'You're the one who called this morning. Was there some complaint
about that tow job?' Mandel asked. 'I'm not responsible for . . .'

'No,' Robert reassured him. 'Not at all. I'm conducting a survey and
I'm interested in the driver of the car.'

'Come into the office.'

The two men went into the small office and Mandel opened a file
cabinet. 'Last Sunday, you said?'

'That's right.'

Mandel took out a card. '*Ja*. That was the *Arschficker* who took our
picture in front of that UFO.'

Robert's palms felt suddenly moist. 'You saw the UFO?'

'*Ja. Ich bin* almost *umgekippt.*'

'Can you describe it?'

Mandel shuddered. 'It . . . it seemed alive.'

'I beg your pardon?'

'I mean . . . there was a kind of light around it. It kept changing colours. It looked blue . . . then green . . . I don't know. It's hard to describe. And there were these little creatures inside. Not human, but . . .' He broke off.

'How many?'

'Two.'

'Were they alive?'

'They looked dead to me.' He mopped his brow. 'I'm glad you believe me. I tried to tell my friends and they laughed at me. Even my wife thought I had been drinking. But I know what I saw.'

'About the car you towed . . .' Robert said.

'*Ja.* The Renault. It had an oil leak, and the bearings burned out. The tow job cost a hundred and twenty-five francs. I charge double on Sundays.'

'Did the driver pay by cheque or credit card?'

'I don't take cheques and I don't take no credit cards. He paid in cash.'

'Swiss francs?'

'Pounds.'

'Are you sure?'

'Yes. I remember I had to check the rate of exchange.'

'Mr Mandel, do you happen to have a record of the licence number of the car?'

'Of course,' Mandel said. He glanced down at the card. 'It was a rental. Avis. He rented it in Geneva.'

'Would you mind giving me that licence number?'

'Sure, why not?' He wrote the number down on a piece of paper and handed it to Robert. 'What is this all about, anyway? The UFO thing?'

'No,' Robert said, in his sincerest voice. He took out his wallet and pulled out an identification card. 'I'm with the IAC, the International Auto Club. My company is doing a survey on tow trucks.'

'Oh.'

Robert walked out of the garage, and thought dazedly, *It looks like we have a fucking UFO with two dead aliens on our hands*. Then why had General Hilliard lied to him when he knew Robert would discover that it was a flying saucer that had crashed?

There could only be one explanation, and Robert felt a sudden, cold chill.

12

The huge mothership floated noiselessly through dark space, seemingly motionless, travelling at 22,000 miles an hour, in exact synchronization with the orbit of the earth. The six aliens aboard were studying the three-dimensional field-of-view optical screen that covered one wall of the spaceship. On the monitor, as the planet Earth rotated, they watched holographic pictures of what lay below, while an electronic spectrograph analysed the chemical components of the images that appeared. The atmosphere surrounding the land masses they passed over was heavily polluted. Huge factories befouled the air with thick, black, poisonous gases, while unbiodegradable refuse was dumped into landfills and into the seas.

The aliens looked down at the oceans, once pristine and blue, now black with oil and brown with scum. The coral of the Great Barrier Reef was turning bleach-white and fish were dying by the billions. The Amazon rain forest was a huge, barren crater, where the trees had been stripped. The instruments on the spaceship indicated that the earth's temperature had risen since their last exploration three years earlier. They could see wars being waged on the planet below, spewing new poisons into the atmosphere.

The aliens communicated by mental telepathy.

Nothing has changed with the Earthlings.

It is a pity. They have learned nothing.

We will teach them.

Have you tried to reach the others?

Yes. Something is wrong. There is no reply.

You must keep trying. We must find the ship.

On earth, thousands of feet below the spaceship's orbit, Robert placed a call from a secure phone to General Hilliard. He came on the line almost immediately.

'Good afternoon, Commander. Do you have anything to report?'

Yes. I would like to report that you are a lying sonofabitch. 'About that weather balloon, General . . . it seems to have turned out to be a UFO.' He waited.

'Yes, I know. There were important security reasons why I couldn't tell you everything earlier.'

Bureaucratic double-talk. There was a small silence.

General Hilliard said, 'I'm going to tell you something in the strictest

590

confidence, Commander. Our government had an encounter with extra-terrestrials three years ago. They landed at one of our NATO air bases. We were able to communicate with them.'

Robert felt his heart begin to beat faster. 'What . . . what did they say?'

'That they intend to destroy us.'

He felt a shock go through him. '*Destroy us?*'

'Exactly. They said they were coming back to take over this planet and make slaves of us, and that there is nothing we can do to prevent them. Not yet. But we're working on ways to stop them. That's why it's imperative that we avoid a public panic so we can buy time. I think you can understand now why it's so important that the witnesses are warned not to discuss what they saw. If word of the idents, as we refer to them, leaked out, it would be a worldwide disaster.'

'You don't think it would be better to prepare people and . . . ?'

'Commander, in 1938, a young actor named Orson Welles staged a radio broadcast called *War of the Worlds*, about aliens invading the earth. Within minutes, there was panic in cities all over America. An hysterical population tried to flee from the imaginary invaders. The telephone lines were jammed, the highways were clogged. People were killed. There was total chaos. No, we have to be prepared for the aliens before we go public with this. We want you to find those witnesses for their own protection, so we can keep this under control.'

Robert found that he was perspiring. 'Yes. I . . . I understand.'

'Good. I gather you've talked to one of the witnesses?'

'I've found two of them.'

'Their names?'

'Hans Beckerman – he was the driver of the tour bus. He lives in Kappel . . .'

'And the second?'

'Fritz Mandel. He owns his own garage in Bern. He was the mechanic who towed the car of a third witness.'

'The name of that witness?'

'I don't have it yet. I'm working on it. Would you like me to speak with them about not discussing this UFO business with anyone?'

'Negative. Your assignment is simply to locate the witnesses. After that, we'll let their respective governments deal with them. Have you learned how many witnesses there are?'

'Yes. Seven passengers plus the driver, the mechanic and a passing motorist.'

'You must locate them all. Each and every one of the ten witnesses who saw the crash. Understood?'

'Yes, General.'

Robert replaced the receiver, his mind in a whirl. UFOs were real. The aliens were enemies. It was a horrifying thought.

Suddenly the uneasy feeling Robert had had earlier returned in full force. General Hilliard had given him this assignment, but they had not told him everything. What else were they holding back?

The Avis rental car company is located at 44 Rue de Lausanne, in the heart of Geneva. Robert stormed into the office and approached a woman behind the desk.

'May I help you?'

Robert slammed down the piece of paper with the licence number of the Renault written on it. 'You rented this car out last week. I want the name of the person who rented it.' His voice was angry.

The clerk drew back. 'I'm sorry, we are not permitted to give out that information.'

'Well, that's just too bad,' Robert retorted, 'because in that case, I'm going to have to sue your company for a great deal of money.'

'I do not understand. What is the problem?'

'I'll tell you what the problem is, lady. Last Sunday, this car ran into mine on the highway and did a hell of a lot of damage. I managed to get his licence number but the man drove away before I could stop him.'

'I see.' The clerk studied Robert a moment. 'Excuse me, please.' She disappeared into a back room. In a few minutes when she returned, she was carrying a file. 'According to our records, there was a problem with the engine of the car, but there was no report of any accident.'

'Well, I'm reporting it now. And I'm holding your company responsible for this. You're going to have to pay to have my car repaired. It's a brand new Porsche, and it's going to cost you a fortune . . .'

'I'm very sorry, sir, but since the accident was not reported, we cannot take any responsibility for it.'

'Look,' Robert said in a more reasonable tone of voice, 'I want to be fair. I don't want to hold your company responsible. All I want to do is have that man pay for the damage he did to my car. It was a hit and run. I may even have to bring the police into this. If you give me the man's name and address, I can talk directly to him, and we can settle it between us and leave your company out of it. Is that fair enough?'

The clerk stood there, making up her mind. 'Yes. We would much prefer that.' She looked down at the file in her hand. 'The name of the person who rented the car is Leslie Mothershed.'

'And his address?'

'213A Grove Road, Whitechapel, London, East 3.' She looked up. 'You are certain our company will not be involved in any litigation?'

'You have my word on it,' Robert assured her. 'This is a private matter between Leslie Mothershed and me.'

Commander Robert Bellamy was on the next Swissair flight to London.

He sat in the dark alone, concentrating, meticulously going over every phase of the plan, making certain that there were no loopholes, that nothing could go wrong. His thoughts were interrupted by the soft buzz of the telephone.

'Janus here.'

'Janus. General Hilliard.'

'Proceed.'

'Commander Bellamy has located the first two witnesses.'

'Very good. Have it attended to immediately.'

'Yes, sir.'

'Where is the Commander now?'

'On his way to London. He should have number three confirmed shortly.'

'I will alert the committee as to his progress. Continue to keep me informed. The condition of this operation must remain Nova Red.'

'Understood, sir. I would suggest . . .'

The line was dead.

FLASH MESSAGE
TOP SECRET ULTRA
NSA TO DEPUTY DIRECTOR
BUNDESANWALTSCHAFT
EYES ONLY
COPY ONE OF (ONE) COPIES
SUBJECT: OPERATION DOOMSDAY
1. HANS BECKERMAN – KAPPEL
2. FRITZ MANDEL – BERN
END OF MESSAGE

13

At midnight in a small farmhouse fifteen miles from Uetendorf, the Lagenfeld family was disturbed by a series of strange events. The older child was awakened by a shimmering yellow light shining through his bedroom window. When he got up to investigate, the light had disappeared.

In the yard, Tozzi, their German shepherd, began barking furiously, awakening old man Lagenfeld. Reluctantly, the farmer got out of bed to quiet the animal, and when he stepped outside he heard the sound of frightened sheep crashing against their pen, trying to escape. As Lagenfeld passed the trough, which had been filled to the brim by the recent rainfall, he noticed that it was bone dry.

Tozzi came running to his side, whimpering. Lagenfeld absently patted the animal on the head. 'It's all right, boy. It's all right.'

And at that moment, every light in the house went out. When the farmer returned to the house and picked up the telephone to call the power company, the phone was dead.

If the lights had remained on a moment longer, the farmer might have seen a strangely beautiful woman walk out of his barnyard and into the field beyond.

14

The Bundesanwaltschaft – Geneva, 1300 Hours

The government minister seated in the inner sanctum of the head-quarters of the Swiss Intelligence Agency watched the Deputy Director finish reading the message. He put the message in a folder marked Top Secret, placed the folder in the desk drawer and locked the drawer.

'Hans Beckerman *und* Fritz Mandel.'

'*Ja.*'

'No problem, Herr Minister. It shall be taken care of.'

'*Gut.*'

'*Wann?*'

'*Sofort*. Immediately.'

The following morning on his way to work, Hans Beckerman's ulcers were bothering him. *I should have pushed that reporter fellow to pay me for that thing I found on the ground. These magazines are all rich. I probably could have got a few hundred marks. Then I could have gone to a decent doctor and had my ulcers treated.*

He was driving past Turler Lake, when ahead of him, at the side of the highway, he saw a woman waving, trying to get a lift. Beckerman slowed down to get a better look at her. She was young and attractive. Hans pulled over to the side of the road. The woman approached the car.

'*Guten Tag*,' Beckerman said. 'Can I help you?' She was even prettier close up.

'*Danke.*' She had a Swiss accent. 'I had a fight with my boyfriend and he dropped me here in the middle of nowhere.'

'Tsk, tsk. That's terrible.'

'Would you mind giving me a lift into Zürich?'

'Not at all. Get in, get in.'

The hitchhiker opened the door and climbed in beside him. 'This is very kind of you,' she said. 'My name is Karen.'

'Hans.' He started driving.

'I don't know what I would have done if you hadn't come along, Hans.'

'Oh, I'm sure someone else would have picked up a pretty woman like you.'

She moved closer to him. 'But I'll bet he wouldn't have been as good-looking as you.'

He glanced over at her. '*Ja?*'

'I think you are very handsome.'

He smiled. 'You should tell that to my wife.'

'Oh, you're married.' She sounded disappointed. 'Why is it all the wonderful men are married? You look very intelligent, too.'

He sat up straighter.

'To tell you the truth, I'm sorry I ever got involved with my boyfriend.' She shifted around in her seat and her skirt climbed up her thigh. He tried not to look. 'I like older, mature men, Hans. I think they're much more sexy than young men.' She snuggled up against him. 'Do you like sex, Hans?'

He cleared his throat. 'Do I . . . ? Well, you know . . . I'm a man . . .'

'I can see that,' she said. She stroked his thigh. 'Can I tell you something? That fight with my boyfriend made me very horny. Would you like me to make love to you?'

He could not believe his luck. She was a beauty and from what he could see, she had a great body. He swallowed. 'I would, but I'm on my way to work and . . .'

'It will only take a few minutes,' she smiled. 'There is a side road up ahead that leads into the woods. Why don't we stop there?'

He could feel himself getting excited. *Sicher. Wait until I tell the boys at the office about this! They'll never believe it.*

'Sure. Why not?' Hans turned the car off the highway and took the little dirt road that led into a grove where they could not be seen by passing motorists.

She slowly ran her hand up his thigh. '*Mein Gott*, you have strong legs.'

'I was a runner when I was younger,' Beckerman boasted.

'Let's get your trousers off.' She undid his belt and helped him slide his pants down. He was already tumescent.

'*Ach! Ein grosser!*' She began to stroke him.

He moaned, '*Leck mich doch am Schwanz.*'

'You like to be kissed down there?'

'*Ja!*' His wife never did that for him.

'*Gut.* Now just relax.'

Beckerman sighed, and closed his eyes. Her soft hands were caressing his balls. He felt the sharp sting of a needle in his thigh and his eyes flew open. '*Wie . . . ?*'

His body stiffened and his eyes bulged out. He was choking, unable to breathe. The woman watched as Beckerman slumped over the steering wheel. She got out of the car and slid his body into the passenger seat, then got behind the wheel of the car and drove back down the dirt road onto the highway. At the edge of the steep mountain road, she waited until the road was clear, then opened the door, stepped on the gas pedal and as the car started to move, she jumped. She stood there, watching the car tumble down the steep cliff. Five minutes later, a black limousine pulled up beside her.

'*Irgendwelche Probleme?*'

'*Keins.*'

Fritz Mandel was in his office ready to close the garage when two men approached.

'I'm sorry,' he said, 'I'm closing. I can't . . .'

One of the men interrupted. 'Our car is stuck down the highway. *Kaputt!* We need a tow.'

'My wife is waiting for me. We are having company tonight. I can give you the name of another . . .'

'It's worth two hundred dollars to us. We're in a hurry.'

'Two hundred dollars?'

'Yes. And our car is in pretty bad shape. We'd like you to do some work on it. That would probably come to another two, three hundred.'

Mandel was becoming interested. '*Ja?*'

'It's a Rolls,' one of the men said. 'Let's see the kind of equipment you have here.' They walked into the service area and stood at the edge of the pit. 'That's pretty good equipment.'

'Yes, sir,' Mandel said, proudly. 'The very best.'

The stranger took out a wallet. 'Here. I can give you some money in advance.' He removed some bills and handed them to Mandel. As he did so, the wallet slipped out of his hands and fell down into the pit. '*Verflucht!*'

'Don't worry,' Mandel said. 'I'll get it.'

He climbed down into the pit. As he did so, one of the men walked over to the control button that operated the raised hydraulic lift and pressed it. The lift started to descend.

Mandel looked up. '*Be careful! What are you doing?*'

He started to scramble up the side. As his fingers touched the ledge, the second man slammed his foot down on Mandel's hand, smashing it, and Mandel dropped back down into the pit, shrieking. The heavy hydraulic lift was inexorably descending on him.

'Let me out of here!' he cried. '*Hilfe!*'

The lift caught him on his shoulder and began pressing him down into the cement floor. A few minutes later, when the terrible screams had stopped, one of the men pressed the button that raised the lift. His companion went down into the pit and retrieved his wallet, careful not to get blood on his clothes. The two men returned to their car and drove off into the quiet night.

FLASH MESSAGE
TOP SECRET ULTRA
ESPIONAGE ABTEILUNG TO DEPUTY DIRECTOR
NSA
EYES ONLY
COPY ONE OF (ONE) COPIES
SUBJECT:
OPERATION DOOMSDAY
1. HANS BECKERMAN – TERMINATED
2. FRITZ MANDEL – TERMINATED
END OF MESSAGE

Ottawa, Canada, 2400 Hours

Janus was addressing the group of twelve.

'Satisfactory progress is being made. Two of the witnesses have already been silenced. Commander Bellamy is on the trail of a third.'

'Has there been a breakthrough yet on SDI?' The Italian. *Impetuous. Volatile.*

'Not yet, but we're confident that the Star Wars technology will be up and functioning very soon.'

'We must do everything possible to hurry it. If it is a question of money . . .' The Saudi. *Enigmatic. Withdrawn.*

'No. There's just a bit more testing to do.'

'When is the next test taking place?' The Australian. *Hearty. Clever.*

'In one week. We will meet here again in forty-eight hours.'

15

DAY FOUR

London, Thursday, October 18th

Leslie Mothershed's role model was Robin Leach. An avid viewer of *Lifestyles of the Rich and Famous*, Mothershed carefully studied the way Robin Leach's guests walked and talked and dressed, because he knew that one day he would appear on that programme. From the time he was a small boy, he had felt that he was destined to be *somebody*, to be rich and famous.

'You're very special,' his mother would tell him. 'My baby is going to be known all over the world.'

The young boy would go to sleep with that sentence ringing in his ears, until he truly believed it. As Mothershed grew older, he became aware that he had a problem: he had no idea exactly *how* he was going to become rich and famous. For a period of time he toyed with the notion of being a movie star, but he was inordinately shy. He briefly contemplated becoming a soccer star, but he was not athletic. He thought about being a famous scientist, or a great lawyer, commanding tremendous fees. His school grades, unfortunately, were mediocre, and he dropped out of school without being any closer to fame. Life was simply not fair. He was physically unprepossessing, thin, with a pale, sickly complexion, and he was short, exactly five foot five and a half inches. Mothershed always stressed the extra half inch. He consoled himself with the fact that many famous men were short: Dudley Moore, Dustin Hoffman, Peter Falk . . .

The only profession that really interested Leslie Mothershed was photography. Taking photographs was so ridiculously simple. Anyone could do it. One simply pressed a button. His mother had bought him a camera for his sixth birthday and had been wildly extravagant in her praise of the pictures he had taken. By the time he was in his teens, Mothershed had become convinced that he was a brilliant photographer. He told himself that he was every bit as good as Ansel Adams, Richard Avedon or Margaret Bourke-White. With a loan from his mother, Leslie Mothershed set up his own photography business in Whitechapel, in his flat.

'Start small,' his mother told him, 'but think big,' and that is exactly what Leslie Mothershed did. He started very small and thought very big, but unfortunately, he had no talent for photography. He photographed parades and animals and flowers, and confidently sent his pictures off to newspapers and magazines, and they were always returned. Mothershed consoled himself with the thought of all the geniuses who had been rejected before their ability was recognized. He considered himself a martyr to philistinism.

And then, out of the blue, his big opportunity had come. A cousin of his mother's who worked for the British publishing firm of Harper-Collins had confided to Mothershed that they were planning to commission a coffee-table book on Switzerland.

'They haven't selected the photographer yet, Leslie, so if you get yourself over to Switzerland right away, and bring back some great pictures, the book could be yours.'

Leslie Mothershed hurriedly packed up his cameras and headed for Switzerland. He knew – he really knew – that this was the break he had been looking for. At last the idiots were going to recognize his talents. He rented a car in Geneva and travelled around the country, taking pictures of Swiss chalets, waterfalls, and snow-capped peaks. He photographed sunrises and sunsets, and farmers working in the fields. And then, in the middle of all that, fate had stepped in and changed his life. He was on his way to Bern when his motor failed. He pulled over to the side of the highway, furious. *Why me?* Mothershed moaned. *Why do these things always happen to me?* He sat there, fuming, thinking about his precious time lost, the expense it would be to have his car towed. Fifteen kilometres behind him was the town of Thun. *I'll get a tow from there*, Mothershed thought. *That shouldn't cost too much.*

He flagged down a passing gasoline truck. 'I need a tow truck,' Mothershed explained. 'Could you stop at a garage in Thun and have them come and get me?'

The truck driver shook his head. 'It's Sunday, mister. The closest garage that's open will be in Bern.'

'Bern? That's fifty kilometres from here. It will cost me a fortune.'

The truck driver grinned. '*Ja*. There they get you by the Sundays.' He started to drive on.

'Wait.' It was difficult to get the words out. 'I'll . . . I'll pay for a tow truck from Bern.'

'*Gut*. I will have them send someone out.'

Leslie Mothershed sat in his disabled car, cursing. *All I needed was this*, he thought, bitterly. He had already spent much too much money on film and now he would have to pay some bloody thief to tow him to a garage. It took almost two interminable hours for the tow truck to arrive. As the mechanic started to attach the car to his truck, there was a flash of light from across the highway, followed by a loud explosion, and Mothershed looked up to what appeared to be a bright object falling out of the sky. The only other traffic on the highway was a tour bus that had pulled to a stop behind his car. The passengers from the bus were hurrying toward the scene of the crash. Mothershed hesitated, torn between his curiosity and his desire to move on. He turned and followed the bus passengers across the highway. When he reached the scene of the accident, he stood there transfixed. *Holy God*, he thought. *It's unreal.* He was staring at a flying saucer. Leslie Mothershed had heard about flying saucers and had read about them, but he had never believed they existed. He gaped at it, awed by the eerie spectacle. The shell had ripped open and he could see two bodies inside, small, with large skulls, sunken eyes, no ears and almost no chins, and they seemed to be wearing some kind of silver metallic suits.

The group from the tour bus was standing around him, staring in horrified silence. The man next to him fainted. Another man turned away and vomited. There was an elderly priest there, clutching his beads and mumbling incoherently.

'My God,' someone said. 'It's a flying saucer!'

And that was when Mothershed had his epiphany. A miracle had fallen into his lap. *He – Leslie Mothershed – was on the spot with his cameras to photograph the story of the century! There was not a magazine or newspaper in the world that would reject the photographs he was about to take. A coffee-table book about Switzerland? He almost laughed aloud at the idea. He was about to astonish the whole world. All the television talk shows would be begging for him, but he would do Robin Leach's show first. He would sell his photographs to the London* Times, *the* Sun, *the* Mail, *the* Mirror – *all the English newspapers, the foreign papers and magazines.* Le Figaro *and* Paris Match, Oggi *and* Der Tag. Time *and* USA Today. *The press everywhere would be pleading with him for his photographs. Japan and South America, and Russia and China and – there was no end to it.* Mothershed's heart was fluttering with excitement. *I won't give anyone an exclusive. Each one will have to pay me individually. I'll start at a hundred thousand pounds a picture, maybe two hundred thousand. And I'll sell them over and over again.* He began feverishly adding up the money he was going to make.

Leslie Mothershed was so busy adding up his fortune that he almost forgot to take the pictures. 'Oh, my God! Excuse me,' he said to no one in particular, and raced back across the highway to get his camera equipment.

The mechanic had finished hoisting the disabled vehicle in the air, ready to tow it away.

'What's going on over there?' he asked.

Mothershed was busy grabbing his camera equipment. 'Come and see for yourself.'

The two men moved across the highway to the wooded area, and Mothershed pushed his way through the circle of tourists.

'Excuse me,' he said. 'Excuse me.'

He adjusted the focus on his camera and started snapping pictures of the UFO and its eerie passengers. He took pictures in black and white and in colour. As the shutter clicked each time, Mothershed thought, *a million pounds . . . another million pounds . . . another million pounds.*

The priest was crossing himself and saying, 'It's the face of Satan.'

Satan, hell, Mothershed thought exultantly. *It's the face of money. These will be the first pictures that prove that flying saucers really exist.* And then suddenly a terrifying thought occurred to him. *What if the magazines think these pictures are fake? There have been a lot of faked photographs of UFOs.* His euphoria vanished. *What if they don't believe me?* And that was when Leslie Mothershed had his second inspiration.

There were nine witnesses gathered around him. Without knowing it, they were about to lend authenticity to his discovery.

Mothershed turned to face the group. 'Ladies and gentlemen,' he called out. 'If you would all like to have your photographs taken here, just line up and I'll be happy to send each of you a print, free.'

There were excited exclamations. Within moments, the passengers from the tour bus were standing beside the remains of the UFO, except for the priest.

He was reluctant. 'I can't,' he said. 'It's evil!'

Mothershed needed the priest. He would make the most convincing witness of them all.

'That's just the point,' Mothershed said persuasively. 'Don't you see? This will be your testimony about the existence of evil spirits.'

And the priest was finally persuaded.

'Spread out a little,' Mothershed ordered, 'so we can see the flying saucer.'

The witnesses shifted their positions.

'That's it. Very good. Excellent. Hold still, now.'

He snapped half a dozen more pictures and took out a pencil and paper.

'If you'll write down your names and addresses, I'll see to it that each of you gets a print.'

He had no intention of sending any prints. All he wanted was corroborating witnesses. *Let the bloody newspapers and magazines try to get around that!*

And then, suddenly, he noticed that several people in the group had cameras. He couldn't allow any other photographs but his! Only photos that had the credit, 'Photograph by Leslie Mothershed', could exist.

'Excuse me,' he said to the group. 'Those of you who have cameras: if you'll pass them to me, I'll take a few pictures of you so that you'll have some taken with your own cameras.'

The cameras were quickly handed to Leslie Mothershed. As he knelt to frame the first shot, no one noticed that Mothershed clicked open the film compartment with his thumb and held it ajar. *There, a little bit of nice bright sunlight will help those photographs no end. Too bad, my friends, but only professionals are allowed to capture historic moments.*

Ten minutes later Mothershed had all their names and addresses. He took one last look at the flying saucer and thought, exultantly, *Mother was right. I am going to be rich and famous.*

He couldn't wait to return to England to develop his precious photographs.

'What the hell is going on?'

The police stations in the Uetendorf area had been inundated with telephone calls all evening.

'Someone is prowling around my house . . .'

'There are strange lights outside . . .'

'My livestock is going crazy. There must be wolves around . . .'

'Someone drained my watering trough.'

And the most inexplicable telephone call of all:

'Chief, you'd better send a lot of tow trucks out to the main highway right away. It's a nightmare. All traffic has stopped.'

'What? Why?'

'No one knows. The car engines just suddenly went dead.'

It was a night they would never forget.

16

How long is this assignment going to take? Robert wondered, as he strapped himself into his first-class seat on the Swissair flight. As the plane rushed down the runway, its huge Rolls-Royce engines hungrily swallowing the night air, Robert relaxed and closed his eyes. *Was it really just a few years ago that I took this same flight with Susan to London? No. It was more like a lifetime ago.*

The plane touched down at Heathrow at six twenty-nine p.m., on schedule. Robert made his way out of the maze, and took a taxi into the sprawling city. He passed a hundred familiar landmarks, and he could hear Susan's voice, excitedly commenting about them. In those golden days it had never mattered where they were. It was simply enough that they were together. They brought their own happiness with them, their own special excitement in each other. Theirs was the marriage that would have a happy ending.

Almost.

Their problems had started innocently enough with an overseas call from Admiral Whittaker while Robert and Susan were travelling in Thailand. It had been six months since Robert had been discharged from the Navy, and he had not talked to the Admiral in all that time. The call, reaching them at the Oriental Hotel in Bangkok, was a surprise.

'Robert? Admiral Whittaker.'

'Admiral! It's good to hear your voice.'

'It hasn't been easy tracking you down. What have you been up to?'

'Not very much. Just taking it easy. Having a long honeymoon.'

'How is Susan? It *is* Susan, isn't it?'

'Yes. She's fine, thank you.'

'How soon can you get back to Washington?'

'I beg your pardon?'

'It hasn't been announced yet, but I've been given a new assignment, Robert. They've made me Director of 17th District Naval Intelligence. I'd like you to come aboard.'

Robert was taken aback. 'Naval Intelligence? Admiral, I don't know anything about . . .'

'You can learn. You would be doing an important service for your country, Robert. Will you come and discuss it with me?'

'Well . . .'

'Good. I'll expect you in my office Monday morning at 0900. Say hello to Susan for me.'

Robert repeated the conversation to Susan.

'Naval Intelligence? That sounds so exciting.'

'Maybe,' Robert said doubtfully. 'I have no idea what's involved.'

'You must find out.'

He studied her for a moment. 'You want me to take it, don't you?'

She put her arms around him. 'I want you to do whatever you want to do. I think you're ready to go back to work. I've noticed in the last few weeks how restless you've become.'

'I think you're trying to get rid of me,' Robert teased. 'The honeymoon is over.'

Susan put her lips close to his. 'Never. Did I ever tell you how crazy I am about you, sailor? Let me show you . . .'

Thinking about it later – too late – Robert decided that that was the beginning of the end of their marriage. The offer had seemed wonderful at the time, and he had gone back to Washington to meet with Admiral Whittaker.

'This job requires brains, courage and initiative, Robert. You have all three. Our country has become a target for every little tin-horn dictatorship that can breed a terrorist group or build a chemical weapons factory. Half a dozen of those countries are working on atomic bombs at this moment, so that they can hold us at ransom. My job is to build an intelligence network to find out exactly what they're up to and to try to stop them. I want you to help me.'

In the end, Robert had accepted the job with Naval Intelligence, and to his surprise, he found that he enjoyed it and had a natural aptitude for it. Susan found an attractive apartment in Rosslyn, Virginia, not far from where Robert worked, and busied herself furnishing it. Robert was sent to the Farm, the CIA training ground for secret service agents. Located in a heavily guarded compound in the Virginia countryside, the Farm occupies twenty square miles, most of it covered in tall pine forest, with the central buildings in a ten-acre cleared area two miles from the front gate. A network of dirt roads branches off through the woods, with locked swinging barricades, and 'No Entry' signs posted. At a small airfield, unmarked aircraft arrive and depart several times a day. The Farm has a deceptively bucolic setting, with leafy trees, deer running in the fields, and small buildings innocently scattered around the extensive grounds. Inside the compound, however, it is a different world.

Robert had expected to train with other Navy personnel, but to his surprise, the trainees were a mixture of CIA inductees and marines, and Army, Navy and Air Force personnel. Each student was assigned a number and housed in a dormitory-like room in one of several spartan two-storey brick buildings. At the Bachelor Officer Quarters, where Robert stayed, each man had his own room, and shared the bathroom with another. The Mess Hall was across the road from the BOQ cluster.

On the day Robert arrived, he was escorted to an auditorium with thirty other newcomers. A tall, powerfully built black Colonel in Air Force uniform addressed the group. He appeared to be in his middle fifties, and he gave the impression of quick, cold intelligence. He spoke clearly and crisply, with no wasted words.

'I'm Colonel Frank Johnson. I want to welcome you here. During your stay, you will use only your first names. From this moment on, your lives will be a closed book. You've all been sworn to secrecy. I would advise you to take that oath very, very seriously. You are *never* to discuss your work with anyone – your wives, your family, your friends. You've been selected to come here because you have special qualifications. There's a lot of hard work ahead of you to develop those qualifications, and not all of you are going to make it. You're going to be involved in things you have never even heard of before. I cannot stress enough the importance of the work you will be doing when you finish here. It has become fashionable in certain liberal circles to attack our intelligence services, whether it's the CIA, Army, Navy or the Air Force, but I can assure you, gentlemen, that without dedicated people like yourselves, this country would be in one hell of a lot of trouble. It's going to be your job to help prevent that. Those of you who do pass will become Case Officers. To put it bluntly, a Case Officer is a spy. He works under cover.

'While you're here, you're going to get the best training in the world. You'll be trained in surveillance and counter-surveillance. You'll have courses in radio communications, encoding, and weaponry and map reading.

'You'll attend a class in interpersonal relations. You'll be taught how to build a rapport, how to draw out an individual's motivations, how to make your target feel at ease.'

The class was hanging on every word.

'You'll learn how to meet and recruit an agent. You'll be trained in how to make sure meeting places are secure.

'You'll learn about dead drops, how to covertly communicate with your contacts. If you're successful at what you do, you will carry out your assignments unnoticed and undetected.'

Robert could feel the excitement that charged the air.

'Some of you will work under official cover. It could be diplomatic or military. Others will work under non-official cover as private individuals – as a businessman, or archaeologist, or novelist – any profession that will give you access to the areas and types of people likely to have the information you're looking for. And now, I'm going to turn you over to your instructors. Good luck.'

Robert found the training fascinating. The instructors were men who had worked in the field and were experienced professionals. Robert absorbed the technical information easily. In addition to the courses Colonel Johnson had mentioned, there was a brush-up course on languages, and one on cryptic codes.

Colonel Johnson was an enigma to Robert. The rumour circulating about him was that he had strong connections at the White House, and was involved in high-level covert activities. He would disappear from the Farm for days at a time, and suddenly reappear.

An agent named Ron was conducting a class.

'There are six phases to the clandestine operational process. The first is spotting. When you know what information you need, your first challenge is to identify and target individuals who have access to that information. The second phase is assessment. Once you have spotted your target, you have to decide if he really has the information you need, and if he might be susceptible to recruitment. What motivates him? Is he happy in his job? Does he have a grudge against his boss? Is he over his head financially? If the prospect has accessibility and there's a motivation that can be exploited, you move along to phase three.

'Phase three is development. You build up a relationship with a prospect. You manage to run into him as often as possible, and build a rapport. The next phase is recruitment. When you think he is ready, you go to work on him psychologically. You use whatever psychological weapons you've got – revenge against his boss, money, the thrill of it. If a Case Officer has done his job well, the prospect usually says yes.

'So far so good. You have a spy working for you. The next step is handling him. You must protect not only yourself, but him. You will arrange surreptitious meetings, and train him in the use of microfilm and, where appropriate, clandestine radio. You will teach him how to detect surveillance, what to say if questioned, and so on.

'The last phase is disconnecting. After some period of time, perhaps your recruit will be transferred to a different job and no longer have access to the information, or maybe we will no longer need the information to which he does have access. In any case, the relationship is ended but it's important to end it in such a way that the recruit doesn't feel he has been used, and is looking for vengeance . . .'

Colonel Johnson had been right. Not everyone made it through the course. Familiar faces kept disappearing. Washed out. No one knew why. No one asked.

One day, as a group was preparing to go into Richmond for a surveillance exercise, Robert's instructor said, 'We're going to see how good you are, Robert. I'm going to send someone to tail you. I want you to lose him. Do you think you can do that?'

'Yes, sir.'

'Good luck.'

Robert took the bus into Richmond and began strolling the streets. Within five minutes he identified his trackers. There were two of them. One was on foot and one was in an automobile. Robert tried ducking into restaurants and shops and hurrying out back doors, but he was unable to shake them. They were too well trained. Finally, it was almost time to return to the Farm and Robert still had not been able to get away from them. They were watching him too closely. Robert walked into a department store and the two men took up positions where they could cover the entrances and exits. Robert went up the escalator to the men's department. Thirty minutes later, when he came down, he was wearing a different suit, a coat and hat, talking to a woman and carrying a baby in his arms. He walked past his pursuers without being recognized.

He was the only one that day who had successfully avoided surveillance.

The jargon taught at the Farm was a language unto itself.

'You probably won't use all these terms,' the instructor told the class, 'but you had better know them. There are two different kinds of agents; an "agent of influence" and an "agent provocateur". The agent of influence tries to change opinion in the country where he operates. An agent provocateur is sent to stir up trouble and create chaos. "Biographic leverage" is CIA code for blackmail. There are also "black bag jobs", which can range from bribes to burglary. Watergate was a black bag job.'

He looked around to make sure that the class was paying attention. They were spellbound.

'From time to time some of you may need a "cobbler" – that's a man who forges passports.'

Robert wondered whether he would ever use a cobbler.

'The phrase to "demote maximally" is a nasty one. It means to purge by killing. So does the word "terminate". If you hear someone talking about the "Firm", it's the nickname we use to refer to the British Secret Service. If you're asked to "fumigate" an office, you won't be looking for termites, you'll be looking for listening devices.'

The arcane expressions fascinated Robert.

'"Ladies" is a euphemism for females sent to compromise the opposition. A "legend" is the faked biography of a spy, to provide him with a cover. "Going private" means leaving the service.'

The instructor scanned the class. 'Any of you know what a "lion tamer" is?'

He waited for an answer. Silence.

'When an agent is sacked, he sometimes gets upset and may make threats to reveal what he knows. A muscleman, or lion tamer, is called in to soften him up. I'm sure none of you will ever have to deal with one.'

That drew nervous laughter.

'Then, there's the word "measles". If a target dies of measles, it means he was murdered so efficiently that death appeared to be accidental or due to natural causes. One method of inducing measles is tabun. That's a colourless or brownish liquid compound that causes nerve paralysis when absorbed through the skin. If someone offers you a "music box", they're offering you a wireless transmitter. The transmitter operator is called a "musician". In the future, some of you will be operating "naked". Don't rush to take off your clothes, it simply means that you're alone and without any assistance from outside.

'There's one more thing I want to discuss today. Coincidence. In our work, there is no such animal. It usually spells danger. If you keep running into the same person again and again, or you keep spotting the same automobile when you're on the move, cover your ass. You're probably in trouble.

'I think that's enough for today, gentlemen. We will take up where we left off tomorrow.'

From time to time, Colonel Johnson called Robert into his office, 'to have a chat,' as he put it. The conversations were deceptively casual, but Robert was aware of an underlying probing being carried on.

'I understand you're happily married, Robert.'

'That's right.'

They spent the next half hour talking about marriage, fidelity and trust.

Another time: 'Admiral Whittaker thinks of you as a son, Robert. Did you know that?'

'Yes.' The pain of Edward's death was something that would never go away.

They talked about loyalty and duty and death.

'You've faced death more than once, Robert. Are you afraid to die?'

'No.' *But to die for a good reason*, Robert thought. *Not senselessly.*

The meetings were frustrating to Robert, because they were like looking into a trick mirror. Colonel Johnson could see him clearly, but the Colonel remained invisible, an enigma cloaked in secrecy.

The course lasted sixteen weeks, and during that time none of the men was permitted to communicate with the outside world. Robert missed Susan desperately. It was the longest they had ever been apart.

When the four months were up, Colonel Johnson called Robert into his office.

'This is goodbye. You've done an excellent job, Commander. I think you're going to find your future very interesting.'

'Thank you, sir. I hope so.'

'Good luck.'

Colonel Johnson watched Robert leave. He sat there for five minutes without moving, then reached a decision. He walked over to the door and locked it. Then he picked up the telephone and made a call.

Susan was waiting for him. She opened the door of their apartment, wearing a sheer negligée that concealed nothing. She flew into his arms and held him close. 'Hi, sailor. Want to have a good time?'

'I'm having one,' Robert said happily, 'just holding you.'

'God, I missed you so much!' Susan drew back and said, fiercely, 'If anything ever happened to you, I think I would die.'

'Nothing is ever going to happen to me.'

'Promise?'

'Promise.'

She studied him a moment, concerned. 'You look so tired.'

'It was a pretty intensive course,' Robert admitted. He was understating it. With all the texts and manuals to study, in addition to the practical, hands-on lessons, none of the recruits had been able to sleep more than a few hours a night. There was little grumbling, for a very simple reason: they were well aware that what they were learning could one day save their lives.

'I know exactly what you need,' Susan decided.

Robert grinned. 'I'll say.' He reached for her.

'Wait. Give me five minutes. Get undressed.'

He watched her walk away and thought, *How damned lucky can a man get?* He began to get undressed.

Susan returned a few minutes later. She said softly, 'Umm. I like you naked.'

He heard his instructor's voice saying, *'Some of you will be operating naked. It means you're alone and without any assistance.'* *What have I gotten into? What have I gotten Susan into?*

She led him into the bathroom. The tub was filled with warm scented water, and the room was dark except for four candles flickering on the basin.

'Welcome home, darling.' She slipped out of her negligée, and stepped into the bathtub. He followed her.

'Susan . . .'

'Don't talk. Lean back against me.'

He felt her hands gently caressing his back and shoulders and he felt the soft curves of her body against him, and he forgot how tired he was.

They made love in the warm water and when they had dried themselves, Susan said, 'So much for the foreplay. Now, let's get serious.'

They made love again, and later, as Robert fell asleep, holding Susan in his arms, he thought, *It will always be like this. Forever.*

17

The following Monday morning Robert reported for his first day of duty at the 17th District Office of Naval Intelligence at the Pentagon.

Admiral Whittaker said warmly, 'Welcome home, Robert. Apparently you impressed the hell out of Colonel Johnson.'

Robert smiled. 'He's quite impressive himself.'

Over coffee, the Admiral asked, 'Are you ready to go to work?'

'Eager.'

'Good. We have a situation in Rhodesia . . .'

Working in the Office of Naval Intelligence was even more exciting than Robert had anticipated. Each assignment was different, and Robert was given the ones classified 'extremely sensitive'. He brought in a defector who revealed Noriega's drug-smuggling operation in Panama, exposed a mole working for Marcos in the American Consulate in Manila, and helped set up a secret listening post in Morocco. He was sent on missions to South America and to the East Indies. The only thing that disturbed him was the long separations from Susan. He hated to be away from her, and he missed her terribly. He had the excitement of his job to occupy him, but Susan had nothing. Robert's caseload kept increasing. He spent less and less time at home, and that was when the problem with Susan became serious.

Whenever Robert came home, he and Susan would run hungrily into each other's arms and make passionate love. But those times began to be further and further apart. It seemed to Susan that no sooner did Robert return from one assignment, than he was sent away on another.

To make matters worse, Robert could not discuss his work with her. Susan had no idea where he went or what he was doing. She knew only that whatever he was involved in was dangerous, and she was terrified that one day he would leave and never return. She dared not ask him questions. She felt like a stranger, completely shut out of an important part of his life. Of *their* life. *I can't go on like this*, Susan decided.

When Robert returned from a four-week assignment in Central America, Susan said, 'Robert, I think we had better have a talk.'

'What's the problem?' Robert asked. He knew what the problem was.

'I'm frightened. We're slipping away from each other, and I don't want to lose us. I couldn't stand it.'

'Susan . . .'

'Wait. Let me finish. Do you know how much time we've spent

together in the last four months? Less than two weeks. Whenever you come home I feel as though you're a visitor, instead of my husband.'

He took Susan in his arms and held her tightly. 'You know how much I love you.'

She laid her head on his shoulder. 'Please don't let anything happen to us.'

'I won't,' he promised. 'I'll have a talk with Admiral Whittaker.'

'When?'

'Immediately.'

'The Admiral will see you now, Commander.'

'Thank you.'

Admiral Whittaker was seated behind his desk, signing papers. He looked up as Robert entered and smiled. 'Welcome home, Robert, and congratulations. That was an excellent job in El Salvador.'

'Thank you, sir.'

'Sit down. Can I offer you some coffee?'

'No, thank you, Admiral.'

'You wanted to talk to me? My secretary said it was urgent. What can I do for you?'

It was difficult to begin. 'Well, sir, this is personal. I've been married less than two years, and . . .'

'You made a wonderful choice, Robert. Susan's a fine woman.'

'Yes, I agree. The problem is that I'm away most of the time, and she's unhappy about it.' He added quickly, 'And she has every right to be. It isn't a normal situation.'

Admiral Whittaker leaned back in his chair and said, thoughtfully, 'Of course, what you're doing isn't a normal situation. Sometimes sacrifices have to be made.'

'I know,' Robert said stubbornly, 'but I'm not prepared to sacrifice my marriage. It means too much to me.'

The Admiral studied him reflectively. 'I see. What is it you're asking?'

'I was hoping that you could find some assignments for me where I'm not away from home so much. This is such a large operation, there must be a hundred things I could do closer to home.'

'Closer to home.'

'Yes.'

The Admiral said slowly, 'You've certainly earned that. I don't see why something like that can't be arranged.'

Robert smiled in relief. 'That's very good of you, Admiral. I would certainly appreciate it.'

'Yes, I think we can definitely arrange that. Tell Susan for me that the problem is solved.'

Robert stood up, beaming. 'I don't know how to thank you.'

Admiral Whittaker waved a hand of dismissal. 'You're too valuable a piece of manpower for me to let anything happen to you. Now go home to your bride.'

When Robert told Susan the news, she was thrilled. She threw her arms around him. 'Oh, darling, that's wonderful.'

'I'm going to ask him for a couple of weeks off so we can take a trip somewhere. It will be a second honeymoon.'

'I've forgotten what a honeymoon is like,' Susan murmured. 'Show me.'

Robert showed her.

Admiral Whittaker sent for Robert the following morning. 'I just wanted you to know I'm making some arrangements about the matter we discussed yesterday.'

'Thank you, Admiral.' Now was the time to mention taking a leave. 'Sir . . .'

Admiral Whittaker said, 'Something has come up, Robert.' The Admiral began to pace. When he spoke, there was a note of deep concern in his voice. 'I've just been informed that the CIA has been infiltrated. It seems that there has been a steady leak of Top Secret information. All they know about the spy is that his code name is "the Fox". He's in Argentina right now. They need someone outside the Agency to handle the operation. The Deputy Director of the CIA has asked for you. They would like you to track the man down and bring him back. I told them the decision is up to you. Do you want to undertake it?'

Robert hesitated. 'I'm afraid I'll have to pass on it, sir.'

'I respect your decision, Robert. You've been travelling constantly and have never turned down an assignment. I know it hasn't been easy on your marriage.'

'I'd like to take on this job, sir. It's just that . . .'

'You don't have to say it, Robert. My opinion of your work and dedication will always remain the same. I just have one favour to ask of you.'

'What's that, Admiral?'

'The Deputy Director of the CIA asked to meet with you, regardless of your decision. As a courtesy. You don't mind, do you?'

'Of course not, sir.'

Early the next morning Robert drove to Langley for his meeting.

'Sit down, Commander,' the Deputy Director said after Robert entered the large corner office. 'I've heard a lot about you. All good things, of course.'

'Thank you, sir.'

The Deputy Director was a man in his early sixties, reed thin with fine white hair and a small brush moustache that moved up and down as he drew on his pipe. A Yale graduate, he had joined the OSS during World War II and then moved into the CIA when it was formed after the conflict. He rose steadily up the ranks of the most powerful intelligence agency in the world.

'I want you to know, Commander, that I respect your decision.'

'I appreciate that.'

'There is one fact, however, that I feel I should bring to your attention.'

'What's that, sir?'

'The President is personally involved in the operation to unmask the Fox.'

'I didn't know that, sir.'

'He regards it – as I do, too – as one of the most important assignments this agency has had since its inception. I know of your situation at home, and I'm sure the President is sympathetic, too. He's a real family man. But your not taking on this assignment might throw – how should I say it – a *cloud* on ONI *and* Admiral Whittaker.'

'The Admiral had nothing to do with my decision, sir,' Robert said.

'I understand that, Commander, but will the President understand that?'

The honeymoon will have to be postponed, Robert thought.

When Robert broke the news to Susan, he said gently, 'This is my last overseas assignment. After this I'll be home so much you'll get sick of me.'

She smiled up at him. 'There isn't that much time in the world. We're going to be together forever.'

The chase after the Fox was the most frustrating thing Robert had ever experienced. He picked up his trail in Argentina, but missed his quarry by one day. The trail led to Tokyo and China and then Malaysia. Whoever the Fox was, he left just enough of a trail to lead to where he had been, but never to where he was.

The days turned into weeks and the weeks turned into months, and always Robert was just behind the Fox. He called Susan almost every day. In the beginning, it was, 'I'll be home in a few days, darling.' And then, 'I might be home next week.' And then, finally, 'I'm not sure when I'll be back.' In the end, Robert had to give up. He had been on the Fox's trail for two and a half months, with no success.

When he returned to Susan, she seemed changed. A little cooler.

'I'm sorry, darling,' Robert apologized. 'I had no idea it would take so long. It was just . . .'

'They'll never let you go, will they, Robert?'

'What? Of course they will.'

She shook her head. 'I don't think so. I've taken a job at Washington Memorial Hospital.'

He was taken aback. 'You've what?'

'I'm going to be a nurse again. I can't sit around waiting for you to come home to me, wondering where you are, and what you're doing, wondering whether you're dead or alive.'

'Susan, I . . .'

'It's all right, my sweetheart. At least I'll be doing something useful while you're gone. It will make the waiting easier.'

And Robert had no answer to that.

He reported his failure to Admiral Whittaker. The Admiral was sympathetic.

'It's my fault for agreeing to let you do it. From now on, we'll let the CIA handle their own damned problems. I'm sorry, Robert.'

Robert told him about Susan taking a job as a nurse.

'That's probably a good idea,' the Admiral said thoughtfully. 'It will take the pressure off your marriage. If you took on some overseas caseloads now and then, I'm sure it won't matter as much.'

'Now and then' turned out to be almost constantly. That was when the marriage really began to disintegrate.

Susan worked at Washington Memorial Hospital as an operating-room nurse and whenever Robert was home she tried to take time off to be with him, but she was caught up more and more in her work.

'I'm really enjoying it, darling. I feel I'm doing something useful.'

She would talk to Robert about her patients, and he remembered how caring she had been with him, how she had nurtured him back to health, back to life. He was pleased that she was doing important work that she loved, but the fact was, they were seeing less and less of each other. The emotional distance between them was widening. There was an awkwardness now that had not existed before. They were like two strangers trying desperately hard to make conversation.

When Robert returned to Washington from a six-week assignment in Turkey, he took Susan out to dinner at Sans Souci.

Susan said, 'We have a new patient at the hospital. He was in a bad plane crash, and the doctors didn't think he was going to live, but I'm going to see to it that he does.' Her eyes were glowing.

She was like that with me, Robert thought. And he wondered if she had leaned over the new patient and said, 'Get well. I'm waiting for you.' He rejected the thought.

'He's so nice, Robert. All the nurses are crazy about him.'

All the nurses? he wondered.

There was a small, nagging doubt at the back of his mind, but he managed to get rid of it.

They ordered dinner.

The following Saturday, Robert left for Portugal, and when he returned three weeks later, Susan greeted him excitedly.

'Monte walked today for the first time!' Her kiss was perfunctory.

'Monte?'

'Monte Banks. That's his name. He's going to be fine. The doctors couldn't believe it, but we wouldn't give up.'

We. 'Tell me about him.'

'He's really darling. He's always giving us gifts. He's very wealthy. He flies his own plane and he was in a bad crash, and . . .'

'What kind of gifts?'

'Oh, you know, just little things . . . candies and flowers and books and records. He tried to give all of us expensive watches but, of course, we had to refuse.'

'Of course.'

'He has a yacht, polo ponies . . .'

That was the day Robert began calling him 'Moneybags'.

Susan talked about him every time she came home from the hospital.

'He's really dear, Robert.'

Dear was dangerous.

'And he's so thoughtful. Do you know what he did today? He had lunch sent from the Jockey Club for all the nurses on the floor.'

The man was sickening. Ridiculously, Robert found himself getting angry. 'Is this wonderful patient of yours married?'

'No, darling. Why?'

'I just wondered.'

She laughed. 'For heaven's sake, you're not jealous, are you?'

'Of some old man who's just learning to walk? Of course not.' *Like hell I'm not.* But he wouldn't give Susan the satisfaction of saying so.

When Robert was at home, Susan tried not to talk about her patient, but if she did not bring up the subject, Robert would.

'How is old Moneybags doing?'

'His name is not Moneybags,' she chided him. 'It's Monte Banks.'

'Whatever.' *It was too bad the sonofabitch couldn't have died in the plane crash.*

The following day was Susan's birthday.

'I'll tell you what,' Robert said, enthusiastically, 'we'll celebrate. We'll go out and have a wonderful dinner somewhere and . . .'

'I have to work at the hospital until eight.'

'All right. I'll pick you up there.'

'Fine. Monte is dying to meet you. I've told him all about you.'

'I look forward to meeting the old man,' Robert assured her.

When Robert arrived at the hospital, the receptionist said, 'Good evening, Commander. Susan is working in the orthopedic ward on the third floor. She's expecting you.' She picked up the telephone.

When Robert got off the elevator, Susan was waiting for him, wearing her white starched uniform, and his heart skipped a beat. She was, oh, so damned beautiful.

'Hello, gorgeous.'

Susan smiled, strangely ill at ease. 'Hello, Robert. I'll be off duty in a few minutes. Come on. I'll introduce you to Monte.'

I can't wait.

She led him into a large private room filled with books and flowers and baskets of fruit, and said, 'Monte, this is my husband, Robert.'

Robert stood there, staring at the man in the bed. He was three or four years older than Robert and resembled Paul Newman. Robert despised him on sight.

'I'm certainly pleased to meet you, Commander. Susan has been telling me all about you.'

Is that what they talked about when she was at his bedside in the middle of the night?

'She's very proud of you.'

That's it, buddy, throw me a few crumbs.

Susan was looking at Robert, willing him to be polite. He made an effort.

'I understand you'll be getting out of here soon.'

'Yes, thanks mostly to your wife. She's a miracle worker.'

Come on, sailor. Do you think I'm going to let some other nurse have that great body? 'Yes, that's her speciality.' Robert could not keep the bitterness out of his voice.

The birthday dinner was a fiasco. All Susan wanted to talk about was her patient.

'Did he remind you of anyone, darling?'

'Boris Karloff.'

'Why did you have to be so rude to him?'

He said coldly, 'I thought I was very civil. I don't happen to like the man.'

Susan stared at him. 'You don't even know him. What don't you like about him?'

I don't like the way he looks at you. I don't like the way you look at him. I don't like the way our marriage is going to hell. God, I don't want to lose you. 'Sorry. I guess I'm just tired.'

They finished their dinner in silence.

The next morning, as Robert was getting ready to go to the office, Susan said, 'Robert, I have something to say to you . . .'

And it was as though he had been struck in the pit of his stomach. He could not bear to have her put what was happening into words.

'Susan . . .'

'You know I love you. I'll always love you. You're the dearest, most wonderful man I've ever known.'

'Please . . .'

'No, let me finish. This is very hard for me. In the last year we've only spent minutes together. We don't have a marriage anymore. We've drifted apart.'

Every word was a knife stabbing into him.

'You're right,' he said desperately. 'I'll change. I'll quit the Agency. Now. Today. We'll go away somewhere and . . .'

She shook her head. 'No, Robert. We both know that wouldn't work. You're doing what you want to do. If you stopped doing it because of me you would always resent me. This isn't anybody's fault. It just . . . happened. I want a divorce.'

It was as though the world had caved in on him. He felt suddenly sick to his stomach.

'You don't mean that, Susan, we'll find a way to . . .'

'It's too late. I've been thinking about this for a long time. All the while you were away and I sat home alone and waited for you to come back I thought about it. We've been living separate lives. I need more than that. I need something you can't give me anymore.'

He stood there, fighting to control his emotions. 'Does this . . . does this have anything to do with Moneybags?'

Susan hesitated. 'Monte has asked me to marry him.'

He could feel his bowels turning to water. 'And you're going to?'

'Yes.'

It was some kind of crazy nightmare. *This isn't happening*, he thought. *It can't be*. His eyes filled with tears.

Susan put her arms around him and held him close. 'I will never again feel about any man the way I felt about you. I loved you with all my heart and soul. I will always love you. You are my dearest friend.' She pulled back and looked into his eyes. 'But that isn't enough. Do you understand?'

All he understood was that she was tearing him apart. 'We could try again. We'll start over and . . .'

'I'm sorry, Robert.' Her voice was choked. 'I'm so sorry, but it's finished.'

Susan flew to Reno for a divorce, and Commander Robert Bellamy went on a two-week drunk.

Old habits die hard. Robert telephoned a friend at the FBI. Al Traynor

619

had crossed Robert's path half a dozen times in the past, and Robert trusted him.

'Tray, I need a favour.'

'A favour? You need a psychiatrist. How the hell could you let Susan get away?'

The news was probably all over town.

'It's a long, sad story.'

'I'm really sorry, Robert. She was a great lady. I . . . never mind. What can I do for you?'

'I'd like you to run a computer check on someone.'

'You've got it. Give me a name.'

'Monte Banks. It's just a routine inquiry.'

'Right. What do you want to know?'

'He's probably not even in your files, Tray, but if he is . . . did he ever get a parking ticket, beat his dog, run a red light? The usual.'

'Sure.'

'And I'm curious about where he got his money. I'd like a fix on his background.'

'So, just routine, huh?'

'And, Tray, let's keep this between us. It's personal. Okay?'

'No problem. I'll call you in the morning.'

'Thanks. I owe you a lunch.'

'Dinner.'

'You've got it.'

Robert replaced the receiver and thought, *Portrait of a man clutching at straws. What am I hoping for, that he's Jack the Ripper, and Susan will come flying back into my arms?*

Early the following morning, Dustin Thornton sent for Robert. 'What are you working on, Commander?'

He knows perfectly well what I'm working on, Robert thought. 'I'm winding up my file on the diplomat from Singapore, and . . .'

'It doesn't seem to be occupying enough of your time.'

'I beg your pardon?'

'In case you've forgotten, Commander, the Office of Naval Intelligence is not mandated to investigate American citizens.'

Robert was watching him, puzzled. 'What are you . . . ?'

'I've been notified by the FBI that you have been trying to obtain information that is completely out of the jurisdiction of this agency.'

Robert felt a sudden rush of anger. That sonofabitch Traynor had betrayed him. So much for friendship. 'It was a personal matter,' Robert said. 'I . . .'

'The computers of the FBI are not there for your convenience, nor to help you harass private citizens. Do I make myself clear?'

'Very.'

'That's all.'

Robert raced back to his office. His fingers trembled as he dialled 202-324-3000. A voice answered, 'FBI.'

'Al Traynor.'

'Just a moment, please.'

A minute later, a man's voice came on the line. 'Hello. May I help you?'

'Yes. I'm calling Al Traynor.'

'I'm sorry, Agent Traynor is no longer with this office.'

Robert felt a shock go through him. 'What?'

'Agent Traynor has been transferred.'

'Transferred?'

'Yes.'

'To where?'

'Boise. But he won't be up there for a while. A long while, I'm afraid.'

'What do you mean?'

'He was struck by a hit-and-run driver last night while jogging in Rock Creek Park. Can you believe it? Some creep must have been drunk out of his mind. He ran his car right up on the jogging path. Traynor's body was thrown over forty feet. He may not make it.'

Robert replaced the receiver. His mind was spinning. What the hell was going on? Monte Banks, the blue-eyed all-American boy, was being protected. From what? By whom? *Jesus*, Robert thought, *what is Susan getting herself into?*

He went to visit her that afternoon.

She was in her new apartment, a beautiful duplex on 'M' Street. He wondered whether Moneybags had paid for it. It had been weeks since he had seen Susan, and the sight of her took his breath away.

'Forgive me for barging in like this, Susan. I know I promised not to.'

'You said it was something serious.'

'It is.' Now that he was here, he didn't know how to begin. *Susan, I came here to save you?* She would laugh in his face.

'What's happened?'

'It's about Monte.'

She frowned. 'What about him?'

This was the difficult part. How could he tell her what he himself didn't know? All he knew was that something was terribly wrong. Monte Banks was in the FBI computer all right, with a tickler: *No information to be given out without proper authorization.* And the inquiry had been kicked right back to ONI. *Why?*

'I don't think he's . . . he's not what he seems to be.'

'I don't understand.'

'Susan – where does he get his money?'

621

She looked surprised at the question. 'Monte has a very successful import-export business.'

The oldest cover in the world.

He should have known better than to have come charging in with his half-baked theory. He felt like a fool. Susan was waiting for an answer and he had none.

'Why are you asking?'

'I was . . . I just wanted to make sure he's right for you,' Robert said lamely.

'Oh, Robert.' Her voice was filled with disappointment.

'I guess I shouldn't have come.' *You got that right, buddy.* 'I'm sorry.'

Susan walked up to him and gave him a hug. 'I understand,' she said softly.

But she didn't understand. She didn't understand that an innocent inquiry about Monte Banks had been stonewalled, referred to the Office of Naval Intelligence, and that the man who had tried to get that information had been transferred to the boondocks.

There were other ways of obtaining information, and Robert went about them circumspectly. He telephoned a friend who worked for *Forbes Magazine*.

'Robert! Long time no see. What can I do for you?'

Robert told him.

'Monte Banks? Interesting you should mention him. We think he should be on our Forbes Four Hundred wealthiest list, but we can't get any hard information on him. Do you have anything for us?'

A zero.

Robert went to the public library and looked up Monte Banks in *Who's Who*. He was not listed.

He turned to the microfiche, and looked up back issues of the *Washington Post* around the time that Monte Banks had had his plane accident. There was a brief item about the plane crash. It mentioned Banks as an entrepreneur.

It all sounded innocent enough. *Maybe I'm wrong*, Robert thought. *Maybe Monte Banks is a guy in a white hat. Our government wouldn't have protected him if he was a spy, a criminal, into drugs . . . The truth is that I'm still trying to hold onto Susan.*

Being a bachelor again was a loneliness, an emptiness, a round of busy days and sleepless nights. A tide of despair would sweep over him without warning, and he would weep. He wept for himself and for Susan and for everything that they had lost. Susan's presence was everywhere. The apartment was alive with reminders of her. Robert was cursed with total recall, and each room tormented him with memories of Susan's voice, her laughter, her warmth. He remembered the soft hills and valleys of her body as she lay in bed naked, waiting for him, and the ache inside him was unbearable.

His friends were concerned.

'You shouldn't be alone, Robert.'

And their rallying cry became, 'Have I got a girl for you!'

They were tall and beautiful, and small and sexy. They were models and secretaries and advertising executives and divorcees and lawyers. But none of them was Susan. He had nothing in common with any of them, and trying to make small talk with strangers in whom he had no interest only made him feel more lonely. Robert had no desire to go to bed with any of them. He wanted to be alone. He wanted to rewind the film back to the beginning, to rewrite the script. With hindsight, it was so easy to see his mistakes, to see how the scene with Admiral Whittaker should have played.

The CIA has been infiltrated by a man called The Fox. The Deputy Director has asked for you to track him down.

No, Admiral. Sorry. I'm taking my wife on a second honeymoon.

He wanted to re-edit his life, to give it a happy ending. Too late. Life did not give second chances. He was alone.

He did his own shopping, cooked his meals for himself and went to the neighbourbood laundromat once a week when he was home.

It was a lonely, miserable time in Robert's life. But the worst was yet to come. A beautiful designer he had met in Washington telephoned him several times to invite him to dinner. Robert had been reluctant, but he had finally accepted. She prepared a delicious candlelight dinner for the two of them.

'You're a very good cook,' Robert said.

'I'm very good at everything.' And there was no mistaking her meaning. She moved closer to him. 'Let me prove it to you.' She put her hands on his thighs and ran her tongue around his lips.

It's been a long time, Robert thought. *Maybe too long.*

They went to bed, and to Robert's consternation, it was a disaster. For the first time in his life, Robert was impotent. He was humiliated.

'Don't worry, darling,' she said. 'It will be all right.'

She was wrong.

Robert went home feeling embarrassed, crippled. He knew that in some crazy, convoluted way, he had felt that making love to another woman was a betrayal of Susan. *How stupid can I get?*

He tried to make love again, several weeks later, with a bright secretary at ONI. She had been wildly passionate in bed, stroking his body and taking him inside her hot mouth. But it was no use. He wanted only Susan. After that, he stopped trying. He thought of consulting a doctor, but he was too ashamed. He knew the answer to his problem, and there was no solution. He poured all his energy into work.

Susan called him at least once a week. 'Don't forget to pick up your shirts at the laundry,' she would say. Or: 'I'm sending over a maid to clean up the apartment. I'll bet it's a mess.'

Each call made the loneliness more intolerable.

She had called him the night before her wedding.

'Robert, I want you to know I'm getting married tomorrow.'

It was difficult for him to breathe. He began to hyperventilate.

'Susan . . .'

'I love Monte,' she said, 'but I love you, too. I'll love you until the day I die. I don't want you ever to forget that.'

What was there to say to that?

'Robert, are you all right?'

Sure. I'm great. Except that I'm a fucking eunuch. Scratch the adjective.

'Robert?'

He could not bear to punish her with his problem. 'I'm fine. Just do me a favour, will you, baby?'

'Anything I can.'

'Don't . . . don't let him take you on your honeymoon to any of the places we went to.'

He hung up and went out and got drunk again.

That had been a year earlier. That was the past. He had been forced to face the reality that Susan now belonged to someone else. He had to live in the present. He had work to do. It was time to have a chat with Leslie Mothershed, the photographer who had the photographs and names of the witnesses Robert had been assigned to track down on what was going to be his last assignment.

18

Leslie Mothershed was in a state beyond euphoria. The moment he had returned to London, clutching his precious film, he had hurried into the small pantry he had converted into a darkroom and checked to make sure he had everything on hand: film-processing tank, thermometer, spring-type clothes pins, four large beakers, a timer, and developer, stop-bath solutions, and fixer. He turned out the light and switched on a small red overhead lamp. His hands were trembling as he opened the cartridges and removed the film. He took deep breaths to control himself. *Nothing must go wrong this time*, he thought. *Nothing. This is for you, Mother.*

Carefully, he rolled the film into reels. He placed the reels in the tank and filled it with developer, the first of the liquids he would use. It would require a constant temperature of 68°F and periodic agitation. After eleven minutes, he emptied the contents and poured the fixer over the reels.

He was getting nervous again, terrified of making a mistake. He poured off the fixer for the first wash and then let the film sit in a tankful of water for ten minutes. This was followed by two minutes of constant agitation in a hypocleansing agent and twelve more minutes in water. Thirty seconds in photo-flo solution ensured there would be no streaks or flaws in the negatives. Finally, very, very carefully, he removed the film, hung it up with clothes pins, and used a squeegee to remove the last drips from the film. He waited impatiently for the negatives to dry.

It was time to examine the negatives. Holding his breath, heart pounding, Mothershed picked up the first strip of negatives and held it up to the light. *Perfect. Absolutely perfect!*

Each one was a gem, a picture that any photographer in the world would be proud to have taken. Every detail of the strange spacecraft was outlined, including the bodies of the two alien forms lying inside.

Two things he had not noticed before caught Mothershed's eye, and he took a closer look. Where the spaceship had cracked open he could see three narrow couches inside the ship – and yet there were only two aliens. The other thing that was strange was that one of the alien's hands had been severed. It was nowhere to be seen in the photograph.

Maybe the creature had only one hand, Mothershed thought. *My God, these pictures are masterpieces! Mother was right. I'm a genius.* He looked around the tiny room and thought, *The next time I develop my films, it will be in a big, beautiful darkroom in my mansion in Eaton Square.*

He stood there fingering his treasures like a miser fingering his gold. There wasn't a magazine or newspaper in the world that wouldn't kill to get these pictures. All these years the bastards had rejected his photographs, with their insulting little notes. 'Thank you for submitting the photos which we are herewith returning. They do not fit our present needs.' And, 'Thank you for your submission. They are too similar to pictures we have already printed.' Or simply, 'We are returning the photographs you sent us.'

For years he had gone begging to the creeps for jobs, and now they were going to crawl to him, and he was going to make them pay through the nose.

He could not wait. He had to start immediately. Since bloody British Telecom had shut off his phone merely because he happened to be a few weeks late making his last quarterly payment, Mothershed had to go outside to find a phone. On an impulse, he decided to go to Langan's, the celebrity hangout, and treat himself to a much deserved lunch. Langan's was well beyond his means, but if there was ever a time to celebrate, this was it. Wasn't he on the verge of becoming rich and famous?

A maître d' seated Mothershed at a table in a corner of the restaurant, and there, at a booth not ten feet away, he saw two familiar faces. He suddenly realized who they were, and a little thrill ran through him. Michael Caine and Roger Moore, in person! He wished his mother were still alive so he could tell her about it. She had loved reading about movie stars. The two men were laughing and having a good time, not a care in the world, and Mothershed could not help staring. Their glances moved past him. *Smug bastards,* Leslie Mothershed thought angrily. *I suppose they expect me to come over and ask for their autographs. Well, in a few days they're going to be asking for mine. They'll be falling all over themselves to introduce me to their friends. 'Leslie, I want you to meet Charles and Di, and this is Fergie and Andrew. Leslie, you know, is the chap who took those famous photos of the UFOs.'*

When Mothershed finished his lunch, he walked past the two stars, and went upstairs to the phone booth. Directory Inquiries gave him the number of the *Sun.*

'I'd like to speak to your picture editor.'

A male voice came on the line. 'Chapman.'

'What would it be worth to you to have photographs of a UFO with the bodies of two aliens in it?'

The voice at the other end of the phone said, 'If the pictures are good enough, we might run them as an example of a clever hoax, and . . .'

Mothershed said waspishly, 'It so happens that this is no hoax. I have the names of nine reputable witnesses who will testify that it's real . . . including a priest.'

626

The man's tone changed. 'Oh? And where were these pictures taken?'

'Never mind,' Mothershed said cagily. He was not going to let them trick him into giving away any information. 'Are you interested?'

The voice said cautiously, 'If you can prove that the pictures are authentic, yes, we would be very interested.'

Damn right you would, Mothershed thought gleefully. 'I'll get back to you.' He hung up.

The other two phone calls were just as satisfactory. Mothershed had to admit to himself that getting the names and addresses of the witnesses had been a stroke of pure genius. There was no way now that anyone could accuse him of trying to perpetrate a fraud. These pictures were going to appear on the front pages of every important newspaper and magazine in the world. *With my credit: Photographs by Leslie Mothershed.*

As Mothershed left the restaurant he could not resist walking up to the booth where the two stars were seated. 'Excuse me, I'm sorry to bother you, but would you give me your autographs?'

Roger Moore and Michael Caine smiled up at him pleasantly. They scribbled their names on pieces of paper and handed them to the photographer.

'Thank you.'

When Leslie Mothershed got outside, he savagely tore up the autographs and threw them away.

Screw them! he thought. *I'm more important than they are.*

19

Robert took a taxi to Whitechapel. They drove through the City, the business section of London, heading east until they reached the Whitechapel Road, the area made infamous a century earlier by Jack the Ripper. Along the Whitechapel Road were dozens of outside stalls selling everything from clothing to fresh vegetables, to carpets.

As the taxi neared Mothershed's address, the neighbourhood became more and more dilapidated. Graffiti was scrawled all over the peeling, brownstone buildings. They passed the Weaver's Arms pub. *That would be Mothershed's local*, Robert thought. Another sign read: 'Walker Bookmaker' . . . *Mothershed probably places his bets on horses there*.

They finally reached 213A Grove Road. Robert dismissed the taxi and studied the building in front of him. It was an ugly two-storey building that had been converted into small flats. Inside was the man who had a complete list of the witnesses Robert had been sent to find.

Leslie Mothershed was in the living room, poring over his windfall, when the doorbell rang. He looked up, startled, filled with a sudden inexplicable fear. The ring was repeated. Mothershed scooped up his precious photographs and hurried into the converted darkroom. He slipped the pictures into a pile of old prints, then walked back into the living room and opened the front door. He stared at the stranger who stood there.

'Yes?'

'Leslie Mothershed?'

'That's right. What can I do for you?'

'May I come in?'

'I don't know. What is this about?'

Robert pulled out a Defence Ministry identification card and flashed it. 'I'm here on official business, Mr Mothershed. We can either talk here or at the Ministry.' It was a bluff. But he could see the sudden fear on the photographer's face.

Leslie Mothershed swallowed. 'I don't know what you're talking about, but . . . come in.'

Robert entered the drab room. It was shabby-genteel, dreary, not a place where anyone would live by choice.

'Would you kindly explain what you're doing here?' Mothershed put the proper note of innocent exasperation in his voice.

'I'm here to question you about some photographs you took.'

He knew it! He had known it from the moment he heard the bell. *The bastards are going to try to take my fortune away from me. Well, I'm not going to let them do it.* 'What photographs are you talking about?'

Robert said patiently, 'The ones you took at the site of the UFO crash.'

Mothershed stared at Robert for a moment as though caught by surprise, and then forced a laugh. 'Oh, *those*! I wish I had them to give to you.'

'You *did* take those pictures?'

'I tried.'

'What do you mean . . . you tried?'

'The bloody things never came out.' Mothershed gave a nervous cough. 'My camera fogged. That's the second time that's happened to me.' He was babbling now. 'I even threw out the negatives. They were no good. It was a complete waste of film. And you know how expensive film is these days.'

He's a bad liar, Robert thought. *He's on the edge of panic*. Robert said sympathetically, 'Too bad. Those photographs would have been very helpful.' He said nothing about the list of passengers. If Mothershed lied about the photographs, he would lie about the list. Robert glanced around. The photographs and the list had to be hidden here somewhere. *They shouldn't be difficult to find*. The flat consisted of the small living room, a bedroom, a bathroom and what looked like a door to a utility closet. There was no way he could force the man to hand over the material. He had no real authority. But he wanted those photographs and the list of witnesses before the SIS came and took them away. He needed that list for himself.

'Yes,' Mothershed sighed. 'Those pictures would have been worth a fortune.'

'Tell me about the spaceship,' Robert said.

Mothershed gave an involuntary shudder. The eerie scene was fixed in his mind forever. 'I'll never forget it,' he said. 'The ship seemed to . . . to pulsate, like it was alive. There was something evil about it. And then there were these two dead aliens inside.'

'Can you tell me anything about the passengers on the bus?'

Sure I can, Mothershed gloated to himself. *I have all their names and addresses*. 'No, I'm afraid I can't.' Mothershed went on, talking to conceal his nervousness. 'The reason I can't help you about the passengers is that I wasn't on that bus. They were all strangers.'

'I see. Well, thank you for your cooperation, Mr Mothershed. I appreciate it. Sorry about your pictures.'

'So am I,' Mothershed said. He watched the door close behind the stranger and thought, happily, *I've done it! I've outsmarted the sonsofbitches*.

Outside in the hall, Robert was examining the lock on the door. A

Chubb. And an old model. It would take him seconds to open it. He would start surveillance in the middle of the night and wait for the photographer to leave the flat in the morning. *Once I have the list of passengers in my possession, the rest of the assignment will be simple.*

Robert checked into a small hotel near Mothershed's flat, and telephoned General Hilliard.

'I have the name of the English witness, General.'

'Just a moment. All right. Go ahead, Commander.'

'Leslie Mothershed. He lives in Whitechapel. 213A Grove Road.'

'Excellent. I'll arrange for the British authorities to speak to him.'

Robert did not mention the passenger list or the photographs. Those were his aces in the hole.

Reggie's Fish and Chip Shop was located in a little cul de sac off the Brompton Road. It was a small establishment with a clientele made up mainly of clerks and secretaries who worked in the neighbourhood. Its walls were covered with football posters and the parts that were exposed had not seen fresh paint since the Suez conflict.

The phone behind the counter rang twice before it was answered by a large man dressed in a greasy wool sweater. The man looked like a typical East Ender except for a gold-rimmed monocle fixed tightly in his left eye. The reason for the monocle was apparent to anyone who looked closely at the man – his other eye was made of glass and of a colour blue that was generally seen on travel posters.

'Reggie here.'

'This is the Bishop.'

'Yes, sir,' said Reggie, his voice dropping to a whisper.

'Our client's name is Mothershed. Christian tag Leslie. Resides at 213A Grove Road, E3. We need this order filled quickly. Understood?'

'Consider it done, sir.'

20

Leslie Mothershed was lost in a golden daydream. He was being interviewed by the world press. They were asking him about the huge castle he had just bought in Scotland, his château in the South of France, his enormous yacht. *'And is it true that the Queen has invited you to become the official Royal photographer?' 'Yes. I said I would let her know. And now, ladies and gentlemen, if you will all excuse me, I'm late for my show at the BBC . . .'*

His reverie was interrupted by the sound of the doorbell. He looked at his watch. Eleven o'clock. *Has that man returned?* He walked over to the door and cautiously opened it. In the doorway stood a man shorter than Mothershed (that was the first thing he noticed about him) with thick glasses and a thin, sallow face.

'Excuse me,' the man said diffidently. 'I apologize for disturbing you at this hour. I live just down the block. The sign outside says you're a photographer.'

'So?'

'Do you do passport photos?'

Leslie Mothershed do passport photos? The man who was about to own the world? That would be like asking Michelangelo to paint the bathroom.

'No,' he said, rudely. He started to close the door.

'I really hate to bother you, but I'm in a terrible jam. My plane leaves for Tokyo at eight o'clock in the morning and a little while ago when I took out my passport, I saw that somehow my photograph had been torn loose. It's missing. I've looked everywhere. They won't let me on the plane without a passport photo.' The little man was near tears.

'I'm sorry,' Mothershed said. 'I can't help you.'

'I'd be willing to pay you a hundred pounds.'

A hundred pounds? To a man with a castle and a château and a yacht? It was an insult.

The pathetic little man was going on. 'I could go even higher. Two hundred or three hundred. You see, I really must be on that plane or I'll lose my job.'

Three hundred pounds to take a passport picture? Forgetting the developing, it would take about ten seconds. Mothershed began to calculate. That came to eighteen hundred pounds a minute. Eighteen hundred pounds a minute was one hundred and eight thousand pounds an hour. If he worked an eight-hour day, that would be eight hundred and sixty-four thousand pounds a day. In one week that would come to . . .

'Will you do it?'

Mothershed's ego jockeyed with his greed, and greed won out. *I can use a bit of pocket money.*

'Come in,' Mothershed said. 'Stand against that wall.'

'Thank you. I really appreciate this.'

Mothershed wished he had a Polaroid camera. That would have made it so simple. He picked up his Vivitar and said, 'Hold still.'

Ten seconds later it was done.

'It will take a while to develop it,' Mothershed said. 'If you come back in . . .'

'If you don't mind, I'll wait.'

'Suit yourself.'

Mothershed took the camera into the darkroom, put it into the black bag, turned out the overhead light, switched on the red light and removed the film. He would do this in a hurry. Passport pictures always looked terrible, anyway. Fifteen minutes later, as Mothershed was timing the film in the developer tanks, he began to smell smoke. He paused. Was it his imagination? No. The smell was getting stronger. He turned to open the door. It seemed to be stuck. Mothershed pushed against it. It held fast.

'Hello,' he called out. 'What's happening out there?'

There was no response.

'Hello?' He pressed his shoulder against the door, but there seemed to be something heavy on the other side of it, keeping it closed. 'Mister?'

There was no answer. The only sound he could hear was a loud crackling noise. The smell of smoke was becoming overpowering. The flat was on fire. *That was probably why the man had left. He must have gone to get help.* Leslie Mothershed slammed his shoulder against the door, but it would not budge. 'Help!' he screamed. 'Get me out of here!'

Smoke was starting to pour under the door, and Mothershed could feel the heat of the flames beginning to lick at it. It was getting difficult to breathe. He was starting to choke. He tore at his collar, gasping for air. His lungs were burning. He was beginning to lose consciousness. He sank down on his knees. 'Oh, God, please don't let me die now. Not now that I'm going to be rich and famous . . .'

'Reggie here.'

'Was the order filled?'

'Yes, sir. A bit overcooked but delivered on time.'

'Excellent.'

When Robert arrived at Grove Road at two o'clock in the morning, to begin his surveillance, he was confronted with an enormous traffic jam. The street was filled with official vehicles, a fire engine, ambulances and three police cars. Robert pushed his way through the crowd of bystanders and hurried over to the centre of activity. The whole building had been engulfed by the fire. From the outside he could see that the first-floor flat occupied by the photographer had been completely gutted.

'How did it happen?' Robert asked a fireman.

'We don't know yet. Stand back, please.'

'My cousin lives in that flat. Is he all right?'

'I'm afraid not.' His tone became sympathetic. 'They're just taking him out of the building now.'

Robert watched as two ambulance attendants pushed a stretcher carrying a body into the ambulance.

'I was staying with him,' Robert said. 'All my clothes are in there. I'd like to go in and . . .'

The fireman shook his head. 'It wouldn't do you any good, sir. There's nothing left of the flat but ashes.'

Nothing left but ashes. Including the photographs and the precious list of passengers with their names and addresses.

So much for fucking serendipity, Robert thought bitterly.

In Washington, Dustin Thornton was having lunch with his father-in-law, in Willard Stone's offices, in his lavish private dining room. Dustin Thornton was nervous. He was always nervous in the presence of his powerful father-in-law.

Willard Stone was in a good mood. 'I had dinner with the President last evening. He told me that he's very pleased with your work, Dustin.'

'I'm very gratified.'

'You're doing a fine job. You're helping to protect us against the hordes.'

'The hordes?'

'Those who would try to bring this great country to its knees. But it is not just the enemy outside the walls we have to beware of. It is those who pretend to be serving our country, who fail to do their duty. Those who do not carry out their orders.'

'The mavericks.'

'That's right, Dustin. The mavericks. They must be punished. If . . .'

A man walked into the room. 'Excuse me, Mr Stone. The gentlemen have arrived. They're waiting for you.'

'Yes.' Stone turned to his son-in-law. 'Finish your lunch, Dustin. I have something important to take care of. One day, I may be able to tell you about it.'

21

The streets of Zürich were filled with weird-looking creatures with odd shapes, misshapen giants with large, grotesque bodies and tiny eyes, with skin the colour of boiled fish. They were meat eaters, and she hated the fetid smells they exuded from their bodies. Some of the females wore animal skins, the remains of the creatures they had murdered. She was still stunned by the terrible accident that had taken away the life essence of her companions.

She had been on earth for four cycles of what these beings called *luna*, and she had not eaten in all that time. She was faint from thirst. The only water she had been able to drink was the fresh rain water in the farmer's trough, and it had not rained since the night she arrived. The other water on earth was undrinkable. She had gone into an alien feeding place, but she had been unable to stand the stench. She had tried to eat their raw vegetables and fruit, but they were tasteless, not like the succulent food at home.

She was called the Graceful One, and she was tall and stately and beautiful, with luminous green eyes. She had adopted the appearance of an Earthling after she left the site of the crash, and she walked through the crowds unnoticed.

She was seated at a table in a hard, uncomfortable chair that had been built for the human body, and she read the minds of the creatures around her.

Two of the beings were seated at a table near her. One was speaking aloud. 'It's the chance of a lifetime, Franz! For fifty thousand francs you can get in at the start. You've got fifty thousand francs, haven't you?' She read the loud thoughts in his head. *Come on, you swine. I need the commission.*

'Sure, but I don't know . . .' *I'll have to borrow it from my wife.*

'Have I ever given you bad investment advice?' *Make up your mind.*

'It's a lot of money.' *She'll never give it to me.*

'What about the potential? There's a chance to make millions.' *Say yes.*

'All right. I'm in.' *Maybe I can sell some of her jewellery.*

I have him! 'You'll never regret it, Franz.' *He can always take a tax loss.*

The Graceful One had no idea what the conversation meant.

At the far end of the restaurant, a man and woman were seated at a table. They were talking in low voices. She stretched her mind to hear them.

'Jesus Christ!' the man said. 'How the hell could you get pregnant?' *You stupid bitch!*

'How do you think I got pregnant?' *Your cock did it!*

Pregnant was how these beings gestated, procreating clumsily with their genitals, like their animals in the fields.

'What are you going to do about it, Tina?' *You've got to get an abortion.*

'What do you expect me to do? You said you were going to tell your wife about me.' *You lying bastard.*

'Look, honey, I am, but this is a bad time.' *I was crazy to ever get involved with you. I should have known you were trouble.*

'It's a bad time for me, too, Paul. I don't even think you love me.' *Please tell me you do.*

'Of course I love you. It's just that my wife is going through a rough period right now.' *I don't intend to lose her.*

'I'm going through a rough period right now, too. Don't you understand? I'm having your baby.' *And you're damn well going to marry me.* Water was coming from her eyes.

'Calm down, honey. I tell you, everything is going to be fine. I want the baby as much as you do.' *I'll have to talk her into an abortion.*

At a table next to them, a male creature was seated alone.

They promised me. They said the race was fixed, that I couldn't lose, and like a fool, I turned all my money over to them. I've got to find a way to put it back before the auditors come. I couldn't stand it if they put me in jail. I'll kill myself first. I swear to God, I'll kill myself.

At another table, a male and female were in the middle of a discussion.

'. . . it's nothing like that. It's just that I've got this beautiful chalet in the mountains and I thought it would be good for you to get away for a weekend and relax.' *We'll spend a lot of time relaxing in my bed, chérie.*

'I don't know, Claude. I've never gone away with a man before.' *I wonder if he believes that.*

'*Oui*, but this is not a sex thing. I just thought of the chalet because you said you needed a rest. You can think of me as your brother.' *And we will try some good, old-fashioned incest.*

The Graceful One was unaware that the various people were speaking in different languages, for she was able to filter them all through her consciousness and understand what they were saying.

I must find a way to get in touch with the mothership, she thought. She took out the small, hand-held silver coloured transmitter. It was a divided neuro-net system, half of it consisting of living organic material and the other half a metallic compound from another galaxy. The organic material contained thousands of single cells, so that as they died off, others would multiply, keeping the connections constant. Unfortunately, the dilitheum crystal that activated the transmitter had broken off, and was lost. She had tried to communicate with her ship, but the transmitter was useless without it.

She tried to eat another leaf of lettuce but she could no longer stand the stench. She rose and started toward the door. The cashier called out after her, 'Just a minute, miss. You haven't paid for your meal.'

'I'm sorry. I do not have your medium of exchange.'

'You can tell that to the police authorities.'

The Graceful One stared into the cashier's eyes, and watched her go limp. She turned and walked out of the feeding place.

I must find the crystal. They are waiting to hear from me. She had to concentrate to focus her senses. But everything seemed blurred and distorted. Without water, she knew she was going to die soon.

22

DAY FIVE

Bern, Switzerland

Robert had come to a dead end. He had not realized how much he had counted on obtaining Mothershed's list of names. *Up in smoke*, Robert thought. *Literally.* The trail was cold now. *I should have gotten the list when I was in Mothershed's flat. That will teach me to . . . teach.* Of course! A thought that had been in the back of his mind suddenly came into focus. Hans Beckerman had said, *Affenarsch! All the other passengers were excited about seeing the UFO and those dead creatures in it, but this old man kept complaining about how we had to hurry up to get to Bern because he had to prepare some lecture for the University.* It was a long shot, but it was all Robert had.

He rented a car at the Bern airport and headed for the University. He turned off Rathausgasse, the main street of Bern, and drove to Länggass-Strasse, where the University of Bern was located. The University is composed of several buildings, the main one a large four-storey stone building with two wings, and large stone gargoyles adorning the roof. At each end of the courtyard in front of the building are glass skylights over classrooms, and at the rear of the University is a large park overlooking the Aare River.

Robert walked up the front steps of the Administration Building and entered the reception hall. The only information Beckerman had given him was that the passenger was German, and that he was preparing his lecture for Monday.

A student directed him to the Office of the Administration. The woman seated behind the desk was a formidable figure. She had on a severely tailored suit, black-framed spectacles, and she wore her hair in a bun. She looked up as Robert entered her office.

'*Bitte?*'

Robert pulled out an identification card. 'Interpol. I'm conducting an investigation, and I would appreciate your cooperation, Miss . . .'

'Frau. Frau Schreiber. What kind of investigation?'

'I'm looking for a professor.'

She frowned. 'His name?'

'I don't know.'

'You do not know his name?'

'No. He's a visiting professor. He gave a lecture here a few days ago. *Montag.*'

'Many visiting professors come here every day to give lectures. What is his discipline?'

'I beg your pardon?'

'What does he teach?' Her tone was growing impatient. 'What subject did he lecture on?'

'I don't know.'

She let her exasperation show. '*Tut mir leid.* I can't help you. And I am too busy for frivolous questions like this . . .' She started to turn away.

'Oh, it's not frivolous,' Robert assured her. '*Es ist sehr dringend.*' He leaned forward and said, in a low voice, 'I'm going to have to take you into my confidence. The professor we're looking for is involved in a prostitution ring.'

Frau Schreiber's mouth made a small 'o' of surprise.

'Interpol has been on his trail for months. The current information we have on him is that he is German and that he gave a lecture here on the fifteenth of this month.' He straightened up. 'If you don't want to help, we can conduct an official investigation of the University. Of course, the publicity . . .'

'*Nein, nein!*' she said. 'The University must not be involved in anything like this.' She looked worried. 'You say he lectured here on – what day?'

'The fifteenth. Monday.'

Frau Schreiber rose and walked over to a filing cabinet. She pulled it open and scanned some papers. She extracted several sheets from a folder. 'Here we are. There were three guest professors who gave lectures here on the fifteenth.'

'The man I want is German.'

'These are all German,' Frau Schreiber said stiffly. She shuffled the papers in her hand. 'One of the lectures was on economics, one on chemistry and one on psychology.'

'May I see those?'

Reluctantly, she handed the reports to Robert.

He studied the sheets. Each one had a name written down with a home address and a telephone number.

'I can make a copy of these for you, if you wish.'

'No, thank you.' He had already memorized the names and numbers. 'None of these is the man I'm looking for.'

Frau Schreiber gave a sigh of relief. 'Well, thank God for that. Prostitution! We would never be involved in such a thing.'

'I'm sorry I troubled you for nothing.' Robert left and headed for a telephone booth in town.

The first telephone call was to Berlin. 'Professor Streubel?'

'*Ja.*'

'This is the Sunshine Tours Bus Company. You left a pair of glasses on our bus last Sunday when you were touring with us in Switzerland and . . .'

'I do not know what you are speaking about.' He sounded annoyed.

'You were in Switzerland on the fourteenth, were you not, Professor?'

'No. On the fifteenth. To give a lecture at the University of Bern.'

'And you did not take our bus tour?'

'I have no time for such foolishness. I'm a busy man.' And the professor hung up.

The second call was to Hamburg. 'Professor Heinrich?'

'This is Professor Heinrich.'

'This is the Sunshine Tours Bus Company. You were in Switzerland on the fourteenth of this month?'

'Why do you wish to know?'

'Because we found a briefcase of yours on one of our buses, Professor, and . . .'

'You have the wrong person. I have been on no tour buses.'

'You did not take a tour of ours to the Jungfrau?'

'I just told you, no.'

'I'm sorry to have bothered you.'

The third call was to Munich. 'Professor Otto Schmidt?'

'Yes.'

'Professor Schmidt, this is the Sunshine Tours Bus Company. We have a pair of your glasses that you left on our bus a few days ago, and . . .'

'There must be some mistake.'

Robert's heart sank. He had struck out. There was nowhere left to go.

The voice went on. 'I have my glasses here. I have not lost them.'

Robert's spirits soared. 'Are you sure, Professor? You *were* on the Jungfrau trip on the fourteenth, were you not?'

'Yes, yes, but I told you, I have not lost anything.'

'Thank you very much, Professor.' Robert replaced the receiver. *Jackpot!*

Robert dialled another number and within two minutes he was speaking with General Hilliard.

'I have two things to report,' Robert said. 'The witness in London I told you about?'

'Yes?'

'He died in a fire last night.'

'Really? Too bad.'

'Yes, sir. But I believe I've located another witness. I'll let you know as soon as I check him out.'

'I'll wait to hear from you, Commander.'

General Hilliard was reporting to Janus.

'Commander Bellamy has located another witness.'

'Good. The group is getting restless. Everyone is worried that this story will surface before SDI is operational.'

'I'll have more information for you soon.'

'I don't want information, I want results.'

'Yes, Janus.'

Plattenstrasse, in Munich, is a quiet residential street with drab brownstone buildings huddled together as though for protection. Number five was identical to its neighbours. Inside the vestibule was a row of mailboxes. A small card below one of them read 'Professor Otto Schmidt'. Robert rang the bell.

The apartment door was opened by a tall, thin man with an untidy mop of white hair. He was wearing a tattered sweater and smoking a pipe. Robert wondered whether he had created the image of an archetypical college professor, or whether the image had created him.

'Professor Schmidt?'

'Yes?'

'I wonder if I might talk to you a moment. I'm with . . .'

'We have already talked,' Professor Schmidt said. 'You are the man who telephoned me this morning. I am an expert at recognizing voices. Come in.'

'Thank you.' Robert entered the living room. The walls were crowded from floor to ceiling with bookcases filled with hundreds of volumes. Books were stacked everywhere; on tables, on the floor, on chairs. The sparse furniture in the room seemed to be an afterthought.

'You're not with any Swiss tour bus company, are you?'

'Well, I . . .'

'You are American.'

'Yes.'

'And this visit has nothing to do with my lost glasses that were not lost.'

'Well . . . no, sir.'

'You are interested in the UFO I saw. It was a very upsetting experience. I always believed they might exist, but I never thought I would see one.'

'It must have been a terrible shock.'

'It was.'

'Can you tell me anything about it?'

'It was . . . it was almost alive. There was a kind of shimmering light around it. Blue. No, maybe more of a grey. I . . . I'm not sure.'

He remembered Mandel's description: *It kept changing colours. It looked blue . . . then green.*

'It had broken open, and I could see two bodies inside. Small . . . big eyes. They were wearing some kind of silver suit.'

'Is there anything you can tell me about your fellow passengers?'

'My fellow passengers on the bus?'

'Yes.'

The professor shrugged. 'I know nothing of them. They were all strangers. I was concentrating on a lecture I was going to give the next morning, and I paid very little attention to the other passengers.'

Robert watched his face, waiting.

'If it will help you any,' the professor said, 'I can tell you what countries some of them came from. I teach chemistry, but the study of phonetics is my hobby.'

'Anything you can remember would be appreciated.'

'There was an Italian priest, a Hungarian, an American with a Texan accent, an Englishman, a Russian girl . . .'

'Russian?'

'Yes. But she was not from Moscow. From her accent, I would say Kiev, or very near there.'

Robert waited, but there was only silence. 'You didn't hear any of them mention their names or talk about their professions?'

'I'm sorry. I told you, I was thinking about my lecture: it was difficult to concentrate. The Texan and the priest sat together. The Texan never stopped talking. It was very distracting. I don't know how much the priest even understood.'

'The priest . . .'

'He had a Roman accent.'

'Can you tell me anything more about any of them?'

The professor shrugged. 'I'm afraid not.' He took another puff of his pipe. 'I'm sorry I can't be of any help to you.'

A sudden thought came to Robert. 'You said you're a chemist?'

'Yes.'

'I wonder if you would mind taking a look at something, Professor.' Robert reached in his pocket and pulled out the piece of metal Beckerman had given him. 'Can you tell me what this is?'

Professor Schmidt took the object in his hand, and as he examined it, his expression changed. 'Where . . . where did you get this?'

'I'm afraid I can't say. Do you know what it is?'

'It appears to be part of a transmitting device.'

'Are you sure?'

He turned it over in his hand. 'The crystal is dilitheum. It's very rare. See these notches here? They suggest that this fits into a larger unit. The metal itself is . . . My God, I've never seen anything like it!' His voice was charged with excitement. 'Can you let me have this for a few days? I would like to do some spectrographic studies on it.'

'I'm afraid that's impossible,' Robert said.

'But . . .'

'Sorry.' Robert took back the piece of metal.

The professor tried to conceal his disappointment. 'Perhaps you can bring it back. Why don't you give me your card? If I think of anything more, I'll call you.'

Robert fumbled in his pockets for a moment. 'I don't seem to have any of my cards with me.'

Professor Schmidt said slowly, 'Yes, I thought not.'

'Commander Bellamy is on the line.'

General Hilliard picked up the telephone. 'Yes, Commander?'

'The latest witness's name is Professor Schmidt. He lives at Plattenstrasse 5 in Munich.'

'Thank you, Commander. I'll notify the German authorities immediately.'

Robert was on the verge of saying, 'I'm afraid that's the last witness I'll be able to find,' but something held him back. He hated to admit failure. And yet, the trail had become cold. A Texan and a priest. The priest was from Rome. Period. Along with a million other priests. And there was no way to identify him. *I have a choice*, Robert thought. *I can give up and go back to Washington, or I can go to Rome and give it one last try . . .*

Bundesverfassungsschutzamt, the headquarters of the Office for the Protection of the Constitution, is located in central Berlin on Neumarkterstrasse. It is a large, grey, nondescript building, indistinguishable from the buildings around it. Inside, on the second floor, in the conference room, the chief of the department, Inspector Otto Joachim, was studying a message. He read it twice, then reached for the red telephone on his desk.

DAY SIX

Munich, Germany

The following morning, as Otto Schmidt headed for his chemistry lab, he was thinking about the conversation he had had with the American the evening before. Where could that piece of metal have come from? It was astonishing, beyond anything in his experience. And the American puzzled him. *He said he was interested in the passengers on the bus. Why? Because they had all been witnesses to the flying saucer? Were they going to be warned not to talk? If so, why had not the American warned him? There was something strange going on*, the professor decided. He entered the laboratory and took off his jacket and hung it up. He put on an apron to keep his clothes from getting soiled and walked over to the table where he had been working for many weeks on a chemical experiment. *If this works*, he thought, *it could mean a Nobel prize*. He lifted the beaker of sterile water and started to pour it into a container filled with a yellow liquid. *That's strange. I don't remember it being such a bright yellow.*

The roar of the explosion was tremendous. The laboratory erupted in a gigantic blast, and pieces of glass and human flesh spattered the walls.

FLASH MESSAGE
TOP SECRET ULTRA
BFV TO DEPUTY DIRECTOR NSA
EYES ONLY
COPY ONE OF (ONE) COPY
SUBJECT: OPERATION DOOMSDAY
4. OTTO SCHMIDT – TERMINATED
END OF MESSAGE

Robert missed the news of the professor's death. He was aboard an Alitalia plane, on his way to Rome.

23

Dustin Thornton was getting restless. He had power now, and it was like a drug. He wanted more. His father-in-law, Willard Stone, kept promising to bring him into some mysterious inner circle, but so far, he had failed to fulfil that promise.

It was by pure chance that Thornton learned that his father-in-law disappeared every Friday. Thornton had called to have lunch with him.

'I'm sorry,' Willard Stone's personal secretary said, 'but Mr Stone is away for the day.'

'Oh, too bad. What about lunch next Friday?'

'I'm sorry, Mr Thornton. Mr Stone will be away next Friday, also.'

Strange. And it became even stranger, because when Thornton called two weeks later, he received the same reply. *Where did the old man disappear to every Friday?* He was not a golfer, or a man to indulge in any hobbies.

The obvious answer was a woman. Willard Stone's wife was very social and very rich. She was an imperious woman, almost as strong in her way as her husband. She was not the sort of woman who would tolerate her husband having an affair. *If he is having an affair,* Thornton thought, *I've got him by the balls.* He knew he had to find out.

With all the facilities at his command, Dustin Thornton could have found out very quickly what his father-in-law was up to, but Thornton was no fool. He was well aware that if he made one misstep, he would be in big trouble. Willard Stone was not the kind of man to brook any interference in his life. Thornton decided to investigate the matter himself.

At five a.m., on the following Friday, Dustin Thornton was slumped behind the wheel of an inconspicuous Ford Taurus, half a block from Willard Stone's imposing mansion. It was a cold, miserable dawn, and Thornton kept asking himself what he was doing there. There was probably some perfectly reasonable explanation for Stone's odd behaviour. *I'm wasting my time*, Thornton thought. But something kept him there.

At seven o'clock, the driveway gates opened and a car appeared. Willard Stone was at the wheel. Instead of his usual limousine, he was in a small, black van used by the household staff. A feeling of exultation spread through Thornton. He knew he was on to something. People lived according to their pattern, and Stone was breaking the pattern. It *had* to be another woman.

Driving carefully, and staying well behind the van, Thornton followed his father-in-law through the streets of Washington to the road that led to Arlington.

I'll have to handle this very delicately, Thornton thought. *I don't want to push him too hard. I'll get all the information I can about his mistress, and then I'll confront him with it. I'll tell him my only interest is in protecting him. He'll get the message. The last thing he wants is a public scandal.*

Dustin Thornton was so wrapped up in his own thoughts that he almost missed the turn that Willard Stone had taken. They were in an exclusive residential district. The black van abruptly disappeared up a long, tree-shaded driveway.

Dustin Thornton stopped the car, deciding the best way to proceed. Should he face Willard Stone with his infidelity now? Or should he wait until Stone left and then talk to the woman first? Or should he quietly gather all the information he needed, and then have a talk with his father-in-law? He decided to reconnoitre.

Thornton parked his car on a side street and walked around to the alley at the back of the two-storey house. A wooden fence blocked off the back of the yard, but that was no problem. Thornton opened the gate, and stepped inside. He was facing huge, beautiful, manicured grounds with the house at the rear.

He moved quietly in the shadow of the trees that lined the lawn, and stood at the back door, deciding what his next move should be. He needed proof of what was going on. Without it, the old man would laugh at him. Whatever was happening inside at this moment could be the key to his future. He had to find out.

Very gently, Thornton tried the back door. It was unlocked. He slipped inside, and found himself in a large, old-fashioned kitchen. There was no one around. Thornton moved toward the service door, and pushed it open slightly. He was facing a large reception hall. At the far end was a closed door that could have led to a library. Thornton walked toward it, moving quietly. He stood there, listening. There was no sign of life in the house. *The old man was probably upstairs in the bedroom.*

Thornton walked toward the closed door and opened it. He stood in the doorway, staring. There were a dozen men seated in the room around a large table.

'Come in, Dustin,' Willard Stone said. 'We've been expecting you.'

24

Rome proved to be difficult for Robert, an emotional ordeal that drained him. He had honeymooned there with Susan, and the memories were overpowering. Rome was Roberto, who managed the Hassler Hotel for his mother, and who was partially deaf but could lip-read in five languages. Rome was the gardens of Villa d'Este in Tivoli, and the Ristorante Sibilla and Susan's delight at the one hundred fountains created by the son of Lucrezia Borgia. Rome was Otello at the bottom of the Spanish Steps, and the Vatican, and the Colosseum and the Forum and Michelangelo's Moses. Rome was sharing *tartufi* at Tre Scalini and the sound of Susan's laughter, and her voice saying, 'Please promise me we'll always be this happy, Robert.'

What the hell am I doing here? Robert wondered. *I don't have any idea who the priest is, or whether he's even in Rome. It's time to retire, to go home and forget all this.*

But something inside him, some stubborn streak inherited from a long-dead ancestor, would not let him. *I'll give it one day,* Robert decided. *Just one more day.*

The Leonardo da Vinci airport was crowded, and it seemed to Robert that every other person was a priest. He was looking for one priest in a city of – what? Fifty thousand priests? A hundred thousand? In the taxi on the way to the Hassler Hotel, he noticed crowds of robed priests on the streets. *This is impossible*, Robert thought. *I must be out of my mind.*

He was greeted in the lobby of the Hassler Hotel by the assistant manager.

'Commander Bellamy! What a pleasure to see you again.'

'Thank you, Pietro. Do you have a room for me for one night?'

'For you – of course. Always!'

Robert was escorted to a room he had occupied before.

'If there's anything you need, Commander, please . . .'

I need a bloody miracle, Robert thought. He sat down on the bed and lay back, trying to clear his mind.

Why would a priest from Rome travel to Switzerland? There were several possibilities. He might have gone on vacation, or there might have been a convocation of priests. He was the only priest on the tour bus. What did that signify? Nothing. Except, perhaps, that he was not travelling with a group. So it could have been a trip to visit his friends or family. Or maybe he *was* with a group, and they had other plans that day. Robert's thoughts were going around in a futile circle.

Back to the beginning. How did the priest get to Switzerland? The chances are pretty good that he doesn't own a car. Someone could have given him a lift, but more probably he travelled by plane or train or took a bus. If he were on vacation, he wouldn't have a lot of time. So let's assume he took a plane. That line of reasoning led nowhere. Airlines did not list the occupations of their passengers. The priest would be yet another name on the passenger manifest. But if he were part of a group . . .

The Vatican, the official residence of the Pope, rises majestically on Vatican Hill, on the west bank of the Tiber, in the northwest end of Rome. The dome of St Peter's Basilica, designed by Michelangelo, towers over the huge piazza, filled day and night with avid sightseers of all faiths.

The piazza is surrounded by two semicircular colonnades completed in 1667 by Bernini, with 284 columns of travertine marble placed in four rows and surmounted by a balustrade on which stand 140 statues. Robert had visited there a dozen times, but each time the sight took his breath away.

The interior of the Vatican, of course, was even more spectacular. The Sistine Chapel and the museum and the Sala Rotonda were indescribably beautiful.

But on this day, Robert had not come here to sightsee.

He found the Office of Public Relations for the Vatican in the wing of the building devoted to secular affairs. The young man behind the desk was polite.

'May I help you?'

Robert flashed an identification card. 'I'm with *Time* magazine. I'm doing an article on some priests who attended a convocation in Switzerland in the past week or two. I'm looking for background information.'

The man studied him for a moment, then frowned. 'We had some priests attend a convocation in Venice last month. None of our priests was in Switzerland recently. I'm sorry, I'm afraid I can't help you.'

'It's really very important,' Robert said earnestly. 'How would I go about getting that information?'

'The group you are looking for . . . what branch of the Church do they represent?'

'I beg your pardon?'

'There are many Roman Catholic Orders. There are Franciscans, Marists, Benedictines, Trappists, Jesuits, Dominicans, and several others. I suggest you go to the Order they belong to and inquire there.'

Where the hell is 'there'? Robert wondered. 'Do you have any other suggestions?'

647

'I'm afraid not.'

Neither have I, Robert thought. *I found the haystack. I can't find the needle.*

He left the Vatican and wandered through the streets of Rome, heedless of the people around him, concentrating on his problem. At the Piazza del Popolo, he sat down at an outdoor café and ordered a Cinzano. It sat in front of him, untouched.

For all he knew, the priest could still be in Switzerland. *What Order does he belong to? I don't know. And I have only the professor's word that he was Roman.*

He took a sip of his drink.

There was a late afternoon plane to Washington. *I'm going to be on it*, Robert decided. *I give up.* The thought galled him. *Out, not with a bang, but with a whimper.* It was time to leave.

'*Il conto, per favore.*'

'*Si, signore.*'

Robert's eyes swept idly around the piazza. Across from the café, a bus was loading passengers. In the line were two priests. Robert watched as the passengers paid their fares and moved toward the back of the bus. When the priests reached the conductor, they smiled at him and took their seats without paying.

'Your check, *signore*,' the waiter said.

Robert didn't even hear him. His mind was racing. Here, in the heart of the Catholic Church, priests had certain privileges. It was possible, just possible . . .

The offices of Swissair are located at 10 Via Po, five minutes from the Via Veneto. Robert was greeted by a man behind the counter.

'May I see the manager, please?'

'I am the manager. Can I help you?'

Robert flashed an identification card. 'Michael Hudson. Interpol.'

'What can I do for you, Mr Hudson?'

'Some international carriers are complaining about illegal price discounting in Europe – in Rome, particularly. According to international convention . . .'

'Excuse me, Mr Hudson, but Swissair does not give discounts. Everyone pays the posted fares.'

'Everyone?'

'With the exception of employees of the airline, of course.'

'Don't you have a discount for priests?'

'No. On this airline, they pay full fare.'

On this airline. 'Thank you for your time.' And Robert was gone.

His next stop – and his last hope – was Alitalia. 'Illegal discounts?' The manager was staring at Robert, puzzled. 'We give discounts only to our employees.'

'Don't you give discounts to priests?'

The manager's face brightened. 'Ah, that, yes. But that is not illegal. We have arrangements with the Catholic Church.'

Robert's heart soared. 'So, if a priest wanted to fly from Rome, say – to Switzerland, he would use this airline?'

'Well, it would be cheaper for him. Yes.'

Robert said, 'In order to bring our computers up-to-date, it would be helpful if you could tell me how many priests have flown to Switzerland in the past two weeks. You would have a record of that, wouldn't you?'

'Yes, of course. For tax purposes.'

'I would really appreciate that information.'

'You wish to know how many priests have flown to Switzerland in the past two weeks?'

'Yes. Zürich or Geneva.'

'Just a moment. I will talk to our computers.'

Five minutes later, the manager returned with a computer printout. 'There was only one priest who flew Alitalia to Switzerland in the past two weeks.' He consulted the printout. 'He left Rome on the seventh, and flew to Zürich. His return flight was booked for two days ago.'

Robert took a deep breath. 'His name?'

'Father Romero Patrini.'

'His address?'

He looked down at the paper again. 'He lives in Orvieto. If you need any further . . .' He looked up.

Robert was gone.

25

DAY SEVEN

Orvieto, Italy

He stopped the car on a hairpin bend on Route S-71, and there across the valley, high on a rise of volcanic rock, was a breathtaking view of the city. It was an ancient Etruscan centre, with a world-famous cathedral, and half a dozen churches, and a priest who had witnessed the crash of a UFO.

The town was untouched by time, with cobblestone streets and lovely old buildings, and an open-air market where farmers came to sell their fresh vegetables and chickens.

Robert found a parking place in the Piazza del Duomo, across from the cathedral, and went inside. The enormous interior was deserted except for an elderly priest who was just leaving the altar.

'Excuse me, Father,' Robert said. 'I'm looking for a priest from this town who was in Switzerland last week. Perhaps you . . .'

The priest drew back, his face hostile. 'I cannot discuss this.'

Robert looked at him in surprise. 'I don't understand. I just want to find . . .'

'He is not of this church. He is from the church of San Giovenale.' And the priest hurried past Robert. *Why was he so unfriendly?*

The church of San Giovenale was in the Quartiere Vecchio, a colourful area with medieval towers and churches. A young priest was tending the garden next to it. He looked up as Robert approached.

'*Buon giorno, signore.*'

'Good morning. I'm looking for a priest who was in Switzerland last week. He . . .'

'Yes, yes. Poor Father Patrini. It was a terrible, terrible thing that happened to him.'

'I don't understand. What terrible thing?'

'Seeing the devil's chariot. It was more than he could stand. The poor man had a nervous breakdown.'

'I'm sorry to hear that,' Robert said. 'Where is he now? I would like to talk to him.'

650

'He's in the hospital near the Piazza di San Patrizin, but I doubt if the doctors will allow anyone to see him.'

Robert stood there, troubled. A man suffering a nervous breakdown was not going to be much help. 'I see. Thank you very much.'

The hospital was an unpretentious one-storey building, near the outskirts of the city. He parked the car and walked into the small lobby. There was a nurse behind the reception desk.

'Good morning,' Robert said. 'I would like to see Father Patrini.'

'*Mi scusi, ma* . . . that is impossible. He cannot speak with anyone.'

Robert was determined not to be stopped now. He had to follow up the lead Professor Schmidt had given him. 'You don't understand,' Robert said smoothly. 'Father Patrini *asked* to see me. I've come to Orvieto at his request.'

'He *asked* to see you?'

'Yes. He wrote to me in America. I've come all this way just to see him.'

The nurse hesitated. 'I do not know what to say. He is very ill. *Molto.*'

'I'm sure it would cheer him up to see me.'

'The doctor is not here . . .' She made a decision. 'Very well. You may go into his room, *signore*, but you may only stay a few minutes.'

'That's all I'll need,' Robert said.

'This way, *per piacere.*'

They walked down a short corridor with small, neat rooms on either side. The nurse led Robert to one of the doors.

'Only a few minutes, *signore.*'

'*Grazie.*'

Robert entered the little room. The man in the bed looked like a pale shadow lying on the white sheets. Robert approached him and said softly, 'Father . . .'

The priest turned to look up at him and Robert had never seen such agony in a man's eyes.

'Father, my name is . . .'

He grabbed Robert's arm. 'Help me,' the priest mumbled. 'You must help me. My faith is gone. All my life I have preached of God and the Holy Spirit and now I know that there is no God. There is only the devil and he has come for us . . .'

'Father, if you . . .'

'I saw it with my own eyes. There were two of them in the devil's chariot, but, oh, there will be more! Others will come! Wait and see. We are all doomed to hell.'

'Father – listen to me. What you saw was not the devil. It was a space vehicle that . . .'

The priest let go of Robert and looked at him with sudden clarity. 'Who are you? What do you want?'

Robert said, 'I'm a friend. I came here to ask you about the bus trip you took in Switzerland.'

'The bus. I wish I had never gone near it.' The priest was becoming agitated again.

Robert hated to press him, but he had no choice.

'You sat next to a man on that bus. A Texan. You had a long conversation with him, remember?'

'A conversation. The Texan. Yes, I remember.'

'Did he mention where he lived in Texas?'

'Yes, I remember him. He was from America.'

'Yes. From Texas. Did he tell you where his home was?'

'Yes, yes. He told me.'

'Where, Father? Where is his home?'

'Texas. He talked of Texas.'

Robert nodded encouragingly. 'That's right.'

'I saw them with my own eyes. I wish God had blinded me. I . . .'

'Father – the man from Texas. Did he say where he was from? Did he mention a name?'

'Texas, yes. The Ponderosa.'

Robert tried again. 'That's on television. This was a real man. He sat next to you on . . .'

The priest was becoming delirious again. 'They're coming! Armageddon is here. The Bible lies! It is the devil who will invade the earth.' He was shouting loudly now. 'Look out! Look out! I can see them!'

The nurse came hurrying in. She looked at Robert reprovingly. 'You will have to leave, *signore*.'

'I need just one more minute . . .'

'*No, signore. Adesso!*'

Robert took one last look at the priest. He was raving incoherently. Robert turned to go. There was nothing further he could do. He had gambled on the priest giving him a lead to the Texan, and he had lost.

Robert returned to his car and headed back toward Rome. It was finally over. The only clues he had left – if they could be called clues – were the mention of a Russian woman, a Texan, and a Hungarian. But there was no way to pursue them any further. *Check and checkmate.* It was frustrating to have come this far and then to be stopped. If only the priest had remained coherent long enough to give him the information he needed! He had been so close. What was it the priest had said? *The Ponderosa.* The old priest had been watching too much television, and in his delirium, he had obviously associated Texas with the once popular TV show, *Bonanza.* The Ponderosa, where the mythical Cartwright family lived. *The Ponderosa.* Robert slowed the car, and pulled over to the side of the road, his mind racing. He made a U-turn and sped back toward Orvieto.

Half an hour later, Robert was talking to the bartender in a small trattoria in the Piazza della Republica. 'You have a beautiful town here,' Robert said. 'It's very peaceful.'

'Oh, *si, signore*, we are quite content here. Have you visited Italy before?'

'I spent part of my honeymoon in Rome.' *You make all my dreams come true, Robert. I've wanted to see Rome ever since I was a little girl.*

'Ah, Rome. Too big. Too noisy.'

'I agree.'

'We live simple lives here, but we are happy.'

Robert said casually, 'I noticed television antennas on many of the roofs here.'

'Oh, yes, indeed. We are quite up-to-date in that respect.'

'One can see that. How many television channels does the town receive?'

'Only one.'

'I suppose you get a good many American shows?'

'*No, no.* This is a government channel. Here we receive only shows made in Italy.'

Bingo! 'Thank you.'

Robert placed a call to Admiral Whittaker. A secretary answered the phone. 'Admiral Whittaker's office.'

Robert could visualize the office. It would be the kind of anonymous cubbyhole they kept for non-persons the government no longer had any use for.

'Could I speak to the Admiral, please? Commander Robert Bellamy calling.'

'Just a moment, Commander.'

Robert wondered whether anybody bothered to keep in touch with the Admiral now that the once powerful figure was part of the mothball fleet. Probably not.

'Robert, it's very good to hear from you.' The old man's voice sounded tired. 'Where are you?'

'I can't say, sir.'

There was a pause. 'I understand. Is there something I can do for you?'

'Yes, sir. This is rather awkward because I've been ordered not to communicate with anyone. But I need some outside help. I wonder if you could check on something for me?'

'I can certainly try. What would you like to know?'

'I need to know whether there's a ranch anywhere in Texas called The Ponderosa.'

'As in *Bonanza*?'

'Yes, sir.'

'I can find out. How will I reach you?'

'I think it would be better if I called you, Admiral.'

'Right. Give me an hour or two. I'll keep this just between ourselves.'

'Thank you.'

It seemed to Robert that the tiredness had gone out of the old man's voice. He had, at last, been asked to do something, even if it was as trivial as locating a ranch.

Two hours later, Robert telephoned Admiral Whittaker again.

'I've been waiting for your call,' the Admiral said. There was a satisfied note in his voice. 'I have the information you wanted.'

'And?' Robert held his breath.

'There *is* a Ponderosa ranch in Texas. It's located just outside of Waco. It's owned by a Dan Wayne.'

Robert heaved a deep sigh of relief. 'Thank you very much, Admiral,' he said. 'I owe you a dinner when I get back.'

'I'll be looking forward to that, Robert.'

Robert's next call was to General Hilliard. 'I located another witness in Italy. Father Patrini.'

'A priest?'

'Yes. In Orvieto. He's in the hospital, very ill. I'm afraid the Italian authorities won't be able to communicate with him.'

'I'll pass that on. Thank you, Commander.'

Two minutes later, General Hilliard was on the line to Janus.

'I've heard from Commander Bellamy again. The latest witness is a priest. A Father Patrini in Orvieto.'

'Take care of it.'

FLASH MESSAGE
TOP SECRET ULTRA
NSA TO DEPUTY DIRECTORY SIFAR
EYES ONLY
COPY ONE OF (ONE) COPIES
SUBJECT: OPERATION DOOMSDAY
5. FATHER PATRINI – ORVIETO
END OF MESSAGE

The headquarters of SIFAR is on Via della Pineta, on the southernmost outskirts of Rome, in an area surrounded by farm-houses. The only thing that would cause a passer-by to give a second glance at the inno-cent, industrial-looking stone buildings occupying two square blocks would be the high wall surrounding the complex, topped by barbed wire, with security posts at each corner. Hidden in a military compound, it is one of the most secretive security agencies in the world, and one of the least known. There are signs outside the compound reading: *Vietare passare oltre i limiti.*

Inside a spartan office on the first floor of the main building, Colonel Francesco Cesar was studying the flash message he had just received. The Colonel was a man in his early fifties with a muscular body, topped by a pitted, bulldog face. He read the message for the third time.

So, Operation Doomsday is finally happening. È una bella fregatura. It is good that we have prepared for this, Cesar thought. He looked down at the cable again. A priest.

It was after midnight when the nun walked past the desk of the night duty nurses at the little hospital in Orvieto.

'I guess she's going to see Signora Fillipi,' said Nurse Tomasino.

'Either her or old man Rigano. They're both on their last legs.' The nun glided silently round the corner and walked directly into the priest's room. He was sleeping peacefully, his hands gathered almost as if in prayer, on his chest. A wedge of moonlight sliced through the blinds, casting a golden band across the priest's face.

The nun removed a small box from beneath her habit. Carefully, she took out a beautiful cut-glass rosary, and placed it in the old priest's hands. As she adjusted the beads, she drew one of them quickly across his thumb. A thin line of blood appeared. The nun took a tiny bottle from the box, and with an eye dropper, delicately squeezed three drops into the open cut.

It only took a few minutes for the deadly, fast-acting poison to work. The nun sighed as she made the sign of the cross over the dead man. She left as silently as she had come in.

FLASH MESSAGE
TOP SECRET ULTRA
SIFAR TO DEPUTY DIRECTOR NSA
EYES ONLY
COPY ONE OF (ONE) COPIES
SUBJECT: OPERATION DOOMSDAY
5. FATHER PATRINI – ORVIETO –
TERMINATED
END OF MESSAGE

26

Frank Johnson was recruited because he had been a Green Beret in Vietnam and was known among his comrades as 'the killing machine'. He loved to kill. He was motivated, and highly intelligent.

'He's perfect for us,' Janus said. 'Approach him carefully. I don't want to lose him.'

The first meeting took place in an Army barracks. A Captain was talking to Frank Johnson.

'Don't you worry about our government?' the Captain asked. 'It's being run by a bunch of bleeding hearts who are giving the store away. This country needs nuclear power, but the damned politicians are stopping us from building new plants. We depend on the damn Arabs for oil, but will the government let us do our own off-shore drilling? Oh, no. They're more worried about the fish than they are about us. Does that make sense to you?'

'I see your point,' Frank Johnson said.

'I knew you would, because you're intelligent.' He was watching Johnson's face as he spoke. 'If Congress won't do anything to save our country, then it's up to some of us to do something.'

Frank Johnson looked puzzled. 'Some of *us*?'

'Yeah.' *Enough for now*, the Captain thought. 'We'll talk about it later.'

The next conversation was more specific. 'There's a group of patriots, Frank, who are interested in protecting our world. They're pretty high-powered gentlemen. They've formed a committee. The committee may have to bend a few laws to get its work done, but in the end, it will be worth it. Are you interested?'

Frank Johnson grinned. 'I'm very interested.'

That was the beginning. The next meeting took place in Ottawa, Canada, and Frank Johnson met some of the members of the committee. They represented powerful interests from a dozen countries.

'We're well organized,' a member explained to Frank Johnson. 'We have a strict chain of command. There's a Propaganda Division, Recruiting, Tactics, Liaison . . . and a Death Squad.' He went on: 'Almost every intelligence organization in the world is part of this.'

'You mean the heads of . . . ?'

'No, not the heads. The deputies. The hands-on people who know what's going on, who know what danger our countries are in.'

The meetings took place all over the world – Switzerland, Morocco, China – and Johnson attended all of them.

It was six months before Colonel Johnson met Janus. Janus had sent for him.

'I've been given excellent reports about you, Colonel.'

Frank Johnson grinned. 'I enjoy my work.'

'So I've heard. You're in an advantageous position to help us.'

Frank Johnson sat up straighter. 'I'll do anything I can.'

'Good. At the Farm, you're in charge of supervising the training of secret agents in the various services.'

'That's right.'

'And you get to know them and their capabilities.'

'Intimately.'

'What I would like you to do,' Janus said, 'is to recruit those who you feel would be most helpful to our organization. We're interested only in the best.'

'That's easy,' Colonel Johnson said. 'No problem.' He hesitated a moment. 'I wonder . . .'

'Yes?'

'I can do that with my left hand. I'd really like to do something more, something bigger.' He leaned forward. 'I've heard about Operation Doomsday. Doomsday is right up my alley. I'd like to be a part of that, sir.'

Janus sat there, studying him a moment. Then he nodded. 'Very well, you're in.'

Johnson smiled. 'Thank you. You won't be sorry.' Colonel Frank Johnson left the meeting a very happy man. Now he would have a chance to show them what he could do.

27

DAY EIGHT

Waco, Texas

Dan Wayne was not having a good day. As a matter of fact, he was having a dreadful day. He had just returned from the Waco county courthouse where he was facing bankruptcy proceedings. His wife, who had been having an affair with her young doctor, was divorcing him, intent on getting half of everything he had (which could be half of nothing, he had assured her lawyer). And one of his prize bulls had to be destroyed. Dan Wayne felt that fate was kicking him in the balls. He had done nothing to deserve all this. He had been a good husband and a good rancher. He sat in his study contemplating the gloomy future.

Dan Wayne was a proud man. He was well aware of all the jokes about Texans being loud-mouthed, larger-than-life braggarts, but he honestly felt he had something to brag about. He had been born in Waco, in the rich agricultural region of the Brazos River Valley. Waco was modern, but it still retained a flavour of the past, when the five Cs had been its support: cattle, cotton, corn, collegians and culture. Wayne loved Waco with all his heart and soul, and when he had met the Italian priest on the Swiss tour bus, he had spent almost five hours going on about his home town. The priest had told him he wanted to practise his English, but actually, as he thought back on it, Dan had done almost all the talking.

'Waco has everything,' he had confided to the priest. 'Our climate's great. We don't allow it to get too hot or too cold. We have twenty-three schools in the school district, and Baylor University. We have four newspapers, ten radio stations and five television stations. We have a Texas Ranger Hall of Fame that will knock you out. I mean, we're talking *history*. If you like fishing, Father, Brazos River is an experience you'll never forget. Then, we have a safari ranch and a big art centre. I tell you, Waco is one of the unique cities of the world. You must come and pay us a visit.'

And the little old priest had smiled and nodded, and Wayne wondered how much English he really understood.

Dan Wayne's father had left him a thousand acres of ranch land, and the son had built up his cattle herd from two thousand to ten thousand.

There was also a prize stallion that was going to be worth a fortune. And now, the bastards were trying to take it all away from him. It wasn't his fault that the cattle market had gone to hell, or that he had gotten behind with his mortgage payments. The banks were closing in for the kill, and his only chance to save himself was to find someone who would buy the ranch, pay off his creditors, and leave him with a little profit.

Wayne had heard about a rich Swiss who was looking for a ranch in Texas, and he had flown over to Zürich to meet him. In the end, it had turned out to be a wild goose chase. The dude's idea of a ranch was an acre or two with a nice little vegetable garden. *She-eet!*

That was how Dan Wayne had happened to be on the tour bus when that extraordinary thing occurred. He had read about flying saucers, but he had never believed in them. Now, by God, he certainly did. As soon as he returned home, he had called the editor of the local newspaper.

'Johnny, I just saw an honest-to-God flying saucer with some dead, funny-looking people in it.'

'Yeah? Did you get any pictures, Dan?'

'No. I took some, but they didn't come out.'

'Never mind. We'll send a photographer out there. Is it on your ranch?'

'Well, no. As a matter of fact, it was in Switzerland.'

There was a silence.

'Oh. Well, if you happen to come across one on your ranch, Dan, give me another call.'

'Wait! I'm being sent a picture by some fellow who saw the thing.' But Johnny had already hung up.

And that was that.

Wayne almost wished that there *would* be an invasion of aliens. Maybe they would kill off his damned creditors. He heard the sound of a car coming up the drive and rose and walked over to the window. Looked like an easterner.

Probably another creditor. These days they were coming out of the woodwork.

Dan Wayne opened the front door.

'Howdy.'

'Daniel Wayne?'

'My friends call me Dan. What can I do for you?'

Dan Wayne was not at all what Robert had expected. He had envisioned a stereotype of a burly Texan. Dan Wayne was slight and aristocratic-looking, with an almost shy manner. The only thing that gave away his heritage was his accent.

'I wonder if I might have a few minutes of your time?'

'That's about all I've got left,' Wayne said. 'By the way, you're not a creditor, are you?'

'A creditor? No.'

'Good. Come on in.'

The two men walked into the living room. It was large and comfortably furnished with western-style furniture.

'This is a nice place you have here,' Robert said.

'Yeah. I was born in this house. Can I offer you anything? A cold drink, maybe?'

'No, thanks. I'm fine.'

'Have a seat.'

Robert sat down on a soft leather couch.

'What did you want to see me about?'

'I believe you took a bus tour in Switzerland last week?'

'That's right. Is my ex-wife having me followed? You don't work for her, do you?'

'No, sir.'

'Oh.' He suddenly understood. 'You're interested in that UFO thing. Damnedest thing I ever saw. It kept changing colours. And those dead aliens!' He shuddered. 'I keep dreaming about it.'

'Mr Wayne, can you tell me anything about the other passengers who were on that bus?'

'Sorry, I can't help you out there. I was travelling alone.'

'I know, but you spoke to some of the other passengers, didn't you?'

'To tell you the truth, I had a lot on my mind. I wasn't paying much attention to anyone else.'

'Do you remember anything about any of them?'

Dan Wayne was silent for a moment. 'Well, there was an Italian priest. I talked to him quite a bit. He seemed like a nice fellow. I want to tell you something, that flying saucer thing really shook him up. He kept talking about the devil.'

'Did you speak to anyone else?'

Dan Wayne shrugged. 'Not really . . . wait a minute. I talked a little bit to some fellow who owns a bank in Canada.' He ran his tongue across his lips. 'To tell you the truth, I'm having a little financial problem here with the ranch. It looks as though I might lose it. I hate goddamn bankers. They're all blood-suckers. Anyway, I thought this fellow might be different. When I found out he was a banker, I talked to him about trying to work out some kind of loan arrangement here. But he was just like all the rest of them. He couldn't have been less interested.'

'You said he was from Canada.'

'Yeah, Fort Smith, up in the Northwest Territories. I'm afraid that's about all I can tell you.'

Robert tried to conceal his excitement. 'Thank you, Mr Wayne, you've been very helpful.' Robert rose.

'That's it?'

'That's it.'

'Would you like to stay for supper?'

660

'No, thanks. I have to be on my way. Good luck with the ranch.'

'Thanks.'

Fort Smith, Canada, Northwest Territories.

Robert waited until General Hilliard came on the line.

'Yes, Commander?'

'I found another witness. Dan Wayne. He owns The Ponderosa, a ranch outside of Waco, Texas.'

'Very good. I'll have our office in Dallas speak to him.'

FLASH MESSAGE
TOP SECRET ULTRA
NSA TO DEPUTY DIRECTOR DCI
EYES ONLY
COPY ONE OF (ONE) COPIES
SUBJECT: OPERATION DOOMSDAY
6. DANIEL WAYNE – WACO
END OF MESSAGE

In Langley, Virginia, the Deputy Director of the Central Intelligence Agency studied the transmission thoughtfully. *Number six.* Things were going well. Commander Bellamy was doing an extraordinary job. The decision to select him had been a wise one. Janus had been right. The man was always right. And he had the power to have his wishes carried out. So much power . . . The Director looked at the message again. *Make it look like an accident,* he thought. *That shouldn't be difficult.* He pressed a buzzer.

The two men arrived at the ranch in a dark blue van. They parked in the courtyard and got out of the car, carefully looking around. Dan Wayne's first thought was that they had come to take possession of the ranch. He opened the door for them.

'Dan Wayne?'

'Yes. What can I . . . ?'

That was as far as he got.

The second man had stepped behind him and hit him hard across the skull with a blackjack.

The larger of the two men slung the unconscious rancher over his shoulder and carried him outside to the barn. There were eight horses in the barn. The men ignored them and walked to the last stall at the back. Inside was a beautiful black stallion.

The large man said, 'This is the one.' He put Wayne's body down.

The second man picked up a cattle prod from the ground, stepped up to the stall door, and hit the stallion with the electric prod. The stallion whinnied and reared up. The man hit him again hard across the nose. The stallion was bucking wildly now, confined in the small space, smashing against the walls of the stall, his teeth bared and the whites of his eyes flashing.

'Now,' the smaller man said. His companion lifted the body of Dan Wayne and tossed it over the half door into the stall. They watched the bloody scene for several moments, then, satisfied, turned and left.

FLASH MESSAGE
TOP SECRET ULTRA
DCI TO DEPUTY DIRECTOR NSA
EYES ONLY
COPY ONE OF (ONE) COPIES
SUBJECT: OPERATION DOOMSDAY
6. DANIEL WAYNE – WACO – TERMINATED
END OF MESSAGE

28

DAY NINE
Fort Smith, Canada

Fort Smith, in the Northwest Territories, is a prosperous town of two thousand people, most of them farmers and cattle ranchers, with a sprinkling of merchants. The climate itself is demanding, with long and rigorous winters, and the town is living proof of Darwin's theory of the survival of the fittest.

William Mann was one of the fit ones, a survivor. He had been born in Michigan, but in his early thirties he had passed through Fort Smith on a fishing trip and had decided that the community needed another good bank. He had seized the opportunity. There was only one other bank there, and it took William Mann less than two years to put his competitor out of business. Mann ran his bank the way a bank should be run. His god was mathematics, and he saw to it that the numbers always came out to his benefit. His favourite story was the joke about the man who went to a banker pleading for a loan so that his young son could have an immediate operation to save his life. When the applicant said he had no security, the banker told him to get out of his office.

'I'll go,' the man said, 'but I want to tell you that in all my years, I've never met anyone as coldhearted as you are.'

'Wait a minute,' the banker replied. 'I'll make you a sporting proposition. One of my eyes is a glass eye. If you can tell me which one it is, I'll give you the loan.'

Instantly, the man said, 'Your left one.'

The banker was amazed. 'No one knows that. How could you tell?'

The man said, 'That's easy. For a moment, I thought I detected a gleam of sympathy in your left eye, so I knew it must be your glass eye.'

That, to William Mann, was a good businessman's story. One did not conduct business based on sympathy. You had to look at the bottom line. While other banks in Canada and the United States were toppling like tenpins, William Mann's bank was stronger than ever. His philosophy was simple: no loans to start up businesses; no investments in junk bonds; no loans to neighbours whose children might desperately need an operation.

Mann had a respect that bordered on awe for the Swiss banking

663

system. The gnomes of Zürich were bankers' bankers. So, one day, William Mann decided to go to Switzerland to speak to some of the bankers there to learn if there was anything he was missing, any way he could squeeze more cents out of the Canadian dollar. He had been received graciously, but in the end he had learned nothing new. His own banking methods were admirable, and the Swiss bankers had not hesitated to tell him so.

On the day he was to leave for home, Mann decided to treat himself to a tour of the Alps. He had found the tour boring. The scenery was interesting, but no prettier than the scenery around Fort Smith. One of the passengers, a Texan, had dared try to persuade him to make a loan on a ranch that was going into bankruptcy. He had laughed in the man's face. The only thing about the tour that was of any interest was the crash of the so-called flying saucer. Mann had not believed in the reality of that for an instant. He was sure it had been staged by the Swiss government to impress tourists. He had been to Disney World and he had seen similar things that looked real, but were faked. *It's Switzerland's glass eye*, he thought sardonically.

William Mann was happy to return home.

Every minute of the banker's day was meticulously scheduled, and when his secretary came in and said that a stranger wished to see him, Mann's first instinct was to dismiss him. 'What is it he wants?'

'He says he wants to do an interview with you. He's writing an article about bankers.'

That was a different matter entirely. Publicity of the right kind was good for business. William Mann straightened his jacket, smoothed down his hair, and said, 'Send him in.'

His visitor was an American. He was well dressed, which indicated that he worked for one of the better magazines or newspapers.

'Mr Mann?'

'Yes.'

'Robert Bellamy.'

'My secretary tells me you want to do an article about me.'

'Well, not entirely about you,' Robert said. 'But you'll certainly be prominent in it. My newspaper . . .'

'Which newspaper is that?'

'The *Wall Street Journal*.'

Ah, yes. This was going to be excellent.

'The *Journal* feels that most bankers are too isolated from what's going on in the rest of the world. They seldom travel, they don't go to other countries. You, on the other hand, Mr Mann, have the reputation of being very well travelled.'

'I suppose I am,' Mann said modestly. 'As a matter of fact, I came back from a trip to Switzerland just last week.'

'Really? Did you enjoy it?'

'Yes. I met with several other bankers there. We discussed world economics.'

Robert had pulled out a notebook and was making notes. 'Did you have any time for pleasure?'

'Not really. Oh, I took a little tour on one of those buses. I had never seen the Alps before.'

Robert made another note. 'A tour. Now that's exactly the kind of thing we're looking for,' Robert said, encouragingly. 'I imagine you met a lot of interesting people on the bus.'

'Interesting?' He thought about the Texan who had tried to borrow money. 'Not really.'

'Oh?'

Mann looked at him. The reporter obviously expected him to say more. *You'll certainly be prominent in the article.* 'There was this Russian girl.'

Robert made a note. 'Really? Tell me about her.'

'Well, we got to talking, and I explained to her how backward Russia was and what terrible trouble they were heading for unless they changed.'

'She must have been very impressed,' Robert said.

'Oh, she was. Seemed like a bright girl. For a Russian, that is. They're all pretty insulated, you know.'

'Did she mention her name?'

'No. Wait. It was Olga something.'

'Did she happen to say where she was from?'

'Yes. She works as a librarian at the main branch in Kiev. It was her first trip abroad, I guess because of *glasnost*. If you want my opinion . . .' he stopped to make sure Robert was writing it down, 'Gorbachev sent Russia to hell in a hand basket. East Germany was handed to Bonn on a plate. On the political front Gorbachev moved too fast, and on the economic front he moved too slowly.'

'That's fascinating,' Robert murmured. He spent another half hour with the banker, listening to his opinionated comments on everything from the Common Market to arms control. He was able to get no further information about other passengers.

When Robert returned to his hotel, he telephoned General Hilliard's office.

'Just a moment, Commander Bellamy.'

He heard a series of clicks, and then General Hilliard was on the line.

'Yes, Commander?'

'I've traced another passenger, General.'

'The name?'

'William Mann. He owns a bank in Fort Smith, Canada.'

'Thank you. I'll have the Canadian authorities speak to him right away.'

'By the way, he gave me another lead. I'll be flying to Russia this evening. I'll need a visa from Intourist.'

'Where are you calling from?'

'Fort Smith.'

'Stop at the Visigoth Hotel in Stockholm. There will be an envelope for you at the desk.'

'Thank you.'

FLASH MESSAGE
TOP SECRET ULTRA
NSA TO DEPUTY DIRECTOR CGHQ
EYES ONLY
COPY ONE OF (ONE) COPIES
SUBJECT: OPERATION DOOMSDAY
7. WILLIAM MANN – FORT SMITH
END OF MESSAGE

At eleven o'clock that evening William Mann's doorbell rang. He was not expecting anyone, and he disliked unannounced callers. His housekeeper had retired, and his wife was in her room upstairs, asleep. Annoyed, Mann opened the front door. Two men dressed in black suits stood in the doorway.

'William Mann?'

'Yes.'

One of the men pulled out an identification card. 'We're from the Bank of Canada. May we come in?'

Mann frowned. 'What's this about?'

'We would prefer to discuss that inside if you don't mind.'

'Very well.' He led the men into the living room.

'You were recently in Switzerland, were you not?'

The question threw him off guard. 'What? Yes, but what on earth . . . ?'

'While you were gone we had your books audited, Mr Mann. Are you aware that there is a shortage in your bank of one million dollars?'

William Mann looked at the two men, aghast. 'What are you talking about? I check those books every week myself. There has never been one penny missing!'

'One million dollars, Mr Mann. We think you're responsible for embezzling it.'

His face was turning red. He found himself sputtering. 'How . . . how dare you! Get out of here before I call the police.'

'That won't do you any good. What we want you to do is repent.'

He was staring at them now, confused. 'Repent? Repent *what*? You're crazy!'

'No, sir.'

One of the men pulled out a gun. 'Sit down, Mr Mann.'

Oh, my God! I'm being robbed. 'Look,' Mann said, 'take whatever you want. There's no need for violence and . . .'

'Sit down, please.'

The second man walked over to the liquor cabinet. It was locked. He smashed the glass and pulled the cabinet open. He picked up a large water glass, filled it with scotch, and carried it over to where Mann was seated.

'Drink this. It will relax you.'

'I . . . I never drink after dinner. My doctor . . .'

The other man put the gun to William Mann's temple. 'Drink it or the glass is going to be full of your brains.'

Mann understood now that he was in the hands of two maniacs. He took the glass in his shaking hand and took a sip.

'Drink it down.'

He took a larger swallow. 'What . . . what is it you want?' He raised his voice, hoping that his wife might hear and come downstairs, but it was a vain hope. He knew what a sound sleeper she was. The men were obviously here to rob the house. *Why don't they just get on with it?*

'Take anything,' he said. 'I won't stop you.'

'Finish up what's in the glass.'

'This isn't necessary. I . . .'

The man punched him hard above his ear. Mann gasped with pain. 'Finish it.'

He swallowed the rest of the whisky in one gulp, and felt it burning as it went down. He was beginning to feel giddy. 'My safe is upstairs in the bedroom,' he said. His words were beginning to slur. 'I'll open it for you.' Maybe that would wake his wife and she could call the police.

'There's no hurry,' the man with the gun said. 'You have plenty of time for another drink.'

The second man went back to the liquor cabinet and filled the glass to the brim again. 'Here.'

'No, really,' William Mann protested. 'I don't want it.'

The glass was shoved into his hand. 'Drink it down.'

'I really don't . . .'

A fist slammed into the same spot above his ear. Mann almost fainted from the pain.

'Drink it.'

Well, if that's what they want, why not? The quicker this nightmare is over with, the better. He took a big swallow and gagged.

'If I drink any more, I'm gonna be sick.'

The man said quietly, 'If you get sick, I'll kill you.'

Mann looked up at him and then at his partner. There seemed to be two of everybody.

'What do all of you want?' he mumbled.

'We told you, Mr Mann. We want you to repent.'

William Mann nodded drunkenly. 'Okay, I repent.'

The man smiled. 'You see, that's all we ask. Now . . .' He put a piece of paper in Mann's hand. 'All you have to do is write, "I'm sorry. Forgive me."'

William Mann looked up blearily. 'Tha's all?'

'That's all. And then we'll leave.'

He felt a sudden sense of elation. *So that was what this was all about. They were religious fanatics.* As soon as they left he would call the police and have them arrested. *I'll see to it that the bastards are hanged.*

'Write, Mr Mann.'

It was difficult for him to focus. 'What did you say you want me to write?'

'Just write, "I'm sorry. Forgive me."'

'Right.' He had difficulty holding the pen. He concentrated very hard and began to write. *I'm sorry. Forgive me.*

The man took the paper from Mann's hand, holding it by the edges. 'That's very good, Mr Mann. See how easy that was?'

The room was beginning to spin around. 'Yeah. Thank you. I've repented. Now would you leave?'

'I see that you're left-handed.'

'What?'

'You're left-handed.'

'Yes.'

'There's been a lot of crime around here lately, Mr Mann. We're going to give you this gun to keep.'

He felt a gun being placed in his left hand.

'Do you know how to use a gun?'

'No.'

'It's very simple. You use it like this . . .' The man lifted the gun to William Mann's temple and squeezed Mann's finger on the trigger. There was a muffled roar. The bloodstained note dropped to the floor.

'That's all there is to it,' one of the men said. 'Good night, Mr Mann.'

FLASH MESSAGE
TOP SECRET ULTRA
CGHQ TO DEPUTY DIRECTOR NSA
EYES ONLY
COPY ONE OF (ONE) COPIES
SUBJECT: OPERATION DOOMSDAY
7. WILLIAM MANN –
FORT SMITH –
TERMINATED
END OF MESSAGE

DAY TEN
Fort Smith, Canada

The following morning, the bank examiners reported a million dollars missing from Mann's bank. The police listed Mann's death as a suicide.

The missing money was never found.

29

DAY ELEVEN

Brussels, 0300 Hours

General Shipley, the Commandant at NATO Headquarters, was awakened by his adjutant.

'I'm sorry to wake you up, General, but we seem to have a situation on our hands.'

General Shipley sat up, rubbing the sleep from his eyes. He had had a late night entertaining a group of visiting senators from the United States. 'What's the problem, Billy?'

'I just received a call from the radar tower, sir. Either all our equipment has gone crazy or we're having some strange visitors.'

General Shipley pushed himself out of bed. 'I'll be there in five minutes.'

The darkened radar room was filled with enlisted men and officers gathered around the lighted radar screens in the centre of the room. They turned and sprang to attention as the General entered.

'At ease.' He walked over to the officer in charge, Captain Muller. 'What's going on here, Lewis?'

Captain Muller scratched his head. 'It beats me. Do you know any plane that can travel 22,000 miles per hour, stop on a dime, and go into reverse?'

General Shipley was staring at him. 'What are you talking about?'

'According to our radar screens, that's what's been going on for the last half hour. At first, we thought it might be some kind of electronic device that's being tested, but we checked with the Russians, the British and the French, and they're picking up the same thing on their radar screens.'

'So, it couldn't be something in the equipment,' General Shipley said heavily.

'No, sir. Not unless you want to assume that all the radar in the world has suddenly gone crazy.'

'How many of these have appeared on the screen?'

'Over a dozen. They move so fast that it's hard to even keep track of them. We pick them up and they disappear again. We've eliminated atmospheric conditions, meteors, fireballs, weather balloons, and any kind of flying machine known to man. I was going to scramble some planes, but these objects – whatever they are – are flying so damned high that we'd never be able to get near them.'

General Shipley walked over to one of the radar screens. 'Is anything coming in on your screens now?'

'No, sir. They're gone.' He hesitated a moment. 'But, General, I have a terrible feeling they'll be coming back.'

30

Ottawa, 0500 Hours

When Janus finished reading General Shipley's report aloud, the Italian stood up and said, excitedly, 'They are getting ready to invade us!'

'They have already invaded us.' The Frenchman.

'We are too late. It is a catastrophe.' The Russian. 'There is no way . . .'

Janus interrupted. 'Gentlemen, it is a catastrophe we can prevent.'

'How? You know their demands.' The Englishman.

'Their demands are out of the question.' The Brazilian. 'It's no business of theirs what we do with our trees. The so-called greenhouse effect is scientific garbage, totally unproven.'

'And what about us?' The German. 'If they force us to clean up the air over our cities, we would have to shut down our factories. We would have no industries left.'

'And we would have to stop manufacturing cars,' the Japanese said. 'And then where would the civilized world be?'

'We are all in the same position.' The Russian. 'If we have to stop all pollution, as they insist, it would destroy the world's economies. We must buy more time until Star Wars is ready to take them on.'

Janus said crisply, 'We are agreed on that. Our immediate problem is to keep our people calm, and avoid the spread of panic.'

'How is Commander Bellamy progressing?' The Canadian.

'He's making excellent progress. He should be finished in the next day or two.'

31

Kiev, The Soviet Union

Like most of her countrywomen, Olga Romanchanko had become disenchanted with *perestroika*. In the beginning, all the promised changes that were going to happen in Mother Russia sounded so exciting. The winds of freedom were blowing through the streets, and the air was filled with hope. There were promises of fresh meat and vegetables in the shops, pretty dresses and real leather shoes and a hundred other wonderful things. But now, six years after it had all begun, bitter disillusion had set in. Goods were scarcer than ever. It was impossible to survive without the black market. There was a shortage of virtually everything, and prices had soared. The main streets were still filled with *rytvina* – huge potholes. There were protest marches in the streets, and crime was on the increase. Restrictions were more severe than ever. *Perestroika* and *glasnost* had begun to seem as empty as the promises of the politicians who promoted them.

Olga had worked at the library in Lenkomsomol Square, in the centre of Kiev, for seven years. She was thirty-two years old, and had never been outside the Soviet Union. Olga was reasonably attractive, a bit overweight, but in Russia that was not considered a disadvantage. She had been engaged twice to men who had moved away and deserted her; Dmitri, who had left for Leningrad, and Ivan, who had moved to Moscow. Olga had tried to move to Moscow to be with Ivan, but without a *propiska*, a Moscow residence permit, it was not possible.

As her thirty-third birthday approached, Olga was determined that she was going to see something of the world before the Iron Curtain closed around her once again. She went to the head librarian, who happened to be her aunt.

'I would like to take my vacation, now,' Olga said.

'When do you want to leave?'

'Next week.'

'Enjoy yourself.'

It was as simple as that. In the days before *perestroika*, taking a vacation would have meant going to the Black Sea or Samarkand or Tbilisi, or any one of a dozen other places inside the Soviet Union. But now, if she were quick about it, the whole world was open to her. Olga took an atlas from the library shelf and pored over it. There was such a big world out there! There was Africa and Asia, and North and South America . . . she was afraid to venture that far. Olga turned to the map of Europe. *Switzerland*, she thought. *That's where I'll go.*

She would never have admitted it to anyone in the world, but the main reason Switzerland appealed to her was because she had once tasted Swiss chocolate, and she had never forgotten it. She loved sweets. The candy in Russia – when one could get it – was sugarless and tasted terrible.

Her taste for chocolate was to cost Olga her life.

The journey on Aeroflot to Zürich was an exciting beginning. She had never flown before. She landed at the international airport in Zürich, filled with anticipation. There was something in the air that was different. *Maybe it is the smell of real freedom*, Olga thought. Her finances were strictly limited, and she had made reservations at a small, inexpensive hotel, the Leonhare, at Limmatquai 136.

Olga checked in at the reception desk. 'This is my first time in Switzerland,' she confided to the clerk, in halting English. 'Could you suggest some things for me to do?'

'Certainly. There is much to do here,' he told her. 'Perhaps you should start with a tour of the city – I will arrange it.'

'Thank you.'

Olga found Zürich extraordinary. She was awed by the sights and sounds of the city. The people on the street were dressed in such fine clothes, and drove such expensive automobiles. It seemed to Olga that everyone in Zürich must be a millionaire. And the stores! She window-shopped along Bahnhofstrasse, the main shopping street of Zürich, and she marvelled at the incredible cornucopia of goods in the windows: there were dresses and coats and shoes and lingerie and jewellery and dishes and furniture and automobiles and books and television sets and radios and toys and pianos. There seemed to be no end to the goods for sale. And then Olga stumbled across Sprüngli's, famous for their confections and chocolates. And what chocolates! Four large store-front windows were filled with a dazzling array of them. There were huge boxes of mixed chocolates, chocolate bunnies, chocolate loaves, chocolate-covered nuts. There were chocolate-covered bananas and chocolate beans filled with liqueurs. It was a feast just to look at the display in the windows. Olga wanted to buy everything, but when she learned the prices, she settled for a small box of assorted chocolates and a large candy bar.

Over the next week, Olga visited the Zürichhorn Park and the Rietberg Museum and the Gross Münster, the church erected in the eleventh century, and a dozen other wonderful tourist attractions. Finally, her time was running out.

The hotel clerk at the Leonhare said to her, 'The Sunshine Tours Bus Company has a fine tour of the Alps. I think you might enjoy that before you leave.'

'Thank you,' Olga said. 'I will try it.'

When Olga left the hotel, her first stop was to visit Sprüngli's again, and the next stop was at the office of the Sunshine Tours Bus Company, where she arranged to go on a tour. It had proved to be most exciting. The scenery was breathtaking, and in the middle of the tour they had seen the explosion of what she thought was a flying saucer, but the Canadian banker she was seated next to explained that it was merely a spectacle arranged by the Swiss government for tourists, that there were no such things as flying saucers. Olga was not completely convinced. When she returned home to Kiev she discussed it with her aunt.

'Of course there are flying saucers,' her aunt said. 'They fly over Russia all the time. You should sell your story to a news paper.'

Olga had considered doing it, but she was afraid that she would be laughed at. The Party did not like its members to get publicity, especially the kind that might subject them to ridicule. All in all, Olga decided that, Dmitri and Ivan aside, her vacation had been the highlight of her life. It was going to be difficult to settle down to work again.

The ride from the airport into the centre of Kiev took the Intourist bus one hour, driving along the newly built highway. It was Robert's first time in Kiev, and he was impressed by the ubiquitous construction along the highway, and the large apartment buildings that seemed to be springing up everywhere. The bus pulled up in front of the Dnieper Hotel and disgorged its two dozen passengers. Robert looked at his watch. Eight p.m. The library would be closed. His business would have to wait until morning. He checked into the huge hotel, where a reservation had been made for him, had a drink at the bar and went into the austere whitewashed dining room for a dinner of caviar, cucumbers and tomatoes, followed by a potato casserole flavoured with tiny bits of meat and covered with heavy dough, all accompanied by vodka and mineral water.

His visa had been waiting for him at the hotel in Stockholm, as General Hilliard had promised. *That was a quick bit of international cooperation*, Robert thought. *But no cooperation for me. 'Naked' is the operational word.*

After dinner, Robert made a few inquiries at the desk, and meandered over to Lenkomsomol Square. Kiev was a surprise to him. One of the oldest cities in Russia, it was an attractive, European-looking city, situated on the Dnieper River, with green parks and tree-lined streets. Churches were everywhere and they were spectacular examples of religious architecture: there were the Churches of St Vladimir's and St Andrew's and St Sophia's, the last completed in 1037, pure white with its soaring blue bell tower, and the Pechersk Monastery, the tallest structure in the city. *Susan would have loved all this*, Robert thought. She had never been to Russia. He wondered if she had returned from Brazil yet. On an impulse, when he returned to his hotel room, he telephoned her, and to his surprise the call was put through almost immediately.

'Hello?' *That throaty, sexy voice.*

'Hi. How was Brazil?'

'Robert! I tried to telephone you several times. There was no answer.'

'I'm not home.'

'Oh.' She had been trained too well to ask where he was. 'Are you feeling well?'

For a eunuch, I'm in wonderful shape. 'Sure. Great. How's Money . . . Monte?'

'He's fine. Robert, we're leaving for Gibraltar tomorrow.' *On Moneybags' fucking yacht, of course. What was the name of it? Ah, yes. The* Halcyon. 'The yacht?'

'Yes. You can call me on it. Do you remember the call letters?'

He remembered. *WS 337. What did the WS stand for? Wonderful Susan . . . Why separate . . . Wife stealer?*

'Robert?'

'Yes, I remember. Whiskey Sugar 337.'

'Will you call? Just to let me know you're all right.'

'Sure. I miss you, baby.'

A long, painful silence. He waited. What did he expect her to say? *Come rescue me from this charming man who looks like Paul Newman and forces me to go on his 250-foot yacht and live in our squalid little palaces in Monte Carlo, and Morocco, and Paris, and London, and God alone knew where else.* Like an idiot, he found himself half hoping she would say it.

'I miss you, too, Robert. Take care of yourself.' And the connection was broken. He was in Russia, alone.

DAY TWELVE

Early the following morning, ten minutes after the library opened, Robert walked into the huge, gloomy building and approached the reception desk.

'Good morning,' Robert said.

The woman behind the desk looked up. 'Good morning. Can I help you?'

'Yes. I'm looking for a woman who I believe works here, Olga . . .'

'Olga? Yes, yes.' She pointed to another room. 'She will be in there.'

676

'Thank you.'

It had been as easy as that. Robert walked into the other room, past groups of students solemnly studying at long tables, *preparing for what kind of future?* Robert wondered. He reached a smaller reading room and walked inside. A woman was busily stacking books.

'Excuse me,' Robert said.

She turned. 'Yes?'

'Olga?'

'I am Olga. What do you wish with me?'

Robert smiled disarmingly. 'I'm writing a newspaper article on *perestroika* and how it affects the average Russian. Has it made much difference in your life?'

The woman shrugged. 'Before Gorbachev, we were afraid to open our mouths. Now we can open our mouths, but we have nothing to put in them.'

Robert tried another tactic. 'Surely, there are some changes for the better. For instance, you are able to travel now.'

'You must be joking. With a husband and six children, who can afford to travel?'

Robert ploughed on. 'Still, you went to Switzerland, and . . .'

'Switzerland? I have never been to Switzerland in my life.'

Robert said slowly, 'You've never been to Switzerland?'

'I just told you.' She nodded toward a dark-haired woman who was collecting books from the table. 'She's the lucky one who got to go to Switzerland.'

Robert took a quick look. 'What's her name?'

'Olga. The same as mine.'

He sighed. 'Thank you.'

A minute later, Robert was in conversation with the second Olga.

'Excuse me,' Robert said. 'I'm writing a newspaper article on *perestroika* and the effect that it's had on Russian lives.'

She looked at him warily. 'Yes?'

'What's your name?'

'Olga. Olga Romanchanko.'

'Tell me, Olga, has *perestroika* made any difference to you?'

Six years earlier, Olga Romanchanko would have been afraid to speak to a foreigner, but now it was allowed. 'Not really,' she said carefully. 'Everything is much the same.'

The stranger was persistent. 'Nothing at all has changed in your life?'

She shook her head. 'No.' And then added patriotically, 'Of course we can travel outside the country now.'

He seemed interested. 'And have you travelled outside the country?'

'Oh, yes,' she said proudly. 'I have just returned from Switzerland. Is a very beautiful country.'

'I agree,' he said. 'Did you get a chance to meet anyone on the trip?'

'I met many people. I took a bus and we went through high mountains. The Alps.' Suddenly Olga realized she shouldn't have said that because the stranger might ask her about the spaceship, and she did not want to talk about that. It could only get her into trouble.

'Really?' asked Robert. 'Tell me about the people on the bus.'

Relieved, Olga responded. 'Very friendly. They were dressed so . . .' She gestured. 'Very rich. I even met man from your capital city, Washington, DC.'

'You did?'

'Yes. Very nice. He gave me card.'

Robert's heart skipped a beat. 'Do you still have it?'

'No. I threw it away.' She looked around. 'Is better not keep things like that.'

Damn!

And then she added, 'I remember his name. Parker, like your American pen. Kevin Parker. Very important in politics. He tells senators how vote.'

Robert was taken aback. 'Is that what he told you?'

'Yes. He takes them on trips and gives gifts, and then they vote for things his clients need. That is the way democracy works in America.'

A lobbyist. Robert let Olga talk for the next fifteen minutes, but he got no further useful information about the other passengers.

Robert telephoned General Hilliard from his hotel room.

'I found the Russian witness. Her name is Olga Romanchanko. She works in the main library in Kiev.'

'I'll have a Russian official speak to her.'

FLASH MESSAGE
TOP SECRET ULTRA
NSA TO DEPUTY DIRECTOR GRU
EYES ONLY
COPY ONE OF (ONE) COPIES
SUBJECT: OPERATION DOOMSDAY
8. OLGA ROMANCHANKO – KIEV
END OF MESSAGE

That afternoon Robert was on an Aeroflot Tupolev Tu – 154 jet to Paris. When he arrived three hours and twenty-five minutes later, he transferred to an Air France flight to Washington, DC.

At two a.m. Olga Romanchanko heard the squeal of brakes as a car pulled up in front of the apartment building where she lived, on Vertryk Street. The walls of the apartment were so thin that she could hear voices outside on the street. She got out of bed and looked out of the window. Two men in civilian clothes were getting out of a black Chaika, the model used by government officials. They were approaching the entrance to her apartment building. The sight of them sent a shiver through her. Over the years, some of her neighbours had disappeared, never to be seen again. Some of them had been sent to the Gulag in Siberia. Olga wondered who the secret police were after this time, and even as she was thinking it, there was a knock on her door, startling her. *What do they want with me?* she wondered. *It must be some mistake.*

When she opened the door, the two men were standing there.

'Comrade Olga Romanchanko?'

'Yes.'

'Glavnoye Razvedyvatelnoye Upravleniye.'

The dreaded GRU.

They pushed their way past her into the room.

'What . . . what is it you want?'

'We will ask the questions. I am Sergeant Yuri Gromkov. This is Sergeant Vladimir Zemsky.'

She felt a sudden sense of terror. 'What's . . . what's wrong? What have I done?'

Zemsky pounced on it. 'Oh, so you know you have done something wrong!'

'No, of course not,' Olga said, flustered. 'I do not know why you are here.'

'Sit down,' Gromkov shouted. Olga sat.

'You have just returned from a trip to Switzerland, *nyet*?'

'Y . . . yes,' she stuttered, 'but it . . . it was . . . I got permission from . . .'

'Espionage is not legal, Olga Romanchanko.'

'Espionage?' She was horrified. 'I don't know what you are talking about.'

The larger man was staring at her body, and Olga suddenly realized she was wearing only a thin nightgown.

'Let's go. You are coming with us.'

'But there is some terrible mistake. I'm a librarian. Ask anybody here who . . .'

He pulled her to her feet. 'Come.'

'Where are you taking me?'

'To headquarters. They want to question you.'

They allowed her to put on a coat over her nightgown. She was shoved down the stairs and into the Chaika. Olga thought of all the people who had ridden in cars like this before and had never returned, and she was numb with fear.

The larger man, Gromkov, was driving. Olga was seated in the back with Zemsky. He somehow seemed less frightening to her, but she was petrified by who they were and what was going to happen to her.

'Please believe me,' Olga said earnestly. 'I would never betray my . . .'

'Shut up,' Gromkov barked.

Vladimir Zemsky said, 'Look, there's no reason to be rough with her. As a matter of fact, I believe her.'

Olga felt her heart leap with hope.

'Times have changed,' Comrade Zemsky went on. 'Comrade Gorbachev doesn't like us to go around bothering innocent people. Those days are past.'

'Who said she's innocent?' Gromkov growled. 'Maybe she is, maybe she isn't. They'll find out soon enough at headquarters.'

Olga sat there listening to the two men discussing her as though she were not there.

Zemsky said, 'Come now, Yuri, you know that at headquarters she will confess, whether she's guilty or not. I don't like this.'

'That's too bad. There's nothing we can do about it.'

'Yes, there is.'

'What?'

The man next to Olga was silent for a moment. 'Listen,' he said. 'Why don't we just let her go? We could tell them she was not at home. We'll put them off for a day or two, and they will forget all about her because they have so many people to question.'

Olga tried to say something, but her throat was too dry. She desperately wanted the man beside her to win the argument.

Gromkov grumbled. 'Why should we risk our necks for her? What do we get out of it? What is she going to do for us?'

Zemsky turned to look at Olga questioningly. Olga found her voice. 'I have no money,' she said.

'Who needs your money? We have plenty of money.'

Gromkov said, 'She has something else.'

Before Olga could reply, Zemsky said, 'Wait a minute, Yuri Ivanovich, you can't expect her to do that.'

'That's up to her. She can either be nice to us or go down to headquarters and get beaten up for a week or two. Maybe they'll keep her in a nice *shizo*.'

Olga had heard about *shizos*. Unheated four-by-eight-foot cells with wooden plank beds and no blankets. *Be nice to us*. What did that mean?

'It's up to her.'

Zemsky turned to Olga, 'What do you want to do?'

'I . . . I don't understand.'

'What my partner is saying is that if you're nice to us we could just drop this whole thing. In a little while they'll probably forget about you.'

'What . . . what would I have to do?'

Gromkov grinned at her in the rear-view mirror. 'Just give us a few minutes of your time.' He remembered something he had once read, *Just lie there and think of the Czar*. He giggled.

Olga suddenly understood what they were getting at. She shook her head. 'No, I could not do that.'

'Right.' Gromkov started speeding up. 'They'll have a good time with you at headquarters.'

'Wait!' She was in a panic, not knowing what to do. She had heard horror stories of what had happened to people who had been arrested and become *zeks*. She had thought that that was all finished, but now she could see that it was not. *Perestroika* was still just a fantasy. They would not allow her to have an attorney, or talk to anyone. In the past, friends of hers had been raped and murdered by the GRU. She was trapped. If she went to jail they could keep her for weeks, beating her and raping her, maybe worse. With these two men, at least it would be over in a few minutes and then they would let her go. Olga made her decision.

'All right,' she said miserably. 'Do you wish to go back to my apartment?'

Gromkov said, 'I know a better place.' He turned the car around.

Zemsky whispered, 'I'm sorry about this, but he's in charge. I can't stop him.'

Olga said nothing.

They drove past the bright red Shevchenko Opera House, and headed for a large park bordered by trees. It was completely deserted at this hour. Gromkov drove the car under the trees and turned off the lights and engine.

'Let's get out,' he said.

The three of them got out of the car.

Gromkov looked at Olga. 'You're lucky. We're letting you off easy. I hope you appreciate it.'

Olga nodded, too frightened to speak.

Gromkov led them to a small cleared area. 'Get undressed.'

'It's cold,' Olga said, 'couldn't we . . . ?'

Gromkov slapped her hard across the face. 'Do as you're told before I change my mind.'

Olga hesitated an instant, and as his arm drew back to hit her again, she started unbuttoning her coat.

'Take it off.'

She let it drop to the ground.

'Now the nightgown.'

Slowly, Olga lifted the nightgown over her head and pulled it off, shivering in the cold night air, standing naked in the moonlight.

'Nice body,' Gromkov said. He squeezed her nipples.

'Please . . .'

'You make one sound, and we take you to headquarters.' He pushed her to the ground.

681

I won't think about this. I'll pretend I'm in Switzerland on the bus tour, looking at all the beautiful scenery.

Gromkov had dropped his pants and was spreading Olga's legs apart.

I can see the Alps covered with snow. There is a sleigh going by with a young boy and girl in it.

She felt him place his hands under her hips, and he shoved his maleness into her, hurting her.

There are beautiful cars along the highway. More cars than I have ever seen in my life. In Switzerland everybody has a car.

He was plunging into her harder now, pinching her, making wild, animal noises.

I will have a little home in the mountains. What do the Swiss call them? Chalets. And I will have chocolates every day. Boxes of them.

Gromkov was withdrawing now, breathing heavily. He stood up and turned to Zemsky. 'Your turn.'

I will get married and have children, and we will all go skiing in the Alps in winter.

Zemsky had zipped open his pants and was climbing on top of her.

It will be such a wonderful life. I will never return to Russia. Never. Never. Never.

He was inside her now, hurting her more than the other man had, squeezing her buttocks, and pushing her body into the cold ground until the pain was almost unbearable.

We will live on a farm, where it's quiet and peaceful all the time, and we will have a garden with beautiful flowers.

Zemsky finished with her and looked up at his companion. 'I bet she enjoyed it,' he grinned.

He reached down for Olga's neck and broke it.

The following day there was an item in the local paper about a librarian who had been raped and strangled in the park. There was a stern warning from the authorities that it was dangerous for young women to go to the park alone at night.

FLASH MESSAGE
TOP SECRET ULTRA
DEPUTY DIRECTOR GRU TO DEPUTY
DIRECTOR NSA
EYES ONLY
COPY ONE OF (ONE) COPIES
SUBJECT: OPERATION DOOMSDAY
8. OLGA ROMANCHANKO – KIEV –
TERMINATED
END OF MESSAGE

32

Willard Stone and Monte Banks were natural enemies. They were both ruthless predators, and the jungle they prowled was the stone canyons of Wall Street, with its high-powered takeovers, leveraged buy-outs and stock deals.

The first time the two men clashed was during the attempted takeover of a huge utility company. Willard Stone made the first bid, and anticipated no problem. He was so powerful, and his reputation so fearsome, that very few people dared challenge him. It was a great surprise then when he learned that a young upstart named Monte Banks was contesting his bid. Stone was forced to raise his own bid, and the ante kept going up. Willard Stone finally acquired control of the company, but at a much higher price than he had anticipated paying.

Six months later, in a takeover bid for a large electronics firm, Stone was confronted again by Monte Banks. The bidding kept escalating, and this time, Banks won.

When Willard Stone learned that Monte Banks intended to compete with him for control of a computer company, he decided it was time to meet with his competitor. The two men met on neutral ground in Paradise Island, in the Bahamas. Willard Stone had had a thorough investigation made of his competitor and had learned that Monte Banks came from a wealthy oil family, and had brilliantly managed to parlay his inheritance into an international conglomerate.

The two men sat down to lunch. Willard Stone, old and wise, Monte Banks, young and eager.

Willard Stone opened the conversation. 'You're becoming a pain in the ass.'

Monte Banks grinned. 'Coming from you, that's a big compliment.'

'What is it you want?' Stone asked.

'The same as you. I want to own the world.'

Willard Stone said thoughtfully, 'Well, it's a big enough world.'

'Meaning?'

'There's room enough for both of us.'

That was the day they became partners. Each ran his own business separately but when it came to new projects – timber and oil and real estate – they went into deals together, instead of competing with each other. Several times the Anti-Trust Division of the Justice Department tried to stop their deals, but Willard Stone's connections always prevailed. Monte Banks owned chemical companies responsible for massive pollution of lakes and rivers, but when he was indicted, the indictment was mysteriously dropped.

The two men had a perfect symbiotic relationship.

Operation Doomsday was a natural for them, and they were heavily involved in it. They were on the verge of closing a deal to purchase ten million acres of lush, tree-rich land in the Amazon. It was going to be one of the most profitable deals they had ever gone into.

They could not afford to let anything stand in their way.

33

DAY THIRTEEN
Washington, DC

The Senate of the United States was in plenary session. The junior senator from Utah had the floor.

'. . . and what is happening to our ecology is a national disgrace. It is time that this great body realized that it is its sworn duty to preserve the precious heritage that our forefathers entrusted to us. It is not only our sworn duty but our privilege to protect the land, the air and the seas against those vested interests that are selfishly destroying it. And are we doing this? Are we in all conscience doing our best? Or are we allowing the voice of Mammon to influence us . . . ?'

Kevin Parker, seated in the visitors' gallery, glanced at his watch for the third time in the past five minutes. He wondered how much longer the speech was going to last. He was sitting through this only because he was having lunch with the senator, and he needed a favour from him. Kevin Parker enjoyed walking through the corridors of power, hobnobbing with congressmen and senators, dispensing largesse in return for political favours.

He had grown up poor in Eugene, Oregon. His father was an alcoholic who had owned a small lumber yard. An inept businessman, he had turned what should have been a thriving business into a disastrous failure. The young boy had to work from the age of fourteen, and because his mother had run away with another man years earlier, he had no home life at all. He could easily have become a drifter and ended up like his father, but his saving grace was that he was extraordinarily handsome and personable. He had wavy blond hair and fine aristocratic features that he must have inherited from some long-forgotten ancestor. A few affluent townspeople took pity on the boy, giving him jobs, encouragement, and going out of their way to assist him. The wealthiest man in town, Jeb Goodspell, was particularly eager to help Kevin, and gave him a part-time job with one of his companies. A bachelor, Goodspell often invited young Parker to join him for dinner at his home.

'You can *be* somebody in this life,' Goodspell told him, 'but you can't make it without friends.'

'I know that, sir. And I certainly appreciate your friendship. Working for you is a real life saver.'

'I could do a lot more for you,' Goodspell said. They were seated on the couch in the living room, after dinner. He put his arm around the young boy. 'A *lot* more.' He squeezed the boy's shoulder. 'You have a good body, do you know that?'

'Thank you, sir.'

'Do you ever get lonely?'

He was lonely all the time. 'Yes, sir.'

'Well, you don't have to be lonely anymore.' He stroked the boy's arm. 'I get lonely, too, you know. You need someone to hold you close and comfort you.'

'Yes, sir.'

'Have you ever had any girls?'

'Well, I went with Sue Ellen for a while.'

'Did you sleep with her?'

The boy blushed. 'No, sir.'

'How old are you, Kevin?'

'Sixteen, sir.'

'It's a great age. It's an age when you should be beginning to start a career.' He studied the boy a moment. 'I'll bet you'd be darn good in politics.'

'Politics? I don't know anything about that, sir.'

'That's why you're going to school, to learn things. And I'm going to help you.'

'Thank you.'

'There are plenty of ways of thanking people,' Goodspell said. He rubbed his hand along the boy's thigh. 'Many ways.' He looked into Parker's eyes. 'You know what I mean?'

'Yes, Jeb.'

That was the beginning.

When Kevin Parker was graduated from Churchill High School, Goodspell sent him to the University of Oregon. The boy studied political science, and Goodspell saw to it that his protégé met everybody. They were all impressed with the attractive young man. With his connections, Parker found that he was able to do favours for important people, and to bring people together. Becoming a lobbyist in Washington was a natural step, and Parker was good at the job.

Goodspell had died two years earlier, but Parker had by then acquired a talent and a taste for what his mentor had taught him. He liked to pick up young boys and take them to out-of-the-way hotels where he would not be recognized.

The senator from Utah was finally finishing. '. . . and I say to you now that we must pass this bill if we want to save what is left of our ecology. At this time, I would like to ask for a roll call vote.'

Thank God, the endless session was almost over. Kevin Parker

686

thought about the evening that lay ahead of him, and he began to get an erection. The night before, he had met a young man at Danny's 'P' Street Station, a well-known gay bar. Unfortunately, the young man had been with a companion. But they had eyed each other during the evening, and before he left, Parker had written a note and slipped it into the young man's hand. It said simply, 'Tomorrow night.' The young man had smiled and nodded.

Kevin Parker was hurriedly getting dressed to go out. He wanted to be at the bar when the boy arrived. The young man was much too attractive, and Parker did not want him picked up by someone else. The front doorbell rang. *Damn.* Parker opened the door.

A stranger stood there. 'Kevin Parker?'

'Yes . . .'

'My name is Bellamy. I'd like to talk to you for a minute.'

Parker said, impatiently, 'You'll have to make an appointment with my secretary. I don't discuss business outside of office hours.'

'This isn't exactly business, Mr Parker. It concerns your trip to Switzerland a couple of weeks ago.'

'My trip to Switzerland? What about it?'

'My agency is interested in some of the people you might have met over there.' Robert flashed his false CIA identification.

Kevin Parker studied the man more carefully. What could the CIA want with him? They were so goddamn nosey. *Have I covered my ass?*

There was no point in antagonizing the man. He smiled. 'Come in. I'm late for an appointment, but you said this won't take more than a minute?'

'No, sir. I believe you took a bus tour out of Zürich?'

So that's what this is all about. That flying saucer business. It had been the goddamnedest thing he had ever seen. 'You want to know about the UFO, don't you? Well, I want to tell you, it was a weird experience.'

'It must have been, but, frankly, we at the Agency don't believe in flying saucers. I'm here to find out what you can tell me about your fellow passengers on the bus.'

Parker was taken aback. 'Oh. Well, I'm afraid I can't help you there. They were all strangers.'

'I understand that, Mr Parker,' Robert said patiently, 'but you must remember *something* about them.'

Parker shrugged. 'Well, a few things . . . I remember exchanging a few words with an Englishman who took our pictures.'

Leslie Mothershed. 'Who else?'

'Oh, yes. I talked a little to a Russian girl. She seemed very pleasant. I think she said she was a librarian somewhere.'

Olga Romanchanko. 'That's excellent. Can you think of anyone else, Mr Parker?'

'No, I guess that's about . . . oh, there were two other men. One was an American, a Texan.'

Dan Wayne. 'And the other one?'

'He was a Hungarian. He owned a carnival or circus or something like that in Hungary.' He remembered. 'It was a carnival.'

'Are you sure about that, Mr Parker?'

'Oh, yes. He was telling me some stories about the carnival business. He was certainly excited seeing that UFO. I think if he could have, he would have put it in his carnival as a sideshow. I must admit, it was a pretty awesome sight. I would have reported it, but I can't afford to get mixed up with all the weirdos who claim they saw flying saucers.'

'Did he happen to mention his name?'

'Yes, but it was one of these unpronounceable foreign names. I'm afraid I don't remember it.'

'Do you remember anything else about him?'

'Only that he was in a hurry to get back to his carnival.' He glanced at his watch. 'Is there anything else I can do for you? I'm running a little late.'

'No, thank you, Mr Parker. You've been very helpful.'

'My pleasure.' He flashed Robert a beautiful smile. 'You must drop by my office and see me sometime. We'll have a nice chat.'

'I'll do that.'

So it's nearly over, Robert thought. *They can take my job and shove it. It's time to pick up the pieces of my life and start over.*

Robert placed a call to General Hilliard. 'I've just about wrapped it up, General. I found Kevin Parker. He's a lobbyist in Washington, DC. I'm on my way to check out the last passenger.'

'I'm very pleased,' General Hilliard said. 'You've done an excellent job, Commander. Get back to me as quickly as you can.'

'Yes, sir.'

FLASH MESSAGE
TOP SECRET ULTRA
NSA TO DEPUTY DIRECTOR CIA
EYES ONLY
COPY ONE OF (ONE) COPIES
SUBJECT: OPERATION DOOMSDAY
9. KEVIN PARKER – WASHINGTON, DC
END OF MESSAGE

When Kevin Parker arrived at Danny's 'P' Street Station, he found it even more crowded than it had been the evening before. The older men

688

were dressed in conservative suits, while most of the younger men were in Levis, blazers and boots. There were a few who looked out of place, in black leather outfits, and Parker thought that this element was disgusting. Rough trade was dangerous, and he had never gone in for that sort of bizarre behaviour. *Discretion*, that had always been his motto. *Discretion*. The handsome young boy was not there yet, but Parker had not expected him to be. He would make his entrance later, beautiful and fresh, when the others in the bar would be tired and sweaty. Kevin Parker walked up to the bar, ordered a drink and looked around. Television sets on the walls were playing MTV stations. Danny's was an S and M – stand and model – bar. The younger men would assume poses that made them appear as attractive as possible, while the older men – the buyers – would look them over and make their selections. The S and M bars were the classiest. There were never any fights in them, for most of the customers had capped teeth, and they could not afford to chance having them knocked out.

Kevin Parker noticed that many of the patrons had already selected their partners. He listened to the familiar conversations going on around him. It fascinated him that the conversations were always the same, whether they took place in leather bars, dance bars, video bars or underground clubs that changed their locations every week. There was an indigenous argot.

'That queen is nobody. She thinks she's Miss Thing . . .'

'He went off on me for no reason. He gets so terribly upset. Talk about sensitive . . .'

'Are you a top or a bottom?'

'A top. I have to give the orders, girl.' Snapping his fingers.

'Good. I like taking them . . .'

'He read me for filth . . . Just stood there criticizing me . . . my weight, my complexion, my attitude. I said "Mary, it's over between us". But it hurt. That's why I'm here tonight . . . trying to forget him. Could I have another drink . . . ?'

At one a.m., the young boy walked in. He looked around, saw Parker and walked over to him. The boy was even more beautiful than Parker had remembered.

'Good evening.'

'Good evening. Sorry I'm late.'

'That's all right. I didn't mind waiting.'

The young man took out a cigarette and waited while the older man lit it for him.

'I've been thinking about you,' Parker said.

'Have you?'

The boy's eyelashes were incredible.

'Yes. Can I buy you a drink?'

'If it will make you happy.'

Parker smiled. 'Are you interested in making me happy?'

The boy looked him in the eyes and said softly, 'I think so.'

'I saw the man you were here with last night. He's wrong for you.'

'And you're right for me?'

'I could be. Why don't we find out? Would you like to go for a little walk?'

'Sounds good.'

Parker felt a tingle of excitement. 'I know a cosy place where we can be alone.'

'Fine. I'll skip the drink.'

As they started toward the front door, it suddenly opened and two large young men entered the bar. They stepped in front of the boy, blocking his way. 'There you are, you sonofabitch. Where's the money you owe me?'

The young man looked up at him, bewildered. 'I don't know what you're talking about. I've never seen you be . . .'

'Don't give me that shit.' The man grabbed him by the shoulder and started marching him out to the street.

Parker stood there, furious. He was tempted to interfere, but he could not afford to get involved in anything that might turn into a scandal. He stayed where he was, watching the boy disappear into the night.

The second man smiled at Kevin Parker sympathetically.

'You should choose your company more carefully. He's bad news.'

Parker took a closer look at the speaker. He was blond and attractive, with almost perfect features. Parker had a feeling that the evening might not be a total loss, after all. 'You could be right,' he said.

'We never know what fate has in store for us, do we?' He was looking into Parker's eyes.

'No, we don't. My name's Tom. What's your name?'

'Paul.'

'Why don't you let me buy you a drink, Paul?'

'Thank you.'

'Do you have any special plans for tonight?'

'That's up to you.'

'How would you like to spend the night with me?'

'That sounds like fun.'

'How much money are we talking about?'

'I like you. For you, two hundred.'

'That seems reasonable.'

'It is. You won't be sorry.'

Thirty minutes later Paul was leading Kevin Parker into an old apartment building on Jefferson Street. They walked upstairs to the third floor, and entered a small room. Parker looked around. 'It's not much, is it? A hotel would have been nicer.'

Paul grinned. 'It's more private here. Besides, all we need is the bed.'

'You're right. Why don't you get undressed? I want to see what I'm buying.'

'Sure.' Paul started stripping. He had a great body.

Parker watched him and he felt the old familiar urge beginning to build.

'Now, you get undressed,' Paul whispered. 'Hurry, I want you.'

'I want you, too, Mary.' Parker began to take off his clothes.

'What do you like?' Paul asked. 'Lips or hips?'

'Let's make it a cocktail. Excuse the pun. We've got all night.'

'Sure. I'm going into the bathroom,' Paul said. 'I'll be right back.'

Parker lay on the bed naked, anticipating the exquisite pleasures that were about to happen. He heard his companion come out of the bathroom and approach the bed.

He held out his arms. 'Come to me, Paul,' he said.

'I'm coming.'

And Parker felt a burst of agony as a knife slashed into his chest. His eyes flew open. He looked up, gasping. 'My God, what . . . ?'

Paul was getting dressed. 'Don't worry about the money,' he said. 'It's on the house.'

FLASH MESSAGE
TOP SECRET ULTRA
CIA TO DEPUTY DIRECTOR NSA
EYES ONLY
COPY ONE OF (ONE) COPIES
SUBJECT: OPERATION DOOMSDAY
9. KEVIN PARKER – WASHINGTON, DC –
TERMINATED
END OF MESSAGE

Robert Bellamy missed the late news bulletin because he was on a plane to Hungary to find a man who owned a carnival.

34

DAY FOURTEEN

Budapest

The flight from Paris to Budapest on Malév Airlines took two hours and five minutes. Robert knew very little about Hungary except that during World War II it had been a partner in the Axis, and had later become a Russian satellite. Robert took the airport bus to the centre of Budapest, impressed by what he saw. The buildings were old and the architecture classic. The Parliament House on the Rudolph Quay was a huge, Neo-gothic structure that dominated the city, and high on Castle Hill above the city was the Royal Palace. The streets were crowded with automobiles and shoppers.

The bus stopped in front of the Hotel Duna Intercontinental. Robert walked into the lobby and approached the concierge.

'Excuse me,' Robert said. 'Do you speak English?'

'*Igan*. Yes. What may I do for you?'

'A friend of mine was in Budapest a few days ago, and he told me he saw a wonderful carnival. I thought as long as I was in town, I might take a look at it. Can you tell me where I might find it?'

The concierge frowned. 'Carnival?' He pulled out a sheet of paper and scanned it. 'Let's see. In Budapest at the present time, we have an opera, several theatre productions, ballet, night and day tours of the city, excursions in the country . . .' He looked up. 'I'm sorry. There are no carnivals.'

'Are you sure?'

The concierge handed the list to Robert. 'See for yourself.' It was written in Hungarian.

Robert handed it back. 'Right. Is there anyone else I might talk to about this?'

The concierge said, 'The Ministry of Culture might be able to help you.'

Thirty minutes later, Robert was speaking to a clerk in the office of the Ministry of Culture.

'There is no carnival in Budapest. Are you sure your friend saw it in Hungary?'

'Yes.'

'But he did not say where?'

'No.'

'I am sorry. I cannot help you.' The clerk was impatient. 'If there is nothing else . . .'

'No.' Robert rose to his feet. 'Thank you.' He hesitated. 'I do have one more question. If I wanted to bring a circus or a carnival into Hungary, would I have to get a permit?'

'Certainly.'

'Where would I go for that?'

'To the Budapest Administration of Licences.'

The licences building was located in Buda near the medieval city wall. Robert waited for thirty minutes before he was ushered into the office of a formal, pompous official.

'Can I help you?'

Robert smiled. 'I hope so. I hate to take up your time with something as trivial as this, but I'm here with my young son, and he heard about a carnival playing somewhere in Hungary and I promised to take him to see it. You know how kids are when they get an idea in their heads.'

The official stared at Robert, puzzled. 'What is it you wanted to see me about?'

'Well, to tell you the truth, no one seems to know where the carnival is, and Hungary is such a big and beautiful country . . . Well, I was told that if anyone knew what was going on in Hungary, it would be you.'

The official nodded. 'Yes. Nothing like that is permitted to open without being issued a licence.' He pressed the buzzer and a secretary came in. There was a rapid exchange in Hungarian. The secretary left and came back two minutes later with some papers. She handed them to the official. He looked at them and said to Robert, 'In the past three months, we have issued two permits for carnivals. One closed a month ago.'

'And the other?'

'The other is currently playing in Sopron. A little town near the German frontier.'

'Do you have the owner's name?'

The official consulted the paper again. 'Bushfekete. Laslo Bushfekete.'

Laslo Bushfekete was having one of the best days of his life. Few people are lucky enough to spend their lives doing exactly what they want to do and Laslo Bushfekete was one of those fortunate few. Bushfekete was a big man, six foot four, weighing three hundred pounds. He sported a diamond wristwatch, diamond rings, and a large gold bracelet. His father had owned a small carnival, and when he died, the son had taken it over. It was the only life he had ever known.

Laslo Bushfekete had grandiose dreams. He intended to expand his little carnival into the biggest and best in Europe. He wanted to be known as the P. T. Barnum of carnivals. At the moment, however, he could only afford the usual sideshow attractions: the Fat Lady and the Tattooed Man, the Siamese Twins and the Thousand-Year-Old Mummy 'dug up from the bowels of the tombs of ancient Egypt'. Then there were the Sword Swallower and the Flame Eater, and the cute little Snake Charmer, Marika. But in the end, all they really added up to was just another travelling carnival.

Now, overnight, all that was going to change. Laslo Bushfekete's dream was about to come true.

He had gone to Switzerland to audition an escape artist he had heard about. The *pièce de résistance* of the act was a routine where the performer was blindfolded, handcuffed, locked in a small trunk, then locked in a larger trunk, and finally lowered into a tank of water. It had sounded fantastic over the telephone, but when Bushfekete flew to Switzerland to see it, he found that there was one insurmountable problem: it took the escape artist thirty minutes to escape. No audience in the world was going to stay around staring at a trunk in a tank of water for thirty minutes.

It had looked as though the trip had been a complete waste of time. Laslo Bushfekete had decided to take a tour to kill the day until it was time to catch his plane. As it turned out, that ride changed his life.

Like his fellow passengers, Bushfekete had seen the explosion and raced across the field to try to help any survivors in what they all thought was a plane crash. But the sight that had confronted him was incredible. There was no question but that it was a flying saucer, and in it were two strange-looking little bodies. The other passengers stood there, gaping at it. Laslo Bushfekete had walked around to see what the back of the UFO looked like, and then he had stopped, staring. About ten feet behind the wreck, lying on the ground out of sight of the others, was a tiny severed hand, with six fingers and two opposing thumbs. Without even thinking, Bushfekete had taken out his handkerchief, scooped up the hand and slipped it into his pocket. His heart was beating wildly. He had in his possession the hand of a genuine extraterrestrial! *From now on you can forget all your Fat Ladies, Tattooed Men, Sword Swallowers and Flame Eaters*, he thought. *Step right up, ladies and gentlemen, for the thrill of a lifetime. What you're about to see is a sight that no mortal has ever seen before. You are looking at one of the most incredible objects in the universe. It's not an animal. It's not a vegetable. It's not a mineral. What is it? It's part of the remains of an extraterrestrial . . . A creature from outer space . . . This is not science fiction, ladies and gentlemen, this is the real thing . . . For 500 forints you can have your photograph taken with the . . .*

And that reminded him. He hoped that the photographer who had been at the crash site would remember to send the photograph he had promised. He would have it blown up and put next to the exhibit. That would be a neat touch. *Showmanship. That's what life was all about. Showmanship.*

He could not wait to return to Hungary and start to fulfil his grandiose dream.

When he arrived home and unwrapped the handkerchief, he noticed that the hand had shrivelled. But when Bushfekete rinsed off the dirt, amazingly, it regained its original firmness.

Bushfekete had hidden the hand safely away and had ordered an impressive glass case with a special humidifier built for it. When he was through exhibiting it in his carnival, he planned to travel with it all over Europe. All over the world. He would set up exhibits in museums. He would have private showings for scientists, perhaps, even heads of state. And he would charge them all. There was no end to the fabulous fortune that lay ahead.

He had told no one about his good luck, not even his sweetheart, Marika, the sexy little dancer who worked with cobras and puff adders, two of the most dangerous of the species *Ophidia*. Of course, their poison sacs had been removed but the audience did not know that because Bushfekete also kept a cobra, its poison sac intact, which he displayed free of charge to the public, who watched it kill rats. It wasn't surprising that people got a thrill out of watching the beautiful Marika let her pet snakes slither across her sensuous, half-naked body. Two or three nights a week, Marika came into Laslo Bushfekete's tent and crawled across his body, her tongue flicking in and out, like her pets. They had made love the night before, and Bushfekete was still exhausted from Marika's incredible gymnastics. His reminiscences were interrupted by a visitor.

'Mr Bushfekete?'

'You're talking to him. What can I do for you?'

'I understand you were in Switzerland last week.'

Bushfekete was instantly wary. *Had someone seen him pick up the hand?* 'What . . . what about it?'

'You went on a bus tour last Sunday?'

Bushfekete said cautiously, 'Yes.'

Robert Bellamy relaxed. It was finally over. This was the last witness. He had taken on an impossible assignment and he had done a good job. *A damned good job, if I say so myself. We have no idea where they are.* And he had found them all. He felt as though a tremendous burden had been lifted from his shoulders. He was free now. Free to return home and begin a new life.

'What about my trip, mister?'

'It's not important,' Robert Bellamy assured him. And it wasn't, not any longer. 'I was interested in your fellow passengers, Mr Bushfekete, but now I think I have all the information I need, so . . .'

'Oh, hell, I can tell you all about them,' Laslo Bushfekete said. 'There was an Italian priest from Orvieto, Italy, a German – I think he was a chemistry professor from Munich – some Russian girl who worked in the library in Kiev, a rancher from Waco, Texas, a Canadian banker from the territories and some lobbyist named Parker from Washington, DC.'

My God, Robert thought. *If I had gotten to him first, I could have saved a lot of time. The man is amazing. He recalled them all.* 'You have quite a memory,' Robert said.

'Yeah.' Bushfekete smiled. 'Oh, and there was that other woman.'

'The Russian woman.'

'No, no, the *other* woman. The tall, thin one, who was dressed in white.'

Robert thought for a moment. None of the others had mentioned a second woman. 'I think you must be mistaken.'

'No, I'm not.' Bushfekete was insistent. 'There were two women there.'

Robert made a mental count. It simply did not add up. 'There couldn't have been.'

Bushfekete was insulted. 'When that photographer fellow took the pictures of all of us in front of that UFO, she was standing right next to me. She was a real beauty.' He paused. 'The funny part is I don't recall seeing her on the bus. She was probably in the back somewhere. I remember she seemed kind of pale. I was a little worried about her.'

Robert frowned. 'When all of you returned to the bus, was she with you?'

'Come to think of it, I don't remember seeing her after that. But I was so excited by that UFO thing, I wasn't paying much attention.'

There was something here that did not fit. *Could there have been eleven witnesses instead of ten? I'll have to check that out*, Robert thought. 'Thank you, Mr Bushfekete,' he said.

'My pleasure.'

'Good luck.'

Bushfekete grinned. 'Thanks.' He didn't need luck. Not any more. Not with the hand of a real genuine alien in his possession.

That night Robert Bellamy made his final report to General Hilliard. 'I have his name. It's Laslo Bushfekete. He runs a carnival, outside of Sopron, Hungary.'

'That's the last of the witnesses?'

Robert hesitated an instant. 'Yes, sir.' He had started to mention the eighth passenger, but he decided to wait until he had verified it. It seemed too improbable.

'Thank you, Commander. Well done.'

FLASH MESSAGE
TOP SECRET ULTRA
NSA TO DEPUTY DIRECTOR HRQ
EYES ONLY
COPY ONE OF (ONE) COPIES
SUBJECT: OPERATION DOOMSDAY
10. LASLO BUSHFEKETE – SOPRON
END OF MESSAGE

They arrived in the middle of the night when the carnival was shut down. They left fifteen minutes later, as silently as they had come.

Laslo Bushfekete dreamed he was standing at the entrance to the large white tent, watching the huge crowd lined up at the box office to buy their 500-forint tickets.

Come right this way, folks. See the genuine body part of an alien from outer space. Not a drawing, not a photograph, but an actual part of an actual ET. Only 500 forints for the thrill of a lifetime, a sight you will never forget.

And then he was in bed with Marika, and they were both naked, and he could feel her nipples pressing against his chest and her tongue slithering across his body and she was crawling all over him, and he got an erection, and he reached for her and his hands closed over something cold and slimy, and he woke up and opened his eyes and screamed, and that was when the cobra struck.

They found his body in the morning. The cage for the poisonous snake was empty.

FLASH MESSAGE
TOP SECRET ULTRA
HRQ TO DEPUTY DIRECTOR NSA
EYES ONLY
COPY ONE OF (ONE) COPIES
SUBJECT: OPERATION DOOMSDAY
10. LASLO BUSHFEKETE – SOPRON –
TERMINATED
END OF MESSAGE

General Hilliard made a call on the red phone. 'Janus, I've received the final report from Commander Bellamy. He's found the last of the witnesses. They've all been taken care of.'

697

'Excellent. I'll inform the others. I want you to proceed at once with the rest of our plan.'

'Immediately.'

FLASH MESSAGE
TOP SECRET ULTRA
NSA TO DEPUTY DIRECTORS:
SIFAR, MI6, GRU, CIA, COMSEC, DCI,
CGHQ, BFV EYES ONLY
COPY ONE OF (ONE) COPIES
SUBJECT: OPERATION DOOMSDAY
11. COMMANDER ROBERT
BELLAMY –
TERMINATE
END OF MESSAGE

BOOK TWO
The Hunted

35

DAY FIFTEEN

Robert Bellamy was in a dilemma. *Could there have been an eleventh witness? And if there was, why hadn't any of the witnesses mentioned her before?* The clerk who sold the bus tickets had told him there were only seven passengers. Robert was convinced that the Hungarian carnival owner had made a mistake. It would have been easy to ignore it, to assume that it was untrue, but Robert's training would not permit it. He had been too well disciplined. Bushfekete's story had to be checked out. *How?* Robert thought about it. *Hans Beckerman. The bus driver will know.*

He placed a call to Sunshine Tours. The office was closed. There was no listing in Kappel for a Hans Beckerman. *I'm going to have to go back to Switzerland and settle this,* Robert thought. *I can't leave any loose ends.*

It was late at night when Robert arrived in Zürich. The air was cold and crisp and there was a full moon. Robert rented a car and took the now familiar drive to the little village of Kappel. He drove past the church and pulled up in front of Hans Beckerman's home, convinced that he was on a wild goose chase. The house was dark. Robert knocked on the door and waited. He knocked again, shivering in the cold night air.

Mrs Beckerman finally answered the door. She was wearing a faded flannel robe. '*Bitte?*'

'Mrs Beckerman, I wonder if you remember me? I'm the reporter who's writing an article on Hans. I'm sorry to bother you so late, but it's important that I speak to your husband.'

His words were greeted with silence. 'Mrs Beckerman?'

'Hans is dead.'

Robert felt a small shock go through him. 'What?'

'My husband is dead.'

'I . . . I'm sorry. How?'

'His car went over the side of the mountain.' Her voice was filled with bitterness. 'The *Dummkopf Polizei* said it was because he was full of drugs.'

'Drugs?' *I'm sorry I cannot offer you a drink. Ulcers. The doctors cannot even give me drugs to relieve the pain. I am allergic to all of them.*

'The police said it was an accident?'

'*Ja.*'

'Did they perform an autopsy?'

'They did, and they found drugs. It makes no sense.'

He had no answer. 'I'm terribly sorry, Mrs Beckerman. I . . .'

The door closed, and Robert stood there, alone in the cold night.

One witness was gone. No . . . two. Leslie Mothershed had died in a fire. Robert stood there for a long time. Two witnesses dead. He could hear the voice of his instructor at the Farm: *There's one more thing I want to discuss today. Coincidence. In our work, there is no such animal. It usually spells danger. If you keep running into the same person again and again, or if you keep spotting the same automobile when you're on the move, cover your ass. You're probably in trouble.*

Probably in trouble. Robert was caught up in a series of conflicting emotions. What had happened *had* to be coincidences, and yet . . . *I've got to check out the mystery passenger.*

His first call was to Fort Smith, Canada. A distraught woman's voice answered the telephone. 'Yes?'

'William Mann, please.'

The voice said, tearfully, 'I'm sorry. My husband is . . . is no longer with us.'

'I don't understand.'

'He committed suicide.'

Suicide? That hard-headed banker? What the hell is going on? Robert wondered. What he was thinking was inconceivable, and yet . . . He began making one phone call after another.

'Professor Schmidt, please.'

'*Ach*! The professor died in an explosion in his laboratory . . .'

'I'd like to speak to Dan Wayne.'

'Poor devil. His prize stallion kicked him to death last . . .'

'Laslo Bushfekete, please.'

'The carnival's closed. Laslo is dead . . .'

702

'Fritz Mandel, please.'
   'Fritz was killed in a freak accident . . .'
The alarms were going full blast now.

'Olga Romanchanko.'
   'The poor girl. And she was so young . . .'

'I'm calling to check on Father Patrini.'
   'The poor soul passed away in his sleep.'

'I have to speak to Kevin Parker.'
   'Kevin was murdered . . .'

Dead. Every one of the witnesses dead. And he was the one who had found them and identified them. Why had he not known what was going on? Because the bastards had waited until he was out of each country before executing their victims. The only one he had reported to was General Hilliard. *We must not involve anyone else in this mission . . . I want you to report your progress to me every day.*

They had used him to finger the witnesses. *What was behind all this?* Otto Schmidt had been killed in Germany, Hans Beckerman and Fritz Mandel in Switzerland. Olga Romanchanko in Russia, Dan Wayne and Kevin Parker in America, William Mann in Canada, Leslie Mothershed in England, Father Patrini in Italy, and Laslo Bushfekete in Hungary. That meant that the security agencies in more than half a dozen countries were engaged in the biggest cover-up in history. Someone at a very high level had decided that all the witnesses to the UFO crash must die. *But who? And why?*

It was an international conspiracy and he was in the middle of it.

Priority: get under cover. It was hard for Robert to believe that they intended to kill him, too. He was one of them. But until he knew for certain, he could not take any chances. The first thing he had to do was to get a phony passport. That meant Ricco in Rome.

Robert caught the next plane out and found himself fighting to stay awake. He had not realized how exhausted he was. The pressure of the last fifteen days, in addition to all the jet lag, had left him drained.

He landed at the Leonardo da Vinci airport, and when he walked into the terminal, the first person he saw was Susan. He stopped, in shock. Her back was to him and for a moment he thought he might be mistaken. And then he heard her voice.

'Thank you. I have a car picking me up.'

Robert moved to her side. 'Susan . . .'

She turned, startled. 'Robert! What . . . what a coincidence! But what a lovely surprise.'

'I thought you were in Gibraltar,' Robert said.

She smiled uneasily. 'Yes. We're on our way there. Monte had some business here to take care of first. We're leaving tonight. What are you doing in Rome?'

Running for my life. 'I'm finishing up on a job.' *It's my last. I've quit, darling. We can be together from now on, and nothing will ever separate us again. Leave Monte and come back to me.* But he could not bring himself to say the words. He had done enough to her. She was happy in her new life. *Leave it alone,* Robert thought.

She was watching him. 'You look tired.'

He smiled. 'I've been running around a little.'

They looked into each other's eyes, and the magic was still there. The burning desire, and the memories, and the laughter, and the yearning.

Susan took his hand in hers and said softly, 'Robert. Oh, Robert. I wish we . . .'

'Susan . . .'

And at that moment, a burly man in a chauffeur's uniform walked up to Susan. 'The car is ready, Mrs Banks.' And the spell was broken.

'Thank you.' She turned to Robert. 'I'm sorry. I have to go now. Please take care of yourself.'

'Sure.' He watched her leave. There were so many things he wanted to say to her. *Life has a lousy sense of timing.* It had been wonderful seeing Susan again but what was it that was troubling him? Of course! *Coincidence. Another coincidence.*

He took a taxi to the Hassler Hotel.

'Welcome back, Commander.'

'Thank you.'

'I'll have a bellman take up your bags.'

'Wait.' Robert looked at his watch. Ten p.m. He was tempted to go upstairs and get some sleep, but he had to arrange his passport first.

'I won't be going to my room right away,' Robert said. 'I would appreciate it if you would have my bags sent up.'

'Of course, Commander.'

As Robert turned to leave, the elevator door opened and half a dozen Shriner fraternity men came pouring out, laughing and chattering. They had obviously had a few drinks. One of them, a stout, red-faced man, waved to Robert.

'Hi there, buddy . . . having a good time?'

'Wonderful,' Robert said. 'Just wonderful.'

Robert walked through the lobby to the taxi stand outside. As he started to get into the taxi, he noticed an inconspicuous grey Opel parked across the street. It was too inconspicuous. It stood out among the large, luxurious automobiles around it.

'Via Monte Grappa,' Robert told the taxi driver. During the drive, Robert looked out of the rear window. No grey Opel. *I'm getting jumpy,* he thought. When they arrived at Via Monte Grappa, Robert got out at the corner. As he started to pay the driver, he saw, out of the corner of his eye, the grey Opel half a block down the street, yet he could have sworn it had not followed him. He started walking, moving away from the car, strolling slowly, stopping to look in shop windows. In the reflection of a store window, he saw the Opel, moving slowly behind him. When Robert reached the next corner, he noticed that it was a one-way street. He turned into it, going against the heavy traffic. The Opel hesitated at the corner, then sped away to pick Robert up at the other end. Robert reversed direction and walked back to Via Monte Grappa. The Opel was nowhere in sight.

Robert hailed a taxi. 'Via Monticelli.'

The building was old and unprepossessing, a relic of better days. Robert had visited it many times before, on various missions. He walked down three basement steps and knocked on the door. An eye appeared at the peephole, and a moment later the door was flung open.

'Roberto!' a man exclaimed. He threw his arms around Robert. 'How are you, *mio amico*?'

The speaker was a fat man in his sixties with white, unshaven stubble, thick eyebrows, yellowed teeth and several chins. He closed the door behind him and locked it.

'I'm fine, Ricco.'

Ricco had no second name. *For a man like me,* he liked to boast, *one name is enough. Like Garbo.* 'What can I do for you today, my friend?'

'I'm working on a case,' Robert said, 'and I'm in a hurry. Can you fix me up with a passport?'

Ricco smiled. 'Is the Pope Catholic?' He waddled over to a cabinet in the corner and unlocked it. 'What country would you like to be from?' He pulled out a handful of passports with different-coloured covers, and sorted through them. 'We have a Greek passport, Turkish, Yugoslavian, English . . .'

'American,' Robert said.

Ricco pulled out a passport with a blue cover. 'Here we are. Does the name of Arthur Butterfield appeal to you?'

'Perfect,' Robert said.

'If you'll stand over by the wall, I will take your picture.'

Robert moved over to the wall. Ricco opened a drawer and took out a Polaroid camera. A minute later, Robert was looking at a picture of himself.

'I wasn't smiling,' Robert said.

Ricco looked at him, puzzled. 'What?'

'I wasn't smiling. Take another one.'

Ricco shrugged. 'Sure. Whatever you say.'

Robert smiled while the second passport picture was taken. He looked at it and said, 'That's better.' He casually slipped the first picture into his pocket.

'Now comes the high-tech part,' Ricco announced. Robert watched as Ricco walked over to a work bench where there was a laminating machine. He placed the picture on the inside of the passport.

Robert moved to a table covered with pens, ink and other paraphernalia, and slipped a razor blade and a small bottle of glue into his jacket pocket.

Ricco was studying his handiwork. 'Not bad,' he said. He handed the passport to Robert. 'That will be five thousand dollars.'

'And well worth it,' Robert assured him, as he peeled off ten five-hundred-dollar bills.

'It's always a pleasure doing business with you people. You know how I feel about you.'

Robert knew exactly how he felt. Ricco was an expert cobbler who worked for half a dozen different governments, and was loyal to none. He put the passport in his pocket.

'Good luck, Mr Butterfield.' Ricco smiled.

'Thanks.'

The moment the door closed behind Robert, Ricco reached for the telephone. Information was always worth money to someone.

Outside, twenty yards down the street, Robert took the new passport out of his pocket and buried it in a trash can. *Chaff.* The technique he had used as a pilot to lay false trails for enemy missiles. *Let them look for Arthur Butterfield.*

The grey Opel was parked half a block away. Waiting. *Impossible.* Robert was sure that the car was the only tail they had on him. He was certain the Opel had not followed him, and yet it kept finding him. They had to have some way of keeping track of him. There was only one answer: they were using some kind of homing device. And he had to be carrying it. Attached to his clothes? No. They had had no opportunity. Captain Dougherty had stayed with him while he packed, but he would not have known what clothes Robert would take. Robert made a mental inventory of what he was carrying . . . cash, keys, a wallet, handkerchief, credit card. *The credit card! I doubt if I'll need that, General. Take it. And keep it with you at all times.*

The sneaky sonofabitch. No wonder they had been able to find him so easily.

The grey Opel was no longer in sight. Robert took out the card and examined it. It was slightly thicker than an ordinary credit card. By squeezing it, he could feel an inner layer. They would have a remote control to activate the card. *Good,* Robert thought. *Let's keep the bastards busy.*

There were several trucks parked along the street, loading and unloading goods. Robert examined the licence plates. When he came to a red truck with French plates, he looked around to make sure he was not observed, and tossed the card in the back of the truck.

He flagged down a taxi. 'Hassler, *per favore.*'

In the lobby, Robert approached the concierge. 'See if there's a flight out of here tonight to Paris, please.'

'Certainly, Commander. Do you prefer any particular airline?'

'It doesn't matter. The first flight out.'

'I will be happy to arrange it.'

'Thank you.' Robert walked over to the hotel clerk. 'My key, please. Room 314. And I'll be checking out in a few minutes.'

'Very good, Commander Bellamy.' The clerk reached in a pigeonhole and pulled out a key and an envelope. 'There's a letter here for you.'

Robert stiffened. The envelope was sealed, and addressed simply: *Commander Robert Bellamy.* He fingered it, feeling for plastique or any metal inside. Carefully, he opened it. Inside was a printed card advertising an Italian restaurant. It was innocent enough. Except, of course, for his name on the envelope.

'Do you happen to remember who gave you this?'

'I'm sorry,' the clerk said apologetically, 'but we have been so busy this evening . . .'

It was not important. The man would have been faceless. He would have picked up the card somewhere, slipped it into the envelope and stood by the desk, watching to see the room number of the slot that the envelope was placed in. He would be upstairs now, in Robert's room, waiting. It was time to see the face of the enemy.

Robert became aware of raised voices and turned to watch the Shriners he had seen earlier, entering the lobby, laughing and singing. They had obviously had a few more drinks. The portly man said, 'Hi there, pal. You missed a great party.'

Robert's mind was racing. 'You like parties?'

'Hoo hoo!'

'There's a real live one going on upstairs,' Robert said. 'Booze, girls – anything you want. Just follow me, fellows.'

'That's the American spirit, pal.' The man clapped Robert on the back. 'You hear that, boys? Our friend here is throwing a party!'

They crowded into the elevator together and rode up to the third floor.

The Shriner said, 'These Italians sure know how to live it up. I guess they invented orgies, huh?'

'I'm going to show you a *real* orgy,' Robert promised.

They followed him down the hall to his room. Robert put the key in the lock and turned to the group. 'Are you all ready to have some fun?'

There was a chorus of 'yeses' . . .

Robert turned the key, pushed the door open, and stepped to one side. The room was dark. He snapped on the light. A tall, thin stranger was standing in the middle of the room with a Mauser, equipped with a silencer, half drawn. The man looked at the group with a startled expression, and quickly shoved the gun back in his jacket.

'Hey! Where's the booze?' one of the Shriners demanded.

Robert pointed to the stranger. 'He has it. Go get it.'

The group surged toward the man. 'Where's the liquor, buddy? . . . Where are the girls? . . . Let's get this party on the road . . .'

The thin man was trying to get through to Robert, but the crowd was blocking his way. He watched helplessly as Robert bolted out of the door. He took the stairs two at a time.

Downstairs in the lobby, Robert was moving toward the exit when the concierge called out, 'Oh, Commander Bellamy, I made your reservation for you. You are on Air France flight 312 to Paris. It leaves at one a.m.'

'Thanks,' Robert said hurriedly.

He was out of the door, into the small square overlooking the Spanish Steps. A taxi was discharging a passenger. Robert stepped into it. 'Via Monte Grappa.'

He had his answer now. They intended to kill him. *They're not going to find it easy.* He was the hunted now instead of the hunter, but he had one big advantage. They had trained him well. He knew all their techniques, their strengths, and their weaknesses, and he intended to use that knowledge to stop them. First, he had to find a way to throw them off his trail. The men after him would have been given a story of some kind. They would have been told he was wanted for smuggling drugs, or for murder, or espionage. They would have been warned: *He's dangerous. Take no chances. Shoot to kill.*

Robert said to the taxi driver, 'Roma Termini.' They were hunting for him, but they would not have had enough time to disseminate his photograph. So far, he was faceless.

The taxi pulled up at Via Giovanni Giolitti 36, and the driver announced, 'Stazione Termini, *signore*.'

'Let's just wait here a minute.' Robert sat in the taxi, studying the front of the railway station. There seemed to be only the usual activity. Everything appeared to be normal. Taxis and limousines were arriving and departing, discharging and picking up passengers. Porters were loading and unloading luggage. A policeman was busily ordering cars to move out of the restricted parking zone. But something was disturbing Robert. He suddenly realized what was wrong with the picture. Parked directly in front of the station, in a no-parking zone, were three unmarked sedans, with no one inside. The policeman ignored them.

'I've changed my mind,' Robert said to the driver. 'Via Veneto 110/A.' It was the last place anyone would look for him.

The American Embassy and consulate are located in a pink stucco building facing the Via Veneto, with a black wrought-iron fence in front of it. The embassy was closed at this hour, but the passport division of the consulate was open on a twenty-four-hour basis, to handle emergencies. In the foyer on the first floor, a marine sat behind a desk.

The marine looked up as Robert approached. 'May I help you, sir?'

'Yes,' Robert said. 'I want to inquire about getting a new passport. I lost mine.'

'Are you an American citizen?'

'Yes.'

The marine indicated an office at the far end. 'They'll take care of you in there, sir. Last door.'

'Thank you.'

There were half a dozen people in the room applying for passports, reporting lost passports, and getting renewals and visas.

'Do I need a visa to visit Albania? I have relatives there . . .'

'I need this passport renewed by tonight. I have a plane to catch . . .'

'I don't know what happened to it. I must have left it in Milan . . .'

'They grabbed my passport right out of my purse . . .'

Robert stood there, listening. Stealing passports was a thriving cottage industry in Italy. Someone here would be getting a new passport. At the head of the line was a well-dressed, middle-aged man being handed an American passport.

'Here is your new passport, Mr Cowan. I'm sorry you had such a bad experience. I'm afraid there are a lot of pickpockets in Rome.'

'I'll sure see to it that they don't get hold of this one,' Cowan said.

'You do that, sir.'

Robert watched Cowan put the passport in his jacket pocket and turn to leave. Robert stepped ahead of him. As a woman brushed by, Robert lunged into Cowan, as though he had been pushed, almost knocking him down.

'I'm terribly sorry,' Robert apologized. He leaned over and straightened the man's jacket for him.

'No problem,' Cowan said.

Robert turned and walked into the public men's room down the hall, the stranger's passport in his pocket. He looked around to make sure he was alone, then went into one of the booths. He took out the razor blade and bottle of glue he had stolen from Ricco. Very carefully, he slit the top of the plastic and removed Cowan's photograph. Next, he inserted the picture of himself that Ricco had taken. He glued the top of the plastic slot closed, and examined his handiwork. Perfect. He was now Henry Cowan. Five minutes later, he was out in the Via Veneto, getting into a taxi. 'Leonardo da Vinci.'

It was twelve thirty when Robert arrived at the airport. He stood outside, looking for anything unusual. On the surface, everything appeared to be normal. No police cars, no suspicious-looking men.

Robert entered the terminal, and stopped just inside the door. There were various airline counters scattered around the large terminal. There seemed to be no one loitering or hiding behind posts. He stayed where he was, wary. He could not explain it, even to himself, but somehow, everything seemed *too* normal.

Across the room was an Air France counter. *You are on Air France flight 312 to Paris. It leaves at one a.m.* Robert walked past the counter and approached a woman in uniform behind the Alitalia counter. 'Good evening.'

'Good evening. Can I help you, *signore*?'

'Yes,' Robert said. 'Would you please page Commander Robert Bellamy to come to the courtesy telephone?'

'Certainly,' she said. She picked up a microphone.

A few feet away, a fat middle-aged woman was checking a number of suitcases, heatedly arguing with an airline attendant about overweight fees. 'In America, they never charged me for overweight.'

'I'm sorry, madam. But if you wish all these bags to go on, you must pay for excess baggage.'

Robert moved closer. He heard the attendant's voice over the loudspeaker. 'Will Commander Robert Bellamy please come to the white courtesy telephone. Commander Robert Bellamy, please come to the white courtesy telephone.' The announcement echoed throughout the airport.

A man holding a carry-on bag was walking past Robert. 'Excuse me . . .' Robert said.

The man turned. 'Yes?'

'I hear my wife paging me but . . .' he indicated the woman's bags, 'I can't leave my luggage.' He pulled out a ten-dollar bill and handed it to the man. 'Would you please go over to that white telephone and tell her I'll pick her up at our hotel in an hour? I'd really appreciate it.'

The man looked at the ten-dollar bill in his hand. 'Sure.'

Robert watched him walk over to the courtesy telephone and pick it up. He held the receiver to his ear and said, 'Hello . . . hello . . . ?'

The next moment, four large men in black suits appeared from nowhere and closed in, pinning the hapless man to the wall.

'Hey! What is this?'

'Let's do this quietly,' one of the men said.

'What do you think you're doing? Get your hands off me!'

'Don't make a fuss, Commander. There's no point . . .'

'*Commander?* You've got the wrong man! My name is Melvyn Davis. I'm from Omaha!'

'Let's not play games.'

'Wait a minute! I've been set up. The man you want is over there!' He pointed to where Robert had been standing.

There was no one there.

Outside the terminal, an airport bus was getting ready to depart. Robert boarded it, mingling with the other passengers. He sat at the back of the bus, concentrating on his next move.

He was desperate to talk to Admiral Whittaker, to try to get answers about what was going on, to learn who was responsible for killing innocent people because they had witnessed something they were not supposed to have seen. Was it General Hilliard? Dustin Thornton? Or Thornton's father-in-law, Willard Stone, the man of mystery? Could he be involved in this in some way? Was it Edward Sanders, the Director of NSA? Did it go as high as the President? Robert needed answers.

The bus trip into Rome took an hour. When the bus stopped in front of the Eden Hotel, Robert disembarked.

I've got to get out of the country, Robert thought. There was only one man in Rome he could trust. Colonel Francesco Cesar, head of SIFAR, the Italian Secret Service. He was going to be Robert's escape from Italy.

Colonel Cesar was working late. Messages had been flashing back and forth among foreign security agencies, and they all involved Commander Robert Bellamy. Colonel Cesar had worked with Robert in the past and he was very fond of him. Cesar sighed as he looked at the latest message in front of him. *Terminate.* And as he was reading it, his secretary came into the office.

'Commander Bellamy is on line one for you.'

Colonel Cesar stared at her. 'Bellamy? Himself? Never mind.' He waited until the secretary left the room, then snatched up the telephone. 'Robert?'

'*Ciao*, Francesco. What the hell is going on?'

'You tell me, *amico*. I've been getting all kinds of urgent communiqués about you. What have you done?'

'It's a long story,' Robert said. 'And I haven't time. What have you heard?'

'That you've gone private. That you've been turned, and are singing like a canary.'

'*What?*'

'I heard you've made a deal with the Chinese and . . .'

'*Jesus Christ.* That's ridiculous!'

'Is it? Why?'

'Because an hour later they'd be hungry for more information.'

'For God's sake, Robert, this is nothing to joke about.'

'Tell me about it, Francesco. I've just sent ten innocent people to their deaths. I'm scheduled to be number eleven.'

'Where are you?'

'I'm in Rome. I can't seem to get out of your fucking city.'

'*Cacatura!*' There was a thoughtful silence. 'What can I do to help?'

'Get me to a safe house where we can talk, and I can figure out how to get away. Can you arrange that?'

'Yes, but you must be careful. Very careful. I will pick you up myself.'

Robert breathed a deep sigh of relief. 'Thanks, Francesco. I really appreciate it.'

'As you Americans say, you owe me one. Where are you?'

'The Lido bar in Trastevere.'

'Wait right there. I'll see you in exactly one hour.'

'Thanks, *amico*.' Robert replaced the receiver. It was going to be a long hour.

Thirty minutes later, two unmarked cars coasted to a stop ten yards from the Lido bar. There were four men in each car and they were all carrying automatic weapons.

Colonel Cesar got out of the first car. 'Let's do this quickly. We don't want anyone else to get hurt. *Andate al dietro, subito.*'

Half the men silently went around to cover the back of the building.

Robert Bellamy watched from the rooftop of the building across the street as Cesar and his men raised their weapons and charged into the bar.

All right, you bastards, Robert thought grimly, *we'll play it your way.*

36

DAY SIXTEEN

Rome, Italy

Robert placed a call to Colonel Cesar from a phone booth in the Piazza del Duomo. 'Whatever happened to friendship?' Robert asked.

'Don't be naïve, my friend. I'm under orders, just as you are. I can assure you, there is no use in your running. You're at the head of every intelligence agency's most wanted list. Half the governments of the world are looking for you.'

'Do you believe I'm a traitor?'

Cesar sighed. 'It doesn't matter what I believe, Robert. This is nothing personal. I have my orders.'

'To take me out.'

'You can make it easier by turning yourself in.'

'Thanks, *paesano*. If I need more advice, I'll call Dear Abby.' He slammed down the receiver.

Robert was aware that the longer he was at large, the greater the danger he was in. There would be security agents closing in on him from half a dozen countries.

There has to be a tree, Robert thought. The line came from a legend about a hunter who was relating an experience he had on safari. 'This huge lion was racing toward me, and all my gun bearers had fled. I had no gun, and there was nowhere to hide. Not a bush or a tree in sight. And the beast was charging straight at me, coming closer and closer.' 'How did you escape?' a listener asked. 'I ran over to the nearest tree and climbed it.' 'But you said there were no trees.' 'You don't understand. There *has* to be a tree!' *And I have to find it*, Robert thought.

He looked around the piazza. It was almost deserted at this hour. He decided it was time to have a talk with the man who had started him on this nightmare, General Hilliard. But he would have to be careful. Modern electronic phone tracing was almost instantaneous. Robert observed that the two telephone booths next to the one he was in were both empty. *Perfect*. Ignoring the private number General Hilliard had given him, he dialled the switchboard of NSA. When an operator answered, Robert said, 'General Hilliard's office, please.'

A moment later, he heard a secretary's voice. 'General Hilliard's office.'

Robert said, 'Please hold for an overseas call.' He dropped the receiver and hurried into the next booth. He quickly redialled the number. A different secretary answered, 'General Hilliard's office.'

'Please hold for an overseas call,' Robert said. He let the receiver hang and walked into the third booth, and dialled. When another secretary answered, Robert said, 'This is Commander Bellamy. I want to speak to General Hilliard.'

There was a gasp of surprise. 'Just a moment, Commander.' The secretary buzzed the intercom. 'General, Commander Bellamy is on line three.'

General Hilliard turned to Harrison Keller. 'Bellamy is on line three. Start a trace, fast.'

Harrison Keller hurried over to a telephone on a side table, and dialled the Network Operations Centre, manned and monitored twenty-four hours a day. The senior officer on duty answered. 'NOC. Adams.'

'How long will it take to do an emergency trace on an incoming call?' Keller whispered.

'Between one and two minutes.'

'Start it. General Hilliard's office, line three. I'll hang on.' He looked over at the General and nodded.

General Hilliard picked up the telephone.

'Commander . . . is that you?'

In the Operations Centre, Adams punched a number into a computer. 'Here we go,' he said.

'I thought it was time you and I had a talk, General.'

'I'm glad you called, Commander. Why don't you come in and we can discuss the situation? I'll arrange a plane for you, and you can be here in . . .'

'No thanks. Too many accidents happen in airplanes, General.'

In the communications room, ESS, the electronic switching system, had been activated. The computer screen began lighting up. *AX121-B . . . AX122-C . . . AX123-C . . .*

'What's happening?' Keller whispered into the phone.

'The Network Operations Centre in New Jersey is searching the Washington, DC trunks, sir. Hold on.'

The screen went blank. Then the words: *OVERSEAS TRUNK LINE ONE* flashed onto the screen.

'The call is coming from somewhere in Europe. We're tracing the country . . .'

General Hilliard was saying, 'Commander Bellamy, I think there's been a misunderstanding. I have a suggestion . . .'

Robert replaced the receiver.

General Hilliard looked over at Keller. 'Did you get it?'

Harrison Keller talked into the phone to Adams. 'What happened?'

'We lost him.'

Robert moved into the second booth and picked up the telephone.

714

General Hilliard's secretary said, 'Commander Bellamy is calling on line two.'

The two men looked at each other. General Hilliard pressed the button for line two.

'Commander?'

'Let *me* make a suggestion,' Robert said.

General Hilliard put his hand over the mouthpiece. 'Get the trace working again.'

Harrison Keller picked up the telephone and said to Adams, 'He's on again. Line two. Move fast.'

'Right.'

'My suggestion, General, is that you call off all your men. And I mean *now*.'

'I think you misunderstand the situation, Commander. We can work this problem out if . . .'

'I'll tell you how we can work it out. There's a termination order out on me. I want you to cancel it.'

In the Network Operations Centre, the computer screen was flashing a new message: *AX155-C Subtrunk A21 verified. Circuit 301 to Rome. Atlantic Trunk 1.*

'We've got it,' Adams said into the phone. 'We've traced the trunk to Rome.'

'Get me the number and location,' Keller told him.

In Rome, Robert was glancing at his watch. 'You gave me an assignment. I carried it out.'

'You did very well, Commander. Here is what I . . .'

The line went dead.

The General turned to Keller. 'He hung up, again.'

Keller spoke into the phone. 'Did you get it?'

'Too quick, sir.'

Robert moved into the next booth and picked up the tele phone.

General Hilliard's secretary's voice came over the intercom. 'Commander Bellamy is on line one, General.'

The General snapped, 'Find the bastard!' He picked up the telephone. 'Commander?'

'I want you to listen, General, and listen closely. You've murdered a lot of innocent people. If you don't call off your men, I'm going to the media to tell them what's going on.'

'I wouldn't advise you to do that, unless you want to start a worldwide panic. The aliens are real, and we're defenceless against them. They're getting ready to make their move. You have no idea what would happen if word of this leaked out.'

'Neither have you,' Bellamy retorted. 'I'm not giving you a choice. Call off the contract on me. If there's one more attempt made on my life, I'm going public.'

'All right,' General Hilliard said. 'You win. I'll call it off. Why don't we do this? We can . . .'

'Your trace should be working pretty good, now,' Robert said. 'Have a good day.'

The connection was broken.

'Did you get it?' Keller barked into the phone.

Adams said, 'Close, sir. He was calling from an area in Central Rome. He kept switching numbers on us.'

The General looked over at Keller. 'Well?'

'I'm sorry, General. All we know is that he's somewhere in Rome. Do you believe his threat? Are we going to call off the contract on him?'

'No. We're going to eliminate him.'

Robert went over his options again. They were pitifully few. They would be watching the airports, railroad stations, bus terminals and car rental agencies. He could not check into a hotel because SIFAR would be circulating red notices. Yet he had to get out of Rome. He needed a cover. A companion. They would not be looking for a man and a woman together. It was a beginning.

A taxi was standing at the corner. Robert mussed his hair, pulled down his tie, and staggered drunkenly toward the taxi. 'Hey, there,' he called. 'You!'

The driver looked at him, distastefully.

Robert pulled out a twenty-dollar bill and slapped it into the man's hand. 'Hey, buddy, I'm lookin' a'get laid. You know what tha' means? D'you speak any goddamn English?'

The driver looked at the bill. 'You wish a woman?'

'You got it, pal. I wish a woman.'

'*Andiamo*,' the driver said.

Robert lurched into the cab, and it took off. He looked back. He was not being followed. The adrenalin was pumping. *Half the governments in the world are looking for you.* And there would be no appeal. Their orders were to assassinate him.

Twenty minutes later they had reach Tor di Ounto, Rome's red light district, populated by whores and pimps. They drove down Passeggiata Archeologica, and the driver pulled to a stop at a corner.

'You will find a woman here,' he said.

'Thanks, buddy.' Robert paid the amount on the meter, and stumbled out of the taxi. It pulled away with a squeal of tyres.

Robert looked around, studying his surroundings. No police. A few cars and a handful of pedestrians. There were more than a dozen whores cruising the street. In the spirit of 'let's round up the usual suspects', the police had conducted their bi-monthly sweep to satisfy the voices of morality, and moved the city's prostitutes from the Via Veneto, with its high visibility, to this area where they would not offend the dowagers taking tea at Doney's. For that reason, most of the ladies were attractive

716

and well dressed. There was one in particular who caught Robert's eye.

She appeared to be in her early twenties. She had long, dark hair and was dressed in a tasteful black skirt and white blouse, covered by a camelhair coat. Robert guessed that she was a part-time actress or model. She was watching Robert.

Robert staggered up to her. 'Hi, baby,' he mumbled. 'D'you speak English?'

'Yes.'

'Good. Le's you an' me have a party.'

She smiled uncertainly. *Drunks could be trouble.* 'Maybe you should go sober up first.' She had a soft Italian accent.

'Hey, I'm sober enough.'

'It will cost you a hundred dollars.'

'Tha's okay, honey.'

She made her decision. '*Va bene.* Come. There is a hotel just around the corner.'

'Great. What's your name, baby?'

'Pier.'

'Mine's Henry.' A police car appeared in the distance, headed their way. 'Let's get outta here.'

The other women cast envious glances as Pier and her American customer walked away.

The hotel was no Hassler, but the pimply-faced boy at the desk downstairs did not ask for a passport. In fact, he barely glanced up as he handed Pier a key. 'Fifty thousand lire.'

Pier looked at Robert. He took the money from his pocket and gave it to the boy.

The room they entered contained a large bed in the corner, a small table, two wooden chairs and a mirror over the basin. There was a clothes rack behind the door.

'You must pay me in advance.'

'Sure.' Robert counted out one hundred dollars.

'*Grazie.*'

Pier began to get undressed. Robert walked over to the window. He pushed aside a corner of the curtain and peered out. Everything appeared to be normal. He hoped that by now the police were following the red truck back to France. Robert dropped the curtain and turned around. Pier was naked. She had a surprisingly lovely body. Firm, young breasts, rounded hips, a small waist and long, shapely legs.

She was watching Robert. 'Aren't you going to get undressed, Henry?'

This was the tricky part. '. . . tell you the truth,' Robert said, 'I think I had a little too much to drink. I can't give you any action.'

She was regarding him with wary eyes. 'Then why did you . . . ?'

'If I stay here and sleep it off, we can make love in the morning.'

She shrugged. 'I have to work. It would cost me money to . . .'

'Don't worry. I'll take care of that.' He pulled out several hundred-dollar bills and handed them to her. 'Will that cover it?'

Pier looked at the money, making up her mind. It was tempting. It was cold outside, and business was slow. On the other hand, there was something strange about this man. First of all, he did not really seem to be drunk. He was nicely dressed and for this much money he could have checked them into a fine hotel. *Well*, Pier thought, *what the hell? Che cazzo me ne frega?* 'All right. There's only this bed for the two of us.'

'That's fine.'

Pier watched as Robert walked over to the window again and moved the edge of the curtain aside.

'You are looking for something?'

'Is there a back door out of the hotel?'

What am I getting myself into? Pier wondered. Her best friend had been murdered, hanging out with mobsters. Pier considered herself wise in the ways of men, but this one puzzled her. He did not seem like a criminal, but still . . . 'Yes, there is,' she said.

There was a sudden scream, and Robert whirled around.

'*Dio! Dio! Sono venuta tre volte!*' It was a woman's voice, coming from the next room through the paper-thin walls.

'What's that?' Robert's heart was pounding.

Pier grinned. 'She's having fun. She said she just came for the third time.'

Robert heard the creaking of bed springs.

'Are you going to bed?' Pier stood there naked, unembarrassed, watching him.

'Sure.' Robert sat down on the bed.

'Aren't you going to get undressed?'

'No.'

'Suit yourself.' Pier moved over to the bed and lay down beside Robert. 'I hope you don't snore,' Pier said.

'You can tell me in the morning.'

Robert had no intention of sleeping. He wanted to check the street during the night, to make sure they did not come to the hotel. They would get around to these small, third-class hotels eventually, but it would take them time. They had too many other places to cover first. He lay there, feeling bone-tired, and closed his eyes for a moment to rest. He slept. He was back home, in his own bed, and he felt Susan's warm body next to his. *She's back*, he thought, happily. *She's come back to me. Baby, I've missed you so much.*

718

DAY SEVENTEEN

Rome, Italy

Robert was awakened by the sun hitting his face. He sat up abruptly, looking around for an instant in alarm, disorientated. When he saw Pier, memory flooded back. He relaxed. Pier was at the mirror, brushing her hair.

'*Buon giorno*,' she said. 'You do not snore.'

Robert looked at his watch. Nine o'clock. He had wasted precious hours.

'Do you want to make love now? You have already paid for it.'

'That's all right,' Robert said.

Pier walked over to the bed, naked and provocative. 'Are you sure?' *I couldn't if I wanted to, lady.* 'I'm sure.'

'*Va bene*.' She began to dress. She asked casually, 'Who is Susan?'

The question caught him off guard. 'Susan? What made you ask?'

'You talk in your sleep.'

He remembered his dream. Susan had come back to him. Maybe it was a sign. 'She's a friend.' *She's my wife. She's going to get tired of Moneybags and return to me some day. If I'm still alive, that is.*

Robert walked over to the window. He lifted the curtain and looked out. The street was crowded now with pedestrians and merchants opening up their shops. There were no signs of danger.

It was time to put his plan into motion. He turned to the girl. 'Pier, how would you like to go on a little trip with me?'

She looked at him with suspicion. 'A trip . . . where?'

'I have to go to Venice on business, and I hate travelling alone. Do you like Venice?'

'Yes . . .'

'Good. I'll pay you for your time, and we'll have a little holiday together.' He was staring out of the window again. 'I know a lovely hotel there. The Cipriani.' Years ago, he and Susan had stayed at the Royal Danieli, but he had been back since, and it had become sadly run-down, and the beds were impossible. The only thing that remained of the hotel's former elegance was Luciano, at the reception desk.

'It will cost you a thousand dollars a day.' She was ready to settle for five hundred.

'It's a deal.' Robert said. He counted out two thousand dollars. 'We'll start with this.'

Pier hesitated. She had a premonition that something was wrong. But the start of the movie she had been promised a bit part in had been delayed, and she needed the money. 'Very well,' she said.

'Let's go.'

Downstairs, Pier watched him scan the street carefully before stepping out to hail a taxi. *He's a target for somebody*, Pier thought. *I'm getting out of here.*

'Look,' Pier said, 'I'm not sure I should go to Venice with you. I . . .'

'We're going to have a great time,' Robert told her.

Directly across the street he saw a jewellery store. He took Pier's hand. 'Come on. I'm going to get you something pretty.'

'But . . .'

He led her across the street to the jewellery store.

The clerk behind the counter said, '*Buon giorno, signore*. Can I help you?'

'Yes,' Robert said. 'We're looking for something lovely for the lady.' He turned to Pier. 'Do you like emeralds?'

'I . . . yes.'

Robert said to the clerk, 'Do you have an emerald bracelet?'

'*Si, signore*. I have a beautiful emerald bracelet.' He walked over to a case and took out a bracelet. 'This is our finest. It is fifteen thousand dollars.'

Robert looked at Pier. 'Do you like it?'

She was speechless. She nodded.

'We'll take it,' Robert said. He handed the clerk his ONI credit card.

'One moment, please.' The clerk disappeared into the back room. When he returned, he said, 'Shall I wrap it for you, or . . . ?'

'No. My friend will wear it.' Robert put the bracelet on Pier's wrist. She was staring at it, stunned.

Robert said, 'That will look pretty in Venice, won't it?'

Pier smiled up at him. 'Very.'

When they were out on the street, Pier said, 'I . . . I don't know how to thank you.'

'I just want you to have a good time,' Robert told her. 'Do you have a car?'

'No. I used to have an old one, but it was stolen.'

'Do you still have your driver's licence?'

She was watching him, puzzled. 'Yes, but without a car, what good is a driver's licence?'

'You'll see. Let's get out of here.'

He hailed a taxi. 'Via Po, please.'

She sat in the taxi, studying him. Why was he so anxious for her company? He had not even touched her. *Could he be . . . ?*

'*Qui!*' Robert called to the driver. They were a hundred yards away from Maggiore's Car Rental Agency.

'We're getting out here,' Robert told Pier. He paid the driver and waited until the taxi was out of sight. He handed Pier a large bundle of bank notes. 'I want you to rent a car for us. Ask for a Fiat or an Alfa Romeo. Tell them we'll want it for four or five days. This money will cover the deposit. Rent it in your name. I'll wait for you in the bar across the street.'

Less than eight blocks away, two detectives were questioning the hapless driver of a red truck with French licence plates.

'*Vous me faites chier.* I have no idea how the fuck that card got in the back of my truck,' the driver screamed. 'Some crazy Italian probably put it in there.'

The two detectives looked at each other. One of them said, 'I'll phone it in.'

Francesco Cesar sat at his desk, thinking about the latest development. Earlier, the assignment had seemed so simple. '*You won't have any trouble finding him. When the time comes, we will activate the homing device, and it will lead you right to him.*' Someone had obviously under-estimated Commander Bellamy.

Colonel Frank Johnson was seated in General Hilliard's office, his huge frame filling the chair.

'We have half the agents in Europe looking for him,' General Hilliard said. 'So far, they've had no luck.'

'It's going to take more than luck,' Colonel Johnson said. 'Bellamy's good.'

'We know he's in Rome. The sonofabitch just charged a bracelet for fifteen thousand dollars. We have him bottled up. There's no way he can get out of Italy. We know the name he's using on his passport – Arthur Butterfield.'

Colonel Johnson shook his head. 'If I know Bellamy, you haven't a clue about what name he's using. The only thing you can count on is that Bellamy won't do what you count on him to do. We're after a man who's as good as the best in the business. Maybe better. If there's any place to run, Bellamy will run there. If there's any place to hide, he'll hide there. I think our best bet is to bring him out in the open, smoke him out. Right now, he's controlling all the moves. We have to take the initiative away from him.'

'You mean, go public? Give it to the press?'

'Exactly.'

General Hilliard pursed his lips. 'That's going to be touchy. We can't afford to expose ourselves.'

'We won't have to. We'll put out a release that he's wanted on a drug-smuggling charge. That way we can get Interpol and all the police departments in Europe involved without tipping our hand.'

General Hilliard thought about it for a moment. 'I like it.'

'Good. I'm leaving for Rome,' Colonel Johnson said. 'I'm going to take charge of the hunt myself.'

When Colonel Frank Johnson returned to his office, he was in a thoughtful mood. He was playing a dangerous game. There was no question about it. He had to find Commander Bellamy.

37

Robert listened to the phone ring again and again. It was six a.m. in Washington. *I'm always waking the old man up,* Robert thought.

The Admiral answered on the sixth ring. 'Hello . . .'

'Admiral, I . . .'

'Robert! What . . . ?'

'Don't say anything. Your phone is probably bugged. I'm going to make this fast. I just wanted to tell you not to believe anything they're saying about me. I'd like you to try to find out what's going on. I may need your help later.'

'Of course. Anything I can do, Robert.'

'I know.'

'I'll call you later.'

Robert replaced the receiver. No time for a trace. He saw a blue Fiat pull up outside the bar. Pier was at the wheel.

'Move over,' Robert said. 'I'll drive.'

Pier made room for him as he slid in behind the wheel.

'Are we on our way to Venice?' Pier asked.

'Uh huh. We have a couple of stops to make first.' It was time to spread some more chaff around. He turned onto Viale Rossini. Ahead was the Rossini Travel Service. Robert pulled over to the kerb. 'I'll be back in a minute.'

Pier watched him walk into the travel agency. *I could just drive away,* she thought, *and keep the money, and he would never find me. But the damn car is rented in my name. Cacchio!*

Inside the agency, Robert walked up to the woman behind the counter.

'Good day. May I help you?'

'Yes. I'm Commander Robert Bellamy. I'm going to do a bit of travelling,' Robert told her. 'I'd like to make some reservations.'

She smiled. 'That's what we are here for, *signore.* Where are you planning to go?'

'I'd like a first-class airline ticket to Beijing, one way.'

She made a note. 'And when would you like to leave?'

'This Friday.'

'Very good.' She pressed some keys on the computer. 'There's an Air China flight leaving at seven forty p.m. Friday night.'

'That will do nicely.'

She pressed some more keys. 'There we are. Your reservation is confirmed. Will that be cash or . . . ?'

'Oh, I'm not through yet. I want to reserve a train ticket to Budapest.'

'And when would that be, Commander?'

'Next Monday.'

'And in what name?'

'The same.'

She looked at him strangely. 'You are flying to Beijing on Friday and . . .'

'I'm not finished,' Robert said pleasantly. 'I want a one-way airline ticket to Miami, Florida, on Sunday.'

Now she was openly staring at him. '*Signore*, if this is some kind of a . . .'

Robert pulled out his ONI credit card and handed it to her. 'Just charge the tickets to this card.'

She studied it a moment. 'Excuse me.' She went into the back office and came out a few minutes later. 'That will be perfectly all right. We will be happy to make the arrangements. Do you wish all the reservations under one name?'

'Yes. Commander Robert Bellamy.'

'Very good.'

Robert watched as she pressed more buttons on the computer. A minute later, three tickets appeared. She tore them off the printer.

'Please put the tickets in separate envelopes,' Robert said.

'Of course. Would you like me to send them to . . . ?'

'I'll take them with me.'

'*Si, signore.*'

Robert signed the credit card slip and she handed him his receipt.

'There you are. Have a nice trip . . . trips . . . er . . .'

Robert grinned. 'Thanks.' A minute later he was behind the wheel of the car.

'Are we going now?' Pier asked.

'We have just a few more stops to make,' Robert said.

Pier watched him carefully scan the street again before pulling out.

'I want you to do something for me,' Robert told her.

Now it's coming, Pier thought. *He's going to ask me to do something terrible*. 'What is it?' she asked.

They had stopped in front of the Hotel Victoria. Robert handed Pier one of the envelopes. 'I want you to go to the desk and reserve a suite in the name of Commander Robert Bellamy. Tell them you're his secretary and that he'll be arriving in an hour, but that you want to go up to the suite and approve it. When you get inside, leave this envelope on a table in the room.'

She looked at him, puzzled. 'That's all?'

'That's all.'

The man made no sense at all. '*Bene*.' She wished she knew what the crazy American was up to. *And who is Commander Robert Bellamy?* Pier got out of the car and walked into the lobby of the hotel. She was

724

a bit nervous. In the course of practising her profession, she had been thrown out of a few first-class hotels. But the clerk behind the desk greeted her politely. 'May I help you, *signora*?'

'I am the secretary to Commander Robert Bellamy. I wish to reserve a suite for him. He will be here in an hour.'

The clerk consulted the room chart. 'We do happen to have one very nice suite available.'

'May I see it, please?' Pier asked.

'Certainly. I'll have someone show it to you.'

An assistant manager escorted Pier upstairs. They walked into the living room of the suite and Pier looked around. 'Will this be satisfactory, *signora*?'

Pier had not the faintest idea. 'Yes, this will be fine.' She removed the envelope from her purse and laid it on a coffee table. 'I will leave this here for the Commander,' she said.

'*Bene.*'

Curiosity got the better of Pier. She opened the envelope. Inside was a one-way plane ticket to Beijing in the name of Robert Bellamy. Pier put the ticket back in the envelope, left it on the table and went downstairs.

The blue Fiat was parked in front of the hotel.

'Any problem?' Robert asked.

'No.'

'We have just two more stops to make, and then we're on our way,' Robert said cheerfully.

The next stop was the Hotel Valadier. Robert handed Pier another envelope. 'I want you to reserve a suite here in the name of Commander Robert Bellamy. Tell them he'll be checking in within an hour. Then . . .'

'I leave the envelope upstairs.'

'Right.'

This time Pier walked into the hotel with more confidence. *Just act like a lady,* she thought. *You've got to have dignity. That's the fucking secret.*

There was a suite available in the hotel.

'I would like to look at it,' Pier said.

'Of course, *signora*.'

An assistant manager escorted Pier upstairs. 'This is one of our nicest suites.' It was beautiful.

Pier said haughtily, 'I suppose it might do. The Commander is very particular, you know.' She took the second envelope out of her purse, opened it, and glanced inside. It contained a train ticket to Budapest in the name of Commander Robert Bellamy. Pier stared at it, confused. *What kind of game is this?* She left the ticket by the bed stand.

When Pier returned to the car, Robert asked, 'How did it go?'

'Fine.'

'Last stop.'

This time it was the Hotel Leonardo da Vinci. Robert handed Pier the third envelope. 'I would like you to . . .'

'I know.'

Inside the hotel, a clerk said, 'Yes, indeed, *signora*, we have a lovely suite. When did you say the Commander will be arriving?'

'In an hour. I would like to examine the suite to see if it is satisfactory.'

'Of course, *signora*.'

The suite was more lavish than the other two Pier had looked at. The assistant manager showed her the huge bedroom with a large canopied bed in the centre. *What a waste*, Pier thought. *In one night, I could make a fortune here*. She took out the third envelope and looked inside. It contained an airplane ticket to Miami, Florida. Pier left the envelope on the bed.

The assistant manager escorted Pier back to the living room. 'We have colour TV,' he said. He walked over to the television set and turned it on. A picture of Robert leaped onto the screen. The anchorman's voice was saying: '. . . and Interpol believes that he is presently in Rome. He is wanted for questioning in an international drug-smuggling operation. This is Bernard Shaw for CNN News.' Pier was staring at the screen, transfixed.

The assistant manager turned off the television set. 'Is everything satisfactory?'

'Yes,' Pier said slowly. *A drug smuggler!*

'We'll be looking forward to seeing the Commander.'

When Pier joined Robert in the car downstairs, she looked at him with different eyes.

'Now we're ready,' Robert smiled.

At the Hotel Victoria, a man in a dark suit was studying the guest register. He looked up at the clerk. 'What time did Commander Bellamy check in?'

'He has not been here yet. His secretary reserved the suite. She said he would be here within the hour.'

The man turned to his companion. 'Have the hotel staked out. Get reinforcements. I'll wait upstairs.' He turned to the clerk. 'Open the suite for me.'

Three minutes later the clerk was opening the door to the suite. The man in the dark suit moved in cautiously, gun in hand. The suite was empty. He saw the envelope on the table and picked it up. The front of it read: 'Commander Robert Bellamy'. He opened the envelope and glanced inside. A moment later he was dialling the headquarters of SIFAR.

Francesco Cesar was in the middle of a meeting with Colonel Frank Johnson. Colonel Johnson had landed at Leonardo da Vinci airport two hours earlier, but he showed no signs of fatigue.

'As far as we know,' Cesar was saying, 'Bellamy is still in Rome. We've had more than thirty reports on his whereabouts.'

'Any of them check out?'

'No.'

The phone rang. 'It's Luigi, Colonel,' the voice on the telephone said. 'We've got him. I'm in his hotel suite at the Hotel Victoria. I have his airline ticket to Beijing. He is planning to leave Friday.'

Cesar's voice filled with excitement. 'Good! Stay there. We will be right over.' He hung up and turned to Colonel Johnson. 'I'm afraid your journey was for nothing, Colonel. We've got him. He's registered at the Hotel Victoria. They found an airline ticket in his name for Beijing on Friday.'

Colonel Johnson said mildly, 'Bellamy registered at the hotel in his own name?'

'Yes.'

'And the plane ticket is in his name?'

'Yes.' Colonel Cesar rose. 'Let's get on over there.'

Colonel Johnson shook his head. 'Don't waste your time.'

'What?'

'Bellamy would never . . .'

The telephone rang again. Cesar snatched it up. A voice said, 'Colonel? This is Mario. We've located Bellamy. He's at the Hotel Valadier. He's taking a train Monday to Budapest. What do you want us to do?'

'I'll get back to you,' Colonel Cesar said. He turned to look at Colonel Johnson. 'They found a train ticket to Budapest in Bellamy's name. I don't understand what . . .'

The telephone rang again.

'Yes?' His voice was pitched higher.

'It's Bruno. We've located Bellamy. He's registered at the Hotel Leonardo da Vinci. He's planning to leave Sunday for Miami. What shall I . . . ?'

'Come back here,' Cesar snapped. He slammed down the phone. 'What the hell is his game?'

Colonel Johnson said grimly. 'He's seeing to it that you're wasting a lot of manpower, isn't he?'

'What do we do now?'

'We trap the bastard.'

They were driving on the Via Cassia, near Olgiata, headed north toward Venice. The police would be covering all the major exits from Italy, but they would be expecting him to go west, to head for France or

Switzerland. *From Venice*, Robert thought, *I can take the hydrofoil to Trieste and make my way up to Austria. After that . . .*

Pier's voice interrupted his thoughts. 'I'm hungry.'

'What?'

'We haven't had any breakfast or lunch.'

'I'm sorry,' Robert said. He had been too preoccupied to think about eating. 'We'll stop at the next restaurant.'

Pier watched him as he drove. She was more puzzled than ever. She lived in a world of pimps and thieves, and drug smugglers. This man was no criminal.

They stopped at the next town in front of a small trattoria. Robert pulled into the parking lot and he and Pier got out of the car.

The restaurant was crowded with patrons, and noisy with conversation and the clatter of dishes. Robert found a table against the wall, and took a seat facing the door. A waiter approached and handed them menus.

Robert was thinking: *Susan should be on the boat by now. This may be my last chance to talk to her.* 'Look over the menu.' Robert rose. 'I'll be right back.'

Pier watched him walk over to the public telephone near their table. He put a coin in the slot.

'I would like to talk to the marine operator in Gibraltar. Thank you.'

Who is he calling in Gibraltar? Pier wondered. *Is that his get-away?*

'Operator, I want to place a collect call to the American yacht, *Halcyon*, off Gibraltar. Whiskey Sugar 337. Thank you.'

A few minutes passed while the operators talked to each other and his call was accepted.

Robert heard Susan's voice on the telephone.

'Susan . . .'

'Robert! Are you all right?'

'I'm fine. I just wanted to tell you . . .'

'I know what you want to tell me. It's all over the radio and television. Why is Interpol hunting you?'

'It's a long story.'

'Take your time. I want to know.'

He hesitated. 'It's political, Susan. I have evidence that some governments are trying to suppress. That's why Interpol is after me.'

Pier was listening intently to Robert's end of the conversation.

'What can I do to help?' Susan asked.

'Nothing, honey. I just called to hear your voice once more in case . . . in case I don't get out of this.'

'Don't say that.' There was panic in her voice. 'Can you tell me what country you're in?'

'Italy.'

There was a brief silence. 'All right. We're not far from you. We're just off the coast of Gibraltar. We can pick you up at any place you say.'

'No, I . . .'

'Listen to me. It's probably your only chance of escape.'

'I can't let you do that, Susan. You'd be in jeopardy.'

Monte had walked into the saloon in time to hear part of the conversation. 'Let me talk to him.'

'Just a moment, Robert, Monte wants to speak to you.'

'Susan, I haven't . . .'

Monte's voice came over the line. 'Robert, I understand you're in serious trouble.'

The understatement of the year. 'You might say that.'

'We'd like to help you out. They won't be looking for you on a yacht. Why don't you let us pick you up?'

'Thanks, Monte, I appreciate it. The answer is no.'

'I think you're making a mistake. You'll be safe here.'

Why was he so eager to help? 'Thanks, anyway. I'll take my chances. I'd like to speak to Susan again . . .'

'Of course.' Monte Banks handed the phone to Susan. 'Talk him into it,' he urged.

Susan spoke into the phone. 'Please let us help you.'

'You have helped me, Susan.' He had to stop for a moment. 'You're the best part of my life. I just want you to know that I'll always love you.' He gave a little laugh. 'Although *always* may not be such a big deal anymore.'

'Will you call me again?'

'If I can.'

'Promise me.'

'All right. I promise.'

He slowly replaced the receiver. *Why did I do that to her? Why did I do that to myself? You're a sentimental idiot, Bellamy.* He walked back to the table.

'Let's eat,' Robert said. They ordered.

'I heard your conversation. The police are looking for you, aren't they?'

Robert stiffened. *Careless. She was going to be trouble.* 'It's just a little misunderstanding. I . . .'

'Don't treat me like a fool. I want to help you.'

He was watching her warily. 'Why should you help me?'

Pier leaned forward. 'Because you've been generous to me. And I hate the police. You don't know what it's like to be out on the streets, hounded by them, treated like dirt. They arrest me for prostitution, but they take me to their back rooms and pass me around. They are animals. I would do anything to get even with them. Anything. I can help you.'

'Pier, there's nothing you . . .'

'In Venice the police will catch you easily. If you stay at a hotel, they

729

will find you. If you try to get on a ship, they will trap you. But I know a place where you will be safe from them. My mother and brother live in Naples. We can stay at their house. The police will never look for you there.'

Robert was silent for a moment, thinking about it. What Pier said made a good deal of sense. A private house would be much safer than any other place, and Naples was a big port. It would be easy to get a ship out of there. He hesitated before he answered. He did not want to put Pier in danger.

'Pier, if the police find me, they have orders to kill me. You would be considered an accomplice. You could be letting yourself in for trouble.'

'It's very simple.' Pier smiled. 'We won't let them find you.'

Robert returned her smile. He made up his mind. 'All right. Eat your lunch. We're going to Naples.'

Colonel Frank Johnson said, 'Your men have no idea where he is headed?'

Francesco Cesar sighed. 'Not at the moment. But it is only a matter of time before . . .'

'We don't have time. Have you checked the whereabouts of his ex-wife?'

'His ex-wife? No. I don't see what . . .'

'Then you haven't done your homework,' Colonel Johnson snapped. 'She's married to a man named Monte Banks. I would suggest that you locate them, and fast.'

38

She wandered down the broad boulevard, barely conscious of where she was going. How many days had it been since the terrible crash? She had lost count. She was so tired that it was difficult for her to concentrate. She desperately needed water; not the polluted water that the Earthlings drank, but fresh, clear rain water. She needed the pure fluid to revive her life essence, to gain the strength to find the crystal. She was dying.

She staggered and bumped into a man.

'Hey! Watch where . . .' The American salesman took a closer look at her and smiled. 'Hi, there. Imagine bumping into you like this!' *What a doll.*

'Yes, I can imagine that.'

'Where are you from, honey?'

'The seventh sun of the Pleiades.'

He laughed. 'I like a gal with a sense of humour. Where you headed?'

She shook her head. 'I do not know. I am a stranger here.'

Jesus, I think I'm on to something. 'Have you had dinner?'

'No. I cannot eat your food.'

I've got a real weirdo here. But a beauty. 'Where are you staying?'

'I am not staying anywhere.'

'You don't have a hotel?'

'A hotel?' She remembered. *Boxes for travelling strangers.* 'No. I must find a place to sleep. I am very tired.'

His smile broadened. 'Well, Papa can take care of that. Why don't we go up to my hotel room? I've got a nice, big comfortable bed there. Would you like that?'

'Oh, yes, very much.'

He could not believe his good luck. 'Wonderful!' *I'll bet she's great in the hay.*

She looked at him, puzzled. 'Your bed is made of hay?'

He was staring at her. 'What? No, no. You like your little jokes, don't you?'

She could barely keep her eyes open. 'Could we go to bed now?'

He rubbed his hands together. 'You bet! My hotel is just around the corner.'

He picked up his key at the desk and they took the elevator to his floor. When they got to his room, the man asked, 'Would you like a little drink?' *Let's loosen you up.*

She wanted one desperately, but not the liquids the Earthlings had to offer. 'No,' she said. 'Where is the bed?'

My God, she's a hot little thing. 'In here, honey.' He led her into the bedroom. 'You're sure you wouldn't like a drink?'

'I am sure.'

He licked his lips. 'Then why don't you – er – get undressed?'

She nodded. It was an Earthling custom. She removed the dress she was wearing. She was wearing nothing underneath. Her body was exquisite.

The man stared at her and said, happily, 'This is my lucky night, honey. Yours, too.' *I'm going to fuck you like you've never been fucked before.* He tore off his clothes as fast as he could and jumped into bed beside her. 'Now!' he said. 'I'm going to show you some real action.' He glanced up. 'Damn! I left the light on.' He started to get up.

'Never mind,' she said sleepily. 'I will turn it off.'

And as he watched, her arm reached out, out, across the wide room, and her fingers became leafy green tendrils as they brushed against the light switch.

He was alone in the dark with her. He screamed.

39

They were travelling at high speed on the Autostrada del Sole, the freeway to Naples. They had been driving in silence for the last half hour, each preoccupied with his own thoughts.

Pier broke the silence. 'How long would you like to stay at my mother's house?' she asked.

'Three or four days, if that's all right.'

'That will be fine.'

Robert had no intention of staying there for more than one night, two at the most. But he kept his plans to himself. As soon as he found a ship that was safe, he would be on his way out of Italy.

'I'm looking forward to seeing my family,' Pier said.

'You have just one brother?'

'Yes. Carlo. He is younger than me.'

'Tell me about your family, Pier.'

She shrugged. 'There is not much to tell. My father worked at the docks all his life. A crane fell on him and killed him when I was fifteen. My mother was ill, and I had to support her and Carlo. I had a friend at Cinecittà studios and he got me bit parts. They paid very little and I had to sleep with the assistant director. I decided I could make more money on the streets. Now I do a little of both.' There was no self-pity in her voice.

'Pier . . . are you sure your mother won't object to your bringing a stranger home?'

'I am sure. We are very close. Mother will be happy to see me. Do you love her very much?'

Robert glanced over at her in surprise. 'Your mother?'

'The woman you were talking to on the telephone in the restaurant – Susan.'

'What makes you think I love her?'

'The tone of your voice. Who is she?'

'A friend.'

'She is very lucky. I wish I had someone who cared for me like that. Is Robert Bellamy your real name?'

'Yes.'

'And are you a commander?'

That was more difficult to answer. 'I'm not sure, Pier,' he said. 'I used to be.'

'Can you tell me why Interpol is after you?'

He said carefully, 'It's better if I don't tell you anything. You could be in enough trouble just being with me. The less you know the better.'

'All right, Robert.'

He thought about the strange circumstances that had brought the two of them together. 'Let me ask you something. If you knew that there were aliens coming down to earth in spaceships, would you panic?'

Pier studied him a moment. 'Are you serious?'

'Very.'

She shook her head. 'No. I think it would be exciting. Do you believe such things exist?'

'There's a possibility,' he said cautiously.

Pier's face lit up. 'Really? Do they have real . . . I mean . . . are they built like men?'

Robert laughed. 'I don't know.'

'Does this have anything to do with why the police are after you?'

'No,' Robert said quickly. 'Nothing.'

'If I tell you something, will you promise not to be angry with me.'

'I promise.'

When she spoke, her voice was so low he could hardly hear her. 'I think I am falling in love with you.'

'Pier . . .'

'I know. I am being foolish. But I have never said that to anyone before. I wanted you to know.'

'I'm flattered, Pier.'

'You're not making fun of me?'

'No. I'm not.' He looked at the gas gauge. 'We'd better find a filling station soon.'

They came to a service station fifteen minutes later. 'We'll fill the tank here,' Robert said.

'Fine,' Pier smiled. 'I can call my mother and let her know that I am bringing home a handsome stranger.'

Robert drove up to the gas pump and said to the attendant, '*Fate il pieno, per favore.*'

'*Si, signore.*'

Pier leaned over and gave Robert a kiss on the cheek. 'I will be right back.'

Robert watched her walk into the office and get change for the telephone. *She's really very pretty,* Robert thought. *And intelligent. I must be careful not to hurt her.*

Inside the office, Pier was dialling. She turned to smile and wave at Robert. When the operator came on, Pier said, 'Get me Interpol. *Subito!*'

734

40

From the moment Pier had seen the news broadcast about Robert Bellamy, she had known she was going to be rich. If Interpol, the international criminal police force, was looking for Robert, there had to be a huge reward out for him. And she was the only one who knew where he was! The reward would be all hers. Persuading him to go to Naples, where she could keep an eye on him, had been a stroke of genius.

A man's voice on the telephone said, 'Interpol. May I help you?'

Pier's heart was pounding. She glanced out of the window to make sure Robert was still at the gas pump. 'Yes. You are looking for a man named Commander Robert Bellamy, yes?'

There was a moment of silence. 'Who is calling, please?'

'Never mind. Are you after him or not?'

'I'll have to transfer you to someone else. Will you hold the line, please?' He turned to his assistant. 'Put a trace on this. *Pronto!*'

Thirty seconds later, Pier was speaking with a senior official. 'Yes, *signora*. Can I help you?'

No, you fool. I'm trying to help you. 'I have Commander Robert Bellamy. Do you want him, or don't you?'

'But, yes, *signora*, we want him very much. And you say you have him?'

'That's right. He's with me now. How much is he worth to you?'

'Are you speaking of a reward?'

'Of course I'm speaking of a reward.' She glanced out of the window again. *What kind of idiots are these?*

The official signalled to his assistant to move faster.

'We have not yet set a price on him, *signora*, so . . .'

'Well, set one now. I'm in a hurry.'

'How much of a reward are you expecting?'

'I don't know.' Pier thought for a moment. 'Would fifty thousand dollars be all right?'

'Fifty thousand dollars is a lot of money. If you tell me where you are, we could come to you and negotiate a deal that . . .'

He must think I'm pazza. 'No. You either agree to pay me what I want now or . . .' Pier looked up and saw Robert approaching the office. 'Hurry! Yes or no?'

'Very well, *signora*. Yes. We will agree to pay you . . .'

Robert came through the door, moving toward her.

Pier said into the telephone, 'We should be there in time for dinner,

Mama. You will like him. He is very nice. Good. We will see you later. *Ciao*.'

Pier replaced the receiver and turned to Robert. 'Mother is dying to meet you.'

At Interpol headquarters, the senior official said, 'Did you trace the call?'

'Yes. It came from a filling station on the Autostrada del Sole. It looks like they're on their way to Naples.'

Colonel Francesco Cesar and Colonel Frank Johnson were studying a map on the wall of Cesar's office.

'Naples is a big city,' Colonel Cesar was saying. 'There are a thousand places for him to hide there.'

'What about the woman?'

'We have no idea who she is.'

'Why don't we find out?' Johnson asked.

Cesar looked at him, puzzled. 'How?'

'If Bellamy needed a woman companion in a hurry, as a cover, what would he do?'

'He would probably pick up a whore.'

'Right. Where do we start?'

'Tor di Ounto.'

They drove down the Passeggiata Archeologica and watched the streetwalkers peddling their wares. In the car with Colonel Cesar and Colonel Johnson was Captain Bellini, the police supervisor of the district.

'This is not going to be easy,' Bellini said. 'They're all in competition with one another, but when it comes to the police, they're like blood sisters. They won't talk.'

'We'll see,' Colonel Johnson said.

Bellini ordered the driver to pull over to the kerb and the three men got out of the car. The prostitutes were eyeing them warily. Bellini walked up to one of the women. 'Good afternoon, Maria. How's business?'

'It will be better when you leave.'

'We're not planning to stay. I just want to ask you a question. We're looking for an American who picked up one of the girls last night. We think they are travelling together. We want to know who she is. Can you help us?' He showed her a photograph of Robert.

Several other prostitutes had gathered around to listen to the conversation.

'I can't help you,' Maria said, 'but I know someone who can.'

Bellini nodded approvingly. 'Good. Who?'

Maria pointed to a store-front across the street. A sign in the window read: 'Fortune Teller – Palm Reader'. 'Madam Lucia might help you.'

The girls laughed appreciatively.

Captain Bellini looked at them, and said, 'So you like jokes, do you? Well, we're going to play a little joke I think you're going to love. These two gentlemen are very anxious to have the name of the girl who went off with the American. If you don't know who she is, I suggest you talk to your friends, find someone who does know, and when you have the answer, give me a call.'

'Why should we?' one of them asked defiantly.

'You'll find out.'

One hour later the prostitutes of Rome found themselves under siege. Patrol wagons swept the city, picking up all the women working the streets, and their pimps. There were screaming protests.

'You can't do this . . . I pay police protection.'

'This has been my beat for five years . . .'

'I've been giving it to you and your friends for free. Where's your gratitude . . . ?'

'What do I pay you protection for . . . ?'

By the following day, the streets were virtually empty of prostitutes, and the jails were full.

Cesar and Colonel Johnson were sitting in Captain Bellini's office. 'It's going to be difficult to keep them in jail,' Captain Bellini warned. 'I might also add that this is very bad for tourism.'

'Don't worry,' Colonel Johnson said, 'someone will talk. Just keep the pressure on.'

Their break came late in the afternoon. Captain Bellini's secretary said, 'There's a Mr Lorenzo to see you.'

'Send him in.'

Mr Lorenzo was dressed in a very expensive suit, and wore diamond rings on three fingers. Mr Lorenzo was a pimp.

'What can I do for you?' Bellini asked.

Lorenzo smiled. 'It's what I can do for *you* gentlemen. Some of my associates inform me that you are looking for a particular working girl who left town with an American, and since we are always eager to cooperate with the authorities, I thought I would give you her name.'

Colonel Johnson said, 'Who is she?'

Lorenzo ignored the question. 'Naturally, I'm sure you would want to express your appreciation by releasing my associates and their friends.'

Colonel Cesar said, 'We are not interested in any of your whores. All we want is the name of the girl.'

'That is very gratifying news, sir. It's always a pleasure to deal with reasonable men. I know that . . .'

'Her name, Lorenzo.'

'Yes, of course. Her name is Pier. Pier Valli. The American spent

737

the night with her at the L'Incrocio Hotel, and the next morning they took off. She is not one of my girls. If I may say so . . .'

Bellini was already on the telephone. 'Bring up the records on a Pier Valli. *Subito!*'

'I hope you gentlemen are going to show your gratitude by . . .'

Bellini looked up, and then said into the phone, 'And cancel Operation Puttana.'

Lorenzo beamed. '*Grazie.*'

Pier Valli's records were on Bellini's desk five minutes later. 'She started streetwalking when she was fifteen. She has been arrested a dozen times since then. She . . .'

'Where does she come from?' Colonel Johnson interrupted.

'Naples.' The two men looked at each other. 'She has a mother and brother living there.'

'Can you find out where?'

'I can check it out.'

'Do that. *Now.*'

41

They were approaching the suburbs of Naples. Old apartment houses lined the narrow streets, with laundry hanging out of almost every window, making the buildings look like concrete mountains flying colourful flags.

Pier asked, 'Have you ever been to Naples?'

'Once.' Robert's voice was tight. *Susan was sitting beside him, giggling. I heard Naples is a wicked city. Can we do a lot of wicked things here, darling?*

We're going to invent some new things, Robert promised.

Pier was watching him. 'Are you all right?'

Robert brought his mind back to the present. 'I'm fine.'

They were driving along the bay of the Castel Dell' Ovo, the old abandoned castle near the water.

When they arrived at Via Toledo, Pier said, excitedly, 'Turn here.'

They were approaching Spaccanapoli, the old section of Naples.

Pier said, 'It's just up ahead. Turn left onto Via Benedetto Croce.'

Robert made the turn. The traffic here was heavier, and the noise of horns deafening. He had forgotten how noisy Naples could be. He slowed the car down to avoid hitting the pedestrians and dogs that ran in front of the car as though they were blessed with some kind of immortality.

'Turn right here,' Pier directed, 'into Piazza del Plebiscito.' The traffic was even worse here, and the neighbourhood more run down.

'Stop!' Pier cried out.

Robert pulled over to the kerb. They had stopped in front of a row of seedy shops.

Robert glanced around. 'This is where your mother lives?'

'No,' Pier said. 'Of course not.' She leaned over and pressed the horn. A moment later, a young woman came out of one of the shops. Pier got out of the car and raced to greet her. They hugged each other.

'You look wonderful!' the woman exclaimed. 'You must be doing very well.'

'I am.' Pier held out her wrist. 'Look at my new bracelet!'

'Are those real emeralds?'

'Of course they are real.'

The woman yelled at someone inside the store, 'Anna! Come on out. Look who is here!'

Robert was watching the scene, unbelievingly. 'Pier . . .'

'In a minute, darling,' she said. 'I have to say hello to my friends.'

Within minutes, half a dozen women were clustered around Pier, admiring her bracelet, while Robert sat there helplessly, gritting his teeth.

'He is crazy about me,' Pier announced. She turned to Robert, 'Aren't you, *caro*?'

Robert wanted to strangle her, but there was nothing he could do. 'Yes,' he said. 'Can we go now, Pier?'

'In a minute.'

'*Now!*' Robert said.

'Oh, very well.' Pier turned to the women. 'We must leave now. We have an important appointment. *Ciao!*'

'*Ciao!*'

Pier got into the car beside Robert, and the women stood there, watching them drive away.

Pier said happily. 'They are all old friends.'

'Wonderful. Where's your mother's house?'

'Oh, she doesn't live in the city.'

'*What?*'

'She lives outside, in a little farmhouse, half an hour from here.'

The farmhouse was on the southern outskirts of Naples, an old stone building set off from the road.

'There it is!' Pier exclaimed. 'Isn't it beautiful?'

'Yes.' Robert liked the fact that the house was away from the centre of town. There would be no reason for anyone to come looking for him here. *Pier was right. It's a perfect safe house.*

They walked up to the front door, and before they reached it the door flew open and Pier's mother stood there, smiling at them. She was an older version of her daughter, thin and grey-haired, with a lined, careworn face.

'Pier, *cara! Mi sei mancata!*'

'I've missed you, too, Mama. This is the friend I telephoned you about that I was bringing home.'

Mama did not miss a beat. 'Ah? *Si*, you are welcome Mr . . . ?'

'Jones,' Robert said.

'Come in, come in.'

They entered the living room. It was a large room, comfortable and homey, crammed with furniture.

A boy in his early twenties entered the room. He was short and dark, with a thin, sullen face and brooding brown eyes. He wore jeans and a jacket with the name *Diavoli Rossi* sewn on it. His face lit up when he saw his sister. 'Pier!'

'Hello, Carlo.' They hugged.

'What are you doing here?'

'We came to visit for a few days.' She turned to Robert. 'This is my brother, Carlo. Carlo, this is Mr Jones.'

'Hello, Carlo.'

Carlo was sizing Robert up. 'Hello.'

Mama said, 'I will fix a nice bedroom for you two lovebirds, in the back.'

Robert said, 'If you don't mind . . . that is, if you have an extra bedroom, I'd prefer a room to myself.'

There was an awkward pause. The three of them were staring at Robert.

Mama turned to Pier. *'Omosessuale?'*

Pier shrugged. *I don't know.* But she was sure he was not a homosexual.

Mama looked at Robert. 'As you wish.' She hugged Pier again. 'I'm so happy to see you. Come into the kitchen. I will make some coffee for us.'

In the kitchen, Mama exclaimed, *'Benissimo!* How did you meet him? He looks very rich. And that bracelet you are wearing. It must have cost a fortune. My goodness! Tonight I will cook a big dinner. I will invite all the neighbours so they can meet your . . .'

'No, Mama. You must not do that.'

'But, *cara*, why should we not spread the news of your good luck? All our friends will be so pleased.'

'Mama, Mr Jones just wants to rest for a few days. No party. No neighbours.'

Mama sighed, 'All right. Whatever you wish.'

I'll arrange for him to be picked up away from the house, so that Mama will not be disturbed.

Carlo had noticed the bracelet, too. 'That bracelet. Those are real emeralds, huh? Did you buy that for my sister?'

There was an attitude about the boy that Robert did not like. 'Ask her.'

Pier and Mama came out of the kitchen. Mama looked at Robert. 'You are sure you do not want to sleep with Pier?'

Robert was embarrassed. 'Thank you. No.'

Pier said, 'I'll show you your bedroom.' She led him toward the back of the house, to a large, comfortable bedroom with a double bed in the middle of the room.

'Robert, are you afraid of what Mama might think if we slept together? She knows what I do.'

'It's not that,' Robert said. 'It's . . .' There was no way he could explain. 'I'm sorry, I . . .'

Pier's voice was cold. 'Never mind.'

She felt unreasonably offended. Twice now he had refused to sleep

741

with her. *It serves him right that I am turning him over to the police,* she thought. And yet she felt a small, nagging sense of guilt. He was really very nice. But fifty thousand dollars was fifty thousand dollars.

At dinner, Mama was talkative, but Pier and Robert and Carlo were silent and preoccupied.

Robert was busily working out his plan of escape. *Tomorrow,* he thought, *I'll go down to the docks and find a ship out of here.*

Pier was thinking about the phone call she was planning to make. *I'll call from town, so the police cannot trace it here.*

Carlo was studying the stranger his sister had brought to the house. He should be an easy mark.

When dinner was over, the two women went into the kitchen. Robert was alone with Carlo.

'You're the first man my sister has ever brought here,' Carlo said. 'She must like you a lot.'

'I like her a lot.'

'Do you? Are you going to take care of her?'

'I think your sister can take care of herself.'

Carlo smirked. 'Yeah. I know.' The stranger seated across from him was well dressed and obviously rich. Why was he staying here when he could have stayed at some fancy hotel? The only reason Carlo could think of was that the man was in hiding. And that brought up an interesting point. When a rich man was in hiding, somehow, some way, there was money to be made from the situation.

'Where are you from?' Carlo asked.

'From no place in particular,' Robert said pleasantly. 'I travel a lot.'

Carlo nodded. 'I see.' *I'll find out from Pier who he is. Somebody will probably be willing to pay a lot of money for him, and Pier and I can split it.*

'Are you in business?' Carlo asked.

'Retired.'

It would not be hard to force this man to talk, Carlo decided. Lucca, the leader of the Diavoli Rossi, could crack him open in no time.

'How long will you be staying with us?'

'It's hard to say.' The boy's curiosity was beginning to get on Robert's nerves.

Pier and her mother came out of the kitchen.

'Would you like some more coffee?' Mama asked.

'No, thank you. That was a delicious dinner.'

Mama smiled. 'That was nothing. Tomorrow I will prepare a feast for you.'

'Good.' He would be gone by then. He stood up. 'If you don't mind, I'm rather tired. I'd like to turn in.'

'Of course,' Mama said. 'Good night.'

'Good night.'

They watched Robert as he walked toward the bedroom.

Carlo grinned. 'He doesn't think you're good enough to sleep with him, eh?'

The remark stung Pier, as it was meant to. She would not have minded it, if Robert were a homosexual, but she had heard him talk to Susan, and she knew better. *I'll show the* stronzo.

Robert lay in bed, thinking about his next move. Laying a false trail with the homing device that had been hidden in the credit card would give him a little time, but he was not depending too much on it. They probably would have caught up with the red truck by now. The men who were after him were ruthless and smart. Were heads of world governments involved in the massive cover-up? Robert wondered. Or was it an organization within an organization, a cabal in the intelligence community acting illegally on its own? The more Robert thought about it, the more feasible it seemed that the heads of state might be unaware of what was going on. And a thought struck him. It had always seemed odd to him that Admiral Whittaker had suddenly been retired from ONI and relegated to some Siberia. But if someone had *forced* him out because they knew he would never be part of the conspiracy, then it began to make sense. *I have to contact the Admiral*, Robert thought. He was the only one he could trust to get to the truth of what was happening. *Tomorrow*, he thought. *Tomorrow*. He closed his eyes, and slept.

The creaking of the bedroom door awakened him. He sat up in bed, instantly alert. Someone was moving toward the bed. Robert tensed, ready to spring. He smelled her perfume then, and felt her slide in bed beside him.

'Pier . . . What are you . . . ?'

'Ssh.' Her body pressed against his. She was naked. 'I got lonely,' she whispered. She snuggled closer to him.

'I'm sorry, Pier, I . . . I can't do anything for you.'

Pier said, 'No? Then let me do something for you.' Her voice was soft.

'It's no use. You can't.' Robert felt a deep frustration. He wanted to spare both of them the embarrassment of what was not going to happen.

'Don't you like me, Robert? Do you not think I have a beautiful body?'

'Yes.' And she did. He could feel the warmth of her body pressing closer.

She was stroking him gently, rippling her fingers up and down his chest, moving lightly toward his groin.

He had to stop her before the humiliating fiasco was repeated. 'Pier, I can't make love. I haven't been able to be with a woman since . . . for a long time.'

'You don't have to do anything, Robert,' she said. 'I just want to play. Do you like being played with?'

He felt nothing. *Goddamn Susan!* She had taken more than herself away from him, she had taken a part of his manhood.

Pier was sliding down his body now. 'Turn over,' she said.

'It's no use, Pier. I . . .'

She rolled him over and he lay there cursing Susan, cursing his impotence. He could feel Pier's tongue moving along his back, making tiny, delicate circles, moving lower and lower. Her fingers were gently flicking over his skin.

'Pier . . .'

'Ssh.'

He felt her tongue spiralling down deeper and deeper, and he began to feel aroused. He started to move.

'Ssh. Lie still.'

Her tongue was soft and warm, and he could feel her breasts trailing along his skin. His pulse began to quicken. *Yes*, he thought. *Yes! Oh, yes!* His tumescence grew until he became rock-hard, and when he could stand it no longer, he grabbed Pier and turned her over.

She felt him and gasped, 'My God, you're enormous. I want you inside me.'

And a moment later Robert plunged into her, again and again, and it was as if he had been reborn. Pier was skilful and wild, and Robert revelled in the dark cave of her velvety softness. They made love three times that night. Finally, they slept.

DAY EIGHTEEN

Naples, Italy

In the morning, as the pale light was coming through the window, Robert awakened. He held Pier close in his arms and whispered, 'Thank you.'

Pier smiled mischievously. 'How do you feel?'

'Wonderful,' Robert said. And he did.

Pier snuggled against him. 'You are an animal!'

Robert grinned. 'You're good for my ego,' he said.

Pier sat up and said seriously, 'You are not a drug smuggler, are you?'

It was a naïve question. 'No.'

'But Interpol is after you.'

That hit closer to home. 'Yes.'

Her face lit up. 'I know! You're a spy!' She was as excited as a child.

Robert had to laugh. 'Am I?' And he thought, *Out of the mouths of babes.*

'Admit it,' Pier insisted. 'You're a spy, aren't you?'

'Yes,' Robert said gravely. 'I'm a spy.'

'I knew it!' Pier's eyes were glowing. 'Can you tell me some secrets?'

'What kind of secrets?'

'You know, spy secrets . . . codes and things like that. I love to read spy novels. I read them all the time.'

'Do you?'

'Oh, yes! But they're just made-up stories. You know all the real things, don't you? Like the signals that spies use. Are you allowed to tell me one?'

Robert said seriously, 'Well, I really shouldn't, but I suppose *one* would be all right.' *What can I tell her that she'll believe?* 'There's the old window shade trick.'

She was wide-eyed. 'The old window shade trick?'

'Yes.' Robert pointed to a window in the bedroom. 'If everything is under control, you leave the shades up. But if there's trouble, you pull one shade down. That's the signal to warn your fellow agent away.'

Pier said excitedly, 'That's wonderful! I've never read that in a book.'

'You won't,' Robert said. 'It's very secret.'

'I won't tell anyone,' Pier promised. 'What else?'

What else? Robert thought for a moment. 'Well, there's the telephone trick.'

Pier snuggled closer to him. 'Tell me about that.'

'Er . . . let's say a fellow spy telephones you to find out if everything is all right. He'll ask for Pier. If everything is fine, you say, "This is Pier." But if there is any problem, you say, "You have the wrong number."'

'That's wonderful!' Pier exclaimed.

My instructors at the Farm would have a heart attack if they heard me talking this nonsense.

'Can you tell me anything else?' Pier asked.

Robert laughed. 'I think those are enough secrets for one morning.'

'All right.' She rubbed her body along his body.

'Would you like to take a shower?' Pier asked.

'Love to.'

They soaped each other under the warm water, and as Pier spread Robert's legs and began to wash him, he became tumescent again.

They made love in the shower.

While Robert was getting dressed, Pier put on a robe and said, 'I'll see about breakfast.'

Carlo was waiting for her in the dining room.

'Tell me about your friend,' he said.

'What about him?'

'Where did you meet him?'

'In Rome.'

'He must be very rich to have brought you that emerald bracelet.'

She shrugged. 'He likes me.'

Carlo said, 'Do you know what I think? I think your friend is running away from something. If we told the right party, there could be a big reward in it.'

Pier moved over to her brother, her eyes blazing. 'Stay out of this, Carlo.'

'So, he *is* running away.'

'Listen, you little *piscialetto*, I'm warning you – mind your own business.' She had no intention of sharing the reward with anyone.

Carlo said reproachfully, 'Little sister, you want it all for yourself.'

'No. You don't understand, Carlo.'

'No?'

Pier said earnestly, 'I'll tell you the truth. Mr Jones is running away from his wife. She has hired a detective to find him. That's all there is to it.'

Carlo smiled. 'Why didn't you tell me this before? Then it's no big deal, I'll forget about it.'

'Good,' Pier said.

And Carlo thought, *I've got to find out who he really is.*

Janus was on the telephone. 'Have you any news yet?'

'We know that Commander Bellamy is in Naples.'

'Do you have any assets there?'

'Yes. They're looking for him now. We have a lead. He's travelling with a prostitute who has a family in Naples. We think they may have gone there. We're following through on it.'

'Keep me informed.'

In Naples, the Bureau of Municipal Housing was busily trying to track down the whereabouts of Pier Valli's mother.

A dozen security agents and the Naples police force were scouring the city for Robert.

Carlo was busily making his own plans for Robert.

Pier was getting ready to telephone Interpol again.

42

The danger in the air was almost palpable and Robert felt he could reach out and touch it. The waterfront was a beehive of activity, with cargo ships busily loading and unloading. But another element had been added: there were police cars cruising up and down the quay, and uniformed policemen and obvious-looking detectives questioning dock workers and sailors. The concentrated manhunt took Robert by complete surprise. It was almost as though they had known he was in Naples, for it would have been impossible for them to be conducting this intense a search for him in every major city in Italy. He did not even bother to get out of the car. He turned around and headed away from the docks. What he had thought would be an easy plan – to board a cargo ship bound for France – had now become too dangerous. Somehow, they had managed to track him here. He went over his options again. Travelling any distance by car was too risky. There would be roadblocks around the city by now. The docks were guarded. That meant the railroad station and airport would be covered, as well. He was in a vice, and it was closing in on him.

Robert thought about Susan's offer. *We're just off the coast of Gibraltar. We can pick you up at any place you say. It's probably your only chance of escape.* He was reluctant to involve Susan in his danger, and yet he could think of no other alternative. It was the only way out of the trap he was in. They would not be looking for him on a private yacht. *If I can find a way to get to the* Halcyon, he thought, *they could drop me off near the coast near Marseilles, and I can get ashore by myself. That way, they won't be in danger.*

He parked the car in front of a small trattoria on a side street, and went inside to make the call. In five minutes, he was connected with the *Halcyon*.

'Mrs Banks, please.'

'Who shall I say is calling?'

Monte has a fucking butler to answer his phone on the yacht. 'Just tell her an old friend.'

A minute later he heard Susan's voice. 'Robert . . . is that you?'

'The bad penny.'

'They . . . they haven't arrested you, have they?'

'No. Susan.' It was difficult for him to ask the question. 'Is your offer still open?'

'Of course it is. When . . . ?'

'Can you reach Naples by tonight?'

Susan hesitated. 'I don't know. Hold on a moment.' Robert heard talking in the background. Susan came on the line again. 'Monte says we have an engine problem, but we can reach Naples in two days.'

Damn. Every day here increased the chances of his getting caught. 'All right. That will be fine.'

'How will we find you?'

'I'll contact you.'

'Robert, please take care of yourself.'

'I'm trying. I really am.'

'You won't let anything happen to you?'

'No, I won't let anything happen to me.' *Or to you.*

When Susan replaced the receiver, she turned to her husband and smiled. 'He's coming aboard.'

One hour later, in Rome, Francesco Cesar handed a cablegram to Colonel Frank Johnson. It was from the *Halcyon*. It read: 'Bellamy coming aboard *Halcyon*. Will keep you informed.' It was unsigned.

'I've made arrangements to monitor all communication to and from the *Halcyon*,' Cesar said. 'As soon as Bellamy steps aboard, we've got him.'

43

The more Carlo Valli thought about it, the more certain he was that he was about to make a big score. Pier's fairy tale about the American running away from his wife was a joke. Mr Jones was on the run, all right, but he was running from the police. There was probably a reward out for the man. Maybe a big reward. This had to be handled very delicately. Carlo decided to discuss it with Mario Lucca, the leader of the Diavoli Rossi.

Early in the morning, Carlo got on his Vespa motor scooter and headed for Via Sorcella, behind the Piazza Garibaldi. He stopped in front of a run-down apartment building, and pressed the bell on a broken mailbox marked 'Lucca'.

A minute later a voice yelled out, 'Who the fuck is it?'

'Carlo. I have to talk to you, Mario.'

'It better be good at this hour of the morning. Come on up.'

The door buzzer sounded, and Carlo went upstairs.

Mario Lucca was standing at an open door, naked. At the end of the room Carlo could see a girl in his bed.

'*Che cosa?* What the hell are you doing up so early?'

'I couldn't sleep, Mario. I'm too excited. I think I'm on to something big.'

'Yeah? Come in.'

Carlo entered the small, messy apartment. 'Last night my sister brought home a mark.'

'So what? Pier's a whore. She . . .'

'Yeah, but this one is rich. And he's in hiding.'

'Who is he hiding from?'

'I don't know. But I'm going to find out. I think there might be a reward out for him.'

'Why don't you ask your sister?'

Carlo frowned. 'Pier wants to keep it all for herself. You should see the bracelet he bought her – emeralds.'

'A bracelet? Yeah? How much is it worth?'

'I'll let you know. I'm going to sell it this morning.'

Lucca stood there, thoughtful. 'I'll tell you what, Carlo. Why don't we have a talk with your sister's friend? Let's pick him up and take him over to the club this morning.' The club was an empty warehouse in Pascalone Quartiere Sanita, with a room that was soundproof.

Carlo smiled. '*Bene*. I can get him down there easy enough.'

'We'll be waiting for him,' Lucca said. 'We'll have a little talk with him. I hope he has a nice voice, because he's going to sing for us.'

When Carlo returned to the house, Mr Jones was gone. Carlo panicked.

'Where did your friend go?' he asked Pier.

'He said he had to go into town for a little while. He'll be back. Why?'

He forced a smile. 'Just curious.'

Carlo waited until his mother and Pier were in the kitchen preparing lunch, then hurried into Pier's room. He found the bracelet hidden under some lingerie in a dresser drawer. He swiftly pocketed it and was on his way out when his mother came out of the kitchen.

'Carlo, aren't you staying for lunch?'

'No. I have an appointment, Mama. I'll be back later.'

He got on his Vespa and headed toward the Quartiere Spagnolo. *Maybe the bracelet is phony*, he thought. *It could be paste. I hope I don't make a fool of myself with Lucca*. He parked the motorbike in front of a small jewellery store that had a sign in front that read: '*Orologia*'. The owner, Gambino, was an elderly, wizened man, with an ill-fitting black wig and a mouthful of false teeth. He looked up as Carlo entered.

'Good morning, Carlo. You're out early.'

'Yeah.'

'What have you got for me today?'

Carlo took out the bracelet and laid it on the counter. 'This.'

Gambino picked it up. As he studied it, his eyes widened. 'Where did you get this?'

'A rich aunt died and left it to me. Is it worth anything?'

'It could be,' Gambino said cautiously.'

'Don't fuck around with me.'

Gambino looked hurt. 'Have I ever cheated you?'

'All the time.'

'You boys are always kidding around. I'll tell you what I will do, Carlo. I'm not sure I can handle this by myself. It's very valuable.'

Carlo's heart skipped a beat. 'Really?'

'I'll have to see if I can lay it off somewhere. I'll give you a call tonight.'

'Okay,' Carlo said. He snatched up the bracelet. 'I'll keep this until I hear from you.'

Carlo left the shop, walking on air. So, he had been right! The sucker was rich, and he was also crazy. *Why else would someone give an expensive bracelet to a whore?*

In the store, Gambino watched Carlo leave. He thought, *What the hell have those idiots got themselves into?* From under the counter, he picked up a circular that had been sent to all pawn shops. It had a description of the bracelet he had just seen, but at the bottom, instead of the usual police number to call, there was a special notice: 'Notify SIFAR immediately'. Gambino would have ignored an ordinary police circular, as he had hundreds of times in the past, but he knew enough about SIFAR to know that one never crossed them. He hated to lose the profit on the bracelet, but neither did he intend to put his neck in a noose. Reluctantly, he picked up the telephone and dialled the number on the circular.

44

It was the season of fear, of swirling, deadly shadows. Years earlier, Robert had been sent on a mission to Borneo and had gone into the deep jungle after a traitor. It had been in October, during *musim takoot*, the traditional head-hunting season, when the jungle natives lived in terror of *Balli Salang*, the spirit that sought out humans for their blood. It was a season of murders, and now for Robert, Naples had suddenly become the jungles of Borneo. Death was in the air. *Do not go gentle into the fucking night*, Robert thought. *They'll have to catch me first.* How had they traced him here? *Pier*. They must have tracked him down through Pier. *I have to get back to the house and warn her*, Robert thought. *But first I have to find a way out of here.*

He drove toward the outskirts of the city, to where the autostrada began, hoping that by some miracle, it might be clear. Five hundred yards before he reached the entrance, he saw the police roadblock. He turned around and headed back toward the centre of the city.

Robert drove slowly, concentrating, putting himself into the minds of his pursuers. They would have all avenues of escape out of Italy blocked. Every ship leaving the country would be searched. And a plan suddenly came to him. They would have no reason to search ships *not* leaving Italy. *It's a chance*, Robert thought. He headed for the harbour again.

The little bell over the door of the jewellery shop rang, and Gambino looked up. Two men in dark suits walked in. They were not customers.

'Can I help you?'

'Mr Gambino?'

He exposed his false teeth. 'Yes.'

'You called about an emerald bracelet.'

SIFAR. He had been expecting them. But this time he was on the side of the angels. 'That's right. As a patriotic citizen, I felt it was my duty . . .'

'Cut the bullshit. Who brought it in?'

'A young boy named Carlo.'

'Did he leave the bracelet?'

'No, he took it with him.'

'What's Carlo's last name?'

Gambino lifted a shoulder. 'I don't know his last name. He's one of the boys in the Diavoli Rossi. That's one of our local gangs. It's run by a kid named Lucca.'

'Do you know where we can find this Lucca?'

Gambino hesitated. If Lucca found out that he had talked, he would have his tongue cut out. If he did *not* tell these men what they wanted to know, he would have his brains bashed in. 'He lives on Via Sorcella, behind the Piazza Garibaldi.'

'Thank you, Mr Gambino. You've been very helpful.'

'I'm always happy to cooperate with . . .'

The men were gone.

Lucca was in bed with his girlfriend when the two men shoved open the door to his apartment.

Lucca leaped out of bed. 'What the hell is this? Who are you?'

One of the men pulled out his identification.

SIFAR! Lucca swallowed. 'Hey, I haven't done anything wrong. I'm a law-abiding citizen who . . .'

'We know that, Lucca. We're not interested in you. We're interested in a boy named Carlo.'

Carlo. So that was what this was about. That fucking bracelet! What the hell had Carlo got himself into? SIFAR did not send men around looking for stolen jewellery.

'Well . . . do you know him or don't you?'

'I might.'

'If you aren't sure, we'll refresh your memory down at headquarters.'

'Wait! I do remember, now,' Lucca said. 'You must mean Carlo Valli. What about him?'

'We'd like to have a talk with him. Where does he live?'

Every member of the Diavoli Rossi had to swear a blood oath of loyalty, an oath that they would die before they would betray a fellow member. That was what made the Diavoli Rossi such a great club. They stuck together. One for all and all for one.

'Do you want to take that trip downtown?'

'What for?' Lucca shrugged. He gave them Carlo's address.

Thirty minutes later, Pier opened the door to find two strangers standing there.

'Signorina Valli?'

Trouble. 'Yes.'

'May we come in?'

She wanted to say no, but she did not dare. 'Who are you?'

One of the men pulled out a wallet and flashed an identification card. *SIFAR.* These were not the people she had made her deal with. Pier

753

felt a sense of panic that they were going to try to cheat her out of her reward. 'What do you want with me?'

'We'd like to ask you a few questions.'

'Go ahead. I have nothing to hide.' *Thank God*, Pier thought, *Robert is out. I can still negotiate.*

'You drove down from Rome yesterday, didn't you.' It was a statement.

'Yes. Is that against the law . . . was I speeding?'

The man smiled. It did nothing to change the expression on his face. 'You had a companion with you?'

Pier answered carefully. 'Yes.'

'Who was he, *signorina*?'

She shrugged. 'Some man I picked up on the road. He wanted a ride to Naples.'

The second man asked, 'Is he here with you now?'

'I don't know where he is. I dropped him off when we got into town and he disappeared.'

'Was your passenger's name Robert Bellamy?'

She knitted her brow in concentration. 'Bellamy? I don't know. I don't think he told me his name.'

'Oh, we think he did. He picked you up on the Tor di Ounto, you spent the night with him at the L'Incrocio Hotel, and the next morning he bought you an emerald bracelet. He sent you to some hotels with airline and train tickets, and you rented a car and you came down to Naples, right?'

They know everything. Pier nodded, her eyes filled with fear.

'Is your friend coming back, or has he left Naples?'

She hesitated, deciding which was the best answer. If she told them that Robert had left town, they would not believe her, anyway. They would wait here at the house and when he turned up, they could accuse her of lying for him and hold her as an accomplice. She decided that the truth would serve her better. 'He's coming back,' Pier said.

'Soon?'

'I'm not sure.'

'Well, we'll just make ourselves comfortable. You don't mind if we look around, do you?' They opened their jackets, exposing their guns.

'N . . . no.'

They fanned out, moving through the house.

Mama walked in from the kitchen. 'Who are these men?'

'They are friends of Mr Jones,' Pier said. 'They have come to see him.'

Mama beamed. 'Such a nice man. Would you like some lunch?'

'Sure, Mama,' one of the men said. 'What are we having?'

Pier's mind was in a turmoil. *I have to call Interpol again*, she thought. *They said they would pay fifty thousand dollars.* Meanwhile, she had to keep Robert away from the house until she could make arrangements to turn him in. But how? She suddenly remembered their conversation that morning. *If there's trouble you pull one shade down.* The two men were seated at the dining-room table, eating a bowl of *capellini*.

'It's too bright in here,' Pier said. She rose and walked into the living room and pulled down the window shade. Then she went back to the table. *I hope Robert remembers about the warning.*

Robert was driving toward the house, reviewing his plan of escape. *It's not perfect*, he thought, *but at least it should get them off the trail long enough to buy me some time.* He was approaching the house. As he neared it, he slowed down and looked around. Everything appeared to be normal. He would warn Pier to get out, and then take off. As Robert started to park in front of the house, something struck him as odd. One of the front shades was down. The others were up. It was probably a coincidence, but still . . . an alarm bell sounded. Could Pier have taken his little game seriously? Was it meant to be a warning of some kind? Robert stepped on the accelerator and kept driving. He could not afford to take any chances, no matter how remote. He drove to a bar a mile away, and went inside to use the telephone.

They were seated at the dining-room table when the telephone rang. The men tensed. One of them started to rise.

'Would Bellamy be calling here?'

Pier gave him a scornful look. 'Of course not. Why should he?' She rose and walked over to the telephone. She picked up the receiver. 'Hello?'

'Pier? I saw the window shade and . . .'

All she had to do was say that everything was all right, and he would come back to the house. The men would arrest him, and she could demand her reward. But would they merely arrest him? She could hear Robert's voice saying: *If the police find me, they have orders to kill me.*

The men at the table were watching her. There was so much she could do with fifty thousand dollars. There were beautiful clothes to buy, cruises to take, a pretty little apartment in Rome . . . and Robert would be dead. Besides, she hated the goddamned police. Pier said into the telephone, 'You have the wrong number.'

Robert heard the click of the receiver and stood there, stunned. She had believed the tall tales he had told her and it had probably saved his life. *Bless her.*

Robert turned the car around and headed away from the house, toward the docks, but instead of going to the main part of the port that serviced the freighters and ocean liners leaving Italy, he drove to the other side, past Santa Lucia, to a small pier where the sign over a kiosk read: 'Capri and Ischia'. Robert parked the car where it could easily be spotted, and walked up to the ticket seller.

'When does the next hydrofoil leave for Ischia?'

'In thirty minutes.'

'And for Capri?'

'Five minutes.'

'Give me a one-way ticket to Capri.'

'*Si, signore.*'

'What's this *"si signore"* crap?' Robert said in a loud voice. 'Why don't you people speak English like everybody else?'

The man's eyes widened in shock.

'You goddamn guineas are all alike. Stupid! Or, as you people would say, *stupido*.' Robert shoved some money at the man, grabbed the ticket and walked toward the hydrofoil.

Three minutes later he was on his way to the island of Capri. The boat started out slowly, making its way cautiously through the channel. When it reached the outer limits, it surged forward, rising out of the water like a graceful porpoise. The ferry was full of tourists from a variety of countries, happily chattering away in different tongues. No one was paying any attention to Robert. He made his way to the small bar where they served drinks. He said to the bartender, 'Give me a vodka and tonic.'

'Yes, sir.'

He watched the bartender mix the drink. 'There you are, *signore*.'

Robert picked up the glass and took a swallow. He slammed the glass back down on the bar. 'You call this a drink for Christ's sakes?' he said. 'It tastes like horse piss. What's the matter with you goddamn Italians?'

People around him were turning to stare.

The bartender said, stiffly, 'I'm sorry, *signore*, we use the best . . .'

'Don't give me that shit!'

An Englishman nearby said stiffly, 'There are ladies present. Why don't you watch your language?'

'I don't have to watch my language,' Robert yelled. 'Do you know who I am? I'm Commander Robert Bellamy. And they call this a boat? It's a piece of junk!'

He made his way to the bow and sat down. He could feel the eyes of the other passengers on him. His heart was hammering, but the charade was not over yet.

When the hydrofoil docked at Capri, Robert walked over to the ticket booth at the entrance to the funicular. An elderly man was in the booth selling tickets.

'One ticket,' Robert yelled. 'And hurry up! I don't have all day. You're too old to be selling tickets, anyway. You should stay home. Your wife is probably screwing all your neighbours.'

The old man started to rise in anger. Passers-by were giving Robert furious glances. Robert grabbed the ticket and stepped into the crowded funicular. *They'll remember me*, he thought grimly. He was leaving a trail that no one could miss.

When the funicular came to a stop, Robert shoved his way through the crowd. He walked up the winding Via Vittorio Emanuele, to the Quisisana Hotel.

'I need a room,' Robert told the clerk behind the desk.

'I'm sorry,' the clerk apologized, 'but we are fully booked. There is . . .'

Robert handed him sixty thousand lire. 'Any room will do.'

'Well, in that case, I think we can accommodate you, *signore*. Would you register, please?'

Robert signed his name. Commander Robert Bellamy.

'How long will you be staying with us, Commander?'

'One week.'

'That will be fine. May I have your passport?'

'It's in my luggage. It'll be here in a few minutes.'

'I will have a bellboy show you to your room.'

'Not now. I have to go out for a few minutes. I'll be right back.'

Robert stepped out of the lobby, into the street. Memories hit him like a blast of cold air. He had walked here with Susan, exploring the little side streets, and strolled down Via Ignazio Cerio and Via di Campo. It had been a magic time. They visited the Grotta Azzurra, and had morning coffee at the Piazza Umberto. They took the funicular up to Anacapri, and rode donkeys to Villa Jovis, Tiberius's villa, and swam in the emerald green waters at the Marina Piccola. They shopped along Via Vittorio Emanuele and took the chair lift to the top of Monte Solaro, their feet skimming over the vine leaves and leafy trees. Off to the right they could see the houses sprinkled down the hillside toward the sea, yellow broom covering the ground, an eleven-minute ride through a colourful fairyland of green trees, white houses and, in the distance, the blue sea. At the top, they had coffee at the Barbarossa Ristorante, and then went into the little church in Anacapri to thank God for all their blessings, and for each other. Robert had thought then that the magic was Capri. He had been wrong. The magic was Susan, and the magician had left the stage.

Robert went back to the funicular station at the Piazza Umberto, and took the tram down, quietly mingling with the other passengers. When the funicular arrived at the bottom, he walked out, carefully avoiding the ticket seller. He went over to the kiosk at the boat landing. In a heavy Spanish accent, Robert asked, '*A que hora sale el barco a Ischia?*'

'*Sale en treinta minutos.*'

'*Gracias.*' Robert bought a ticket.

He walked into a bar at the waterfront, took a seat in the back and nursed a scotch. By now they would have undoubtedly found the car, and the hunt for him would narrow. He spread out the map of Europe in his mind. The logical thing for him to do would be to head for

England, and find a way to get back to the States. It would make no sense for him to return to France. *So, France it is,* Robert thought. A busy seaport to leave Italy from. *Civitavecchia. I have to get to Civitavecchia. The* Halcyon.

He got change from the owner of the bar, and used the telephone. It took the marine operator ten minutes to put his call through. Susan was on the line almost immediately.

'We've been waiting to hear from you. *We.* He found that interesting. 'The engine is fixed. We can be in Naples early in the morning. Where shall we pick you up?'

It was too risky for the *Halcyon* to come here. Robert said, 'Do you remember the palindrome? We went there on our honeymoon.'

'The what?'

'I made a joke about it because I was so exhausted.'

There was a silence on the other end of the line. Then Susan said softly, 'I remember.'

'Can the *Halcyon* meet me there tomorrow?'

'Hold on a moment.'

He waited.

Susan returned to the telephone. 'Yes, we can be there.'

'Good.' Robert hesitated. He thought of all the innocent people who had already died. 'I'm asking a lot of you. If they ever found out you helped me, you could be in terrible danger.'

'Don't worry. We'll meet you there. Be careful.'

'Thanks.'

The connection was broken.

Susan turned to Monte Banks. 'He's coming.'

At SIFAR headquarters in Rome they were listening to the con versation. There were four men in the room. The radio operator said, 'We've recorded it, if you would like to hear it again, sir.'

Colonel Cesar looked at Frank Johnson questioningly.

'Yes. I'm interested in hearing the part about where they're going to meet. It sounded like he said Palindrome. Is that somewhere in Italy?'

Colonel Cesar shook his head. 'I never heard of it. We'll check it out.' He turned to his aide. 'Look it up on the map. And keep monitoring all transmissions to and from the *Halcyon*.'

'Yes, sir.'

At the farmhouse in Naples, the phone rang. Pier started to get up to answer it.

'Hold it,' one of the men said. He walked over to the phone and picked it up. 'Hello?' He listened for a moment, then threw the phone

758

down and turned to his companion. 'Bellamy took the hydrofoil to Capri. Let's go!'

Pier watched the two men hurry out of the door, and thought: *God never meant me to have so much money, anyway. I hope he gets away.*

When the ferry boat to Ischia arrived, Robert mingled with the crowd boarding it. He kept to himself, avoiding eye contact. Thirty minutes later, when the boat docked at Ischia, Robert disembarked and walked over to the ticket booth on the pier. A sign announced that the ferry to Sorrento was due in ten minutes.

'A round trip ticket to Sorrento,' Robert said.

Ten minutes later he was on his way to Sorrento, back to the mainland. *With a little luck, the search will have shifted to Capri,* Robert thought. *With a little luck.*

The food market at Sorrento was crowded. Farmers had come in from the countryside bringing fresh fruit and vegetables and sides of beef that lined the meat stalls. The street was thronged with vendors and shoppers.

Robert approached a husky man in a stained apron, loading a truck. '*Pardon, monsieur . . .*' Robert spoke with a perfect French accent. 'I'm looking for transportation to Civitavecchia. Would you happen to be going that way?'

'No. Salerno.' He pointed to a man loading another truck nearby. 'Giuseppe might be able to help you.'

'*Merci.*'

Robert moved over to the next truck. '*Monsieur*, would you be going to Civitavecchia by any chance?'

The man said, noncommittally, 'I might be.'

'I would be glad to pay you for the ride.'

'How much?'

Robert handed the man a hundred thousand lire.

'You could buy yourself a plane ticket to Rome for that much money, couldn't you?'

Robert instantly realized his mistake. He looked around nervously. 'The truth is, I have some creditors watching the airport. I'd prefer to go by truck.'

The man nodded. 'Ah. I understand. All right, get in. We're ready to leave.'

Robert yawned. 'I am *très fatigué*. How do you say? – tired. Would you mind if I slept in the back?'

'It's going to be a bumpy ride, but suit yourself.'

'*Merci.*'

The back of the truck was filled with empty crates and boxes. Giuseppe watched Robert climb in, and he closed up the tailgate. Inside, Robert concealed himself behind some crates. He suddenly realized how exhausted he really was. The chase was beginning to wear him down. How long had it been since he had slept? He thought of Pier and how she had come to him in the night and had made him feel whole again, a man again. He hoped she was all right. Robert slept.

In the cab of the truck, Giuseppe was thinking about his passenger. The word was out about an American the authorities were looking for. His passenger had a French accent, but he looked like an American and he dressed like an American. It would be worth checking out. There might be a nice reward.

One hour later, at a truck stop along the highway, Giuseppe pulled up in front of a gas pump. 'Fill it up,' he said. He walked around to the back of the truck and peered inside. His passenger was asleep.

Giuseppe went inside the restaurant and made a telephone call to the local police.

45

The call had been routed to Colonel Cesar. 'Yes,' he said to Giuseppe, 'that sounds very much like our man. Listen carefully. He is dangerous, so I want you to do exactly as I tell you. Do you understand?'

'Yes, sir.'

'Where are you now?'

'At the AGIP truck stop on the highway to Civitavecchia.'

'And he's in the back of your truck now?'

'Yes.' The conversation was making him nervous. *Maybe I should have minded my own business.*

'Don't do anything to make him suspicious. Get back in your truck and keep driving toward Civitavecchia. Give me your licence number and a description of your truck.'

Giuseppe gave it to him.

'Fine. We will take care of everything. Now get moving.'

Colonel Cesar turned to Colonel Johnson and nodded. 'We have him. I'll have a roadblock set up. We can be there by helicopter in thirty minutes.'

'Let's go.'

When Giuseppe replaced the receiver, he wiped his sweaty palms on his shirt, and headed for the truck. *I hope there won't be a shoot-out. Maria would kill me. On the other hand, if the reward is large enough . . .* He climbed into the cab of the truck and headed for Civitavecchia.

Thirty-five minutes later, Giuseppe heard the sound of a helicopter overhead. He looked up. It had the markings of the State Police. Ahead of him on the highway, he saw two police cars lined up next to each other, forming a roadblock. Behind the cars were policemen with automatic weapons. The helicopter landed at the side of the road, and Cesar and Colonel Frank Johnson stepped out.

As he neared the roadblock, Giuseppe slowed the truck down. He shut off the ignition and jumped out, running toward the officers. 'He's in the back!' he shouted.

The truck rolled to a stop. Cesar shouted, 'Close in.'

The policemen converged on the truck, weapons ready.

'Don't shoot,' Colonel Johnson yelled. 'I'll take him.' He moved toward the back of the truck. 'Come on out, Robert,' Colonel Johnson called, 'it's over.'

There was no response.

'Robert, you have five seconds.'

Silence. They waited.

Cesar turned to his men and nodded.

'No!' Colonel Johnson yelled. But it was too late.

The police began firing into the back of the truck. The noise of the automatic fire was deafening. Splinters of crates began flying into the air. After ten seconds, the firing ceased. Colonel Frank Johnson jumped into the back of the truck and moved the crates and boxes out of his way.

He turned to Cesar. 'He's not here.'

DAY NINETEEN

Civitavecchia, Italy

Civitavecchia is the ancient seaport for Rome, guarded by a massive fort completed by Michelangelo in 1537. The port is one of the busiest in Europe, servicing all sea-going traffic to and from Rome and Sardinia. It was early in the morning, but the port was already alive with noisy activity. Robert made his way past the railroad yards and stepped into a small trattoria filled with pungent cooking odours and ordered breakfast.

The *Halcyon* would be waiting for him at the appointed place, Elba. He was grateful that Susan had remembered it. On their honeymoon, they had stayed in their room there for three days and nights, making love. Susan had said, 'Would you like to go for a swim, darling?'

Robert had shaken his head. 'No. I can't move. "Able was I, ere I saw Elba."' And Susan had laughed and they had made love again. *And bless her, she had remembered the palindrome.*

Now all he had to do was to find a boat to take him to Elba. He walked down the streets leading to the harbour. It was bustling with maritime activity, crowded with freighters, small motor boats and private yachts. There was a landing for a ferry boat. Robert's eyes lit up when he saw it. *That would be the safest way to get over to Elba.* He would be able to lose himself in the crowds.

As Robert started toward the ferry landing, he noticed a dark, unmarked sedan parked half a block away, and he stopped. It had official licence plates. There were two men seated inside the car watching the docks. Robert turned and walked in the other direction.

Scattered among the dockworkers and tourists, he spotted plain-clothes detectives trying to look unobtrusive. They stood out like beacons. Robert's heart began to pound. How could they possibly have tracked him here? And then he realized what had happened. *My God, I told the truck driver where I was going! Stupid! I must be very tired.*

He had fallen asleep in the truck, and the absence of movement had awakened him. He had got up to look out, and had seen Giuseppe go into the gas station and make a phone call. Robert had slipped out of the truck and climbed into the back of another truck headed north toward Civitavecchia.

He had trapped himself. They were looking for him here. A few hundred yards away were dozens of boats that could have afforded him an escape. Not any longer.

Robert turned away from the harbour and walked toward town. He passed a building with a huge colourful poster on the wall. It read: 'Come to the Fairgrounds. Fun for All! Food! Games! Rides! See the Big Race!' He stopped and stared.

He had found his escape.

46

At the fairgrounds, five miles outside of Civitavecchia, were a dozen large, colourful balloons spread across the field, looking like round rainbows. They were moored to trucks while ground crews were busily filling their envelopes with cold air. Half a dozen chase cars stood by, ready to track the balloons, two men in each car, the driver and the spotter.

Robert walked up to a man who seemed to be in charge. 'It looks like you're getting ready for the big race,' Robert said.

'That's right. Ever been in a balloon?'

'No.'

They were skimming over Lake Como and he dropped the balloon down until it touched the water. 'We're going to crash,' Susan screamed. He smiled. 'No, we're not.' The bottom of the balloon was dancing on the waves. He threw out a sandbag and the balloon began to lift again. Susan laughed and hugged him and said . . .

The man was speaking. 'You should try it sometime. It's a great sport.'

'Yeah. Where is the race heading?'

'Yugoslavia. We have a nice easterly wind. We'll be taking off in a few minutes. It's better to fly early in the morning when the wind is cool.'

'Really?' Robert said politely. He had a quick flash of a summer day in Yugoslavia. *We have four people to smuggle out of here, Commander. We must wait until the air is cooler. A balloon that can lift four people in the winter air can only lift two people in the summer air.*

Robert noticed that the crews were finishing filling the balloons with air and starting to light the large propane burners, pointing the flame into the envelope opening, to warm the air inside. The balloons, which were lying on their sides, began to rise until the baskets stood upright.

'Mind if I look around?' Robert asked.

'Go ahead. Just stay out of everyone's way.'

'Right.' Robert walked over to a yellow and red balloon that was filled with propane gas. The only thing holding it to the ground was a rope attached to one of the trucks.

The crewman who had been working on it had wandered off to talk to someone. There was no one else near.

Robert climbed into the basket of the balloon, and the huge envelope seemed to fill the sky above him. He checked the rigging and equipment, the altimeter, charts, a pyrometer to monitor the temperature of the envelope, a rate of climb indicator, and a tool kit. Everything was in order. Robert reached into the tool kit and pulled out a knife. He sliced into the mooring rope, and a moment later, the balloon started to ascend.

'Hey!' Robert yelled. 'What's going on here? Get me down!'

The man he had spoken to was gaping up at the runaway balloon. '*Figlio d'una mignotta!* Don't panic,' he shouted. 'There's an altimeter on board. Use your ballast and stay at one thousand feet. We'll meet you in Yugoslavia. Can you hear me?'

'I hear you.'

The balloon was rising higher and higher, carrying him east, away from Elba, which was to the west. But Robert was not concerned. The wind changed direction at varying altitudes. None of the other balloons had taken off yet. Robert spotted one of the chase cars start up, moving to track him. He dropped ballast and watched the altimeter climb. Six hundred feet . . . seven hundred feet . . . nine hundred feet . . . eleven hundred feet . . .

At fifteen hundred feet the wind began to weaken. The balloon was almost stationary now. Robert dropped more ballast. He used the stair step technique, stopping at different altitudes to check the wind direction.

At two thousand feet, Robert could feel the wind begin to shift. It swayed in the turbulent air for a moment, then slowly began to reverse direction and move west.

In the distance far below, Robert could see the other balloons rising and moving east toward Yugoslavia. There was no sound at all except for the soft whispering of the wind. *It's so quiet, Robert. It's like flying on a cloud. I wish we could stay up here forever.* She had held him close. *Have you ever made love in a balloon? she murmured. Let's try it.*

And later, *I'll bet we're the only people in the world who have made love in a balloon, darling.*

Robert was over the Tyrrhenian Sea now, heading northwest toward the coast of Tuscany. Below, a string of islands stretched in a circle off the coast, with Elba the largest.

Napoleon had been exiled here, and he had probably chosen it because on a clear day, Robert thought, *he could see his beloved island of Corsica. In exile, Napoleon's one thought was how to escape and get to France. Mine, too. Only Napoleon didn't have Susan and the* Halcyon *to rescue him.*

In the distance, Monte Capanne suddenly loomed up, rising three thousand feet into the sky. Robert pulled the safety line that opened the valve at the top of the balloon to allow the hot air to escape, and the balloon began to descend. Below him, Robert could see the lush pink and green of Elba, the pink that came from the granite outcrops and Tuscan houses, and the green of the heavy forests. Below, pristine white beaches were scattered around the edges of the island.

He landed the balloon at the base of the mountain, away from the city, to attract as little attention to himself as possible. There was a road not far from where he had landed and he walked over to it and waited until a car came by.

'Could you give me a lift into town?' Robert called.

'Certainly. Jump in.'

The driver appeared to be somewhere in his eighties, with an old, wrinkled face.

'I could have sworn I saw a balloon in the sky a little while ago. Did you see it, mister?'

'No,' Robert said.

'Visiting?'

'Just passing through. I'm on my way to Rome.'

The driver nodded. 'I was there once.'

The rest of the ride was made in silence.

When they reached Portoferraio, the capital and only city of Elba, Robert stepped down from the car.

'Have a nice day,' the driver said in English.

My God, Robert thought, *Californians have been here.*

Robert walked along Via Garibaldi, the main street, crowded with tourists, mostly families, and it was as though time had stood still. Nothing had changed; *except that I've lost Susan, and half the governments in the world are trying to assassinate me. Otherwise,* Robert thought wryly, *everything is exactly the same.*

He bought binoculars in a gift shop, and walked to the waterfront and sat at a table outside the Stella Mariner Restaurant, where he had a clear view of the harbour. There were no suspicious cars, no police boats, and no policemen in sight. They still thought they had him bottled up on the mainland. It would be safe for him to board the *Halcyon*. All he had to do now was wait for it to arrive.

He sat there sipping *procanico*, the delicate native white wine, watching for the *Halcyon*. He went over his plan again. The yacht would drop him off near the coast of Marseilles, and he would make his way to Paris where he had a friend, Li Po, who would help him. It was ironic. He heard Francesco Cesar's voice saying: *I've heard you've made a deal with the Chinese.*

He knew that Li Po would help him, because Li had once saved Robert's life, and according to ancient Chinese tradition, he had become responsible for Robert. It was a matter of *win yu* – honour.

Li Po was with the Guojia Anquanbu, the Chinese Ministry of State Security that dealt with espionage. Years earlier, Robert had been caught while trying to smuggle a dissident out of China. He had been sent to Qincheng, the top security prison in Beijing. Li Po was a double agent who had worked with Robert before. He managed to arrange for Robert to escape.

At the Chinese border, Robert had said, 'You should get out of this while you're still alive, Li. Your luck won't last forever.'

Li Po had smiled. 'I have *ren* – the ability to endure, to survive.'

One year later, Li Po had been transferred to the Chinese Embassy in Paris.

Robert decided that it was time to make his first move. He left the restaurant and wandered down to the waterfront. It was crowded with large and small boats leaving from Portoferraio.

Robert approached a man polishing the hull of a sleek motor boat. It was a Donzi, powered by a V-8 351 inboard engine.

'Nice boat,' Robert said.

The man nodded. '*Merci.*'

'I wonder if I could rent it to take a little cruise around the harbour?'

The man stopped what he was doing and studied Robert. 'That might be possible. Are you familiar with boats?'

'Yes. I have a Donzi back home.'

The man nodded approvingly. 'Where are you from?'

'Oregon,' Robert said.

'It will cost you four hundred francs an hour.'

Robert smiled. 'That's fine.'

'And a deposit, of course.'

'Of course.'

'She's ready to go. Would you like to take her out now?'

'No, I have some errands to run. I thought tomorrow morning.'

'What time?'

'I'll let you know,' Robert said.

He handed the man some money. 'Here's a partial deposit. I'll see you tomorrow.'

He had decided it would be dangerous to let the *Halcyon* come into port. There were formalities. The *capitano di porto* – the harbourmaster – issued each yacht an *autorizzazione* and recorded its stay. Robert intended for the *Halcyon* to be as little involved with him as possible. He would meet it at sea.

In the office of the French Marine Ministry, Colonel Cesar and Colonel Johnson were talking to the marine operator. 'Are you sure there has been no further communication with the *Halcyon*?'

'No, sir, not since the last conversation I reported to you.'

'Keep listening.' Colonel Cesar turned to Colonel Johnson and smiled. 'Don't worry. We'll know the moment Commander Bellamy boards the *Halcyon*.'

'But I want to get him before he's aboard.'

The marine operator said, 'Colonel Cesar, there is no Palindrome listed on the map of Italy. But I think we've pinned it down.'

'Where is it?'

'It's not a place, sir. It's a word.'

'*What?*'

'Yes, sir. A palindrome is a word or sentence that is spelled the same forward or backward. For example, 'Madam I'm Adam'. We've run some through our computers.' He handed him a long list of words.

Colonel Cesar and Colonel Johnson scanned the list. 'Kook . . . deed . . . bib . . . bob . . . boob . . . dad . . . dud . . . eve . . . gag . . . mom . . . non . . . noon . . . Otto . . . pop . . . sees . . . tot . . . toot . . .' Cesar looked up. 'It's not much help, is it?'

'It might be, sir. They were obviously using some kind of code. And one of the most famous palindromes was supposedly said by Napoleon: "Able was I ere I saw Elba."'

Colonel Cesar and Colonel Johnson looked at each other. '*Elba*. Jesus Christ! That's where he is!'

DAY TWENTY

The Island of Elba

It first appeared as a faint speck on the horizon, rapidly looming larger in the early morning light. Through the binoculars, Robert watched it materialize into the *Halcyon*. There was no mistaking the ship. There were not many at sea like it.

Robert hurried down to the beach where he had arranged to rent the motor boat.

'Good morning.'

The owner of the boat looked up. '*Bonjour, monsieur*. Are you ready to take it out?'

Robert nodded. 'Yes.'

'How long will you want it for?'

'No more than an hour or two.'

Robert gave the man the rest of the deposit, and stepped down into the boat.

'Take good care of it,' the man said.

'Don't worry,' Robert assured him, 'I will.'

The owner untied the painter, and moments later the boat was headed out to sea, racing toward the *Halcyon*. It took Robert ten minutes to reach the yacht. As he approached it, he saw Susan and Monte Banks standing on the deck. Susan waved to him and he could see the anxiety in her face. Robert manoeuvred the small boat next to the yacht and tossed a line to a deckhand.

'Do you want to bring it aboard, sir?' the man called.

'No, let it go.' The owner would find it soon enough.

Robert walked up the ladder to the spotless teak deck. Susan had once described the *Halcyon* to Robert, and he had been impressed, but in actuality it was even more impressive. The *Halcyon* was two hundred and eighty feet long, with a luxurious owner's cabin, eight double suites for guests, and cabins for a crew of sixteen. It had a drawing room, a dining room, an office, a saloon and a swimming pool.

The ship was propelled by two 1250 horsepower sixteen-cylinder turbo-charged caterpillar D399 diesel engines, and carried six tenders. The interior design had been done in Italy by Luigi Sturchio. It was a floating palace.

'I'm glad you made it,' Susan said.

And Robert had the impression that she was ill at ease, that something was wrong. Or was it just his nerves?

She looked absolutely beautiful, and somehow, he was disappointed. *What the hell had I expected? That she would look pale and miserable?*

He turned to Monte. 'I want you to know how much I appreciate this.'

Monte shrugged. 'Glad to help you out.'

The man was a saint.

'What's your plan?'

'I'd like you to turn and head due west to Marseilles. You can drop me off the coast and . . .'

A man in a crisp white uniform approached. He was in his fifties, heavyset, with a neatly trimmed beard.

'This is Captain Simpson. This is . . .' Monte Banks looked at Robert for help.

'Smith. Tom Smith.'

Monte said, 'We'll be heading for Marseilles, Captain.'

'We're not going into Elba?'

'No.'

Captain Simpson said, 'Very well.' He sounded surprised.

Robert scanned the horizon. All clear.

'I'd suggest we go below,' Monte Banks said.

When the three of them were seated in the saloon, Monte asked, 'Don't you think you owe us an explanation?'

'Yes, I do,' Robert said, 'but I'm not going to give you one. The less you know about this whole affair the better. I can only tell you that I'm innocent. I'm involved in a political situation. I know too much, and I'm being hunted. If they find me, they'll kill me.'

Susan and Monte exchanged a look.

'They have no reason to connect me with the *Halcyon*,' Robert went on. 'Believe me, Monte, if there were any other way for me to escape, I would have taken it.'

Robert thought of all the people who had been killed because he had tracked them down. He could not bear to have anything happen to

769

Susan. He tried to keep his voice light. 'I would appreciate it for your own sakes, if you didn't mention that I was ever aboard this ship.'

'Of course not,' Monte said.

The yacht had slowly swung around and was heading west.

'If you'll excuse me, I have to have a word with the captain.'

Dinner was an awkward affair. There were strange undercurrents that Robert did not understand, a tension that was almost tangible. Was it because of his presence? Or was it something else? Something between the two of them? *The sooner I get away from here, the better*, Robert thought.

They were in the saloon having an after-dinner drink when Captain Simpson came into the room.

'When will we reach Marseilles?' Robert asked.

'If the weather holds, we should be there tomorrow afternoon, Mr Smith.'

There was something about Captain Simpson's manner that irritated Robert. The captain was gruff, almost to the point of being rude. *But he must be good*, Robert thought, *or Monte would not have hired him. Susan deserves this yacht. She deserves the best of everything.*

At eleven o'clock Monte looked at his watch and said to Susan, 'I think we had better turn in, darling.'

Susan glanced at Robert. 'Yes.'

The three of them rose.

Monte said, 'You'll find a change of clothes in your cabin. We're about the same size.'

'Thank you.'

'Good night, Robert.'

'Good night, Susan.'

Robert stood there, watching the woman he loved going off to bed with his rival. *Rival? Who the hell am I kidding? He's the winner. I'm the loser.*

Sleep was an elusive shadow, dancing just out of reach. Lying in his bed, Robert was thinking that on the other side of the wall, only a few feet away, was the woman he loved more than anyone in the world. He thought of Susan lying in her bed, naked . . . *she never wore a nightgown* . . . and he felt himself beginning to get an erection. *Was Monte making love to her at this moment or was she alone? . . . and was she thinking of him and remembering all the great times they had had together? Probably not. Well, he would be out of her life soon. He would probably never see her again.*

770

It was dawn before he closed his eyes.

In the communications room at SIFAR, radar was tracking the *Halcyon*. Colonel Cesar turned to Colonel Johnson, and said, 'Too bad we couldn't intercept him at Elba, but we've got him now! We have a cruiser standing by. We're just waiting word from the *Halcyon* to board her.'

DAY TWENTY-ONE

Early in the morning Robert was on deck, looking out over the calm sea. Captain Simpson approached him. 'Good morning. It looks like the weather is going to hold, Mr Smith.'
'Yes.'
'We'll be in Marseilles by three o'clock. Will we be staying there long?'
'I don't know,' Robert said pleasantly. 'We'll see.'
'Yes, sir.'
Robert watched Simpson stride off. *What was there about the man?*
Robert walked back to the stern of the yacht and scanned the horizon. He could see nothing, and yet . . . In the past, his instincts had saved his life more than once. He had long ago learned to rely on them. Something was wrong.

Over the horizon out of sight, the Italian Navy cruiser *Stromboli* was stalking the *Halcyon*.

When Susan appeared for breakfast, she looked pale and drawn.
'Did you sleep well, darling?' Monte asked.
'Fine,' Susan said.
So they didn't share the same cabin! Robert felt an unreasonable sense of pleasure from that knowledge. He and Susan had always slept in the same bed, her naked, nubile body spooning into his. *Jesus, I've got to stop thinking like this.*

Ahead of the *Halcyon*, on the starboard bow, was a fishing boat from the Marseilles fleet, bringing in a fresh catch.
'Would you like some fish for lunch?' Susan asked.
Both men nodded. 'Fine.'
They were almost abreast of the fishing boat.

As Captain Simpson walked by, Robert asked, 'What is our ETA to Marseilles?'

'We'll be there in two hours, Mr Smith. Marseilles is an interesting port. Have you ever been there?'

'It *is* an interesting port,' Robert said.

In the communications room, at SIFAR, the two colonels were reading the message that had just come in from the *Halcyon*. It read simply: '*Now*.'

'What's the *Halcyon*'s position?' barked Colonel Cesar.

'They're two hours out of Marseilles, heading for the port.'

'Order the *Stromboli* to overtake and board her immediately.'

Thirty minutes later, the Italian Navy cruiser *Stromboli* was closing in on the *Halcyon*. Susan and Monte were at the fantail of the yacht, watching the warship racing toward them.

A voice came over the cruiser's loudspeaker. 'Ahoy, *Halcyon*. Heave to. We're coming aboard.'

Susan and Monte exchanged a look. Captain Simpson came hurrying toward them.

'Mr Banks . . .'

'I heard it. Do as they say. Stop the engines.'

'Yes, sir.'

A minute later, the pulse of the engines stopped, and the yacht lay still in the water. Susan and her husband watched as armed sailors from the Navy cruiser were lowered into a dinghy.

Ten minutes later a dozen sailors were swarming up the ladder of the *Halcyon*.

The naval officer in charge, a lieutenant commander, said, 'I'm sorry to trouble you, Mr Banks. The Italian government has reason to believe that you are harbouring a fugitive. We have orders to search your ship.'

Susan stood there watching, as the sailors started spreading out, moving along the deck and going below to search the cabins.

'Don't say anything.'

'But . . .'

'Not a word.'

They stood on the deck in silence, watching the search go on.

Thirty minutes later they were assembled again on the main deck.

'There's no sign of him, Commander,' a sailor reported.

'You're certain of that?'

'Absolutely, sir. There are no passengers aboard, and we have identified each member of the crew.'

The Commander stood there a moment, frustrated. His superiors had made a serious mistake.

He turned to Monte and Susan and Captain Simpson. 'I owe you an apology,' he said. 'I'm terribly sorry to have inconvenienced you. We'll leave now.' He turned to go.

'Commander . . .'

'Yes?'

'The man you're looking for got away on a fishing boat half an hour ago. You should have no trouble picking him up.'

Five minutes later, the *Stromboli* was speeding toward Marseilles. The Lieutenant Commander had every reason to be pleased with himself. Half the governments of the world had been pursuing Commander Robert Bellamy, and he was the one who had found him. *There could be a nice promotion in this,* he thought.

From the bridge, the navigation officer called out, 'Commander, could you come up here, please?'

Had they spotted the fishing boat already? The Lieutenant Commander hurried up to the bridge.

'Look, sir!'

The Commander took one look and his heart sank. In the distance ahead, covering the horizon, was the entire Marseilles fishing fleet, a hundred identical boats returning to port. There was no way in the world to identify the one Commander Bellamy was on.

47

He stole a car in Marseilles. It was a Fiat 1800 Spider convertible, parked on a dimly lit side street. It was locked and there was no key in the ignition. No problem. Looking around to make sure he was not observed, Robert made a rip in the canvas top and shoved his hand inside to unlock the door. He slid inside the car, reached under the dashboard and pulled out all the wires of the ignition switch. He held the thick red wire in one hand while, one by one, he touched the other wires to it until the dashboard lit up. He hooked two wires together, and touched the remaining ones to the two wires hooked together until the engine began to turn over. He pulled out the choke and the engine roared into life. A moment later, Robert was on his way to Paris.

His first priority was to get hold of Li Po. When he reached the Paris suburbs, he stopped at a phone booth. He telephoned Li's apartment and heard the familiar voice on the answering machine: *Zao, mes amis . . . Je regrette que je ne sois pas chez moi mais il n'y a pas du danger que je ne réponde pas à votre coup de téléphone. Prenez garde que vous attendiez le signal de l'appareil.*

Good morning. I regret I am not home, but there is no danger of my not returning your call. Be careful to wait for the tone. Robert counted out the words in their private code. The key words were: Regret . . . danger . . . careful.

The phone was tapped, of course. Li had been expecting his call, and this was his way of warning Robert. He had to get to him as quickly as possible. He would use another code they had employed in the past.

Robert walked along the Rue St Honoré. He had walked this street with Susan. She had stopped in front of a shop window and posed like a mannequin. *Would you like to see me in that dress, Robert? No, I'd prefer to see you out of it.* And they had visited the Louvre, and Susan had stood transfixed in front of the Mona Lisa, her eyes brimming with tears . . .

Robert headed for *Le Matin*. Half a block from the newspaper office, he stopped a teenager on the street.

'Would you like to make fifty francs?'

The boy looked at him suspiciously. 'Doing what?'

Robert scribbled something on a piece of paper and handed it to the boy with a fifty-franc note.

'Just take this into *Le Matin* to the Want Ads desk.'

'*Bon, d'accord.*'

Robert watched the boy go into the building. The ad would get in in time to make next morning's edition. It read: 'Tilly. Dad very ill, needs you. Please meet with him soon. Mother.'

There was nothing to do now but wait. He dared not check into a hotel because they would all have been alerted. Paris was a ticking time bomb.

Robert boarded a crowded tour bus and sat at the back, keeping a low, silent profile. The tour group visited the Luxembourg Gardens, the Louvre, Napoleon's Tomb in Les Invalides, and a dozen other monuments. And always, Robert managed to lose himself in the middle of the crowd.

He bought a ticket for the midnight show at the Moulin Rouge as part of another tour group. The show started at two a.m. When it was over, he filled in the rest of the night moving around Montmartre, going from small bar to small bar.

DAY TWENTY-TWO

Paris, France

The morning papers would not be out on the streets until five a.m. A few minutes before five, Robert was standing near a newspaper stand, waiting. A red truck drove up and a boy threw a bundle of papers onto the pavement. Robert picked up the first one. He turned to the Want Ads. His ad was there. Again there was nothing to do but wait.

At noon, Robert wandered into a small tobacconist shop, where dozens of personal messages were tacked to a board. There were help-wanted ads . . . advertisements for apartments to let . . . students seeking roommates . . . bicycles for sale . . . In the middle of the board, Robert found the message he was looking for. 'Tilly eager to see you. Call her at 50 41 26 45.'

Li Po answered on the first ring. 'Robert?'

'*Zao*, Li.'

'My God, man, what is happening?'

'I was hoping you could tell me.'

'My friend, you're getting more attention than the President of France. The cables are burning up about you. What have you done? No, don't tell me. Whatever it is, you're in serious trouble. They've tapped the phone at the Chinese Embassy, my phone at home is tapped, and they're watching my flat. They've been asking me a lot of questions about you.'

'Li, do you have any idea what this is all . . . ?'

'Not over the phone. Do you remember where Sung's apartment is?' *Li's girlfriend.* 'Yes.'

'I'll meet you there in half an hour.'

'Thanks.' Robert was keenly aware of what jeopardy Li Po was putting himself in. He remembered what had happened to Al Traynor, his friend at the FBI. *I'm a fucking Jonah. Everyone I come near dies.*

The apartment was on Rue Benouville in a quiet arrondissement of Paris. When Robert reached the building, the sky was heavy with rain clouds, and he could hear the distant rumble of thunder. He walked into the lobby and rang the doorbell of the apartment. Li Po opened the door at once.

'Come inside,' he said. 'Quickly.' He closed the door behind Robert and locked it. Li Po had not changed since the last time Robert had seen him. He was tall and thin, and ageless.

The two men clasped hands.

'Li, do you know what the hell is going on?'

'Sit down, Robert.'

Robert sat.

Li studied him for a moment. 'Have you ever heard of Operation Doomsday?'

Robert frowned. 'No. Does it have anything to do with UFOs?'

'It has everything to do with UFOs. The world is facing disaster, Robert.'

Li Po began to pace. 'Aliens are coming to earth to destroy us. Three years ago they landed here and met with government officials to demand that all the industrial powers close down their nuclear plants and stop burning fossil fuel.'

Robert was listening, puzzled.

'They demanded a stop to the manufacturing of petroleum, chemicals, rubber, plastics . . . That would mean the closing down of thousands of factories all over the world. Automobile and steel plants would be forced to shut down. The world economy would be a shambles.'

'Why should they . . . ?'

'They claim we're polluting the universe, destroying the earth and the seas . . . they want us to stop making weapons, to stop waging war.'

'Li . . .'

'A group of powerful men from a dozen countries got together – top industrialists from the United States, Japan, Russia, China . . . A man with the code name of Janus organized intelligence agencies around the world to form Operation Doomsday, to stop the aliens.' He turned to Robert. 'You've heard of SDI?'

'Star Wars. The satellite system to shoot down Soviet intercontinental ballistic missiles.'

Li shook his head. 'No. That was a cover. SDI was not created to fight the Russians. It is being designed for the specific purpose of knocking down UFOs. It's the only chance there is of stopping them.'

Robert sat there in stunned silence, trying to absorb what Li Po

776

was saying, while the rumble of thunder grew louder. 'You mean, the governments are behind . . . ?'

'Let's say, there are cabals within each government. Operation Doomsday is being run privately. Do you understand now?'

'My God! The governments aren't aware that . . .' He looked up at Li. 'Li – how did you learn all this?'

'It's very simple, Robert,' Li said quietly, 'I'm the Chinese connection.' There was a Beretta in his hand.

Robert stared at the gun. 'Li . . . !'

Li squeezed the trigger, and the sound of the shot mingled with a sudden deafening crack of thunder and a flash of lightning outside the window.

48

The first few drops of clean rain water awakened her. She was lying on a park bench, too exhausted to move. For the last two days, she had felt her life energy flowing out of her. *I am going to die here on this planet.* She drifted into what she thought would be her last sleep. And then, the rain came. The blessed rain. She could hardly believe it. She lifted her head to the sky and felt the cool drops running down her face. It began to rain harder, and harder. Fresh, pure liquid. She stood up then, and raised her hands high, letting the water pour over her, giving her new strength, bringing her back to life. She let the rain water fill her body, absorbing it into her very essence, until she began to feel her tiredness vanish. She felt herself growing stronger and stronger, until finally, she thought, *I am ready. I can think clearly. I know who can help me find my way back.* She took out the small transmitter, closed her eyes, and began to concentrate.

49

It was the lightning streak that saved Robert's life. At the instant that Li Po started to squeeze the trigger, the sudden flash of light outside the window distracted him for a moment. Robert moved, and the bullet hit him in his right shoulder instead of his chest.

As Li raised the gun to fire again, Robert gave a side-thrust kick, knocking the gun out of Li's hand. Li spun forward and punched Robert hard in his wounded shoulder. The pain was excruciating. Robert's jacket was covered with blood. He lashed out with a forward elbow smash. Li grunted with pain. He riposted with a deadly *shuto* chop to the neck, and Robert evaded it. The two men circled each other, both of them breathing hard, looking for an opening. They fought silently in a deadly ritual older than time, and each knew that only one of them would come out of this alive. Robert was weakening. The pain in his shoulder was increasing, and he could see his blood dripping to the floor.

Time was on Li Po's side. *I've got to end this quickly*, Robert thought. He moved in with a front snap kick. Instead of evading it, Li took the full force of it, and was close enough to Robert to drive his elbow into Robert's shoulder. Robert staggered. Li moved in with a spin and back kick, and Robert faltered. Li was on top of him in an instant, pummelling him, pounding his shoulder again and again, backing him across the room. Robert was too weak to stop the rain of punishing blows. His eyes began to dim. He fell against Li, grabbing him, and the two men went down, smashing a glass table, shattering it. Robert lay on the floor, powerless to move. *It's over*, he thought. *They've won.*

He lay there, half-conscious, waiting for Li to finish him off. Nothing happened. Slowly, painfully, Robert lifted his head. Li lay next to him on the floor, his eyes opened wide, staring at the ceiling. A large shard of glass, like a transparent dagger, protruded from his chest.

Robert struggled to sit up. He was weak from the loss of blood. His shoulder was an ocean of pain. *I have to get to a doctor*, he thought. *There was a name . . . someone that the Agency used in Paris . . . someone at the American Hospital. Hilsinger. That was it. Leon Hilsinger.*

Dr Hilsinger was ready to leave his office for the day when the telephone call came in. His nurse had already gone home, so he picked up the phone. The voice at the other end of the phone was slurred.

'Dr Hilsinger?'

'Yes.'

'This is Robert Bellamy . . . need your help. I've been badly hurt. Will you help me?'

'Of course. Where are you?'

'Never mind that. I'll meet you at the American Hospital in half an hour.'

'I'll be there. Go right to the Emergency Room.'

'Doctor – don't mention this call to anyone.'

'You have my word.' The line went dead.

Dr Hilsinger dialled a number. 'I just heard from Commander Bellamy. I'm meeting him at the American Hospital in half an hour . . .'

'Thank you, Doctor.'

Dr Hilsinger replaced the receiver. He heard the reception door open and looked up. Robert Bellamy was standing there with a gun in his hand.

'On second thoughts,' Robert said, 'it might be better if you treated me here.'

The doctor tried to conceal his surprise. 'You . . . you should be in a hospital.'

'Too close to the morgue. Patch me up and make it fast.' It was difficult to talk.

Dr Hilsinger started to protest, then thought better of it. 'Yes. Whatever you say. I'd better give you an anaesthetic. It will . . .'

'Don't even think about it,' Robert said. 'No tricks.' He was holding the gun in his left hand. 'If I don't get out of here alive, neither do you. Any questions?' He felt faint.

Dr Hilsinger swallowed. 'No.'

'Then get to work.'

Dr Hilsinger led Robert into the next room, an examining room filled with medical equipment. Slowly and carefully, Robert slipped out of his jacket. Holding the gun in his hand, he sat down on the table. Dr Hilsinger had a scalpel in his hand. Robert's fingers tightened on the trigger.

'Relax,' Dr Hilsinger said nervously. 'I'm just going to cut your shirt.'

The wound was raw and red, and seeping blood. 'The bullet is still in there,' Dr Hilsinger said. 'You won't be able to stand the pain unless I give you . . .'

'No!' He was not going to let himself be drugged. 'Just take it out.'

'Whatever you say.'

Robert watched the doctor walk over to a sterilizing unit and put in a pair of forceps. Robert sat on the edge of the table, fighting off the dizziness that threatened to engulf him. He closed his eyes for a moment, and Dr Hilsinger was standing in front of him, the forceps in his hand.

'Here we go.' He pushed the forceps into the raw wound and Robert

780

screamed aloud with the pain. Bright lights flashed in front of his eyes. He started to lose consciousness.

'It's out,' Dr Hilsinger said.

Robert sat there for a moment, trembling, taking deep breaths, fighting to regain control of himself.

Dr Hilsinger was watching him closely. 'Are you all right?'

It took Robert a moment to find his voice. 'Yes . . . patch it up

The doctor poured peroxide into the wound, and Robert started to pass out again. He gritted his teeth. *Hang on. We're almost there.* And finally, blessedly, the worst was over. The doctor was strapping a heavy bandage across Robert's shoulder.

'Give me my jacket,' Robert said.

Dr Hilsinger stared at him. 'You can't go out now. You can't even walk.'

'Bring me my jacket.' His voice was so weak he could hardly talk. He watched the doctor walk across the room to get his jacket, and there seemed to be two of him.

'You've lost a lot of blood,' Dr Hilsinger cautioned. 'It would be dangerous for you to leave.'

And more dangerous for me to stay, Robert thought. Carefully, he slipped his jacket on and tried to stand. His legs began to buckle. He grabbed the side of the table.

'You'll never make it,' Dr Hilsinger warned.

Robert looked up at the blurry figure in front of him. 'I'll make it.'

But he knew that the moment he left, Dr Hilsinger would be on the phone again. Robert's eyes fell on the spool of heavy surgical tape Dr Hilsinger had used.

'Sit in the chair.' His words were slurred.

'Why? What are you . . . ?'

Robert raised the gun. 'Sit down.'

Dr Hilsinger sat. Robert picked up the roll of tape. It was awkward, because he only had the use of one hand. He pulled the end of the wide tape loose and began to unroll it. He moved over to Dr Hilsinger. 'Just sit quietly and you won't get hurt.'

He fastened the end of the tape to the arm of the chair, and then started winding it around the doctor's hands.

'This really isn't necessary,' Dr Hilsinger said. 'I won't . . .'

'Shut up.' Robert continued to bind the doctor to the chair. The effort had started the rivers of pain flowing again. He looked at the doctor and said quietly, 'I'm not going to faint.'

He fainted.

He was floating in space, drifting weightlessly through white clouds, at peace. *Wake up.* He did not want to wake up. He wanted this wonderful feeling to go on forever. *Wake up.* Something hard was pressing against his side. Something in his jacket pocket. With his eyes still closed, he reached in and held it in his hand. It was the crystal. He drifted back to sleep.

Robert. It was a woman's voice, soft and soothing. He was in a lovely green meadow, and the air was filled with music, and there were bright lights in the sky overhead. A woman was moving toward him. She was tall and beautiful, with a gentle, oval face and a soft, almost translucent complexion. She was dressed in a snow-white gown. Her voice was gentle and hushed.

No one's going to hurt you anymore, Robert. Come to me. I'm waiting here for you.

Slowly, Robert opened his eyes. He lay there for a long moment, then sat up, filled with a sudden sense of excitement. He knew now who the eleventh witness was, and he knew where he was to meet her.

50

DAY TWENTY-THREE
Paris, France

He telephoned Admiral Whittaker from the doctor's office.

'Admiral. Robert.'

'Robert! What's going on? They told me . . .'

'Never mind that now. I need your help, Admiral. Have you ever heard of the name Janus?'

Admiral Whittaker said slowly, 'Janus? No. I never heard of him.'

Robert said, 'I've found out he's heading some kind of secret organization that's killing innocent people, and now he's trying to kill me. We have to stop him.'

'How can I help?'

'I need to get to the President. Can you arrange a meeting?'

There was a moment of silence. 'I'm certain I can.'

'There's more. General Hilliard is involved.'

'What? How . . . ?'

'And there are others. Most of the intelligence agencies in Europe are in it, too. I can't explain any more now. I want you to call Hilliard. Tell him I've found an eleventh witness.'

'I don't understand. An eleventh witness to what?'

'I'm sorry, Admiral, but I can't tell you. Hilliard will know. I want him to meet me in Switzerland.'

'Switzerland?'

'Tell him I'm the only one who knows where the eleventh witness is. If he makes one wrong move, the deal is off. Tell him to go to the Dolder Grand in Zürich. There will be a note waiting for him at the desk. Tell him I also want Janus in Switzerland, in person.'

'Robert, are you certain you know what you're doing?'

'No, sir, I'm not. But this is the only chance I've got. I want you to tell him my conditions are not negotiable. Number one, I want safe passage to Switzerland. Number two, I want General Hilliard and Janus to meet me there. Number three, after that, I want a meeting with the President of the United States.'

'I will do everything I can, Robert. How will I get in touch with you?'

'I'll call you back. How much time will you need?'

'Give me one hour.'

'Right.'

'And Robert . . .'

He could hear the pain in the old man's voice. 'Yes, sir?'

'Be careful.'

'Don't worry, sir. I'm a survivor. Remember?'

One hour later Robert was speaking to Admiral Whittaker again.

'You have a deal. General Hilliard seemed shaken by the news of another witness. He's given me his word you will not be harmed. Your conditions will be met. He's flying to Zürich and will be there tomorrow morning.'

'And Janus?'

'Janus will be on the plane with him.'

Robert felt a surge of relief. 'Thank you, Admiral. And the President?'

'I spoke to him myself. His aides will arrange a meeting for you whenever you're ready.'

Thank God!

'General Hilliard has a plane to fly you to . . .'

'No way.' He was not going to let them get him into a plane. 'I'm in Paris. I want a car and I'll drive it myself. I want it left in front of the Hotel Littré in Montparnasse within half an hour.'

'I'll see to it.'

'Admiral?'

'Yes, Robert?'

It was difficult to keep his voice steady. 'Thank you.'

He walked down Rue Littré, moving slowly because of the pain. He approached the hotel cautiously. Parked directly in front of the building was a black Mercedes sedan. There was no one inside. Across the street was a blue and white police car, with a uniformed policeman behind the wheel. On the sidewalk, two men in civilian clothes stood watching Robert approach. *French Secret Service.*

Robert found that he was having trouble breathing. His heart was pounding. Was he stepping into a trap? The only insurance he had was the eleventh witness. Did Hilliard believe him? Was it enough?

He walked toward the sedan, waiting for the men to make a move. They stood there, silently watching him.

Robert moved toward the driver's side of the Mercedes and looked inside. The keys were in the ignition. He could feel the eyes of the men fastened on him as he opened the door and slid into the driver's seat. He sat there a moment, staring at the ignition. *If General Hilliard had double-crossed Admiral Whittaker, this was the moment when everything would end in a violent explosion.*

784

Here goes. Robert took a deep breath, reached down with his left hand and turned the key. The motor purred into life. The Secret Service men stood there, watching him drive away. As Robert approached the intersection, a police car pulled in front of his car, and for a moment, Robert thought he was going to be stopped. Instead, the police turned on their red flashing light, and the traffic seemed to melt away. *They're giving me a fucking escort!*

Overhead Robert heard the sound of a helicopter. He glanced up. The side of the helicopter was marked with the insignia of the French National Police. General Hilliard was doing everything possible to see that he arrived in Switzerland safely. *And after I show him the last witness*, Robert thought grimly, *he thinks he's going to kill me. But the General is in for a surprise.*

Robert reached the Swiss border at four o'clock in the afternoon. At the border, the French police car turned back, and a Swiss police car became his escort. For the first time since the affair had started, Robert began to relax. *Thank God Admiral Whittaker had friends in high places.* With the President expecting a meeting with Robert, General Hilliard would not dare to harm him. His mind turned to the woman in white, and at that instant, he heard her voice. The sound of it reverberated through the car.

Hurry, Robert. We are all waiting for you.

All? Was there more than one? I'll find out soon enough, Robert *All? Was there more than one? I'll find out soon enough*, Robert thought.

In Zürich, Robert stopped at the Dolder Grand Hotel and wrote a note at the desk for the General.

'General Hilliard will ask for me,' Robert told the clerk. 'Please give this to him.'

'Yes, sir.'

Outside, Robert walked over to the police car that had been escorting him. He leaned down to talk to the driver. 'From here on in, I want to be on my own.'

The driver hesitated. 'Very well, Commander.'

Robert got back in his car and started driving toward Uetendorf and the scene of the UFO crash. As he drove, he thought of all the tragedies that had occurred because of it and all the lives that had been taken. *Hans Beckerman and Father Patrini; Leslie Mothershed and William Mann; Daniel Wayne and Otto Schmidt; Laslo Bushfekete and Fritz Mandel; Olga Romanchanko and Kevin Parker. Dead. All of them dead.*

I want to see the face of Janus, Robert thought, *and look into his eyes.*

The villages seemed to race by, and the pristine beauty of the Alps belied all the bloodshed and terror that had started here. The car approached Thun, and Robert's adrenalin began to flow. Ahead was the field where he and Beckerman had found the weather balloon, where the nightmare had begun. Robert pulled the car over to the side of the road and switched off the engine. He said a silent prayer. Then he got out of the car, crossed the highway and went into the field.

A thousand memories flashed through Robert's mind. The phone call at four in the morning. *You are ordered to report to General Hilliard at National Security Agency Headquarters at Fort Meade at 0600 this morning. Is the message understood, Commander?*

How little he had understood it then. He recalled General Hilliard's words: *You must find those witnesses. All of them.* And the search had led from Zürich to Bern, London, Munich, Rome and Orvieto; from Waco to Fort Smith; from Kiev to Washington, and Budapest. Well, the bloody trail had finally come to an end, here, where it had all begun.

She was waiting for him, as Robert had known she would be, and she looked exactly as she had appeared in his dream. They moved toward each other, and she seemed to be floating toward him, a radiant smile on her face.

Thank you for coming, Robert.

Had he actually heard her speak, or was he hearing her thoughts? How did one talk to an alien being?

'I had to come,' he said simply. There was a totally unreal quality to the scene. *I'm standing here speaking with someone from another world! I should be terrified, but in my whole life, I've never felt more at peace.* 'I have to warn you,' Robert said. 'Some men are coming here who want to harm you. It would be better if you left before they arrive.'

I cannot leave.

And Robert understood. He reached in his pocket with his left hand and pulled out the small piece of metal containing the crystal.

Her face lit up. *Thank you, Robert.*

He handed it to her and watched her fit it into the piece she held in her hand.

'What happens now?' Robert asked.

Now I can communicate with my friends. They will be coming for me.

Was there something ominous in that sentence? Robert recalled General Hilliard's words: *They intend to take over this planet and make slaves of us.* What if General Hilliard was right? What if the aliens did intend to take over the earth? Who was going to stop them? Robert looked at his watch. It was almost time for General Hilliard and Janus to arrive, and even as Robert thought it, he heard the sound of a giant Huey helicopter approaching from the north.

Your friends are here.

Friends. They were his mortal enemies, and he was determined to expose them as murderers, to destroy them.

The grass and flowers in the field began to flutter wildly as the helicopter came to a landing.

He was about to come face to face with Janus. The thought of it filled him with a murderous rage. The door of the helicopter opened.

Susan stepped out.

51

In the mothership, floating high above earth, there was great joy. All the lights on the panels were flashing green.

We have found her!

We must hurry.

The huge ship started to hurl itself toward the planet far below.

52

For a single instant, time was frozen, and then it shattered into a thousand pieces. Robert watched, stunned, as Susan stepped out of the helicopter. She stood there for a second, and then started toward Robert, but Monte Banks who was right behind her, grabbed her and held her back.

'Run, Robert! Run! They're going to kill you!'

Robert took a step toward her, and at that moment, General Hilliard and Colonel Frank Johnson stepped out of the helicopter.

General Hilliard said, 'I'm here, Commander. I've kept my part of the bargain.' He walked over to Robert and the woman in white. 'I assume this is the eleventh witness. The missing alien. I'm sure we'll find her very interesting. So it's finally finished.'

'Not yet. You said you would bring Janus.'

'Oh, yes. Janus insisted on coming to see you.'

Robert turned toward the helicopter. Admiral Whittaker was standing in the doorway.

'You asked to see me, Robert?'

Robert stared at him, unbelievingly, and there was a red film before his eyes. It was as though his world had collapsed. 'No! Why . . . ? *Why* in God's name?'

The Admiral was moving toward him. 'You don't understand, do you? You never did. You're worried about a few meaningless lives. We're worried about saving our world. This earth belongs to us, to do with as we please.'

He turned to stare at the woman in white. 'If you creatures want war, you're going to get war. And we'll beat you!' He turned back to Robert. 'You betrayed me. You were my son. I let you take Edward's place. I gave you a chance to serve your country. And how did you repay me? You came whining to me to let you stay home so you could be with your wife.' His voice was filled with contempt. 'No son of mine would ever do that. I should have seen then how distorted your values were.'

Robert stood there, immobile, too shocked to speak.

'I broke up your marriage because I still had faith in you, but . . .'

'You broke up my . . . ?'

'Remember when the CIA sent you after the Fox? I arranged that. I hoped it would bring you to your senses. You failed because there was no Fox. I thought I had straightened you out, that you were one of us. And then you told me you were going to quit the Agency. That's when I knew you were no patriot, that you had to be eliminated, destroyed. But first you had to help us with our mission.'

'Your *mission*? To kill all those innocent people? You're insane!'

'They had to be killed to stop them from spreading panic. We're ready now for the aliens. All we needed was a little more time, and you've given it to us.'

The woman in white had stood there listening, saying nothing, but now her thoughts floated into the minds of those standing in the field. *We have come here to prevent you from destroying your planet. We are all part of one universe. Look up.*

Their heads turned toward the sky. There was an enormous white cloud overhead, and as they stared up at it, it seemed to change before their eyes. They were looking at a vision of a polar ice cap, and as they watched, it began to melt, and the water came pouring through the rivers and oceans of the world, flooding London and Los Angeles, New York, and Tokyo, and coastal cities around the world in a dizzying montage. The vision changed to an enormous vista of desolate farmlands, with crops burnt to cinders under a broiling, merciless sun, and the corpses of dead animals strewn across the landscape. The scene before their eyes changed again, and they saw riots in China, and famines in India, and a devastating nuclear war, and finally, people living in caves. The vision slowly disappeared.

There was a moment of awed silence. *That is your future if you go on as you are.*

Admiral Whittaker was the first to recover. 'Mass hypnosis,' he snapped. 'I'm sure you can show us other interesting tricks.' He moved toward the alien. 'I'm taking you back to Washington with me. We have a lot of information to get from you.' The Admiral looked at Robert. 'You're finished.' He turned to Frank Johnson. 'Take care of him.'

Colonel Johnson removed his pistol from his holster.

Susan broke away from Monte, and ran to Robert's side. 'No!' she screamed.

'Kill him!' Admiral Whittaker said.

Colonel Johnson was pointing a gun at the Admiral. 'Admiral – you're under arrest.'

Admiral Whittaker was staring at him. 'What . . . What are you saying? I told you to kill him. You're one of us.'

'You're wrong. I never have been. I infiltrated your organization a long time ago. I was looking for Commander Bellamy not to kill him, but to save him.' He turned to Robert. 'I'm sorry I couldn't get to you sooner.'

Admiral Whittaker's face had turned ashen. 'Then you'll be destroyed too. Nobody can stand in our way. Our organization . . .'

'You no longer have an organization. At this moment, all the members are being rounded up. It's finished, Admiral.'

Overhead, the sky seemed to be vibrating with light and sound. The huge mothership was floating down directly above them, bright green lights flashing from its interior. They stared in awe as they watched it land. A smaller spaceship appeared, and then another, and then two more and another two, until the sky seemed to be filled with them, and there was a great roar in the air that became a glorious music that echoed throughout the mountains. The door of the mothership opened and an alien appeared.

The woman in white turned to Robert. *I am leaving now.* She moved toward Admiral Whittaker, General Hilliard, and Monte Banks. *You shall come with me.*

Admiral Whittaker drew back. 'No! I won't go!'

Yes. We will not hurt you. She held out her hand, and for an instant nothing happened. Then, as the others watched, the three men began slowly moving toward the spaceship in a hypnotic daze.

Admiral Whittaker screamed, 'No!'

He was still screaming when the three men disappeared inside the spaceship.

The woman in white turned to the others. *They will not be harmed. They have much to learn. When they have learned, they will be brought back here.*

Susan was holding Robert tightly.

Tell people they must stop killing this planet, Robert. Make them understand.

'I'm only one man.'

There are thousands of you. Every day your numbers grow. One day there will be millions, and you must all speak with one strong voice. Will you do it?

'I'll try. I'll try.'

We are leaving now. But we will be watching you. And we will be back.

The woman in white turned and entered the mothership. The lights inside began to glow brighter and brighter, until they seemed to light up the entire sky. Suddenly, without warning, the mothership took off, followed by the smaller ships, until finally they all vanished from sight.

Tell the people they must stop killing the planet. Right, Robert thought. *I know now what I'm going to do with the rest of my life.*

He looked at Susan and smiled.

THE BEGINNING

791

AUTHOR'S NOTE

In researching this novel, I have read numerous books, and magazine and newspaper articles citing astronauts who had reportedly had extra-terrestrial experiences: Colonel Frank Borman on *Gemini 7* supposedly took pictures of a UFO that followed his capsule. Neil Armstrong on *Apollo 11* saw two unidentified spacecraft when he landed on the moon. Buzz Aldrin photographed unidentified spacecraft on the moon. Colonel L. Gordon Cooper, on a Project Mercury flight, encountered a large UFO over Perth, Australia, and recorded voices speaking languages later found to belong to no known earth language.

I talked to these men, as well as to other astronauts, and each one assured me that the stories were apocryphal, rather than apocalyptic, that they had had no experiences of any kind with UFOs. A few days after my telephone conversation with Colonel Gordon Cooper, he called me back. I returned his call, but he had suddenly become unavailable. One year later, I managed to acquire a letter written by him, dated November 9th, 1978, discussing UFOs.

I telephoned Colonel Cooper again to ask him if the letter was authentic. This time, he was more forthcoming. He informed me that it was, and that on his journeys into space he had personally witnessed several flights of UFOs. He also mentioned that other astronauts had had similar experiences that they were warned not to discuss.

I have read a dozen books that prove conclusively that flying saucers exist. I have read a dozen books that prove conclusively that flying saucers do *not* exist. I have run video tapes purporting to be photographs of flying saucers, and have met with therapists in the United States and abroad who specialize in hypnotizing people who claim to have been taken up into UFOs. The therapists say that they have handled hundreds of cases in which the details of the victims' experiences are startlingly similar, including identical, unexplainable marks on their bodies.

An Air Force general in charge of the Blue Book project – a US government group formed to investigate flying saucers – assured me that there has never been any hard evidence of flying saucers, or of aliens.

Yet, in the foreword to *Above Top Secret*, a remarkable book by Timothy Good, Lord Hill-Norton, Admiral of the Fleet and British Chief of Defence Staff from 1971 to 1973, writes:

> The evidence that there are objects which have been seen in our atmosphere, and even on terra firma, that cannot be accounted for

either as man-made objects or as any physical force or effect known to our scientists seems to me to be overwhelming . . . A very large number of sightings have been vouched for by persons whose credentials seem to me unimpeachable. It is striking that so many have been trained observers, such as police officers and airline or military pilots . . .

In 1933, the 4th Swedish Flying Corps began an investigation of mysterious unmarked aircraft appearing over Scandinavia, and on April 30th, 1934, Major-General Erik Reuterswaerd issued the following statement to the press:

Comparisons of these reports show that there can be no doubt about illegal air traffic over our secret military areas. There are many reports from reliable people which describe close observation of the enigmatic flier. And in every case, the same remark can be noted; no insignias or identifying marks are visible on the machines . . . the question is: Who or what are they, and why have they been invading our air territory?

In 1947, Professor Paul Santorini, a leading Greek scientist, was asked to investigate missiles flying over Greece. 'We soon established that they were not missiles. But, before we could do any more, the Army, after conferring with foreign officials, ordered the investigation stopped. *Foreign scientists flew to Greece for secret talks with me.*' [Emphasis added.] The professor confirmed that a 'world blanket of secrecy' surrounded the UFO question because, among other reasons, the authorities were unwilling to admit the existence of a force against which there was 'no possibility of defence'.

From 1947 to 1952, ATIC (Air Technical Intelligence Centre) received approximately 1,500 official reports of sightings. Of these the Air Force carries 20 per cent as unexplained.

Air Chief Marshal Lord Dowding, Commander-in-Chief of RAF Fighter Command during the Battle of Britain in 1940, wrote:

More than 10,000 sightings have been reported, the majority of which cannot be accounted for by any 'scientific explanation'. They have been tracked on radar screens . . . and the observed speeds have been as great as 9,000 miles an hour . . . I am convinced that these objects do exist and that they are not manufactured by any nation on earth. I can therefore see no alternative to accepting the theory that they come from an extraterrestrial source . . .

Recently, in Elmwood, Wisconsin, the entire town watched as flying saucers moved across their skies for several days.

General Lionel Max Chassin, who rose to the rank of Commanding General of the French Air Forces and served as General Air Defence Co-ordinator, Allied Air Forces, Central Europe (NATO), wrote:

> That strange things have been seen is now beyond question . . . The number of thoughtful, intelligent, educated people in full possession of their faculties who have 'seen something' and described it grows every day.

Then there was the famous Roswell Incident, in 1947. According to eyewitness reports, on the evening of July 2nd, a bright disc-shaped object was seen over Roswell, New Mexico. The following day, widely scattered wreckage was discovered by a local ranch manager and his two children. The authorities were alerted and an official statement was released confirming that the wreckage of a flying disc had been recovered.

A second press statement was immediately issued stating that the wreckage was nothing more than the remains of a weather balloon, which was dutifully displayed at a press conference. Meanwhile the real wreckage was reported to have been sent to Wright Field. The bodies were described by one witness as 'like human but they were not humans. The heads were round, the eyes were small, and they had no hair. Their eyes were widely spaced. They were quite small by our standards and their heads were larger in proportion to their bodies. Their clothing seemed to be one-piece and grey in colour. They seemed to be all males and there were a number of them . . . Military personnel took over and we were told to leave the area and not to talk to anyone about what we had seen.'

According to a document acquired from an intelligence source in 1984, a highly secret panel, code-named 'Majestic 12' or 'MJ-12', was formed by President Truman in 1947 to investigate UFOs and report its findings to the President. The document, dated November 18th, 1952 and classified TOP SECRET/MAJIC/EYES ONLY, was allegedly prepared by Admiral Hillenkoetter for President-elect Dwight Eisenhower, and includes the astonishing statement that the remains of four alien bodies were recovered two miles from the Roswell wreckage site.

Five years after the panel was formed, the committee wrote a memo to then President-elect Eisenhower about the UFO project and the need for secrecy:

> Implications for the National Security are of continuing importance, in that motives and ultimate intentions of these visitors remain completely unknown . . . It is for these reasons, as well as the obvious international technological considerations and the ultimate need to avoid a public panic at all costs, that the Majestic 12 Group remains of the unanimous opinion that imposition of the strictest security

precautions should continue without interruption into the new administration.

The official explanation of denial is that the document's authenticity is questionable.

The National Security Agency is reported to be withholding more than one hundred documents relating to UFOs, the CIA approximately fifty documents, and the DIA six.

Major Donald Keyhoe, a former aide to Charles Lindbergh, publicly accused the US government of denying the existence of UFOs, in order to prevent public panic.

In August 1948, when a top secret 'Estimate of the Situation' by the Air Technical Intelligence Centre offered its opinion that UFOs were interplanetary visitors, General Vandenberg, Air Force Chief of Staff at the time, ordered the document burned.

Is there a worldwide government conspiracy to conceal the truth from the public?

In the short space of six years, twenty-three English scientists who worked on Star-Wars-type projects have died under questionable circumstances. All of them had worked on different facets of electronic warfare, which includes UFO research.

A list of the deceased and the dates and circumstances of their deaths follows.

1982. Professor Keith Bowden, killed in auto crash.

July 1982. Jack Wolfenden, died in a glider accident.

November 1982. Ernest Brockway, suicide.

1983. Stephen Drinkwater, suicide by strangulation.

April 1983. Lieutenant Colonel Anthony Godley, missing, declared dead.

April 1984. George Franks, suicide by hanging.

1985. Stephen Oke, suicide by hanging.

November 1985. Jonathan Wash, suicide by jumping from a building.

1986. Dr John Brittan, suicide by carbon monoxide poisoning.

October 1986. Arshad Sharif, suicide by placing a rope around his neck, tying it to a tree and then driving away at high speed. Took place in Bristol, one hundred miles away from his home in London.

October 1986. Vimal Dajibhai, suicide by jumping from a bridge in Bristol, one hundred miles away from his home in London.

January 1987. Avtar Singh-Gida, missing, declared dead.

February 1987. Peter Peapell, suicide after crawling under car in garage.

March 1987. David Sands, suicide by driving car into café at high speed.

April 1987. Mark Wisner, death by self-strangulation.

April 10th, 1987. Stuart Gooding, killed in Cyprus.
April 1987. Shani Warren, suicide by drowning.
May 1987. Michael Baker, killed in auto crash.
May 1988. Trevor Knight, suicide.
August 1988. Alistair Beckham, suicide by self-electrocution.
August 1988. Brigadier Peter Ferry, suicide by self-electrocution.
Date unknown. Victor Moore, suicide.
Coincidences?

In the past three decades, there have been at least 70,000 reports of mysterious objects in the sky and countless more sightings, perhaps ten times as many, that have gone unreported.

Reports of UFOs have come from hundreds of countries all over the globe. In Spain, UFOs are known as *Objetos Foladores No Identificados* . . . in Germany, they are *Fliegende Untertassen* . . . in France, *Soucoupes Volantes* . . . in Czechoslovakia, *Letajici Talire*.

The eminent astronomer Carl Sagan has estimated that our Milky Way galaxy alone may contain some 250 billion stars. About a million of these, he believes, may have planets capable of supporting some form of civilization.

Our government denies the existence of extraterrestrial intelligence, yet on Columbus Day, in 1992, in California and Puerto Rica, NASA will activate radio telescopes equipped with special receivers and computers capable of analysing tens of millions of radio channels at once, to search for signs of intelligent life in the universe.

NASA has nicknamed the mission 'MOP' for Microwave Observing Project, but astronomers refer to it as 'SETI', for Search for Extraterrestrial Intelligence.

I have asked two former presidents of the United States whether they have any knowledge of UFOs or aliens, and their responses were negative. Would they have told me if they had had any information? Given the blanket of secrecy that seems to surround the subject, I think not.

Do flying saucers really exist? Are we being visited by aliens from another planet? With new technology probing deeper and deeper into the universe, looking for signs of intelligent life in space, perhaps we will have the answer much sooner than we expect.

There are many working in space exploration, astronomy and cosmology who, not content to wait for that answer, put themselves out on a limb and make a prediction of their own. Jill Tartar, an astrophysicist and SETI project scientist at NASA's Ames Research Centre, in Ames, Iowa, is among them.

There are 400 billion stars in the galaxy. We're made of stardust, really common stuff. In a universe filled with stardust, it's hard to believe that we are the only creatures who could be.

Text of a letter from Colonel L. Gordon Cooper to Ambassador Griffith

Ambassador Griffith
Mission of Grenada to the United Nations
866 Second Avenue
Suite 502
New York, New York 10017

Dear Ambassador Griffith:

I wanted to convey to you my views on our extraterrestrial visitors popularly referred to as 'UFOs', and suggest what might be done to properly deal with them.

I believe that these extraterrestrial vehicles and their crews are visiting this planet from other planets, which obviously are a little more technically advanced than we are here on earth. I feel that we need to have a top level, coordinated program to scientifically collect and analyze data from all over the earth concerning any type of encounter, and to determine how best to interface with these visitors in a friendly fashion. We may first have to show them that we have learned to resolve our problems by peaceful means, rather than warfare, before we are accepted as fully qualified universal team members. This acceptance would have tremendous possibilities of advancing our world in all areas. Certainly then it would seem that the UN has a vested interest in handling this subject properly and expeditiously.

I should point out that I am not an experienced UFO professional researcher. I have not yet had the privilege of flying a UFO, nor of meeting the crew of one. I do feel that I am somewhat qualified to discuss them since I have been into the fringes of the vast areas in which they travel. Also, I did have occasion in 1951 to have two days of observation of many flights of them, of different sizes, flying in fighter formation, generally from east to west over Europe. They were at a higher altitude than we could reach with our jet fighters of that time.

I would also like to point out that most astronauts are very reluctant to even discuss UFOs due to the great numbers of people who have indiscriminately sold fake stories and forged documents abusing their names and reputations without hesitation. Those few astronauts who have continued to have a participation in the UFO field have had to do so very cautiously. There are several of us who do believe in UFOs and who have had occasion to see a UFO on the ground, or from an airplane.

If the UN agrees to pursue this project, and to lend their credibility to it, perhaps many more well qualified people will agree to step forth and provide help and information.

I am looking forward to seeing you soon.

Sincerely,

L. Gordon Cooper
Col. USAF (kct)
Astronaut